HUMANITY'S CHAMPION

Ajela's face was animated now. The feeling in her reached and caught up Hal as music might have caught him up.

'By the time I was nine I knew I had to come here; and by the time I was eleven, they let me come – on Tam's personal responsibility.' She smiled suddenly. 'It seemed,' she said, 'Tam was intrigued by someone only my age who could be so set on getting here; and I found out later, partly he hoped I might hear the voices, as you and he did. But I didn't.'

'So it's because of Tam you're still here?' Hal asked.

'I came because of him, yes,' she said. 'But since then I've come to see what he sees in the Encyclopedia – what *you* should see in it. How, even if there weren't any Tam Olyn, I'd still be here. It's the hope of the race,' she said to him. 'Their one hope. I don't believe any longer that the answer can lie with our Exotics, or anyone else. It's here – here! No place else. And only Tam's been able to keep it alive. He needs you . . .'

Also by Gordon R. Dickson in Sphere Books:

The Final Encyclopedia

GORDON R. DICKSON

SPHERE BOOKS LIMITED

First published in Great Britain by
Sphere Books Ltd 1985
27 Wright's Lane, London W8 5SW
Copyright © 1984 by Gordon R. Dickson
Published in the USA by Tom Doherty Associates 1984
Reprinted 1986

TRADE
MARK

Set in 9/9½ pt Plantin

Printed and bound in Great Britain by
Cox & Wyman Ltd, Reading

The Final Encyclopedia, and the Childe Cycle of books of which it is a part, are dedicated to my mother, Maude Ford Dickson, who in her own way in ninety-five years has achieved far greater things.

Star Map
WORLDS OF THE CHILDE CYCLE

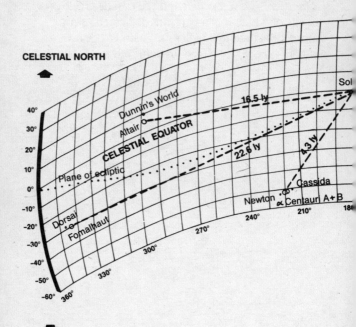

CELESTIAL NORTH

CELESTIAL SOUTH

Sol

Dunnin's World

16.5 ly

Altair

CELESTIAL EQUATOR

22.6 ly

4.3 ly

Plane of ecliptic

Cassida

Newton

α Centauri A+B

Dorsai

Fomalhaut

40°
30°
20°
10°
0°
-10°
-20°
-30°
-40°
-50°
-60°

360°
330°
300°
270°
240°
210°
18(

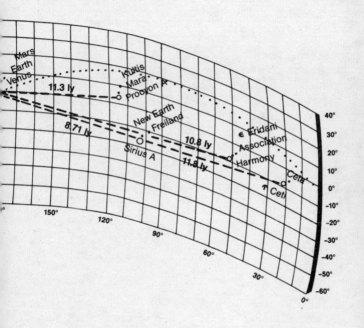

Mars
Earth
Venus
11.3 ly
Kutis
Mara
Procyon A
8.71 ly
New Earth
Freiland
10.8 ly
Sirius A
11.8 ly
ε Eridani
Association
Harmony
Ceta
τ Ceti

40°
30°
20°
10°
0°
-10°
-20°
-30°
-40°
-50°
-60°

150°   120°   90°   60°   30°   0°

○ Star
● Planet
..... Plane of Sol's Ecliptic
– – – Distance from Sol in
         light years

(not to scale)

CHAPTER ONE

The low-angled daylight dimmed suddenly on the page of a poem by Alfred Noyes that Walter the InTeacher was reading. It was as if a little cloud had passed over the face of the late afternoon sun that was slanting its rays through the library window beside him. But when Walter glanced up, Earth's star shone bright and round in the sky. There was no cloud.

He frowned, set the antique book aside and reached into his now old-fashioned Maran robes to take out a small, transparent cube filled with liquid, within which normally drifted a thin pink strip of semi-living tissue. It was a cube sent to him here on Earth fourteen years back, from what remained of the old Splinter Culture of the men and women of Mara – that with Kultis had been the two Exotic Worlds. In all those years, as often as he had looked at it, the appearance of the strip had never changed. But now he saw it lying shriveled and blackened and curled as if burned, at the bottom of the liquid enclosing it. And from the implications of this it came to Walter then, coldly and like something he had been half-expecting for some time, that the hour of his death was upon him.

He put the cube away and got swiftly to his feet. At ninety-two he was still tall, spare and active. But he did not know how long the life gauge had been shriveled, or how much time remained. He went quickly, therefore, along the library and out through a tall french window onto the flagstone terrace, flanked at each end by heavy-blossomed lilac bushes and standing a sheer forty feet above the half mile of lake enclosed by the Mayne estate.

On the terrace, legs spread and big hands locked together behind him, Malachi Nasuno, once an officer and man of the Dorsai, but now a tutor like Walter, stood watching an eggshell plastic canoe and the canoeist in it, paddling toward the house. It was almost sunset. The sun, dropping rapidly behind the sharp peaks of the Sawatch range of the Rocky Mountains around them, was growing a shadow swiftly across the lake from its further end. This shadow the canoeist was racing, just ahead of its edge on the dark blue water.

Walter wasted no time, but hurried to the flagstaff at one end of the terrace. He loosened the cord on the staff; the sun-warmed, flexible length of it ran through his fingers, burning them lightly, and the flag with its emblem of a hawk flying out of a wood fluttered to the terrace stones.

Out on the lake, the canoeist's paddle beat brightly once more in the sunlight and then ceased. The living figure vanished overside. A moment later, the canoe itself heaved up a little, filled and sank, as if it had been ripped open from beneath and pulled down into the depths. A second later the advancing edge of darkness upon the water covered the spot where the craft had been.

Walter felt the breath of Malachi Nasuno suddenly warm against his left ear. He turned to face the heavy-boned, deep-lined features of the old professional soldier.

'What is it?' asked Malachi, quietly. 'Why alarm the boy?'

'I wanted him to get away – if he can,' answered Walter. 'The rest of us are done for.'

Malachi's craggy, hundred-year-old face hardened like cooling metal and the grey thickets of his brows pulled close together.

'Speak for yourself,' he said. 'When I'm dead, I'm dead. But I'm not dead yet. What is it?'

'I don't know,' said Walter. He lifted the cube from his robes and showed it. 'All I know is I've had this warning.'

'More of your Exotic hocus-pocus,' growled Malachi. But the growl was only half disdainful. 'I'll go warn Obadiah.'

'There's no time.' Walter's hand on a still-massive forearm stopped the ex-soldier. 'Obadiah's been ready to meet that personal God of his for years now, and any minute we're liable to have eyes watching what we do. The less we seem to be expecting anything, the better Hal's chance to get away.'

Far up along the shadowed margin of the lake, the gaudy shape of a nesting harlequin duck, disturbed from some tall waterweeds below overhanging bushes, burst suddenly into the open, crying out, and fluttered, half-running, half-flying, across the darkened surface of the water to another part of the shore. Walter breathed out in relief.

'Good lad,' he said. 'Now, if he'll just stay hidden.'

'He'll stay,' said Malachi, grimly. 'He's not a lad now, but a man. You and Obadiah keep forgetting that.'

'A man, at sixteen?' said Walter. The ready tears of age were unexpectedly damp against the outer corners of his eyes. 'So soon?'

'Man enough,' grunted Malachi. 'Who's coming? Or what?'

'I don't know,' answered Walter. 'What I showed you was just a device to warn of a sharp pressure increase of the ontogenetic energies, moving in on us. You remember I told you one of the last things I was able to have them do on Mara was run calculations on the boy; and the calculations indicated high probability of his intersection with a pressure-climax of the current historical forces before his seventeenth year.'

2

'Well, if it's only energies –' Malachi snorted.

'Don't fool yourself!' said Walter, almost sharply for a Maran. 'There'll be men or things to manifest its effect when it gets here, just as a tornado manifests a sudden drop in air pressure. Perhaps –' He broke off. Malachi's gaze had moved away from the Maran. 'What is it?'

'Others, perhaps,' said Malachi, quietly. His generous nostrils spread, almost sniffing the cooling air, tinged now by the sky-pink of the sunset that was beginning to flood between the white-touched mountain peaks.

'Why do you say that?' Walter glanced covertly around, but saw nothing.

'I'm not sure. A hunch,' said Malachi.

Walter felt coldness within him.

'We've done wrong to our boy,' he almost whispered. Malachi's eyes whipped back to focus on him.

'Why?' demanded the Dorsai ex-soldier.

'We've trained him to meet men – men and women at most,' whispered Walter, crouching under his feeling of guilt. 'And these devils are loose now on the fourteen worlds.'

'The Others aren't "devils"!' snapped Malachi, not bothering to keep his voice down. 'Mix your blood and mine, and Obadiah's in with it – mix together blood of all the Splinter Cultures if you want to, and you still get men. Men make men – nothing else. You don't get anything out of a pot you don't put into it.'

'Other Men and Women. Hybrids.' Walter shivered. 'People with half a dozen talents in one skin.'

'What of it?' growled Malachi. 'A man lives, a man dies. If he lives well and dies well, what difference does it make what kills him?'

'But this is our Hal –'

'Who has to die someday, like everyone else. Straighten up!' muttered Malachi. 'Don't they grow any backbones on the Exotics?'

Walter pulled himself together. He stood tall, breathed deeply and with control for a few seconds, then put on peace like a cloak.

'You're right,' he said. 'At least Hal's had all we could give him, the three of us, in skill and knowledge. And he's got the creativity to be a great poet, if he lives.'

'Poet!' said Malachi, bleakly. 'There's a few thousand more useful things he could do with his life. Poets –'

He broke off. His eyes met Walter's with abrupt warning.

Walter's eyes acknowledged the message. He folded his hands in the wide sleeves of his blue robe with a gesture of completion.

'But poets are men, too,' he said, as cheerfully and casually as someone making light argument for its own sake. 'That's why, for example, I think so highly of Alfred Noyes, among the nineteenth century poets. You know Noyes, don't you?'

'Should I?'

'I think so,' said Walter. 'Of course, I grant you no one remembers anything but *The Highwayman*, out of all his poems, nowadays. But *Tales of a Mermaid Tavern*, and that other long poem of his – *Sherwood* – they've both got genius in them. You know, there's that part where Oberon, the king of elves and fairies, is telling his retainers about the fact Robin Hood is going to die, and explaining why the fairies owe Robin a debt –'

'Never read it,' grunted Malachi, ungraciously.

'Then I'll quote it for you,' said Walter. 'Oberon is talking to his own kind and he tells about one of them whom Robin once rescued from what he thought was nothing worse than a spider's web. And what Noyes had Oberon say is – listen to this now –

' ". . . He saved her from the clutches of that Wizard,
'That Cruel Thing, that dark old Mystery,
'Whom ye all know and shrink from . . .!" '

Walter broke off, for a thin, pale-faced young man in a dark business suit, holding a void pistol with a long, narrow, wire-coil-shielded barrel, had stepped from the lilac bushes behind Malachi. A moment later another gunman joined him. Turning, Walter saw yet two more had appeared from the bushes at his end of the terrace. The four pistols covered the two old men.

' ". . . Plucked her forth, so gently that not one bright rainbow gleam upon her wings was clouded. . . ." ' A deep, vibrant voice finished the quotation, and a very tall, erect man with dark hair and lean, narrow-boned face, carrying the book Walter had just been reading with one long finger holding a place in its pages, stepped through the same french window from which Walter had come a few moments before.

'. . . But you see?' he went on, speaking now to Walter, 'how it goes downhill, gets to be merely pretty and ornate, after that first burst of strength you quoted? Now, if you'd chosen instead the song of Blondin the Minstrel, from that same poem –'

His voice took on sudden strength and richness – half-chanting the quoted lines in the fashion of the plainsong of the medieval monks.

'Knight on the narrow way,
Where wouldst thou ride?
"Onward," I heard him say,
"Love, to thy side!" '

'. . . then I'd have had to agree with you.'

Walter bent his head a little with bare politeness. But there was a traitorous stir in his chest. The magnificent voice, the tall, erect figure before him, plucked at Walter's senses, trained by a lifetime of subtleties, with the demand for appreciation he would have felt toward a Stradivarius in the hands of some great violinist.

4

Against his will, Walter felt the pull of a desire – to which, of course, yielding was unthinkable – to acknowledge the tall man as if this other was a master, or a king.

'I don't think we know you,' said Walter slowly.

'Ahrens is my name. Bleys Ahrens,' said the tall man. 'And you needn't be worried. No one's going to be hurt. We'd just like to use this estate of yours for a short meeting during the next day or two.'

He smiled at Walter. The power of his different voice was colored by a faint accent that sounded like archaic English. His face held a straight-boned, unremarkable set of features that had been blended and molded by the character lines around the mouth and eyes into something like handsomeness. The direct nose, the thin-lipped mouth, the wide, high forehead and the brilliant brown eyes were all softened by those lines into an expression of humorous kindness.

Beneath that face, his sharply square and unusually wide shoulders, which would have looked out of proportion on a shorter man, seemed no more than normal above the unusual height of his erect, slim body. That body stood relaxed now, but unconsciously balanced, like the body of a yawning panther. And the pale-faced young gunmen gazed up at him with the worshipping gaze of hounds.

'We?' asked Walter.

'Oh, a club of sorts. To tell you the truth, you'd do better not to worry about the matter at all.' Ahrens continued to smile at Walter, and looked about at the lake and the wooded margin of it that could be seen from the terrace.

'There ought to be two more of you here, shouldn't there?' he said, turning to Walter again. 'Another tutor your own age, and your ward, the boy named Hal Mayne? Where would they be, now?'

Walter shook his head, pleading ignorance. Ahrens' gaze went to Malachi, who met it with the indifference of a stone lion.

'Well, we'll find them,' said Ahrens lightly. He looked back at Walter. 'You know, I'd like to meet that boy. He'd be . . . what? Sixteen now?'

Walter nodded.

'Fourteen years since he was found . . .' Ahrens' voice was frankly musing. 'He must have some unusual qualities. He'd have had to have them – to stay alive, as a child barely able to walk, alone on a wrecked ship, drifting in space for who-knows-how-long. Who were his parents – did they ever find out?'

'No,' said Walter. 'The log aboard showed only the boy's name.'

'A remarkable boy . . .' said Ahrens again. He glanced out around the lake and grounds. 'You say you're sure you don't know where he is now?'

'No,' answered Walter.

Ahrens glanced at Malachi, inquiringly.

'Commandant?'

5

Malachi snorted contemptuously.

Ahrens smiled as warmly on the ex-soldier as he had at Walter, but Malachi was still a stone lion. The tall man's smile faded and became wistful.

'You don't approve of Other Men like me, do you?' he said, a little sadly. 'But times have changed, Commandant.'

'Too bad,' said Malachi, dryly.

'But too true,' said Ahrens. 'Did it ever occur to you your boy might be one of us? No? Well, suppose we talk about other things if that suggestion bothers you. I don't suppose you share your fellow tutor's taste for poetry? Say, for something like Tennyson's *Morte D'Arthur* – a piece of poetry about men and war?'

'I know it,' said Malachi. 'It's good enough.'

'Then you ought to remember what King Arthur has to say in it about changing times,' said Ahrens. 'You remember – when Arthur and Sir Bedivere are left alone at the end and Sir Bedivere asks the King what will happen now, with all the companionship of the Round Table dissolved, and Arthur himself leaving for Avalon. Do you remember how Arthur answers, then?'

'No,' Malachi said.

'He answers –' and the voice of Ahrens rang out in all its rich power again, '*The old order changeth, giving place to new . . .*' Ahrens paused and looked at the old ex-soldier significantly.

'– *And God fulfills himself in many ways – lest one good custom should corrupt the world*,' interrupted a harsh, triumphant voice.

They turned, all together. Obadiah Testator, the third of Hal Mayne's tutors, was being herded out through the french window into their midst, at the point of a void pistol by a fifth young gunman.

'You forgot to finish the quotation,' rasped Obadiah at Ahrens. 'And it applies to your kind too, Other Man. In God's eye you, also, are no more than a drift of smoke and the lost note of a cymbal. You, too, are doomed at His will – like that!'

He had come on, farther than his young guard had intended, to snap his bony fingers with the last word, under the very nose of Ahrens. Ahrens started to laugh and then his face changed suddenly.

'Posts!' he snapped.

Tension sprang like invisible lightning across the terrace. Of the four gunmen already there, three had left off covering Walter and Malachi to aim at Obadiah, as he snapped his fingers. One only still covered Malachi. Now, at the whip of Ahrens' voice, the errant gunmen pulled their weapons almost in panic back to their original targets.

'Oh, you fools, you young fools!' said Ahrens softly to them. 'Look at me!'

Their pale and guilty glances sidled back to his face.

'The Maran –' Ahrens pointed at Walter, 'is harmless. His people taught him that violence – and any violence – would cripple his thinking processes. And the Fanatic here is worth perhaps one gun. But you see that old man there?'

He pointed at the unmoved Malachi.

'I wouldn't lock one of you, armed as you are, with him, unarmed, in an unlighted room, and give a second's hope to the chance of seeing you alive again.'

He paused, while the gunmen cringed before him.

'Three of you cover the Commandant,' he went on at last, quietly. 'And the other two watch our religious friend here. I'll –' he smiled softly at them, 'undertake to try to defend myself against the Maran.'

The aim of the pistols shifted obediently, leaving Walter uncovered. He felt a moment's pang of something like shame. But the fine engine of that mind of his, to which Ahrens had referred, had come to life; and the unprofitable emotion he had briefly felt was washed away by a new train of thought. Meanwhile, Ahrens had looked back at Obadiah.

'You're not exactly a lovable sort of man, you know,' he told the Friendly.

Obadiah stood, unawed and unchangeable. Fanatic against fanaticism, apostate to the totalitarian hyper-religiosity of the Splinter Culture that had birthed him, the Friendly loomed almost as tall as Ahrens. But from that point on any comparisons between them went different ways.

Face to face with the obvious necessity now of his own death to protect the boy he had tutored – for Obadiah was no fool and Walter, from fourteen years of living with the Fanatic, saw that the other had already grasped the situation – Obadiah was regarding the terminal point of his life neither with the workmanlike indifference of Malachi, nor with the philosophical acceptance of Walter, but with a fierce, dark, and burning joy.

Grim-countenanced, skull-featured and lath-thin from a life of self-discipline, nothing was left of Obadiah in his eighty-fourth year but a leathery and narrow lantern of gray-black skin and bones. It was a lantern illuminated by an all-consuming inner faith in his individually-conceived God – the God who in gentleness and charity was the direct antithesis of the dark and vengeful Lord of Obadiah's Culture, and the direct, acknowledged antithesis of Obadiah, himself.

Oblivious now to Ahrens' humor, as to all other unimportant things, he folded his arms and looked directly into the taller man's eyes.

'Woe to you,' he said, calmly, 'to you, Other Man, and all of your breed. And again I say, woe unto you!'

For a second, meeting the deep-sunk, burning eyes in that dark, bony face, Ahrens frowned slightly. His gaze turned and went past Obadiah to the gunman covering him.

'The boy?' Ahrens asked.

'We looked . . .' the young man's voice was husky, almost

7

whispering. 'He's nowhere . . . nowhere around the house.'

Ahrens wheeled sharply to look at Malachi, and Walter.

'If he was off the grounds one of you'd know it?'

'No. He . . .' Walter hesitated uncertainly, 'might have gone for a hike, or a climb in the mountains . . .'

He saw Ahrens' brown eyes focus upon him. As he looked, without warning the dark pupils of them seemed to grow and swell, as if they would finally fill the whole field of Walter's vision. Again, the emotional effect of the strange voice and commanding presence rang in his memory.

'Now, that's foolish of you,' said Walter, quietly, making no effort to withdraw his attention from the compelling gaze of Ahrens. 'Hypnotic dominance of any form needs at least the unconscious cooperation of the subject. And I am a Maran Exotic.'

The pupils were suddenly normal again. This time, however, Ahrens did not smile.

'There's something going on here . . .' he began, slowly. But Walter had already recognized the fact that time had run out.

'All that's different,' he interrupted, 'is that you've been underestimating me. The unexpected, I think some general once said, is worth an army –'

And he launched himself across the few feet of distance separating them, at Ahrens' throat.

It was a clumsy charge, made by a body and mind untrained to even the thought of physical violence; and Ahrens brushed it aside with one hand, the way he might have brushed aside the temper tantrum of a clumsy child. But at the same time the gunman behind Obadiah fired; it felt as if something heavy struck Walter in the side. He found himself tumbling to the terrace.

But, useless as his attack had been, it had distracted at least the one armed guard; and in that split second of distraction, Obadiah hurled himself – not at either of the gunmen guarding him, but at one of those covering Malachi.

Malachi himself had been in movement from the first fractional motion of Walter's charge. He was on one of the two still holding pistols trained on him, before the first man could fire. And the charge from the gun of the other passed harmlessly through the space the old soldier had occupied a second before.

Malachi chopped down the gunman he had reached as someone might chop a flower stalk with one swipe of an open hand. Then he turned, picked up the man who had missed him, and threw that gunman into the fire-path of the discharge from the pistols of the two who had been covering Obadiah – just as the remaining armed man, caught in Obadiah's grasp, managed to fire twice.

In that same moment, Malachi reached him; and they went down together, the gunman rolling on top of the old man.

From the level of the terrace stones, lying half on his side, Walter stared at the ruin his charge had made. Obadiah lay fallen with his head twisted around so that his open and unmoving eyes stared blankly in Walter's direction. He did not move. No more did the man Malachi had chopped down, nor the other gunman the ex-soldier had thrown into the fire from his companions' pistols. One other gunman, knocked down by the thrown man, was twitching and moaning strangely on the terrace.

Of the two guards remaining, one lay still on top of Malachi, who had ceased to move, and the other was still on his feet. He turned to face Ahrens and cringed before the devastating blaze of the Other Man's gaze.

'You fools, you fools!' said Bleys softly. 'Didn't I just get through telling you to concentrate on the Dorsai?'

The remaining gunman shrank in on himself in silence.

'All right,' said Bleys, sighing. 'Pick him up.' He indicated the moaning man and turned to the gunman on top of the silent figure of Malachi.

'Wake up.' Bleys prodded the man on top with his toe. 'It's all over.'

The man he had prodded rolled off Malachi's body and sprawled on the stones with his head at an odd angle to his body. His neck was broken. Bleys drew in a slow breath.

'Three dead – and one hurt,' he said as if to himself. 'Just to destroy three unarmed old teachers. What a waste.' He shook his head and turned back to the gunman who was lifting the moaning man.

They think I'm already dead, too, then, thought Walter, lying on the flagstones.

The realization came to him without much surprise. Bleys was already holding open the french window so that the wounded man could be half-carried inside the library by his companion. Bleys followed, his finger still marking a place in the volume of Noyes' poetry Walter had originally been reading. The french window closed. Walter was left alone with the dead, and the dying light of day.

He was aware that the charge from the void pistol had taken him in the side; and a certain feeling of leakage inside him confirmed his belief that the wound was mortal. He lay waiting for his personal end and it grew in him after a moment that it was something of a small victory that neither Ahrens nor the surviving gunman had realized he was still alive.

He had stolen several minutes more of life. That was a small victory, to add to the large victory that there was now no one from whom the lightning of Bleys' multi-talented mind could deduce the unique value of Hal. A value that, since it was connected to a possible pressure climax of the ontogenetic energies, could be as dangerous to the Other Men as they would be to Hal once they realized he might pose a threat to them.

It was this awareness of Hal as a possible danger that Walter had been so concerned to hide from Ahrens. Now he had done so. Now, they would probably search the grounds for the boy, but not with any particular urgency; and so, perhaps, Hal could escape. Walter felt a modest surge of triumph.

But the sunset was red, and deepening around him as well as around the other silent bodies; and the feeling of triumph faded. His life was leaking fast from him, and he realized now, for the first time, that he had never wanted to die. If only, he thought, I could have lived to think a little longer.

He felt a moment's unutterable and poignant feeling of regret. It seemed to him suddenly that if he had existed only a few more hours, some of the answers he had sought all his life might have come to him. But then that feeling, too, faded; the light seemed to darken swiftly about him, and he died.

The sun was now setting. Shortly, its rays left the stone terrace and even the dark slates of the house rooftop. Darkness brimmed in the area below the mountains, and the french windows above the terrace flagstones glowed yellow from the lights in the library. For a little while the sky, too, was light; but this also went, and left only the brilliant pinpoints of gleaming stars in a velvet-black, moonless sky.

Down by the margin of the lake, the tall weeds rising out of the black water by the shore stirred. Nearly without a sound, the tall, sapling-thin, shadowy figure of a sixteen-year-old boy hoisted itself up on the grassy bank and stood erect there, dripping and shivering, staring at the terrace and the lighted house.

CHAPTER TWO

For a moment only he stood staring. He felt numb, set apart from reality. Something had happened up on the terrace. He had witnessed it, but there was a barrier, a wall in his mind that blocked him off from remembering exactly what had taken place. In any case, there was no time now to examine it. An urgency implanted long since against just such a moment as this was pushing him hard, urging him along a path toward certain rehearsed actions that had been trained in him against this time when even thought would be impossible. Obeying that urging, he slipped back out of sight among the greenery that surrounded the lake.

Here, in the dimness, he went swiftly around the lake until he came to a small building. He opened its door and stepped into its unlighted interior.

It was a toolshed full of equipment for keeping the grounds in order; anyone unfamiliar with it would have tripped over any of several dozen pieces of such equipment within two steps beyond the door. But Hal Mayne, although he turned on no illumination, moved lightly among them without touching anything, as if his eyes could see in this kind of darkness.

It had been, in fact, one small part of his training – finding his way blindfolded about the interior of this shed. Certainly now, by practice and touch alone, he found a shelf against the wall, turned it on a hidden pivot at its midpoint and opened a shallow, secret compartment between two studs of the building's back wall. Five minutes later, he slipped back outdoors with the compartment reclosed behind him. But now he wore dry clothes, gray slacks and blue half-jacket. He carried a small travel bag, and had tucked into an interior pocket of the half-jacket papers that would authorize him to travel to any of the fourteen inhabited worlds, plus the cards and vouchers that would make available to him enough Earth and interplanetary funds to get him to a number of off-world destinations.

He went now, among the night-dark trees and bushes once more, in the direction of the house. He was deliberately not thinking – he had not thought from the moment he had seen the flag dipped and had responded by hiding in the lake. Thought was trying to come back, but training still held it at bay; and for the moment there was no

11

will or urge in him to break through the wall in his mind.

He was not thinking, only moving – but he moved like a wisp of mist over the night ground. His lessons had begun as soon as he could walk, at the hands of three experts who had literally lived for him and had poured into him everything that they had to teach. From his standpoint, it had all seemed merely natural and normal, that he should come to know what he knew and be able to do what he did. It was without effort, almost unconsciously, that he went through the dark woods so easily and silently, where almost anyone else would have blundered and made noise.

He came at last to the terrace, now deep in shadow – too buried in darkness to show what still lay there, even though light shone from the library windows at its inner edge. His training kept him apart from the shadow, he did not look into it, did not investigate. Instead, he went toward the edge of one of the windows of the house, from which he could look down into the library itself.

The floor of the library was nearly two meters below the level of the terrace; so that, from within, the window he looked through was high in an outer wall. The room itself was both long and high, its floor-to-ceiling bookshelves warmly stuffed with some thousands of antique, printed and bound volumes holding works like those poems of Alfred Noyes which Walter the InTeacher had been fond of reading. In the fireplace at one end a fire had just been lit, to throw the ruddy, comforting light of its flames upon the heavy furniture, the books, and the ceiling. The two men in the room stood talking. They were both so tall that their shoulders were almost on a level with Hal's feet. They stood face to face; and there was a certain tenseness about the two of them, like partners who might at any moment become adversaries.

One was the tall man he had seen earlier on the terrace. The other was a man nearly the same height, but outweighing the slim man by half again as much. Not that the other man was fat. He was merely powerfully built, with the sort of round, thick arms and body that, even in lesser proportion on someone of normal height, would have made him seem formidable. His face was round and cheerful under a cap of curly, jet-black hair, and he smiled merrily. Facing the taller, slimmer man, he appeared coarse-bodied, almost untidy, in the soft material of the slacks and cloth jacket that made up the maroon business suit he wore. In contrast, the taller man – in gray slacks and black half-cape – seemed tailored and remote.

Hal moved close to the edge of the pane to see if he could hear their talk; and the words inside came faintly through the insulated glass to his ear.

'. . . tomorrow, at the latest,' the tall man was saying. 'They should all be here, then.'

'They'd better be. I hold you responsible, Bleys.' It was the big, black-haired man speaking.

'When didn't you, Dahno?'

Distantly, a point of information clicked in the back of Hal's mind. Dahno, or Danno – it was spelled various ways – was the one usually spoken of as the leader of the loose Mafia-sort of organization by which the Other People were said to be increasing their hold upon the inhabited worlds. The Others tended to be known to their people by first names only – like kings. Bleys . . . that would be Bleys Ahrens, one of the lesser leaders of the Others.

'Always, Bleys. As now. Your dogs made something of a mess taking over here.'

'Your dogs, Dahno.'

The thick-bodied giant brushed the answer away.

'The dogs I lent you. It was your job to set up for the Conference here, Mr. Vice-Chairman.'

'Your dogs aren't trained, Mr. Chairman. They like killing because they think it proves their value in our eyes. That makes them unreliable with void pistols.'

Dahno chuckled again. His eyes were hard and bright.

'Are you pushing me, Bleys?'

'Pushing back.'

'All right – within limits. But there'll be fifty-three of us here by tomorrow. The bodies don't matter as long as they're cleaned up, out of the way. Then we can forget them.'

'The boy won't,' said Bleys.

'Boy?'

'The ward these three were raising and tutoring.'

Dahno snorted faintly.

'You're worried about a boy?' he said.

'I thought you were the one who talked about neatness, Dahno. The old men died before they could tell us about him.'

Dahno brushed the air again – a little impatiently. Hal watched him, standing in darkness outside the swath of light from the window.

'Why would the dogs think to keep them alive?'

'Because I didn't tell them to kill.' Bleys' voice did not seem to have been raised, but it came with peculiar clearness to Hal's ears through the glass. Dahno cocked his head to look at the slim man, his face for a moment not cheerful, but merely watching.

'Aside from that,' he said, his own voice unchanged, 'what could they tell us?'

'More.' Bleys' voice was again as it had been earlier. 'Didn't you look at the prospectus on holding our Conference here? This place was set up under a trust established from the sale of an unregistered interstellar courier-class ship, which was found drifting near Earth, with the boy in it as a two-year-old child, or younger. No one else was aboard. I don't like mysteries.'

13

'It's all that Exotic blood in you that doesn't like mysteries,' Dahno said. 'Where would we be if we took the time to try to understand every mystery we came across? Our game is controlling the machinery, not understanding it. Tell me about another way a few thousand of us can hope to run fourteen worlds.'

'You could be right,' said Bleys. 'But still it's a careless attitude.'

'Bleys, my buck,' said Dahno. His voice changed only as slightly as Ahrens' had a moment before, but his eyes reflected the red light of the fire. 'I'm never careless. You know that.'

The night breeze freshened off the lake and a sudden small gust sent the branches of a lilac bush lashing against the pane of another of the library windows. Both of the men inside looked toward the sound at once. Hal stepped back noiselessly from the window, deeper into the shadow.

His training was urging him away, now. It was time to go. He half-swung toward the terrace, still not forming clearly in his mind the true picture of what was there, but with the empty feeling that what he was leaving was something to which he would never have a chance to return. But his training had anticipated that feeling also, and overrode it. He turned away from terrace and house alike, and moved off through the surrounding trees at a silent trot.

There were gravel-bed roads in the area for the traffic of air-cushion vehicles, but the way he took avoided them. He ran steadily, easily, through the pine-scented night air of the forest, his footsteps silent on the dead conifer needles underfoot and making only little more sound on the patches of bare rock and hard earth. His pace was a steady twelve kilometers an hour, and, in a little less than an hour and a half, he reached the small commercial center known as Thirkel. There were a dozen other such centers and two small towns that he could have reached in less distance and time; but an unconscious calculation from his training had led him to choose Thirkel.

Thanks to that calculation, at Thirkel he had only a fourteen minute wait before a regularly scheduled autobus stopped on its way into Bozeman, Montana. He was the only passenger boarding in the soft mountain night. He stepped aboard and displayed one of the credit tabs he now carried to the automatic control unit of the bus. The unit noted the charge for his travel, closed the doors behind him with a soft breath of air, and lifted the vehicle into the air again.

He came into Bozeman shortly after midnight and caught a shuttle to Salt Lake Pad. Then, as the early dawn was pinkening the sky beyond the surrounding mountains, he lifted in an orbital jitney on its run from that Pad to the gray-clad globe that was the Final Encyclopedia, swimming in orbit around Earth at sixteen hundred kilometers from its surface.

The jitney carried no more than fifty or sixty passengers – all of them having passed pre-clearance at the Earth end of the trip.

14

Among Hal's papers had been a continually-renewed scholar's passport for a single visit, under his own name. Earth, the Dorsai, Mara and Kultis were the only four worlds where the Others had not yet gotten control of the internal government. But on Earth, only the records of the Final Encyclopedia could be regarded as secure from prying by the Others; and so all credit and record transactions Hal had made since leaving his home had been achieved with papers or tabs bearing the name of Alan Semple. These he now destroyed, as the jitney lifted, and he was left carrying nothing to connect him with the false name he had temporarily used. The automated records at the Final Encyclopedia would be too well informed for him to hope to use a false name; but, in them, his real name would be safe.

Twelve hundred kilometers out from Earth's surface the jitney began its approach to the Final Encyclopedia. On the screen of his seat compartment Hal saw it first as a silver crescent, expanding as they moved out of Earth's shadow, to a small silver globe of reflected sunlight. But as they came closer, the small globe grew inexorably and the great size of the Encyclopedia began to show itself.

It was not just its size, however, that held Hal fixed in his seat, his attention captured by the screen as the massive sphere on it swelled and swelled. Unlike the other passengers aboard this jitney, he had been trained by Walter to a special respect for what the Encyclopedia promised. He had gazed at it countless times on screens like this one, but never when he himself was about to set foot in it.

The jitney was slowing now, matching velocities as it approached the sphere. Now that they were closer, Hal could see its surface looking as if it were shrouded in thick gray fog. This would be a result of the protective force-panels that interlocked around the Encyclopedia – a derivation of the phase-shift that had opened up faster-than-light communication and transportation between the worlds, four hundred years before. The force-panels were a discovery, and a closely guarded secret, of those on the Encyclopedia. It had been these which had given the structure the silvery appearance from a distance – as the gray mist of dawn close above the water of a lake seems silvered by the early light of day.

Within those panels, the Encyclopedia was invulnerable to any physical attack. Only at points where the panels joined were there soft spots that had to be conventionally armored; and it was to one of these soft spots the jitney was now headed to find a port in which to discharge its passengers.

Hidden within the shield provided by those panels, was the physical shape of the Encyclopedia: a structure of metal and magic – the metal from the veins of Earth and the magic of that same force that made possible the phase drive and the panels – so that there was no way for anyone to tell from observation alone what was material and what was force-panel about the corridors and rooms that made up the

15

Encyclopedia's interior. People within that structure did not move about as much as they were moved. The room they were occupying, on proper command, would become next door to the room to which they wished to go. Yet, also if they wished, there were distances of seemingly solid corridors to traverse and solid doors to open on places within the structure. . . .

Metal and magic . . . as a boy Hal Mayne had been led to an awe of the Encyclopedia, from as far back as he could remember. For the moment now, that awe reinforced the wall protecting him from what he might otherwise remember from only a few hours before. He remembered how it had been an Earthman, Mark Torre, who had conceived the Encyclopedia. But Mark Torre, and even Earth would never have managed to get it built on its own. A hundred and thirty years had been required to bring it to completion, and all the great wealth that the two rich Exotic Worlds of Mara and Kultis could spare for its construction. Its beginnings had been put together on the ground, just within the Exotic Enclave at the city of St. Louis, in North America. A hundred and two years later, the half-finished structure had been lifted into its first orbital position only two hundred and fifty kilometers above the Earth. Twelve years after that, the last of the work on it had been finished, and it had been placed here, in its final orbit.

Mark Torre's theory had postulated a dark area always existing in Man's knowledge of himself, an area where self-perception had to fail, as the perception of any viewing mechanism fails in the blind area where it, itself, exists. In that area, ran Torre's theory, the human race would at last find something which had been lost in the people of the Splinter Cultures on the younger worlds; and this, once found, would be the key to the race's last and greatest growth.

There was a largeness of dream and purpose about that theory, and the Encyclopedia itself, that had always resonated powerfully within Hal. That resonance touched him now as the jitney reached the point where the corners of four of the huge, insubstantial force-panels came together, and the jointure where their forces met dilated to reveal an aperture into the docking area that awaited them.

The jitney drifted in, very slowly it seemed, and settled into the cradle that waited for it. Abruptly, they were enclosed by a blaze of light. The aperture that had seemed so tiny as they had approached, now revealed itself to have the diameter of a chamber that dwarfed the jitney and was aswarm with human workers and machines.

Hal got to his feet and joined the procession of passengers moving to the exit port of the jitney. He stepped through the port, onto a sloping ramp and into a roar and clangor of sound, as the busy machines moved about the jitney on the metal floor and walls. Metal and magic . . . he went down the slope of the ramp and through a faintly hazy circle that was an entrance to the interior parts of the

Encyclopedia. As he stepped through that circle, all the noise behind him was cut off. He found himself being carried forward by a movable floor, down a corridor walled in soft light, in a muted hush that welcomed him after the noise he had just left, and seemed to soften even the low-voiced conversations of his fellow passengers.

The line slowed, stopped, moved forward a couple of paces, stopped again, moved, stopped. The passengers ahead were displaying their clearance papers to a wall screen from which a thin-faced, black-haired young man looked out at them.

'Fine. Thank you.' The young man nodded at the passenger ahead of Hal, and the passenger moved on. As Hal stepped level with the screen, the man moved aside out of camera range and a lively female face under a cloud of bright blonde hair, young enough to be that of a girl rather than of a woman, took the vacated space. Under the bright gold hair, she had a round, laughing expression and brown eyes with flecks of green swimming in their irises.

'I see . . .' She looked at Hal's papers as he held them up to the screen, then back to him. 'You're Hal Mayne? Fine.'

It seemed to Hal that her eye met his with a particular friendliness; and a comfort came to him from seeing her that for a second dangerously weakened the wall that hid things in the back of his mind. Then he moved on.

The corridor continued. The people in front of him were moving more quickly now, single file down it. Ahead, a voice was speaking to them out of nowhere in particular.

'. . . If you'll please pause at the point where the corridor widens, and listen. Tell us if you hear anything. This is the Transit Point, at the center of the Index Room. You are now at the exact center of the communication system of the Encyclopedia. We do not expect you to hear anything; but if any of you do, will you speak up. . . .'

More magic . . . they had moved what seemed like only a hundred meters; but now they were at the very center of the sphere that was the Encyclopedia. But neither Walter the InTeacher nor anyone else had ever mentioned to him anything about a Transit Point. He was not yet at the wide stationary spot that had been spoken of, but he found himself listening, as if there might be something he could hear even before he reached it. Vaguely, he felt the request to listen as if it had been a challenge. If there was something to hear there, he should be able to pick it up. He found himself straining to hear.

Almost – he could see the wide, unmoving spot now and he was only two people back from it – he could imagine that he was hearing something. But it was probably only the people who had already passed the Transit Point, discussing it among themselves. There was something familiar about their voices. He could not identify them but there was still a feeling of familiarity, although they seemed to be speaking a language he did not know. He had been trained to break

17

down unfamiliar languages into familiar forms. If it was Indo-European . . . yes, it seemed to be a Romance tongue of some sort, one of the modern derivatives of Latin.

But their conversations were very loud now, and there seemed to be a number of them all talking at once. There was a single person left in front of him before he would reach the Transit Point. How could they expect anyone to hear anything at the Point if they were talking like this ahead of it – and behind, too, for that matter? The voices were all around him. Everybody in the line must be talking. The man just ahead of him stepped on, clearing the Transit Point. Hal stepped into it, stopped there, and the voices exploded.

Not tens of them, not hundreds or thousands, or even millions – but billions and trillions of voices in countless languages, arguing, shouting, calling to him. Only, they did not merge into one great, voiceless roar, like the radio roar of a universe. They each remained distinct and separate – unbelievably, he heard each one; and among them there were three he knew, calling out to him, warning him. The voice of Walter the In Teacher, of Malachi Nasuno, of Obadiah Testator – and with his identification of those three voices, the mental wall that had been protecting him finally crumbled and went down.

The Transit Point whirled around him. He was conscious, as of something heard from a little distance, of a sound coming from his own throat. He spun, staggered, and would have fallen – but he was caught and held upright. It was the young woman from the screen, the one with the green flecks in her eyes, who was holding him. Somehow she was here, physically, beside him; and she was not as small as he had thought her to be when he had seen her face on the screen. Still, his awkward, long-boned length was not easy to support; and, almost immediately, there were two men with her.

'Easy . . . hold him . . .' said one man; and something touched deep inside him, triggering a darkness like the spreading stain of biologic ink pushed out by a fleeing octopus. It flooded all through him, hiding all things in utter darkness, even his memory of what had happened on the terrace.

Gradually he roused once more, to silence and to peace. He was alone, naked, in a bed in a room walled by slowly changing, pastel colors. Besides the bed, and the table-surface beside it, there were a couple of chair floats hanging in the air, a desk, and a small pool with blue sides and floor that made the water in it seem much deeper than he guessed it actually to be. He propped himself up on one elbow and looked about him. The room had a disconcerting property of seeming to expand in the direction in which he was looking, although he was not conscious of any actual movement of its walls or floor. He looked around and then back at the bed in which he lay.

It had never really occurred to him as an important fact –

although he had always been aware of it – that he had been raised under conditions that were deliberately spartan and archaic. It had always seemed only natural to him that the books he read should be heavy things of actual paper, that there should be no moving walkways in his home, or that the furniture there should be uniformly of solid, material construction, with physical legs that supported it upon the floor, rather than devices that appeared to float in midair, and to appear out of that same air of dissolve back into it at the touch of a control.

This was the first time he had ever awakened in a force bed. He knew what it was, of course, but he was totally unprepared for the comfort of it. To the eye, he seemed to lie half-immersed in a white cloud perhaps twenty centimeters thick, which floated in the air with its underside an equal distance above the floor of the room. The white cloud-stuff wrapped him in warmth against the cooler air, and that portion of it which was underneath him became firm enough to support him in whatever position he took. Right now the elbow on which he leaned was upheld as if by a warm cupped hand, although to his eye it was merely buried to the depth of half his forearm in the thick mist.

He sat up, swinging his legs over the side of the bed – and with that movement, memory came back completely, like a silent body blow. He saw the terrace and what had happened there in the eye of his mind, as he had watched it all through the screen of lakeside branches. Overcome, he huddled on the edge of the bed, his face in his hands; and for a moment the universe rocked around him and his mind ran screaming from what it now saw.

But there was no longer any wall to hold it back from him, and after a while he came to some sort of terms with it. He lifted his face from his hands again. The color had gone out of the walls of the room. The sensors in them had read the changes in the temperature and humidity of his skin, as well as half a hundred other tiny signals of his body, and accurately reflected his change in emotion. Now the color of the room was a dull, utilitarian gray, as bleak as a chamber carved from rock.

A terrible feeling of rebellion erupted in him, a fury that such a thing as had happened should have been allowed to take place; and riding the energy wave of that fury as the wall glowed into the redness of heated iron around him, his training was triggered again, and pushed him to a further action.

Under the force of his will his consciousness gathered itself, focused on the glint of a single point of light from one corner of a float and closed in on that point until it was the only thing he saw. Through that point, as through a doorway, his mind moved with its Exotic training into a discipline that was partly self-hypnosis, partly a freeing of a direct channel from his awareness into his own

19

unconsciousness. His vision moved back and out, away once more from the point of light, and he saw all the room again. Only now, there seemed to be three figures sitting in the available floats; and they were Walter, Malachi and Obadiah.

The men who had raised and tutored him were not really there, of course. He knew that. Even as he spoke to them now, he knew that it was not actually they who answered, but constructs of them, created by his imagination from his countless memories of the attitudes and reactions he had observed in them during their lives together. It was, in fact, his own knowledge of them that was answering him, with their voices, uttering the words that he knew they would say if they could be here with him now. The technique was a discipline that had been instilled against a moment just like this one, a moment in which he would need their help and they would no longer be around to give it. But in that first second as he looked at them, it was not a cry for help he threw at them, but an accusation.

'You didn't have to!' He was half-sobbing. 'You let them kill you and leave me alone; and you didn't have to!'

'Oh, Hal!' Pain was strong in Walter's voice. 'We had to protect you.'

'I didn't ask you to protect me! I don't want to be protected. I wanted you alive! And you let them shoot you!'

'Boy,' said Malachi, gruffly, 'you were prepared for this day. We taught you that something like what happened could happen, and what you must do if it did.'

Hal did not answer. Now that he had opened the door to his grief it took possession of him utterly. He huddled on the edge of the bed, facing them, weeping.

'I didn't know . . .' he sobbed.

'Child,' said Obadiah, 'you've been taught how to handle pain. Don't fight it. Accept it. Pain alters nothing for him who is beyond such things.'

'But I'm not beyond it.' Hal was rocking in his misery, rhythmically rocking on the edge of the bed, backward and forward.

'Obadiah is right, Hal,' said Walter, softly. 'You were taught; and you know how to handle this moment.'

'You don't care, none of you . . . you don't understand!' Hal rocked back and forth.

'Of course we understand.' Walter's voice sounded the note of the suffering in him, evoked by the suffering in Hal. 'We were the only family you had; and now it seems to you you've got no one. You feel as if everything's been taken away. But it's not like that. You still have a family – an enormous family, made up of everyone else in the human race.'

Hal shook his head – back and forth, back and forth – as he rocked.

'But you do,' said Walter. 'Yes, I know. Right now you think there's no one on the fourteen worlds could take the place of those you've lost. But there will be. You'll find all things in people. You'll find those who hate you and those who love you – and those you'll love. I know you can't believe that, now; but it will be.'

'And there's more than love,' said Malachi, suddenly. 'You'll find that out. In the end you may have to do without love to get done what you have to do.'

'That will come,' said Obadiah, 'if God wills. But there's no reason the child should have to face that test, yet. Leave it to the future, Malachi.'

'The future is here,' growled Malachi. 'He won't survive the forces against him by sitting on a bed and crying. Boy, straighten up –' The command was harsh, but the tone in which it was uttered was not. 'Try to take hold. You have to plan what to do. The dead are dead. The living owe their concern to the living, even if the living are themselves.'

'Hal,' said Walter, still gently, but insistently. 'Malachi is right. Obadiah is right. By clinging to your grief, now, you only put off the moment when you have to think of more important things.'

'No,' said Hal, shaking his head. 'No.'

He shut his mind against them. It was unthinkable that he should let go any of the grief inside him. To do so, even in the smallest way, threw the earth of certainty upon the doubtless unmarked graves of these three he had loved and still loved. But they continued to talk, saying the things he had heard them say so many times, in the ways he remembered them saying such things; and gradually he began, in spite of himself, to listen.

The shock of what had happened had driven him nearly back into being a very young child again, with all the terrible helplessness of the young. But now, as the familiar voices spoke back and forth around him, he began to come back up to the relative maturity of his sixteen years.

'. . . he must hide somewhere,' Walter was saying.

'Where?' said Malachi.

'I'll go to the Exotics,' Hal surprised himself by saying. 'I could pass for a Maran – couldn't I, Walter?'

'What about that?' Malachi demanded of the InTeacher, 'Would your people give him up to the Others?'

'Not willingly,' said Walter. 'But you're right. If the Others located him there and put pressure on, they couldn't keep him. The Exotics are free of Other control on their own worlds, but their interplanetary connections are vulnerable – and two worlds have to take precedence in importance over one boy.'

'He could hide on Harmony or Association,' Obadiah said. 'The Other People control our cities, but outside those cities there are those who will never work with the Belial-spawn. Such people of mine would not give him up.'

'He'd have to live like an outlaw,' Walter said. 'He's too young to fight yet.'

'I can fight!' said Hal. 'Others, or anyone else!'

'Be quiet, boy!' growled Malachi. 'They'd have you on toast for breakfast without getting up off their chairs. You're right, Walter. The Friendly Worlds aren't safe for him.'

'Then, the Dorsai,' said Hal. Malachi's gray thickets of eyebrows frowned at him.

'When you're ready and able to fight, then go to the Dorsai,' the old man said. 'Until that day, there's nothing they can do for you there.'

'Where, then?' said Obadiah. 'All other worlds but Earth are already under Other control. They'd only have to sniff him there, and he'd be gone with no one to aid him.'

'Still,' said Walter. 'It has to be one of the other worlds. Earth, here, is also no good. They'll be looking for him as soon as they unravel the full story of his life and our teaching. There're Exotic mixed breeds among them, like that tall man who was there at our death; and they, like me – like all of us trained on Mara or Kultis – know onto-genetics. They're a historic force, the Other People, and they'll know that for any such force there must be a counter-force. They'll have been watching for its appearance among the rest of the race, from the beginning. They'll take no chances of leaving Hal alive once they have his full story.'

'Newton, then,' said Obadiah. 'Let him hide among the laboratories and the ivory towers.'

'No,' said Malachi. 'They're all turtles, there, all clams. They pull back into their shell and pull the shell in after them. He'd stick out like a sore thumb among such people.'

'What about Ceta?' said Obadiah.

'That's where the Others are thickest – where the banking and the threads of interstellar trade are pulled,' said Malachi, irritably. 'Are you mad, Obadiah? Anyway, all of these unspecialized worlds, as well as old Venus and Mars, are places where none of the machinery of society is under any control but that of the Others. One slip and it'd be over for our boy.'

'Yes,' said Walter slowly. 'But Obadiah, you said all worlds but the Dorsai, the Exotics, the Friendlies and Earth were already under Others' control. There's one exception. The world they can't be bothered with because there's no real society there for them to want to control. Coby.'

'The mining world?' Hal stared at Walter. 'But there's nothing there for me to do but work in the mines.'

'Yes,' said Walter.

Hal continued to stare at the InTeacher.

'But . . .' words failed him. Mara, Kultis, the Friendly Worlds of Harmony and Association, and the Dorsai were all places to which he had longed to go. Any beyond these, any of the Younger Worlds were unknown, interesting places. But Coby. . . .

'It's like sending me to prison!' he said.

'Walter,' Malachi was looking at the InTeacher, 'I think you're right.'

He swung to face Hal.

'How old are you now, boy? You're due to turn seventeen in a month or so, aren't you?'

'In two weeks,' said Hal, his voice thinning at the sudden surge of old memories, of early birthday parties and all the years of his growing up.

'Seventeen –' said Malachi, looking again at Walter and at Obadiah. 'Three years in the mines and he'd be almost twenty –'

'Three years!' The cry broke from Hal.

'Yes, three years,' said Walter softly. 'Among the nameless and lost people there, you can do a better job of becoming nameless and lost, yourself, than you can do on any other world. Three years will bury you completely.'

'And he'll come out different,' said Obadiah.

'But I don't want to be different!'

'You must be,' said Malachi to him. 'That is, at least, if you're to survive.'

'But, three years!' said Hal again. 'That's nearly a fifth of my life so far. It's an eternity.'

'Yes,' said Walter; and Hal looked at him hopelessly. Walter, the gentlest of his three tutors, was the least likely to be moved once he had come to a decision. 'And it's because it'll be an eternity for you, Hal, that it'll be so useful. With all we tried to do for you, we've still raised you off in a corner, away from ordinary people. There was no choice for us, but still you're crippled by that. You're like a hothouse plant that can wither if it's suddenly set out in the weather.'

'Hothouse plant?' Hal appealed to Malachi, to Obadiah. 'Is that all I am? Malachi, you said I was as good as an average Dorsai my age, in my training. Obadiah, you said –'

'God help you, child,' said Obadiah, harshly. 'In what you are and in what we tried to make of you, you're a credit to us all. But the ways of the worlds are some of the things you do not know; and it's with those ways that you'll have to live and struggle before God brings you at last to your accomplishment and your rest. Your way cannot be in corners and byways any more – and I should have realized that when I suggested Newton as a place for you to go. You have to go out among your fellow men and women from now on and begin to learn from them.'

'They won't want to teach me,' said Hal. 'Why should they?'

'It's not for them to teach, but for you to learn,' said Obadiah.

'Learn!' said Hal. 'That's all you ever said to me, all of you – learn this! Learn that! Isn't it time I was doing something more than learning?'

'There is nothing more than learning,' said Walter; and in the InTeacher's voice Hal heard the absolute commitment of the three facing him that he should go to Coby. It was not something that he could argue against successfully. He was not being faced with an opinion by three other people, but by the calculation that was part of the pattern trained in him. That calculation had surveyed the options open to him and decided that his most secure future for the upcoming years lay on Coby.

Still, he was crushed by that decision. He was young and the thirteen other inhabited worlds of mankind glittered with promise like tempting jewels. As he had said, going into the mines would be like going to prison, and the three years – to him – would indeed be an eternity.

CHAPTER THREE

Hal did not know at what point the shades of his tutors left him. Simply, after a while, the floats were empty and he was alone once more. His mind had wandered from his need for them, and they had gone, back into the land of his memories, like the flames of blown-out candles.

But he felt better. Even with the dreary prospect of Coby facing him, he felt better now. Purpose had come back to life in him; and the evocation of the attitudes and certainties of his dead tutors had given him a certain amount of strength. Also, though he was not consciously aware of this, the basic vitality of his youth was lifting his spirits whether he wanted them lifted or not. He had too much sheer physical energy to do nothing but sit and mourn, in spite of the severity of the emotional wound their deaths had dealt him.

He dressed, examined the controls of his room and ordered in some food. He was eating this when his annunciator chimed.

He keyed the screen on his bedside table-surface; and the bright and cheerful face of the young woman from the Transit Point took shape in it.

'Hal Mayne?' she said. 'I'm Ajela, Special Assistant to Tam Olyn.'

There was a split-second before the second name she had mentioned registered on him. Tam Olyn was the Director of the Encyclopedia – had been its Director for eighty-odd years. He had originally been a top-level interplanetary newsman; but he had abandoned that as suddenly as a man might turn from the world into the seclusion of a monastery to step in, almost at the moment of his entrance there, to being the supreme authority of the Encyclopedia. Hal had learned all about the man in his studies; but he had never thought that he might someday be talking directly to one of the Director's close assistants.

'I'm honored to meet you,' he said automatically to the screen.

'Can I drop in on you?' Ajela asked. 'There's something we should talk about.'

Caution laid its hand on him.

'I'm just here temporarily,' he said. 'I'll be going out to one of the younger worlds as soon as I can get passage.'

'Of course,' she said. 'But meanwhile, if you wouldn't mind talking to me . . .'

'Oh, no. No, of course not.' He was aware that he fumbled, and he felt embarrassment kindle in him. 'Come along right now, if you want.'

'Thank you.'

The screen lost its image, returning to a uniform pearl gray without depth. Hastily, he finished his meal and pushed his emptied utensils down the disposal slot. They had hardly disappeared when the annunciator chimed again.

'Can I come in?' asked the voice of Ajela, from the blank screen.

'Certainly. Come along –' he went to the door but it opened before he could reach it, and she stepped through it.

She was wearing a loose saffron robe that tied at the waist and reached to her knees. In spite of her youth, she was clearly an Exotic; and she seemed to have the Exotic ability to make everything about her seem as if it could never have been otherwise. So the saffron robe seemed to him, in that first moment in which he really looked at her, as if it was the only thing she should ever wear. Her impact on him was so profound that he almost drew back defensively. He might, indeed, have been even more wary of her than he was; but the open, smiling face and disregard of pretense reassured his prickly young male fear of making the wrong move, suddenly finding himself face to face with a startlingly beautiful woman – he, who had had so little normal acquaintance with women of any age until now.

'You're all right now?' she asked him.

'Fine,' he said. 'I – thank you.'

'I'm sorry,' she said. 'If we could have warned you, we would have. But the way it is with the Transit Point, if we warn people, we'd never know . . . it's all right if I sit down?'

'Oh, of course!' He backed away and they sat down in facing floats.

'What wouldn't you know?' he asked, his unquenchable curiosity rising even above his feelings of social awkwardness.

'We'd never be sure that they weren't imagining what they said they heard.'

Hal shook his head.

'There wasn't any imagination in what I heard,' he said.

'No.' She was looking closely at him. 'I don't believe there was. What exactly did you hear?'

He looked at her closely, cautiously.

His mind was now almost completely recovered from the unsureness he had felt on first talking to her.

'I'd like to know more of what this is all about,' he said.

'Of course you would,' she said warmly. 'All right, I'll tell you. The fact is, early in the building of the Final Encyclopedia they discovered by accident that someone stepping into the Transit Point for the first time might hear voices. Not voices speaking to them –'

26

She stopped to gaze closely at him. 'Just voices, as if they were over-hearing them. Mark Torre, in his old age, was the first to hear them. But only Tam Olyn, the first time he stepped into the Encyclopedia, heard them so plainly that he collapsed – the way you did.'

Hal stared at her. All his training had ingrained in him the principle of going cautiously, the more unknown or strange the territory. What Ajela had just said was so full of unknown possibilities that he felt a danger in showing any reaction at all before he had had time to under-stand the matter. He waited, hoping she would simply talk on. But she did not. She only waited in her turn.

'Tam Olyn,' he said at last.

'Yes.'

'Just Tam Olyn and me? In all these years?'

'In all these years,' she said. Her voice had a note in it he could not interpret, a note that was almost sad, for no reason that he could under-stand. She watched him, he thought, with an odd sympathy.

'I think,' he said carefully, 'you ought to tell me all about this; and then give me a chance to think about it.'

She nodded.

'All right,' she said. 'Mark Torre conceived of the Encyclo-pedia – you know that. He was Earth-born, no Exotic, but the Exotics found his conception so in agreement with ontogenetics and our other theories of human and historical evolution that we ended by financing the building of this –' she gestured at the structure around them.

Hal nodded, waited.

'As I said, it was in his late years Mark Torre first heard the voices at the Transit Point.' She looked at him with a seriousness that was almost severity. 'He theorized then that what he'd heard was just the first evidence of the first small use by any individual of the potential of the Encyclopedia. It was as if someone who'd had no knowledge of what to listen for had suddenly tuned in to all the radio noise of the universe. Sorting out the useful information from that roar of noise, Torre said, would take experience.'

Again she paused, almost frowning at him. Hal nodded again, to show his appreciation of the importance of what she was saying.

'I see,' he said.

'This idea,' she went on, 'is what meshed with some of our theories on the Exotics, because it seemed to say that using the Encyclopedia the way Mark Torre dreamed of it being used – as a new sort of tool for the human mind – called for some special ability, an ability not yet to be found in all of the human race. Torre died without making any sense out of what he heard. But he was convinced someone would eventually. After him, Tam took charge here; but Tam's lived in the Encyclopedia all these years without learning how to handle or use what he hears.'

'Not at all?' Hal could not help interrupting.

'Not at all,' Ajela said, firmly.

27

'But, like Mark Torre, he's been certain that sooner or later some-one would come along who could; and when that finally happens the Encyclopedia is at last going to be put to use as what it was built to be, a tool to unravel the inner universe of the race – that inner universe that's been a dark and fearful mystery since people first started to be conscious of the fact they could think.'

Hal sat looking at her.

'And now,' he said, 'you – and Tam Olyn – you think I might be the one to use it?'

She frowned at him.

'Why are you so cautious . . . so fearful?' she asked.

He could not tell her. The implication he thought he heard in her voice was one of cowardice. He bristled instinctively.

'I'm not fearful,' he said, sharply. 'Just careful. I was always taught to be like that.'

She reacted instantly.

'I'm sorry,' she said with unexpected softness; and her eyes made him feel as if he had made a most unjustified inference from what she had said. 'Believe me, neither Tam nor I are trying to push you into anything. If you stop and think, you'll realize that what Mark Torre and Tam were thinking was something that never could be forced on anyone in any case. It'd be as impossible to force that as it'd be impossible to force someone to produce great art. A thing that'd be as great and new as that couldn't ever be forced into existence. It can only come out of some person willing to give her or his life to it.'

These last words of hers echoed with a particular power in his mind. In his heart he had never yet been able to delude himself that he was adult, in any ordinary social sense. Even though he was taller than most men already and had already packed into his sixteen years more learning than a normal person would have pushed upon him by twice that time, secretly, and inwardly, he had never been able to convince himself that he was grown up yet. Because of this he had been very conscious of the fact that she was probably a year or two older than he was, and had suspected her of being contemptuous of him, of looking down on him because of it. In a way, the capability of his three tutors had so overshadowed him that they had kept him feeling like a child beyond his years.

But now, for the first time in talking to her, he began to be conscious also of an independence and a strength that he had never felt before. He found himself looking on her and thinking of her, and all the rest of them in this Encyclopedia, with possibly the exception of Tam Olyn, as potential equals, rather than superiors; and, thinking this, he found himself – although the thought did not surface as such in his conscious mind – beginning to fall in love with Ajela.

'I told you, though,' he said to her, suddenly conscious of the silence between them, 'I'm on my way out. So it doesn't matter whether I heard anything or not.'

She sat looking at him penetratingly for a long, silent moment.

'At least,' she said at last, 'you can take the time to come and talk to Tam Olyn. You and he have something very rare in common.'

The point she made was not only effective, but flattering. He was aware she had intended it to be that, but he could not help responding. Tam Olyn was a fabulous name. For his own to be matched with it was ego-building. For just that moment his private grief and loss were forgotten and he thought only that he was being invited to meet Tam Olyn face to face.

'Of course. I'll be honored to talk to him,' he said.

'Good!' Ajela got to her feet.

He stared up at her.

'You mean – right now?'

'Why not?'

'No reason not – of course.' He got up, in his turn.

'He wants very much to talk to you,' she said. She turned, but not toward the door. Instead, she stepped to the bedside tablefloat and the panel of controls there. Her fingers tapped out some code or other.

'We'll go right over,' she said.

He was not aware of any feeling of the room's movement; but after a moment's wait she turned toward the door, walked across and opened it, and instead of the corridor he had expected to see, he found himself looking into another, much larger room. Another space, in fact, was a better word for it; it seemed to be not so much a room as a forest glade with comfortable, heavily padded chairfloats scattered up and down its grassy floor along the banks of a small stream that murmured away out of sight between the trunks of a pine forest at the near end of the room and flowed from the base of a small waterfall at the other. A summer midday sky seemed to be overhead.

Behind a desk by the stream, down a little distance from the waterfall, sat the room's single occupant. He looked up as Hal and Ajela approached, pushing aside some time-yellowed and brittle-looking papers that he had been examining on his desk. To Hal's private surprise, he was not the frail-looking centenarian Hal had expected. He was aged – no doubt about it – but he looked more like an eighty-year-old in remarkably good physical condition than someone of his actual years. It was only when they came forward, and Hal met the eyes of the Director of the Final Encyclopedia for the first time, that he felt the full impact of the man's age. The dark gray eyes sunken in wrinkles chilled him with a sense of experience that went beyond any length of the years that Hal could imagine living.

'Sit down,' Tam said. His voice was hoarse and old and deep.

Hal walked forward and took a float directly in front of Tam Olyn.

Ajela, however, did not sit down. She continued walking forward, and turned to stand beside and partly behind the back of the padded float in which he sat. With one arm she leaned on the top of the float back, the other dropped so that the tips of her fingers rested lightly on Tam's shoulder, as lightly as the lighting of a butterfly. She looked out over Tam's head at Hal, but spoke to the older man.

'Tam,' she said, 'this is Hal Mayne.'

Her voice had a different tone in it that touched Hal for a moment almost with jealousy and with a certain longing.

'Yes,' said Tam.

His voice was indeed old. It was hoarse and dry. All his hundred and twenty-plus years echoed in it. His eyes continued to hold Hal's.

'When I first met Mark Torre, after hearing the voices,' Tam said slowly, 'he wanted to touch my hand. Let me have your hand, Hal Mayne.'

Hal got up and extended his hand over the desk. The light, dry fingers of the old man, like twigs covered in thin leather, took it and held it for a second – then let it go.

'Sit down,' said Tam, sinking back into his seat.

Hal sat.

'Mark Torre felt nothing when he touched me,' Tam said, half to himself, 'and I felt nothing now. It doesn't transfer . . . only, now I know why Mark hoped to feel something when he touched me. I've come to want it, too.'

He drew a slow breath through his nostrils.

'Well,' he said, 'that's it. There's nothing to feel. But you did hear the voices?'

'Yes,' said Hal.

He found himself awed. It was not just the ancientness of Tam Olyn that touched him so strongly. There was something beyond that, something that must have been there all of Tam Olyn's life – an elemental force for either good or evil, directed these last eighty-odd years to one purpose only. That time, that distance, that fixity of purpose towered over everything Hal had ever experienced like a mountain over someone standing at the foot of it.

'Yes. I didn't doubt you,' Tam was saying, now. 'I just wanted the pleasure of hearing you tell me. Did Ajela tell you how rare you are?'

'She mentioned that you and Mark Torre were the only ones who'd heard the voices,' Hal answered.

'That's right,' Tam Olyn said. 'You're one of three. Mark, myself . . . and now you.'

'I . . .' Hal fumbled as he had fumbled earlier with Ajela, 'I'm honored.'

'Honored?' There was a dark, angry flash in the eyes set so deeply beneath the age-heavy brow. 'The word "honored" doesn't begin to describe it. Believe me, who used to make my living from words.'

Ajela's fingertips pressed down a little, lightly upon the shoulder they touched. The dark flash passed and was gone.

'But you don't understand, of course,' Tam said, less harshly. 'You think you understand, but you don't. Think of my lifetime and Mark Torre's. Think of the more than a century it took to build this, all around us. Then think deeper than that. Think of all the lifetime of the human race, from the time it began to walk on two legs and dream of things it wanted. Then, you might start to understand what it means to the human race for you to hear the voices at the Transit Point the way you did.'

A strange echo came to Hal's mind as he sat under the attack of these words – and it was a curiously comforting echo. Abruptly, it seemed to him he heard in Tam Olyn's voice the trace of an element of another, loved harshness of expression – which had been Obadiah's. He stared at Tam. His studies had always told him that the other was pure Earthman – full-spectrum Earth stock; but what Hal had thought he had heard just now was the hard ring of Friendly thinking – of pure faith, unselfsparing and uncompromising. How could the Director of the Final Encyclopedia have come to acquire some of the thought-ways of a Faith-holder?

'I suppose I can't appreciate it as much as you do,' Hal said. 'But I can believe it's a greater thing than I can imagine – to have done it.'

'Yes. Good,' said Tam, nodding. 'Good.'

He leaned forward over his desk.

'Ajela tells me your clearance request states that you're simply passing through,' he said. 'We'd like you to stay.'

'I can't,' answered Hal, automatically. 'I've got to go on, as soon as I can find a ship.'

'To where?' The commanding old voice, the ancient eyes held him pinned. Hal hesitated. But if it was not safe to speak to Tam Olyn, who could he speak to?

'To Coby.'

'Coby? And you're going to do what, on Coby?'

'I'm going to work there,' Hal said, 'in the mines – for a while.'

'A while?'

'A few years.'

Tam sat looking at him.

'Do you understand you could be here instead, with all it means to have heard the voices, and following to whatever great discovery they might lead you to?' he demanded. 'You realize that?'

'Yes.'

'But you're going to go to Coby to do mining, anyway?'

'Yes,' said Hal, miserably.

'Will you tell me why?'

'No,' said Hal, feeling the hand of trained caution on him again, 'I . . . can't.'

There was another long moment in which Tam merely sat watching him.

'I assume,' Tam said at the end of that time, 'you've understood all I've told you. You know the importance of what hearing the voices implies. Ajela and I, here and now, probably know more about you – thanks to the records of the Encyclopedia – than anyone alive, except your three tutors. I assume they agreed to this business of your going to Coby?'

'Yes. They –' Hal hesitated. 'It was their idea, their decision.'

'I see.' Another long pause. 'I also assume there're reasons, for your own good, to make you go; and it's these you aren't free to tell me.'

'I'm sorry,' said Hal. 'That's right. I can't.'

There rose once again in his mind the remembered image of his three tutors and the still semi-obscured memory of what he had watched on the terrace only the day before. A pressure grew in his chest until it threatened to choke him. It was rage, a rage against the people who had killed those whom he loved. There would be no peace for him, anywhere, until he had found the tall man, and everyone connected with him who had brought Walter, Malachi, and Obadiah to their deaths. Something hard and old and cold had been waked in him by their slaying. He was going to Coby only to grow strong, so that in the end he could bring retribution to that tall man and the others. There was no way he could stay here at the Final Encyclopedia or anywhere else. If he were to be held prisoner here, he knew, he would find some way to break loose and go to Coby.

He became aware that Tam was talking again.

'Well then,' said Tam, 'I'll respect the privacy of your reasons. But I'll ask you one thing in return – remember. Remember our need of you here. This –'

He gestured at everything around him.

'– this is the most precious thing ever produced by the human race. But it needs someone to direct it. It had Mark Torre in the beginning. It's had me since. But now I'm old, too old. Understand – I'm not offering you the Directorship. You'd only qualify for that later on, if you showed you could do the job, and after a great deal of time and work. But there isn't any other prospect but you; and past indications are there aren't likely to be, in the time I've got left.'

He stopped. Hal did not know what to say, so he said nothing.

'Have you any conception of what it's like to have a tool like the Encyclopedia at your fingertips?' Tam said suddenly. 'You know scholars use it as a reference work; and the overwhelming majority of people think it's nothing more than that – a large library, nothing else. But that use is like using a human being for a beast of burden when he or she could be a doctor, a scientist, or an artist! The Encyclopedia's not here just to make available what's already known. It's been built at all this great cost and labor for something more, something far more important.'

He paused and stared at Hal, the deep lines of his face deeper with emotion that could either be of anger or anguish.

'Its real purpose – its only true purpose –' he went on, 'is to explore the unknown. For that it needs a Director who understands what that means, who won't lose sight of that purpose. You can be that person; and without you, all the potential value of the Encyclopedia to the human race can be lost.'

Hal had not planned to argue; but his instincts and training led him to question instinctively.

'If it's that important,' he said, 'what's wrong with waiting however long it takes? Inside the force panels nothing can touch the Encyclopedia. So why not just keep on waiting until someone else who can hear the voices comes along, someone who's free?'

'There're no denotations in reality, only connotations,' said Tam harshly. The command in his dark eyes held Hal almost physically in his seat. 'Since time began people have given words arbitrary definitions. They created logical structures from those same definitions, and thought that they'd proved something, in terms of the real universe. Safe physically doesn't mean totally safe. There're non-material ways in which the Encyclopedia is vulnerable to destruction; and one of them's an attack on the minds directing it. Marvelous as it is, it's still only a tool, needing the human intellect to put it to work. Take that human intellect from it and it's useless.'

'But that's not going to happen,' said Hal.

'It's not?' Tam's voice grew even harsher. 'Look around you at the fourteen worlds. Do you know the old Norse legends, the term "Ragnarok"? It means the end of the world. The doom of Gods and Men.'

'I know,' said Hal. 'First came the Frost Giants and Fimbulwinter, then Ragnarok – the last great battle between Gods and Giants.'

'Yes,' said Tam. 'But you don't know that Ragnarok – or Armageddon, the real Armageddon, if you like that word better – is on us now?'

'No,' said Hal; but the words in the old, hoarse voice jarred him deeply, and he felt his heart pumping strongly in his chest.

'Then take my word for it. It is. Hundreds of thousands – millions of years it's taken us to build our way up from the animal level to where we could spread out among the stars. Unlimited space. Space for everyone. Space for each individual to emigrate to, to settle down on and raise those of the same mind as himself or herself. And we did it. We paid the cost and some survived. Some even matured and flowered, until we had a few special Splinter Cultures, like the Exotic, the Dorsai, and the Friendly. Some didn't. But so far we've never been tested as a whole race, a whole race inhabiting more than one world. The only enemies we met were natural forces and each other, so we've built up worlds; and we've built this Encyclopedia.'

A sudden coughing interrupted him. For a little while his voice had strengthened and cleared as he spoke until it nearly lost its hoarseness and sounded young again. But then it had hoarsened rapidly once more, and now the coughing took him. Ajela massaged his neck with the fingertips of both her hands until the fit stopped and he lay back in the float breathing deeply.

'And now,' he went on, slowly and throatily after a long moment, 'the work of all our centuries has borne its fruit – just before the frost. The peak of the harvest season is on us and the unpicked fruit will rot on the trees. We've found out the Splinter Cultures can't survive on their own. Only full-spectrum humans survive. Now, the most specialized of our Splinter Cultures are dying; and there's a general social breakdown preparing us for the end. Where the physical laws of the universe have tried and failed to defeat us, we've done it to ourselves. The pattern of life's become fouled and sterile; and there's a new virus spreading among us. The cross-breeds among the Splinter Cultures are a sickness to our whole race as they try to turn it into a mechanism for their own personal survival. Everywhere, everywhere – the season of our times is going downhill into a winter-death.'

He stopped and stared fiercely at Hal for a moment.

'Well? Do you believe me?' he demanded.

'I suppose so,' said Hal.

The fierceness that had come into Tam's face relaxed.

'You,' he went on, looking at Hal, 'of all people, have to understand this. We're dying. The race is dying. Look, and you have to see it! The people on all the fourteen worlds don't realize it yet because it's coming too slowly, and because they're blinded by the limited focus of their attitudes toward time and history. They only look as far as their own lifetime. No, they don't even look that far. They only look at how things are for their own generation. But to us, up here, looking down at the original Earth and all the long pattern of the centuries, the beginnings of decay and death are plain to see. The Others are going to win. You realize that? They'll end up owning the rest of the race, as if all other humans were cattle – and from that day on there'll be no one left to fight them. The race as a whole will start to die, because it'll have stopped growing – stopped going forward.'

Tam paused again.

'There's only one hope. One faint hope. Because even if we could kill off all the Others now, this moment, it wouldn't stop what's coming. The race'd only find some other disease to die of. The cure has to be a cure of the spirit – a breaking out into some new, vaster area for all of us to explore and grow in. Only the Encyclopedia can

34

make that possible. And maybe only you can make it possible for the Encyclopedia, and push back the shadows that are falling, falling in now over all of us.'

His voice had run down in strength toward the end of his words until it was almost inaudible to Hal. He stopped talking; and this time he did not start again. He sat still behind his desk, looking down at the top of it. Ajela stood silently behind him, soothingly massaging his neck; and Hal sat still. It seemed to Hal, although the little stream ran unchanged beside them, the pseudo-sky overhead was still as blue and the appearance of the pine forest around them was still as green and lovely, that a coldness had crept into the room they occupied, and that all the colors and softnesses in it had become dulled and hardened and old.

'In any case,' Ajela said, into the new silence, 'I can show Hal around the Encyclopedia during the time he's got before he has to go.'

'Yes.' Tam lifted his eyes to look at the two of them once more. 'Show him around. Give him a chance to see as much as he can, while he can.'

CHAPTER FOUR

Back in Hal's room, Ajela played with the controls bank; and a lean-faced man with grizzled hair appeared on the screen.

'Ajela!' he said.

'Jerry,' she told him, 'this is Hal Mayne, who just came in yesterday. He wants to go out to Coby as soon as he can. What have you got as possibilities?'

'I'll look.' The screen went blank.

'A friend of yours?' Hal asked.

She smiled.

'There're less than fifteen hundred of us on permanent staff, here,' she said. 'Everybody knows everybody.'

The screen lit up again with the face of Jerry.

'There's a liner outbound to New Earth, due to hit orbit here in thirty-two hours, eighteen minutes,' he said. 'Hal Mayne?'

'Yes?' Hal moved up to where he could be seen on Jerry's screen.

'From New Earth in two days you can transship by cargo ship to Coby itself. That should put you on Coby in about nine days, subjective time. Will that do you?'

'That's fine,' said Hal.

'You've got your credit papers on file, here?'

'Yes.'

'All right,' said Jerry. 'I can just go ahead and book it for you, if you want.'

Hal felt a touch of embarrassment.

'I don't want any special favors –' he was beginning.

'What favors?' Jerry grinned. 'This is my job, handling traffic for our visiting scholars.'

'Oh, I see. Thanks,' said Hal.

'You're welcome.' Jerry broke the connection.

Hal turned back to Ajela.

'Thank you for doing the calling, though,' he said. 'I don't know your command codes here at all.'

'Neither does anyone who's non-permanent personnel. You could have found out from the Assistance Operator, but this saves time. You do think you'd like to have me show you around the Encyclopedia?'

'Yes. Absolutely –' Hal hesitated. 'Could I actually work with the Encyclopedia?'

'Certainly. But why don't you leave that until last? After you've seen something of it, working with it will make more sense to you. We could go back to the Transit Point and start from there.'

'No.' He did not want to hear the voices again – at least, not for a while. 'Can we get some lunch first?'

'Then suppose I take you first to the Academic control center – I mean after the dining room, of course.'

They left their table, walked out of the dining room, down what seemed like a short corridor, and entered through a dilated aperture into a room perhaps half the size of the dining room. Its walls were banked with control consoles; and in mid-air in the center of the room floated what looked like a mass of red, glowing cords, making a tangle that was perhaps a meter thick, from top to bottom, and two meters wide by three long. Ajela led him up to it. The cords, he saw from close-up, were unreal – visual projections.

'What is it?' he asked.

'The neural pathways of the Encyclopedia currently being activated as people work with them.' She smiled sympathetically at him. 'It doesn't seem to make much sense, does it?'

He shook his head.

It takes a great deal of time to learn to recognize patterns in it,' she said. 'The technicians that work with it get very good. But, actually only Tam can look at it and tell you at a glance everything that's being done with it.'

'How about you?' he asked.

'I can recognize the gross patterns – that's about all,' she said. 'I'll need ten more years to begin to qualify myself for even the beginning technician level.'

He looked at her with a touch of suspicion.

'You're exaggerating,' he said. 'It won't take you that long.'

She laughed, and he felt gratified.

'Well, maybe not.'

'I'd guess you must be pretty close to being level with a beginning technician right now,' he said. 'You're pulling that Exotic trick of talking yourself down. You wouldn't have gone from nowhere to becoming Tam's special assistant in six years, if you weren't unusual.'

She looked at him, suddenly sober.

'Plainly,' she said, 'you're a little unusual yourself. But, of course, you'd have to be.'

'I would? Why?'

'To hear the voices at the Transit Point.'

'Oh,' he said. 'That.'

37

She took him up close to the glowing, air-borne mass of red lines, and began to trace individual ones, explaining how one was clearly a tap from the Encyclopedia's memory-area of history over to the area of art, which meant that a certain scholar from Indonesia had found a connection to a new sidelight on the work he was doing; and how another line showed that the Encyclopedia itself was projecting related points to the research another person was doing – in effect suggesting avenues of exploration.

'Is this all just what Tam called "library" use of the Encyclopedia?' Hal asked.

'Yes.' Ajela nodded.

'Can you show me what the other kind would look like in these neural pathways?' he asked.

She shook her head.

'No. The Encyclopedia's still waiting for someone who can do that.'

'What makes Tam so sure it's possible?'

She looked gravely at him.

'He's Tam Olyn. And he's sure.'

Hal reserved judgment on the question. She took him next to the mechanical heart of the Encyclopedia, the room containing the controls for the solar power it stored and used, to run the sphere and to drive the force-panels that protected it. The panels actually used little of the power. Like the phase-shift from which they were derived, they were almost non-physical. Where the phase-shift drive did not actually move a spaceship as much as it changed the description of its location, the protective panels in effect set up an indescribably thin barrier of no-space. Just as a spaceship under phase drive at the moment of shift was theoretically spread out evenly throughout the universe and immediately reassembled at some other designated spot than that from which it started, so any solid object attempting to pass the curtain of no-space in the panels became theoretically spread out throughout the universe, without hope of reassembling.

'You know about this?' Ajela asked Hal as they stood in the mechanicals control room.

'A little,' he said. 'I learned, the way everybody does, how the shift was developed from the Heisenberg Uncertainty Principle.'

'Not everybody,' she said. He frowned at her.

'Oh?'

She smiled. 'You'd be surprised what percentage of the total race has no idea of how space vessels move.'

'I suppose,' he said, a little wistfully. 'But anyway, the force-panels don't seem that hard to understand. Essentially, all they do is what a spaceship does, if a one-in-a-million chance goes wrong. It's just that after things are spread out they're never reassembled.'

'Yes,' she said, slowly. 'People talk about phase-shift errors as if they were something romantic – a universe of lost ships. But it's not romantic.'

He gazed closely at her.

'Why does that make you so sad?' he asked, deeply moved to see her cheerfulness gone.

She stared at him for a second.

'You're sensitive,' she said.

Before he could react to that statement, however, she had gone on.

'But shouldn't I be sad?' she asked. 'People have died. To them there was nothing romantic about it. People have been destroyed or lost forever, who might have changed the course of the race if they'd lived. How about Donal Graeme, who brought the fourteen worlds to the closest thing to a unified political whole that they'd ever known – just a hundred years or so ago? He was only in his thirties when he left the Dorsai for Mara, and never got there.'

Hal shrugged. He knew the bit of history she referred to. But in spite of the sensitivity she had just accused him of having, he could not work up much sympathy for Dona Graeme, who after all had had nearly a third of a normal lifetime before he was lost. He became aware that Ajela was staring at him.

'Oh, I forgot!' she said. 'You were almost lost that way. It was just luck you were found. I'm sorry. I didnt' think when I brought the subject up.'

It was like her, he thought – already he was thinking of ways in which she was like, although he had only known her a matter of hours – to put the kindest possible interpretation on his indifference to what moved her deeply.

'I don't remember any of it,' he said. 'I was under two years old when they found me. As far as I'm concerned, it could just as well have happened to someone else.'

'Haven't you ever been tempted to try and establish who your parents were?'

Internally, he winced. He had been tempted, hundreds of times. He had woven a thousand fantasies in which by chance he discovered them, still alive somewhere.

He shrugged again.

'How'd you like to go down to the Archives?' she asked. 'I can show you the facsimiles of all the art of the race from the paleolithic cave paintings of the Dordogne, up until now; and every weapon and artifact and machine that was ever made.'

'All right,' he said; and with an effort hauled himself off thoughts of his unknown parents. 'Thanks.'

They went to the Archives, which were in another room-area just under the actual metal skin of the Encyclopedia. All the permanent rooms made a layer of ten to twenty meters thick just inside that skin.

With the force-panels outside it, that location was as safe as any-where within the sphere itself; and this arrangement left the great hollow interior free for the movable rooms to shift about it.

As Ajela explained, the rooms were in reality always in motion, being shuttled about to make way for the purposeful movement of other rooms as they were directed into proximity with one another. In the gravityless center of the sphere, with each room having its own interior gravity, this motion was all but unnoticeable, said Ajela; though in fact Hal had already come to be conscious of it – not the movement itself, but the changes in direction. He supposed that long familiarity with the process had made permanent personnel like Ajela so used to it that they did not notice it any more.

He let her talk on, although the facts she was now telling him were some he had learned years ago from Walter the InTeacher. He was aware that she was talking to put him at his ease, as much as to inform him.

The Archives, when they came to them, inhabited a very large room made to seem enormous, by illusion. It had to be large to appear to hold the lifesize and apparently solid, three-dimensional images of objects as large as Earth's Roman Colosseum, or the Symphonie des Flambeaux which Newton had built.

He had not expected to be deeply moved by what he would see there, most of which he assumed he had seen in image form before. But as it turned out, he was to betray himself into emotion, after all.

'What would you like to see first?' she asked him.

Unthinkingly, his head still full of the idea of testing the useful-ness of the Encyclopedia, he mentioned the first thing he could think of that legitimately could be here, but almost certainly would not.

'How about the headstone on Robert Louis Stevenson's grave?' he asked.

She touched the studs on her bank of controls, and almost within arm's length of him the transparent air resolved itself into an upright block of gray granite with words cut upon it.

His breath caught. It was an image copy only, his eyes told him, but so true to actuality it startled him. He reached out to the edge of the imaged stone and his fingers reported a cold smoothness, the very feel of the stone itself. He, with all the response to poetry that had always been in him, had always echoed internally to this before all other epitaphs, the one that Stevenson had written for himself when he should be laid in a churchyard.

He tried to read the lines of letters cut in the stone, but they blurred in his vision. It did not matter. He knew them without seeing them:

Under the wide and starry sky,
Dig the grave and let me lie.

Glad did I live and gladly die,
And I laid me down with a will.

This be the verse you grave for me:
Here he lies where he longed to be;
Home is the sailor, home from the sea,
And the hunter home from the hill.

The untouchable words woke again in him the memory of the three who had died on the terrace, and kindled a pain inside him so keen that he thought for a second or two he would not be able to bear it. He turned away from the stone and Ajela; and stood, looking at nothing, until he felt her hand on his shoulder.

'I'm sorry,' she said. 'But you asked. . . .'

Her voice was soft, and her touch on his shoulder so light he could barely sense it; but together they made a rope by which he was able to haul himself once more back up from the bitter ache of the personal loss.

'Look,' she said, 'I've got something else for you. Look!'

Reluctantly, he turned and found himself looking at a bronze sculpture no more than seven inches in height. It was the sculpture of a unicorn standing on a little patch of ground with tight-petalled roses growing near his feet. His neck was arched, his tail in an elegant circle, his mane flying and his head uptilted roguishly. There was a look in his eye and a twist to his mouth that chortled at the universe.

It was *The Laughing Unicorn*, by Darlene Coltrain. He was unconquerable, sly, a dandy – and he was beautiful. Life and joy bubbled up and fountained in every direction from him.

It was impossible for pain and such joy to occupy the same place; and after a moment the pain began to recede from Hal. He smiled at the unicorn in spite of himself; and could almost convince himself that the unicorn smiled back.

'Do you have the originals of any of these facsimiles?' he asked Ajela.

'Some,' she said. 'There's the problem of available storage space – let alone that you can't buy things like this with credit. What we do have are those that have been donated to us.'

'That one?' he asked, pointing at *The Laughing Unicorn*.

'I think . . . yes, I think that's one we do,' she said.

'Could I see it? I'd like to actually handle it.'

She hesitated, then slowly but plainly shook her head.

'I'm sorry,' she said. 'No one touches the originals but the archivists – and Tam.'

She smiled at him.

'If you ever get to be Director, you can keep him on your desk, if you want.'

Ridiculously, inexpressibly, he longed to own the small statuette; to take it with him for comfort when he went out alone between the stars and into mines on Coby. But of course that was impossible. Even if he did own the original himself, it was too valuable to be carried in an ordinary traveller's luggage. Its loss or theft would be a tragedy to a great many people besides himself.

He lost himself after that in looking at a number of other facsimiles of art, all sorts of works, books and other artifacts that Ajela summoned up with her control bank. In an odd way, a barrier had gone down between the two of them with the emotions that had just been evoked in him, first by the Robert Louis Stevenson gravestone and then by the *Laughing Unicorn*. By the time they were done, it was time for another meal. This time they ate in another dining room – this one imaged and decorated to give the appearance of a beer hall, full of music, loud talk, and the younger inhabitants of the Encyclopedia – although few of these were as young as Ajela, and none as young as Hal. But he had learned that when he remembered to act soberly and trade on his height he could occasionally be taken for two or three years older than he actually was. No one, at least, among those that stopped by the booth where they sat, showed any awareness that he was two years younger than she.

But the food and drink hit him like a powerful drug, after the large events of the last two days. An hour or so in the dining room, and he could barely keep his eyes open. Ajela showed him how to code for his own room on the booth's control bank, and led him down another short corridor outside the dining room to a dilating aperture that proved, indeed, to be the door to his own quarters.

'You think there'll be time for me to work with the Encyclopedia tomorrow?' he said as she left.

'Easily,' she said.

He slept heavily, woke feeling happy, then remembered the deaths on the terrace – and grief rushed in on him again. Again he watched through the screen of the bush at the edge of the pond and saw what happened. The pain was unendurable. It was all too close. He felt he had to escape, the way a drowning man might feel, who had to escape from underwater up to where there was air and light. He clutched frantically for something other to cling to, and fastened on the recollection that today he would have a chance to work with the Encyclopedia itself. He clung to this prospect, filling his mind with it and with what he had done the day before when Ajela had taken him around.

Still thinking of these things he got up, ordered breakfast, and an hour later Ajela called to see if he was awake yet. Finding him up, she came to his room.

'Most people work with the Encyclopedia in their rooms,' she told him. 'But if you like I can add a carrel to this room, or set one up for you elsewhere.'

'Carrel,' he echoed. He had assumed for some years now that there were no words worth knowing he did not know, but this was new to him.

'A study-room.'

She touched the controls on his desk and a three-dimensional image formed in the open center of his quarters. It showed something not much larger than a closet holding a single chair float and a fixed desk surface with a pad of control keys. The walls were colorless and flat; but as she touched the controls in Hal's room again, they dissolved into star filled space, so that float and desk seemed now to be adrift between the stars. Hal's breath caught in his throat.

'I can have the carrel attached to my room here?' he asked.

'Yes,' she said.

'Then I think that's what I'd like.'

'All right.' She touched the control. The light shimmer of the wall opposite the door that was the entrance to his room moved back to reveal another door. As he watched it opened and he saw beyond it the small room she had described as a carrel. He went to and into it, like a bee drawn to a flower blossom. Ajela followed him and spent some twenty minutes teaching him how to call up from the Encyclopedia whatever information he might want. At last she turned to leave him.

'You'll make better use of the resources of the Encyclopedia,' she said, 'if you've got a specific line of inquiry or investigation to follow. You'll find it'll pay you to think a bit before you start and be sure you're after information that needs to be developed from the sources it'll give you, rather than just a question that can be simply answered.'

'I understand,' he said, excitement moving in him.

But once she had gone and he was alone again, the excitement hesitated and the grief in him, together with the cold ancient fury toward Bleys Ahrens he had felt earlier, threatened to wake in him once more. Resolutely he shoved it back down inside him. He pressed the control set in the arm of his chair that sealed the room about him and set its walls to an apparent transparency that left him seemingly afloat in space between the stars. His mind hunted almost desperately, knowing that he must find something to occupy it or else it would go back to the estate again, to the lake and the terrace. The words of Malachi's evoked image came back to him.

'. . . *the concerns of the living, must be with the living, even if the living are themselves . . .*'

He made a powerful effort to think only of the here and now. What would he want if he was simply here at the Final Encyclopedia in this moment and nothing at all had happened back at his home? Reaching out, his mind snatched again at the dreams built up from his reading. He had asked to see the gravestone of Robert Louis

Stevenson yesterday. Perhaps he should simply ask for whatever else the Encyclopedia had to tell him about Stevenson that he had never known before? But his mind shied away from that idea. The image of Stevenson was now tied in his mind to the image of a gravestone, and he did not want to think of gravestones.

He flung his mind wide. The Three Musketeers? D'Artagnan? What about Nigel Loring, the fictional hero of two of the historical novels by the inventor of Sherlock Holmes, Conan Doyle – the novels *Sir Nigel* and *The White Company*.

The idea of Sir Nigel, the small but indomitable hero of those two novels of the days of men in iron and leather welcomed his imagination like a haven. Nigel Loring was a character who had always glowed with an unusual light and color in his imagination. Perhaps Conan Doyle had even started a third novel about him, and never finished it? No, not likely. If that had been true he would almost undoubtedly have run across some word of it before now. He pressed the query key of the keypad on the arm of his chair and spoke aloud to the Encyclopedia.

'List for me all that Conan Doyle ever wrote about the character Nigel Loring, who appears in the novels *The White Company* and *Sir Nigel* by Conan Doyle.'

A hard copy coiled up out of the void into existence and dropped in his lap. At the same time a soft bell note chimed and a voice replied to him in pleasant female tones.

'Data from sources delivered in hard copy. Would you also like biographical details about the historical individual who is antecedent?'

Hal frowned, puzzled.

'I'm not asking for data on Conan Doyle,' he said.

'That's understood. The historical individual referred to was the actual Nigel Loring, knight, of the fourteenth century AD.' Hal stared at the stars. The words he had just heard echoed in his head and a bubble of excitement formed within him. Almost fearful that it would turn out there had been some mistake, he spoke again.

'You're telling me there actually was someone named Nigel Loring in England in the fourteenth century?'

'Yes. Do you want biographical details on this person?'

'Yes, please. All possible details –' he added hastily, 'and will you list references to the real Nigel Loring in documents of the time and after. I want copies of these last, if you can give them to me.'

Another coil of hard copy emerged from the desktop, followed by a number of paper sections and pictures. Hal ignored the hard copy but picked up the second half of the delivery and went quickly through it. There was an amazing number of things, running from excerpts from the *Chronicles* of Jean Froissart; an account list of presents given by Edward, the Black Prince of England, to courtiers

44

in his train; and ending with an image of a stall in a chapel. With the image of the chapel stall was a printed description identifying it, which Hal found the most fascinating of all the material.

The stall, he read, still existed. Nigel Loring had been one of the charter members of the Order of the Garter. The chapel was St. George's Chapel, in the English palace of Windsor. The existing chapel now, he learned, was not, however, the original chapel. The original chapel had been built by Edward the Third and its rebuilding was begun by Edward IV and probably finished in the reign of Henry VIII. Work had gone on at night with many hundreds of candles burning at the time in order to get it ready at Henry's express order for one of his marriages.

For a moment the terrace and its happenings were forgotten. The actual historical Nigel Loring and Doyle's fictional character slid together in Hal's mind. It seemed to him that he reached across time to touch the actual human being who had been Nigel Loring. For a moment it was possible to believe that all the people in the books he had read might have been as alive and touchable as any real person, if only he knew where and how to reach out for them. Fascinated, he pulled another character out of his mind almost at random, and spoke to the Encyclopedia.

'Tell me,' he asked, 'was the character Bellarion, in the novel *Bellarion* by Raphael Sabatini also inspired by a real historical person of the same name?'

'No,' answered the Final Encyclopedia.

Hal sighed, his imagination brought back to the practical Earth. It would have been too good to be true to have had Bellarion also an actual character in history.

'. . . however,' the Encyclopedia went on, 'Sabatini's Bellarion draws strongly upon the military genius of the actual fourteenth century condottiere, Sir John Hawkwood, from whom Conan Doyle also drew to some extent in the writing of the books that contain the character of Sir Nigel. It is generally accepted that John Hawkwood was in part a model for both fictional characters. Would you like excerpts of the critical writings reaching this conclusion?'

'Yes – NO!' Hal shouted aloud. He sat back, nearly quivering with excitement.

John Hawkwood was someone about whom he knew. Hawkwood had caught his imagination early, not only from what Hal had read about him, but because Malachi Nasuno had spoken of him, referring to him as the first modern general. Cletus Graeme also had cited Hawkwood's campaigns a number of times in Cletus's multivolumed work on strategy and tactics – that same Cletus Graeme who had been the great-grandfather of Donal Graeme of whom Ajela had spoken. Donal Graeme had ended up enforcing a peace on all the fourteen worlds. In Hal's mind, suddenly, a line led obviously from

Donal to Cletus Graeme and back through the warrior elements of western history to Hawkwood.

Hawkwood had come out from the village of Sible Hedingham in the rural England of the early fourteenth century, had fought his way up through the beginnings of the Hundred Years War in France and ended as Captain General of Florence, Italy. He had died at last in his bed at a probable age of over eighty, after a life of frequent hand-to-hand armed combat. He had been called 'the first of the modern generals' by others before Malachi; and he had introduced longbowmen from England into the Italian warfare of the fourteenth century with remarkable results.

Hal had been fascinated by him on first discovery. Not merely because of the clangor and color of Hawkwood's life, as seen from nearly a thousand years later, but because in the Englishman's lifetime, going from Sible Hedingham in his youth to Florence in his later years, he had effectively travelled from the society of the deep Middle Ages into the beginnings of the modern era. The flag that had been flying over Hal's terrace, and that Walter InTeacher had lowered to warn him, the flag of a hawk flying out of a wood, had been made by Hal himself with a device out of his imagination after a thorough search through the books in the library of the estate had failed to have any information on Hawkwood's coat of arms – on sudden impulse Hal spoke again to the Encyclopedia.

'What was the coat of arms borne by Sir John Hawkwood?'

There was a brief pause.

'Sir John Hawkwood's arms were: argent, on a chevron sable three escallops of the field.'

The screen showed a shield with a silver background, crossed by a thick v-shaped black band, called a 'chevron,' point upwards in the middle of the ground, and with three silver cockle shells spaced out upon the black chevron.

Why the cockles? Hal wondered. The only connection he could think of to cockle shells was St. James of Compostela, in Spain. Could Hawkwood at the time have been in Compostela? Or might the cockles in the arms mean something else? He queried the Final Encyclopedia.

'The cockle shells are common to many coats of arms,' answered the Encyclopedia, 'I can furnish you with details if you like. They appear, for example, on some of the oldest arms, such as those of the Graemes, and on the arms borne by many of the septs of the Graeme family, such as the well known arms of Dundee and Dunbar. Do you wish details, a full report on cockles as a device on coats of arms during past centuries?'

'No,' said Hal.

He sat back, thinking. Something in the deepest depths of his mind had been triggered by this discovery that the real Hawkwood lay in some manner behind the fictional characters of Doyle's Nigel Loring and Sabatini's Bellarion, something that continued backward to tie into this business of the cockle shells and Hawkwood. The cockle shells and Hawkwood somehow fitted together; they linked and evoked something. He could feel the mental chemistry of their interaction like a stirring in his unconscious, it was a sensation which he knew, it was the sort of deep excitement that came on just before he began to envision a poem. The chain of logic that ran from these things to whatever was now building in his creative unconscious was not one his conscious mind could see or follow, but experience had taught him the futility of trying. He felt its workings there, now, as someone might feel conflicting winds blowing upon him in the absolute darkness of night. It was a pressure, a fever, an imperative. Something about this search and discovery had touched on a thing that was infinitely more compelling, was much larger, than what he had sat down here with the expectation of discovering, as an ocean is larger than a grain of sand on one of its shores. It reached out to touch him like a call, like a trumpet note reaching out, reaching all the way through him to summon him to a thing more important than anything he had felt in all his sixteen years before.

The sensation was powerful. It was almost with relief that he found the lines of a poem beginning to stir in his head, forming out of the mists of his discovery, strange, archaic sounding lines. . . . His fingers groped automatically for the keypad that was on the arm of his chair, not to summon the Encyclopedia back for another question or command but simply to resolve the poetic images forming inside him into words. Those words, as he pressed the keys, began to take visible shape, glowing like golden fire against the starscape before him.

À OUTRANCE

Within the ruined chapel, the full knight
Woke from the coffin of his last-night's bed;
And clashing mailed feet on the broken stones—

His fingers paused on the keys. A chill, damp wind seemed suddenly to blow clear through him. He shook off the momentary paralysis and wrote on . . .

Strode to the shattered lintel and looked out.

A fog lay holding all the empty land
A cloak of cloudy and uncertainness,
That hid the earth; in that enfoliate mist
Moved voices wandered from a dream of death.

It was a wind of Time itself, the thought came to him unexpectedly, that he felt now blowing through him, blowing through flesh

47

and bones alike. It was the sound of that wind he heard and was now rendering into verse. He wrote . . .

A warhorse, cropping by the chapel wall,
Raised maul-head, dripping thistles on the stones;
And struck his hooves; and jingled all his gear.
'Peace . . .' said the Knight. 'Be still. Today, we rest.

'The mist is hiding all the battlefield.
'The wind whips on the wave-packs of the sea.
'Our foe is bound by this no less than we.
'Rest,' said the Knight. 'We do not fight today.'

The warhorse stamped again. And struck his hooves.
Ringing on cobbled dampness of the stones.
Crying – 'Ride! Ride! Ride!' And the Knight mounted him,
Slowly. And rode him slowly out to war.

. . . The chime of the room phone catapulted him out of his thoughts. He had been sitting, he realized, for some time with the written poem before him, his thought ranging on journeys across great distances. He reached out reflexively to the control keys.

'Who is it?'

'It's Ajela.' From behind the void and the glowing lines of his poem, her voice came clearly and warmly, bringing back with it all of the reality he had abandoned during his recent ranging. 'It's lunch time – if you're interested.'

'Oh. Of course,' he said, touching the keypad. The lines of verse vanished, to be replaced by the image of her face, occulting the imaged stars.

'Well,' she said, smiling at him, 'did you have a useful session with the Encyclopedia?'

'Yes,' he said. 'Very much.'

'And where would you like to eat?'

'Any place,' he said – and hastily amended himself. 'Any place quiet.'

She laughed.

'The quietest place is probably right where you are now.'

'– any quiet place except my room, then.'

'All right. We'll go back to the dining room I took you to the first time. But I'll arrange for a table away from other people where no one will be sent to sit near us,' she said. 'Meet you at the entrance there in five minutes.'

By the time he figured out the controls to move his room close to the dining room, and got to the dining room entrance, Ajela was already there and waiting for him. As he came down the short length of corridor that was now between his room's front door and the entrance to the dining room, he was aware suddenly that this was probably the last time he would see her before he left. The two days just past had done a good deal to shift her in his mind from the category of someone belonging to the Encyclopedia, and therefore beyond his understanding, into someone he knew – and for whom he felt.

The result was that his perceptions were now sharpened. As far back as he could remember, his tutors had trained him to observe; as he met her now, spoke to her, and was led by her to a table in one deserted corner of the room, he saw her as perhaps he should have seen her from the start.

It was as if his vision of her had focused. He noticed now how straight she stood and how she walked with something like an air of command – certainly with an air of firmness and decision that was almost alien in an Exotic – as she led the way to their table. She was dressed in green today, a light green tunic that came down to mid-thigh, hugging her body tightly, over an ankle-length skirt that was slit all the way up the sides, revealing tight trousers of a darker green with the parting of the slits at each stride.

The tunic's green was that of young spring grass. There was a straightness to her shoulders, seen against the distant pearl-gray of the light-wall at the far end of the dining room. Her bright blonde hair was gathered into a pony-tail by a polished wooden barrette that showed the grain of the wood. The pony-tail danced against the shoulders of her tunic as she strode, echoing in its movements the undulations of her skirt. She reached their table, sat down, and he took the float opposite her.

She asked him again about his morning with the Encyclopedia as they decided what to eat, and he answered briefly, not wanting to go into details of how what he had learned had struck so deep a chord of response within him. Watching her now, he saw in the faint narrowing of her eyes that she had noticed this self-restraint.

'I don't mean to pry,' she said. 'If you'd rather not talk about it –'

'No – no, it's not that,' he answered quickly. 'It's just that my mind's everywhere at once.'

She flashed her sudden smile at him.

'No need to apologize,' she said. 'I was just mentioning it. As for the way you feel – the Encyclopedia affects a lot of scholars that way.'

He shook his head, slowly.

'I'm no scholar,' he answered.

'Don't be so sure,' she said gently. 'Well, have you thought about whether you still want to go ahead and leave, the way you planned, in just a few hours?'

He hesitated. He could not admit that he would prefer to stay, without seeming to invite her to argue for his staying. He understood himself, starkly and suddenly. His problem was a reluctance to tell her he must leave, that there was no choice for him but to leave. Caught between answers, neither of which he wanted to give, he was silent.

'You've got reasons to go. I understand that,' she said, after a moment. She sat watching him. 'Would you like to tell me about them? Would you like to talk about it, at all?'

He shook his head.

'I see,' she said. Her voice had gentled. 'Do you mind, anyway, my telling you Tam's side of it?'

'Of course not,' he replied.

Their plates, with the food they had ordered, were just rising to the surface of the table. She looked down at hers for a moment, and then looked back up at him levelly.

'You've seen Tam,' she said as they began to eat, and the gentleness in her voice gave way to a certainty that echoed the authority of her walk. 'You see his age. One year, several years, might not seem so much to you; but he's old. He's very old. He has to think about what will happen to the Encyclopedia if there's no one to take charge of it after . . . he steps down as Director.'

He was watching her eyes, fascinated, as she spoke. They were a bluish green that seemed to have depths without end and reflected the color of her clothing.

He said, after a second, since she had paused as if waiting response from him, 'Someone else would take over the Encyclopedia, wouldn't they?'

She shook her head.

'No one person. There's a Board of Directors who'll step in, and stay in. The Board was scheduled to take over after Mark Torre's death. Then Mark found Tam and changed that part of the plan. But now, if Tam dies without a successor, the Board's going to take over, and from then on the Encyclopedia will be run by committee.'

'And that's something you don't want to happen?'

'Of course I don't!' Her voice tightened. 'Tam's worked all his life to point the Encyclopedia toward what it really should do, rather than let it turn into a committee-run library! What would you think I'd want?'

Her eyes were now full green, as green as the rare tinge that can color the wood flames of an open camp fire. He waited a second more to let her hear the echo of her words in her ears before he answered.

'You should want whatever it is you want,' he said, echoing what he had been taught and believed in. Her eyes met his for a second more, burningly, then dropped their gaze to her plate. When she spoke again, the volume of her voice had also dropped.

'I . . . you don't understand,' she said slowly. 'This is very hard for me –'

'But I do understand,' he answered. 'I told you, one of my tutors was an Exotic. Walter the InTeacher.'

What she had meant, he knew from Walter's teachings, was that it was difficult for her to plead with him to stay at the Encyclopedia, much as she plainly wanted to. As an Exotic, she would have been conditioned from childhood never to try to influence other people. This, because of the Exotic belief that participation in the historical process, even in the smallest degree, destroyed the clear-sightedness of a separate and dispassionate observer; and the Exotics' main reason for existence was to chart the movements of history, separately and dispassionately. They dreamed only of an end to which those movements could lead. But she was, he thought, as she had more or less admitted already, a strange Exotic.

'Actually,' he told her, 'you argue better for my staying here when you don't argue, than you could if you used words.'

He smiled, to invite her to smile back, and was relieved when she did. What he said had been said clumsily; but all the same, it was a truth she was too intelligent not to see. If she had argued, he would have had someone besides himself to marshal his own arguments against. This way, he was left to debate with his own desires; which, she might have guessed, could make an opponent far harder for him to conquer than she was.

But his conscience sank its teeth into him, now. He was, he knew, leading her on to hope – which was an unfair thing to do. He must not give in and stay here. But, because she was an Exotic and because he knew what that meant as far as her beliefs were concerned, he could think of no way to explain this to her that would not either wound or baffle her. He did not, he thought almost desperately, know enough about her – enough about her as the unique individual she was – to talk to her. And there was no time to learn that much about her.

'You're from – where? Mara? Kultis?' he asked, striking out at random. 'How did you happen to end up here?'

She smiled, unexpectedly.

'Oh, I was a freak,' she said.

'A freak?' Privately he had sometimes called himself that. But he could not imagine applying it to someone like her.

'Well, say I was one of the freaks, then,' she answered. 'We called ourselves that. Did you ever hear of a Maran Exotic called Padma?'

'Padma . . .' He frowned.

The name had a strange echo of familiarity, as if he had indeed heard Walter or one of his other tutors mention it, but nothing more. His memory, like the rest of him, had been trained to a fine point. If he had been told of such a man, he should be able to remember it. But nowhere, searching his memory now, could he find any clear reference to someone called Padma.

'He's very old now,' she said. 'But he's been an Outbond, from either Mara or Kultis, at one time or another, to every important culture on the fourteen worlds. He goes clear back to the time of Donal Graeme. In fact – that's why I'm here.'

'He's that old?' Hal stared at her. 'He must be older than Tam.'

She sobered, suddenly. The smile left her face and went out of her voice as well.

'No. He's younger – but just by a few years.' She shook her head. 'Even when he was a very young man, he had an ageless look, they say. And he was brilliant, even then – even among his own generation on the Exotics. But you're almost right. When I got here, I found out even Tam had thought Padma was older than he was. But it's not true. There's been no one Tam's age; and no one like him – ever. Even Padma.'

He looked at her half-skeptically.

'There are fourteen worlds,' he said.

'I know,' she said. 'But the Final Encyclopedia's got no record of anyone else much more than a hundred and eighteen years old just now. Tam's a hundred and twenty-four. It's his will that keeps him going.'

He could hear in her voice an appeal to him to understand Tam. He wanted to tell her that he would try, but once more he did not trust himself to put the assurance into words he could trust her to believe.

'But you were telling me how you got here,' he said, instead. 'You were saying you were one of the freaks. What did you mean? And what's Padma got to do with it?'

'It was his conscience created us – me, and the others –' she said. 'It all goes back long ago to something that happened between him and Donal Graeme, back when Donal was alive and Padma was still young. Later, what passed between them brought Padma to feel that he'd been too young and sure of himself, to notice something important – that Donal had something Padma should have been aware of and made use of; something critical, he said, to the search we've been engaged in on the Exotics for three centuries now. Those are Padma's own words, to an Assembly of both the Exotic worlds forty years ago. Padma came finally to think that Donal might have been a prototype of the very thing we'd been searching for, the evolved form of human being we've always believed the race will finally produce.'

He frowned at her, reaching out to understand. Donal he knew of through general history and the tales of Malachi. But he had never been too impressed with Donal, in spite of Donal's triumphs. Ian and Kensie, Donal's uncles; and Eachan Khan, Donal's grim, war-crippled father, had caught more at his imagination, among the Graemes of Foralie on the Dorsai. But the uneasy feeling that he should recognize the name continued to nag at him on a low level of consciousness.

'Padma,' Ajela was going on, 'felt we Exotics had to look for what he might have missed seeing in Donal; and because Padma was enormously *respected* – if you had an Exotic teacher, you know what the word *respected* means on Mara and Kultis – and because he suggested a way that had never been tried, it was agreed he could make an experiment. I – and some others like me – were the elements of the experiment. He chose fifty of the brightest Exotic children he could find and arranged to have us brought up under special conditions.'

Hal frowned again at her.

'Special conditions?'

'Padma's theory was that something in our own Exotic society was inhibiting the kind of personal development that had made someone like Donal Graeme possible. Whatever else was true about him, no one could deny Donal had abilities no Exotic had ever achieved. That pointed to a blindness somewhere in our picture of ourselves, Padma said.'

She was carried away now on the flood of what she was telling him. Her eyes were blue-green and depthless once more.

'So,' she went on, 'he got a general agreement to let him experiment with the fifty of us – Padma's Children, they called us, then – and he saw to it we were exposed, from as soon as we were able to understand, not only to the elements of our own culture, but to those in the Dorsai and the Friendly cultures which our Exotic thinking had always automatically rejected. You know how our family structure on Mara and Kultis is much looser than on the Dorsai or the Friendlies. As children, we treat all adults almost equally as parents or near relatives. No one forced the fifty of us in any particular direction, but we were given more freedom to bond emotionally to individuals, to indulge in romantic, rather than logical thinking. You see – a romantic attitude was the one common element permitted Dorsai and Friendly children, which we on the Exotics had always been steered away from.'

He sat, studying her as she talked. He did not yet see where her words were headed, but he could feel strongly across the short physical distance separating them that what she was saying was not only something of intense importance to her, but something that it was difficult for her to say to him. He nodded now, to encourage her to go on; and she did.

'To make the story short,' she said, 'we were set free to fall in love with things we ordinarily would've been told were unproductive subjects for such attention; and in my case what I fell in love with, when I was barely old enough to learn about it, was the story of Tam Olyn – the brilliant, grim, interstellar newsman who tried and almost succeeded in a personal vendetta to destroy the Friendly culture, only to change his mind suddenly and completely, to come back to Earth and take on all the responsibility of the Final Encyclopedia, where he'd been the only person except Mark Torre to hear the voices at the Center point.'

Her face was animated now. The feeling in her reached and caught up Hal as music might have caught him up.

53

'This man, who still controls the Final Encyclopedia,' she went on animatedly, 'holding it in trust all these years for the race, and refusing to let any other person or power control it. By the time I was nine I knew I had to come here; and by the time I was eleven, they let me come – on Tam's personal responsibility.'

She smiled suddenly.

'It seemed,' she said, 'Tam was intrigued by someone only my age who could be so set on getting here; and I found out later, partly he hoped I might hear the voices, as you and he did. But I didn't.'

She stopped speaking, suddenly, with her last three words. The smile went. She had hardly touched the small salad she had ordered; but Hal recognized with surprise that his own plate was utterly empty – and yet he could not remember eating as he listened to her.

'So it's because of Tam you're still here?' he said, finally, when it seemed she would not go on. She had started to poke at her salad, but when he spoke she put her fork down and looked levelly across the table at him.

'I came because of him, yes,' she said. 'But since then I've come to see what he sees in the Encyclopedia – what you should see in it. Now, even if there weren't any Tam Olyn, I'd still be here.'

She glanced down at her salad and pushed the transparent bowl that held it away from her. Then she looked back at him, again.

'It's the hope of the race,' she said to him. 'Their one hope. I don't believe any longer that the answer can lie with our Exotics, or anyone else. It's here – here! No place else. And only Tam's been able to keep it alive. He needs you.'

The tone of her voice on her last words tore at him. He looked at her and knew finally that he could not give her a flat no, not here, not now. He took a deep, unhappy breath.

'Let me think about it – a little longer,' he said. Suddenly, he felt a desperate need to get away from her before he made her some promise that was neither true nor possible to keep. He pushed his float back from the table, still unable to keep his eyes off her face. He would tell her later, he told himself, call her from his room, and tell her that eventually he would be back. Even with their phone screens on, there would be a psychic distance between them that would lessen the terrible power of persuasion he felt coming at him from her now, and make it possible for him to reassure her he would someday return.

'I'll go back to my room and think about it, now,' he said.

'All right,' she said without moving. 'But remember, you heard the voices. You have to understand; because there's only the three of us who do. You, Tam and I. Remember what you risk if you leave, now. If you go, and while you're gone Tam reaches the point where he can't go on being Director any longer, by the time you come back the Board will be in charge; and they won't want to give up control. If you go now, you may lose your chance here, forever!'

He nodded and stood up. Slowly, she stood up on the other side of the table and together, not saying anything more to each other, they went out of the dining room. At its entrance, Ajela touched a control pad set in the wall, and the same short corridor formed with a door at the end that would be the entrance to his own quarters.

'Thank you,' he said, hardly looking at her. 'I'll call you – as soon as I've got something to tell you.'

After a moment more he met her eyes with his own. Her naked gaze seemed to go through him effortlessly.

'I'll wait for you to call,' she said.

He went down the corridor, still feeling her standing watching him from behind, as he had felt the piercing strength of her gaze. Not until the door of his room closed behind him did he feel free of her. He dropped into a float opposite his bed.

There was an empty loneliness and a longing in him. What he needed desperately, he told himself, was some point outside the situation that now held him, where he could stand and look at it – and at her expectations and Tam's. Of course, she would see no sense in his going. From her standpoint, the Encyclopedia was so much beyond Coby in what it had to offer him that any comparison of the two was ridiculous. All Coby had to offer was someplace to hide.

The Encyclopedia offered him not only that, but the shield of the force panels, the protection of those who belonged to the single institution that the Others probably would never be able to control, and quite possibly would have no interest in controlling. In fact, as long as he stayed and worked with the Final Encyclopedia, here, what sort of threat did he pose to the Others? It would be only out in their territory, on the younger worlds, that he posed a possible threat to them. Even if they discovered him here, it might well be that they would simply decide to leave him alone.

Meanwhile, there was all that the Encyclopedia had to offer him. Walter the InTeacher had been fond of saying that the pursuit of knowledge was the greatest adventure ever discovered by the human race. The degree to which Ajela had touched Hal just now had almost swept him away beyond the power of any personal choice. To be able to work with the Encyclopedia as he had done for a short while was like having the Universe handed to him for a plaything. It was more than that –

It was, thought Hal suddenly, like being able to play God.

On Coby he would be a stranger among strangers – and probably among strangers who were the sweepings of the fourteen worlds, for who would go and work in the mines of Coby if he could be someplace else? Here, he already knew Ajela . . . and Tam.

And her last words had struck him forcefully. She was right in the fact that if he went now and Tam died or stopped being Director, Hal's own chances at that post with the Encyclopedia could be lost forever. His mind shied from the responsibility of the prospect. But it was a great and almost unheard-of thing, to be someone who could be considered as a successor to the Director of the Encyclopedia. Tam seemed a crusty sort of individual – age might have something to do with that, or it might be his natural pattern – but Ajela obviously found him to be someone she could love; and, in fact, Hal had found himself warming to the old man, also, even during their brief meeting.

It might also be his resemblance to Obadiah. Perhaps Hal was deliberately making himself see Obadiah in the Director, and this was giving him a greater feeling of closeness to Tam than the situation actually justified. But it really did not matter whether Tam and he were close or not. The overwhelmingly important thing was the Encyclopedia itself and that it have a continuity of Directors; and if Hal was indeed a serious possibility to take control from Tam's hands eventually, then. . . .

Hal's mind drifted into a dark, but comfortable dream of the Encyclopedia, as it might be after he had been here some years and was finally in control as Director. Ajela could probably be brought to agree to stay on with him, in something like the relationship that she had with Tam – of course she could, for the Encyclopedia's sake, if nothing else. And, if they should really agree well together. . . .

He looked at the chronometer on his wrist. The ring that was set to local time showed a little less than an hour and a half before his ship was scheduled to lift from its docking, just under the metal and force-panel skin of the Encyclopedia. His mind still caught in his dark dream, he got up and went across the room, to find the travel bag with which he had come to the Encyclopedia. He was holding it in his hands before he realized what he was doing.

He laughed.

He was on his way to Coby.

The recognition came like a dull, but expected, shock. Abruptly, then, he realized; it was not the dead hands of Walter, Malachi and Obadiah reaching out to control him against his will. It was not even the calculation of his training that had implemented its decision by some sort of conditioned lever upon his will. It was simply that he, for reasons he could not clearly enunciate, knew that he had to go; and, far from weakening that certainty, what he had heard from Ajela and experienced in his earlier work with the Encyclopedia that morning had confirmed it.

Heavily, he began to do what little gathering of papers and possessions was necessary. He had been deluding not only Ajela, but himself, by pretending that the question of his staying was still open.

He had not been able to face Ajela with that truth over the lunch table. She would not have pressed him for reasons, he knew, being an Exotic; but she would have – and still did – deserve some. Only, he would not be able to give her any. So he would simply sneak out of the Encyclopedia, after all, as he had, in effect, sneaked in; and he would send both her and Tam a message afterwards, once he was irrevocably on his way among the stars.

He finished up, coded the number of his exit port into the room control, and stepped out the dilated entrance into a short corridor that took him down and through another entrance, past another screen from which an elderly woman perfunctorily scanned his papers, and into the port chamber.

There was a forty minute wait before he could board the ship. But five minutes later he was in his compartment, and forty minutes after that, the ship sealed and lifted. An annunciator woke over his head.

'First phase shift in two hours,' it said. 'First phase shift in two hours. There will be a meal service immediately after the shift. All portside compartments, first seating; all starboardside compartments, second seating.'

He was in a portside compartment; but he was not hungry – although in two hours, knowing himself, he would probably be starving, as usual. He sat down on that one of the two fixed seats in the compartment that was below the bed folded up against the bulkhead.

Once they had phase-shifted, there would be no direct communication possible with the Encyclopedia. At once, they would be light-years distant; and a message physically carried by a ship inbound to Earth would be the quickest way of getting in touch. He did not feel up to talking face to face with Ajela, in any case; but something in him rebelled at waiting to tell her until he was well away. She would be looking at the time and thinking that he had decided against going, and was working with the Encyclopedia – and she would hear from him about dinner time.

He roused himself, stepped across to the tiny desk against the wall of his compartment opposite the bed, sat down on the other seat, and coded a call to the ship's communications center. The screen lit up with a heavy man in ship's whites.

'I'd like to send a message back to the Encyclopedia,' he said.

'Certainly. Want the message privacy coded? And written or spoken?'

'Spoken,' he said. 'Never mind the privacy code. It's to Ajela, Special Assistant to the Director. "Ajela. I'm sorry. I had to go." '

His own voice repeated itself back at him from the screen.

'*Ajela. I'm sorry. I had to go.*'

'That's all?' said the shipman.

'Yes. Sign it – my name's Hal Mayne –' he checked himself. 'Wait, add on . . . "I'll see you both again, as soon as I can." '

'*Ajela. I'm sorry. I had to go. I'll see you both again, as soon as I can. Hal Mayne.*' The screen gave his words back to him once more.

'All right? Or did you want that last sentence as a p.s.?' asked the shipman.

'No, that's fine. Thank you.'

Hal broke the connection and got up from the seat. He pulled the bed down into position and stretched out on it. He lay on his back, looking at the ceiling and bulkheads of his compartment, which showed the same flat brown color everywhere he looked. A faint vibration through the fabric of the ship around them was the only sign that they were under way; it would be the only sensation of movement to be felt – and not even that during phase shift – until they went into docking mode in New Earth orbit.

There had never been any possible decision except that he should go on to Coby. But it had taken the Encyclopedia to help him see the inevitability of it; and even then the recognition had come in through the back door of his mind. It had been the poem that had told him, its images speaking from his unconscious, as surely as the images of Walter, Malachi and Obadiah had spoken from it on his first night in the great sphere. He was the knight and was summoned in one direction only.

The poem had been no more than a codification of that oceanic feeling he had touched when he worked with the Encyclopedia. Blindly there, he had felt something, some great effort, that rang its particular call trumpet-like, reading back through him. For a little while, unknowing, he had touched what could be – and it was so large in promise that it dwarfed all other things. But the way to it did not lie through a dusty scholar's cell, or even by way of Tam's desk in the Encyclopedia. At least, not yet. There were things within him that would have to grow to match in size what he had felt in the Encyclopedia; and some deep-buried instinct had come to tell him clearly that these would not grow in a sterile, protected environment. It was out among the materials of which the race was made that he must find the particular strength he would need to use the mighty lever that was the Encyclopedia. And, once he had found it, he would be back – whether he was wanted or not.

The faint vibration of the ship thrummed all through him as he lay. He felt caught, like someone apart, suspended between all worlds, waiting.

CHAPTER FIVE

As the spaceship to New Earth pulled away from Earth orbit preparatory to its first phase shift into interstellar space, the awareness of his utter loneliness moved in on Hal all at once. In the Final Encyclopedia, thanks to Tam and Ajela, he had not felt completely alone; and until he had gotten to the Final Encyclopedia the anesthesia of shock and his training had held the realities of his new orphan's status at a numb distance from his emotions. But now, unexpectedly, a full appreciation of it flooded him.

That first night on shipboard he dreamed a vivid, colorful dream in which it turned out that the events on the terrace and the deaths of Malachi, Obadiah and Walter had been nothing but a nightmare from which he had just awakened. He felt foolish, but inexpressibly relieved to discover that the three of them were still alive and all was well.

Then he awoke to reality, and lay in the darkness, listening to the faint breathing of the ventilating system of the ship, echoing out through the grille on the near wall of his stateroom. Emptiness and desolation filled him. He pulled the bedcovers over his head like a very young child, and lay there, cold, in his misery, until, at some unknown, later time, he fell asleep again, to other dreams he did not remember on awakening.

But from then on the awareness of his isolation and vulnerability was always with him. He was able to push it into a back corner of his mind, but there it settled, as if in some dark corner, where Bleys and the rest of the Others seemed also to crouch, waiting. He realized now that he had made a serious mistake in not asking that this passage from the Encyclopedia be booked for him under a false name.

The situation was not completely irreparable, of course. Once he got to New Earth, he could cancel the reservations made under the name of Hal Mayne, and then make new reservations to Coby under an alias. At most, then, this ship's records would only show Hal Mayne as going no farther than New Earth. But the record of his having been outbound from Old Earth aboard this ship would remain, for the Others to find.

A cooler part of his mind told him that even travelling under his real name as he was now, the passenger record would not be easy for Bleys to run down. It was not that ship's records were not kept and that the Others could not eventually get access to them all. It was simply that, given the mass of interstellar shipping and the complexity of individual records on fourteen worlds, it became a statistical nightmare to search through all of these in an attempt to trace or locate a single individual.

Nonetheless, he made up his mind to be as inconspicuous as possible until he reached Coby and, once there, to lose himself under a completely false identity. Being inconspicuous would mean, of course, that he should restrict his contacts with other people aboard, as much as possible; but that was a small hardship. At this moment he felt no great desire to make the acquaintances of his fellow passengers, or those who staffed the ship.

It was a prudent decision, but in making it he had not considered how much such solitary behavior would leave him to his own thoughts and feelings during the days that followed. At times he would find himself unexpectedly immersed in grief, an unbearable grief that would mutate gradually into an icy, compelling rage, that in its own strange way seemed familiar, although he could not recall having felt anything like it before. It made him shiver, thinking of Bleys and the Others, and all their kind. A desire to destroy them and everything connected with them would seize him so powerfully that he could think of nothing else.

As ye have done to me and mine . . .

The words seemed to arise out of some ancient part of him like a stained and weathered carving on the stone of his soul. He would follow the advice of the ghosts of Malachi, Obadiah, and Walter to hide until he was strong enough to fight back against those who had done this; and then he would destroy them as they had destroyed all those he had ever loved. Just as Ajela had reminded him that Tam Olyn had once set out to destroy the entire Friendly culture. Tam had changed and turned back from what he had started to accomplish, but Hal would never do so.

Walter's teaching had warned against letting destructive emotions grow and take charge of him; and he had been trained in ways to control them. But he found now that in the worst moments of his grief, the rage was the only thing that could push it from him – and at such times the grief seemed too great to be borne.

Still, in all, the trip to New Earth was not that long in actual subjective, shipboard time. Most of the passengers on board were bound beyond that world, to Freiland, which was now the richer and more commercially active of the two worlds under the star of Sirius. But the ships stopped at New Earth first, because New Earth was the major transshipment point for that solar system; and, like Hal, all those who were going on to other destinations would be making their change to other vessels there, rather than at Freiland.

Hal had hoped to find at least one other person aboard who was going to Coby, or who had known that planet first hand, so that he could ask what the life there was actually like for miners. But none of the other transshipping passengers were bound in his direction – he had asked the purser to check the ship's list to make sure. In the end, when he took the jitney down to New Earth City for the three days he must wait for his vessel to Coby, he was as much alone and knew as little as he had when he had come on board.

But New Earth City itself caught his attention, even driving the memory of the events on the terrace and the Encyclopedia temporarily into the background of his thoughts. It was a space-base city, which meant it had its primary commercial activity in off-world shipping. The sky was busy with passenger and cargo jitneys going to and from parking orbit; the streets were equally full of a multitude of shipping agents. He had no trouble finding passage under a different name on a ship headed for Coby, after he had cancelled his original reservations.

The city, itself, lay in the uplands of the north temperate zone of that world, in mid-continent, at the confluence of the two large rivers that together with their tributaries provided a watershed for nearly one-third of the continent's land mass. Hal remembered from his geography studies that the city was supposed to be very cold in winter. But now it was mid-summer, the air dusty and windy with the odor unique to vegetation of that latitude on the planet. He sat in sidewalk restaurants, drinking the local fruit and vegetable juices and watching the people who passed.

In spite of his training, the romantic part of him had always clung to the thought that there would be markedly noticeable differences to be seen in the people on the younger inhabited planets. But New Earth was an unspecialized world and the majority of the people on it looked as much like full-spectrum humans as those of Earth. They looked the same; essentially, they talked the same; and, with slight variations in cut and style, they wore the same sort of clothes. Only occasionally did he see an individual who dressed and acted as if he or she clearly belonged to one of the true Splinter Cultures – Friendly, Exotic, or Dorsai – and these stood out sharply from those about them.

Nonetheless, it was a strange and foreign place, New Earth City – the sunlight, the smells, the activity, all had differences about them that caught at his imagination and compelled it. He could see no signs of the decay Tam Olyn had spoken of, the approach of an Armageddon, an end to present civilization, or even to the human race itself. Dismissing the puzzle at last from his mind, he turned to a more immediate question. He tried telling those he met that he was a University-level student from Earth on a thesis-trip, testing his ability to pass for someone in his late teens or early twenties, and was gratified when no one questioned this.

Part of him, he had found out long since, was a chameleon; an imaginative actor who could be seduced by an infinite number of roles. He had three days, local time, to pass before his new transport to Coby would be leaving orbit; and, even in three days, he came close to being strongly tempted to stay where he was for a month or two, learning to fit in with what he saw around him and experiencing New Earth living from within its society.

But the thought that Bleys might already have set – no matter how idly – a search in progress for him, plus the pull of that same amorphous, oceanic purpose in him which had set him unthinkingly to packing as the time approached to board the jitney to the New Earth-bound ship; these sent him up to the ship to Coby in time; and a few hours later, he was once more between the stars, heading toward the first phase shift that would bring him eventually to work in the mines of that airless world.

The ship he travelled on now was not a passenger liner, like the one on which he had left Earth orbit, but a cargo vessel that carried a small complement of passengers in accommodations comparable to those of the ship's officers. The only other passengers were three commercial representatives who spent all their time gambling with gravityless shotballs in the lounge. The officers and crew were indifferent to conversation with the passengers. They had their own professional clubbishness, and except at meals he never saw them; and so, at the end of five days, they came to Coby.

– Not just to an orbit around Coby, however. At the mining world, it developed, spaceships did not park in orbit and wait for jitneys from the surface. They not only went down like military craft, directly to the surface, they went one step further. They descended below the world's surface. Everything built on Coby had been built underground, and as the ship Hal was on gingerly nudged its way close to the Moon-like landscape of the planet, that landscape developed a crack before them from which light shone upward. Barely hovering, it seemed, on its maneuvering powerways, the ship slid into an opening, as the jitney from Earth had slipped into the opening of the port of the Final Encyclopedia.

The moment they were inside, the opening closed again behind them. With pressure barriers, there had been minimal loss of air; but for a world that needed to make all its air and water out of crustal chemicals, even small losses would be important, Hal thought. But then he forgot problems having to do with the crustal extraction of chemicals; for the place into which they had come was another matter entirely than the entry port of the Encyclopedia.

This was like nothing so much as a full-sized surface military or commercial spaceport, hollowed out of the solid stuff of the world, with a spacepad of remarkable dimensions, its edges thick with fitting yards. In the viewing screen of his room, with which Hal was watching their landing, spaceships could be seen lying in the cradles of those yards and being fitted with the metal parts and fabrications that Coby could supply more cheaply than any of the other worlds.

It had been ironic, Obadiah had said once, harshly, that the human race had been so slow to realize how favored was the planet of its birth. Not only in terms of air, water, climate and the wealth of its ecology – but in the availability of its metals. The first people settling on the younger worlds had been quick to discover that the metals they needed were neither so available in that quantity that Earth had accustomed them to, nor so cheaply easy to extract from the rocky mantle of their planets. On twelve of the fourteen worlds, the human race had metal-hungry societies; and on a few of those worlds, like both of the Friendly planets and on the Dorsai, that poverty was so great that they could not have existed in a modern interstellar community if they had not been able to buy much of what they needed for their technological life off-planet. The fourteen worlds could only remain one community if they could trade together; and the one currency they had in common was professional skills, packaged in the minds and bodies of their own people. So the worlds had specialized.

Physicians and specialists in the soft sciences came from schools on the Exotics. Statisticians from the Friendlies. Professional military from the Dorsai. An individual working on a world other than his or her own earned not only a personal income in that planet's local currency, but interstellar credit for the world that had raised and trained her or him. And on the basis of that interstellar credit metal-poor worlds like New Earth bought what they needed from Coby. . . .

Their cargo spaceship was already settling onto the field below; and with the other passengers, Hal left the ship. He found immigration officials waiting at the foot of the landing stair; but the checks made were brief and simple.

'Visa?' The heavy-bodied, gray-haired official who greeted him took the visa he had purchased on New Earth, under the name of Tad Thornhill, from Hal's hand. 'Visiting or staying?'

'Staying,' Hal said. 'I want to look for a job here.'

The woman ran the papers through the transverse slot of her desk and passed them back to Hal. Endless repetitions of the same words had worn her voice to a near-monotone.

'Check the directory in the Terminal for the nearest Assignments Office outside of the port area,' she said. 'If you change your mind or for any reason stay in the port area, you must register and leave Coby again within eight days, or face deportation. If you leave the port area, you may only return on pass from your work superiors. Next!'

63

Hal moved on and the commercial representatives behind him took his place.

Inside the terminal building, the directory – when he queried its console – printed in its screen the words: *Halla Station Assignment Office, Halla Station: Tube Line C: report for job interview at destination.* It also extruded a small hard-copy card with the same information printed on it.

Hal took the card and tucked it into his bag. The port area looked interesting, especially the fitting yards. He thought of trying to get a job there, rather than in the mines. But a little more thought brought back to mind the fact that he was here to become invisible to the Others; and in a port area, pinned down by job-required identification and security observation, would not be the best place to hide.

In fact, he thought, remembering the lessons that had been drilled into him, he would undoubtedly minimize the danger of being traced here by the Others if he got out of the port area as fast as possible. He went searching for, and found the subway-like station that was the terminal of Tube C, took passage in one of the long, silver cars that floated there in their magnetic rings, and an hour and a half later got out two thousand kilometers away, at Halla Station Terminal.

The Assignment Office was in one corner of the Terminal, four desks in an open area. Three had no one at them. One had a man interviewing another man, who by his appearance and the travel bag on the floor beside his chair was a job applicant like Hal. Hal waited until the other applicant had finished and been sent out through a rear door in the Terminal. Then he came up to the desk, handed his papers to the interviewer and sat down without waiting to be asked.

The man behind the desk did not seem to resent Hal's not waiting for an invitation. He scanned the papers, made out in the name of Tad Thornhill, ran them through the slot on his desk and then looked over at Hal. He was in his early thirties, a short, slim individual with a narrow, white face and a shock of red hair – the sort of face that might have been friendly, if it had not been for an expression of indifference that seemed to have worn lines in it.

'You're sure you want to work in the mines?' he asked.

'I wouldn't be here if I didn't,' Hal said.

The interviewer rattled busily away at the keys of his console and a hard copy document emerged from his desk top.

'Sign here, and here. If you change your mind in less than a week, you will be charged for food and lodging and any other expenses incurred by you. Do you understand?'

'Yes.' Hal reached out to put his thumbprint in the signature area. The interviewer blocked the motion with his own hand.

'Are you aware that the society here on Coby is different from what you may have encountered on any of the other worlds? That, in particular, the process of laws is different?'

64

'I've read about it,' said Hal.

'On Coby,' went on the interviewer, as if Hal had not spoken, 'you are immune to off-world deportation by reason of legal papers of any kind originating other than on this planet. However, all legal power here is vested in the management of the Company you work for and in the Planetary Consortium of Companies to which the Company you will work for belongs. The legal authority to whom you will be directly responsible for your actions is the Company Judge-Advocate, who combines in himself the duties of criminal investigator, prosecutor, judge and jury. If you are cited by him, you are presumed guilty until you can prove your innocence. You will be held wholly at his disposal for whatever length of time he desires, and you are liable to questioning by any means he wishes to use in an effort to elicit whatever information he needs. His judgment on your case is final, not subject to review and may include the death penalty, by any process he may specify; and the Company is under no obligation to notify anyone of your death. Do you understand all this?'

Hal stared at the man. He had read all this before as part of his studies, everything that the interviewer had just told him. But it was an entirely different matter to sit here and have these statements presented to him as present and inescapable realities. A cool breeze seemed to breathe on the back of his neck.

'I understand,' he said.

'Very good. You'll remember then,' said the interviewer, 'that what you may have been accustomed to as personal rights no longer exist for you once you have put your thumbprint on this contract. I have offered you terms for a minimum work commitment of one standard Coby year at apprentice wages. There are no shorter work commitments. Do you wish to contract for a longer term?'

'No,' said Hal. 'But I can renew my contract at the end of a year without losing anything, can't I?'

'Yes.' The interviewer took his guarding hand away from the signature area. 'Your thumbprint here, please.'

Hal looked at the man. There is a unique human being within each sane member of the human race, Walter the InTeacher used to say. Try, and you can reach him, or her. He thought of trying to make the effort now, but he could find nothing in the man before him to touch.

He reached out, put this thumbprint on the contract and signed.

'This is your copy,' said the interviewer, detaching it from his desk and passing it to him. 'Go out the door to the rear and follow the signs in the corridor to the office of the Holding Area.'

Hal followed the directions. They led him down a well-lighted tunnel about four meters wide to a much wider entrance in the right wall of the tunnel. Turning in at the entrance, he saw what appeared to be an enclosed office to his right, and a considerably larger enclosed area to his left, through the doorless entrance of which came the sound of music and voices. Straight ahead, but further on, he could see what seemed to be a double row of large cages made of floor to ceiling metal bars, but with their doors, for the most part, standing open.

He assumed that the office on the right was the one he had been directed to in the Holding Area; but curiosity led him toward the doorway of the place opposite, with the noisy interior. He automatically approached its doorway from an angle, out of training, and stopped about three meters away to look in; but he need not have been cautious. None of those inside were paying any attention to anything outside.

Apparently, it was simply a recreation place. It was well-filled with people, but with only one woman visible, and the rest men. There was a bar and most of those there seemed to be drinking out of silvery metal mugs that must have held at least half a liter. On any other world, such mugs would have been expensive items indeed – perhaps here they were simply a cheap way to cut down on breakage.

Hal turned back to the office, knocked on its door when he could find no annunciator stud, and – when he heard nothing – let himself in.

Within was a wall to wall, waist-high counter dividing the room crosswise, with two desks behind it. Only one desk was occupied, and the man at it was middle-aged, balding and heavy-set. He had the look of someone who did little but sit at desks. He glanced up at Hal.

'We don't knock here,' he said. He extended his hand without getting up. 'Papers.'

Hal leaned over the counter and managed to pass them over without taking his feet off the floor. The man behind the counter accepted them and ran them through the slot in his desk.

'All right,' he said, handing them back – Hal had to stretch himself across the counter once more to retrieve them – 'find yourself a bunk out back. Rollcall and assignments at eight-thirty in the morning. My name's Jennison – but you call me Superintendent.'

'Thank you,' said Hal, reflexively, and for the first time Jennison lifted his gaze from his desk and actually looked at him.

'How old are you?' he asked.

'Twenty,' said Hal.

'Sure.' Jennison nodded.

'Is there any place I could get something to eat?' Hal asked.

'I'll sell you a package meal,' Jennison said. 'Got credit?'

'You just saw my papers.'

Jennison punched his key pad and looked into the screen on his desk.

'All right,' he said. 'I've debited you the cost of one package meal.'

He swiveled his float around and touched the wall behind him, which opened to show a food storage locker. He took a white, sealed package from the locker and tossed it to Hal.

'Thanks,' said Hal.

'You'll get out of that habit,' said Jennison.

'What habit?' asked Hal.

Jennison snorted a short laugh and went back to his work without answering.

Hal took his package and his bag and went out of the office, and into the back area, among the cages. When he came to them he found that each one held two double-decker bunks on each side of the cage, so that each had sleeping space for eight individuals. The bunks stood against the side walls of the cage with a little space of the wall of bars before them, and beyond them to where the cell ended in the solid wall that must be backed by the rock of the cave excavated to make this area. The first few cages he came to had two or three occupants in each, all of them sleeping heavily. He continued on back until he could see that there was no cage without at least one person in it.

He finally chose a cage in which the only occupant was a man sitting on one of the bottom bunks toward the back. The cage door was open and Hal came in, a little hesitantly. The man, a leathery-looking individual in his late thirties or early forties, had been carving on a piece of what looked like gray metal, but which must have been quite soft. Now, the knife and the metal bar hung motionless in his hands as he watched Hal enter. His face was expressionless.

'Hello,' said Hal. 'I'm Tad Thornhill. I just signed a contract for work, here.'

The other did not not say anything. Hal gestured toward the bottom bunk opposite the one on which the man sat.

'Is this taken?' he asked.

The man stared at him a second longer, still without expression, then he spoke.

'That one?' he said. His voice was hoarse, as if disuse had left it rusty. 'No, that doesn't belong to anybody.'

'I'll take it then.' Hal tossed his bag to the head end of the bunk, in the corner against the back wall. He sat down, and began to open the sealed meal package. 'I haven't eaten since I left the ship.'

The other man again said nothing, but went back to his carving. Hal spread the package open and saw through the transparent seal that it was some kind of stew with a baked vegetable that looked like a potato in its skin, some bread, and a small bar of what looked like chocolate, but certainly must be synthetic. He could feel the package heating automatically in his hands, now that the outer seal had been broken. He waited the customary sixty seconds, broke the transparent inner seal, and began eating. The food was tasteless and without much texture, but the heat of it was good, and it filled his empty stomach. He suddenly realized he had forgotten to ask Jennison for something to drink.

He looked across at the other man, busy shaping his piece of soft metal into something that looked like a statuette of a man.

'Is there anything to drink around here?' he asked.

'Beer and liquors up in the canteen, front, if you've got the credit,' said the other without looking up.

'I mean something like fruit juice, coffee, water – something like that,' said Hal.

The other looked at him and jerked his knife up and to his right, pointing chest-high on the wall just beyond them. Rising, Hal found an aperture in the wall, and a stud beside it. He looked about for something to use as a cup, found nothing and finally ended up folding a crude cup out of the outer shell of the meal package. He pressed the stud, and water fountained up in a small arc. He caught it in his jury-rigged cup and drank. It tasted strongly of iron.

He sat down again, finished his meal with the help of several more cupfuls of the water, then bundled the package and containers in his hands and looked around him.

'Throw it under the bunk,' said the man across from him.

Hal stared; but the other was bent over his carving and paying no attention. Reluctantly, for it was hard for him to believe that the advice was correct, he finally did as the man had suggested. Then he lay down on the bunk, with his bag prudently between his head and the wall of bars that separated him from the next cages, and gazed at the dark underside of the bunk above him.

He was about to drop off to sleep when the sound of footsteps made him open his eyes again and look toward his feet. A short, somewhat heavy man was just entering the door of the cage. This newcomer stopped just inside the door and stared at Hal.

'He asked me if that bunk was anybody's,' said the man doing the carving. 'I told him no, it wasn't anybody's.'

The other man laughed and climbed up into the top bunk next to the one below which the carver sat. He thrashed around momentarily, but ended up on his side, looking down into the cage, and lay there with his eyes open.

Hal closed his eyes again, and tried to sleep; but with the arrival of the second man, his mind had started to work. He made himself lie still and willed his arms, legs, and body to relax, but still he did not sleep. The powerful feeling of grief and loneliness began to take him over once more. He felt naked in his isolation. This place was entirely different from the Final Encyclopedia where he had at least found intelligent, responsible people like those with whom he had grown up; and where he had even found those who could be friends, like Ajela and Tam. Here, he felt almost as if he had been locked into a cage with wild animals, unpredictable and dangerous.

He lay watching as other men came into the cage from time to time, and took bunks. Out of the habits of his training, he kept automatic count, and even though his eyes were half-closed, he knew after a while that all the other bunks had been filled. By this time there was a good deal of low-voiced conversation amongst the other occupants of the cage, and from the cages on either side of them. Hal tried to pay no attention. He made, in fact, an effort to block the voices out; and he was beginning at last to think that he might be on the verge of drifting off to sleep when his outer leg was sharply poked.

'You!' He recognized the rusty voice of the man on the lower bunk opposite and opened his eyes. 'Sit up and talk for a minute. Where you from?'

'Earth,' said Hal. 'Old Earth.' Effortfully, he pulled himself up and swung his legs over the edge to sit on the side of the bunk.

'Old Earth, is it? This is the first time you've been on Coby?'

'Yes,' said Hal. Something about this conversation was wrong. There was a falseness about the other man's tone that triggered off all the alertness that Malachi had trained into him. Hal could feel his heartbeat accelerating, but he forced himself to yawn.

'How d'you like it here?'

The carver had shifted his position to the head of his bed, so that he now sat with his back braced against one of the upright posts at the end of his bunk, the darkness of the solid rock wall half a meter behind him. He continued to carve.

'I don't know. I haven't seen much of it, here,' Hal said. He turned, himself, so as to face more directly the man and the end wall behind him. He did not want to make enemies in this new environment, but the feeling of uneasiness was strong, and he wished the other would come to the point of this sudden impulse to make conversation.

'Well, you've got a lot to see. A lot,' said the carver. 'If you've never been here before, and haven't seen much, I take it you've never been down in a mine, either.'

'No,' said Hal. 'I haven't.'

He was conscious that the conversation had died in the other bunks. The rest of the men in the cage must either be asleep, or listening. Hal felt the concentration of attention upon him. Like a wild animal, himself, or like a very young child, he was paying less attention to what the man was saying to him, than he was to how the other was saying it – the tone of voice, the way the man sat, and all the other non-verbal signals he was broadcasting.

'. . . you're in for something you'll never forget, first time you go down in a mine,' the carver was saying. 'Everybody thinks we just punch buttons down there, nowdays. Hell, no, we don't punch

69

buttons. On Coby we don't just punch buttons. You'll see.'

'What do you mean?' Hal asked.

'You'll see –' said the carver. One of the other occupants of the room, in an upper bunk near the door, unexpectedly began to whistle, and the carver raised his voice. 'Most of the time you're working in a stope so tight you can't stand up in it, carving out the ore, and the heat from the rock gas your torch's boiling off as it cuts builds up until it could cook you.'

'But that sort of work's easily done by machines,' said Hal, remembering part of his studies. 'All it needs –'

'Not on Coby,' said the carver. 'On Coby, you 'n' me are cheaper than machines. You'll see. They hang a man here for being late to work too many times.'

Hal stared at the other. He could not believe what he had just heard.

'That's right, you think about it,' said the carver, whittling away. 'You think all that they told you about the Judge-Advocate can't be true? Listen, he can pull your fingernails out, or anything else, to make you talk. It's legal here; and they do it just on general principles in case you've got something to tell them they don't know about, once you're arrested. Three days under arrest and I've seen a man age twenty years –'

It all happened very quickly. Later on, Hal was to guess that the uneasy animal/child part of him must have caught some slight sound that warned him; but at the time all he knew was that something made him glance around suddenly, toward the entrance end of the cage. In the instant, he saw the faces of all the other occupants looking over the edges of their bunks, watching avidly; and, almost upon him from the entrance, coming swiftly, a tall, rawboned man in his forties, with a wedge-shaped face twisted with insane fury, one of the metal mugs held high in one hand, sweeping toward the back of Hal's head.

Hal reacted as instinctively as he might have put out a hand to keep himself from falling. From a time before he could remember, he had exercised under the direction of Malachi; and his exercises had long since lost all conscious connection with the real purpose for which they had originally been designed. They were simply physical games that made him feel good, the way swimming or running did. But now, when there was no time for thought, his body responded automatically.

There was a suddenness of action; no blurring – everything very clear and very fast. He had risen, turned and caught hold of the oncoming man before he had hardly realized it himself, levering and carrying the heavy attacking body forward into the air on its own momentum, to smash against the rock wall. The man struck with a heavy, sodden sound and collapsed at the foot of the wall, to lie there without any motion whatsoever.

Again, with no conscious time lag, Hal found himself turned back and watching all the others in the cage, wire-taut, balanced and waiting. But the rest lay as they had been, motionless, some still with the avid look not yet gone from their faces. But, as he watched, it faded where it still existed, leaving them all looking at him, dull-faced and stupid with astonishment.

Hal continued to stand, motionless, where he was. He felt nothing, but he would have reacted at the slightest movement from any of them; and each of them there seemed to understand this. They breathed through open mouths without sound, watching him . . . and the moment stretched out, and stretched out, as some of the tension in the cage began to trickle away like sands from a broken hourglass.

Gradually, the man on the bottom bunk farthest from Hal on his right slowly put one leg out and lowered a foot to the floor, slowly followed it with the second, and gradually stood up. Carefully, he backed away until he had passed out through the door of the cage. Then he turned and walked away swiftly. Hal stayed as he was, without moving, while, one by one, the others cautiously departed in turn. He was left at last alone, with the motionless figure on the floor.

The occupants of the other cages around him were utterly silent. He looked right and left and everyone he saw was looking away from him. He turned to stare down again at the body lying huddled against the wall. For the first time it occurred to him that the man might be dead. He had been flung head-first against a stone wall – it could be that his neck had broken.

All emotion in Hal was still lost in wariness and tension, but now, gradually, his mind was beginning to work again. If the man who had attacked him was dead . . . Hal had only been defending himself. But if the others who had been in the cage should all testify that he had been the aggressor. . . .

Plainly, he understood now that they all must have known that the man was coming, and that he would be likely to attack anyone using his bunk. He had been drunk, drugged or paranoid, possibly all three; and they had all been waiting for his return and probable attack on Hal. Perhaps, thought Hal emptily, they were all friends of his. Possibly they had even sent word to him that some stranger had taken his place – since obviously the carver had deliberately lied to Hal and even tried to set him up to be hit from behind, by moving so that Hal would have to turn his back to the cage entrance.

If the others should now all swear that Hal had picked a fight and killed this man deliberately . . . no, it was impossible. Justice, even here, could not be that unreasonably blind.

But the thought again of the right of the Judge-Advocate to use any means he wished to extract answers from someone under arrest returned to him, prickling the skin on the back of his neck.

Could he get back to the port, and off-planet? Not without using his visa as Tad Thornhill, and the moment he did that, he would undoubtedly arrested.

Common sense came suddenly like a cooling draft of air into his fevered mind. He squatted down and put his fingers on the neck of the man on the floor, feeling for the left carotid artery. It pulsed strongly against his fingertips; and when he put his hand over the other's mouth, he could feel the stir of breath against his palm. A deep sigh came out of him. The attacker had only been knocked out, after all. Hal's knees weakened with relief.

But, on the heels of that relief came a strong urge to get out of this place enclosing him. He turned quickly, and went out the door and up between the row of cages. The people in them had begun talking after their immediate moment of silence following the attack. But they stopped talking again now, as he passed, and this time their eyes watched him as he went by. When he reached the front of the area the canteen was still as noisy as ever, but the office was now dark, and looked as if it had been locked for the night. He hesitated, then walked on and out into the corridor, turning down it in the opposite direction to that from which he had come.

This way, the corridor seemed to run on forever in a straight line ahead of him, and there was nobody within sight in it, as far as his eye could see. He picked up speed as he went along until his long legs were swinging him forward at a rate of nearly seven kilometers an hour.

He had no idea yet where he was going, or why he was going there. He was driven only by an instinct to get away; and he was still charged to the teeth with the adrenaline his body had released in him under his instinct to defend himself. Even now, there was no fury in him, only a steady, sick feeling; and the sole relief from that feeling was to keep striding on, kilometer after kilometer, forcing his body into a mode that would make it forget the fight-or-flight reaction.

Time went by, and, little by little, the sick feeling began to fade. He was left with only a dullness, an empty sort of feeling such as might come after recovery from a hard blow in the solar plexus. He felt hollow inside. His mind brought him no solutions to the situation in which he now supposed he was. Whether his attacker had been insane or not, he had to assume that the others in the cage might well be his friends and would lie about what had happened, if only to protect themselves. They might even be waiting to revenge themselves on Hal when he got back – and there were six of them, not counting whoever else there might be in the other cages who might also know them and want to help them. Nor, probably, could he look for any protection from Jennison, who had given a strong impression of holding himself apart from Hal and everyone else in the Holding Area.

72

But there was no safe place to go to, except off-Coby. He had been warned that he could not return to the port area without the permission of his superiors. But they might not yet know at the port that he had signed a contract, and he could buy passage on some outbound ship. Otherwise – in this owned and artificial environment, there would be no such thing as existence outside of the social order. And there was no other place for him to go that he knew of, although presumably this corridor led to somewhere else on Coby.

Probably the best thing he could do was to keep on walking. This corridor had to lead someplace. Once there, with authorities who might be at least neutral about what had happened back at Halla Station Holding Area, he could plead his case and perhaps get a fair hearing. . . .

He stopped suddenly, his nerves wire-tight. As he strained to listen, he could now pick up a faint noise coming from ahead of him; and his eyes, now that he tried to see as far as possible down the corridor ahead, seemed to make out something like a dancing dot. He held still, closed his eyes for three counted seconds and then slowly opened them again, comparing the first moment of sight with the last thing he had seen before closing his eyelids. There was no doubt that the dot was there.

Something was coming his way, making a faint humming noise as it did so. Even in his present state, a corner of Hal's mind paused to puzzle over the sound, for it was like no noise he had heard before; but at the same time it had a ring of familiarity that he could not pin down.

In any case, there was nothing he could do but wait for its coming. The dot was expanding at a rate that implied it was coming faster than he could run from it. Hal stood where he was; and, after a little, the puzzle of the sound was solved, for as it came closer, it changed; and he both identified it and realized why he had not been able to identify it earlier.

What he was hearing was simply the sound of an air-cushion vehicle moving toward him. But by some freak of acoustics in the long, straight tunnel, the breathy whisper of the underjets was changed and amplified into a resonance that from a distance rang like a musical humming. The tunnel was acting like the pipe of a flute or the drone on a bagpipe. Now, however, as the vehicle came closer, the humming note began to be lost in the normal, breathy sound of the downward air-rush of the jets, and the total noise became identifiable for what it was.

At the same time, the vehicle itself was growing large enough to be recognized. As with sound, vision was evidently subject to tricks played on it by a corridor of this sort. The still, horizontal layers of air about him, extended into the distance, seemed to have an effect something like that of the heated air of the daytime desert. Even though the vehicle and its rider were now close enough to be seen for what they were – a simple four-place open truck and driver – still their outlines seemed to waver and change as if Hal was looking at a mirage. On impulse he started to walk again, toward the oncoming vehicle, and the outlines began to firm up.

Hal and the truck drew together. As they got close enough that the distortions of air in the corridor no longer bent the truck and its operator into odd shapes, the driver was revealed to be a man at least in his sixties, wearing a gray coverall and a gray cap. Below the cap his face was a remarkably young face grown old. At first glance it looked ancient, but then something almost boyish would glint out from among the lines and leathery skin. Truck and Hal came level, and the driver brought the vehicle to a stop.

Hal also stopped; and looked warily back at the man.

'What are you doing here?' the driver spoke in a half-shout; and his voice was the battered remnant of a tenor.

'Walking,' said Hal.

'Walking!' The driver stared at Hal. 'How long?'

'I don't know,' said Hal. He had to make an effort to remember. 'An hour, maybe two.'

'An hour! Two hours!' The driver was still in a half-shout, still staring at him. 'You know you're nearly twenty kilometers from Halla Station? That's where you're from, aren't you – Halla Station?'

Hal nodded.

'Then where d'you think you're walking to?'

'The next station,' said Hal.

'Next station's a hundred and twenty kilometers!'

Hal said nothing. The driver considered him for a few seconds more.

'You'd better get in. I'll take you back to Halla Station. Get in, now!'

Hal considered. A hundred and twenty kilometers without food, and above all without water, was something he could not hope to walk. He went slowly around the rear end of the truck and came up to find the driver trying to lever a large package out of the front seat beside him, into the back part of the vehicle.

Hal pushed it over for him and climbed up into the open seat. The driver started up again.

'I'm Hans Sosyetr,' the driver said. 'Who're you?'

'Tad Thornhill,' said Hal.

'Just got here, didn't you? Brand new, aren't you?'

'Yes,' said Hal.

They drove along for a little while in silence.

'How old are you?' said the driver.

'Twenty,' said Hal – and remembered he was no longer on Earth – 'standard years.'

'You aren't twenty,' said the driver.

Hal said nothing.

'You aren't nineteen. You aren't eighteen. How the hell old really are you?'

'Twenty,' said Hal.

Hans Sosyetr snorted. They drove along in silence for a way. The truck breathed steadily under them.

'What happened?' Sosyetr said. 'Some damn thing happened, don't tell me it didn't. You were at the Holding Area and something happened. So what was it?'

'I almost killed a man,' said Hal. The sick feeling returned to his stomach as the whole moment came alive for him briefly, once more.

'Did you kill him?'

'No,' said Hal. 'He was just knocked out.'

'What happened?'

'I looked around and saw him starting to hit me with one of those metal mugs from the canteen,' Hal said. He was surprised that he was answering this man so freely; but there was now an exhausted feeling coming over him, and, besides, Hans Sosyetr's age and direct questions seemed to make it hard not to answer the older man.

'So?'

'I threw him against a wall. It knocked him out.'

'So you started to walk to Moon Transfer?'

'Moon Transfer?' Hal looked at him. 'Is that the name of the next station?'

'What else? So you started to walk there. Why? Somebody chasing you?'

'No. They all got up and went out of the cage after it happened. They backed out and went away.'

'Backed away?' Sosyetr looked over at him. 'Who was this kip you threw against the wall?'

'I don't know,' said Hal.

'What's he look like?'

'About my height,' said Hal. 'No, maybe a little taller. And heavier, of course. About thirty or forty standard years. Dark face, wide at the top and narrow at the bottom.'

'And you threw him against a wall?' said Sosyetr. 'Bigger and older than you, and you just threw him against a wall. How'd you manage to do a thing like that?'

Hal was suddenly cold and tight inside with caution.

'It just happened,' he said. 'I was lucky.'

'Luckiest twenty-year-old I ever ran into. Why don't you tell me the whole thing?'

Hal hesitated; and then the wall of caution inside him unexpectedly dissolved. He felt a sudden, desperate urge to explain the whole thing to someone, and he found himself telling the older man about everything that had happened, from the time he stepped into the cage and asked the man carving metal if the bunk was empty.

'So,' said Sosyetr, when he was done. 'Why'd you leave? Why'd you start walking out that way?'

'Those others in the cage had to be friends of whoever it was I threw against the wall,' said Hal.

'Friends? In a Holding Area? And I thought you said they ran like rabbits.'

'I didn't say they all ran like rabbits . . . the point is, if they are his friends, they might swear I started it.'

'Swear? Who to?'

'The Judge-Advocate.'

'What's the Judge-Advocate to do with all this?'

Hal turned his head to stare at the old face beside him. 'I hurt a man pretty badly. I could have killed him.'

'So? In a Holding Area? They haul people out of there every morning.'

Hal continued to stare. After a moment he managed to get his voice to work.

'You mean – nobody cares?'

Sosyetr laughed, a laugh high in his throat.

'Nobody important. What those kips do, or what happens to them, is their own business. Once they get on a payroll, if they make trouble, Judge-Advocate might take an interest.'

He looked over at Hal.

'Judge-Advocate's pretty important. About the only law you're likely to have anything to do with is Mine Personnel Manager, or maybe company police.'

Hal sat, gradually absorbing this new information. There was a hard core forming in him now around the wariness that the attack in the cage had woken in him.

'If there's no law to speak of in a Holding Area,' he said, 'it was a good thing I left. There'd be nothing to keep his friends from doing anything they want to me.'

Sosyetr laughed again.

'Don't sound to me like friends – or that they'd much want to do anything to you, the way you say they ran off.'

'I told you,' said Hal. 'They didn't run.'

'Six of them, and they left? If they went then, I don't think you got much to worry about when you go back.'

'No,' said Hal. 'I'm not going back. Not tonight, anyway.'

Sosyetr blew a breath out, gustily.

'All right,' he said. 'You wait while I unload this stuff in Halla Station, maybe give me a hand unloading, and I'll sign for you to get a room at the Guest House until morning. You can give me a debit tab against your first wages. You want to be back at the Holding Area for job assignment at eight-thirty a.m., though.'

Hal looked at the older man with abrupt astonishment and gratitude, but Sosyetr was scowling at the front of the truck with his head cocked on one side as if listening for some noise in the underjets that should not have been there. Hal sat back in his truck seat, a sense of relief making him feel limp. Out of the wariness in him, out of what he had just learned from Sosyetr, from the attack of the man with the metal mug, and from the behavior of the other six men in the cage, a new awareness was just beginning to be born in him.

For the moment, he was only aware of this as a general feeling. But, in a strange way, as it grew and began to come to focus in him, the images of Malachi, Walter and Obadiah seemed to move back a little. Time and experience were already beginning to come between him and his recent memories of them – when he had as yet not really come to accept the fact that they were gone. A sadness too deep for expression moved in him, and held its place there all the rest of the silent ride with Sosyetr into Halla Station.

CHAPTER SIX

The Guest House in Halla Station proved to be a form of barracks for those who were not employees of local companies or offices. Hal learned, somewhat grimly, that the Guest House had been open to him all the time, since he had credit to pay for it. The Holding Area was only for job seekers, or former miners rehiring who had no credit. Everything at the Area, including the beer in the canteen, was free. This also included the package of food Jennison had charged him for. The Holding Area, in short, was for the Coby version of indigents – or those who knew no better, like himself.

'Hell,' said Sosyetr, as they sat over a late meal in the clean and comfortable meal room of the Guest House, 'didn't you ever think to ask the interviewer at Halla Station what you could buy?'

'No,' said Hal. 'I just took for granted he'd tell me whatever I needed to know. I was stupid.'

'Sure,' said Sosyetr, nodding. 'You were stupid, all right. Stupid-est twenty-year-old I ever met.'

Hal looked up quickly from the chunk of processed meat he was cutting. But if there had been a grin on the older man's face, he had been too slow to surprise it.

He finished eating – Sosyetr had already finished a much smaller meal and was sitting with a cup of Coby coffee, watching him – and pushed the plate aside.

'Sost,' he said, for the other had said this was the version he preferred to hear of a last name most people mispronounced – and he was not partial to Hans – 'what happens from the time I report for job assignment to roll-call?'

This time he did see Sost grin.

'Going to ask some questions now?'

'From now on,' said Hal.

Sost nodded.

'All right,' he said. He drank from his coffee cup and set it down again. 'You'll show up there tomorrow morning and everybody who can stand on their feet'll be out in front of the office. Agent'll call the roll, mark off anyone not there, and hand out assignments on the basis of the work orders he got since roll call the morning before. That's about it.'

'Then what? What if I'm called for a work assignment?'

'Then you get travel papers with directions and travel passes credited against your new job; and you take off for whatever company needed you enough to hire you.'

'And when I get there?'

'You'll be assigned to a team on one of the shifts – unless the team captain throws you back. If that happens, they'll bounce you around until they find a team that'll take you.'

'What if no one wants me?'

'You?' Sost looked at him. 'Not likely. But if they did the company'd give you a week's wages and dump you at the nearest Holding Area. You get to start all over again.'

He got up to get himself another cup of coffee from the wall dispenser and sat back down at the table they were sharing.

'Sost,' said Hal, 'what are the things that make you think I'm younger than twenty?'

Sost stared at him for a long moment.

'You want to know what to look out for?' he said at last. 'I'll tell you. The first thing is, keep your mouth shut. Sure, I know your voice changed four-five years ago; but every time you say something you talk like a kid. Hell, you think like a kid. So don't talk, if you can help it.'

Hal nodded.

'All right,' he said 'I won't.'

'And take your time,' said Sost. 'Don't start talking to everyone you meet like he was an old friend. I don't mean act suspicious all the time, either. Just – hold back a little. Wait a bit. Don't go jumping around with your body, either. You get a little older, you won't have that kind of energy to waste. Sit still when you sit. But the big thing is – watch that talking. Just get in the habit of not doing it.'

'You talk a fair amount,' Hal said.

'There you go,' Sost said. 'That's just the sort of thing a kid would say. That's just the wrong thing. What's it change things for you, what I do? As far as me talking, I know what to say. I can make noise with my mouth all day long and not give anything away I don't want to. You, you give everything you've got away, every time you open your lips.'

Hal nodded.

'All right,' he said.

'That's better,' said Sost. 'Now, what're you planning to do tomorrow?'

'Wait and see,' said Hal.

'All right.' Sost nodded, in his turn. 'Good for you. You're learning. But I mean, what're you going to do about those kips back at the Holding Area?'

Hal shrugged.

79

'That's even better. You'll do,' said Sost. He got up. 'I'm folding up. That's another difference. You grow up, and you know there's a next day coming. You don't forget it.'

After the older man had left, Hal sat for a little while, enjoying the clean smells and the privacy of the dining room, in which he was now alone. Then he went to bed behind a locked door in the comfortable room his credit had been able to provide for him.

A knocking at his door seemed to wake him the minute he had closed his eyes. He got up, unlocked and opened the door, and found Sost dressed and waiting.

'What time is it?' Hal asked thickly.

'Seven-thirty,' Sost said. 'Or don't you want breakfast?'

They had breakfast in the same meal room and Sost drove him out to the Holding Area.

'I'll wait,' said Sost, parking the truck when they got there just at the 8:30 roll-call time. 'You're a natural to get assigned today. But if you don't, I can give you a lift back to the Guest House before I go on.'

Hal started to get out of the truck to join the men standing before the office.

'Sit still,' said Sost, under his breath. 'What the hell, you can hear from here, can't you? What'd I tell you last night about jumping?'

Hal settled back in his seat in the truck. He sat silently with Sost, waiting with the standing crowd for Jennison to put in an appearance. He had time to study the others who were waiting; and he found himself looking for the man who had attacked him. But the wedge-shaped face and long body did not seem to be there. Perhaps the other man had been hurt more badly than Hal had thought. . . . The thought chilled him, but after Sost's words the night before, he did not say anything to the older man.

He started to get out of the truck again.

'Sit still, I said,' growled Sost softly.

'I've got to get my bag – if it's still there.'

'After.'

Hal sank back in his seat. He went back to searching the crowd for faces he could recognize. He picked out the man who had been doing the carving, but was not able to identify certainly any of the others from the cage. He gradually became aware that none of those in the crowd were meeting his eyes. In fact, the carver had turned away when Hal had started watching him.

Experimentally, he picked out a man he was sure he had never seen before and stared only at him. The man, apparently casually, first turned away from Hal's gaze; then, when Hal continued to watch, the other moved deeper into the crowd, stepping behind other, taller individuals and using them as screens until they moved, until he had been herded by Hal's unrelenting watch to the far edge of the crowd.

The door opened finally, and Jennison appeared. It was almost a quarter to nine. He was carrying a hard copy printout in his hand, and without looking at the crowd he began to read off names. Hal's was the third to be read. When Jennison had finished, he looked up and saw the truck with the two of them in it.

'Sost!' he called, and waved. Sost waved back. Jennison turned and went back into the office.

'You know him?' Hal asked.

'No,' said Sost. 'Looks like he knows me, though. Lots do.'

The crowd before the office was beginning to disintegrate slowly as disappointed members of it began to break off toward the cages or the canteen and those whose names had been called moved up to cluster just outside the door.

'No hurry,' Sost said, as Hal again started to get out of the truck. 'Let the others go in first. Now's a good time to get that bag of yours.'

'If it's still there,' said Hal again, glumly.

Sost laughed, but said nothing.

Hal got out of the truck and, tensing instinctively, approached the men, who were still in a loose gathering before the office. They parted unobtrusively to let him through, with none of them looking directly at him in the process. Beyond them, the corridor between the rows of cages was empty, and the cages themselves were deserted except for a heavily inert body here and there on a bunk. He went to the cage he had been in the night before, stepped inside, and looked for the bunk he had occupied.

His bag was there, just where he had left it. He took it back to the truck. There were still a number of men waiting before the office door and as he came through the space before the building, one came out and another entered. Hal climbed back into the truck.

'It was there, all right,' he said. 'I can't believe it.'

Sost chuckled, this time quietly.

'Who of them'd take it?' he asked.

Hal looked curiously at the older man; but playing his new game of speaking as little as possible, he waited, instead of asking what the older man had meant. Either Sost would tell him before the older man left, or the answer would emerge otherwise.

He sat comfortably with Sost until the last man had come out of the office, then got down from the truck and crossed the space to the office door, himself. He stepped in and found Jennison in position at his desk behind the counter. But this time Jennison got up, smiling, and came to the other side of the counter.

'Here's your assignment papers,' Jennison said, handing them over. 'You're hired by the Yow Dee Mine, Templar Mining Company. You ought to be there in two hours by tube. I gave you a good assignment.'

Hal did not answer immediately. He had not liked Jennison on first encounter. He liked him no more now; and he was certain that the apparent generosity and friendliness must tie in with some advantage Jennison was hoping to gain from him. The thing would be to try and find out what that advantage was. 'Such situations,' Walter had told him once, 'always develop into bargaining sessions. And the first secret of successful bargaining is to make the other party do the proposing.'

'You charged me for a meal, last night,' Hal said, picking up the assignment papers.

'That's right, I did,' said Jennison. He leaned on the counter and continued to smile. 'Officially, of course, I shouldn't have done it. If I'd known more about you, I wouldn't have. But in a job like this, you take what you can. I wouldn't do it again; but now the credit's entered with central bookkeeping, it'd be a little awkward to fix it without upsetting the accountants at headquarters. And I get along by getting along with people. Now, I did you a big favor with the mine I assigned you to – ask your friend Sost about that if you don't believe me. Why don't you do me the small favor of forgetting that small charge to your credit? Maybe someday we can do a little business, and I can knock the amount of it off a price.'

'And maybe we won't do any business,' said Hal.

Jennison laughed.

'On Coby everybody does business with everybody. As I say, ask your friend Sost.'

'Maybe I'm different,' said Hal.

He had chosen the words at random; but his senses, stretched to their greatest alertness, suddenly convinced him that he had triggered a reaction from Jennison with that last answer. Of course, Jennison could be interpreting what he had just said as a threat . . . Hal suddenly remembered that he had come here to Coby to hide, and he was abruptly conscious of the danger of insisting too much on any difference he might have. He spoke again quickly.

'Anyway, I don't expect to come through here again.'

'There's always a chance,' said Jennison. 'I don't know myself what might bring us to talking again; but I always like to part friends with everybody. All right?'

'I don't make friends that easily.'

Jennison showed a trace of impatience.

'I'm just pointing out I may be able to do you some good, someday!' he said. 'You'll maybe find out you want to do business with me, after all. It'll work a lot better then if we're already – all right, not friends, then – but at least friendly.'

Hal watched the man closely. Jennison was sounding sincere. Hal could check with Sost, but he was beginning to be strongly convinced that the agent must have some specific stock-in-trade which the events here had convinced him he might be able to sell to Hal, someday; and he was trying to pave the way for that sale, in advance.

Hal put the assignment papers safely in an inside jacket pocket.

'What happened to that man who jumped me last night?' he asked.

'Who?' Jennison raised an eyebrow, turned about and ran his eye down a list of what seemed to be names on a printout on his desk. '. . . Khef? Oh, yes, Khef. He's all right. In the infirmary. Slight concussion; probably be back here in a day or two – though they say they may want to hold him for some psychiatrics.'

Hal turned and went out the door. He had to struggle against a lifetime of training to keep from saying goodbye; but he managed it.

Outside, the space between the canteen and the office was now empty. Things seemed to be going full blast once more in the canteen. He walked over and got in the truck with Sost.

'What does "psychiatrics" mean here?' he asked.

'Head-tests. For crazies.' Sost looked at him. 'What's your assignment?'

'Yow Dee Mine,' said Hal. 'Jennison seemed to think he'd done me a particular favor.'

Sost whistled briefly.

'Could be,' he said. 'It's a good mine. Honest management. Good team leaders – or used to be good team leaders, last I heard, anyway.'

Sost raised the truck from the ground on its air jets and turned it back toward Halla Station.

'What are team leaders?' Hal asked.

'Six to ten men to a team. One man leads them. You'll be taking the tube. I'll run you over to it.'

'You mean, working down in the mine, they work in teams?'

Sost nodded.

'What's the procedure when I get there? Are they going to stick me on a team – do I go right down the mine and to work? Or is there some sort of training I'll have to get first?'

'Your team leader'll train you – all the training you'll get,' said Sost. 'But they don't just stick you on. Like I say, the team captain can turn you down if he wants to. They don't do it too much, though. A team captain that hard to please wears out the patience of management, pretty fast. Probably they'll send you down on your first shift the day after you get there, but if they want to, they can tell you to suit up, hand you a torch and walk you right out of the hiring yard into the skip.'

'Skip? That's what you called the others back at the Holding Area, wasn't it?'

'No – kip. A kip – that's what you're going to be – is the last man joined onto the team. He's got to run all the errands for the rest of them. A skip – that's the car you go down into the mine in. Like an elevator.'

'Oh,' said Hal. He continued to ask questions, however, until Sost dropped him off at the tube platform.

'Just do what it says on your travel orders,' said Sost, finally. 'I got to get to work. So long.'

He turned the truck abruptly on its own long axis and began to drive off.

'Wait!' Hal called after him. 'When am I going to run into you again? How do I find you?'

'Just ask anybody!' Sost called back without turning his head. He lifted one hand briefly in farewell and drove around a corner out of sight of the platform and the tube tunnel.

It was some twenty minutes later that the train Hal was waiting for came through and he got on board. The mine that he had been assigned to was south of Halla Station but back towards the port city, almost half the distance Hal had originally come out. The tube car he was riding was almost empty of other passengers, and none of these showed any eagerness to socialize, which relieved him of the need to discourage conversation. He was free to sit by himself and think; and he did.

He was feeling curiously empty and lonely. Once again, he had met someone he liked, only to leave him behind. Except that, in the case of Sost, he still had the other's advice for a companion. Though it was not easy advice to follow. Hal would not have thought of himself as someone who jumped around physically and talked too much. His own self-image was of someone almost too quiet and almost too silent. But if he had struck Sost as being overactive and talkative, he must be doing more moving about and talking than he should, or else the other man would not have chosen those characteristics to pick on.

But advice alone was a cold companion. He thought now that he seemed fated to end up alone in the universe. Maybe it was necessary for things to happen that way to him now that his life had turned out the way it had. Certainly, if he was going to become invisible to the Others who might be looking for him, he probably could not afford the risk of having friends. He had been brought up, particularly by Walter the InTeacher, to reach out automatically and make connection with all other human beings around him. But now he would have to practice, not merely at not making friends, but rebuffing anyone who might try to make a friend of him.

To turn himself into a close-lipped solitary individual was one way to make sure nobody else would care much to be close to him. The ghosts of Walter, Malachi, and Obadiah had been right. His first imperative was to survive – by any means possible – until he was old enough and strong enough to defend himself against Bleys Ahrens and Dahno.

In any case, whatever method he chose to survive, one thing was sure. From now on, he could not afford the luxury of letting things happen to him. He would have to take control of his life and steer it the way he wanted it to go. To leave it any longer to circumstance and the will of others was a certain invitation to disaster. He had no idea yet how to go about taking such control, but he would learn.

It came to him, riding the strong wave of loneliness and unhappiness in him, that this was evidently what adulthood was mean to be – the taking on of the necessity of doing things he had no idea of how to do, and carrying the responsibility alone because now there was no one else to trust with it. He would have to become, he thought, like an armed ship belonging to no nation, travelling always alone, and running out his weapons at the first sight of any other vessel that ventured closed to him.

But he had to do it. Sitting on the soft train seat, soothed by the minute vibrations of the car he was in, as it flew through endless tunnels in the planetary crust of Coby, he drifted off toward sleep, telling himself that he must find out how to do it, some way. . . .

He woke shortly before he got to his destination, and was reasonably alert by the time the car slowed for his stop. He roused himself to get up and step down onto the station platform, and went on into the station, to the area where, as at Halla Station, a single interviewer sat at one of several available desks.

'Papers,' said the interviewer as he came up, automatically extending a hand.

Hal made no move to produce his papers.

'Where's the Guest House?' he asked.

The interviewer's arm slowly sank back onto the desk top. He looked at Hal for a long moment, uncertainly.

'Guest House?' he answered at last. 'Out the back door and two streets to your right. You'll see the sign.'

Hal went toward the door, feeling the eyes of the interviewer following him. The man would have no way of knowing whether or not Hal was a new employee under assignment; and plainly the other was not sure enough of himself to check and find out. Sost's advice had been good.

Hal found the Guest House and walked inside to its lobby, which was identical in every way with the lobby of the Guest House in Halla Station. But there was a short young woman behind the registration counter instead of the elderly man he had encountered at the Guest House at Halla Station. Hal put down his bag and signed in, passing his credit and employment papers over.

'I've been hired by the Yow Dee Mine,' he said to her. 'Is there some way I can get a ride out to it, if it's some ways to go?'

The Guest House manager had brown hair and a cheerful, acorn-shaped face.

'You won't want to wait in the terminal until all the other hirees are in, and then ride out in Company transportation, will you?' she said. 'No, I thought not. You're all to be added to teams on the day shift, so they won't be holding showup until this evening, after dinner. You might as well be comfortable here until then; and our on-duty maintenance worker'll run you out for a small charge.'

'Thanks,' said Hal, gratefully; and was immediately angry with himself for not succeeding in being more taciturn and unsociable. But it was hard to adjust all at once.

Later, the maintenancer – a girl younger than he was – drove him out to the mine. Its main area was a very large cave-space holding the pit-head, a number of structures built of what looked like concrete, including the offices and the bunkhouse – the maintenancer pointed out and named them for him – clustered around three sides of an open space that looked to be half recreation area, half marshalling yard, in which a number of people were already gathered.

'Looks like they're all ready to start your showup,' the maintenancer said, as Hal got down from the small duty truck in which she had run him out. 'On the side over at the left there, those six you see, they're the other kips like you.'

Hal took his bag and walked over. He was conscious that a number of the men in the crowd of miners standing around – he could see no women – turned to look at him as he came. He made it a point to ignore this and go straight to the six people the maintenancer had pointed out. One of these was a lean, brown-haired, snub-nosed woman in her early twenties, wearing the same sort of hard-finish work jacket and slacks that a number of the men in the watching crowd also wore. She gazed at Hal, frowning a little.

He had barely joined these others when a tall, rawboned miner, at least in his fifties, came over from the watching crowd, took Hal roughly by the elbow and turned him around, so that they were face to face.

'You just in from Halla Station?'

The man had some of the rhythms of someone from one of the Friendly Worlds in his voice, although nothing else about him looked as if he came from the same Splinter Culture that had produced Obadiah.

'Yes,' said Hal, looking directly back, almost on a level, into his face. The other released him and went back into the crowd without saying anything more.

There was a stir among those watching and faces turned to the door of what the maintenancer had pointed out as the Management Office. A very erect, thick-stomached man with wavy gray hair and an impatient face came out of the door there and stood at the top of the three steps that led down into the walled area.

'All right, team leaders,' he called, his dry, harsh baritone carrying out over the other sounds of the crowd. 'Where are you? Who's short?'

The general crowd moved back, leaving four men standing each a little apart from the other. One was the rawboned fifty-year-old who had spoken to Hal. The others were between that age and thirty; one, a lean, dark man in his forties; one who looked like a somewhat younger version of Sost – a burly blond-headed individual in his thirties; and a short, very wide-bodied and powerful-looking individual with a round head and jet-black hair who could have been any age between thirty and sixty.

'All right. Who's got priority for first assignment?' called the man on the steps. 'You – Beson, isn't it?'

'Me,' said the lean, dark man.

'All right.' The man on the steps looked at a piece of printout in his hand. 'Tonina Wayle!'

With a satisfied look on her face, the one woman among the kips, who had been continuing to watch Hal, crossed over to Beson. Several of the men from the crowd behind the four team leaders greeted her as if she was an old acquaintance.

'Next? Charlei?' The burly, Sost-like man nodded. 'You draw Morgan Amdur. Morgan Amdur, which one are you?'

The man next to Hal stepped forward a little.

'All right,' said the burly man, dryly. The man next to Hal crossed over.

'Anyo Yuan. Step out there!'

The man farthest from Hal among the kips took a pace forward.

'John, he's yours.'

'All right,' said the wide-bodied leader with the black hair. Anyo Yuan, who was evidently as new to this as Hal, hesitated, looking around him uncertainly.

'Go on over to John Heikkila, Yuan,' said the man on the step. 'Tad Thornhill.'

Hal stepped forward.

'Will, he's yours. Thornhill, your leader is Will Nann –'

'Don't want him!' The words from the tall, rawboned man were loud enough to echo from the walls of the surrounding buildings. Hal felt the sick drop of stomach that comes with the sudden fall of a fast elevator.

CHAPTER SEVEN

'Cause or peremptory?' the gray-haired man was demanding.

'I hear he's a trouble-maker.' Once more, Will Nanne's voice was painfully clear over all the open area.

'All right,' said the man on the steps. 'Thornhill, you step back. Wallace Carter?'

The smallest of the kips stepped out as Hal retreated.

'Yours, Charlei.'

'All right.'

'Johannes Hevelius.'

'Yours, Beson.'

'He'll do.'

The other two crossed over. Hal was left standing nakedly alone.

'All right. Last call on Thornhill. You're all still short at least one worker. Will Nanne, you don't want him?'

'No.'

'Beson?'

'Not for me.'

'Charlei?'

'Not for me.'

'John? Last chance.'

The powerful, short man turned and walked with a rolling gait over to Will Nanne.

'Tell me what you heard about him,' he said.

Nanne leaned down and spoke quietly in Heikkila's ear. The shorter man listened, nodded, and turned to the man on the step.

'I'll take him.'

Hal moved slowly across the flat surface of the space toward John Heikkila. The powerful-looking leader who had claimed him was talking to Anyo Yuan. Hal stood waiting until the conversation was done, and then Heikkila turned and saw him.

'You come with me,' he said.

He led Hal, not toward the bunkhouse, to which everyone else was now moving – the man on the steps having gone back into the Management Office – but in the opposite direction, across to an empty far corner of the enclosure. Then he stopped and turned to face Hal. He looked at Hal in silence for a moment.

'You like to fight?' he said. His voice was tenor-toned, but hard.

'No,' said Hal. He was torn between his desire to sound convincing to Heikkila and his attempt to maintain the tight-lipped taciturn image Sost had urged on him.

'That's not what I hear. Will tells me you put a man in the infirmary down at Halla Station Holding Area, yesterday.'

'He tried to hit me with a metal mug when I wasn't looking,' said Hal. 'It was just an accident he ended up in the hospital.'

Heikkila stared at him coldly for an extended moment.

'You think you could put me in the infirmary?'

Hal stared at him, suddenly weary with a weariness much older than his years. The other was standing with his face barely eight inches from Hal's. The round, black hair of his head came barely to Hal's eye-level; but his great chest and arms seemed to blot out half the scene behind him. He would carry nearly as much weight again as Hal, in experienced adult bone and muscle; and there was a dangerousness about the way he stood that marked plain upon him the fact that he was something more than a merely ordinarily competent fighter. Someone like this – again, the knowledge, like the answer, came from a time older than Hal's years, older than the lessons of Malachi – would have to be killed, killed quickly, by someone as light and young as Hal if there was to be any hope of stopping him at all. He was waiting now for assurance that Hal would know better than to pick a fight with him. Hal did – but he could not lie in answering. Not if he was to work and live with this man from now on.

'If you came for me the way that man at the Holding Station did,' Hal said heavily, 'I'd have to try. But I don't want to fight – anybody.'

Heikkila continued to stare harshly. Slowly, then, the harshness went and something a little like puzzlement came into the round face.

'It's a good thing, then,' he said slowly, at last. 'Because there's no fighting on my team. We don't have time to fight. We don't have time for anything but getting the ore out. You understand me?'

Hal nodded. Unexpectedly, he found he wanted to be on this man's team rather than that of any other leader he had seen there.

'If you'll give me a chance,' he told Heikkila, 'you'll see I'm telling the truth. I'm not a troublemaker.'

Heikkila watched him for a second more.

'You calling Will Nanne a liar?'

'I don't know what he heard,' said Hal. 'But whatever it was he can't have heard it as it happened.'

'That so?' Heikkila still stared at him; but the last of the dangerousness Hal had felt like a living presence in the team leader was gone. 'Damn if I understand. How big was this kip you laid out?'

'About my height,' said Hal, 'but older.'

'Oh. Real old?'

'Not real old . . .' said Hal – and then suddenly realized he might be implying too much in an opposite direction. 'But he came at me without any warning, from behind. I was just trying to save myself. He hit a wall.'

'You're saying he put himself in the infirmary?'

'Yes . . . in a way.'

Heikkila nodded.

'Damn,' he said, again. He studied Hal. 'How old are you?'

'Twenty.'

'Twenty!' Heikkila snorted.

'– next year,' said Hal, desperately.

'Sure,' said Heikkila. 'Sure you are.'

He sighed gustily, from the depths of his wide chest.

'All right, come on with me, then,' he said. 'But it's rough working in the mines. You better know that.'

He turned and led the way across the open space toward the bunkhouse.

'That woman, the first one to get picked. She's been a miner, before, hasn't she?' asked Hal, catching up with him.

'Sure,' said Heikkila. 'Right here at the Yow Dee.'

'If she can do it,' Hal said, thinking of her relative smallness, 'I can.'

Heikkila snorted again. It was almost a laugh.

'You think so?' he said. 'Well, you just worry about showing me you're willing to work, or you'll be off my team after the first shift. My team bids top quota at this mine. You make it through the first shift and I'll give you two weeks to toughen in. If you don't do it by then – out!'

As they got close to the bunkhouse, Hal found himself at last identifying something that had bothered him from first landing on Coby. Because the habitable area of the planet was underground, there was no real outdoors. Odors and sunlight and a dozen other small, natural signals did not intrude their differences here to remind him that he was no longer on Earth. In spite of this, an unrelenting sense of alienness had been with him from the first moment of his leaving the ship. Now, suddenly, he realized the cause of it.

There were almost no shadows. Here in this open space, a thousand sources of illumination in the cave roof far overhead gave a light that came from all angles and did not change. Even where there were shadows, these, too, were permanent. Here, there would be neither night nor day. It occurred to him suddenly that it might be almost a relief to go down into the mine and get away from this upper area where time seemed forever at a standstill.

They had reached the bunkhouse. He followed John Heikkila in, through a lounge area into a narrow corridor, with lines of doors in each wall, some open but most closed, entrances to what seemed to be a series of single person rooms. They continued along to the end of the corridor before John stopped and let them both into a room which was half again as large as the ones Hal had glimpsed through open doors as they walked down the corridor. This room held not only a bed, a couple of comfortable chair floats and a small writing desk, as the other rooms had, but also a large, business-style desk; and it was at this desk that Heikkila now sat down, extended one square, thick hand, and said the word that Hal was coming to hear even in his sleep.

'Papers.'

Hal got them out and passed them over. The leader passed them through the transverse slot in his desk, fingered some code on his pad of keys, beside the slot, and returned the papers to Hal. A hard-copy of a single printed page came up through the slot and he handed this also to Hal.

'You're hired as kip,' said John. 'One-fiftieth team share and an open charge against all necessary equipment, supplies and living expenses.'

He held out his hand to Hal, who gripped it automatically. 'I'm John,' he said. 'You're Tad. Welcome to the team.'

'John . . .' said Hal. He looked at the hard copy in his hand.

'I don't understand,' he said. 'Doesn't the mine management hire me –'

'We bid and sub-contract here, team by team, just like most of the honest mines do,' said John, looking up at him. 'You work for the team. I work for the team. The only difference between you and me is I'm leader – I do all the paperwork and make all the decisions. And I get the biggest share.'

He got to his feet.

'We're on day shift for the rest of this two-week,' he said. 'Another pair of three-days. Better set your caller for four-thirty, if you want to make breakfast by five hundred hours and lineup by five-thirty with all your equipment. Come on, I'll show you your place.'

He got up from the desk, and led the way out into the hall and down to one of the doors. Opening it, he revealed a room in which everything was neat and ready for occupancy.

'Bunkhouse maintenance takes care of ordinary cleanup,' he said. 'You make an unusual mess, you settle it with them; whether you clean up yourself, or pay them extra out of your own account. Better settle it yourself, because if they come to me with it, it's going to cost you even more.'

Hal nodded. He laid his bag down on the bed. The sheets, he saw, were synthetic fabric knits.

John looked at him. The team leader's dark brown eyes were as bleak as an arctic night; and there was no way to tell if there had ever been any emotion in them or not.

'Better get some sleep,' John said. He went out, closing the door behind him.

Hal put his travel bag in the small closet and stretched out on top of the bed's coverings.

He felt in him a desperate need for time to sort out in his own mind what had happened to him. Evidently, the Leader called Will Nanne had gotten word of what had happened at the Holding Area of Halla Station; and if that was so, this world of mines must be an incredible whispering gallery. How could word travel so fast? And why?

He puzzled over it, but found himself drifting off to sleep in spite of the questions in his mind. He was just about lost to slumber when it occurred to him that it might be one of Jennison's sources of income, selling information on the men he assigned to the team leaders at the mines he assigned them to. But Jennison had seemed to want to be on Hal's side, the last time Hal had talked to him – the assignment man had flatly said that he expected them to do some business together in the future. If so, why would he pass on a report that had come very close to costing Hal the job he, Jennison, had assigned him to?

Sost had said that if Hal was not hired, he would be sent back to the nearest Holding Area to be processed again. In this case, would the Holding Area have been Halla Station again? And if so, could Jennison have set the whole thing up to impress Hal with his power to produce or withhold good jobs?

Hal was dropping into sleep with this question, too, unanswered, when a knock at the door jarred him into instant, wary wakefulness.

'Thornhill?' said a woman's voice through the panel. 'You in there? Can I come in?'

He got up and opened the door. Tonina Wayle was standing outside; and as if she assumed that the opened door was an invitation, she walked in, closed it firmly behind her and sat on the float closest to his bed.

'Thought I'd say a word or two to you,' she said.

She stared at him, almost the way John had, for a second without saying anything more. Then she spoke again.

'You're from Old Earth, aren't you?'

'You can tell?' he said. She laughed, surprising him; for the laugh was not unkindly.

'I can guess – now,' she said. 'Maybe a lot of the others couldn't. Give you another two weeks here and nobody'll be able to guess.'

She sobered, suddenly.

'You've never been in a mine before, have you?' she asked.

No.'

'Well, you're not starting too badly. John Heikkila's one of the best. I'm on Beson McSweeney's team now, so I won't say anything one way or another between them; but you can be proud of being on John's.'

'That story,' said Hal, 'of what I did to that man who jumped me down at the Holding Area – it was an accident he got hurt, actually. I told Heikkila – John – that, but I don't know if he believed me.'

'If it's the truth, he'll end up believing it,' said Tonina. She ran her eyes over him. 'I don't find it too easy to believe, myself. How –'

'I'm twenty,' said Hal, quickly. 'I just look young for my age.'

Tonina shrugged.

'Well, as I say, you'll get a fair shake from John. He wants production, but so does any other Leader,' she said. 'Did he tell you what you'd be doing?'

'No,' said Hal.

'I thought not,' she said. 'There's none better, but he's been in the mines so long he forgets there're people who don't know. Well, he won't expect much of you your first shift tomorrow, anyway, so there's no need to worry.'

'What do I do?'

'You'll be mucking out behind the men with torches,' she said. 'They'll be cutting ore from the rockface, and it'll be up to you to get what they cut out sorted and back into the carts.'

She paused and looked at him.

'You don't even follow that much, do you?' she said. 'When you and your team go down into the mine, the skip'll take you to the level your team's working on. After you leave the skip you'll ride the carts – they're like a train without tracks to run on, a train with cars that look like open metal bins. They'll each carry two men at once. You'll ride the carts back through the levels – tunnels to you – until you come to the end of the one where your team's bid to work on a section of the vein. The vein's the way the ore with the metal in it runs through the rock. It never runs level, so you're nearly always working on what's called a stope, that's sort of like a step up or a step down to get at the ore, and you cut out what's there until you have to go on and make another stope.'

He nodded, fascinated.

'But what's "mucking out"?' he asked.

'The top men in the team'll be carving rock – working ahead in the stope with laser torches –'

She laughed at the look on his face.

'Yes, real laser torches, right out of three hundred years ago. Here on Coby's the only place on all the worlds where miners cost less than equipment; and a laser's the only safe type of torch for anyone to use for cutting. You'll be behind the top men, gathering up the ore they've cut out of the rock. Just be damn sure you do two things. Keep the gloves of your suit on, no matter how you sweat inside your suit. You start handling a rock barehanded and get burned, you'll know it. And be God damn sure you don't take your helmet off, ever!'

Her last word came with a vehemence that startled him.

'All right,' he said. 'I won't.'

'You'll see the lead people, and maybe some of the others, throwing their helmets back from time to time. But don't you do it. They know when it's safe, because they know what they've just been cutting. You don't. I don't care how miserable it gets inside that headpiece, you keep it on. Otherwise you'll see them take theirs off, you'll take yours off, and then all of a sudden they've got theirs back on; but by then it's too late for you. You'll've inhaled some of the hot gases the torches boil out when they cut the rock; and it's too late.'

'I see,' said Hal.

'You better.' She got to her feet. 'Well, I've got to turn in myself. We work a twenty-hour day here, three days on, three days off; and on a three-day stint you better learn to sleep any time you can. You can catch up on your threes-off. I guess John'll keep an eye on you, this first day at least, about taking off your helmet. But nobody can watch you all the time; so you better get in the habit of taking care of yourself.'

She went toward the door. Hal stood up.

'Wait –' he said. All his resolution about being taciturn and reserved had slipped away from him. She had been the first person to show anything like kindness to him at this mine, and he felt he could not let her go without knowing her better. 'Uh – you used to work at this mine before, John Heikkila said.'

'Yes,' she replied, with the door half open.

'You must have liked it here, or you wouldn't have come back.'

'Wrong,' she said, and almost grinned. 'The other way around. They liked me here. That meant better shares in a team; and people I could trust, down in the mine, when I worked with them.'

'Why'd you leave?'

The humor went out of her face suddenly.

'I left to go down to the main infirmary with someone,' she said.

'Your husband?'

'Husband?' For a moment she looked startled. 'No, my brother.'

'Oh,' said Hal. Some inner part of his emotional sensitivities was beginning to fly warning signals, but he blundered on. 'Did your brother work here before you did?'

'No. I got him the job.' She hesitated. 'He was my younger brother. He was bound to go working in the mines after knowing I was. He was about your age when I first got him in here.'

She looked at him grimly, again.

'Your real age,' she said.

'And he's working in some other mine now?'

Her face was wiped clean of expression.

'He's dead.'

'Oh.' Hal felt the way someone teetering on the edge of a precipice might feel, hearing the ground break suddenly under his feet. He stammered, lamely, 'I'm sorry.'

'He took his damn helmet off. I'd told him a million times not to!'
She turned and went out, the door closing hard behind her.

He stood for a long moment, then slowly turned and began undressing for bed.

He woke to the sound of his alarm in the morning, dressed and stumbled down the hall, following the foot-traffic there, until it led him to the dining hall. The room was a place of long tables, loaded with eggs, fried vegetables, breads and what must certainly be processed meats in the forms of sausages and steaks. Evidently people simply took whatever seat was vacant, as they came in. It was not a time of conversation but of stoking up. Grateful for the silence, he surrounded an excellent and gargantuan meal, wistfully realizing even as he finally pushed his plate away from him, that – even with this – he would probably be starving again long before the lunch break came.

Something seemed to have happened overnight. This morning was all business, and the feeling he had had earlier of being shunned by everyone there no longer seemed to hold. No one paid any particular attention to him but no one avoided him, either. As he was leaving the dining hall, John Heikkila came and found him.

'You come with me,' John said.

He led Hal off into the crowd of men who were heading for the far end of the bunkhouse. They emerged into a room filled with racks from which hung what looked like heavy cloth coveralls with boots, gloves and helmets, each helmet containing a wide transverse window for vision. John took him to the end of one rack, glanced at him, selected one of the coveralls and threw it at him.

'This is yours from now on,' he said. 'Come to me when we get off shift and I'll show you how to check it for leaks. You got to check after every shift. Now get it on, and come along with the rest on our team.'

Hal obeyed. With the coverall on, it was not as easy to pick out the people he recognized, among the identically-clad figures around him. But John's wide, short shape was unmistakable. Hal followed it; and ended moving in a mass of bodies out through a farther tunnel that echoed and roared to the sound of their thick-soled boots, until they came to an open area where the walls were naked rock. In the center of the floor of the area was the large mouth of a steeply inclined shaft, surrounded by machinery. As Hal watched, there was a puff of what looked like white dust from the hole; and a second later, the cage of some sort of elevator rose through the opening until its floor stood level with that of the stone underfoot around it.

'Everybody in!' said John, his voice booming out with metallic echoes through the speaker valve of his helmet. They crowded clumsily into the cage. There was room for all of them, but they ended up pressed tightly together. Within the enclosed confines of his own suit, Hal could hear the loud sound of his own breathing; as if he panted, except that he had no reason to pant.

'You, Thornhill, stand clear of the side of the skip!'

It was John's voice again, booming out. Obediently, Hal pressed inward upon the bodies about him, and away from the metal bars that separated him from the roughly-cut rock walls of the inclined shaft.

'All right. All down!' boomed John.

The cage dropped suddenly, and kept dropping. Hal pressed against the bodies around him as he almost became airborne. He was already beginning to sweat inside his suit; but, curiously, there was an unexpected feeling of satisfaction in him.

He was being dropped rapidly into the deep rock of Coby. There was no longer any choice about what he was doing. He was committed. He was, in fact, a miner; one of the miners that surrounded him. Their work was the work he would be doing. He could imagine it coming, in time, to be second nature to him; and even now he seemed to feel the beginnings of a familiarity with it.

He had achieved at last what he had begun when he had run from Ahrens and Danno; and from what had happened on the terrace. He had hidden himself from the Others and taken charge of his own life. No one but he had brought himself to this point. No one but he would be directing himself from now on. He would be all by himself, apart and isolated from those around him, which was a sad and lonely thought. But at the same moment, for the first time, his survival and his future would be in his own hands alone. From this moment forward there was no going back. One way or another he would survive – and grow – and finally return to bring retribution to Bleys and the Others.

The realization was cold but strongly attractive. There was almost a feeling of triumph in him. The hidden, oceanic purpose that he felt at times, hidden deep in his mind, seemed content.

CHAPTER EIGHT

The skip dropped swiftly between the close, rough-cut rock walls, its interior lights illuminating the brown of their igneous rock, shot through with the occasional flicker of white that was the gold-bearing quartz. It was gold and sometimes silver that they dug for at the Yow Dee Mine, according to the information in Hal's employment papers. He tried to watch the swiftly passing rock to get a glimpse of whether the quartz he was seeing was indeed visibly veined with gold; but the skip was going down too quickly. He found himself up against the bars of the cage and, remembering John Heikkila's orders to stand away from these, stepped guiltily back.

He felt a hard jab in the center of his spine.

'Who in hell you think you're standing on, kip?'

He turned clumsily in his protective suit and found himself looking through his face shield at another face shield and the features of a lean, big-nosed man in not more than his early twenties, slightly shorter than Hal himself, with straight black hair and an angry expression.

'I'm sorry,' he said. 'I was just –'

'Sorry don't make it. Just stay off my foot.'

Hal had not stepped on any foot. The years of exercises had trained him to be aware at all times of the balance of his own body and the character of what he supported himself on. If he had felt a foot beneath his own, he would have shifted clear of it instinctively before his weight had fully come down upon it. He stared into the other face, baffled; and stopped himself just before he protested that the other had imagined being stepped on.

'I will,' he said.

The man growled something at him that was lost in its passage through the speaker valve of his suit and the pickups of Hal's. Hal backed a few inches toward the bars and the other turned away.

The skip's floor began to press up against their feet as its descent slowed. It came to a stop, and the gates by which they had entered it swung open. Following the other miners, the last one out because he had been farthest from the gates, Hal stepped from the overhead gloom of the skip shaft into a large, brilliantly-lit, high-ceilinged chamber that seemed to be the terminal for a number of trains of small cars, each train pointing through one of the many openings in the circular wall of the chamber. The crowd that had filled the skip was now breaking up into smaller groups, each heading toward a different train of waiting cars, in a general mutter of conversation, from which he was sharply conscious of being apart. Some of the cars were already filled with miners from what must be previous skip-loads. With some relief, Hal saw that the black-haired individual who had complained about being stepped on in the skip was headed toward a partly-loaded train beside which Will Nanne waited.

Hal woke suddenly to the fact that he was being left alone by the skip. He looked for John Heikkila and located him, finally, heading with a contingent of miners toward a string of six cars. Hal hurried to catch up.

By the time he did, the others were already climbing into the cars. These were little more than open metal boxes on soft-tired wheels, their four sides sloping outward from above those wheels; wheels, sides and all painted green. Hal was the last to board of the twelve miners who apparently made up the Heikkila team, with the exception of John himself, who had stood frowning by the head car as everyone else climbed in.

'Come on, Tad!' he called, now. 'Work-time's counting.'

Hal climbed into the next to the last car, which he had to himself, the other miners in John's team having filled the first four cars, with the exception of a space for John in the first car. John, seeing Hal in, climbed in himself, and with a chorus of metallic clankings the train of cars jerked into movement without any command from John that Hal could make out.

They trundled into one of the openings, which turned out to be the end of a tunnel. Here, the sounds of their travel picked up, echoing into a roar cast back by the close rock walls. The floor of the car Hal was in bumped and jibed under him. The tunnel floor was plainly level, but not smooth, as the floor of the larger, terminal chamber had been; and the cars were without springs. Hal, who had sat down unthinkingly in his car, hastily moved to imitate the other miners in the cars ahead, whom he now saw were squatting, knees under their chins. This was a more comfortable, if less balanced way to travel, and he found that it paid to cross his arms and press his hands against the sides of the car to brace himself.

All the same, the ride was fascinating. Now that they were well into the tunnel, the train of cars was picking up speed. They swayed and lurched thunderously along between rocky walls, here less than two meters apart, their way illuminated every ten meters or so by what looked like thousand-year lights stuck to the naked rock of the ceiling, another two meters overhead. Once more, Hal searched the rock to see if he could see any signs of visible gold in the quartz veining. But here, he was not even able to discover any streaks of the quartz itself. He strained his eyes through the window of his suit – and suddenly became aware that in the cars ahead of him all the others had the hoods of their suits thrown back.

He hesitated, remembering Tonina's warning about taking off his helmet, then reminded himself she had been talking about not exposing himself to possibly lethal gases when the other miners were using their torches. Here in the tunnel it ought to be safe, since all the others had theirs off. He threw his own headgear back and peered at the passing rock. But it still appeared as he had seen it through the window of the suit. There was no veining of quartz visible in the granite of the rock.

But it was a relief to have the hood off. The air blowing past his face with the movement of their passage was cold and damp with a faintly musty, acidic smell. He began to have some notion of what it was going to be like to work and sweat sealed in his suit, if this was the way he felt after only a matter of minutes in it, with no exertion.

But there was an eeriness, a magic to being underground like this, rolling through the tunnelled rock at a speed that seemed to threaten to scrape them against the walls on curves. He thought of the story of Peer Gynt in the hall of the Mountain King, from the long poem by Henrik Ibsen; and the music Edvard Grieg had written for that scene thundered and pounded in his memory over the hum of the tires on the rock and the metallic clanking and creaking of the connected cars as they fled down the tunnel.

The cars of the train turned off abruptly into a narrower tunnel. They clanked along another short distance at reduced speed, then came out into a slightly enlarged area where a ramp led from the level they were on to another level about a meter and a half higher, like one step of a giant stairs. The cars rolled up the ramp, straight ahead for a few feet, then up another ramp, and so continued, mounting or descending ramps at small intervals until they stopped so suddenly that Hal was thrown against the front end of his car.

Ahead of the front car they seemed to have come to a solid wall of granite; but since everyone in the cars ahead was getting out, Hal could not be sure at first glance. He climbed out himself and went forward to discover that the front car had come to a stop with its front wheels almost touching a meter and a half rise of rock. It was another of the giant stairsteps, but this time there was no ramp rising to it, and the space at its top barely gave standing room before it reached a wall of stone scored up and down and crosswise until it looked as if someone had made a clumsy attempt at a vertical chessboard.

In an untidy pile at the foot of the meter-and-a-half step were various tools, which the other members of the team were already taking up. Hal watched curiously. Most of the tools were stubby, thick-bodied devices like handguns with thick, short barrels, which Hal guessed to be the torches Tonina Wayles had spoken of; and what seemed to be an equal number of prosthetic-like apparatuses, fitted onto a left-handed glove with the fingers ending in five long, metal spines which curved inward until their points almost touched.

These made no sense. Then, Hal saw those who had put them on beginning to manipulate them. The spines spread open and closed, apparently independently of any action by the gloved fingers. In some cases their needle-sharp points glowed cherry red for a second, then white, then dulled back to ordinary metal color. Each of the miners who put these on tested them several times, looking like creatures half-human, half-insect, groping at thin air; then climbed up onto the step of rock and faced the scored wall.

The rest of the team, except for the six now on the ledge and John Heikkila, had gone back past Hal about ten meters down the tunnel and sat down with their helmets thrown back. John, standing by the front car below the ledge, looked about and saw Hal.

'All right, kip!' he said. 'Over here!'

Hal went forward to him, wondering.

'Put your helmet on. Keep it on.'

In spite of himself, Hal glanced back at the six other team members who were sitting with their backs to the rock and talking, farther back in the tunnel. He put the helmet on and John's voice came to him through the earphones of his head-covering with the slight unnaturalness of sounds heard over the phone circuits between the two closed suits.

'You don't know anything about this, do you, Thornhill?'

'No,' said Hal.

'All right. Your job's to muck out while the torches are working.' John reached up and closed his own helmet over his head. Up on the ledge, the six torch-bearers had had their helmets closed for some time. They were standing looking down at John and Hal, obviously waiting.

'Ordinarily, I'd be up there with the first shift with the torches,' John said. 'But I'll stay down here with you until you get the hang of it. Now, the blocks are going to come off the the ledge as they cut them out, until the ledge gets wide enough so they can't sling them all the way back off the edge. When that happens, we'll cut a ramp and you'll be going up to work right behind the torchers. But for now, the blocks'll be coming off the stops to you, and you want to keep your feet out from under. You understand?' He paused.

Hal nodded.

'Yes,' he said.

'All right. The other thing to look out for is that the blocks'll still be hot when they come. So don't try to handle them except with tongs. These are tongs. . . .'

He picked up a couple of the spined apparatuses.

'Hold out your hands.'

Hal did, and John pushed one of the devices onto the end of each of Hal's gloves. There was a hand-shaped indentation in the end of each device, Hal discovered, into which his suit glove fitted; thumb, forefinger, middle finger, and the last two fingers as a unit – each slipped into one of the four indentations. Experimentally, he flexed the fingers of his right hand and the four clawlike extensions spread and closed in response.

'Waldos,' he said.

'No, they're tongs,' said John. 'Now you use them to pick up the blocks. Watch me. All right, Torchers, get moving!'

He was fitting a pair of the devices onto the gloves of his own suit as he spoke. He barely had them on before the hiss and crackle of the torches burning into the rock exploded up on the ledge; and a moment or two later one of the torchers kicked a block of granite about the size of a grapefruit back over the edge to fall almost at Hal's feet. Easily, John scooped it up in the four pincers of his tongs. He held it out before Hal.

'Don't touch it,' he said. 'Just look at it. See the vein in it?'

Hal looked. He could see a line of quartz streaking through the piece of granite.

'Is there gold in that?' he asked, fascinated.

'You're damn right,' said John, 'and probably some silver, but you can't see traces of that. Look, you see the color in the quartz, there?'

Hal squinted at the quartz, uncertain as to what he should be looking for.

'I think so,' he said. John tossed the block into the first car.

'You'll learn,' he said.

Several more chunks of rock carved from the wall had landed at their feet while they had been talking. John scooped them up, showed them momentarily to Hal and then tossed them into the car. The next one, however, he again held out to Hal for more extended examination.

'See?' he said. 'No veining. Those you ditch.'

With a flip of his tongs, he threw the last block over against the wall of the tunnel.

'That's sorting,' he said, continuing to work steadily now, for now the blocks were coming in a continuous stream off the ledge. 'It'll take you a while to learn it, but you'll get it. The team only gets paid for the good ore it brings back. Any dead rock just takes up space in the cars and cuts our production for the day. But don't sweat it to begin with. Just do the best you can for now. The quicker you learn, though, the better off the team's going to be and the more the rest of us are going to like you. Now, you try it with some of these blocks.'

Hal tried it. It took no great skill to learn to use the tongs, though it was a little tricky at first, getting a good grip on the blocks without the feeling in his fingers to guide him; and the waldo controls into

101

which his gloves fitted were so responsive that he overcontrolled at first. But within a dozen minutes he was picking up the blocks with fair skill and dropping them into the cars. Sorting, however, was another matter. Whenever he paused to examine the blocks closely, John snapped at him to keep going.

While he was learning, John kept helping him. But Hal picked up speed in handling the blocks swiftly, although he was very aware that he was still rejecting only about one block in ten, whereas John was rejecting more like one in five. Still, the team leader seemed satisfied with just his handling ability; and gradually he let Hal take over more and more of the work until finally he himself was only standing and watching.

'All right,' he said at last. 'Just keep doing it that way. But take a break now and we'll change crews.'

He turned and called up at the crew on the ledge.

'Change!'

The torches hissed and crackled down into silence. Those on the ledge dropped off it and those who had been seated back in the tunnel came forward, pulling their helmets into place and taking the torches from the first workers, climbing up on the ledge to take their place. This time, John was among the torchers, his own helmet pulled into position. He paused for a second, looking over his shoulder, down at Hal.

'Keep your helmet on, until I tell you to take it off,' he said. 'You hear that?'

'Yes,' said Hal.

'All right!' John turned to face the wall and the rest of his crew turned with him. 'Let's go!'

So the workshift began. At first Hal sweated over the prospect of handling the stream of blocks without John to back him up. But if there was anything at all in which life had supplied him with experience, it was the process of learning anything new. He quickly became practiced at seizing the blocks firmly with the tongs, so that they did not slip from his grasp or skitter out of reach when he tried to lift them into the cars; and after a while even his choice of the ore-filled blocks, as opposed to those that should be discarded, seemed to improve.

As the shift wore on, the torchers themselves picked up speed. Hal had to struggle anew to not let the blocks coming off the ledge get ahead of him. He succeeded, becoming faster himself. But as he did, the unaccustomed use of the muscles involved in bending and lifting began to build up on him.

Fortunately, he had a chance to stop and catch his breath every fifteen minutes or so when the crews changed. But even with these breaks, as the first half of the shift wore on he began to tire and slow. The lunch break came just in time to save him from getting badly behind the torchers, but food and rest revived him. He started out the second half of the shift keeping up almost easily; but this burst of strength turned out to be temporary. He tired more quickly now than he had in the morning; and to his deep embarrassment the blocks finally got ahead of him to the point where even by working right through a break time, he was losing ground to the torchers.

Sweating, gasping for air inside his suit, he looked longingly every so often at the miners at the rock wall, whom he could see occasionally throwing back their helmets for a brief breath of fresher air. A hundred times he was tempted to lift his own helmet for a second, but the discipline worked into him in his early years helped him to fight off the temptation. Nonetheless, he was literally staggering on his feet, when he finally felt a hand on his shoulder and turned to see John standing beside him.

CHAPTER NINE

'Go take a break,' said John. He gave Hal a light shove away from the blocks with which Hal had been working and bent to the task of handling the blocks himself.

On rubbery legs, Hal walked back down the tunnel and slid down the wall into a sitting position on the tunnel floor. He lifted his helmet and breathed more deeply than he could ever remember breathing in his life before.

He had thought John was merely taking over for him. But now he saw not only John, but all the current torchers, knocking back their helmets and coming down off the ledge, which was already too deep to be properly called only a ledge. As he watched, they were joined by the resting crew of torchers and the whole team together began to cut a ramp to the ledge.

They had almost completed this when a train of five empty cars rolled in to join them, with only one passenger aboard; a great, spiderous old man with his helmet thrown back to show oriental features, and tongs at the end of both the long arms depending from his massive, bowed shoulders. This new train braked to a halt beside their own and the old man hopped out. John went over to speak to him; and Hal, too far away to make out what was being said, saw the old man listening with his face at right angle to John's, nodding occasionally and twitching the tongs at the ends of his arms as if impatient to have the conversation over. John finished finally and turned away. The old man took one step to the chunks of rejected rock lying along the base of the rock wall where Hal had thrown them, and attacked them with both sets of tongs.

Attack was the proper word. Hal had thought that John was fast and experienced with the tongs; but this old man was unbelievable. He faced the wall, using both arms at once, and slung the chunks of dead rock behind him without looking. Not only did they all land in the empty car just behind him, but when the car was full, he seemed to know it by instinct and moved on, still without turning to look, to begin filling the car next in line. Hal watched him, fascinated.

'All right, Tad. Let's go.'

Hal looked up to see John standing over him and scrambled hastily to his feet, ready to go back to work. Then he realized that the cutting of the ramp was completed but the torchers had not gone back up on the higher level to resume work, themselves. Instead, everyone was climbing into the cars of their own train, perching on top of the ore there.

'Are we through?' Hal said, unable to believe it.

'We're through,' said John. 'Get aboard.'

Lost in his fog of effort, it had not registered on Hal that all the cars of their train were now filled with ore. He glanced once more at the old man and saw that the other had almost finished picking up, in minutes, the rejected rock that Hal had worked a full shift to accumulate.

'What's he doing?' asked Hal, dazedly, as he turned toward the last car of their own train.

'Slag-loading,' said John. 'Clean-up. He'll take the dead rock for a last sort, in case anything worthwhile's been missed, and pile it at the minehead for pickup and dumping topside on the surface. Get in there, now.'

'I can't believe the shift's over,' said Hal. He climbed into the last car.

'It's over,' said John. He went up and got into the lead car. Hal did not see what controls he used, but as soon as John was aboard the train started moving, backing and filling several times to make the tight turn in the narrow space that would allow it to head back the way they had come.

They hummed and clanked through the tunnels. Perched on the ore in his own half-filled car, Hal abandoned himself to the luxury of being through with the day's work. He felt worn out, but not uncomfortable. In fact, there was a half-pleasant exhausted warmth to his body, now that the labor was done with and he had had some small time to rest. It had been explained to him by Malachi Nasuno within the past year that his immature muscles could not yet be expected to deliver the power that an equal weight of them could provide once he had stopped growing; but that, on the other hand, his recovery rate from exertion would be correspondingly faster than that of an equivalent, older individual – and the older the other individual, the greater Hal's advantage. As he rode the swaying car now, he could feel strength being reborn in him; and this, together with the satisfaction of having gotten through the shift without trouble, left him feeling more secure and comfortable than he had felt at any time since he had left his home on Earth.

It seemed to him that there was now a bond of identity with the other miners riding the ore train back to the skip. He was suddenly close to them. The dark colors and the enclosing walls of the tunnels made one family of them all. For the first time since he had left Earth, he had a sensation of being accepted and belonging somewhere in the universe.

He was still in the warm grasp of this feeling when they reached the terminus room and the bottom of the skip. Other trains, also loaded with ore, were already there, or just pulling in ahead of theirs. They stopped and everyone in Hal's team piled off the loaded cars – Hal following suit. Only John stayed aboard, and when they were all off, he put the train in motion again, driving it off through a tunnel opening beyond the skip.

'What do we do now?' Hal asked one of the other team members, for they were making no move to go toward the skip, which was standing open and waiting at the bottom of its shaft.

'Wait for John,' said the team member, a short, lean man in his mid-twenties with a piratical black mustache drooping its ends around the corners of his lips.

Hal nodded. He stood waiting with the rest; and after three or four minutes, John came walking back out of the tunnel into which he had driven the train and rejoined them.

'Half ton over quota,' he said, holding a printed slip before tucking it into a chest pocket of his suit. There was a mutter of approval from the other team members.

'Hey, with a new kip! Good!' The miner Hal had spoken to punched Hal's shoulder in friendly fashion – or rather, tried to, for Hal reflexively swayed away from the fist, riding the blow so that the other's gloved knuckles barely touched him. The other did not seem to notice that his punch had not landed.

'Let's ride up!' said John, and led the way toward the skip, which was half full of men from other teams ready to go up as John led his own people on to it.

'Watch it!' a voice called almost in Hal's ear as he stepped aboard. 'Watch your feet. We got a new kip with big boots and no manners.'

Hal turned and found himself looking across only inches of space into the face of the lean, big-nosed young miner who had complained about his foot being stepped on by Hal on the way down.

'What's the matter with you, Neif?' said the black-mustached miner from Hal's team. 'It's his first day.'

'I'm not talking to you, Davies.' The miner called Neif glanced at Hal's team member. 'Let him answer for himself, if he thinks he belongs down in a mine.'

The skip closed its door and started upwards with a jerk.

'I didn't touch your foot,' said Hal to Neif.

Neif pushed his face close.

'I'm a liar, am I?'

'What's going on over there?' the voice of John Heikkila reached them through the mass of packed bodies. Hal looked away from Neif and said nothing.

The skip rose. When they reached the top and the gates opened, Hal stepped out quickly and moved away from the bodies behind him. In spite of the close-packed ride to the minehead, some of the warmth and identity with his team members while riding the ore cars back to the terminus had now gone from him.

'This way,' he heard John's voice in his ear. 'We slip these suits, and I'll show you how to check yours for leaks.'

Hal followed him back to the room where he had first been given the suit. There, at John's direction, he took it off and watched as John hooked up to the suit a small hose hanging from the wall below a vernier-shaped scale. John sealed the coveralls, tightened the hose about a valve near the suit's belt level and squeezed the tube. The coveralls inflated.

'Fine,' said John after a second, deflating the suit. 'No leaks. Never forget to do that after every shift. You won't get a second chance. The first time you inhale hot gases downstairs is it.'

'I'll remember,' said Hal. 'Now what –'

'Dinner in forty minutes,' John answered without waiting for the question to be finished. 'Why don't you go outside – oh, here's someone looking for you.'

The someone was Tonina. John went off and Tonina came forward to stand and look Hal up and down.

'How'd you get back before we did?' Hal asked. 'I didn't even see you in the skip this morning.'

'The shifts are staggered,' she said, 'so the slag loaders can have a regular round for clean-up. Beson and the rest of us went down before you, so we came back up before you.'

'Oh,' said Hal. She had led off and he was automatically following her. 'Where are we going?'

'Outside,' she said. 'I want a look at you under the high lights.'

They emerged through a door into the open staging area with its flat and dusty surface bright under the ceiling lights far overhead in the general cavern. What looked to Hal to be most of the other miners not on shift were milling around, talking in groups and obviously waiting for the dinner hour.

'Now stop,' said Tonina, once they were well out under the ceiling lights, which had the apparent brightness of the noonday sun on Earth. She squinted up at him. 'You look good. All right! I heard you did fine down there.'

'I did?' said Hal. 'But I kept falling behind. The shift ended just in time or John would have had to have helped me.'

'That's still good,' said Tonina. 'You worked clear through your first shift down. Almost nobody new to the mines does that. It doesn't matter what kind of shape they were in when they got here, either. You use a different set of muscles on the tongs and everybody gets wrung out to start with.'

'Hey, you – big foot kip!' said a voice Hal had come to recognize. He turned to see Neif bearing down on them. Now, out of his suit, the other man was less impressive. He was a good half a head shorter than Hal and he looked lean, but Hal's training told him that the other would probably outweigh him by a good twenty per cent more of mature bone and muscle. In the open v-neck of his loose shirt, his neck and chest area showed a deep tan that could only have been achieved here by the use of special tanning lamps. His shoulders were square and broad, his waist narrow, and his eyes very dark.

'I want a couple more words with you,' he said.

'Get away from him, Neif,' said Tonina. 'He's brand new. Pay no attention to him, Tad.'

'You stay out of this, Tonina,' said Neif. 'I'm talking to you, kip. I don't like my foot tramped on and I don't like being called a liar.'

There was a sick feeling in Hal. Other miners, attracted by the raised voices, had begun to drift into a circle around them.

'Don't tell me what to do, Neif!' Tonina shoved herself between the two of them, facing Neif. 'You ought to know better than to take off on someone new. Where's John? John Heikkila, this bastard here's trying to be a big man by taking off on your kip!'

Her voice carried.

'What is it?' said John, a moment later, shoving through the crowd to join them. 'What's your problem, Neif?'

'None of your business,' said Neif. 'This kip of yours rode my foot all the way down in the skip today, then called me a liar when I told him not to do it.'

John looked at Hal. Hal shook his head.

Hal's feeling of sickness increased. He was here to be inconspicuous and with every moment this business with Neif was making him more conspicuous. It seemed to him as if everyone at the mine was becoming involved.

'I wasn't on his foot,' he said, 'but it's all right –'

'You say you weren't on his foot. All right. Then there's no problem,' said John. He stood facing Neif like a human tank. But Neif's face twisted.

'You're not my leader. If this kip can't take care of himself what's he doing here?'

'Go crawl in a hole!' Tonina broke in, fiercely. 'You heard he had a rep and you want to get a piece of it, that's all.'

Neif ignored her. He was looking at John.

'I said, you're not my leader.'

'Sure,' said John. He looked around at the crowd. 'Will?'

Will was standing in the front rank to John's left.

'What about it?' Will said to John, without moving. 'We heard he's a troublemaker. You knew that when you took him on. If he isn't, let him stand up for himself. If that rep's true, he maybe engineered this fight himself to show off.'

'It's all right,' said Hal, hastily. 'John, it's all right. I didn't step on his foot, but if he thinks I did, I'm sorry –'

'Sorry, hell!' said Neif. 'You think you can call me a liar and just walk away. Either stand up for yourself or get out of the mine.'

'John!' said Tonina.

John shrugged and stepped back. The circle of people around them were moving back until Hal and Neif were at the center of a large open space. Tonina waited for a moment longer, then she, too, stepped back.

Hal stood looking at Neif, feeling despair now. The light was very bright and the air was dry and hot about him. The surrounding miners seemed far away and alien. He was as isolated in his own mind as if he stood in the midst of a pack of wolves. He stared at the face of Neif and saw no reasonableness there.

Let him, he thought suddenly to himself. I'll let him do what he wants. That's the only way out of this mess. If he beats me up, then maybe they'll forget that reputation business. . . .

He could see Neif beginning to step toward him, the other man's right shoulder dropping as his fist clenched. Hal's body cried out to move into any one of a dozen defensive postures from his training, but he held it prisoner with his mind. He only put up his fists in what he hoped was a clumsy and amateurish fashion.

Neif came toward him. I will stand still, Hal told himself. He forced himself to stand without moving as Neif stepped close.

. . . Hal was confused. Something was wrong, but he could not immediately remember what it was. He was on the ground and certain of only one thing, and that was that he had been attacked. He saw a figure of a man over him, stepping toward him and shifting his body weight in a way that announced a kick was coming.

Instinctively his own body reacted, gathering itself up, somersaulting backward to roll on and up once more onto its feet, facing the attacker. He was remembering now that this was the man called Neif; and that he had intended to let the other do what he wanted; but his mind was still fogged and strange and he could not remember why he should do that.

At the same time, Neif was coming on again, after a slight, startled pause at seeing Hal move so swiftly from a helpless position on the ground to his feet and ready to react. Neif came in swiftly, swinging his right first for Hal's adam's apple.

Shaky and weak, but automatically responding, Hal turned his body sideways to let the fist go by and made one sweeping step forward and around the other as Neif staggered, off-balance from his unsuccessful punch. He stood, facing the back of the other man. Automatically, without conscious thought, Hal pumped two short, twisting blows with right and left hand fists into the kidney areas of the back before him. Neif dropped.

Hal took a step away and stood looking down at the other. His head was clearing rapidly now, and as it did the feeling of sickness came back on him.

It was no use. He could not make himself simply stand there and take whatever punishment Neif wanted to hand out. He simply could not make himself do it. That first blow that had made him momentarily unconscious had awakened a primitive fear and instinct for survival within him. But the other man was down now, and unmoving. Maybe that would be the end of it.

He started to move away . . . and Neif stirred. His arms tensed, pulled his hands back alongside his body, and pushed himself up on one knee, facing away from Hal. He rose uncertainly to his feet and turned around. He came toward Hal.

If I could just knock him out, Hal thought. . . .

But his head was still not completely clear and Neif was almost on top of him. Hal raised his two arms, trapped the arm that was attempting to hit him, and, turning, knelt, so that Neif cartwheeled over Hal's right shoulder to land heavily on his back. Again, he lay still for a moment, the breath knocked out of him. But once more, after a few seconds, he began to stir, to turn and climb to his feet.

Hal's head was almost clear now and bleakly he faced the impossibility of what he had been thinking of doing. There was no way just to knock Neif out, harmlessly. That was the stuff of romantic adventures found in the bound volumes of the library that Walter InTeacher had made available to him – not the reality of what Malachi had taught him. Only in fiction could someone be hit so cleverly with fists or club that he was knocked briefly unconscious, but otherwise put into no danger of real damage. In real life the same impact that would only render one person unconscious could kill another of the same weight, size and general physical condition.

No, the only blows he knew that he could be sure would put Neif down to stay were all killing blows. Someone with the experience of Malachi Nasuno might have risked using one of them with just the right amount of force only to stun, but Hal was neither strong enough nor skilled enough to risk it.

He felt despair. Neif was coming at him again, a crazy expression around his eyes. Once more Hal faded away before the other's attack, caught him, led him off balance and threw him. Once more, after a second, Neif struggled back to his feet and attacked again. Hal threw him once more; and still, again, Neif climbed back to his feet and came on. Hal threw him.

The man was plainly in superb physical condition from his hard work in the mines; and also he was obviously not going to give up until he was stopped. The internal sickness came again to fill Hal completely. The crowd watching seemed very far away. The world about him was a place of rock and light; dry, dusty and empty except for the unending necessity to deal with this attacker who would not

110

lie down, would not leave him alone, and who forced him to continue handing out punishment.

Please, make him stay down! . . . the prayer repeated itself, over and over in Hal, as Neif continued to climb back to his feet and come again. In his mind, long ago, Hal had stopped reacting; in his mind, he was trying to leave himself for Neif to do anything the other man wanted to do to him. But the fear still with him overrode and ignored his mind; and refused to let the other man close.

In his imagination Hal saw the other lying still – too still – on the ground; and inside himself he shuddered away from the image. This could not go on. With a sudden spasm of desperate self-control, Hal succeeded in forcing himself to stand still with his arms down; and Neif finally reached him, grappled with him, and pulled him to the stony floor on which they fought.

But the miner was a man with his strength almost gone. Nothing was truly left in him but the blind will to keep fighting as long as he was alive. Neif's fingers fumbled up Hal's cheeks to gouge at his eyes, but Hal dodged them – and was suddenly filled with hope born of inspiration.

Lying on the ground with the other man on top of him, he slid his hands up to hold the other's shoulders, and under the pretense of trying to push the other away, pressed his thumbs into the carotid arteries on each side of Neif's neck. In the same moment Neif's fingers finally found Hal's eye-sockets.

Desperately Hal bowed his head on his neck so that most of the pressure was taken by his cheekbones. His mind counted slowly as Neif continued to try to sink his fingers into Hal's eye-sockets . . . one thousand . . . one thousand one . . . one thousand two . . . he pressed his face as close as possible to Neif's dusty hair and continued counting as he held the pressure on the other's arteries.

As he counted one thousand forty-three, Neif's fingers began to relax and at one thousand sixty they fell away entirely; and the miner lay motionless. Hal crawled out from under the other man's body and looked down. Neif continued to lie still.

Hal turned and walked, stumblingly, away from the motionless man toward the wall of bodies between himself and the bunkhouse. He could see Tonina directly ahead of him, her face for some reason in focus where the faces around her were featureless blurs. The surface on which he walked seemed constructed rather of pillows than of the hard rock and packed dust.

A sudden, swelling murmur went through the crowd. They were looking past him. He stopped and turned exhaustedly to look.

Neif was up on one elbow, looking around him. He was obviously conscious again; but, just as Hal had lost orientation after absorbing the other's first blow, so Neif's temporarily blood-starved brain cells were for the moment confused, and he would not be sure just why he was lying where he was.

Hal turned away again and plodded on toward the ring of faces and Tonina. He reached them; and, as he did so, the ring broke up, the miners in it streaming past him to surround Neif, help him to his feet and assist him to his room. Tonina was suddenly before Hal and she caught him strongly around the waist with one arm, as he tripped and almost fell.

'It's all right,' she said. 'It's all right. It's over now. I'll take you in. Where are you hurt?'

He stared down at her. He was suddenly conscious of the aching of his eyes and jaw, and the bruises and scrapes of the hard rock on which he and Neif had wrestled. But he wanted to tell her that there was nothing really wrong with him, nothing but exhaustion; that outside of that first blow, Neif had done nothing to him. But the sickness in him mounted, and his throat was clenched as tightly shut against it as if a pipe wrench had been tightened upon it. He could only stare at her.

'Lean on me,' she said.

She turned and half-led, half-carried him toward the bunkhouse. Her arm around his waist was incredibly strong – stronger by far, a portion of his mind thought bitterly, than his own. He let himself be taken away in silence and brought to his own room, dropped on his bed and undressed. Lying on the bed, he began to shiver violently and uncontrollably.

Tonina wrapped the bedcover tightly around him and turned its controls to heat, but he still shivered. Hastily, she shrugged out of her own outer clothes and slipped in under the blanket with him. She put her hard, strong arms around him and held his trembling body to her, warming it with her own body heat.

Gradually, his shuddering ceased. Warmth was born in him again and flooded out through all his limbs. He lay relaxed. He still breathed deeply and tremblingly for a while longer, but finally even that slowed. Instinctively, his arms closed around Tonina, drawing her even more closely to him, running his hands over her body.

For a moment she tensed and resisted him. Then the tightness went out of her and she let him pull her to him.

CHAPTER TEN

A month and a half later Sost showed up unexpectedly at the mine with a delivery, pulling into the staging area just as dinner was ending for the teams that ate with John Heikkila's. Hal wandered comfortably out of the door of the dining hall and saw a familiar-looking truck shape before the office building and an even more familiar human shape getting out of it.

Hal started toward the truck, picking up speed as he went. Sost, however, disappeared into the office building carrying a large package before Hal got there, and Hal stood waiting until the older man came out again.

'Hey there,' said Sost when he emerged, as casually as if they had parted fifteen minutes before. He rambled down the steps and came up to offer Hal a square, thick hand. 'How's the Yow Dee been doing for you?'

'I like it here,' said Hal, taking the hand. 'Come on over to the canteen and sit down.'

'Won't refuse,' said Sost.

The canteen was half full of off-shift miners. Hal looked around for Tonina or anyone from his team, but saw none of them.

'Here,' said Hal, finding them seats at an empty table with six places. 'What would you like? There's only food-drinks and coffee, because of the mine regulations.'

'Coffee's fine,' said Sost, taking a seat.

Hal got them both coffee – or what was called coffee on Coby – and brought it back to their table in copper mugs with ceramic rims at the top so that lips would not be burned on the hot metal when the cups were filled.

'I didn't know you came way over here,' he said to Sost.

'I'm liable to end up anywhere,' Sost said, drinking from his own cup. 'Like it here, do you?'

Just then Tonina came in the door.

'Tonina!' he called. She looked around, saw him, and Sost, and headed toward them. 'Yes, it's a good mine . . . Tonina, sit down. I'd like you to meet Sost. Do you want something to drink?'

'Not right now,' she said, joining them at the table. She and Sost looked at each other.

'I've heard the name,' she said.

'I get around,' said Sost. 'I met the boy, here, just outside his holding station. Stupidest twenty-year-old I ever saw; and I told him so. We ended up getting on real well.'

'Ah,' said Tonina. She relaxed. Hal had noticed before how quick she was to tense up in any unusual situation. Normally she did not relax this quickly. 'He's getting brighter every day.'

'Don't say?' said Sost, drinking coffee.

'I do say,' Tonina said. 'He's rating right at the top among the muckers-out and he's only been here a little over a month.'

'Six weeks,' said Hal.

'I remember you now,' Tonina said to Sost, 'you used to come in regularly to the old Trid Mine. Nearly two years ago. I got started there. You remember Alf Sumejari, the head cook. . . .'

They talked about people whose names were unknown to Hal. But he did not feel uncomfortable at being left out of the conversation. He sat listening comfortably, and when John Heikkila walked through the entrance a few minutes later he called the team leader over to join them.

'He's doing all right,' John told Sost, whom he had evidently met before.

'About time then, isn't it?' said Sost.

'I'll be the judge of that,' said John. 'Are you going to be coming in here regularly, then?'

'Not on a regular schedule,' Sost said. 'But I'll be working this territory generally for quite a while. There'll be things to bring me to the Yow Dee.'

He pushed his empty coffee mug away from him and stood up. John and Tonina were also getting to their feet and Hal scrambled to his. He had the sudden, sharp feeling that something he had not understood had gone on about him.

'You're leaving right away?' he said to Sost. 'I thought we could take a few hours –'

'Got to keep schedule,' said Sost. He nodded at John and Tonina. 'See you in Port, sometime.'

He went out the door. John and Tonina were already moving away in different directions into the room. Hal looked after them for a second, then followed Sost out.

'But when'll I see you again?' he asked Sost as the older man climbed into his truck.

'Any time. Not too long,' said Sost.

He powered up the truck on its fans, turned it on its axis and drove out of the staging area. Hal looked after him for several moments, then turned back to the canteen. He wanted to hear what John and Tonina thought of Sost. But as he got there, John came out and went across toward the office; and a second later Tonina also came out and went toward the bunkhouse.

114

Hal started to follow her, then read in the set of her back and shoulders that she was not in a mood for company. His steps slowed. He felt a little sadness. Since that first night following his fight she had never really let him within arm's length of her, although in all other ways she had been as warmly friendly as ever.

He watched her go. Walter InTeacher had coached him in the Exotic way of empathy, and he could feel deep in Tonina an old unhappiness that she had long ago given up any hope of conquering. She had simply lived with it until it had reached the point where she was all but unaware that it was still there. Still, he could feel how much of everything she did was directed by that ancient pain and the mechanisms she had developed to bury it. She would not have been willing to be helped with it now, even if Hal had known how to help her; and he did not. All he could do was feel the entombed ache in her and ache in sympathy with it.

By the next day, however, his empathic sense found something else to occupy itself as he rode down in the skip with the rest of the team. He could not miss noticing a difference in all of them toward him, today. But it was not an unfriendly difference. Hal shrugged internally; and, since it seemed to be harmless, he put it out of his mind.

When they got to the vein on which they were currently digging, he fitted himself automatically with a pair of tongs on each glove and turned around to the ledge, only to come within inches of bumping into Will Nanne. Hal had not exchanged a word with the other team leader since the day of his arrival; and he stopped, surprised and wary at seeing him here now, in the area of the Heikkila team.

'Well,' said Will. Like Hal and the rest of them at the moment the helmet of his suit was thrown back; and his face was as unsmiling as ever. 'You been here nearly two months now, haven't you?'

'About a month and a half, actually,' said Hal.

'Time enough,' said Will. 'I need another torcher on my team. Want to shift over, and I'll train you?'

'Torcher?'

Hal stared at him. He had been having daydreams of the day when John Heikkila might offer him a chance to try working with a torch; and only a small part of that daydream was concerned with the larger percentage of the team's profits that would be coming to him if he became a torcher. The large part had had to do with the dream of being, in his own eyes as well as in the eyes of the other workers, a full-fledged miner.

For a moment he was strongly tempted; and then the whole weight of the friendships he had made with John and the rest of the team rejected the offer, even as he was voicing his incredulity.

'You don't want *me*?'

'I don't say it twice,' Will said. 'I've offered you a job. Take it or leave it.'

'But you don't like me!' said Hal.

'Didn't. Do now,' said Will. 'Well, how about it? Work time's counting. I can't stand around here all shift waiting for you to make up your mind. Coming with me, or not?'

Hal took a deep breath.

'I can't,' he said. 'Thanks anyway. I'm sorry.'

'You mean you won't.'

'I mean I won't. But thanks for offering me the job –'

A strange thing was happening to Will Nanne's grim face. It was not changing, but laughter was coming out of it. Hal stared at the man, bewildered, and suddenly began to realize that there was merriment all around him. He looked again at Will, at the closed lips and scowling features with the snorts of laughter coming from the long nose. He looked around and saw the rest of his own team in a circle about him, not getting ready for work at all, their helmets all thrown back, and laughing.

John was one of them, standing almost at Hal's right elbow. But when he saw Hal's eyes on him, he sobered in turn and became almost as sour-faced as Will.

'All right, damn it!' he said. 'I guess I got to give you a chance to try torching if everybody's going to be coming around here trying to hire you away from the team. Come on, everyone, let's get to work. Time's counting. Better luck next time, Will.'

'I expect you'll be over to steal one of my team next,' grumped Will; and turning, he went off, still snorting softly to himself.

Hal looked at John and grinned. He was beginning to understand.

'What're you looking so pleased about?' said John. 'For two profit points, I'd fire you now and give you no place to go but with Will. How do I know you haven't been talking to him about changing teams, before this, behind my back?'

Hal only grinned more widely.

'All right,' John said, turning away. 'Let's see how happy you are after a shift of torching. Come on up on the ledge.'

Hal followed him up to join the other torchers. They stood facing the wall, in front of about a body's width of rock apiece. John took a position at the left end of the line next to the stope wall.

'Put your helmet on,' said John. 'No. Put it on, *then* pick up your torch. Always do it that way. Now . . .' his voice came filtered through the suit mechanism, 'watch me. Don't try to do any torching to start with, just watch how I do it. Don't knock your helmet back until you see me take mine off. When you see me put mine back on, put yours back on – and keep watching at all times. You understand?'

'Yes,' said Hal, hearing his own voice hollow with excitement inside the helmet.

He obeyed. The wall before him – before each of them – was scored vertically and horizontally by earlier torch cuts; and its surface was a mosaic of different depths of rock, marking the planes where torch cuts had parted a surface chunk from the granite beneath. His eyes were on John.

John raised his torch to the wall, with its muzzle less than hand's length from the rock. A slim, golden pencil of visible light that was the guide for the cutting beam, which could not be seen, reached out and into the face of the stope before him – and a wave of heat that was like a body blow struck Hal, even through the protection of his suit, as the rock was vaporized in an incredibly thin section by the moving, invisible beam.

As he had grown more expert at mucking-out, there had been more and more occasions when Hal had been caught up with his own work and could simply stand for a moment and watch the torchers; and he had come to the conclusion that their work must be very easy compared to his own. In fact, he had puzzled over why it made sense to have two teams working alternate periods, when it would have seemed to have been more practical simply to work a single crew of six or seven men straight through the shift. He now discovered one reason why. The sudden heat blow from the outburst of hot gases from the vaporized rock was breathtaking, even inside the protective suit; and his first experience of it now explained why the torchers worked in spurts, cutting for a few minutes, then pausing, then cutting again.

It was some moments before he could manage to observe two more new things. One was the fact that John seemed to be cutting in a peculiar pattern that moved his torch about strangely on the face of rock before him, as if the areas to be cut were marked in some complicated sequence; and the other was that he shut his torch off each time before beginning to cut a new chunk. He had barely absorbed these facts when John stopped working abruptly; and simply stood, a mechanical-looking figure in his suit, facing the wall. Hal stared at him, not understanding, then became aware that the hiss and crackle of the torches to his right were also giving way to silence. He looked and saw that all the others of the current crew had stopped cutting, except the miner at the far end of the face. Then that man also shut his torch off.

Hal's glove twitched upward to knock back his helmet and give himself some air as he had seen the current crew do so many times. Then he realized that no one else had yet touched their helmets. He checked his movement and stood, gasping in the closed suit, watching John until John reached up and lifted back his own helmet. Hal imitated him and, looking around, taking deep breaths, saw the other torchers opening up as well.

For a few seconds, he breathed air that was only warm; then he saw John putting his helmet back on and followed suit. The torches took up their hiss and crackle again; and once more Hal watched and sweated under the momentary heat-blows before another helmetless break came. It seemed to last only seconds before they were buttoned up and at work again.

Before it came to be time for the other crew to replace them at the rock wall, Hal was soaked in sweat and as enervated as if he had worked a full half-shift at mucking-out, although he had done nothing but watch. But, as he became more accustomed to the heat-blows and the noise, his observation of the way the work went had been improving. He saw that a chunk would be carved out, wherever possible, by undercutting a projecting piece of rock; and then taking out as many other chunks as possible by cutting vertically down to the horizontal undercut. Where there was no way of undercutting, the torcher made slanting cuts into the face of the rock, until these intersected behind the chunk.

At the first touch of the cutting beam, there would be an explosion of gases from the vaporized rock; and for a moment the seeing was, not exactly foggy, but distorted; as if he was looking at the rock wall through the updrafts of heated gas and air. In the moment following the heat blow and the distortion, the view of the rock became solid again; but for a few seconds after that a sort of silver mist seemed to cling to the face of the rock, before vanishing.

It was not until the second time the crew including John and Hal attacked the wall that Hal put the sight of the silver mist together with the pattern of the torchers in knocking back their helmets. It was never until that haze had completely gone that any of them cracked their suits open. Hal's mind, galloping ahead with that observation, deduced that the silver mist must be condensation of some of the gasified rock, boiled out upon the surface of the face and chilled there by the liquified gas coolant projected around the cutting beam from its reservoir in the heavy body of the torch. Until the mist evaporated, there would be danger of some of the vaporized material being still in gas form, in the atmosphere before the stope wall.

As work wore on, Hal began to pick up more understanding of the pattern in which John was cutting into the rock face. The pattern seemed to be designed to keep him cutting always at the greatest possible distance from where the man on his right was cutting on his own section. Looking down along the face, Hal saw that the same patterning seemed to be at work to keep the others of the crew cutting at as close to maximum distance from each other as possible.

The lunch break finally came. John sat down to eat with his back to the tunnel wall beside Hal.

'Well,' he said, tearing into a sandwich with his teeth, 'how about it? You ready to try it?'

Hal nodded.

'If you think I can.'

'Good,' said John. 'At least, you're not so all-fired sure you can just stand up there and do it. Now, I'll tell you what. Pay no atten-

118

tion to how fast the others are cutting. You cut only when I tell you to, and where I tell you to. Got that?'

'Yes,' said Hal.

'All right.' John finished his sandwich and got back to his feet. 'Let's go, crew!'

He, Hal and the others returned to the face. Davies, who had taken over the mucking-out temporarily while Hal tried out with the torch, winked at Hal as Hal passed. Hal took the wink for encouragement and felt warmed by it.

At the face, guided by John's voice and pointing finger, Hal slowly began to choose and excavate pieces of the rock. He did not do well, in his own estimation. He found himself taking a dozen cuts to loosen a piece of rock that John might have taken out in three. But, gradually, as he worked, he began to get a little more efficient and economical in the use of the torch, although the patterns in which John directed his work remained beyond him.

As the shift wore toward its end the heat seemed to sap the strength out of him; it became enormous effort just to lift the torch and concentrate on the cuts John indicated he was to make. His cuts became clumsier; and, for the first time, he began to realize the danger of losing precise control of the torch, which, waved around carelessly in its *on* mode, could slice through suits, human flesh and bone with a great deal more ease than it could through rock – and the rock offered it no problem.

Through the window of his helmet as he continued cutting, he was aware of John watching him closely. John must know that exhaustion was making him uncertain; and at any minute now the team leader would be taking the torch away from him. Something in Hal surged in rebellion. At the next chance he had to knock back his helmet he deliberately drew a deep breath and let it out in slow, controlled fashion as he had been taught, both by Malachi and by Walter . . . and his mind smoothed out.

He had been letting himself become frantic because he could feel his strength dwindling. That was not the way he had been taught to handle situations like this. There were techniques for operating on only a remaining portion of his strength.

The answer was to concentrate what strength remained on what was essential, and close out his attention on anything unnecessary. It was something like controlled tunnel vision, making the most of what was available over the smallest possible area. Having breathed himself back into self-control, he closed up his suit, addressed the rock face again and let his mind spiral inward, his vision close in . . . until all he saw was the rock before his torch and John's directing hands, until all he heard was John's voice.

The heat became distant and unimportant. The fatigue ceased to exist except as an abstract phenomenon. The stope, the mine itself, the very fact that he was underground, became things unimportant and apart. Even the relief periods were brief, unimportant moments before he was back at the face of rock again. The real universe was restricted to that rock face, the torch, and the directions of John.

His grip on the torch steadied. His cuts regained their precision and certainty. In this smaller universe, his present strength and attention were enough and to spare to get the job done. He worked. . . .

Suddenly, they had all stopped and put back their helmets; and they were not starting again. John and the other torchers were turning away from the rock face. Baffled, Hal opened up his perceptions; and staggered physically as the larger world came back into existence about him, a bone-weariness exploding all through him.

He was conscious of John catching his arm and holding him up, guiding him back from the ledge and down the ramp cut the day before to the level below. His legs were wobbly and the torch he had unthinkingly carried back from the rock face – when he should have left it there for the next day's first crew – seemed to weigh several tons. He laid it against the face of the rise in which the ramp was cut; then, overwhelmed, slid down into a sitting position himself with his back to the rise.

Everybody was gathering around him. In the crowd, strangely, were Tonina and Will Nanne, who had left them hours ago.

'Well,' said Will's harsh voice. 'He did it. I wouldn't have believed it if I hadn't seen it myself.'

'All right,' said John, looking down at Hal. 'I suppose you'll do. I hope you understand the whole team's going to have to carry you and lose production until you learn enough to do a fair shift of work?'

'Oh, leave him alone!' said Tonina. 'Can't you let him be now that he's won the job?'

'I have?' Hal said, foggily.

'Well, you still got to throw a port party for the team,' said Davies.

Escorted back to the skip by them all with Tonina on one side of him and John on the other, acting as bumpers to bounce him back on course when he staggered out of the direct line of march, Hal felt a sense of triumph beginning to rise within him and a deep feeling of affection for those around him. He was one of them at last. They were like family, and he felt for each of them as if each was a brother or a sister.

'Port party tonight,' said an unfamiliar voice in the crowded skip. Evidently the whole mining camp had been in on the plans for his trial as a torcher.

'Wait until you make leader, if you ever do,' said Tonina in his ear. 'Then you have to get the whole crowd of underground workers at the mine drunk.'

As they had left the rock face, Hal had felt that he had hardly the strength left to do anything but fall on his bed and sleep the clock around. But once back in the bunkhouse, showered and dressed for Port, he found himself coming back to life. In the end, as they boarded the subway in a group – the team, Tonina, and Will Nanne, who was evidently entitled to share in the party because of having been one of the actors in the traditional drama in which Hal had been offered his chance to try out as a torcher – Hal found himself feeling as well as ever, except for a slight sensation as if he had lost so much weight he might float off the ground, with any encouragement at all.

CHAPTER ELEVEN

Hal, himself, had not been back to the main Coby spaceport since he had come in to this world; but he had come to know that nearly all the miners headed there in their off-time, particularly on the day and a half off they had between their six and a half day work weeks. The six and a half days came about because every three working days there were twelve extra hours off between work periods in which the slag-loaders did general cleanup and maintenance or other administrative work was carried on down in the mine. Every third week the extra half day of weekend holiday was cancelled out as each shift made a move forward of that many hours into a new work-time slot.

He had been puzzled that the shifts should need to change at all on this world where there was no sun and no natural day or nighttime hours. But he came to learn that a number of the miners had living partners or other personal arrangements in Port, where for administrative purposes day and night were strictly set and held. Certainly, everyone else but he seemed to know their way around Port when their group got there, heading off in one specific direction by unanimous agreement.

'Where are we going?' he asked John.

'The Grotto,' said John. They were walking together in the back of the crowd; and now John took Hal by the elbow and slowed him down until they had fallen several meters behind everyone else. Even Tonina, seeing John holding Hal's arm, had gone on ahead.

'. . . You've got the credit for this, haven't you?'

'Yes,' said Hal.

'All right,' said John. 'If you find yourself getting in too deep, remember I can advance you what you need to make up the difference. You'll have to pay me back as soon as possible, though, or I'll take it out of your profit share, some every week until it's paid back.'

'No, I've really got all the funds I'd need,' Hal said.

'All right.'

John let go of him and moved back up into the crowd ahead. Hal, stretching his own legs to catch up also, felt a twinge of guilt. John, in spite of handling Hal's papers, obviously did not know that Hal had brought in with him probably more in the way of a credit balance than a team leader in the mines could earn in twenty years in the mines – and a good chunk of that amount was in interstellar credits.

Remembering his credit balance started Hal on a new train of thought. The Others were unlikely to trace him here; but that did not mean that they could not, or would not. He might one day have to run for it again; and if he did, it would not help if they had located his funds under his own name and tied them up so that he could not use them to get away. What he needed was interstellar credit hidden away, untraceable to any official eye, but quickly available to him in an emergency. He filed the thought to be acted on as soon as possible.

Meanwhile they had reached their destination; they all poured through an arched entrance in the frontage wall of one of the Port blocks of construction. Above the arch the name GROTTO floated in blue flames.

Within, it was so dark that at first he could see nothing and stumbled as he went forward, before he realized he was walking on some soft surface. As his vision adjusted, he saw that this was a thick carpet of something looking very much like grass and that the illusion overhead was of a night sky with the moon hidden behind clouds.

He followed the others forward, and passed with them through a light curtain into a scene of bright moonlight, seeming so brilliant after the short period of near-darkness that he was startled. The illusion of a moon shone down on the appearance of a tiny bay on the shore of a tropical sea, with actual tables and chair floats intermingled with rocks or ground features that also gave sitting or table space. A surf spoke gently on the sandy beach before them all. Soft, spice-perfumed air blew around them; and a full moon surrounded by innumerable stars was overhead in a now-cloudless sky.

The place had evidently been alerted to their coming, for while there were other patrons, a large section of the beach shore with its seating and serving arrangements was empty. Into this area, the team poured and settled itself. A thin, blond man in his mid-forties, perhaps, got up from one of the tables where he was sitting with one of the other customers and came over to the table to which Hal had been steered, and at which he had been joined by John, Tonina and Will Nanne.

'You're the host, I take it?' he said, smiling at Hal. His teeth were white and even, but he was one of those individuals who actually do better not to smile.

'That's right,' said Hal.

'Could I have your credit number?'

Hal passed over his identity card. The other touched it to his wrist monitor, took it away and glanced at the dial of the monitor, then handed it back.

'Enjoy yourselves,' he said. He smiled at Hal again and went away. About Hal, drinks and other consumables ordered by the rest of them were rising to the tops of the table surfaces.

Hal looked at the others at his table. Tonina had some tall yellow drink in a narrow goblet. Will Nanne and John had steins of what appeared to be – and smelled like – beer. Hal spelled out beer on the tabletop waiter, picked the same name brand that John and Will had ordered, and got a glass just like theirs.

'That'll do for me,' said John. 'The next one's with Will.'

Hal stared at him.

'You got to have one drink with everyone else here before you settle down to your own drinking,' said John, a little grimly. 'That's the way it's done.'

'Oh,' said Hal. It did not require any effort to do the sum in his head. Twelve crew members meant twelve drinks. Will Nanne made that figure thirteen, and if they expected him to drink with Tonina as well, that would make fourteen. He felt uneasy for a moment.

However, there was no acceptable alternative. He put aside his uneasiness, lifted his glass of beer and drank. It was a lightly carbonated brew that did not seem too strong, and it went down easier than he had expected.

'You'd better slow down,' said Tonina. 'At that speed you won't make it to the third table.'

His head felt perfectly clear, and his always-hungry stomach did not feel at all overfilled by the one beer. But she undoubtedly knew what she was talking about. He drank the beer with Will Nanne more slowly. After all, no one had said anything about a time limit in which he had to do all this. Will's beer also went down comfortably. Hal decided he rather liked beer. The only time he had tasted it before was when he had been six years old at a picnic at which Malachi had been drinking some; and at that time he had decided it was bitter, unattractive stuff. But there was a lot of food value in beer, he remembered now. Perhaps that was what made it taste better to him in these, his years of greater appetite.

He looked from his second empty glass to Tonina.

'Why don't you save me for last?' she said.

'All right,' said Hal. He was feeling somewhat carefree. 'Which table do I take first?'

'Doesn't matter,' said Will. 'Take the first one you come to.'

Hal got up and, on second thought, chose first a table of three team members, one of which was Davies.

He found it enjoyable drinking with Davies and the others – although all the drinks they had ordered were strong enough to burn his throat. He was a little surprised when they reminded him that, having drunk with each of them, it was now time for him to move on.

He moved on.

He had not enjoyed himself so much in a long time. At the next table, the drinks were all different again. These also burned his throat, but they did not seem as strong as the drinks had at the table where Davies had sat. Once more he lost track of what he was supposed to be doing and had to be reminded to move on. At some indefinite time later he found himself being piloted back to his original table by people who went along on either side of him. He dropped into his chair and grinned at John, Will and Tonina.

Everyone else in their group, it seemed, was now gathered in a circle around the table, watching him. Tonina had scarcely touched her drink in all this time. Its level was lowered only slightly from what it had been when it had risen through the delivery slot in the table. She pushed it at him.

'You might as well just drink this,' she said.

There was an explosion of protest from around the table.

'Not fair! Cheat! He's got to drink a full one each time. . . .'

'What do you want?' Tonina suddenly flared at them. 'He shouldn't even be conscious, after what you've been feeding him! You want to kill him?'

'All right,' said John. 'All right . . . there's not enough gone from that glass to matter.'

The protests died down. Tonina pushed the glass over in front of Hal. He reached out carefully, closed his hand around it and lifted it to his lips. It was warm, after all this time, and sweeter than he would have preferred; with a thick, lemony taste. But there seemed hardly any alcohol in it at all, as far as his taste buds could tell in their present numb condition. He decided that a thing worth doing was worth doing well and drained it before he put the glass back on the table.

The wall of people around him exploded in noise. He was slapped on the back, shoulder-punched in friendly fashion, congratulated . . . and without warning, his stomach seemed to come loose within him and float upward, queasily.

He kept the grin on his face and tried to order the stomach to stay put. But the physical controls he had learned from Walter and Malachi had deserted him. His stomach surged rebelliously. . . .

'Excuse me. . . .' He pushed himself to his feet, turned from the table and looked around with rising panic.

'Help him!' said Tonina, sharply over the chatter of voices. The voices died. Everyone was turning to look at Hal.

'What'd you order, anyway?' somebody asked her. But Hal did not stay to hear the answer. Davies had him by the arm and was piloting him away from the table.

'This way,' Davies said.

Somehow he made it to the restroom with Davies' help; and there it

125

seemed that not only everything he had drunk tonight, but everything he had eaten and drunk for the past two weeks, came up. A little later, alone, haggard and wan, he made his unsteady way back to his original table.

'Feel better now?' asked Tonina, when he sat down.

'A little,' he said. He stared at her. 'Did you give me something to make me sick?'

'I gave you what I ordered for myself,' said Tonina, 'and a good thing, too. You'd be in the hospital right now, if I hadn't. What made you think you could drink like that?'

'I was doing all right,' said Hal, feebly.

'All right! Most of the alcohol hadn't hit your blood-stream yet. Thirty minutes and they'd have been giving you oxygen, at the rate you drank it. Don't you realize the only way to handle that much drink is to take it so slowly you metabolize most of it as you go?'

She sounded like Malachi.

'I know that,' he said. 'I thought I was going slow.'

'Hah!'

'All the same,' said Will, heavily, 'that's not the way it's supposed to be done. He's supposed –'

'Why?' Tonina turned fiercely on the other team leader. 'What more do you want? He drank everything the team gave him first. I was only along for an extra. And I told you. I only gave him what I ordered for myself. If he hadn't drunk it, I would have. Want me to order one right now and drink it to make you happy?'

'No need for that,' said John, as Tonina's hand shot out to the buttons of the table waiter. 'Will, she's right. He had a drink with everyone on the team, first, and you as well.'

'You forget what he is,' said Tonina. 'For God's sake, you forget what he is! Look at him. Twelve large drinks in less than three hours and he's still not only conscious but halfway sensible. How many grown men do you know who can do that?'

'Not the point . . .' protested Hal, weakly. But Tonina ignored him and the others were not listening either. Sitting in the chair, he felt intolerably tired. His eyes closed in spite of anything he could do. . . .

He woke some time later to find himself sitting at the table alone. He felt as if his bones would creak when he moved; his body in general felt dried out and his mind was dulled. But in a sense he felt better than when he had dropped off to sleep. Looking around, he saw that about half the team had left the Grotto, along with Will Nanne. John and Tonina sat with Davies and a couple of the other team members at a table down near the edge of the illusory ocean.

Hal got up to join them, changed his mind and detoured to the restroom again. There was a water fountain there, and after he had drunk what seemed like several gallons of water he felt better. He went out again, found their table and sat down with them.

'Well! Back from the dead?' said Tonina. He smiled, embarrassed.

'Come on,' she said, standing up, 'I'll steer you home.'

'Hey, he doesn't want to go yet,' protested Davies.

'I don't want to go yet,' said Hal.

She stared at him.

'Well, I'm going,' she said, after a moment. 'I've got to get back. I missed half a shift as it is. Will one of you see him safe home and not try to kill him with drink in the meantime?'

'I'll see him back,' said John.

'All right, then.' She looked at Hal. 'We'll see how you feel about this staying when it comes time for you to go on shift, tomorrow.'

Hal felt uncomfortable; but, stubbornly, he was determined not to go. He watched her leave.

'How do you feel?' Davies asked him.

'Dry,' said Hal.

'Beer,' said Davies. 'That's what's good for that – beer.'

'Take it easy,' said John.

'I'm not forcing him!' said Davies. 'You know he'll feel better with some beer in him.'

John sat back, and Davies coded for a beer from the table waiter.

Hal took it, feeling nowhere near as enthusiastic about it as he had felt about the beers earlier. Nonetheless, it was cold, wet and not too unpleasant to swallow. After he had gotten it down, Davies insisted that he have another.

As he drank the second one, Hal noticed that their original party had been dwindling rapidly since he had woken up. Only two others were left at another table besides Davies, John and himself; and Davies was showing signs of becoming silent and drowsy. The two others moved over to sit and talk with them for a while; and while they talked Davies dozed off in his chair. Then the others finished their drinks and headed off, on their way back to the mine and their rooms in the bunkhouse.

Hal was coming alive again, whether it was the two fresh beers or his own physical ability to bounce back. At the same time, even he could see the sense in going back to their beds, now. But instead of suggesting this, John turned back from watching the two who were just leaving as they walked from the room, then glanced at the still-slumbering Davies. He looked at Hal.

'What did happen at that Holding Station when you first got here?' he asked heavily.

'I came in and the man in charge there – his name was Jennison –' said Hal, 'told me to find myself a bed. So, I went looking . . .'

He ran through the events at the Holding Station, step by step, exactly as they had happened. John listened, without saying anything, sitting back in his seat, one heavy hand holding his beer glass, his eyelids half down over his eyes.

'. . . That was it,' said Hal, finally, when he had finished and John still had not said anything. 'That's all there was to it. They all seemed to think I'd done something unusual in stopping that man who tried to brain me; and then word of it must have got to your mine and Will Nanne before I showed up. I didn't know then how fast word gets around here.'

'It wasn't unusual?' John said, not moving, his eyelids still down over his eyes. 'A grown man, big as you or bigger, heavier than you, and you just tossed him against a wall and laid him out, like that?'

'I . . .' Hal hesitated. 'I had an . . . uncle who taught me a few things. I thought it was playing, mostly, when I was growing up, and I learned how to do them without really thinking. When he came at me, I just acted without thinking.'

'And when you had that little go with Neif? You weren't thinking then, either?'

'I was kind of out on my feet after he hit me hard at first. Things just came to me.'

'Sure,' said John. 'You see me?'

Hal nodded.

John reached out his hand and laid it palm-up on the table. He closed his fingers. He did not close them dramatically or with any great emotion, but the thick fingers, the wide palm, came together with an impression of power that was unmistakable.

'When I was fourteen,' he said, as if talking to himself, 'I was as tall as I am now. I never grew a centimeter after that. But even then I could pick up two grown men at once and carry them around.'

Hal watched him across the table, unable to look away.

'When I came here . . .' said John, and for a moment Hal thought he had stopped talking, 'when I came here, six standard years ago, I was in my twenties; and I hadn't settled down, yet. When you're like I was, then, some people can smell you, a kilometer off, and they come looking for you. I was in a Holding Station, when I first came here; and somebody had to try me and it happened. I broke his back. It was him started it, but I was the one broke his back. When I came to my first mine, my first job, they had me tabbed as somebody who was always like that – a gunfighter.'

He stopped talking again. This time he did not go on.

'Is that why you took me on?' said Hal, at last.

John drew a deep breath and let it out.

'Time we were getting back,' he said. 'Wake him up there.'

Hal got up himself, reached over and shook Davies gently by the shoulder. The other miner opened his eyes.

'Oh?' Davies said. 'Time to go?'

He sat up, took hold of the edge of the table and pulled himself upright.

'I guess I'm late,' said a familiar voice. Hal looked up and saw Sost standing at the end of the table. 'All over, is it?'

'Sit down,' said John. 'We can last for one more drink.'

'Not for me,' said Sost. 'Why don't I take you all home? Talk on the way.'

'Fair enough,' said John, getting to his feet. Hal also stood up. He turned and found a face with an unprepossessing smile at his elbow.

'Come back again,' said the proprietor of the Grotto. 'It was our pleasure to have you.'

'He'll want a bill,' said John. 'Itemized.'

'I'm afraid that'll take a few minutes . . .'

'It shouldn't,' said John.

The proprietor went off and came back in a few seconds with a hard copy, which he handed to Hal. John took it and looked it over.

'Close enough,' he said. 'We'll check it, of course.'

'I'm sure you'll find it the way it should be.'

'Sure. See you again,' said John.

He turned the hard copy back to Hal and led the way out.

'It's been a pleasure for us, serving you,' said the proprietor behind them, as they went.

Outside, Sost's truck was waiting in the street before the Grotto. A Port marshal, with a green sash around his waist, was standing beside it.

'Are you the operator?' he said to Sost, as Sost started to get into the control seat. 'I'll have to summon you for leaving this vehicle here.'

'Send the summons to Amma Wong, then, sonny,' said Sost. He looked around behind him. 'Everybody in?'

John and Davies had climbed into the empty bed of the truck in back and stretched out, closing their eyes. Hal, who was beginning to feel hungry and very much awake, climbed into the other front seat beside Sost.

'Amma Wong?' the marshal was standing absolutely still, his narrow, middle-aged face blank of expression. Sost reached into an inside shirt pocket, brought out a wallet, flipped it open and showed it to the marshal, then put it away again before Hal could see what Sost had shown the man.

The marshal stepped back. Sost lifted the truck on its fans and drove off.

'Who's Amma Wong?' asked Hal, as they turned the corner of the block onto one of the arterial roads.

'Director of Freight Handling at the Port here,' said Sost.

'You know her?'

'I work for her.'

'Oh,' said Hal, not much wiser than he had been before his first question. His stomach once more reminded him of its existence. 'Could we stop and pick up something to eat?'

'Hungry?' Sost looked sideways at him. 'Once I park the truck on the freight car, you can get something to eat from the machine on the subway train.'

Hal stared at him.

'You're taking us all the way back to the mine?' he said. 'You're going to put the truck and all on the subway?'

'Right,' Sost nodded.

They drove along in silence for a minute or two.

'Thought you'd have gone home with Tonina,' said Sost.

'She left early,' said Hal. 'What made you think I'd leave early when it's my party?'

Sost chuckled.

'Drinkingest twenty-year-old I ever saw,' he said, half to himself. He looked at Hal. 'Thought she wanted to talk to you privately about something.'

'She did?' Hal stared back at him. 'But she didn't say anything to me. When did she tell you she wanted to talk to me privately?'

'Saw her in Port, here, last week.'

'Last week?' Hal shook his head. He had not thought Tonina had been in Port in any of the weeks recently. 'What did she want to talk to me about?'

'Didn't say,' answered Sost.

CHAPTER TWELVE

Hal woke the next morning to the alarm of his chronometer and only by the sternest exercise of will got himself out of bed. By the time he was showered and dressed for work, however, he felt a great deal better.

He was digging into breakfast in the cookhall, when he became aware of Davies, across the table staring at him. Davies' face was pale and his eyes were red.

Hal slowed down in the face of that stare and finally stopped completely.

'What is it?' he asked Davies.

'I never,' said Davies, 'in my life saw a man with a hangover eat like that.'

Hal felt embarrassed, as he usually did when people paid attention to his appetite.

'I'm hungry this morning,' he said. It was his usual excuse when the matter came up – hungry this morning, this noon, or this evening.

'How do you feel?' demanded Davies.

Hal stopped to consider himself.

'Sort of washed out,' he said. Actually, there was a curious feeling in him, a sort of feeling of satisfied exhaustion as if he had just finished casting out a gang of inner devils.

'How about your head – your headache?'

'I don't have a headache,' Hal said.

Davies continued to stare at him.

'And you're really hungry.'

'I guess I am,' said Hal.

By this time the rest of the miners within earshot, most of them fellow team members, were listening. Hal had the uncomfortable feeling that once more he had done something to mark himself as different from the rest of them.

He forgot the matter, however, as the day's work started. He was still a complete beginner with the cutting torch and it took all his efforts to do a full shift of work. In the days and weeks that followed that began to improve. It came slowly, but eventually he could cut in patterns that meshed efficiently with those of his neighbors on either hand at the rock face, and still keep up with the rest of them.

131

Some days before he reached that point, however, Tonina had rapped on his door late after one shift was over and drawn him out for a walk on the staging area; now, between shifts, deserted.

Under the high, eternal, ceiling lights of the cavern they paced back and forth together and she looked at him strangely.

'I'm leaving the Yow Dee,' she said. 'Moving to Port. I was going to tell you about it, the night you made torcher, but I didn't get a chance to talk to you.'

'Sost said you might have wanted to talk to me.'

'He did?' Her voice was sharp. 'What did he say?'

'Just that he didn't know why. I thought,' Hal said, 'I shouldn't just go asking, that you'd tell me yourself if you really wanted to.'

'Yes,' her voice and eyes softened. 'You would think like that.'

They walked a little more in silence.

'I'm getting married,' she said. 'I almost got married a couple of months ago. That's why I came to the Yow Dee here. I wasn't sure. Now I am. I'm marrying a man named Blue Ennerson. He's in Headquarters, at Port.'

'Headquarters?' Hal said.

She smiled a little.

'Yow Dee and about three dozen other mines and Port businesses are all part of one company,' she said. 'The Headquarters for that company's in Port. Blue's Section Chief of the Record Section.'

'Oh,' said Hal. He felt inadequate, and not only because of his youth. He had learned that most women miners, who were a minority among the other mine workers, tended to marry upwards, into staff or management. Tonina was evidently going to be one such.

'I'm leaving tomorrow,' she said.

'Tomorrow?'

'I didn't have a chance to tell you before this. You were either working, eating or sleeping, since you've become torcher.'

'Yes.'

There was a bleakness in him. He felt he should say something, but had no idea what was said on occasions like this. Eventually, they went back to their rooms; and before he was up the next morning she was gone.

He had expected that the mine would be hollow and empty without her, and it was – at first. But as the months wore on, it became home in almost a real sense and the other team members, although they changed frequently as some left and new workers joined, became almost the family he had imagined them the day he made torcher. At the same time, he was becoming skilled at his work. Within six months he was offered a chance to compete for the position of leader in the voting among the miners to form a new team. To his own surprise, he won; and it was exactly as Tonina had predicted. He found he was expected to make the whole mine drunk. This time he did not have to drink with everyone else; but he did have to foot the bill.

Happily, there were still the funds he had brought to Coby, to draw upon. The next time he had seen Sost after the night in Port, he had asked the older man's advice on a way to hide his funds; and it had ended as a scheme whereby he transferred them, in installments over a period of months, to Sost himself, who set them up in an account under his own name.

'You're going to have to trust me,' said Sost, bluntly. 'But then, you're going to have to trust somebody if you really want to hide those credits. If you find somebody else you feel safer with, just let me know and we'll make the shift. Won't hurt my feelings.'

'I don't think I'm likely to find anyone else,' said Hal.

It was a true prediction. As a team leader, he was set a little at arm's length, necessarily, from the others on his team. Also, he was thrown more in the company of the other leaders like John and Will. He found that he welcomed the privacy this gave him as he continued to grow up.

And he was, indeed, continuing to grow up. The pretense that he had been twenty when he came had to contend with the fact that he continued growing physically, in all ways. Not only did he put on weight and muscle; in the next two and a half years his height shot up, until by the time he was nearly nineteen he was over two meters in height and evidently still growing.

Still, he looked young. He was still, in spite of his height, in the thinness of youth. The width of his shoulders and the mine-developed strength of his long arms did not make up for the youngness of his face and a certain innocence that also seemed to be an inescapable part of him.

He had not been challenged physically again since his first fight with Neif. The miners on his team, the staff, the business people, the inhabitants of the entertainment places he frequented in Port, all seemed to like him and get on well with him. But he made few casual friends and no more close friends. His regular visits to Port usually were in the company of John, Sost, or one or two of his own team members, when they were in the company of anyone he knew at all. Word about Tonina came to him from time to time, but he had not seen her since she had left the Yow Dee to get married.

More and more, he had fallen into the habit of prowling about in solitary fashion, walking for hours in the Port streets and corridors and dropping in on drinking establishments as the whim took him.

These particular establishments began to seem more and more alike as he got to know them. They all catered to the hunger of the Coby-dwellers for sight of an open sky, for a world with atmosphere and with the growing things of a planetary surface. Whatever else their interior was like, it would almost always offer the illusions of sky and a natural body of water, plus growing plants, real or illusory.

Away from their work the Coby miners were lonely and nostalgic individuals. He had been sitting in one of the bars one time when a miner there passed out, leaving unattended the stubby stringed instrument on which he had been playing; and Hal had discovered for himself the usefulness of such a tool.

Walter InTeacher had taught him the basics of music and given him a nodding acquaintance with several instruments, including the classic Spanish guitar. It had not been hard to retune the stubby device in the bar to a more familiar mode and play it. He discovered that the miners would listen to him as long as he wanted to sing, provided the songs were ballad-like and simple.

After that, with Sost's help, he managed to buy a real guitar to carry around on his bar expeditions. In a sense, that purchase marked his trading of the making of individual friends for the making of friends with a general audience, wherever he went – and this was a change that was becoming necessary.

The reason was that as he grew up it became harder for him to talk on the ordinary level of what passed for conversation among the miners, particularly on their times-off. He had begun to find that whenever he talked he had a tendency to make the others around him uncomfortable. They were not interested in the same topics that he was, or in the questions to which his mind naturally drifted. The singing became something he could hide behind and still be social.

More than that. Once fully launched, he began almost without thinking to start putting much of the classical poetry he knew by heart to music. Much of it was singable – or could be made singable with a little surgery on the words and lines. From there it was only a short step further to start writing poetry again himself, in forms that could be sung.

It was an illusion, he told himself, to think that great art could not find its expression in the simplest of materials. The most complex feelings and thoughts were, in the end, only human feelings and thoughts, and as such, by definition could be rendered in the commonest and most familiar of terms, and still carry the overburden of their theme.

'Your songs are always different,' said a hostess in one of the bars to him, one evening.

He read the message she hardly knew she was giving him. She, too, found him different enough to be attractive from a distance, but too different for comfort, up close. Hostesses like herself were only to be found in the luxury bars and the demand for them among the customers anywhere far exceeded the supply. But they flocked around Hal. Flocked . . . and went away again. Wistfully, he watched them go. He would have given far more than they dreamed to find even one of them with whom he could discover again the closeness he had experienced with Tonina after his fight with Neif. But it was never there. He did not know what was missing and, as far as he could discover, the hostesses did not know either – or perhaps, they knew, but could not tell him.

He found himself growing more and more apart from those around him, with the exception of John and Sost; but did not know what to do about it. Then Neif came back into all their lives.

Neif had left the Yow Dee shortly after losing the fight with Hal. He had evidently worked at a number of mines before drifting back to the Yow Dee, where he found a spot on the team of someone who had not been a leader when Hal had first come there. The shift his team was on was one nearly eight hours at variance with the shift Hal's was on, and Hal hardly saw him. Then, without any hint of any such thing being in the wind, marshals from the headquarters of the company that owned Yow Dee mine showed up and arrested Neif on charges of stealing pocket gold.

Pocket gold was the gold occasionally found in the mines in size larger than that of the tracing in the veins. In effect, pocket gold was any small nugget. The charge against Neif was that he had been doing this for some time.

In all these years, Hal had forgotten how different the legal pattern was on Coby. It was a shock to find himself being herded out of the bunkhouse without warning, the morning after the arrest, by what seemed to be a small army of company marshals equipped not with sidearms, but with cone rifles.

'What's going on?' he asked the first person he had a chance to speak to, one of his own team members.

'They're going to shoot him,' said the miner, a heavy-set, dark man looking stupid with sleep and shock.

'They can't. . . .' Hal's voice stopped in his throat. Now that they were outside, they could see Neif being brought from the office building and positioned with his back to the slag pile on the far side of the staging area.

Neif's hands were not tied, but he moved awkwardly as if in a daze. He was left where he had been placed by the two marshals who had brought him out. Three other marshals with cone rifles formed a line facing him and about ten meters from him, and put their rifles to their shoulders with the unanimity of people who were used to working together.

Something like an earthquake of emotion moved suddenly in Hal. He opened his mouth to cry out; and at the same time started to plunge forward. But neither shout nor plunge was finished.

From behind, two arms like hawsers folded about him and the powerful hand of one of those arms closed about his throat, cutting off his voice. There was nothing amateurish about the actions of those arms and that hand. He stamped backwards with his right heel to break an ankle of whoever was holding him and free himself; but his heel found nothing, and in almost the same second the fingers at his throat pressed on a nerve. He found himself fading into unconsciousness.

He came to, it seemed, only a second later. He was still held – but now held upright – by the powerful arms. Neif lay still, face down on the ground of the staging area. The marshals were bringing up a closed truck for the body, and the crowd was melting away, back into the bunkhouse. He turned furiously and saw facing him not only John, but Sost.

'You just keep your mouth shut,' said Sost, before Hal could get a word out, 'and come with me.'

The years with Malachi had taught Hal when not to stop and ask questions. There was in Sost's expression and voice a difference he had never seen or heard in the truck driver before. He followed without a word, accordingly, as Sost led the way around the end of the cookhouse to where his truck was standing. John had followed them to the truck and stood watching as Sost and Hal climbed into it.

'See you in town,' said John, as Sost lifted the truck on its fans.

'With luck, maybe,' said Sost. He turned the vehicle and drove off, away from the Yow Dee.

He took the corridor toward the nearest station, but branched off before they reached the station, down a tunnel Hal was not acquainted with. For the first time Hal saw him open up the truck. They hummed down the corridor at a speed that turned its walls into tan blurs; and Hal found himself marvelling that someone as old as Sost could have the reflexes to keep the truck from scraping the nearby walls at that speed.

It was the beginning of a breakneck trip to Port. At more than a hundred kilometers of tunnel distance from the Yow Dee, Sost stopped, put Hal in back, covered him up with some old tarpaulins, and pulled that truck aboard a branch of the subway at the next station they came to. Half an hour later the two of them walked into a small bar in Port, one which attempted to look something like a cross between a rathskeller and a jungle clearing. Tonina was already there, waiting for them at a table.

Hal looked at her searchingly as they sat down with her. The years of her marriage seemed not to have made any real difference in her, as far as his eye could tell. Somehow, he had expected that they would.

'Thank God!' she said as they sat down. 'I was beginning to think you hadn't made it.'

'I couldn't risk getting on the subway until I was clear,' said Sost. 'I had to cover more ground on fans than they'd think I could cover, before we could risk taking the train.'

He chuckled.

'Nothing like a reputation for being slow and sure,' he said. 'Always knew the time would be it'd come in handy.'

'Can I ask what all this is about, now?' Hal said.

'Take your drinks, first. Make it look like you're drinking,' said Tonina.

She had been coding at the table waiter as they sat down; and three glasses of beer had already risen to the surface of the table some seconds since. Hal and Sost obeyed her.

'You're going to have to get off Coby,' she told Hal, once he had raised the glass to his lips and set it down again. 'Someone either wants you, or wants you dead. I don't know which, and I don't want to know who; but you're going to have to move fast!'

Hal stared at her. Then his gaze moved to Sost. Even though Hal never explicitly told the older man his name, he had accepted the fact that Sost would have seen it on the credit papers Hal had entrusted to him.

'You told her?' he said.

'Her and thirty-forty other people,' Sost answered. 'Somebody's got to look out for you.'

He grinned a little at Hal.

'Don't take it so hard,' Sost said. 'I didn't let on to anyone, including Tonina, that this Hal Mayne had anything to do with you. But I put the name out in what you might call a sort of spider web to catch any questions about him showing up here on Coby.'

'Only Sost has that kind of connections,' said Tonina, tartly. 'You're lucky.'

'But that means thirty to forty people who can tell whoever's asking that they've heard the name,' said Hal.

'Not before they tell me,' answered Sost. 'And that gives us the head start we need. As Tonina says, I've been around here long enough to have connections – good connections.' He stared for a second directly into Hal's eyes.

'You figure Tonina'd tell whoever was interested about Hal Mayne before she'd tell me?'

'No,' said Hal, ashamed.

Hal sat, saying nothing. A thousand times in his mind he had imagined the moment in which he would learn that the Others had concluded he was on Coby; but the present scene was one he had never imagined. He had taken for granted that when it came time for him to run again, he would have been the one to have discovered danger close upon him; and he would have some idea of the situation in which he was caught. But now, it seemed everyone else knew more than he did.

'What happened?' he asked at last. 'How'd you find out someone was looking for me?'

'An inquiry into the whereabouts of someone named Hal Mayne came into the Record Section of the Company Headquarters where my husband's in charge. It ended up as just one on a list of names sent to him for authorization to release information from Company records, to whoever was inquiring about the names. He recognized

137

your name and checked with me, first. I told him to destroy your records and all record of the inquiry. He's done that. John will destroy all records at the Yow Dee; and no one there will think twice. Miners quit without warning every day.'

'What do I owe your husband?' said Hal. Nearly three years had taught him a great deal of how business was done on Coby.

'Nothing,' said Tonina. 'He did it because I asked him to.'

'Thank you,' said Hal. 'And thank him for me. I'm sorry I suggested –'

'Never mind that,' said Tonina. 'Then I got in touch with Sost and Sost looked into it.'

She nodded at Sost and Hal looked over at the older man.

'I did a little checking through some friends of mine,' Sost said. 'The Port marshals are all looking for you, all right; and they mean business. Someone high up's either had his arm twisted or been paid off handsomely.'

'But if they can't find my records?'

'Even with no records,' said Sost. 'It looks like they know, or they've guessed the time you came to Coby. They do know what mines were hiring then. They're doing things at each of those mines – somebody from off-Coby's coaching them, is my guess – that they think'll smoke you out. They don't know what you look like or anything about you; but it figures they know some things about how you'll act when other things happen. That arrest and execution of Neif was aimed at smoking you out.'

Hal felt a chill. He remembered the power of the arms holding him from crying out, from trying to do something before the cone rifles could fire.

'That's why you and John were right behind me?' he asked.

Sost nodded.

'Right. I just got there a second before. There wasn't time to explain things to you. We just went after you and did what we had to. Lucky John was handy. I'm not as young as I used to be.'

'All right,' said Tonina. 'Now you know. Let's get down to how we get you off-world. The faster you move, the safer you'll be.'

Sost nodded. He reached inside his shirt and came out with three packets of papers, which he dropped on the table before Hal.

'Take your pick,' he said. 'I've been spending some of that credit of yours. Jennison – you remember Jennison?'

Hal nodded. He had never forgotten the man in charge at the Holding Station. Apparently Jennison had known what he was talking about when he had said that Hal would be doing business with him later.

'This is his main business. Running a Holding Station lets him pick up a lot of things. But papers are the most valuable.'

'How does he get them?' Hal asked.

138

'Sometimes someone comes through with more than one set and needs money. Sometimes somebody dies and the papers don't get turned in. Lots of ways.'

'And never mind that,' said Tonina. 'Hal, Jennison sent you three different sets to look at. Pick the one you can get the most use out of.'

'And I'll take the other two back to him,' added Sost.

Hal picked up the packets one by one and looked at them. All were identifications and related papers for men in their early twenties. One was a set from New Earth, a set from Newton, and another from Harmony, one of the two Friendly Worlds. He remembered – in fact, his mind had moved back in time; and, evoked by his early training in recall, he seemed to hear the voices of his tutors again as he had conceived them in his room of the Final Encyclopedia. In particular, he heard the voice of Obadiah saying that there were people of his on Harmony who would never give Hal up.

'This one,' said Hal.

He looked more closely at the Harmony packet as Sost took the other two back. Its papers were for someone twenty-three years old and named Howard Beloved Immanuelson, a tithing member of the Revealed Church Reborn, with an occupation as a semantic interpreter and a specialty in advising off-world personnel divisions of large companies. In one sense, these particular papers were a fortunate find. It was only in the past thirty years that the two Friendly Worlds had – almost inexplicably – reversed a centuries-old pattern of behavior that held those of their natives who chose work off-world as being less than respectable in religious conviction and fervor.

The only really acceptable work for a church member on other worlds was that of mercenary soldier – and then only if you had been sent out at the orders of your church or district. Three hundred years of starving for the interstellar credit that could be gained only by natives who worked on other worlds had not shaken this attitude. But in the last thirty-odd years those from Harmony and Association were suddenly cropping up on all the other inhabited planets in considerable numbers. They were even going to worlds of other cultures with the approval of their authorities, to study for such occupations as that of a semantic interpreter. It was a change that had puzzled the Exotic ontogeneticists, Hal remembered Walter the InTeacher telling him. No adequate socio-historical reason for the sudden change in behavior had yet been established.

It followed therefore that, as Immanuelson, Hal could be expected by fellow-Friendlies to be one of a younger, newer breed, infected with off-world habits and ideas, and not necessarily aware of recent events on Harmony – which could help cover any inconsistencies in his masquerade as the other man. 'Off-world,' as currently used on the two Friendly planets, meant any world but those of Harmony and Association.

Some work, he now saw, had already been done to adjust the papers to him. Each of the spaces for his identifying thumbprint were blank. He proceeded to press down on each of these sensitized squares in turn and watch the whorls of his thumbprints leap into visible existence on the papers as he took his hand away. He was now officially Howard Immanuelson. There was a strange little emotion involved in acknowledging the change. It was a feeling as if some part of him had been lost. Not the Hal Mayne part that was basic to him; but that part of him that had come into existence on Coby, and was now officially being removed from existence.

He put the papers into an inside pocket.

'Here's your credit,' Sost said, passing over another set of papers, 'reassigned to your Harmony name. There's still a lot left.'

'Can you trust Jennison?' Hal asked, taking the credit papers.

'Wouldn't have dealt with him, otherwise,' Sost said. 'Don't worry. Freight Handlers has a lock on him.'

'Can Freight Handlers be trusted?' Hal said; and stared a little as the other two laughed.

'Sost was Freight Handlers before Freight Handlers was invented,' Tonina said. 'He may not have the office and the title, but you don't need to worry about Freight Handlers as long as he's here.'

'I just kept my hand in,' said Sost, 'and over the years you get to know people. Now, give me your own papers.'

'We'd better destroy them,' said Hal, passing them over.

'That's the idea. Now,' said Sost, as he tucked the Tad Thornhill papers away. 'We'll leave here, you and me. You've got passage on a ship to Harmony, and a ticket to Citadel, there. You know anything about Citadel?'

'I studied about it, once,' said Hal. 'It's a fair-sized city on the continent they call South Promise, in the low latitudes of the temperate zone.'

'That's right; and it's the one city-sized place on Harmony this Immanuelson's work record doesn't show him as having been in. Once there you're on your own.' Sost stood up, and Hal and Tonina followed suit. 'We'll get you on board with the freight and slip the whole business of outgoing customs. Come on.'

Hal turned toward Tonina. She had made him uncertain about trying to touch her; but now he would never see her again. He put his arms around her awkwardly and kissed her; and she held him strongly for a moment.

'Get going,' she said, pushing him away.

He went out with Sost. Looking back he saw her still standing upright and motionless by the table, watching them go.

CHAPTER THIRTEEN

Hal sat in the jitney taking him down from orbit around Harmony to the city of Citadel. Curiously, in this moment of stepping into a totally new world, it was not his three years on Coby that were beginning to lose reality in his mind, it was the four days of interstellar space travel, with the frequent psychic shocks of the phase shifts that had brought him here. The trip had had the feel of unreality to it; and now he found it also difficult to think of the Friendly World to which he was rapidly descending as real; although he knew it would be so, for him, soon enough.

Something else was filling his mind and driving out anything else but the years just passed on Coby. For the first time in his life, on the trip from there to here, he had come to a stark understanding of why his three tutors had insisted that he go to the mines and work, instead of hiding on one of the Younger Worlds. Their reason had not been merely a matter of shielding him from the eyes of the Others until he was old enough to protect himself. No, the important factor in their decision had lain in what they had said about his need to grow up, to learn about people before he ventured forth to face his enemies.

Only now, after three years on the mining world, he could realize that he had been – up until the moment of the deaths of Obadiah, Malachi and Walter the InTeacher – a hothouse plant. He had been raised as an unusual boy, by unusual people. He had had no real, day-to-day experience or understanding of ordinary men and women; those who were the root stock of the race itself – those from among whom the unusual people like himself were occasionally produced, simply to be taken and used by the historic pressures of their time. Until Coby, such ordinary people had been as unknown to him as if they had been creatures from the furthest stars. Their goals had never been his goals, their sorrows his sorrows, their natures his nature. His lack of understanding of these differences had been an unacceptable defect; because now it came home to him, unsparingly, that it was these, not the gifted ones like himself and those who had brought him up, whom he would be fighting for in the years ahead.

It had been necessary that he begin by realizing his place among such ordinary people, that he learn to understand and feel with and for them, before he could be of any use to the race as a whole. For they were the race. In the mines he had come face to face with this. He had discovered it in Tonina, in John Heikkila, in Sost – in all of them. He had found unremarkable people there he could care about, and who cared about him – regardless of his abilities. People who, in the end, had made his escape possible when alone, with all his special talents, he would have failed.

The remembrance of that escape now made his eyes burn with regret that he had never told Sost, at least, how much the old man had come to mean to him. The manner of their leave taking had been almost casual. They had driven Sost's truck out to the ship he was now in, ostensibly to deliver a large but lightly sealed package, with Hal seated beside Sost and dressed in the gray coveralls of a freight handler. Together, they had carried the package in through the ship's loading entrance to the number one hold and been met there by the Chief Purser, who had evidently been expecting them.

At his direction Hal had taken off the coveralls, dropped them in a refuse container, and taken leave of Sost. He had followed the Chief to a portside cabin, been ushered in, and left with directions not to leave the cabin until after the first phase shift. He had obeyed; and, in fact, had stayed close to his cabin through the first third of the trip. The solitary hours had offered an opportunity for him to practice casting himself mentally into the persona of a tithe-payer of the Revealed Church Reborn.

He had the role model of Obadiah to draw on. Growing up with his three tutors, he had come, instinctively, to imitate each of them. To be like Obadiah, he had only to imagine himself as Obadiah – but the trick down on the surface of Harmony would be to carry that bit of imagination in his mind so constantly that even under moments of stress he would not slip out of character.

He also practiced on the one fellow-passenger who seemed to have any inclination to talk with him beyond the barest exchange of civilities; and this passenger proceeded to open his eyes to an unsuspected danger. The other was an Exotic named Amid, a small, erect old man with – for an Exotic – a remarkably wrinkled face. Amid was returning from Ceta where he had been as an Outbond, teaching the history of the Splinter Cultures at the University of Ceta, in the city of the same name as that of the planet and the University.

Like most Exotics, he was as at ease with everyone as the other Friendlies and Harmony-bound passengers were stiff and suspicious. He was also, like many teachers, in love with his subject; and Hal found him full of fascinating historical anecdotes out of the history of Harmony and Association that he would not have thought anyone but one of the nativeborn Friendlies could have known, and then only if they were from the area or district of the world with which the anecdote dealt.

'Faith,' said Amid to him, the third day out of Coby, 'in its large sense, is more than just the capacity to believe. What it is, is the concept of a personal identity with a specific, incontrovertible version of reality. True faith is untouchable. By definition anything that attacks it is not only false but doomed to be exposed as such. Which is why we have martyrs. The ultimate that can be offered against any true faith-holder to force him to change his beliefs is a threat to destroy him utterly, to cancel out his universe, leaving only nothingness. But for the true faith-holder, even this threat fails, since he, and that in which he has faith, are one; and, by definition, that in which he has faith is indestructible.'

'But why can't someone who merely believes be just as immune to having his personal universe destroyed?' Hal had asked.

'Because merely believing – if you want to define the word separately – implies something to believe in – that is, something apart from the believer. In other words, we have two things in partnership, the believer and his belief. A partnership can be dissolved. Partners can be divorced. But, as I just pointed out, the faith-holder is his faith. He and it make, not two, but a single thing. Since he and it are one, there's no way to take it from him. That makes him a very powerful opponent. In fact, it makes him an unconquerable opponent; since even death can't touch him in his most important part.'

'Yes,' said Hal, remembering Obadiah.

'That difference,' said Amid, 'between the mere believer and the true faith-holder, is the one thing that has to be grasped, if the peoples of this Culture are to be understood. Paradoxically, it's the hardest distinction for the non-Friendly to grasp – just as the intimate parallel commitments of the Exotic and the Dorsai are also the hardest things for people not of those cultures to understand. In the case of each culture, it's a case of an ordinary human capability – for faith, for courage, or for insight – raised to a near-instinctive level of response.'

Remembering that conversation, now, as the jitney approached the landing area, Hal made an effort to apply the distinction Amid had been talking about to what he knew of the Friendly character. It was not easy, because all he really knew about what made a Friendly a Friendly had been absorbed directly into his unconscious by observing Obadiah as he had been growing up. In short he knew, without having to think, what Obadiah would do in almost any situation, once he had been confronted with it, but he had little conscious understanding of why Obadiah would do just that. Hal was, in fact, in a position very like that of someone who could operate a piece of machinery but had no idea of why or how it worked.

As the jitney touched down, he made a mental note at least not to let himself be lulled into complacency by the fact that the people here might seem at first to take him easily for one of themselves. He would have to make a conscious effort to observe and study those around him, in spite of whatever ability he already had to play the role he had adopted. Otherwise, he could end up making a wrong move without ever knowing he had made it; and the results from that wrong move might result in tripping him up without warning.

The passengers left the jitney and found themselves in a closed tunnel that led for some distance before delivering them into a series of rooms where they were sorted out according to the type of personal papers they were carrying. As someone with Harmony papers Hal was channeled with a couple of dozen other Friendlies into the last room to be reached. Within were a number of desks with Immigration Service officials seated at them.

Hal was a little out of position to be first at the table nearest him. Just ahead of him was a slight, slim, dark-skinned young man. There was a hush-zone around each desk, and Hal stood at such an angle to both his fellow traveller and the official that lip-reading was difficult, so there was no way for him to find out in advance any of the questions he might be asked.

Finally, the man ahead of him was directed onward to a fenced enclosure made of two-meter-high wire mesh and containing physical, straight-backed chairs, watched over by a stocky, middle-aged enlisted man in a black Militia uniform. The dark young man took a chair there, and Hal was beckoned forward to the desk with the official.

'Papers?' said the official, as Hal sat down.

Hal produced them and the official read through them.

'How long had it been since you were on Harmony?' he asked.

Hal took it as a good sign that the other had not addressed him in the canting speech of the ultra-fanatics among the Friendlies. It might indicate that the official was one of the more reasonable sort. In any case, he had his answer ready, having studied the papers he was carrying.

'Four and a half standard years, more or less.'

The official shuffled the papers together and handed them back to him.

'Wait over there,' he said, nodding to the enclosure.

Hal took the papers, slowly. No one else of the native Friendlies except the dark-skinned young man had been sent to wait. The rest, from other desks, were all being directed ahead, through a further doorway and out of the room.

'May I ask why?' he said, standing up.

'Anyone off-planet more than three years is checked.'

He felt grimness as he walked over toward the enclosure. He should have thought of this. Sost should have thought of this. No, it was unfair to blame Sost, who would have had no way of knowing that a special effort should have been made to get Friendly papers

144

that were less than three years off the individual's home world. Naturally, the chances of the papers Jennison dealt in being out of date were likely to be greater rather than lesser.

He took a seat across the enclosure from the dark-skinned man, under the watchful eye of the policeman. It seemed to him that the glance of the dark-skinned man met his own eyes strangely for a fraction of a second; then they were watching nothing, again. It would have been easy to believe that the other man had never glanced at him at all, but one of Hal's earliest teachings by Malachi had been in the art of observation. Now, in his mind Hal replayed the last few minutes of what he had just seen, and his memory produced, beyond argument, the brief moment in which the other's eyes had met his.

It was something that could mean nothing – or a great deal. Hal sat back on the stiff, upright chair and let his body relax. Time went by – more than a standard hour. At the end of that period the room was empty of his fellow travellers, except for those in the enclosure; and there were now five of these, including himself. The other three were unremarkable-looking individuals, obviously Friendlies, all of them at least twenty years older than Hal and the dark-skinned man.

'All of you now,' said the policeman, nasally. 'Come. This way.'

They were taken out of the enclosure and the room they had been in, down another short corridor to an underground garage and a waiting bus. The bus hissed up on its fans and they slid out through the garage, emerging into the nighttime streets of Citadel. It was raining, and the rain streaked the windows of the bus, blurring the gray shapes of the building fronts they passed under the sparse yellow glow of the street lighting. They drove for a little under half an hour, then entered another interior garage, down below the street level.

From the bus in the garage, they were taken upstairs into what seemed at first sight to be an office building. Their papers were taken from them; and there was another long wait on straight chairs in an outer office, with trips to the water tap in one wall and to the rest room, under the eye of their police guard, as the only distractions. Then, one by one, they were called into interior offices that had only a single desk and a single interviewer behind it. Once more, Hal saw the dark-skinned young man called before him.

When Hal's turn came, he found himself sitting down at the side of a desk, facing a small, balding man with an egg-shaped face, unblinking eyes and an almost lipless mouth. The gray man picked up papers that Hal recognized as his from the desk, and read through them with a speed that made Hal suspect the other of being already familiar with their contents. He laid the papers back down and looked at Hal from a bureaucratic distance.

'Your name?'

'Howard Beloved Immanuelson.'

'You're a communicant of the Revealed Church Reborn, born into

145

that Church twenty-three point four standard years ago, in the hamlet of Enterprise?'

'Yes,' said Hal.

'Your father and mother were both communicants of that Church?'

'Yes.'

'You remain a communicant in good standing of that Church?'

'I am,' said Hal, 'by the grace of the Lord.'

'You have just returned from four years of work off-planet as a semantic interpreter, having been employed by various of the unchurched. . . .'

The questioning continued, covering the facts of Howard Immanuelson's life as set forth in the papers Hal had been carrying. Once these had been exhausted, the interviewer pushed the papers from him and stared at Hal with his unchanging eyes.

'Do you keep regular times of prayer?' he asked.

Hal had been expecting this sort of question.

'As far as I can,' he said. 'Travelling about as I do among those who do lack the Word, it isn't always easy to keep regular hours of prayer.'

'Ease,' said the interviewer, 'is not the way of the Lord.'

'I know,' said Hal. 'I know as you do that the fact that regular hours of prayer are difficult to keep is no excuse for laxity. So I've become used to inward communication at my usual times of literal prayer.'

The gray man's upper lip seemed to curl a little, but it was so thin Hal could not be sure.

'How many daily are your times of prayer – when it's convenient for you to pray, that is?'

Hal thought swiftly. He did not know the sectarian rules of the Revealed Church Reborn. But if it was a church in the North Oldcontinent region where Enterprise was located, then it was probably in the so-called 'Old' Tradition, rather than the New. In any case, as the saying went, each Friendly was a sect on his own.

'Seven.'

'Seven?' The interviewer kept his tone level and his face expressionless, but Hal suddenly suspected he was talking to one of those who held to the New Tradition, and believed that more than four times of formal prayer a day were arrogant and ostentatious.

'Matins and lauds, prime, terce, sext, none, vespers and compline,' said Hal.

He saw the hint of an unmistakable sourness on the face of the man before him as he reeled off the Latin names. It was a risk to do something like this deliberately; but he would be out of character if he did not clash with almost any other Friendly on details of religious dogma or observance. At the same time he did not want to goad

146

anyone like this strongly enough to give the other a personal reason to make the conditions and results of this interview more harsh than they might otherwise be.

'Yes,' said the interviewer, harshly. 'But for all those gaudy names you pray secretly, like a coward. Perhaps you belong to that anathema, that new cult among our sinful youth, that professes to believe that prayer is unneccessary if you only live with God and His purposes in mind. There's a great Teacher just arrived here among us who could show you the error of that way. . . .'

The tone of his voice was rising. He broke off abruptly and wiped his lips with a folded white handkerchief.

'Did you have much contact with other churched individuals during your years among the ungodly?' he asked, in a more controlled voice.

'By nature of my work,' said Hal, 'I had little contact with anyone from the Promised Worlds. My associations, of necessity, were with those people of the planets on which I was working.'

'But you met and knew some from Harmony or Association?'

'A few,' said Hal. 'I don't think I can even remember the names of any.'

'Indeed? Perhaps you might remember more than names. Do you recall meeting any of those who style themselves the Children of Wrath, or the Children of God's Wrath?'

'On occasion –' Hal began, but the interviewer broke in.

'I'm not referring merely to those who live in knowledge of, and sometimes admit, that they are deservedly forgotten of God. I'm talking of those who have taken this impious name to themselves as an organization counter to God's churches and God's commandments.'

Hal shook his head.

'No,' he said. 'No, I've never even heard of them.'

'Strange,' the thin upper lip curled visibly this time, 'that so widely traveled a person should be so ignorant of the scourge being visited upon the world of his birth. In all those four years, none of those from Harmony or Association that you met ever mentioned the Children of Wrath?'

'No,' said Hal.

'Satan has your tongue, I see.' The interviewer pressed one of a bank of studs on his desktop. 'Perhaps after you think it over, you may come to a better memory. You can go, now.'

Hal got up and reached for his papers, but the gray man opened a drawer of his desk and swept them in. Hal turned to leave, but discovered when he got to the door that that was as far as the freedom of his permission was extended. He was taken in charge by an armed and uniformed police guard and taken elsewhere in the building.

The two of them went down several floors and through a number of corridors to what now began to strongly resemble a jail rather than an office building. Past a couple of heavy, locked doors they came to a desk behind which another police guard sat; and here all pretence that this was anything but a jail ended. Hal had the personal possessions he was carrying taken from him, he was searched for anything he had not admitted carrying, then taken on by the guard behind the desk, down several more corridors and to a final, heavy metal door that was plainly locked and unlocked only from the outside.

'Could I get something to eat?' said Hal as the guard opened this door and motioned inside. 'I haven't had anything since I landed –'

'Tomorrow's meal comes tomorrow,' said the guard. 'Inside!'

Hal obeyed, hearing the door crash shut and locked behind him.

The place into which he had been put was a large room or cell, with narrow benches attached to its bare concrete walls. The floor was also bare concrete with an unscreened latrine consisting of a stool, a urinal and a washstand occupying one blank corner. There was nothing else of note in the cell, except a double window with its sill two meters above the floor, in the wall opposite the door, and one fellow-prisoner.

CHAPTER FOURTEEN

The other occupant of the room, a man stretched out on one of the benches with his back to the room, was apparently trying to sleep; although this was something of an endeavor in the face of the fact that the room was brightly illuminated by a lighting panel let into the center of its ceiling. Hal recognized the man by the color of his hair and his general shape as the dark-skinned young man who had been in front of him through most of the procedure that had taken place since they had all disembarked from the jitney.

Now, as the door to the cell clanged shut and locked behind Hal, the other came to life, rolled over off the bench on to his feet and walked lightly to the cell door to look out through the small window set in its upper panel. He nodded to himself and, turning back into the room, came soft-footedly to Hal, cupping one hand behind his right ear and pointing at the ceiling warningly.

'These Accursed of the Lord,' he said, clearly, taking Hal's arm and leading him toward the corner containing the latrine, 'they make these places so, deliberately, to rob us of all decency. Might I ask you, out of kindness, to stand where you are over there and turn your back for a moment . . . thank you, brother. I'll do as much for you, whenever you wish . . .'

He had drawn Hal by this time right into the corner where the latrine stood. He turned on the water taps of the washstand, triggered the cleansing unit of the stool, and drew Hal's head down with his next to the spouting taps. He wiggled the fingers of both of his hands before Hal's face. Covered by the sound of the running water, he whispered directly into Hal's right ear.

'Can you talk with your fingers?'

Hal shook his head and turned to whisper in the ear of the other.

'No. But I read lips and I can learn very quickly. If you'll mouth the words and show me enough finger-motions to start with, we can talk.'

The dark-skinned young man nodded. He straightened up; and while they still stood covered by the sound of the water coming from the taps, he formed words with his lips.

'My name is Jason Rowe. What is yours, brother?'

Hal leaned close again to whisper in Jason Rowe's ear.

'Howard Immanuelson.' Jason stared at him. Hal went on. 'And you don't need to make the words slowly and exaggeratedly. Just move your lips as if you're speaking normally, and I can follow you easily. Just don't forget to look at me when you speak.'

Jason nodded in turn. He lifted his right hand with thumb and forefinger spread slightly and the other fingers curled into the palm.

'Yes,' he mouthed at Hal.

Hal nodded, imitating the sign with his own thumb and forefinger.

A few minutes later, when Jason shut off the water coming from the taps and they moved off to take flanking benches in another corner of the room, Hal had already learned the signs for *yes, no, I, you, go, stay, sleep, guard* and half the letters of the alphabet. They moved to that corner of the room that was to the right of the door, so that anyone looking through the window of the door would not be able to see what they were doing.

Seated as they were, on the benches at right angles to each other, they came as close as possible to facing each other. They began to talk, at first slowly, as Hal was put to the problem of spelling out most of the words he needed to use. But he gained speed as Jason would guess the word he was after before it was completely spelled and give him the sign for it. Hal's signing vocabulary grew rapidly, to what he could see was the profound, if silent, surprise of Jason. Hal made no attempt to explain. It would hardly help here to air the fact that his mnemonic and communicative skills owed a debt to the skills of the Exotics. Their conversation seemed headed at first in a strange direction and Hal was grateful that he could hide his ignorance of what the other was talking about behind his ignorance of the sign language.

'Brother,' Jason asked, as soon as they were seated facing each other, 'are you of the faith?'

Hal hesitated only a fraction of a second. On the surface there was no reason why any Friendly should not answer such a question in the affirmative; although what the other might mean specifically could be something very much to be determined.

'Yes,' he signed, and waited for enlightenment from Jason.

'I, also,' said Jason. 'But be of good cheer, brother. I do not think that those holding us here have any idea that we're the very kind they're seeking. This witch-hunt they've swept us up in is just part of a city-wide attempt to make themselves look good, in the eyes of one of the Belial-spawn who's come visiting here.'

'Visiting?' Hal spelled out.

He had gone tense at the last words of the other; and now, for the first time there was a touch of cold sickness in the pit of his stomach. The words 'Belial-spawn' were words he had heard Obadiah use to describe the Others. It was too far-fetched a supposition to imagine

150

that the Other or Others looking for him on Coby had traced the route of his escape and beaten him here to Citadel. But, assuming that they had indeed traced him, a spaceship piloted by someone more inclined to take risks on his phase shifts than the paid master of a freighter could indeed have reached the city here a day or two before him.

'So they say,' Jason answered him with silently-moving lips.

'When did he get here?'

Jason's eyes watched Hal curiously.

'Then you had heard – and knew that it was a man, rather than a woman?'

'I . . .' Hal took advantage of his ignorance of the sign language to cover up his slip, 'assumed they'd probably send a man to a New Tradition city like this.'

'Perhaps that was the reason. Anyway, it seems he's been here in Citadel less than twenty standard hours.' Jason smiled startlingly and suddenly. 'I'm good at getting interrogators to tell me things when they're questioning me. I found out quite a bit. They call him Great Teacher – as the lickspittle way of their kind is; and they'll be planning to fawn on him, offering up some examples of those of the faith as sacrifices to his coming.'

'Why should I be of good cheer if that's the situation?' asked Hal. 'It doesn't sound good to me.'

'Why, because they can't be sure, of course,' said Jason. 'In the end, unless they're certain, they'll delay showing us to him, because they're all like whipped dogs. They cringe at the very thought of his scorn if they're wrong. So, we'll have time; and with that time we'll escape –'

He looked almost merrily at Hal.

'You don't believe me?' he mouthed. 'You can't believe that I'd trust you with the knowledge I was going to escape, just like that? Why do you think I open myself to you like this, brother?'

'I don't know,' said Hal.

'Because it happens I knew the Howard Immanuelson whose papers you carry. Oh, not well; but we were advanced students in the same class in Summercity, before he left for Kultis to qualify himself for off-planet work. I also know when it was he went to Coby, and that he died there. But he was of the faith; and all his moving away from Harmony was to launder himself, so that he could come back and be useful to us here. You got aboard at Coby with his papers. Also, you've picked up the finger speech far too swiftly to be other than someone who has used it all his life – you must watch that, brother, while you're here. Be careful of seeming to know too much, too quickly. Even some of the Traitors to God have the wit to put two and two together. Now, tell me. What's your real name, and your purpose in being here?'

Hal's brain galloped.

'I can't,' he signalled. 'I'm sorry.'

Jason looked at him sadly for a long moment.

'Unless you can trust me,' he said, 'I can't trust you. Unless you can tell me, I can't take you with me when I leave here.'

'I'm sorry,' signed Hal again. 'I don't have the right to tell you.'

Jason sighed.

'So be it,' he said. He got up and went across the cell, lay down with his back to the room in the position he had been in when Hal had entered. Hal sat watching him for a few minutes, then tried to imitate the other man and stretch out himself. But his success was limited. The width of his shoulders was too great for the narrow bench; and the best he could do, lying down, was balance himself so precariously that a second's relaxation would send him tumbling to the floor.

He gave in, finally, and sat upright on the bench, drawing in his legs until he perched in lotus position with his back to the wall. His knees and a good part of his legs projected outward into thin air; but in this position the center of his mass was closer to the edge of the bench that touched the wall behind him and he could relax without falling off. He dropped his hands on his thighs carelessly and hunched his shoulders a little to make it appear to any observer that his position was unthinking and habitual rather than practised. Then he turned his mind loose to drift. Within seconds, the cell faded about him; and, for all physical intents and purposes, he slept. . . .

The cell door clashed open abruptly, waking them. Hal was on his feet by the time the guard came through the open door and he saw out of the corner of his eye that Jason was also.

'All right,' said the man who had entered. He was thin and tall – though not as tall as Hal – with a coldly harsh face, and captain's lozenges on his black Militia uniform. 'Outside!'

They obeyed. Hal's body was still numb from sleep, but his mind, triggered into immediate overdrive, was whirring. He avoided looking at Jason in the interests of keeping up the pretense that they had not talked and still did not know each other; and he noticed that Jason avoided looking at him. Once in the corridor they were herded back the way Hal remembered being brought in.

'Where are we going?' Jason asked.

'Silence!' said the captain softly, without looking at him and without changing expression, 'or I will hang thee by thy wrists for an hour or so after this is over, apostate whelp.'

Jason said no more. They were moved along down several corridors, and taken up a freight lift shaft, to what was again very obviously the office section of this establishment. Their guardian brought them to join a gathering of what seemed to be twenty or more prisoners like themselves, waiting outside the open doors of a room with a raised platform at one end, a desk upon it and an open space before it. The flag of the United Sects, a white cross on a black field, hung limply from a flagpole set upright on the stage.

The captain left them with the other prisoners and stepped a few steps aside to speak to the five other enlisted Militiamen acting as guards. They stood, officer, guards and prisoners alike, and time went by.

Finally, there was the sound of footwear on polished corridor floor, echoing around the bend in the further corridor, and three figures turned the corner and came into sight. Hal's breath hesitated for a second. Two were men in ordinary business suits – almost certainly local officials. But the man between them, tall above them, was Bleys Ahrens.

Bleys ran his glance over all the prisoners as he approached, and his eye paused for a second on Hal, but not for longer than might have been expected from the fact that Hal was noticeably the tallest of the group. Bleys came on the turned into the doorway, shaking his head at the two men accompanying him as he did so.

'Foolish,' he was saying to them as he passed within arm's length of Hal. 'Foolish, foolish! Did you think I was the sort to be impressed by what you could sweep off the streets, that I was to be amused like some primitive ruler by state executions or public torture-spectacles? This sort of thing only wastes energy. I'll show you how to do things. Bring them in here.'

The guards were already moving in response before one of the men with Bleys turned and gestured to the Militia officer. Hal and the others were herded into the room and lined up in three ranks facing the platform on which the two men now stood behind the desk and Bleys himself half-sat, half-lounged, with his weight on the further edge of that piece of furniture. To even this casual pose he lent an impression of elegant authority.

A coldness had developed in the pit of Hal's stomach with Bleys' appearance; and now that feeling was growing, spreading all through him. Sheltered and protected as he had been all his life, he had grown up without ever knowing the kind of fear that compresses the chest and takes strength from the limbs. Then, all at once, he had encountered death and that kind of fear for the first time; and now the reflex set up by that moment had been triggered by a second encounter with the tall, commanding figure on the platform before him.

He was not afraid of the Friendly authorities who were holding him captive. His mind recognized the fact that they were only human; and he had been deeply instructed in the principle that for any problem involving human interaction there was a practical solution to be found by anyone who would search for it. But the sight of Bleys faced him with a being who had destroyed the very pillars of his personal universe. He felt the paralysis of his fear spreading all through him; and the rational part of him recognized that once it had taken him over completely he would throw himself upon the fate that would follow Bleys' identification of him – just to get it over with.

He reached for help; and the ghosts of three old men came out of his memory in response.

'He is no more than a weed that flourishes for a single summer's day, this man you face,' said the harsh voice of Obadiah in his mind. 'No more than the rain on the mountainside, blowing for a moment past the rock. God is that rock, and eternal. The rain passes and is as if it never was. Hold to the rock and ignore the rain.'

'He can do nothing,' said the soft voice of Walter the InTeacher, 'that I've not already shown you at one time or another. He's no more than a user of skills developed by other men and women, many of whom could use them far better than he can. Remember that no one's mind and body are ever more than human. Forget the fact he's older and more experienced than you; and concentrate only on a true image of what he is, and what his limits are.'

'Fear is just one more weapon,' said Malachi, 'no more dangerous in itself than a sharpened blade is. Treat it as you would any weapon. When it approaches, turn yourself to let it pass you by, then take and control the hand that guides it at you. The weapon without the hand is only one more thing – in a universe full of things.'

Up on the platform Bleys looked down at them all.

'Pay attention to me, my friends,' he said softly to the prisoners. 'Look at me.'

They looked, Hal with the rest of them. He saw Bleys' lean, aristocratic face and pleasant brown eyes. Then, as he looked at them, those eyes began to expand until they would entirely fill his field of vision.

Reflexively, out of his training under Walter the InTeacher, he took a step back within his own mind, putting what he saw at arm's length – and all at once it was as if he was aware of things on two levels. There was the level on which he stood with the other prisoners, held by Ahrens like animals transfixed by a bright light in darkness; and there was the level in which he was aware of the assault that was being made on his free will by what was hidden behind that bright light, and on which he struggled to resist it.

He thought of rock. In his mind he formed the image of a mountainside, cut and carved into an altar on which an eternal light burned. Rock and light . . . untouchable, eternal.

'I must apologize to you, my friends and brothers,' Bleys was saying gently to all of them. 'Mistakenly, you've been made to suffer; and that shouldn't be. But it was a natural mistake and small mistakes of your own have contributed to it. Examine your conscience. Is there one of you here who isn't aware of things you know you shouldn't have done. . . .'

Like mist, the beginnings of rain blew upon the light and the altar.

But the light continued to burn, and the rock was unchanged. Bleys' voice continued; and the rain thickened, blowing more fiercely upon the rock and the light. On the mountainside the day darkened, but the light burned on through the darkness, showing the rock still there, still unmarked and unmoved. . . .

Bleys was softly showing all of them the way to a worthier and happier life, a way that trusted in what he was telling them. All that they needed to do was to acknowledge the errors of their past and let themselves be guided in the proper path for their future. His words made a warm and friendly shelter away from all storm, its door open and waiting for all of them. But, sadly, Hal must remain behind; alone, out on the mountainside in the icy and violent rain, clinging to the rock so that the wind could not blow him away; and with only the pure but heatless light burning in the darkness to comfort him.

Gradually, he became aware that the wind had ceased growing stronger, that the rain which had been falling ever heavier was now only steady, that the darkness could grow no darker – and that he, the rock and the light were still there, still together. A warmth of a new sort kindled itself inside him and grew until it shouted in triumph. He felt a strength within him that he had never felt before, and with that strength, he stepped back, merging once more the two levels, so that he looked out nakedly through his own eyes again at Bleys Ahrens.

Bleys had finished talking and was stepping down from the platform, headed out of the room. All the prisoners turned to watch him go as if he walked out of the room holding one string to which all of them were attached.

'If you'll come this way, brothers,' said one of the guards.

They were led, by this single guard only, down more corridors and into a room with desks, where they were handed back their papers.

CHAPTER FIFTEEN

Apparently, they were free to go. They were ushered out of the building and Hal found himself walking down the street with Jason at his side. He looked at the other man and saw him smiling and animated.

'Howard!' Jason said. 'Isn't this wonderful? We've got to find the others and tell them about this great man. They'll have to see him for themselves.'

Hal looked closely into Jason's eyes.

'What is it, brother?' said Jason. 'Is something wrong?'

'No,' said Hal. 'But maybe we should sit down somewhere and make some plans. Is there any place around here where we can talk, away from people?'

Jason looked around. They were in what appeared to Hal to be a semi-industrial section. It seemed about mid-morning, and the rain that had been falling when they had landed the day before was now holding off, although the sky was dark and promised more precipitation.

'This early . . .' Jason hesitated. 'There's a small eating place with booths in its back room; and this time of day, the back room ought to be completely empty, anyway.'

'Let's go,' said Hal.

The eating place did indeed turn out to be small. It was hardly the sort of establishment that Hal would have found himself turning into if he had simply wanted a meal; but its front room held only about six customers at the square tables there and the back room, as Jason had predicted, was empty. They took a booth far back in a corner and ordered coffee.

'What plans did you have in mind to make, Howard?' asked Jason, when the coffee had been brought.

Hal tasted the contents of his cup and set the cup down again on the table between them. Coffee – or rather some imitation of it – was to be found on all the inhabited worlds. But its taste varied widely between any two worlds, and was often markedly different in two widely distant parts of the same world. Hal had spent three years getting used to Coby coffee. He would have to start all over again with Harmony coffee.

'Have you seen this?' he asked, in turn.

From a pocket he brought out a small gold nugget encased in a cube of glass. It was the first piece of pocket gold he had found in the Yow Dee Mine; and, following a Coby custom, he had bought it back from the mine owners and had it encased in transparent plastic, to carry about as a good-luck piece. His fellow team-members would have thought him strange if he had not. Now, for the first time, he had a use for it.

Jason bent over the cube.

'Is that real gold?' he asked, with the fascination of anyone not of either Coby or Earth.

'Yes,' said Hal. 'See the color. . . .'

He reached out across the table and took the back of Jason's neck gently and precisely between the tips of his thumb and middle finger. The skin beneath his fingertips jumped at his touch, then relaxed as he put soft pressure on the nerve endings below it.

'Easy,' he said, 'just watch the piece of gold . . . Jason, I want you to rest for a bit. Just close your eyes and lean back against the back of the booth and sleep for a couple of minutes. Then you can open your eyes and listen. I've got something to tell you.'

Obediently, Jason closed his eyes and leaned back, resting his head against the hard, dark-dyed wooden panel that was the back of the booth. Hal took his hand from the other's neck and Jason stayed as he was, breathing easily and deeply for about a hundred and fifty heart-beats. Then he opened his eyes, stared at Hal as if puzzled for a second, and then smiled.

'You were going to tell me something,' he said.

'Yes,' said Hal. 'And you're going to listen to me all the way through and then not say anything until you've thought about what I've just told you. Aren't you?'

'Yes, Howard,' said Jason.

'Good. Now listen closely,' Hal paused. He had never done anything like this before; and there was a danger, in Jason's present unnaturally receptive state, that some words Hal used might have a larger effect than he had intended them to have. 'Because I want you to understand something. Right now you think you're acting normally and doing exactly what you'd ordinarily want to do. But actually, that's not the case. The fact is, a very powerful person has made you an attractive choice on a level where it's very hard for you to refuse him, a choice to let your conscience go to sleep and leave all moral decisions up to someone else. Because you were approached on that particular level, you've no way of judging whether this was a wise decision to make, or not. Do you follow me so far? Nod your head if you do.'

Jason nodded. He was concentrating just hard enough to bring a small frown line into being between his eyebrows. But otherwise his face was still relaxed and happy.

'Essentially what you've just been told,' Hal said, 'is that the man who spoke to you, or people designated by him, will decide not only what's right for you, but what you'll choose to do; and you've agreed that this would be a good thing. Because of that, you've now joined those who've already made that agreement with him; those who were until an hour ago your enemies, in that they were trying to destroy the faith you've held to all your life. . . .'

The slight frown was deepening between Jason's brows and the happiness on his face was being replaced by a strained expression. Hal talked on; and when at last he stopped, Jason was huddled on the other seat, turned as far away from Hal as the close confines of the booth would allow, with his face hidden in his hands.

Hal sat, feeling miserable himself, because the other man was, and tried to drink his coffee. The silence between them continued, until finally Jason heaved a long, shivering sigh and dropped his hands. He turned a face to Hal that looked as if it had not slept for two nights.

'Oh, God!' he said.

Hal looked back at him, but did not try to say anything.

'I'm unclean,' said Jason. 'Unclean!'

'Nonsense,' said Hal. Jason's eyes jumped to his face; and Hal made himself grin at the other. 'What's that I seem to remember hearing when I was young – and you must remember hearing – about the sin of pride? What makes you feel you're special in having knuckled under to the persuasion of someone like that?'

'I lacked faith!' said Jason. 'I turned and loved that spawn of Belial who spoke to us.'

'We all lack faith to some extent,' Hal said. 'There are probably some men and women so strong in their faith that he wouldn't have been able to touch them. I had a teacher once . . . but the point is, that everyone else in that room gave in to him, just as you did.'

'*You* didn't!'

'I've had special training,' said Hal. 'That's what I was telling you just now, remember? What that man did, he succeeded in doing because he's also had special training. Believe me, someone without training would have had to have been a very remarkable person to resist him. But for someone with training, it was . . . relatively easy.'

Jason drew another deep, ragged breath.

'Then I'm ashamed for another reason,' he said bleakly.

'Why?' Hal stared at him.

'Because I thought you were a spy, planted on me by the dogs of the Belial-spawn, when they decided to hold me captive. When we heard Howard Immanuelson had died of a lung disease in a Holding Station on Coby, we all assumed his papers had been lost. The thought that someone else of the faith could find them and use them – and his doing it would be so secret that someone like myself

158

wouldn't know – that was stretching coincidence beyond belief. And you were so quick to pick up the finger speech. So I was going to pretend I was taken in by you. I was going to bring you with me to some place where the other brothers and sisters of the Children of God's Just Wrath could question you; and find out why you were sent and what you knew about us.'

He stared burningly at Hal.

'And then you, just now, brought me back from Hell – from where I could never have come back without you. There was no need for you to do that if you had been one of the enemy, one of the Accursed. How could I have doubted that you were of the faith?'

'Quite easily,' said Hal. 'As far as bringing you back from Hell, all I did was hurry up the process a little. The kind of persuasion that was used on you only takes permanently with people who basically agree with the persuader to begin with. With those who don't, his type of mind-changing gets eaten away gradually by the natural feelings of the individual until over time it wears thin and breaks down. Since you're someone opposed enough to fight him, the only way he could stop you permanently would be to kill you.'

'Why didn't he then?' said Jason. 'Why didn't he kill all of us?'

'Because it's to his advantage to pretend that he only opens people's eyes to the right way to live,' said Hal, hearing an echo of Walter the InTeacher in the words even as he said them. He had not consciously stopped to think the matter out, but Jason's question had evoked the obvious answer. 'Even his convinced followers feel safer if that particular man is always right, always merciful. What he did with us, there, wasn't because we were important, but because the two men with him on the platform were important – to him. There're really only a handful of what you call the Belial-spawn, compared to the trillions of people on the fourteen worlds. Those like him don't have the time, even if they felt like it, to control everyone personally. So, whenever possible they use the same sort of social mechanisms that've been used down the centuries when a few people wanted to command many.'

Jason sat watching him for a long moment.

'Who are you, Howard?' he asked at last.

'I'm sorry.' Hal hesitated. 'I can't tell you that. But I should tell you you've no obligation to call me brother. I'm afraid I lied to you. I'm not of the faith as you call it. I've got nothing to do with whatever organization you and those with you belong to. But I really am running from those like the man we're talking about.'

'Then you're a brother,' said Jason, simply. He picked up his own cup of cold coffee and drank deeply from it. 'We – those the Accursed call the Children – are of every sect and every possible interpretation of the Idea of God. Your difference from the rest of us isn't any greater than our differences from each other. But I'm glad you told me this; because I'll have to tell the others about you when we reach them.'

'Can we reach them?' asked Hal.

'There's no problem in that,' said Jason. 'I'll make contact in town here with someone who'll know where the closest band of Warriors is, right now; and we'll join them. Out in the countryside, we of the faith still control. Oh, they chase us, but they can't do more than keep us on the move. It's only here, in the cities, that the Belial-spawn and their minions rule.'

He slid to the end of the booth and stood up.

'Come along,' he said.

Out in the coldly damp air of the street, they located a callbox and coded for an autocab. In succession, changing cabs each time, they visited a clothing store, a library and a gymnasium, without Jason recognizing anyone he trusted enough to ask for help. Their fourth try brought them to a small vehicle custom-repair garage in the northern outskirts of Citadel.

The garage itself was a dome-like temporary structure perched in an open field on the city's edge; out where residences gave way to small personal farm-plots rented by city dwellers on an annual basis. It occupied an open stretch of stony ground that was its own best demonstration of why it had not been put to personal farming the way the land around it had. Inside the barely-heated dome, the air of which was thick with the faintly banana-like smell of a local tree oil used for lubrication, hanging like an invisible mist over the half-dismantled engines of several surface vehicles, they found a single occupant – a square, short, leathery man in his sixties, engaged in reassembling the rear support fan of an all-terrain fourplace cruiser.

'Hilary!' said Jason, as they reached him.

'Jase –' said the worker, barely glancing up at them. 'When did you get back?'

'Yesterday,' said Jason. 'The Accursed put us up overnight in their special hotel. This is Howard Immanuelson. Not of the faith, but one of our allies. From Coby.'

'Coby?' Hilary glanced up once more at Hal. 'What did you do on Coby?'

'I was a miner,' said Hal.

Hilary reached for a cleansing rag, wiped his hands, turned about and offered one of them to Hal.

'Long?' he asked.

'Three years.'

Hilary nodded.

'I like people who know how to work,' he said. 'You two on the run?'

'No,' said Jason. 'They turned us loose. But we need to get out into the country. Who's close right now?'

Hilary looked down at his hands and wiped them once more on his rag, then threw it into a wastebin.

'Rukh Tamani,' he said. 'She and her people're passing through, on their way to something. You know Rukh?'

'I know of her,' said Jason. 'She's a sword of the Lord.'

'You might connect up with them. Want me to give you a map?'

'Please,' said Jason. 'And if you can supply us –'

'Clothes and gear, that's all,' said Hilary. 'Weapons are getting too risky.'

'Can you take us close to her, at all?'

'Oh, I can get you fairly well in.' Hilary looked at Hal. 'Jase's no problem. But anything I'll be able to give you in the way of clothes is going to fit pretty tight.'

'Let's try what you've got,' said Jason.

Hilary led them to a partitioned-off corner of his dome. The door they went through let them into a storeroom piled to the ceiling with a jumble of containers and goods of all kinds. Hilary threaded his way among the stacks to a pile of what seemed to be mainly clothing and camping gear, and started pulling out items.

Twenty minutes later, he had them both outfitted with heavy bush clothing including both shoulder and belt packs and camping equipment. As Hilary had predicted, Hal's shirt, jacket and undershirt were tight in the shoulders and short in the sleeves. Otherwise, everything that he had given Hal fitted well enough. The one particular blessing turned out to be the fact that there were bush boots available of the proper length for Hal's feet. They were a little too wide, but extra socks and insoles took care of that.

'Now,' Hilary said when the outfitting was complete. 'When did you eat last?'

Hunger returned to Hal's consciousness like a body blow. Unconsciously, once it had become obvious in the cell that there was no hope of food soon, he had blocked out his need for it – strongly enough that he had even sat in the coffee place with Jason and not thought of food, when he could have had it for the ordering. As it was, Jason answered before he did.

'We didn't. Not since we got off the ship.'

'Then I better feed you, hadn't I?' grunted Hilary. He led them out of the storeroom and into another corner of the dome that had a cot, sink, foodkeeper and cooking equipment.

He fed them an enormous meal, mainly of fried vegetables, local mutton and bread, washed down with quantities of a flat, semi-sweet beer, far removed in flavor from the native Earth product. The heavy intake of food operated on Hal like a sedative; and he reacted, once they had all piled into a battered six-place bush van, by stretching out and falling asleep.

He woke to a rhythmic sound that was the slashing of branch tips against the sides of the van. Looking out the windows on either side, he saw that they were proceeding down a forest track so narrow that bushes on either side barely allowed the van to pass. Jason and Hilary were in mid-conversation in the front seat of the van.

'. . . Of course it won't stop them!' Hilary was saying. 'But if there's anything at all the Belial-spawn are even a little sensitive to, it's public opinion. If Rukh and her Command can take care of the Core Shaft Tap, it'll be a choice for the Others of either starving Hope, Valleyvale, and the other local cities, or shifting the ship outfitting to the core tap center on South Promise. It'll save them trouble to shift. It's a temporary spoke in their wheel, that's all; but what more can we ask?'

'We can ask to win,' said Jason.

'God allowed the Belial-spawn to gain control in our cities,' said Hilary. 'In His time, He'll release us from them. Until then, our job is only to tesify for Him by doing all we can to resist them.'

Jason sighed.

'Hilary,' he said. 'Sometimes I forget you're just like the other old folk, when it comes to anything that looks like an act of God's will.'

'You haven't lived long enough yet,' Hilary said. 'To you, everything seems to turn on what's happened in your own few years. Get older and look around the fourteen worlds, and you'll see that the time of Judgment's not that far off. Our race is old and sick in sin. On every world, things are falling into disorder and decay; and the coming among us of these mixed breeds who'd make everyone else into their personal cattle is only one more sign of the approach of Judgment.'

'I can't take that attitude,' said Jason, shaking his head. 'We wouldn't be capable of hope, if hope had no meaning.'

'It's got meaning,' said Hilary, 'in a practical sense. Forcing the spawn to change their plans to another core tap delays them; and who's to know but that very delay may be part of the battle plan of the Lord, as he girds his loins to fight this last and greatest fight?'

The noise of the branches hitting the sides and windows of the van ceased suddenly. They had emerged into an open area overgrown only by tall, straight-limbed conifers – variforms of some earthly stock – spaced about upon uneven, rocky ground that had hardly any covering beyond patches of green moss and brown, dead needles fallen from the trees. The local sun, for the first time Hal had seen it since he had arrived on Harmony, was breaking through a high-lying mass of white and black clouds, wind-torn here and there to show occasional patches of startling blue and brilliant light. The ground-level breeze blew strongly against the van; and for the first time Hal became aware that their way had been for some time uphill. With that recognition, the realization followed that the plant life and the terrain indicated a considerably higher altitude than that of Citadel.

Hal sat up on the seat.

'You alive back there?' said Hilary.

'Yes,' answered Hal.

'We'll be there in a few minutes, Howard,' said Jason. 'Let me talk to Rukh about you, first. It'll be her decision as to whether you're allowed to join her group, or not. If she won't have you, I'll come back with you, too; and we'll stay together until Hilary can find a group that'll have us both.'

'You'll be on your own, if I have to take you back,' said Hilary. 'I can't afford to keep you around my place for fear of attracting attention.'

'We know that,' said Jason.

The van went up and over a rise in the terrain, and nosed down abruptly into a valley-like depression that was like a knife-cut in the slope. Some ten or twenty meters below was the bed of the valley, with a small stream running through it; the stream itself hardly visible because of the thick cluster of small green-needled trees that grew about its moisture. The van slid down the slope of the valley wall on the air-cushion of its fans, plunged in among the trees, and came to a halt at a short distance from the near edge of the stream. From above, Hal had seen nothing of people or shelters; but suddenly they were in the midst of a small encampment.

He took it in at one glance. It was a picture that was to stay in his mind afterwards. Brightly touched by a moment of the sunlight breaking through the ragged clouds overhead, he saw a number of collapsible shelters like beehives, the height of a grown man, their olive-colored side panels and tops further camouflaged by tree branches fastened about them. Two men were standing in the stream, apparently washing clothes. A woman approaching middle age, in a black, leather-like jacket, was just coming out of the trees to the left of the van. On a rock in the center of the clearing sat a gray-haired man with a cone rifle half-torn-down for cleaning, its parts lying on a cloth he had spread across his knees. Facing him, and turning now to face the van, was a tall, slim, dark young woman in a somber green bush jacket, its many square pockets bulging with their contents. Below the bush jacket, she wore heavy, dark brown bush pants tucked into the tops of short boots. A gunbelt and sidearm were hooked tightly about her narrow waist, the black holster holding the sidearm with its weather flap clipped firmly down.

She wore nothing on her head. Her black hair was cut short about her ears, and her deeply bronzed face was narrow and perfect below a wide brow and brilliant, dark eyes. In that single, arrested moment, the repressed poet in Hal woke, and the thought came into his mind that she was like the dark blade of a sword in the sunlight. Then his attention was jerked from her. In a series of flashing motions the disassembled parts of the cone rifle in the hands of the gray-haired man were thrown back together, ending with the hard slap of a new rod of cones into the magazine slot below the barrel. The man was almost as swift as Hal had seen Malachi in similar demonstrations. The movements of this man did not have the smooth, unitary flow of Malachi's – but he was almost as fast.

'All right,' said the woman in the bush jacket. 'It's Hilary.'

The hands of the gray-haired man relaxed on the now-ready weapon; but the weapon itself still lay on the cloth over his knees, pointing in the general direction of Hal and the other two.

'I brought you a couple of recruits,' said Hilary, as coolly as if the man on the rock was holding a stick of candy. He started to walk forward and Jason moved after him. Hal followed.

'This is Jason Rowe,' said Hilary. 'Maybe you know him. The other's not of the faith, but a friend. He's Howard Immanuelson, a miner from Coby.'

By the time he had finished saying this he was within two meters of the woman and the man. He stopped. The woman glanced at Jason, nodded briefly, then turned her brilliant gaze on Hal.

'Immanuelson?' she said. 'I'm Rukh Tamani. This is my sergeant, James Child-of-God.'

Hal found it hard to look away from her, but he turned his gaze on the face of the gray-haired man. He found himself looking into a rectangular, raw-boned set of features, clothed in skin gone leathery some years since from sun and weather. Lines radiated from the corners of the eyes of James Child-of-God, deep parentheses had carved themselves about his mouth from nose to chin, and the pale blue eyes he fastened on Hal were like the muzzles of armed rifles.

'If not of the faith,' he said now, in a flat tenor voice, 'he hath no right here among us.'

Since he had left his home, Hal had until this moment encountered no Friendly cast in the mold he knew, the mold of Obadiah. Now, he recognized one at last. But this man was Obadiah with a difference.

CHAPTER SIXTEEN

There was a moment of silence. The soft fingers of the breeze came through the trees across the stream, quartering past Rukh Tamani and James Child-of-God, and cooled Hal's left cheek as he stood, still facing them.

'He's not of that special faith that's ours,' said Jason. 'But he's a hunted enemy of the Belial-spawn and that makes him our ally.'

Rukh looked at him.

'And you?'

'I've worked for the faith, these past eight years,' Jason said. 'I was one of the warriors in Charity City, even when I was going to college. Columbine and Oliver McKeutcheon both had me in their Commands at different times –'

He turned to nod at Hilary.

'Hilary know about this. He knows me.'

'He's right,' said Hilary. 'About all he says. I've known him five years or more.'

'But you don't know this other,' said James Child-of-God.

'He said he was a miner on Coby,' said Hilary. 'I've shaken hands with him and felt his calluses. He has them where a miner gets them, holding his torch; and the only place on the fourteen worlds they still use torches are in those mines.'

'He could be a spy.' The voice of James Child-of-God had the flat emotionlessness of someone commenting on statistics.

'He isn't.' Jason turned to Rukh Tamani. 'Can I talk to you privately about him?'

She looked at him.

'You can talk to us both privately,' she said. 'Come along, James.'

She turned away. James Child-of-God got to his feet, still carrying the cone rifle, and, with Jason, followed her to the edge of the clearing. They stopped there, and stood together, talking.

Hal waited. His eyes met Hilary's briefly; and Hilary gave him the ghost of a smile, which could have been intended as reassurance. Hal smiled back and looked away again.

He was conscious of his old, familiar feeling of nakedness and loneliness. It had come back upon him, as keenly as the sensation of someone thinly dressed stepping into the breath of a chill and strong wind. At the same time, the touch of the actual breeze upon him, the scent of the open air – were all acting powerfully upon his feelings. That part of him that had always lived in and by poetry had come suddenly to life again after having slept these last years in the mine; and everything that in this moment was impinging on his mind and senses was registering itself with a sharpness he had not felt since the deaths of Walter, Obadiah and Malachi. Now, all at once, it was once more with him; and he could not imagine how he had been living these past years without it. . . .

Abruptly he woke to the fact that the conversation at the edge of the clearing had finished. Both Jason and James Child-of-God were walking back toward him. Rukh Tamani still stood alone where she had been, and she called to him, her voice carrying clearly across the distance between them.

'Come here, please.'

He walked to her and stopped within arm's length.

'Jason Rowe's told us what he knows about you,' she said. Her eyes were penetrating without hardness, brown with an infinity of depths to them. 'He believes in you, but he could be wrong. There's nothing in what he told us that proves you aren't the spy that James is afraid you might be.'

Hal nodded.

'Have you got any proof you aren't a spy, sent either by the Others or by the Militia to help them trap us?'

'No,' he said.

'You understand,' she said, 'I can't risk my people, even to help someone who deserves help, if there's a danger. There's only one of you, but a number of us; and what we do is important.'

'I know that too,' he said.

They said nothing for a second.

'You don't ask our help, anyway?' she asked.

'There's no point to it, is there?' he said.

She studied him. Her face was like her eyes – unguarded, but showing no hint of what she was thinking. He found himself thinking how beautiful she was, standing here in the sunlight.

'For those of us who've taken up arms against the Others and their slaves,' she said, 'other proofs than paper ones can be meaningful. If that weren't so, we wouldn't be out here, fighting. But we not only don't know you or anything about you, but Jason says you refused to tell him who you really are. Is that right?'

'Yes,' he said. 'That's right.'

Once more she watched him for a moment without speaking.

'Do you want to tell me – who you are and how you come to be here?' she said at last. 'If you do, and I think what you tell me is true, we might be able to let you stay.'

He hesitated. The first and most important principle of all those he had been taught, against the time when he might have to run as he had these last years, was to keep his identity secret. At the same time, something in him – and maybe it was the reawakened poetic response, was urging him strongly to stay in this place, with Rukh and these others, at any cost.

He remembered Obadiah.

'One of those who brought me up,' he said, 'was a man named Obadiah Testator, from Oldcontinent here on Harmony. He said once, talking about me – *my people would never give you up*. He was talking about people like you, not giving me up to the Others. Can I ask – would you give me up, once you'd accepted me? Can you think of any conditions under which you would?'

She gazed at him.

'You aren't really of Harmony or Association, are you?' she said.

'No,' he answered. 'Earth.'

'I thought so. That's why you don't understand. There're those on both of our worlds here who might give you up to the Others; but we don't count them among us. God doesn't count them. Once you were accepted here, not even to save the lives of all the others would we give you up, any more than we'd give up any other member of this Command. I'm explaining this to you because you're not one of us; and it's not your fault you need said what shouldn't need to be. What use would it be – all the rest we do – if we were the kind who'd buy safety or victory at the price of even one soul?'

He nodded again, very slowly.

'This Obadiah Testator of yours,' she said. 'Was he a man strong in his faith?'

'Yes.'

'And you knew him well?'

'Yes,' said Hal; and after all these years suddenly felt his throat contract remembering Obadiah.

'Then you should understand what I'm saying.'

He controlled the reflex in his throat and looked once more into her eyes. They were different than the eyes of Obadiah, but they were also the same. Nor would Obadiah have betrayed him.

'I'll tell you,' he said, 'if no one but you has to know.'

'No one does,' said Rukh. 'If I'm satisfied, the rest will take my word for you.'

'All right, then.'

Standing there at the edge of the clearing, he told her everything, from as far back as he could remember, to this moment. When he came to the deaths of Obadiah, Walter and Malachi, his throat tightened again and for a moment he could not talk about it; then he got his voice under control and went on.

'Yes,' she said, when he was done, 'I see why you didn't want to

167

talk about this. Why did your tutors think the Others would be so determined to destroy you if they knew of you?'

'Walter the InTeacher explained it according to ontogenetics – you know about that Exotic discipline?'

She nodded.

'He said that since some of the Others are of Exotic extraction, they'd understand it, too; and they'd know that according to ontogenetic calculations I could represent a problem to them and what they were after. So to protect themselves, they'd try to destroy me. But if I could survive until I was mature enough to fight back, I could not only protect myself, I might even help stop them.'

'I see.' Rukh's dark eyes were almost luminous in the sunlight. 'If I believe you – and I do – you're also a weapon of the Lord, though in your own way.'

She smiled at him.

'We'll keep you. Come along.'

She led him back to the little knot of standing men that was James Child-of-God, Hilary and Jason.

'Howard Immanuelson will be one of us from now on,' she said to Child-to-God; and turned to face Jason. 'And you, of course, if that's what you want.'

'I do,' said Jason. 'Thank you.'

'If you know the life of a Warrior, as you say you do, you know there's little to give thanks for.' She turned again to Child-of-God. 'James, I've just accepted Howard among us because of some things he told me in confidence, things I can't tell you or the others. But I promise you I trust him.'

Child-of-God's blue eyes, hard as sapphires, fastened on Hal.

'If it is thee who say so, Rukh,' he said; and added, directly to Hal, 'Howard, after Rukh, I am in command here. Thou wilt remember that, at all times.'

'Yes,' said Hal.

'Hilary,' said Rukh, 'will you stay to dinner?'

'Thanks, Rukh,' said Hilary, 'but I'm behind with the work in my shop as it is; to say nothing of the fact I've already missed my prayers twice today getting these men out to you.'

'There'll be prayers before dinner.'

'Twice a day, eh?' said Hilary. 'Morning and evening, and that's it? The Lord'll have a heavy account for you people one day, Rukh.'

'To each his own way,' she said.

'And your way is this new one of letting actions be your prayers, is that it?' Hilary sighed and looked over at Child-of-God. 'How does *your* soul feel with only two moments of prayer a day?'

'I pray when God permits,' said Child-of-God, nasally. 'Six times daily or more, that being my way. But it's speaking to God that matters, not the bended knee or the joined hands – and indeed our Rukh serves the Lord.'

His eyes glinted on Hilary.

'Or would you say that was not so?'

'No, I would not say it was not so; and you know I wouldn't say it was not so,' said Hilary calmly. 'But the time may come when prayer at regular times is completely forgotten on these two worlds of which so much was expected once – and if so, won't we prove to have followed in the way of the Belial-spawn after all?'

'Stay for dinner or not, Hilary,' said Rukh. 'We'd like to have you. But we live too close to the edge of our lives to argue practices in this camp.'

Hilary shrugged.

'Forgive me, Rukh,' he said. 'I'm getting old; and it's hard when you get old to feel your race turning from God when we had such high hopes in our youth that one day all would acknowledge and live in His way. All right, all right, I won't say any more. But I can't stay to dinner. Thank you, anyway. When do you think you'll be out of my district?'

'In two days. Are there others you plan to bring to us?'

'No. I just wanted to know in case of emergency.'

'Two days. We've one more district to sweep for makings. Then we move to supply and prepare ourselves.' Rukh turned to Jason. 'Jason, you take Howard around the camp and explain how we do things. Introduce him and yourself to the other members of the command. Then come back to the cook tent. Both of you can give those on meal duty a hand with the serving of dinner. Jason, have you ever managed donkeys?'

'Yes,' said Jason.

'You'll be able to help us right away, then, when we break camp and move on. In the next few days, try and teach Howard as much as you can about the animals.'

She turned back to Hilary.

'And now, Hilary, we're all going to have to get to work. With luck we'll come past here again before the year's out.'

'Good luck,' said Hilary.

They embraced.

'And good luck to the rest of you, as well,' said Hilary, soberly, sweeping Child-of-God, Jason and Hal with his glance. He turned and walked back to his van, got in and lifted it on its fans. A second later he had spun it end for end and taken it into the trees, on his way back up the slope and out of sight.

Rukh turned away, into conversation with Child-of-God. Hal felt a touch on his elbow. He turned to see Jason.

'Come on, Howard,' said Jason, and led him off toward the far edge of the clearing and into the trees beside the stream there.

CHAPTER SEVENTEEN

In appearance, the men and women of Rukh's command seemed to Hal to be less like guerrilla fighters and more like simple refugees. The strongest impression he received as Jason led him about the confines of the camp was one of extreme poverty. Their beehive-shaped tents were patched and old. Their clothing was likewise patched and mended. Their tools, shelters and utensils, had either the marks of long wear or the unspecific, overall appearance of having been used and used again.

The weapons alone contradicted the refugee appearance, but hardly improved it. If not impoverished fugitives, they were, by all visible signs, at best an impoverished hunting party. There were apparently several dozen of them. Once among the trees, Hal revised his first estimate of their numbers upwards, for the majority of their tents were tucked back in under the greenery in such a way as not to be visible from the edge of the valley cut, above. As Jason led him along upstream to their left, they passed many men and women doing housekeeping tasks, mending, or caring for equipment or clothing.

Those he saw were all ages from late teens to their middle years. There were no children, and no really old individuals; and everyone they passed looked up at them as they went by. Some smiled, but most merely looked; not suspiciously, but with the expressions of those who reserve judgment.

They came, after about a hundred yards, to an area that was not a true opening in the trees, but one sparsely overgrown, so that patches of sunlight struck down between the trees in it, and between trees large patches of sky were visible.

Tethered each beneath a tree, at some little distance from each other, were a number of donkeys cropping the sparse grass and other ground vegetation that the sunlight had encouraged to spring up between the trees. Jason led the way to the nearest animal, patted its head, looked at its teeth and ran his hands over its back and sides.

'In good shape,' he said, stepping back. 'Rukh's command won't have been too hard pressed by the Militia, lately.'

He looked at Hal.

'Did you ever see donkeys before?'

'Once,' said Hal. 'They still have them in the Parks, on Earth, to use for camping trips.'

'Did you ever have anything to do with one of them on a camping trip?' Jason asked.

Hal shook his head.

'I only saw them – and of course, I read about them when I was growing up. But I understand they're a lot like horses.'

Jason laughed.

'For what good that does us,' he said.

'I only meant,' said Hal, 'that since I've had something to do with horses, I might find what I know about them useful with these.'

Jason stared at him.

'When were you on Earth long enough to learn about horses?'

Hal felt suddenly uncomfortable.

'I'm sorry,' he said. 'I ended up telling Rukh more than I'd told you – and I still can't tell you. But I forgot for a moment you didn't know. But I've ridden and handled horses.'

Jason shook his head slowly, wonderingly.

'You actually did?' he said. 'Not variforms – but the original, full-spectrum horses?'

'Yes,' said Hal.

He had let it slip his mind that many of Earth's mammals – even the variforms genetically adapted as much as possible to their destination planet – had not flourished on most of the other worlds. The reasons were still not fully understood; but the indications were that, unlike humans, even the highest orders of animals were less adaptable to different environmental conditions, and particularly to solunar and other cycles that enforced changes on their biorhythms. The larger the animals, the less successful they seemed to be perpetuating their own breed under conditions off-Earth; just as, once, many wild animals were unlikely to breed in zoos on Earth. Horses, unlike the ass family, were almost unknown on other worlds, with the exception of the Dorsai, where for some reason they had flourished.

'Do you know anything about harnesses and loading a pack donkey – I mean a pack animal?' asked Jason.

Hal nodded.

'I used to go off in the mountains by myself,' said Hal, 'with just a riding horse and a packhorse.'

Jason took a deep breath and smiled.

'Rukh'll be glad to hear this,' he said. 'Take a look at these donkeys, then, and tell me what you think.'

Together they examined the whole string of pack beasts. To Hal's eye they were in good, if not remarkable, shape.

'But if they were my animals, back on Earth,' he said, when they were done, 'I'd be feeding them up on grain, or adding a protein supplement to their diet.'

171

'No chance for that here,' said Jason, when Hal mentioned this. 'These have to live like the rest of the Command – off the country, any way they can.'

The light had mellowed toward late afternoon as they made their inspection; and it was just about time for the second of the two meals of the day that would be served in the camp. Jason explained this as he led Hal back toward the main clearing.

'We get up and go to bed with the daylight out here,' Jason said as they went. 'Breakfast is as soon as it's light enough to see what you're eating; and dinner's just before twilight – that's going to vary, of course, if we move into upper latitudes where the day's going to be sixteen hours long in summer.'

'It's spring here now, isn't it?' asked Hal.

'That's right. It's still muddy in the lowlands.'

The kitchen area turned out to be a somewhat larger tent under the trees on the far side of the clearing. It was filled with food supplies and some stored-power cooking units. A serving line of supports for cooking containers were set up just outside the tent. Inside, were the cook – a slim, tow-headed girl who looked barely into her middle teens – and three assistants at the other end of the age scale, a man and two women in their forties or above. The preparations for the meal were almost done, and food odors were heavy on the twilight-still air. Both Jason and Hal were put to work carrying out the large plastic cooking cans, heavily full with the various cooked foods for the meal; and setting these cans up on the supports of the serving line.

By the time this was done and they had also brought out and set up an equally large container of Harmony-style coffee, the members of the command had begun to queue for dinner, each one having brought his or her own eating tray.

They went down the line of food cans, served by the three assistants with the aid of Jason and Hal. Hal found himself with a large soup-ladle in his hand, scooping up and delivering what seemed to be a sort of stiff gray-brown porridge, of about the consistency of turkey stuffing. To his right Jason was ladling up what was either a gravy or some kind of sauce that went over what Hal had just served.

When the last of those who had gathered had gone through the line the assistants took their turn, followed by Jason and Hal with trays they had been given from the supply tent. Last of all to help herself was the cook, whose name apparently was Tallah. She took only a dab of the foods she had just made, and carried it back into her supply tent to eat.

Jason and Hal turned aside from the serving line with loaded trays, looking for a comfortable spot of earth to sit on. Most of the other eaters had carried their trays back to their tents or wherever they had come from.

'Howard, come here, please. I'd like to talk to you.'

The clear voice of Rukh made him turn. She and Child-of-God were seated with their trays, some twenty yards off at the edge of the clearing. Rukh was seated on the large end of a fallen log and Child-of-God was perched on the stump of it, from which age and weather had separated the upper part. Hal went over to them, and sat down crosslegged on the ground, facing them with his tray on his knees.

'Jason showed you around, did he?' Rukh asked. 'Go ahead and eat. We can all talk and eat at the same time.'

Hal dug into his own ladleful of the porridge-like food he had been serving. It did taste a little like stuffing – stuffing with nuts in it. He noticed that Child-of-God's tray held only a single item, a liquid stew of mainly green vegetables; and it occurred to him that only in one of the cans at the serving line had he seen anything resembling meat – and that had been only as an occasional grace note of an ingredient.

'Yes,' he answered Rukh, 'we walked through the camp and had a look at the donkeys. Jason seems to think the fact that I've had something to do with horses on Earth would help me be useful with them.'

Rukh's eyebrows went up.

'It will,' she said. She looked, as Jason had predicted, pleased, and put her fork down. 'As I promised you, I haven't said anything to anyone, including James, of what you told me. Still, James – as second-in-command – needs to know much of what I need to know about your usefulness to us. So I asked him to listen while I ask you some specific questions.'

Hal nodded, eating and listening. The food tasted neither as dull nor as strange as he had been afraid it would when he was helping to serve it; and his ever-ready appetite was driving him.

'I notice you aren't carrying anything in the way of a weapon,' Rukh said. 'Even bearing in mind what you told me, I have to ask if you've got some objection to using weapons?'

'No objection, in principle,' Hal said. 'But I've got to be honest with you. I've handled a lot of weapons and practiced with them. But I've never faced the possibility of using one. I don't know what'll happen if I do.'

'No one knows,' said Child-of-God. Hal looked at the other man and found his eyes watching. It was not a stare that those hard blue eyes bent upon him – it was too open to be a stare. Strangely, Child-of-God looked at him with an unwavering, unyielding openness that was first cousin to the nakedness of gaze found in a very young child. 'When thou hast faced another under conditions of battle, thou and all else will know. Until then, such things are secrets of God.'

'What are the weapons you've practiced with?' asked Rukh.

'Cone rifle, needle rifle, slug-throwers of all kinds, all varieties of power rifles and sidearms, staffs and sticks, knives, axe, sling, spear, bow and crossbow, chain and –' Hal broke off, suddenly self-conscious at the length of the list. 'As I said, though, it was just practice. In fact, I used to think it was just one kind of playing, when I was young.'

Child-of-God turned his head slowly to look at Rukh. Rukh looked back at him.

'I have reason to believe Howard in this,' she said to Child-of-God.

Child-of-God looked back at Hal, then his eyes jumped off to focus on Tallah, who had suddenly appeared at his elbow.

'Give me your tray,' Tallah said, holding out her hand, 'and I'll fill it for you.'

'Thou wilt not,' said Child-of-God. 'I know thee, and thy attempts to lead me into sin.'

'All I was going to do was refill it,' said Tallah, 'with that mess you try to live on. I don't care if you get a vitamin deficiency and die. Why should I care? We can get another second-in-command anywhere.'

'Thou dost not cozen me. I know thy tricks, adding that which I should not eat to my food. I've caught thee in that trick before, Tallah.'

'Well, you just die, then!' said Tallah. She was, Hal saw, very angry indeed. 'Go ahead and die!'

'Hush,' said Rukh to her.

'Why don't you order him to eat?' Tallah turned on her. 'He'd eat some decent food if you ordered him.'

'Would you, James?' Rukh asked the older man.

'I would not,' said Child-of-God.

'He would if you really ordered him.'

'Hush, I said,' said Rukh. 'If it becomes really necessary, James, I may have to order you to eat foods you consider sinful. But for now, at least, you can eat a decent amount of what you will eat. If I refill your tray will you trust me not to put anything in it you wouldn't take yourself?'

'I trust thee, of course,' said Child-of-God, harshly. 'How could it be otherwise?'

'Good,' said Rukh.

She stood up, took the tray from his hand and was halfway to the serving line before he started to his feet and went after her.

'But I need no waiting on –' he called after her. He caught up; and they went to the food container holding his vegetable stew together.

'These old Prophets!' said Tallah, furiously, turning to Hal. She glared at him for a moment, then broke suddenly into a grin. 'You don't understand?'

'I ought to,' Hal said. 'I have the feeling I ought to know what this is all about, but I don't.'

'There aren't many like him left, that's why,' said Tallah. 'Where did you grow up?'

'Not on Harmony,' said Hal.

174

'That explains it. Association's hardly a comparable world of the Lord. James – now don't you go calling him James to his face!'

'I shouldn't?'

'None of us, except Rukh, call him James to his face. Anyway, he's one of those who still hang on to the old dietary rules most of the sects had when we were so poor everyone ate grass and weeds to stay alive – and when anything not optimum for survival was supposed to be flying directly in the face of the Lord's will. There's no human reason now for him to try to live on that antique diet – as if God wouldn't forgive him one step out of the way, after the way he's fought for the faith all his life, let alone he calls himself one of the Elect.'

Hal remembered that the self-designated Elect in any of the sects on Harmony or Association were supposed to be certain of Heaven no matter what they did, simply because they had been specially chosen by God.

'– And we can't, we just can't, get the vegetables he'll eat all the time, on the move as we are. There's no way to give him a full and balanced diet from what we have. Rukh'll just have to end by ordering him to eat.'

'Why hasn't she done it before?' Hal tasted his own portion of the vegetable stew that had been the only thing on Child-of-God's tray. It was strange, peppery and odd-flavored, not hard to eat but hardly satisfying.

'Because he'd still blame himself for breaking his dietary laws even if it wasn't his fault he broke them – here they come, and at least she got his tray decently filled.'

Tallah went off. Rukh and Child-of-God came and sat down again.

'We've got two tasks,' Rukh said to Hal. 'In the coming months we'll be trying to do them while dodging the Militia and covering a couple of thousand kilometers of territory. If we get caught by the Militia, I'll expect you to fight; and if we don't, I'll expect you to work like everyone else in the Command; which means as hard as you can from the time you get up in the morning until you fall into your bedsack at night. In return for this, we'll try to feed you and keep you alive and free. This Command, like all those hunted by the slaves of the Others, doesn't have any holidays, or any time off. It spends all its time trying to survive. Do you understand what you're getting into?'

'I think so,' said Hal. 'In any case, if I was trying to survive out here by myself, it'd be a lot worse for me than what you describe.'

'That's true enough.' Rukh nodded. 'Then, there's two things more. One is, I'll expect you to give instant and unquestioning obedience to any command I give you, or James gives you. Are you capable of that, and agreeable to it?'

'That was one of the first things I learned, growing up,' Hal said. 'How to obey when necessary.'

'All right. One more point. Jason's been with a Command before, and he's also of the faith. You'll notice in the next few weeks that he'll be fitted right in with the rest of us, according to his capacities. You, on the other hand, are a stranger. You don't know our ways. Because of that, you'll find that everyone else in camp outranks you; and one result of that is going to be that almost everyone is going to end up giving you orders at one time or another. Do you think you can obey those orders as quickly and willingly as you can the ones from James and myself?'

'Yes,' said Hal.

'You're going to have to, if you plan to stay with us,' Rukh said, 'and you may find it's not as easy as you think. There'll be times when something like your training with weapons is concerned, when you may be positive you know a good deal more than the person who's telling you what to do. In spite of how you feel then, you're still going to have to obey – or leave. Because without that kind of obedience our Command can't survive.'

'I can do that,' said Hal.

'Good. I promise you, in the long run you'll get credit for every real ability you can show us. But we can't take the time or the risk of accepting you as anything but the last in line, and keeping you that way, until we know better.'

Rukh went back to her eating.

'Is that all?' asked Hal. His own tray was empty and he had visions of not being able to get back to the serving line in time to refill it.

'That's all,' said Rukh. 'After you've finished eating, help the cook people to clean up, then look up Jason. He'll have found a tent and equipment for the two of you. Once you're set up in that respect, if it's already dark, you'd probably better turn in, although you're welcome to join whoever's around the campfire. Think before you stay up too late, though. You've got a long day tomorrow, and every day.'

'Right. Thanks,' said Hal.

He scrambled to his feet and went back to the serving line. There he filled and emptied another trayful of food, then hesitated over taking a third until Tallah saw his uncertainty and told him it was all right to eat as much as he wanted.

'. . . For now, anyway,' she said. 'When the Command's short on rations, you'll know it, everyone'll know it. Right now we're fine. We're in rich country and it's good to see people eat.'

'Rich country?' Hal asked.

She laughed.

'This is a district where there're plenty of the faithful, and they've got food and other things they can afford to share with us.'

'I see.'

'And when you're done, you'd better get busy with these serving

176

cans. Take them down to the stream and wash them. Then you can go.'

Hal ate, cleaned the cans and went. It was unmistakably twilight now. He cast about under the trees for Jason, hoping to find him without having to ask. Finally, he was reduced to querying a nearly-bald, but still young-looking, man, who was seated cross-legged in front of one of the tents, putting new cleats on the bottoms of a pair of boots.

The man spat staples out of his mouth, caught them in the palm of his left hand, shifted his hammer to join them, and reached up with his right hand to clasp Hal's.

'Joralmon Troy,' he said. 'You're Howard Immanuelson?'

'Yes,' said Hal, shaking hands.

'Jason Rowe's set a tent up for the two of you back by the beasts. He's either there now, or still feeding and caring for them. You're not of the faith?'

'I'm afraid not,' said Hal.

'But you're not a scorner of God?'

'From as far back as I can remember I was taught never to scorn anything.'

'Then that's all right,' said Joralmon. 'Since God is all things, one who scorns nothing, scorns not Him.'

He put boots, hammer and staples aside, just inside the front entrance of his tent.

'Time for evening prayers,' he said. 'Some pray separately, but there are those of us who gather, night and morning. You're always welcome if you wish to come.'

He looked up at Hal, getting to his feet as he spoke. There was an openness and simple directness to his gaze that was a less intense version of what Hal had seen in Child-of-God.

'I don't know if I can, tonight,' said Hal.

He went back through the twilit woods toward the area where the donkeys had been tethered. With the shadows growing long all about him the forest seemed vaster, the trees taller, reaching pillar-like up to support the dimming sky. A more chill breath of air wandered among the tree-trunks and cooled him as he went.

He found the tent off to one side of the area where the donkeys were tethered, next to a larger one that had its entrance flaps pressed together and sealed. A faint, musty odor came from the sealed tent.

'Howard!'

Jason came around the far side of the tent, smiling.

'What do you think of it?' he said.

Hal looked at the tent. Back on Earth it would have been inconceivable to house himself in such a structure without either replacing it or remaking it completely. It had been a good example of a beehive tent once, of a size to sleep four people, with their packs and possessions for a two-week trip. Now it was shrunken by virtue of the many repairs that had been made in its skin and looked as if its fabric might split from old age at any minute.

'You've done a good job,' said Hal.

'It was sheer luck they had one to give us,' said Jason. 'I was all prepared to start building a lean-to of branches to tuck our bedsacks under – oh, by the way, they had liners for our bedsacks, too. We'll need them at this altitude.'

'How high are we?' asked Hal, as he ducked his head to follow Jason into the tent. Within, under the patched fabric with its smells of food and weapon oil, Jason had the bedsacks laid out on opposite sides of the equally-patched floor, with the feet meeting underneath the highest arc-point of the tent's main support rib. Their packs and other equipment were near the heads of the sacks, but stowed prudently away from possible condensation on the tent's inner surface. Jason touched a glow-tube fastened to the main rib above the feet of the bedsacks, and a small, friendly yellow light illuminated the shadowy interior.

'A little over two thousand meters,' said Jason. 'We'll be going higher when we leave here.'

He was obviously warm with happiness and pride over their tent; but trying not to lead Hal deliberately into praise and compliments.

'This is very good,' said Hal, looking around him. 'How did you do it?'

'The credit's all due the people of this Command,' said Jason. 'They were able to give us everything. I knew you'd be surprised.'

'I am,' said Hal.

'Well, now you've seen it,' said Jason, 'let's go sit by the main fire for a bit and meet people. We have to help the cook crew, but then we'll be getting ready to move on, tomorrow.'

They extinguished the glow tube and left the tent. The campfire to which Rukh and Joralmon had also referred was in a place away from the rest of the camp, on the bank upstream beyond the far edge of the clearing. It was a large fire and it warmed an equally large dispenser of coffee, Jason explained, which served as a focal point for whoever wished to come by and mingle, after the day's work and prayers were done. When Hal and Jason arrived, there were six men and two women already sitting around drinking coffee and talking with each other; and in the next half hour that number tripled.

The two of them helped themselves to coffee and sat down by the pleasant light and heat of the fire. One by one introductions were exchanged with the others already there, and then the rest went back to the conversations they had been having when Hal and Jason arrived.

'What's in that tent just behind us, here?' Hal asked Jason.

Jason grinned.

'Makings,' he said, in a lowered voice.

'Makings?' Hal waited for Jason to explain, but Jason merely continued to grin.

'I don't understand,' Hal said. 'What do you mean by "makings"?'

'Makings for an experiment. A – a military weapon,' said Jason, still softly. 'Not refined yet.'

Hal frowned. Jason's tone had been reluctant. He looked at the expression on Jason's face, which struck him as most peculiar. Then he remembered Jason's words about the lack of privacy in the latrine corner of their cell in the city Militia Headquarters.

'I can tell by the smell,' he said, 'it's organic matter. What kind is it, in that tent?'

'Shh,' said Jason, 'no need to shout it out. Bodily fluids.'

'Bodily fluids? Which? Urine?'

'Shh.'

Hal stared at him, but obediently lowered his voice.

'Is there some reason I shouldn't –'

'Not at all!' said Jason, still keeping his own voice down. 'But no decent person goes shouting out words like that. It's the only way we can make it; but there're enough dirty jokes and songs about the process as it is.'

Hal changed ground.

'What sort of weapon do you need urine for?' he asked. 'All the weapons I've seen around here have been cone rifles or needle guns – except for a few power sidearms like the one Rukh carries.'

Jason stared at him.

'How do you know it's a power sidearm that Rukh's carrying? She never unsnaps that holster cover unless she has to use the pistol.'

Hal had to stop and think how he did know. The fact that Rukh's sidearm was a power weapon had merely been self-evident until this moment.

'By its weight,' he said, after a second. 'The way it drags on her weapon belt shows its weight. Among weapons, only a powered one weighs in that proportion to its size.'

'Excuse me,' said a voice over their heads. They looked up to see a heavy-bodied, thin-limbed man who looked to be about Child-of-God's age, standing over them in heavy jacket and bush trousers. 'I'm Morelly Walden. I've been out of camp on an errand and I didn't get to meet you two, yet. Which one of you is Jason Rowe?'

'I am,' said Jason as both he and Hal got to their feet and clasped hands in turn with Walden. The other man's rectangular face had few wrinkles, but the skin of it was toughened and dry.

'I knew Columbine, and he mentioned you'd been in his Command once. And you are . . .?'

'Howard Immanuelson.'

'Not from this world? You're from Association?'

'No, as a matter of fact I'm not from either Harmony or Association.'

'Ah. Well, welcome, none the less.'

Walden spoke to Jason about members of Columbine's command. Others also came from time to time and introduced themselves. Jason was kept busy talking to them, but beyond introducing themselves they did not offer to talk at any length with Hal.

He sat listening and watching the fire. The instinct in animals and small children, Walter the InTeacher had told him – the instinct, in fact, of people of any age – was to first circle any stranger and sniff him out, get used to his intrusion into their cosmos; and then, only when they were ready, to make the first move to communicate themselves. When the other members of Rukh's command began to feel comfortable with his presence, Hal assumed, they would find occasion to talk to him.

Meanwhile, he was content. This morning he had been an isolated stranger, adrift in a strange world. Now, he had a place on it. There was a close feeling around the campfire, the atmosphere like that of a family, that he had not felt since his tutors' death, except for that one day in the mine after he had made torcher. A family together at the end of the day. While some of the conversations he heard were purely social, others were discussions of shared responsibilities, or shared problems being discussed by people who had been physically separated by the day's events until now. As more members of the command drifted in around the fire, more wood was added to it. The flames reached up; and their light enlarged the apparent interior area of the globe of night that enclosed them all. The firelight made a room in the darkness. They were private in the midst of the outdoors, housed by immaterial walls of warmth and familiarity and mutual concerns.

Altogether, the situation and the moment once more woke that same urge to poetry in him that had first come back to life with his first sight of Rukh. But it was not the urge to make poetic images that touched him now. It was the memory of poetry in his past.

It is long, the night of our waiting,
But we have a call to stay . . .

They were the first two lines of a poem he had written when he had been ten years old and drunk with the image of the great picture Walter the InTeacher had painted for him; a picture of the centuries-long search of the Exotics for an evolved form of humankind, a better race, grown beyond its present weaknesses and faults. Like most of the poems of extreme youth, what power it possessed had been all in the first couple of lines, and from there it had gone downhill into triteness. Since then, he had learned not to go so fast to the setting down of the first words that came to mind. It took restraint and experience to do deliberately what amateur poets tended to do only unconsciously – carry the poem around in the back of the mind until it was complete and ready to be born.

He lost himself now in just that process – not forcing his mind into any mold, but under the influence of the surrounding darkness and the firelight letting the powerful creative forces of the unconscious drift uncontrolled, forming images and memories, good and bad, recent and distant.

Making mental pictures in the city of the white-red embers glowing beneath the burning logs, he watched armies march and builders build; while Sost and Walter, Malachi and Tonina, mixed and mingled in his thoughts and the ghost of Obadiah stood around the fire, talking with the living bodies with whom Hal shared its warmth.

Now that he stood back and looked at himself, something in him had healed with the three years on Coby; but much else was still either unhealed or unfinished. Somewhere, there was waiting a purpose to his life; but he had let that fact be forgotten, until he had driven into the clearing this afternoon and seen Rukh, Child-of-God, and now these others. There must be a purpose because it was unthinkable that life could be otherwise. . . .

So he continued, sitting, dreaming and thinking, occasionally interrupting himself to reply to an introduction or some brief word from other members of the command, until he was roused by a touch on his arm. He turned and saw Jason.

'Howard,' said Jason. 'I'm turning in. You can keep the fire going here as long as you want, even by yourself, but dawn comes early.'

Hal nodded, suddenly aware that the gathering had shrunk to only a handful of people. Two pairs of individuals, and one group of three, were deep in private conversations. Otherwise, only he and Jason were left.

'No,' he said. 'Thanks, but you're right. I'll fold up too.'

He got to his feet, and they went off into the dark. Away from the fire, the night at first seemed pitch-black, but gradually their eyes adjusted to show the moonlit woods. Even with this, however, the area held a different appearance at night; and they might have wandered indefinitely in search of their tent, if Jason had not produced and lit a pinhole torch. The beam of the torch picked up eye-level reflectors pinned onto trees to mark out the numbered routes throughout the camp. They followed the route that led back to the clearing; and there Jason picked out what was evidently the line of reflectors that would lead them to the tethering place of the donkeys, and their tent.

The tent itself was a welcome place to step into at last; and Hal recognized, as Jason turned out the glowtube and the pulled the hood of his own bedsack into place to keep the top of his head warm, that

181

he was ready and overready for sleep. Exhaustion was like a warm bath relaxing all his limbs; and even while thinking this, he was asleep.

He awoke suddenly, holding somebody's throat in the darkness, so that whoever it was could not cry out or breathe. A twist of his thumbs would have broken the neck he held. But swiftly – though it seemed slowly – the odors of the tent, the smell of the camping gear and clothing, brought him back to a realization of where he was. It was Jason he was holding and strangling.

He let go. He got to his feet; and, reaching out in the darkness, found and turned on the glowtube. Yellow light showed Jason lying on the floor of the tent, breathing now, but otherwise not making a sound, staring up at him with wide-open eyes.

CHAPTER EIGHTEEN

'Are you all right?' said Hal numbly. 'What happened?'

Jason's lips worked without a sound. He lifted a hand and felt his throat. At last his voice came, huskily.

'I woke and heard you breathing,' he said. 'Then, suddenly, your breathing stopped. I called to you to wake you up, but you didn't answer. I crawled over to see if you were still there, and you were – but you weren't breathing at all. I tried to shake your shoulder to wake you. . . .'

His voice ran down.

'And I woke up and grabbed your throat,' said Hal.

Jason nodded, still staring up at him.

'I'm sorry,' said Hal. 'I don't know why I did that. I wasn't even awake. I'm sorry.'

Jason got slowly to his feet. They looked at each other with their faces only a few hands-width's apart in the yellow light of the glow-tube.

'You're dangerous, Howard,' said Jason, in an expressionless voice.

'I know,' said Hal, unhappily. 'I'm sorry.'

'No,' said Jason, 'it's good for this Command to have danger-ousness like that on our side, against our enemies. But what made you attack me?'

'I don't know,'

'It was because I woke you suddenly, wasn't it?'

'I suppose,' said Hal. 'But even then . . . I don't usually go around attacking anyone who wakes me suddenly.'

'Were you dreaming?'

'I don't remember . . .' Hal made an effort to remember. 'Yes.'

'A bad dream?'

'In a way . . .' said Hal.

'A bad dream. It's not surprising,' said Jason. 'Many of us know what it's like to have that sort of dream. It's all right. As long as we're both awake now, let's have some coffee.'

Hal shivered.

'Yes,' he said. 'That's a good idea.'

Jason turned to a corner of the tent and came up with a

temperature-sealed plastic container that looked as if it might hold about a liter of liquid.

'I filled it after dinner – I meant to tell you it was here,' he said, almost shyly. He pressed the thumb-stop to jet a stream of dark liquid, steaming in the chill air of the nighttime tent, into a couple of plastic cups. He handed one filled cup to Hal and got back into the warmth of his own bedsack, sitting up with it around him.

Hal imitated him. They looked at each other across the width of the tent.

'Would you want to tell me what the dream was?' Jason said.

'I don't know if I can,' said Hal. 'It wasn't very clear. . . ."

'Yes. I know that kind, too,' said Jason. He nodded. 'Don't try to talk about it, then. Drink the coffee and lie down again. The thread gets broken that way, and the same nightmare doesn't come back. Tomorrow's another day. Think about tomorrow while you're falling asleep.'

'All right,' said Hal.

Jason finished his cup quickly and lay down again, pulling the hood of his bedsack up close around his head.

'Leave the light on or turn it off, whichever you like,' he said. 'It won't bother me.'

'I'll put it out,' said Hal.

He got up, extinguished the glowtube and crawled back into his bedsack in darkness. He had set his cup to one side of the bedsack and it was still half full. Sitting up, he drank it off, then laid back down himself. The feeling of the dream he had admitted having came back to him. There was nothing he could have told Jason about it that would have made sense out of his murderous response at being wakened, or his earlier unaccountable ceasing to breathe.

. . . He had been riding, armed and armored, on horseback with others. They had ridden out of some trees onto the edge of a vast plain, and halted their horses. Distant in the middle of the otherwise stark emptiness of the plain was a dark, solitary, medieval-looking structure – like a peel tower, narrowing as it reached upward to its crenelated top. There were no other buildings around it, only the tower itself – and it was far off. There was a terrible sense about the tower, of waiting, that held them all silent.

'I'll go alone,' he had said to the others.

He had gotten down from his horse, passed the reins to the man next to him and started out on foot across the endless distance of the plain, toward the tower. At some time later, he had looked back and seen those who had been with him, still sitting their horses, small under the trees which were themselves shrunken with the distance he had put between himself and them. Then he had turned again and continued on toward the tower, to which he seemed hardly to have progressed a step since he had left the edge of the wood; and without warning something he could not see had come up out of the waste-land behind him and touched him on the shoulder.

And that had been all. The next thing he had known was that he was awake with his hands around Jason's throat. Still holding in his mind the dream-memory of the tower as he had last seen it in his dream, he fell asleep again.

He woke to the feel of his foot being moved. He opened his eyes and saw that it was Jason who had hold of it, through the bedsack. Jason squatted at arm's length from the bottom end of the bedsack, at maximum distance from him; and his gaze was anxious.

'Wasn't I breathing again?' Hal said, and grinned at him.

Jason let go of his foot and grinned back.

'You were breathing, all right. But we're due to help with break-fast. You'll have to hurry.'

Hal rolled over, fumbled for and found the bath kit with which Hilary had supplied him, and pulled himself out of the warmth of the bedsack into the chill morning air. He stumbled from the tent toward the nearby stream.

Fifteen minutes later they were walking through the dawn woods toward the cook tent. The light was grayish white and mist was everywhere in wisps between the trees. Sounds came very clearly through the mist, sounds of wood being chopped, people calling back and forth, metal objects clanking against each other. The cold, damp air laved Hal's freshly depilated cheeks and touched deep into his lungs when he drew it in. From dead sleepiness, he was waking powerfully to a sense of being very alive, warm and alive within the protection of his heavy outdoor clothing. He was hollow with hunger.

When they got to the cook shack, however, he and Jason had time only for a hastily-gulped cup of coffee before going to work. But eventually the rest of the Command was fed and they got a chance at their own breakfasts.

'We'll look over the packsaddles, first,' Jason said as they sat eating, perched on some boxes in the cooktent, 'along with the other gear. Then we'll check out the animals and decide which to load first and which to lead unloaded for rotation. I haven't had a chance to look in the load tent, yet; but Rukh said we've already picked up about three-quarters of as much raw makings as we can carry; and we'll get the rest on our way.'

'Our way to where?'

Jason stopped eating for a moment and looked at him.

'No one's said anything?' he said. 'Rukh didn't say?'

'No.'

'Why don't you go ask her what you're supposed to know, then come back and tell me?' Jason looked uncomfortable. 'I don't know what to say and what not.'

'I remember you talking in the van to Hilary about the Coretap –'

'I didn't know you were awake.' Jason's face was stricken.

'I'd just woke.'

'Yes. Well,' said Jason, 'why don't you talk to Rukh? That way we'll all know what we can talk about.'

'All right,' said Hal. 'I will.'

They finished their breakfast and went back to the donkeys and the load tent. All that day they worked over the packsaddles and other carrying gear and practiced loading and unloading. Ten of the donkeys were required to carry the community equipment of the Command, and whatever personal gear a member of the Command was temporarily unable to carry. That left sixteen others to carry what Jason continued to refer to as 'the makings,' and act as replacement animals for any of the other donkeys who fell lame or otherwise needed to be rested from their loads. It was ordinary practice, Hal learned, to rotate the loads on the animals, so that each one of them periodically was led unburdened; and this went beyond keeping the animals in the best possible condition. It had its roots in the idea that it was sinful not to allow the beasts, like humans, periodic rest.

The next day the Command packed up and started out; and with that began some weeks of daily travel through the mountains. They made fifteen to eighteen kilometers a day; and each night when they camped, they would be visited by people living in the vicinity, bringing in donations of food or supplies, or more of the raw materials for the potassium nitrate.

The physical demands of this life were entirely different from those the mines had made on Hal, but he adapted quickly. He was still as lean as a stripped sapling and he suspected he was still adding height; but to a great extent he had begun to develop the strength of maturity, while still having the elasticity of youth. Before they were a week on their way, he was completely acclimated to this new life. Even the local coffee was beginning to taste good to him.

Their weeks were all very much alike; high altitude days full of bright sunshine and wind, with a few small white clouds, the air very clean and light, the water icy cold from the mountain streams and their sleep sudden and sound after days that grew steadily longer as they moved south to meet the advancing summer.

Hal and Jason were up at dawn. They ate, harnessed and packed the donkeys for the day's trek. Two hours later, the Command was on the move, its human members lined out ahead with backpacks containing their immediate personal equipment and followed by Jason at the head of the donkeys carrying the general gear of the Command. At the tail end of the donkey contingent were those animals carrying the makings and the unloaded animals. Last of all came Hal as rearguard on the pack train. It was his job to make sure none of the beasts or people fell behind and got left, meanwhile keeping a wary eye on the donkeys ahead of him to make sure no load had slipped and no animal had gone lame.

It was a duty that called for vigilance rather than activity; and Hal's mind was free. It was the first time he had been able to stop to think since he had run from his home in the Rockies. On Coby the weekday life of the mines and the weekend life in Port had not given him the kind of mental privacy in which he could stand back and take stock. Now, it was amply available. In the solitude of his position at the end of the donkey line, with the long day's walk and the solidity of the mountains all around him, peace flowed into him and he had the chance to think long thoughts.

Now that he could hold it off at arm's length, he recognized that the Coby life had been an artificial one. He had spent the last three years indoors. It had been necessary as a place to hide while he grew up physically; and it had taught him to live, if not be completely comfortable, with strangers. But in a deeper sense, it had been, as planned, only a marking of time while he had grown up. Now, he was like a convict released from prison. He was back out in the universe where things could begin to happen; and he saw matters more in their proper dimensions.

One of the things that he saw most clearly was that it would be easy to underestimate most of the people he was now with. Not Rukh, and not Child-of-God – each of whom radiated power like hot coals inches from the palm of a hand. But most of the rest were so limited in their view of the universe, so steeped in their religious beliefs, and in many ways so unquestioning as to be hardly suspected even of shrewdness.

But there was more to each one of them than those limitations implied. They were, in fact, very like these mountains through which they now trudged, committed to a conflict they did not really understand but which they would pursue while any flicker of life was still in them, in the name of what they believed to be right.

Deep down, there was a great strength in each of them; an innate strength and a search toward something of more meaning than mere survival. This difference in them from the miners of Coby had reawakened Hal to the reasons and purpose his own life should have. He found himself thinking of where he would need to go from this present moment, to what end he should be looking, and planning to meet.

Somewhere in the last few weeks, he had hardened into the resolve to meet the Others head-on as soon as he should be strong enough. Among the complex bundle of attitudes that made him what he was, was one reflex that looked back always to the moment in which Malachi, Obadiah and Walter had died on the terrace; and a feeling, hard and ancient and unsparing, looked also toward Bleys and Dahno and all their kind. But beyond that he felt, without the understanding that would enable him to define it, that oceanic purpose that had always been there behind everything else in him, now developing into something like a powerful commitment only waiting for the hour in which it would be called to action.

Because he could not define it, because it evaded his grasp when he tried to get his mind around it, he drifted off into the area of poetic images which had always acted as translator for him of those things which his conscious mind could not grasp. As he had used his memories of Walter, Obadiah and Malachi in the Final Encyclopedia to give form to his problem of escape from the Others, so he found himself coming to use the making of poetry to reach the formless images and conclusions in the back of his mind.

As he tramped along, he cut the creative part of himself loose to the great winds of awareness that blew invisibly behind all thoughts; and, line by line as he walked behind the donkeys through the bright-cold of the high mountains, he found himself beginning to reach out and build a poem that put a form and a language to that awareness. Line by line it grew; and just before one of the midday halts, it was done.

> *No one is so plastic-fine*
> *That he lacks a brown man.*
> *Twisted core of the old-wood roots.*
> *In blind earth moving.*
>
> *Clever folk with hands of steel*
> *Have built us to a high tower,*
> *Pitched far up from the lonely grass*
> *And the mute stone's crying.*
>
> *Only, when some more wily fist*
> *Shatters that tower uplifted,*
> *We may yet last in the stone and grass*
> *By a brown man's holding.*

The poem sang itself in his head like a repeated melody. It was a song, he thought reasonlessly, to eat up the distance between him and the dark tower of his dream.

With that thought, a vagrant idea came to him of another possible poem waiting to be born about the dark tower of his dream – a poem that charted the path into a new and larger arena of possibilities that was waiting in the back of his mind, somewhere. But it slipped away as he reached for it now. Like his song about the brown man, it bore a relationship to himself and his circumstances in ways he could feel but not yet define. Only, the poem about the tower was massive and touched great forces waiting to be. He forced himself to put aside thinking of it and came back to the brown man song to see what it had to tell him.

Clearly, it was saying that a stage was now past for him, a step was achieved – before he could think any farther into it, he saw Jason standing by the side of the route, holding the halter of one of the donkeys. Hal shooed his own beasts ahead and drew level with Jason and his.

'What's up?' he called.

'A thrown shoe,' said Jason. 'It must have happened right after we started. We'll have to switch the load to another animal.'

CHAPTER NINETEEN

The donkeys were divided into two strings, and the one with the thrown shoe was the first of Jason's string. The path they had been following along the mountain slope was only wide enough for one animal in some places and the whole string was blocked from moving farther until that beast was out of the line.

'Howard, can you take her back?' Jason said. 'I can hold the rest.'

Hal came up and began the job of coaxing the donkey off the solid surface of the trail onto the loose rock of the hillside beneath it, so that she could be turned around and led to the rear.

They were moving through a pass in the mountains along the flank of a steep slope, following a path that evidently had not been used since the fall before. It was covered with a winter's debris; twigs and needles and cones from the imported variform conifers that had come to clothe these high-altitude slopes in the temperate zones of Harmony. But it was a route that looked as if it had existed during some years for use in good weather. It took advantage of natural flat areas along the way, winding up and down as it went, but trending always southward.

Below the solid and flat surface of the narrow path, the gray-brown treeless slope pitched sharply downward for over three hundred meters to a cliff-edge and a vertical drop of as much again to a mountain river, hidden far below. Above the path, the slope became less steep and was consequently treed – sparsely, but enough so that, fifty meters up, vegetation blocked the eye completely from a view of a short stretch of higher horizontal ridge that had been paralleling the path for the last several hundred meters.

At the moment, Rukh's Command was following the outward swell of the mountain's breast. Ahead of Hal and Jason, the slowly-moving line of people disappeared from sight around the curve of it, to their left. Behind them Hal, as he got the donkey turned, could see back for several kilometers of open mountainside, past a vertical fold in the rock that made a dozen-meters-wide indentation where they had just passed, an indentation that narrowed sharply upward until it became first a cleft, then a narrow chimney, rising to the stony surface of the ridge above. Behind them, also, there were fewer trees and the full slope of the mountainside up to the treed ridge above lay open to the eye. The air was dry and clear, so that distances looked less than they actually were, under a sky with only a few swift-moving, small clouds.

'So . . . so . . .' soothed Hal, conning the donkey over the loose shale below the path to a point behind the other animals, where he could lead her back up on to it. He reached that point and got her up, turning to find that Jason had ground-hitched the next donkey in line behind the one just taken out. The whole back half of that particular string was now waiting patiently, and Jason was scrambling rapidly along the shale to join him.

'We can put Delilah back in, to replace her –' Jason began as he reached the path beside Hal – and the air was suddenly full of whistlings.

'Down!' shouted Hal, dragging the other man flat on the mountainside below the lip of the path. Sharp-edged pieces of the loose rock that covered the slope stabbed at Hal through his shirt and slacks. Up on the path, several of the loaded donkeys were staggering down onto the slope, or slowly folding at the knees to lie huddled on the path. The whistling ceased, and the abrupt silence was shocking.

'Cone rifles!' Jason's voice was high-pitched and strange. 'Militia up there!'

His tense face was staring up at the tree-hidden ridge. He scrambled to the next-to-last donkey in line, which carried their own gear, and wrestled with its load until he could tug free the weapon that had been issued to him. He slid back down to lie flat beside Hal once more.

'That won't do you any good at this range,' Hal said. Jason's weapon was an ancient needle gun, inaccurate beyond sixty or seventy meters, and ineffective at less than double that distance.

'I know,' panted Jason, still staring up at the hidden ridge. 'But maybe they'll come down on us.'

'They'd have to lose their heads –' Hal was beginning, out of the lessons he had absorbed as a child, when a crunching of boots in shale to their right brought their heads around. They saw Leiter Wohlen, one of the younger men of the Command, running crouching toward them.

'Seen anything?' he gasped, stopping at last over them.

'Get down!' said Hal – but it was too late. The sound of whistlings filled their ears once more, and Leiter fell, dropping his own needle gun. He started to roll bonelessly away from them down the slope. Hal plunged in pursuit, caught him, and saw that he was undeniably dead. Three cones had torn their way through his chest and one had furrowed across the side of his head. Hal snatched up the fallen gun; and, crouched over to take advantage of the cover of the path above, ran across the slope back the way they had travelled.

'Where are you going?' he heard Jason calling after him, But he had no breath to answer.

He scuttled across the loose scree of the slope until the curve of the mountain began to block the direct line of sight between him and that part of the ridge from which the cones had been sent down upon them. He was back in the indentation, that fold of the mountain rock leading upward to the cleft and the chimney. Safe now from observation by the weapon-holders above, he scrambled back up onto the path, and began to climb directly upward in the cleft.

There were not so many loose stones here. He scrambled upward mostly over bare rock, and he went swiftly, the needle gun bouncing on his back, held there by the strap of its sling across his chest. Sweat sprang out on his face, cooling it so that it felt naked in the dry mountain air. He found himself breathing deeply and steadily. It had been a long time since he had pushed himself physically in just this fashion, and his body felt stiff and awkward. But the early habits of his training lived deeply in him, and he could feel the air being drawn powerfully into his lungs, the hammering of his heart in his chest rapid but steady. He climbed swiftly into the narrow neck of the chimney; and from a scramble on hands and feet up the steep slope, he went to rock climbing.

The chimney was some nine or ten meters in height, narrowing sharply until at the top, just below the upper ridge, it was less than a meter in width. He made himself stop and breathe deeply at the bottom of the climb, willing his heart to slow and refilling his depleted tissues with oxygen for the effort.

The needle gun was the real problem. Ordinary procedure would have been to pull it up after him once he got to the upper ridge. But he had no line to lift it with. He stood for a moment, mentally calculating the distance between the ridge above him and the place farther along it, from which the fire of the cone rifles had come. Unless he was unlucky enough to have one of the Militiamen just above him at this moment, the sound of the weapon falling onto the flat rock of the upper ridge should not carry far enough to attract attention.

He stepped back and down from the base of the chimney to find a place where he could plant his feet firmly, then took the needle gun from his back and checked to make sure that its safety was on. It was, and he took the weapon firmly by the muzzle end of the barrel in both hands, swung it at arm's length, then flung it wheeling upward, until it dropped from sight with a distant crash on the upper ridge.

He stood waiting, listening. But there was no sound of anyone coming to investigate. He began to climb.

It had been over four years since his muscles had done this kind of work, and they were slow to respond to it. He climbed with extreme care, checking and rechecking every handhold and foothold, his eyes on the reddish, weather-smoothed rock only inches before them. Little by little, as he went, the old reflexes came back and the familiar skills. He was soaked with sweat now and his shirt clung to his back and shoulders. He panted heavily as he went. But he was warming to the ascent and something of his earlier pleasure at such conquests of vertical space, arm-reach by arm-reach, woke in him again.

He crawled out at last from the shadow of the chimney into the hot sun of the ledge above him and lay there, panting. After a moment a small breeze came by and chilled him pleasantly. His breathing slowed. He looked around for the needle gun, saw it lying within reach of his left arm and pulled it to him, sitting up.

There was a complete silence around him. He might have been alone in the mountains. For a moment a small finger of panic touched him, the thought that he had taken too much time coming up the chimney and the attackers might already have control of the Command. Then he put the feeling aside. Unprofitable emotion. He could hear the dry voice of Malachi, lecturing now in his memory.

He stood up, lifting the needle rifle with him. His breathing was almost normal again. He began to run, noiselessly, on the carpet of pine needles deep on this upper ledge, in the direction that would place him above the Command, strung out on the lower ridge.

His ears were tuned for any sounds from ahead as he went. After only a short distance, he heard voices and paused to listen. There were three speakers, just beyond a small clump of trees just ahead. He cut to his left up the slope and went on more slowly and even more silently. After a moment he was able to look down into the area beyond the tree clump. He saw three men there with cone rifles, wearing the same black uniforms he had seen on the Militia guards in Citadel.

Automatically, the needle gun in his hands came up into firing position. They were less than twenty meters from him, in clear view, with their backs to him. *Patience*, said the remembered voice of Malachi silently in his ear. He dropped the weapon again to arm's-length and continued moving, parallel to the upper ridge and above it.

He passed two more groups of three men with cone rifles before he came to one with four men seated with their rifles, peering down the slope and occasionally firing, while a thin man with the broad white bar of a Captain's chevron sewed slantwise on the left arm of his battle-jacket stood over them, his back, like theirs, to Hal.

There was an air of relaxation and confidence about the Militiamen that made Hal uneasy. He tried to see over the edge of the ridge to the Command below, but could not. Quietly, he turned and climbed higher on the slope and finally was able to see the line of animals and baggage along the path of the lower ridge. No people were visible at all; and he thought that they had sensibly all taken cover below the edge of the ridge, when he remembered the continued firing of the men he had passed and those just below him.

He shaded his eyes against the brightness of the sky – and for the first time was able to make out movement on the mountainside above the lower ridge. A number of those in the Command were working their way from one point of cover to another, up the slope in an attack upon their attackers; and as he watched he focused in on the movement of one slim, dark-clad figure in particular and realized that it was Rukh herself who was leading them.

It was a desperate response on the part of the Command. The Militiamen could sit and take their time about picking off the climbers as they momentarily exposed themselves; while the Command members were not only under extreme difficulty in firing back, but were being exhausted by the climb. Nonetheless they came on, and suddenly Hal realized what Rukh must have in mind.

He looked to his left, along that part of the upper ridge he had not yet observed, and saw that, a short distance beyond, it tilted abruptly downward, as if aiming itself at a joining with the lower ridge, but thinning out to plain mountainside some fifty meters from that meeting. He stared at this part of the mountainside for some moments before he was able to pick out, among the sparse trees of its slope, the movements he was looking for. But at last he found them. Rukh's frontal assault up the slope directly above her was obviously intended primarily to hold the attention of the Militia while she sent another force around the front end of the upper ridge to attack that way.

It was the only response possible to her; and with that thought, Hal turned sharply back to look down at the standing Militiaman with the white chevron on his sleeve. This Captain must be the Militia officer in charge; and he would be ineffective in the extreme if he had set up this ambush without giving some thought to his left flank.

Hal turned and began to move onward, above that left flank. Shortly, he found himself looking down on a wider spot of the ridge, a slight hollow, fenced with not only a natural stand of trees, but by a rough log barricade, facing in the direction up which Rukh's flank attackers would come. In the hollow were more than twenty of the armed Militiamen, waiting.

Hal squatted on the mountainside above the whole scene, the needle gun across his knees. He felt a tightness in his chest. The only hope he had had for the flank attackers had been destroyed by the sight of those twenty black uniforms. He came back to his position above the four men with the standing officer.

Hal thought for a moment, then went back to his position above the first group he had discovered. Below him as he watched, one of the three raised his rifle, fired; then laughed and pointed. One of the others patted him on the shoulder.

Something old and grim moved in Hal. He sank to his knees, rested the barrel of the needle gun on the half-buried boulder behind which he crouched, and fired three bursts. The needles whispered, lightly as the piping of birds on the mountain air. He lay, listening in the silence that had followed their sound; but there was no reaction from the other Militia positions to indicate that anyone there had heard. He got to his feet again and went softly down the slope.

The forms of the three, when he reached them, lay still in the sunlight. He looked at them, feeling an emptiness in his middle body, like that following some heavy blow or wound, the pain of which was still being held at bay by shock. He gathered up the three cone rifles, carefully, so that their metal parts should not knock noisily together, and carried them with him up the mountainside, high enough so that he could see the slopes up which both attacking groups from the Command were working.

Rukh's group was making slow progress, but the group coming up on the flank was moving swiftly. They should be within point-blank range of the Militiamen waiting in the hollow in another five minutes.

Hal sat down, and took the butt plate off one of the cone rifles to get at the tools in the compartment underneath. Cone rifles were designed to be self-cleaning as they were fired, so that something more than filling the barrels with dirt was called for. He unscrewed the locking gate on the magazine tube underneath the barrel and pried off the last of the cones from the rod of them packed in there. Then, keeping the cone he had pried off, he replaced and rescrewed the locking gate.

He picked up the single cone carefully between thumb and middle finger, being careful not to touch the narrow red rim around the wide upper edge of the cone. The red marked the molding of the propellant, triggered by the rifle's mechanism to drive these self-propelled missiles. Setting the cone gently between his close-held knees, so that the rim touched nothing, he unbreached the firing chamber, opened it, and put the cone into the breach – but facing the rear of the chamber instead of forward into the barrel. Gently, he closed the breach upon it. He performed the same operation with one of the other cone rifles.

Closing the breach of the second rifle, he grinned a trifle bitterly, internally. Some of the Command members, at least, would have a great deal to say, if they knew about his wasting two perfectly good military firearms in this fashion – when they were so short of them. And they would be justified.

He got up, picked up his extra weapons, and moved on until he was at a midpoint above the cliff edge occupied by the other two nests of Militiamen, who were continuing to fire over the edge of the ledge on which they sat, unaware of what he had done to the men in

195

the positions to their right. Here, he built himself a rough barricade of the heavier rocks in the immediate area. Then, kneeling behind this barricade, he took aim at the three black-clad figures in the second nest.

The soft piping of the needles that had cut down the three in the first group had not carried to alarm their fellow soldiers. But the heavier whistlings of the cones Hal now fired brought further heads around to stare in the direction of the second nest, even as the three there fell.

They were not looking up at the slope above them, having no immediate reason to think that whoever had fired from so close was not one of the attackers from the Command who had just achieved the level of the upper ridge. In a second they might think to look up as well as sideways, but in that moment Hal got to his feet; and, swinging the first of the rigged cone rifles around his head, he sent it wheeling to drop into the last manned nest to the right of the one with the Captain, following it with the other rifle among the four men in the other nest, just as the officer was stepping out of it to go in the direction from which he had plainly assumed Hal must be firing.

The first cone rifle hit and the jar set off the reversed cone in its breach. There was the soft *whump* of an explosion and an upward flare of flame as the heat and shock of the reversed cone trying to get out of the breach the wrong way set off the rod of other cones in the magazine – followed by another explosion, which was the second cone rifle, a moment later in the nest from which the officer had just stepped.

For less than a minute dust and air-borne debris hid the scene in both nests, and then the gentle mountain breeze blew it aside to show all the human figures in both nests fallen. Either the shock of the explosion or the shrapnel from the exploding rifles had put them, at least temporarily, out of the fight.

Hal's aim had been to attract the attention of the Militia in the hollow away from the attackers coming up the slope. Following the two explosions there was a moment of appalled silence on the upper ridge and then a babble of shouting voices. Some, at least, of the watchers in the hollow began to run back toward the center of the Militia line. Hastily, Hal went sliding down the slope from the position of his exposed barricade. If he had been seen up there, the small rock shield he had built would have been useful. But since he had not been, there was more safety for him, now, below among the trees and vegetation of the upper slope.

The Militiamen hurrying back from the hollow could not see his descent, but they heard him. Shouts went up – and were echoed unexpectedly by those still in the hollow. The attackers from the Command coming up the ridge had reached the defenders at the tree-trunk barricade.

Lying flat behind a tree on the lower ridge, less than ten meters from the officer who had fallen – and who was now beginning to stir again – outside his nest, Hal traded shots with those Militia who had come back toward him following the explosions.

The cone rifle was warm against his cheek, warm from the sunlight through the trees upon it, as he watched through its sights for movement among the trees before him. The movements became less frequent. The shots coming back at him diminished, and ceased.

He looked about him. Down the slope from him he caught sight of the Militia officer, now on his feet and swaying uncertainly, but moving back into his command nest, where the cone rifles dropped by his men stood waiting him. Evidently, he had been untouched by the flying metal of the rifle and only knocked unconscious by the explosion shock. Hal's rifle muzzle swung automatically to center on the narrow, upright back of the man, and then revulsion took hold. There was no need for any more killing. He got silently to his own feet and half-ran, half-dove down the intervening slope to catch the officer and slam him to the ground.

The other lay still beneath him. Hal rolled off and sat up. He turned the officer over on his back, and saw that he was still conscious. Hal had simply knocked the wind out of him. For a moment the other struggled to get his breath, then gradually breathing returned. Hal stared down at him, puzzled. The thin face below was familiar. For a moment more it baffled him, then memory connected. The man he was looking at had been the one who escorted him, with Jason, to the session with Ahrens. The same one who had threatened to hang Jason by the wrists for several hours if he continued to talk.

The officer stirred. He looked up at the rifle Hal held covering him, and from there to Hal's face; and his own face was transformed suddenly with a lean smile and a sudden glittering of eyes.

'Thou!' he said. 'I have found thee –'

'So, thou art here!' interrupted a harsh voice, and Child-of-God walked from the trees at their left into the nest, and halted. For the first time Hal realized that the shouting and the whistling of cone rifles had diminished. Child-of-God's dark eyes focused on the weapon in Hal's hand.

'And thou, too, hast captured a cone rifle. Good!' His gaze went to the Militia officer and for a moment, as Hal watched, the two gazed at each other, different by twenty years of age, in bone and muscle and clothing, but in all other ways alike as brothers.

'Save thyself trouble,' said the officer. 'Thou knowest as I know, that I will tell thee nothing, whatever thou choosest to do to me.'

Child-of-God breathed out through his nostrils. His cone rifle's muzzle came around so casually to center on the officer that for a moment Hal did not understand what the movement implied.

'No!' Hal knocked the cone rifle up, off target.

Child-of-God's weathered face came about to stare at him. There was little strong expression to be seen on it at most times; but now Hal thought he read incredulity there.

' "No"?' echoed Child-of-God. 'To me?'

'We don't have to kill him.'

Child-of-God continued to stare. Then he took a deep breath.

'Thou art new to us,' he said, almost quietly. 'Such as these must all be killed, before they kill us. Also, what the apostate says is true –'

'Thou art the apostate – thou, the Abandoned of the Lord!' broke in the Militia officer, harshly. Child-of-God paid no attention. His eyes were still on Hal.

'What the apostate says is true,' he repeated slowly. 'It's useless to question such as he, who was once of the Elect.'

'It is thou who art fallen from the Elect! I am of God and remain of God!'

Still, Child-of-God paid no attention.

'He would tell us nothing, as he says. Perhaps there is another still living, who was never of the Elect. Such we can make speak.'

Child-of-God's muzzle swung back toward the officer.

'No, I tell you!' Hal this time caught hold of the rifle barrel; and Child-of-God, his face plainly registering astonishment, turned sharply to him.

'Thou wilt release my weapon now,' he began slowly, 'or –'

There was only the faintest sound of movement to alert them; but when they turned back the Militia Captain was dodging between the trees. All in one movement, Child-of-God dropped on one knee, swung up the cone rifle and fired. Bark flew whitely from a tree-trunk. Slowly, he lowered the weapon, staring into the pines. He turned back toward Hal.

'Thou has let one of those who has destroyed many go free,' he said. 'Free, if we do not gain him again, to kill more of our people.'

His voice was level but his eyes burned into Hal.

'And, by hindering me, who would have sent him to God's judgment, thou hast made his freedom possible. Decision will have to be made on this.'

CHAPTER TWENTY

Moments later, Rukh and the attackers who had been coming directly up the mountainside at the Militia position emerged on the ridge. The shouting and the whistling of the cones had dwindled and now fell silent. The members of the Command gathered rifles and equipment from the fallen enemy and returned to the ridge below. There were no prisoners. Apparently neither the Militia nor the Commands took prisoners unless there was a need to question them. The officer that had escaped when Hal had distracted Child-of-God's attention was not recaptured. Possibly, thought Hal, some of the other Militia might have made good their escape. The Command had neither the time nor the energy to pursue fugitives.

Fourteen of the donkeys had been killed by the cone rifle fire or were so badly injured that they had to be destroyed. Their loads were distributed among packs on the backs of the members of the Command. When they were ready to move again, only Rukh and Child-of-God were not carrying packs.

There were some three hours of light left before sunset. Carrying their dead and wounded, they travelled only an hour and a half before making camp; but this was enough to bring them considerably down and out of the mountain pass and into a foothill valley very like that in which they had been camped when Hal and Jason had first joined them. As soon as they had set up their shelters, a burial service was held in the red light of the sunset for those who had been killed, followed by the first food of the day since they had broken camp that morning.

After the meal, Hal went to help Jason stake out and care for the donkeys that still remained to them. He was busy at this when Rukh appeared.

'I want to talk to you,' she said to Hal.

She led him away from the camp, up the bank of the small stream by which they had camped, until they were out of earshot of Jason, and therefore of everyone else in camp. As he followed her, he found himself caught up again by the particular awareness she evoked in him; and her difference from everyone else he had ever known. There was a unique quality about her, and it chimed deeply off the metal of his own inner differences. It was not because he and she were alike, he thought now; because they were not. It was that the common factor of individual uniqueness drew them together – or, at least, drew him powerfully to her.

At last she stopped in a small open space by the stream bank and turned to face him. The twilight was still bright enough so that her face appeared to stand out with a strange three-dimensional solidity. It came to him that, if he only had the ability, he would like to carve her in dark metal as she stood now, facing him.

'Howard,' she said, 'you and this Command are going to have to come to terms.'

'The Command?' he said. 'Or Child-of-God?'

'James *is* the Command,' she said, 'just as much as I am and every working member of it is. The Command can't survive if those in it don't follow orders. No one gave you any order to attack the Militia position on your own, with only a needle gun that would hardly shoot.'

'I know,' he said, bleakly. 'I learned about orders, and the need for obedience to them, so early that I can't remember not knowing it. But the same man who taught me those things also taught me that, when necessary, you do what needs to be done.'

'But what made you think you'd have a chance of doing anything, armed like that, and alone?'

'I've told you about myself, how I was raised,' he answered. He hesitated, but it needed to be said. 'I never fired at a living person in my life before today. But you have to face something, you and the Command. I'm probably better trained for something like we've just been through than anyone here, except you or Child-of-God.'

He stopped. She said nothing, only watched him. He saw the black-clad soldiers again in his mind's eye – laughing and firing down on the lower ridge.

'I was operating by reflex, most of the way,' he said. 'But I didn't try anything I didn't know I could do.'

Surprisingly, she nodded.

'All right,' she said. 'But tell me – how did you feel when it was all over? How do you feel now?'

'Sick,' he said, bluntly. 'I was numb for a while, after. But now I just feel sick – sick and exhausted. I'd like to go to bed and sleep for a month.'

'We'd all like sleep,' she said. 'But we don't feel the sort of sickness you feel – any of us, except you. Have you asked your friend Jason how he feels?'

'No,' he said.

She looked at him silently for a long moment.

'I killed my first enemy when I was thirteen,' she said. 'I was with my father's Command when it was wiped out by the Militia. I got away, the way that officer got away from you today. You've never

200

been through that sort of thing. We have. Combat skills alone don't put you above anyone in this camp.'

He looked down at her, feeling strangely adrift in the universe. She should be carved, he thought, not in metal, but in some dark, eternal rock – and he suddenly remembered the image of the rock on the hillside with which he had fought the attempt of Bleys Ahrens to control him, in the detention center.

'I suppose you're right,' he said, at last, emptily. 'Yes . . . you're right.'

'We're what we have to be – first,' she said. 'After that we're what we are, naturally. James is what he was born into – and what he has to be now. You've got to understand both aspects of him. There's no other way if you're going to fit in as a member of this Command. You've got to understand him both as he is, and as he has to be – to be my lieutenant. Can you do that, Howard?'

'Hal,' he corrected her without thinking.

'I think,' she said, 'for all our sakes, I'd better go on calling you Howard.'

'All right.' He breathed deeply. *There is no anger – there is no sadness – there is no corrosive emotion,* he heard Walter the InTeacher saying, once more, in his mind – *where there is understanding.* 'Yes, you're right. I should understand him. So I will try.'

He smiled at her, to reassure her.

'You'll have to succeed,' said Rukh. She relaxed. 'But, all right, now that that's settled – you did a great deal for us, today. If we hadn't had your attack on the right of the Militia line, neither James' party nor mine might have won through. And if we'd failed, the enemy would only have had to come down at its leisure and kill those of the Command who were still alive. There's that, and the fact you helped get us a number of good cone rifles and supplies. Under the circumstances, I'm going to let you trade that needle gun in for one of the rifles we just got.'

He nodded.

'And,' she said, 'I think it's time you knew as much as the rest of the Command about what we're about to do.'

'Jason said to ask you,' he said. 'I thought it was better to wait until you were ready to tell me, yourself.'

'He was right,' Rukh said. 'Briefly, from the point where we are now, on this side of the mountains, we're committed. Down on the interior plains there's more of us in the Commands than there are Militia available to hold us down. So they settle for watching key points as well as their personnel allows. There's dozen routes out of these mountains on to the plains. We had a fifty-fifty chance of being challenged, whichever one we took. But now that we've gotten past one of their patrols, we'll be pretty well left alone, as long as they don't know what we're up to.'

201

'Tell me something,' said Hal. 'I know the lack of heavy technology makes aircraft not easy to come by and expensive as well, out here on the Younger worlds. But surely these Militia must have some spotter planes – light aircraft – that could find us, or at least help find us, from the air, even after we're down on the plains?'

'They do have,' said Rukh. 'But they haven't many. They're machines made of wood and cloth that can't take very rough weather – that's to begin with. And the jealousy between Militia outfits means that a unit that has a plane isn't too eager to lend it out to another unit. Fuel isn't easy to come by. Finally, in any case, even if they get one or more craft into the air looking for us, the plains are heavily treed; and we do our travelling under cover ninety per cent of the time. The other ten per cent of the time, when there is no cover, we move in the dark hours when we can't be seen. You must have noticed that, yourself.'

'I have,' said Hal.

'What this all adds up to, as I say,' Rukh went on, 'is that now, once we've made it past that one patrol, we can expect to be pretty well left alone unless we do something to draw Militia attention to us. Remember, their first responsibility remains to act as government police arm, not only in the country-side but in the cities; and the requirements of the cities in that area draw off most of their personnel.'

'All right,' said Hal. 'I believe you. What's the Command up to, then? You were just going to tell me.'

She hesitated.

'There's a certain limit to how much information I can give you, even now,' she said, frankly. 'The identity of our target, for example, has only been known to a few –'

'On the way to your camp where I first met you,' he said, 'I heard Hilary and Jason saying something about a Core Tap power plant.'

She shook her head, a little wearily.

'I remember now,' she said. 'Jason reported you overhearing that. The point is, Jason himself shouldn't have known. Hilary's different, but Jason . . . well, as long as you know that much you might as well hear all the rest of it.'

She took a deep breath.

'We Commands,' she said, 'are only the spearheads of opposition to those controlled by the Others. We'll be experimenting with the makings we've collected. We'll practice making fulminating mercury out of it; then when we've got the technique worked out, we'll pass the information along to sympathizers like Hilary, who'll make more fulminating mercury with which we'll later fuse and explode the fertilizer. A kilogram of that will set off tons of oil-soaked nitrate fertilizer. We hope to collect the fertilizer itself from a farming area storage plant we'll be raiding on the plains; and it should be enough to destroy the Core Tap the Others are using to power the construction area for interstellar ships on this North Continent.'

'Won't any fertilizer storage plant be in the heart of a town?' Hal asked.

'Not quite in the heart of,' she answered. 'But definitely in town limits. As a distraction, at the same time we attack the plant we'll rob a metals bank in the same town. Our people can use any metal we can get away with, if we can just smuggle it back through the mountains to the coast; but the bank raid's still only a cover operation for the fertilizer raid, not vice-versa. After we've got the fertilizer, we'll set fire to the storage area, and hope the destruction will hide the fact we've taken some of their supply.'

'I see,' said Hal, the back of his mind at work with the necessary tactics of such an operation.

'The local Militia unit,' said Rukh, 'will only chase us until we're out of their district – unless they suspect what we've really been after. If they do that, they may guess we're up to something bigger than a metal robbery; in which case they'll put out the word and all the Militia Districts will be actively hunting us instead of just the one with the fertilizer plant. Which may make collecting our explosive in its finished form a little difficult.'

'I can see that,' he said, quietly.

'But, with a lot of luck, we'll blow up and block the shaft of the Core Tap, then outrun the alarm that'll be raised for us after that, and make it back into the mountains with enough of us still alive to carry on as a separate Command. But if our luck's anything less than good, we won't make it back to the mountains; and if anything goes wrong, we'll be wiped out and fail to wreck the Core Tap.'

'Don't your people in this part of the continent depend on the power from that Tap to farm and live?'

'Yes.' She looked him in the eye. 'But so do the Others depend on it for a spaceship fitting-yard, the only one in this northern hemisphere. If we blow it, they'll have to switch all their plans to use the one on South Continent – which is smaller and logistically less practical.'

'You're paying a very high price just to put a spoke in their wheels, aren't you?' he asked.

'All prices are high,' she said.

The light that had lingered in the sky was going swiftly, now. Over them, a full moon had been above the horizon for a couple of hours already; but in the brighter sky it had been hardly noticeable. Now, the first breath of a night wind moved about them, chilling them lightly. In the dimness Rukh's face was still perfectly visible, but remote, as if the oncoming dark had emphasized her isolation, not only from him but from everyone else in the universe. Deeply moved, suddenly, for reasons he could not explain to himself, on impulse he put a hand on each of her shoulders and bent forward to look down closely into her face. For a second their eyes were only inches apart, and unthinkingly, his arms went around her and he kissed her.

For a split-second he felt her shock and surprise, then a fierce response came, pressing her against him. But a second later she had put her hands on his upper arms and pushed him back from her with a strength that startled him.

She let go of him. In the near-darkness they looked at each other.

'Who are you?' she said, in a hard voice, so low he could hardly hear her.

'You know who I am,' he answered. 'I've told you.'

'No,' she spoke in that same low voice, staring at him, 'you're more than that.'

'If I am,' he said – they were like two people trapped by a spell – 'I don't know it.'

'You know it.'

She stared at him for a moment more.

'No,' she said, at last, 'you really don't know it, do you?'

She stepped back, away from him.

'I can't belong to anyone,' she said; and her voice seemed to come almost from a remote distance. 'I'm a Warrior of the Lord.'

He could think of nothing to say.

'You don't understand?' she said, at last.

He shook his head.

'I'm one of the Elect. Like James,' she said. 'Don't you know what that means?'

'One of my tutors was an Elect – originally,' he said, slowly. 'I understand. It means far more than that. It means you're certain of Heaven.'

'It means you've been chosen by God. I do what I must, not what I want.' Her face was all but lost now in the dimness; and her voice softened. 'Forgive me, Hal.'

'For what?' he said.

'For whatever I did.'

'You didn't do anything.' His voice roughened. 'It's me.'

'Perhaps,' she said. 'But it's also me. Only – as long as I have the responsibility of this Command, I can't have anything else.'

'Yes,' he said.

She reached out and touched his forearm. He could feel the pressure of her fingers and he imagined that he could feel the warmth of her hand, even through the rough thickness of his shirt sleeve.

'Come along,' she said. 'We still have to talk to James, you and I.'

'All right,' he answered. She turned and they went back through the woods, close together but careful not to touch each other.

They found Child in his own single-person shelter near the center of the camp. He was apparently just ready to go to bed; and in the light of the lamp hanging from the main rib of the shelter his face looked deeply lined and much older than Hal had seen it appear, before. At their appearance in the entrance, he got up from the sleeping sack he was spreading out.

'I'll come,' he said.

He stepped out of the shelter and they backed away to let him emerge. Outside, the pinned-back flap of the entrance spilled just enough light into the night so that they could see each other's faces without making them out in any detail.

'James,' said Rukh. 'I've talked to Howard, and I think he understands now what we're up against, out here.'

Child-of-God looked at Hal, but said nothing. Remembering his promise to try to understand the older man, Hal fought back the instinct to bristle that came at the sight of the dark shadow pools that hid the other's eyes, turning in his direction.

'Also, since he's to be credited with helping us gain a number of cone rifles in good condition, I've promised him one of them.'

Child-of-God nodded.

'And I've told him in full what our plans are for the next few weeks.'

'Thou art in command,' Child said. He had turned to face her as she spoke of the rifles. Now the blur that was his face swung back to Hal. 'Howard, I am thy officer. From now on, wilt thou obey?'

'Yes,' said Hal.

He was bone-weary. The other two must be, also. They said nothing more. He looked from Rukh to Child. They stood at three points of a triangle with space between them.

'If that's all, then,' said Hal. 'I'll be getting back to my shelter. Good night.'

'Good night,' said Rukh, from where she stood.

'We are in God's hands,' said Child, unmoving.

Hal turned and went. There was no community fire that night, and once he turned his back to the light the camp was lost in darkness. But it was always laid out the same pattern; and as he moved into the darkness his eyes began to adjust until the moonlight was enough to show him the way. He got back to his shelter and found it with the hanging lamp within on its dimmest setting – a glowworm gleam barely illuminating the cold, curving walls of the shelter, once he was inside.

In his bedsack, Jason slept heavily. Hal undressed in silence, turned off the lamp and crawled into his own sack. He lay on his back staring up into the darkness, trapped between sleep and waking. In his mind's eye he replayed the climb up the chimney, his reconnaissance of the Militia position. He saw again the Militiaman in the first nest being slapped on the back by his comrade, and laughing. He pressed the firing button of the needle gun and saw the three men fall. He threw the rigged cone rifles into the enemy nests. He watched the rifle of Child come around to point at the Militia officer, and again he knocked it aside. . . .

He saw Rukh, turning to face him in the twilight. . . .

He squeezed his eyes shut, willing himself to sleep, but for once his mind and body would not obey. He lay there, and the ghosts of three old men came out of his memory and stood around him in the darkness.

'It was his first time,' Malachi said. 'He needed her.'

'No,' said Walter the InTeacher, 'our deaths were his first time. And there was no one there for him then.'

'When we were killed, it wasn't like this,' said Malachi. 'This time it was his doing. If he's not to go down and down from here until he drowns, he needs help.'

'She cannot help him,' said Obadiah. 'She is at God's will, herself.'

'He'll survive,' said Walter. It was one of those rare occasions when the Exotic was the hardest of the three. 'He'll survive without anyone if he has to, without anything. That part of him was in my care; and I promise you he will survive this, and worse.'

'Unless thou art wrong,' said Obadiah, harshly.

'Unless is not permitted,' said Walter, softly. 'Hal, you're not sleeping only because you're choosing not to sleep. All things, even this, are subject to the mind. What can't be mended has to be put aside until some time when it can, if ever. What did I teach you? Choice is the one thing that can never be taken from you, right down to the moment of the ultimate choice of death. So, if you want to lie awake and suffer, do so; but face the fact that it's something you're choosing to do, not something over which you've got no control.'

Hal opened his eyes and made himself breathe out deeply; and found that he was exhaling through teeth clamped tightly together. He made his jaw muscles relax, but still he lay, staring up into darkness.

'I can't,' he said at last, aloud.

'You can,' said the ghost of Walter, calmly. 'This, and more.'

It was like trying to unclench a fist held tight so long that it had forgotten any other attitude, coupled with the deep fear of what might happen to the hand, once it was open, unarmored by tension and bone. But at last the knot within him unwound. The walls of the small, close room he had come to occupy in his mind fell apart, and the universe opened up around him once more.

He slept.

CHAPTER TWENTY-ONE

In the morning they moved on, and by afternoon they were into rolling, nearly level country squared off into farmlands, the fields black from the fresh tilling of spring. It was like coming on an oasis after some long trek through a desert; and the sense of sorrow and loss that had held the Command nearly silent since the attack of the Militia began to lift. Even those who had been wounded cheered up, raising themselves on their elbows in their litters, slung between pairs of the remaining donkeys. Looking about, they breathed the warmer air of the lowlands, occasionally laughed softly as they talked with those carrying packs and walking beside them, as if they had just come into a kinder and better land.

In fact, as Hal had learned in his studies, years before, this area of Harmony came close to being a rich spot on the two impoverished Friendly Worlds. Here, the soil was black and thick and the farms produced a surplus which went to feed hungry mouths in large nearby cities; cities of a size that otherwise could be supported only on Harmony's continental coasts, with their access to the food sources of the oceans.

As soon as they reached the farmlands proper, the Command began to disintegrate. The wounded were taken into the homes of local farmers, to be nursed back to health; and both the remaining beasts and the healthy Command members were organized into small units which would make their way openly on foot to the rendezvous, near their target of the fertilizer plant, at a small city several hundred kilometers in from the mountains.

Hal found himself separated from Jason and assigned to a group of ten headed up by Child. They had been chosen, as had the other small units the Command was now divided into, with an eye to giving the appearance of a single large family, with the ages of its members ranging from grandfather to grown grandchildren. The farms of the central North Continent of Harmony were farmed with donkey and human power alone; and the cultural pattern of the farmers was one of large, compound families, in which sons and daughters married and brought their new mates home so that groups of twenty to sixty people living on a single farm were not unusual.

When such families, or portions of them, travelled they had the appearance of a small clan on the road; and consequently the ten Command members with Child as their family elder were not conspicuous when at last they set out. Dressed in jackets and slacks or skirts of gray, dark blue or black, with white shirts, string ties and black berets, all furnished by local partisan farmers they had encountered, the ten could not be told from ordinary travellers on these interior roads.

With the change of scene, Hal found a change of attitude taking him over. Walking the roads, lifting his beret with the others when they encountered another family group walking in the opposite direction, he discovered that with the change he had both gained and lost something. As the fields and houses had closed about him, the wide-ranging sense of freedom he had sensed in the mountains was gone. He was held close again – not as close as he had felt himself held on Coby, but close enough so that his mind seemed once more on a leash.

The urge to write poetry had once more left him. In its place was an urgency and a responsibility he was not yet able to define. In an odd way, it was as if he had been on vacation when they were in the mountains, and now he was back at work in a universe where the practical aspects of life had to be considered.

The militia attack in the pass, the intimate moment with Rukh and the encounter with Child that had preceded it had made him look again at what was around him. He had become closer to these people – all of them, even in this short time, than he had to those on Coby – even including Sost and Tonina and John Heikkila. It was not just that they had fought the Militia together. These in the Command had a dedication and a purpose that echoed to some urge to dedication and purpose in him. In the long run, on Coby, he had needed Tonina, Sost and John, but they had no real need of him. It was as if he had taken a step closer to the whole human race, here on Harmony. At the same time he was even more aware of the distance separating him from each of them. He found he wanted Rukh desperately and at the same time he did not see how he could ever have her. Also, he was unhappy about Child-of-God. The older man was cut of the same cloth as Obadiah had been; and Hal had loved Obadiah. He should, he thought, be able to at least like Child. He wanted to like Child; and he found he did not.

It was more than a simple desire in him to like the older man. As Obadiah had, Child personified the very heart and core of the Friendly Splinter Culture. Hal responded to the Friendlies, as he had also responded to the Exotic and Dorsai Splinter Cultures. Responded to and felt sad for, because Walter had taught him that, in the long run, all three must disappear.

But still he could not bring himself to like or admire Child. Looked at dispassionately, the other seemed to be little more than an opinionated, unyielding individual with no virtues in him beyond his military skills and the fact that chance had placed him in opposition to the Others, and therefore on the same side as Hal himself in the conflict.

And that brought another matter to mind. He could not simply continue to run blindly as one of Rukh's Command, with the hope of always keeping out of the Others' way. There had to be more to life than that. He needed to make some kind of long range plans. But what plans? He was deep in thought about this for perhaps the hundredth time when an unexpected hail brought him out of it.

It was the end of the third day since they had started out to tramp the road in their small group on their way to rendezvous. They had just topped the crest of a small hill and were headed down into a hollow of land perhaps five kilometers across, filled with the familiar plowed fields and several widely-separated farmhouse complexes surrounded by trees planted for windbreak. Coming toward them up the slope of the road from the nearest of these building clumps was a round-bodied man of close to Child's age, waving and calling to them.

They met him a minute or so later and stopped to talk. His face was rosy with the effort of the fast walk; and he took off his beret, fanning himself with it as he spoke.

'You're Child-of-God and these are the soldiers of the Lord from Rukh Tamani's Command? We just got word you were coming. Will you stop at my farm tonight? It'd be a pleasure under the hand of the Lord to have you; and I've wanted to talk to someone from one of the Commands for some time.'

'We thank God who sent thee,' said Child. 'We will be thy guests.'

His harsh voice made his words on the soft, late afternoon air more like a command than a polite acceptance; but the farmer did not seem offended. He fanned himself twice more and put the beret back on his head.

'Come along,' he said; and he led the way down the slope, talking with Child as he went, unquenched by the short, sharp answers he got in reply.

The farm he led them to was clearly one housing a larger than usual family. The living quarters consisted of at least a dozen interconnected buildings. As they walked into the central yard of this complex, enclosed on three sides by the buildings, thin notes of what sounded like some sort of recorder or flute came from the open doorway of the largest building, to which they were heading.

'Forgive me!' said their host.

He darted ahead, into the dark rectangle of the doorway. The sound of the notes cut off abruptly, and in a moment he was back outside, his face rosy again, as he confronted them where they had stopped.

'I'm sorry.' He spoke again, this time particularly to Child. 'These children – but he's a good boy. He just doesn't realize . . . please excuse it.'

'Praise not the Lord with instruments and other idle toys, for He Himself is not idle, neither will He suffer the same before Him,' said Child, grimly.

'I know, I know. It's the times . . . things are changing so fast, and they don't understand. But come in, come in!'

They followed him into a large, airy room, dark after the still-bright day outside. As Hal's eyes adjusted, he saw a number of chairs and benches scattered around a room with a highly-polished wooden floor and an enormous fireplace at one end of it. An opening in the end opposite the fireplace showed another room, long rather than wide, with a table running the length of it that looked as if it could seat half a hundred people.

'Sit down, sit down,' said their host. 'Excuse me, I should introduce myself. My name's Godlun Amjak; and this is my household. Elder Child-of-God, will you do us the honor of speaking to us at evening service in a few minutes?'

'I am no Elder, nor have I ever sought to be. I am a Warrior of God, and that is sufficient,' said Child. 'Yes, I will speak.'

'Thank you.'

'Thank thy God and mine, rather.'

'Of course, of course. I do. I thank God. You're quite right.'

Younger men and women in the customary dress, white above and dark below, were coming shyly into the room, bringing pitchers of cold water and plates of small dark cakes. Child refused cake but accepted the water. They sat for a short time with food and drink, and then were led back through the house and into a rectangular interior courtyard with a stone floor and white-painted walls, unadorned except for the thin black cross as tall as Hal himself, painted on one of the end walls. In front of the cross was a small platform of dark wood and lectern before it; with, however, nothing on the lectern.

The yard was already full of people – obviously the members of the household of Godlun Amjak standing in two ranked and ordered groups on either side of a central aisle-space. Godlun led the ten from the Command down this aisle to a space which had been left for them in front of the right-hand group and only a few steps from the cross and the lectern. Once they were placed, Godlun mounted the platform and looked down at all of them. The courtyard was deep in shadow from the buildings surrounding it; but in contrast the visible patch of sky above them was still a startlingly bright blue without clouds.

There was a moment's hush, as if everyone in the courtyard was holding his breath. Then Godlun spoke.

'We are privileged before the Lord,' he said, 'in that we have as our guests ten Warriors of God, one of whom is an officer, from the Command of Rukh Tamani. These are those who combat the limbs and demons of Satan himself, the Other People, and their minions – those who would teach us to put our faith and our Lord in second place to them. We are further privileged in that the officer of whom I spoke, Child-of-God, will speak to us at this time of worship. It is a great honor for our family and we will remember it as long as the family lasts.'

He got down from the platform and looked at Child, who left the first row of worshippers and came to the platform. His lean face looked down at them all; and his voice rang out like clashed iron over their heads.

' " . . . And I saw three unclean spirits like frogs come out of the mouth of the dragon, and out of the mouth of the beast, and out of the mouth of the false prophet.

' "For they are the spirits of devils, working miracles, which go forth unto the kings of the earth and of the whole world, to gather them to the battle of that great day of God Almighty. . . ." ' *

He broke off, looking at them all.

'Ye know that passage from the Book of Revelations?'

'We know.' The soft chorus was unanimous from the listeners standing around Hal.

' "And he gathered them together into a place called in the Hebrew tongue Armageddon." ' He paused again.

'Ye also know,' he said, 'that that beast and that false prophet, whose coming was foretold in Revelations, are now among us. Think not that to thou, and thou, and thou, their presence maketh a difference; because to one who testifies for the Living God there is never a difference from that which always was and always will be. There is only one day, the Day of the Lord's; and what hour of that day it is, is of no matter to ye who are known to Him, or chosen to be His servants. Other than such as ye, there are only those who will be cast out in the final hour. But among those not to be cast out, none of ye need ask – "What is the hour and the moment in which I will testify for my God?" For all who serve the Lord will be called upon to testify and it matters not when.'

He paused once more, this time for so long a moment that Hal began to think that he was done and about to step down from the lectern. But he went on.

'Nor does the manner of that testifying matter. Especially wrong is he who hopes that his testimony will be easily given, and he who dreams of a martyr's testimony. It is not the manner of giving but the giving itself, that matters. Remember that for thee, by night or day, waking or sleeping, alone or in the sight of multitudes, when thy testimony is required, only one thing is important and that is whether thou givest it or not. For he who is part of the Living God cannot fail to lift the banner of his faith in that moment; and he who is not will have no strength to do so.'

There was a little sigh from the audience, so faint that it was just barely audible to Hal's ears.

'All are doomed who are not of the Lord. But those who testify do not do so only that they may exist eternally. For thy duty to thy God and His works is beyond thyself. If the Lord should come to thee before the moment of thy testifying and say, "Servant and warrior of mine art thou. But yet for my purposes, thou shalt be cast out with those others who know me not" – then, only if thou art truly of the faith will you answer correctly – "if it be thy will, Lord, so be it. *For that I testify is all I ask . . ."* '

His voice had dropped on the last sentence almost to a whisper, but it was a whisper that reached every wall of the courtyard.

' "For Thou my Lord hast been with me all my days and will be with me forever, nor can that which Thou art be taken from me –" ' and once more, for three words, his voice dropped to that hoarse, penetrating nearwhisper – ' "*Even by Thee*, my God. For as Thou art in me, so am I in Thee, forever and ever, beyond all time and universes; for Thou wert before those things and will be after them; and with Thy people may not be slain, but shall live beyond eternity." '

He stopped speaking, at the last so quietly and so naturally that not only Hal, but the rest of those listening, were unprepared for the fact that he was finished. It was only when he stepped down from the lectern and returned to his place in the front ranks of those standing that they all realized it was over. Godlun went forward, stepped up and turned to face them.

'We will sing *Soldier, Ask Not*,' he said.

They began to sing, without accompaniment but with the harmonious blending of voices long used to sounding together, and Hal sang with them; for this – originally a military hymn of the Friendly mercenary forces drafted to fight on other worlds – was one of those he had learned from Obadiah so early that he could not remember a time when he did not know it.

> *Soldier, ask not – now, or ever –*
> *Where to war your banners go . . .'*

They sang it to the end, standing there quietly in their ordinary, everyday clothes, with the peaceful walls of their home buildings surrounding them; and when they were done Godlun stepped down from the platform. The evening service was over; and above them the sky, still cloudless, had darkened with the fading of the light to a deep, cobalt blue in which it was still too early to see the pinprick lights of the stars.

'Come with me,' Godlun said to Child; and led his guests back inside to seat them in the chairs by the top end of the long dining table. His own seat was the one of two at the very end itself. The other seat remained empty.

'My wife, Meah,' he said to Child, in the first chair at his right, once they were all seated. He nodded his head toward the empty chair as if introducing a ghost to the other man.

'May the Lord keep her always,' said Child.

'In His hands,' said Godlun. 'It's sixteen years now since her death. This large house where we all meet was planned by her.'

Child nodded again, but said nothing.

'You are not married?' Godlun asked him.

'My wife and I lived under God's blessing for two years and five days,' said Child, 'before she was killed by Militia.'

Godlun stared at him and blinked.

'How terrible!'

'God chose it so.'

Godlun turned abruptly to shout back over his shoulder through a farther doorway from which came the noise and odors of a kitchen.

'Come now! Hurry, hurry!'

With that, the adult members of the family flooded in to fill the rest of the seats at the table as far as seats still remained available; and others of them appeared with burdened serving trays from the kitchen.

The meal was remarkable. Hal counted over fifteen separate dishes. Even in comparison with the way they had been fed by the other farm families that had entertained them since they had come down out of the mountains, this was a banquet. Godlun was evidently exerting himself and his resources to the utmost. In particular, there were an unusual number of vegetable dishes prepared in accordance with the strictures that governed what someone like Child-of-God might allow himself to eat. Hal had never seen the older man dine so heartily; and it had the effect of making him unusually sociable. He answered Godlun's questions at greater and greater length; until, at last, when they had all moved to the large sitting room and the two were sitting together, close to the fireplace, painted by the light of the flames of the blaze there that had been raised against the chill of the spring evening, Child was all but conducting a monologue, with only an occasional question from Godlun thrown in from time to time.

'. . . There is no doubt,' he was telling the farmer, 'that the numbers of the Militia grow daily as the ranks of those seduced by the Belial-spawn increase. This is fact we must face; and it is as God wills.'

'But . . .' Godlun hesitated. 'You yourself – you have hope.'

'Hope?' In the firelight the time-carved, lean face of Child stared into the round, anxious one of the other man.

'Hope that eventually the Militia and all other hounds of the Belial-spawn must be conquered, and cleansed from our world.'

213

'It's not my duty to hope,' said Child. 'What is, is what God wills.'

'But He can't will that all we've built here over generations, and on Association as well, should be conquered by such as these? That our churches should be closed, our worshipping voices be silenced and all that we've done go down to dust?' said Godlun.

'Knowest thou the will of the Lord?' said Child. 'It may be just that which is his wish; and if so, who are we to question? Only an hour since did I not hear thee sing with me – *Soldier, ask not, now or ever, where to war your banners go!*'

Godlun shook his head slowly.

'I can't believe He would –'

'Thou art concerned for thy children, and for thy children's children,' said Child, less harshly. 'But remember that even these are not thine. They are only lent thee for a little while by the Lord; and He will use them as He requires.'

'But things aren't that bad,' said Godlun. 'The Militia are a trouble to us, yes; and it's true that, in the cities, those who fawn on the Others have things their own way. But the core of our land, our people and our religion, continues here in the countryside, untouched. We –'

'In thy small corner, thou wouldst say, there is still peace,' interrupted Child. 'But look beyond that corner. When thou art wanted, when thy children and thy fields are desired for purposes of the Others, will they not come and take all these, too, from thee, at their whim? Look not merely at the cities of this world, but at all the cities on all worlds. Everywhere the Belial-spawn move almost without check or hindrance. Those of us who are strong in the Faith they cannot touch; but almost all others see them once, and ever after pant at their heels, following without question for one pat on the head, one word of praise from these, their new, false and painted idols. The beast and the false prophet of which Revelation speaks are already among us, gathering their forces for Armageddon across the face of all the worlds.'

'But God will conquer when Armageddon comes!'

'In His own way.'

Godlun shook his head, and looked away, helplessly into the fire.

'I don't believe this,' he said, low-voiced, to the flames. 'I've heard many say this, but I couldn't believe it; and that was why I had to talk to someone like you. How can you, who've given your life to fighting His enemies, talk as if the final battle might be lost?'

'Man of plows and peace,' said Child, almost sadly, 'look outward at the universe. The battle you talk of is already lost. The times are already changed. Even if these whom God has cursed were to be swept away tomorrow, still the old ways are already gone, and not by their doing – but by ours. All the centuries since Mankind first had life breathed into him are coming now to their end, and all that has been built is crumbling. Did not I hear the lascivious and idle sound of a musical instrument in thy own house, as I came up? Yet, he who played – whoever that may be – is still beneath thy roof. He was without doubt at worship with the rest of us, an hour since. If thy own household be so fallen into the gutters and alleyways of sin, how canst thou hope for the redemption of the worlds of men, when within thy own walls there is none?'

Godlun raised his head from the flames and stared at Child. The tendons in his throat moved and stood out, but he made only a small sound that was not even a word.

'Nay,' said Child, with real gentleness. 'Who am I to blame thee? I only show thee what is. For thousands of years the Earth endured as the cradle of God's children, until it came upon evil ways with the luxury of many tools and instruments. Then might the end have come, at that time. But God gave Man one more chance, and opened these further worlds to him. And all went out, each together with those he thought of as his or her own kind, and tried to build again as they thought best, under different suns. But out of all those efforts were made only three peoples which had never been before; we of Faith, those we called the Deniers of God but who call themselves the Exotics, and those of War known as the Dorsai. And, as time hath shown, none of these were God's answer, however much they might be their own; and from their failure has now come these of mixed breeding whom we call the Others, who would make all the worlds their pleasure garden and all other men and women into slaves. Canst thou look at all this and not see that once more we have thrown away the chance given us; so that nothing now remains but for Him to let us reap the harvest we have sowed; and for all who call themselves Mankind to go down finally into darkness and silence, forever?'

Godlun stared at him.

'But you keep fighting!'

'Of course!' said Child. 'I am of God, whatever or whoever else is not. I must testify to Him by placing my body against the enemy while that body lasts; and by protecting those that my small strength may protect, until my personal end. What is it to me that all the peoples of all the worlds choose to march toward the nether pit? What they do in their sins is no concern of mine. Mine only is concern for God, and the way of God's people of whom I am one. In the end, all those who march pitward will be forgotten; but I and those like me who have lived their faith will be remembered by the Lord – other than that I want nothing and I need nothing.'

Godlun dropped his face into his hands and sat for a moment. When he took his hands away again and raised his head, Hal saw that the skin of his face was drawn and he looked very old.

'It's all right for you,' he whispered.

'It is fleshly loves that concern thee,' said Child, nearly as softly. 'I know, for I remember how it was in the little time I had with my wife; and I remember the children unborn that she and I dreamed of together. It is thy children thou wouldst protect in these dark days to come; and it was thy hope that I could give you reason to think thou couldst do so. But I have no such hope to give. All that thou lovest will perish. The Others will make a foul garden of the worlds of humankind and there will be none to stop them. Turn thee to God, my brother, for nowhere else shalt thou find comfort.'

CHAPTER TWENTY-TWO

Sometime in the depths of that night following the dinner, Hal awoke in the long room that had been given the visitors for a dormitory; and, looking down the double row of mattresses with their sleeping forms, decorated by the lozenges of illumination from the moonlight shining through the uncurtained windows, saw all quiet and still.

He rose on his elbow, troubled by the feeling of uneasiness with which he had wakened, but unable to account for it. Then from a distance came a small, repeated sound that gave his mind no picture of what could be causing it. It came from outside the room, through the open windows at the far end. He got up, walked on unshod feet to the end of the nearest of the open windows and looked out. In the courtyard below him where the service had been held, he saw a man's figure, black in the moonlight, seated on one of the benches with its shoulders hunched. As he watched, the shoulders shook, the right hand of the figure went up to the mouth and the sound came again, recognizable now as coughing. With that recognition, his mind identified the familiar shape of the figure; and he did not have to look back into the room behind him to see what mattress lay under empty covers.

The man down there was Child-of-God. Hal stood watching while two more of the paroxysms of coughing shook the figure, then turned and went back to his own bed. Child-of-God did not come back to the room as long as he lay awake, watching; and after a while, Hal fell asleep once more.

They were on their way the next morning while dawn was still red in the east. Godlun's entire household turned out to see them off and fill their packs with cold foods packaged by the kitchen to see them through until evening and the next family that would put them up for a night. The leavetakings they had been engaged in with members of the family had been as warm as if they had been members of the family itself.

Once on the road, Child took the lead as usual without a word. Watching the older man, Hal could not see anything in the leathery face and swift stride of the older man that might indicate a cause for the moonlit fit of coughing in the courtyard the night before. But he found himself studying Rukh's lieutenant with reawakened interest.

By day, Child showed no sign of weakness or illness. He led them at a steady pace through the next few weeks; and it was not until five days later that Hal, waking in the night, discovered the older man missing once more from the sleeping room assigned to them at that night's farm. Looking outside, Hal once more discovered Child seated like someone waiting out a bout of pain, and occasionally breaking into coughing.

Hal probed the rest of their group with cautious questions; but evidently none of the others had ever heard or seen Child on one of these nighttime excursions; and any suggestion that the Command's Second Officer might be ill was met with the light-hearted belief that he was made of metal and leather and no weakness would dare attack him.

They finally reached their rendezvous. It was the Mohler-Beni farm, a large place operated jointly by two separate families, so that a good hundred and twenty-odd people were normally in residence and the coming and going of the additional near two hundred of the reunited Command would not attract as much attention as their activity would on one of the farms of more average size. They were less than thirty kilometers from Masenvale, the small city that held the metals-storage unit and the fertilizer plant that were their targets.

The group containing Hal and Child was the last to arrive. It was at the end of an unusually warm summer day and after they had stowed their gear in one of the large equipment sheds which were being used as barracks for them, the fresh cool of the evening breeze was pleasant as Hal walked with the others to a late meal in the farm's main kitchen.

After the dinner, Rukh collected not only Child, but Hal, and took them off to her private room in the farmhouse – a guest bedroom now cluttered with papers and supplies.

'Howard,' Rukh said to Hal, once she had shut the door of the room firmly behind them, 'I'm asking you here now, not to discuss plans with James and myself, but to act as a source of information from that early military training of yours.'

Hal nodded.

'Come over here to the map, both of you,' she said.

They followed her to a table set up in front of an open window, the large-scale local map on it anchored with fist-sized polished stones against the newly-awakened evening breeze. There was a moistness and electricity in the air that promised a thunderstorm.

'James, I've just got word from our friends in Masenvale,' she said. 'They've promised at least half a dozen fires and the setting off of burglar alarms in four businesses on the south side to divert local police and Militia away from our targets. We're bound to run into some district police forces at the fertilizer plants, but with any luck the fires and alarms, to start with, and after that the raid by the group you'll be with, Howard, on the metals unit, should keep our opposition at the plant from being reinforced until we've loaded up and gone.'

She turned to the table.

'Now, look here,' she said.

'Here's the Mohler-Beni farm.' Rukh put her finger down on the lower half of the map. 'Almost due southwest is Masenvale with the fertilizer plant on the outskirts, on a direct line between us, here, and the center of the city, where the metals-storage is located. South-southwest . . .' her finger traced a line on the map around and beyond the city area, 'are the foothills of the Aldos mountain range, which is the territory we'll be running for, after we've got the fertilizer –'

She broke off, for the sound of heavy air-cushion vehicles had intruded through the open window upon the conversation. She sighed, relaxing a little; and Hal looked at her, sharply. It was not usual for her to show any sign of emotion, even when gaining something like the transport that was now arriving, and which had been critical to the success of her plans.

'The trucks,' she said.

They had been sweating out the arrival of these vehicles from farmers in the neighborhood well enough off to own them, and committed enough to the Command to risk them in an endeavor like the one Rukh was to lead tomorrow. The raids on the fertilizer plant and on the metals-storage building would have been literally impossible without transport; and there had been, until this moment, no absolute certainty that enough would be volunteered. Now, judging by the sounds that continued to come in the open window, the trucks had appeared in numbers that would be more than adequate to the needs of the Command. Rukh turned back to her map.

'With those here now, and any luck at all,' she said, 'we should be into the back roads of the foothills before the Militia can put any force worth worrying about out after us; and once in the foothills, we can leave them to their regular drivers, off-load the donkeys and lose any pursuit without much trouble –'

'What about the drivers, when the Militia catches them?' Hal asked.

Rukh looked levelly at him.

'I said you weren't here to be involved in the discussion, but only to act as an information source,' she said. 'However – as soon as they let us off, the drivers will split up, each going his own way along the back roads and trails, or even overland. With their trucks empty, there'll be nothing to charge the drivers with; and not even the Militia's going to be heavy-handed about questioning local people unless they've got some evidence. The Others know how necessary

219

this farm belt is to the survival of North Continent, to say nothing of the rest of Harmony. That's why they've let the people in this mid-plains area go so free of the restrictions they've placed on people elsewhere.'

The sound of the incoming trucks outside ceased.

'They are fat here, with the fat that comes from laziness of soul,' said Child. 'Though there are those of faith among them.'

'In any case,' said Rukh, 'I've answered your question, Howard. Don't interrupt again. Look at the Aldos range, on the map, please, both of you. It runs south and east. I think we can follow along it in reasonable safety until we come to the general vicinity of Ahruma, where the Core Tap is, and the energy complex built around it. We'll have to leave the foothills then for the open plain to reach Ahruma; but it's within striking distance. We should be able to make the run to it in a couple of hours, going in, and in another couple, coming out after we've sabotaged the Tap. For that, of course, we'll need trucks again and reinforcements from the local people there – will you shut that window, Howard? They're getting noisy out there.'

Hal moved to shut the window, catching sight as he turned of Child's face, which was stiff and angry, staring at the open window. As Hal's hands touched the hasp fastened to the lower edge of the top-pivoted window, there broke out, over the babble of voices outside, the unexpected wheezy sound of some instrument like a concertina or an accordion. Hal pulled the window closed in the same instant; and, turning, saw Child heading out the door of Rukh's room.

'James –' began Rukh sharply. But her lieutenant was already gone, the door closing behind him. She gave a short, exasperated breath, then straightened and turned back to Hal.

'While I have the chance,' said Hal, swiftly, before she could send him also out of the room, 'can I ask you – is he ill?'

She stood, arrested, one hand still on the map.

'Ill?' she said. 'James?'

'On the way here I got the idea he might be,' Hal said, apologetically. As she stood listening, he told her what he had seen of Child's nocturnal coughing fits. When he was done, she looked at him almost coldly for a few seconds before answering.

'Have you told anyone else about his?' she asked.

'No,' said Hal.

Some of the tension went out of the way she stood.

'Good,' she said. She considered him for a moment. When she spoke again, her voice was flat.

'He's old,' she said, 'too old for this sort of life; and he's driven himself beyond his physical limits since he was a boy. There's no stopping him. His only aim is to use himself up in the service of the Lord in the way he thinks best; and we'd be doing him no kindness to interfere with his doing it.'

'That coughing's just age?' asked Hal.

Her eyes were level and dark on him.

'That coughing comes from fluid seeping into his lungs when he lies flat too long,' she said. 'His heart's worn out; and his body's wearing out. There's nothing to be done for him as long as he goes on putting himself through this like a younger man, and he won't consider stopping. Also – we need him. Moreover his life's the Lord's, first; his own, second; and only after that, anyone else's to dictate.'

'I see,' said Hal. 'But –'

He was interrupted by sudden silence outside as the music broke off, followed by the distant, harsh and angry voice of Child, so blurred by distance and the resonances from surrounding structures that it was impossible to make out what he was saying.

'What if the Command gets into a situation where it's dependent upon his being well enough to do what he'd ordinarily do –' Having begun once more, he broke off again, seeing she was not listening to him but to the sounds from outside. He stood watching her, for a moment, like some unseen observer.

'Read all signals,' Walter the InTeacher had told him, 'not merely what the eyes, the ears and the nose pick up, but what you can read of gestalt patterns of response in those around you. Situations in which you lack experience may be interpretable through observation of those you are with at the time. Learn to read, therefore, at second hand. Animals and children do this all the time. We all know how to do this, instinctively; but habits and patterns of the mature and conscious mind lead us away from it.'

What Hal read now in the attitude of Rukh was an interpretation of the noise outside as a cause of unusual uneasiness – for reasons he himself could not find. But it did not matter that he could not, for in this case it was enough to see the understanding of Rukh.

Abruptly, though there was no difference in Child's voice that Hal could hear, the uneasiness in Rukh changed to alarm – and decision. Without warning she suddenly swung about and headed out the door. He followed.

They came out together into the wide side-yard of the farm, on to a nighttime scene lit by the overhead lights of the buildings surrounding three sides of it. A long row of large, van-type produce trucks were parked along one side of the yard and before these were gathered a number of the younger people of the Command and almost an equal number of young men in local farm clothes, evidently those who had brought the trucks.

They were gathered about one of the truck drivers, who carried an obviously homemade accordion slung by a wide strap over one shoulder. But the accordion was silent; the people there were all silent, except for Child, who addressed them all and had all their eyes upon him. Now that he could see the faces of those here, Hal understood Rukh's reaction, for the expressions of the Command members were embarrassed, and the expressions of the truck drivers ranged from sullenness to open anger.

With the appearance of Rukh, Child fell silent also.

'What's going on here?' she asked.

'Dancing!' he spat out. 'As Whores of Babylon –'

'James!' Rukh's voice snapped. He stopped speaking. She looked over the others, her gaze ending at last on the truck drivers who had drawn closer to each other in a ragged group around the man with the musical instrument.

'This is not a holiday,' she said, clearly, 'or a children's game; no matter what your community here allows you to do. Is that understood by all of you who've volunteered to help us?'

There was a shuffling silence among the truck drivers. The one with the accordion, a broad-chested individual with tightly curled brown hair, shrugged the strap of it off his shoulder, and – catching the strap with his hand – lowered the instrument until it sat on the ground at his feet.

'All right, then,' said Rukh, when there was no further answer. 'You drivers go and stand by your individual trucks. Our Command members have already been organized into truck teams. We'll begin counting from this end of the row of vehicles and the Number One team for the fertilizer plant will use that truck; Number Two, the next, and so on until all the teams for the fertilizer plant are assigned to trucks. Then the Number One team for the valuable-metals raid will take the first succeeding truck, and so on, down the line. Teams get together with your drivers now. I want you to know him, and him to know you, by sight.'

She started to turn away.

'James, Howard!' she said to them. 'Come back upstairs with me and we'll finish what we were doing –'

'Wait a minute!'

It was the voice of the accordionist, interrupting her. She turned back to face the crowd; and the local man, leaving his instrument on the ground, came forward toward her and Hal. The other locals edged after him.

'Him,' said the accordionist, when he stood within arm's length of her, looking past her at Hal. 'He's the one they're looking for, isn't he? If he is, hadn't we ought to be told about that?'

'What are you talking about?' said Rukh.

'This one,' the accordionist pointed to Hal, meeting Hal's eyes squarely. 'Isn't he the one all the fuss is about? And if he is, what's he doing coming along on something like this, when just having him with us can be dangerous?'

'I'll give you one more chance to explain yourself,' said Rukh. 'This is one of our Command members, Howard Immanuelson. If the Militia are looking for him, they're looking for all of us.'

'Not like they're looking for him,' said the accordionist. He glanced aside at Child, who had drawn close on the other side of Rukh. 'They've got his picture up everywhere; and there's a special officer – one of the Elect, about forty years old, named Barbage, spending his time doing nothing but heading up the search. He's got the whole district looking for this Immanuelson. Like I say, it's dangerous just having him here with you, let alone taking him along on a raid. For everybody's sakes, he ought to be cleared out of the territory.'

'This officer whom thou callest of the Elect – although when was one of God's enemies such?' broke in Child. 'Is he taller than I am, with black hair and a way of squeezing his eyes together when he blasphemes in his attempt to use godly speech?'

The accordionist looked at him.

'You know him, then?'

Child looked at Rukh.

'It was the officer who commanded the ambush against us in the pass,' said Child. 'He saw both Howard and myself.'

'But it's Immanuelson he wants,' the accordionist said. 'Ask anyone around here. What's he wanted for?'

'You don't ask that of the Warriors of the Commands,' said Rukh. Her voice was clear and hard.

The other's eyes fell away for a second time from the gaze she bent on him, then raised stubbornly again.

'This isn't just a Command matter,' he said. 'We all came to help you, not knowing you had him with you. I tell you, he's a risk to all of us, just by being here! If you won't tell us why they want him so much, you ought to get rid of him.'

'This Command is my responsibility,' Rukh said. 'If you join us, you take directions. You don't give them.'

She started to turn away once more.

'That's not right!' called out the accordionist; and there was a small mutter from his fellow truck drivers to back him up. She turned back. 'This is our district, Captain! We're the ones who have to put up with the Militia after you've gone and your raid's been made. We don't mind that; we even come to help you make it – like this. But when we're part of what you do we ought to have a say in the way you do it, when you make it risky for us. Why don't we vote on whether he goes or not? Wasn't that the way the Commands always used to operate – just like the mercenary soldiers? They had the right to vote, didn't they, if their leaders wanted to do something the majority of them didn't want?'

For a moment no one said anything in the farmyard.

'The mercenary code,' Hal said, hearing his voice sounding strange in the new silence, 'only allowed troops to vote down their officers when at least ninety-nine per cent of them –'

His words were overridden by a verbal explosion from Child-of-God.

'Ye would vote?'

They all turned to him. He stood, shoulders wide, hands a little raised at his sides and his head jutting forward, staring at the drivers.

'Ye would all vote?' The echoes of his voice cracked off the walls of the buildings surrounding them on three sides. 'Ye, with the milk of your farms wet on your lips, the muck of stables thick on your boots, ye would vote on whether one who has fought for the Lord should be kept or sent away?'

He took two steps toward them. They stood without moving, watching him – almost without breathing.

'Who are ye to talk of voting? Howard Immanuelson hath fought by the side of those in this Command, as ye have not. He hath labored with us, walked with us, gone cold and hungry with us, to oppose the Belial-spawn and their minions; while ye have not, only grown up soft and played and danced under their indulgence. What business is it of such as ye that a Warrior of the Lord is being specially searched for in thy district? Ye are the fat and useless sheep on which our enemies feed. We are the wolves of God – and ye would raise your voice to command us?'

He paused. They stood, unmoving; even the man with the accordion seemed to be caught like a fly in the amber of Child's anger.

'I tell ye all now, so that ye may remember, that what ye fear so has no meaning for us,' he said. 'What is it to us who fight, that this district of thine should be under special search for Howard Immanuelson? What matter if all the districts between these two mountain ranges should be in search for him, or if this continent, this world, and all the worlds at once should be searching for him? Were none but the two hundred of our Command opposed by all other humanity, and should they offer us a choice of immediate destruction or all that we wished to gain, if only we would give up one of us – our answer would be the same as if a child in the roadway asked the same question of us, in our full and weaponed power.'

He paused again. In his lined face, his eyes were dark as starless space.

'Ye so fear, some of ye, to be in the company of Howard Immanuelson?' he went on, at last. 'Then take thy trucks and go. We have no need of such as ye, nor of anything ye have, for we who fight stand in the shadow of the Lord, who is all-sufficient!'

He stopped speaking and this time did not start again. Hal glanced at Rukh, remembering her relief when she had heard the sound of the trucks arriving. But she stood, watching the drivers and saying nothing. Beyond, the other members of the Command also stood and said nothing. Like Child, like Rukh, they waited, their eyes on the truck drivers. At last, one by one, the drivers stirred and began to move away from one another, each of them going to a truck and turning about to wait beside the door on the control side of the cab. Last of all, the man with the accordion dropped his eyes, turned and went to stand by the single vehicle that still lacked someone beside it.

'All right,' said Rukh. She spoke dryly; but in the continued stillness her voice seemed to ring almost as loudly as Child's. 'Teams, gather at your trucks. Team leaders, brief your drivers on where they're to take you and what's expected of them. James, Howard, come with me.'

She led the two of them back to her room and to the interrupted briefing session.

CHAPTER TWENTY-THREE

The metals-storage unit of Masenvale was a windowless concrete box surrounded by a high, static-charged fence and lit at night by floodlights that showed the fortified gatehouse and the heavy locked entrance doors stark against the surrounding darkness. It stood alone, in the warm, lowland spring night following the one on which the trucks had arrived at the Mohler-Beni farm, surrounded by a square, two business blocks from the District Militia Headquarters, in the downtown area of this middle-sized city. The relative darkness inside the windowed gatehouse made the man on guard there invisible to the twelve members of the Command who had been driven to the edge of the square by the man who owned the accordion. He had parked the vehicle around the corner from the square in the shadows between two floating street lights; and his passengers, Hal among them, had quietly slipped out of the van into the shadows, and were now gathered just behind the corner of a building facing on the square. The driver had remained with the truck, the vehicle facing away from the scene, his motor switch on warm, with his finger on the switch and the idle position only a finger-twitch away.

The metals unit and its surrounding fence slept in the unchanging pattern of light and shadow. Beyond its front gates and the gatehouse, the concrete surface of the square graded back into the darker shadow of the building, behind a corner of which they stood.

Hal felt a loosening of the muscles of his shoulders and the coolness of the night air being pulled deep into his lungs; and recognized the adaptations of the body to the expectation of possible conflict. A calmness and a detachment seemed, for the first time, to have come over him from the same source. He looked about for Jason, caught the eye of the smaller man, and led the way out into the square. Talking in low voices, apparently immersed in their conversation, the two of them started across the square on a slant that would take them past the front of the static-charged fence with its gate and gatehouse, guarding the unit.

As they moved down alongside the fence past the gatehouse, Hal was just able to make out through one of its windows the peaked cap of the single civilian guard seated within at his desk. Hal slowed his step, Jason slowed with him, and eventually they came to a halt just outside the gates themselves, apparently deep in conversation.

They talked on, their voices so low that their words would not have been understandable unless a listener was standing almost within arm's length of them. They stood, centimeters from the fence with its static charge that would be released at any contact to stun, if not kill, whoever had touched the metal of the fence. Time went on. After a while, the door to the guardhouse opened and the guard stuck his head out.

'You two out there!' he called. 'You can't stand there. Move on!'

Hal and Jason ignored him.

'Did you hear me? Move on!'

They continued to ignore him.

Boots thumping loudly on the three steps down from the gate-house door to the concrete of the square, the guard came out. The door slammed loudly behind him. He came up to the fence, careless about touching his side of it; for any touch from within deactivated the mechanism producing the static charge.

'Did you hear me?' His voice came loudly at them through the wide openings in the wire mesh, from less than an arm's length away. 'Both of you – move on before I call Militia HQ to come pick you up for disturbance!'

Still they acted as if he was not there. He stepped right up against the fence, grabbed the wire and shouted at them; and as he did so, they stepped away, back along it on their side.

'What's going on here –' the guard began.

He did not finish. There was a distant, twanging noise, a hum in the air, and a second later a crossbow bolt with a blunt and padded head flickered into the lights to strike the side of the guard's head with the impact of a blackjack. The man slumped against the fence and began to sag down it toward the concrete; and, reaching swiftly through a couple of the wide mesh spaces, Hal caught and held him, upright but unconscious, against the fence.

With the fence registering an upright and still-living body pressed against its inner surface, its static charge was quiescent. Reaching through it, past Hal's straining shoulder-muscles, Jason unclipped the picture-crowned identity badge of the guard from the left pocket of his uniform jacket, and carried it over to the sensor plate in the right-hand gatepost. He pressed the face of the badge against the plate. There was a slight pause and then, recognizing the badge, the gates swung smoothly and quietly open.

Jason dodged through and put his hand against the interior control plate on the back of the same gatepost. He held it there and the gates stayed open. Hal let go of the guard, who slid down to lie still at the foot of the fence.

Jason went swiftly to stand at one side of the closed doors of the building, drawing a handgun from under his shirt as he did so. Hal came around to pick up the guard, take him into the gatehouse and immobilize him there with tape and a gag. The other ten Command members flooded smoothly across the square and through the open gate of the fence – which the last of them closed behind him.

Hal came out of the gatehouse, carrying the sidearm from the leg holster of the once more conscious, but trussed and now-undressed, guard. He handed the clothes to the member of the Command they seemed most likely to fit and the man who had taken them put them on, pulling the cap low over his eyes. Tilting his head down to pull his face back into the deep shadow below the visor of the uniform hat, the spurious guard stood directly before the sensor plate to the right of the doors blocking out its view of anything else and pressed the doorcall button.

There was a second's wait.

'Jarvy?' said a voice from a speaker panel above the plate.

The uniformed member grunted wordlessly, still holding his head down.

'What?' demanded the speaker panel.

The spurious guard grunted again.

'I can't hear you, Jarvy – what is it?'

The member said nothing, still looking down with his face in shadow.

'Just a minute,' said the speaker panel. 'There's something wrong with the voice pickup out there –'

The two doors swung open in neat mechanical unison. Framed in the white glare of illumination from the interior of the metals unit stood another guard, peering out into the darkness.

'Jarvy, what –' he began; and then he went down, silenced by hands on his mouth and throat even as he fell under the unified rush of several bodies.

'Where's the metals room?' Jason asked Hal, soft-voiced.

'Straight back,' answered Hal, an image of the plan of the unit's interior which Rukh had shown him clear in his memory. He pointed along the hand-truck-wide corridor they had just entered. 'But the guard-office's to the right. You'd better wait until we clear that.'

Jason nodded and fell back. Hal, with two other men and three women of the Command, all armed now with handguns produced from within their clothing, went swiftly and quietly ahead down the corridor and burst in through the first door to their right, which was standing ajar. But inside there was only a single other guard, sitting on a cot at one end of a small room filled with surveillance screens, a power rifle on his knees.

At the sight of them he stared – grasped the rifle as if he would swing it up into firing position, then dropped it as if it had burned his fingers. Going forward before the protection of the handguns those behind him held levelled on the man, Hal picked up the power rifle and found it, not broken open for cleaning as he had expected, but loaded and ready to use.

'What were you going to do with it?' Hal asked the guard.

'Nothing . . .' The guard stared up at him, hopelessly, with frightened eyes.

'How many other people on duty here, now?' Hal loomed over him.

'Just Ham – just Ham and me, and Jarvy on the gate!' said the guard. He was white-faced and shock was losing out to fear.

'How do you unlock the metals room?'

'We can't,' said the guard. 'Really – we can't. They don't let us. It's a time lock on the door.'

Hal looked down at him through a long moment of silence.

'I'm going to ask you again,' he said. 'This time, forget what they told you to say. How do you open the metals room door?'

The guard stared up at him.

'You're the man they're looking for so hard, aren't you?' he blurted out.

'Never mind that,' said Hal. 'The door to the metals room –?'

'I – code KJ9R on the control keyboard –' The guard nodded almost eagerly toward the other side of the room. 'The one under the large screen, there. That's the truth, that really opens it.'

'We know.' Hal smiled at him. 'I was just checking. Lie down where you are, now, and we'll tie you up. You won't be hurt.'

The other Command members with him converged on the guard; and Hal took the power rifle with him as he went back toward the door. As they began to tie the man up, he stepped to the screen the guard had indicated and keyed in the code the man had given. Rukh had explained to him that the Commands normally had little trouble finding out ahead of time the information they would need for raids on places such as this; but it was the practice to always check such information when that was possible. Holding the power rifle, he went back out to the corridor.

'The metals door ought to be open now,' he told a senior member of the Command, a man named Heidrick Falt. 'The guard gave me the same code Rukh had.'

Falt nodded, his eyes thoughtful upon Hal. Falt had been named group leader for this raid. Rukh's instructions had been to let Hal lead only on the way in. As far as Hal could tell, Falt had not resented that exception to his authority; but it was a relief to hand the command back to the other man, now.

'Good,' said Falt. He had a reedy voice too young for his face and body. 'We'll start to load up. You go back and sit with the driver.'

'Right.' Hal nodded.

He left the building. Outside, the square showed no change. It still seemed to slumber under the same lights and shadows as before; and from the outside the metals unit sat with the same air of impregnability it had seemed to wear earlier. He turned the corner, reached the truck and climbed back into the cab. In the small interior glow of the instrument panel the driver turned a round face toward him in which there was no hint of friendliness.

'Ready to go?' he said.

'A while yet,' Hal answered.

For a moment he played with the idea of trying to break through the shell of enmity in which the other had encased himself. Then he put the thought aside. The driver was too tense to be reached at this moment. The concern here was not with how much he might fear and dislike Hal but with whether, as not infrequently happened with local volunteers, his nerve might snap with the waiting, causing him to drive off and leave the raiding party straded. It was to guard against this that Falt had sent Hal back here. The less said between the two of them right now, the better.

They sat, and the minutes crawled by. The driver shifted position from time to time, sighed, rubbed his nose, looked out of the window then back at the instrument panel, and made a dozen other small movements and sounds. Hal sat still and silent, as he had been taught to do under such conditions, deliberately removing a part of his attention from the present moment and reaching out into the abstract universe of the mind. In the present semi-suspended state of consciousness that resulted, it seemed to him that he could almost feel beside him the presence of Rukh, who would now be at the fertilizer area. He felt her as if she was both there, and here with him at the same moment. It was an eerie but powerful sensation; and a poem began to shape itself about it, in the back of his thoughts.

> *And if it should not be you, after all –*
> *Down the long passage, turning in the hall;*
> *Or slipping at a distance through the light*
> *Of streetlamped corners just within my sight;*
> *I will not then turn back into my room,*
> *Chilled and disheartened wrapped in angry gloom;*
> *But warm myself to think the mind should send*
> *So many shades of you to be my friend . . .*

The poem disturbed him. It was not right, somehow. It was too light and facile, not cast in the way he normally thought or had been taught to think. But at the same time it rang with a sense of something discovered he had not known before. It seemed to echo off things completely removed from his present reality, things half-hidden in corners and cul-de-sacs of personal pain that he had never known and could not now remember – lonelinesses that had no proper part of life as he now knew it. For a moment, something moved far back in his mind; he seemed to feel an echoing, down endless centuries of moments such as this, in all of which he now remembered being isolated and set apart from others. Uneasily, he pushed the memories from him. But they returned, along with barely-registered sensations of pains he did not remember ever feeling, as if he had known them all, and been the one within them all. . . .

The door to the cab opened. Falt looked inside.

'Open the back doors,' he said. 'We're coming in.'

The driver touched a control stud on his instrument panel. Behind them they heard the doors trundle apart. Hal moved back from the cab section into the body of the van to help with the loading of whatever metal the Command had lifted from the unit.

'What are they?' he asked, as heavy, smooth gray ingots began to be passed in to him by those standing on the pavement outside the doors. 'What did you bring?'

'High-tin solder,' panted Jason, passing in his personal burden. 'About forty ingots all told. Not too much to carry, but it ought to convince the authorities this was what we were actually after and the fertilizer warehouse business was the diversion.'

Taking and stacking the ingots, Hal put the poem and the ghost memories firmly from him. He was back now in the ordinary universe, where things were as hard and heavy and real as the ingots of solder.

They finished loading and drove off. Falt took over the passenger seat in the cab, but kept Hal there to talk to him as they went.

'I think we ought to head for the foothills, without trying to rendezvous with the rest at the fertilizer warehouse,' Falt said. 'What do you think?'

'And give up the idea of splitting the metal up among the other trucks, so that if we lose a truck or two, we don't lose it all?'

'That's secondary,' said Falt. 'You know that. Our whole raid was secondary to the fertilizer raid; and we took longer than Rukh estimated to get things done here. No, the main thing is to get as many of us as possible safely back to the Command. I think the hills are safer.'

'A dozen people on foot,' Hal said, 'won't be able to move very far or fast with all those ingots, once we leave the truck. We've gotten away clear. No one's chasing us; and if the rest of you left those guards tied up right it could be hours before the alarm goes out on what we did. I'd say make the rendezvous.'

Falt had been sitting sideways on the seat to look back at Hal, now squatting on the small space of open floor in the cab behind both seats. At Hal's answer, Falt turned his head back to look out the windshield of the truck. They were skimming at good speed above the concrete strip of one of the main routes radiating from the center of the city.

'We must be halfway to the fertilizer warehouse now – isn't that right, driver?' said Hal.

There was a slight pause.

'Almost,' said the driver, slowly.

Falt looked over at him.

'You'd rather head for the foothills now?' he asked.

'Yes!' The answer was explosive.

'We don't know what's happened at the fertilizer area,' Hal said. 'They could need another truck and the help of the extra dozen of us.'

Falt blew out a short breath, staring through the windshield again. Then he looked first back at Hal, then at the driver.

'All right,' he said. 'That's where we'll go.'

When they got to the turnoff from the route that was closest to the fertilizer plant, there was a redness to be seen above the skyline of buildings to their left.

'The place could be swarming with Militia already,' said the driver.

'Just go there.' Falt said.

The driver obeyed. Less than two minutes brought them around the corner of a tall lightless office building and the driver brought the truck to a halt.

Ahead of them was a fenced-in area that looked as if it might encompass several city blocks. Within the fence was one tall, almost windowless cube of a concrete building, and several other long, wide concrete structures with curved roofs like sections of barrels laid lengthwise over the rectangular blocks beneath. One of these was aflame at its far end; and lights and alarm bells within that or other buildings could be heard shrilling in the distance. Beyond two truck-wide gates in the fence, now gaping wide open, the dark shapes of the other van-type trucks the Command had brought stood outlined against the light of the burning structure.

'They're still there,' said Hal.

'Go in,' said Falt to the driver.

'No,' said the driver. 'I'm staying here where I can make a run for it. You go in on foot if you want.'

Falt drew a sidearm from under his shirt and held the muzzle against the driver's right temple.

'Go in,' he said.

The driver started up the truck once more. They drove in. As they got closer to the trucks, a scene of ordered confusion became visible between and about them. Most of the members of the Command were engaged in the carrying of twenty-five kilogram bags of fertilizer on their shoulders, from a stack of them outside the burning building to the vans of individual trucks. The body of a man lay before the firelit front end of one of the trucks; and in the center of the activity stood Rukh, directing it.

Hal and the others left their truck; and, with Falt, Hal came up to

Rukh. The rest of their team went unordered to the necessary business of loading sacks of fertilizer into their own truck.

As he and Falt got close to Rukh, Hal saw her for a moment outlined against the red light of the fire. It was as if she stood darkly untouched in the heart of the flames. Then someone passed beyond her with a sack over her shoulder and the illusion was lost. As they came up, she turned, saw them, and spoke without waiting.

'We've got three wounded,' she told Falt. 'No one killed; and we've chased off the district police for the moment. They'll be back shortly with help, so I'm going to have you take those three and whatever you've already got loaded and leave for the rendezvous ahead of the rest of us. They're all three in Tallah's truck, right now. Send six of your people to carry them over. How'd you do?'

'No one even hurt,' said Falt. 'Typical small-city guards. Not like Militia at all. They practically rolled over and put their paws in the air for us.'

'Good,' said Rukh. 'Get moving, then. We've cut alarm communications and some of the local people are helping to contain information on the fact we're here; but I don't estimate more than another fifteen minutes before we've got Militia around our ears. Howard, if for any reason the wounded have to split off from the rest, you're to stay with them.'

'Right,' said Hal.

CHAPTER TWENTY-FOUR

He and Falt went back to the truck. Falt began reassigning members of their team, as they returned laden, to the job of bringing over the three wounded. Once a sufficient number had been sent, he put the rest as they came in to passing over to other trucks as many of the ingots as could be moved before the three casualties were brought. Five minutes later, they were out of the gates and leaving the red glow behind them; the dark ribbon of the route unwinding before the nose of their truck and the dark shapes of the foothills and further mountains rising on the night horizon under the still starlit sky. The new moon had not yet put in its appearance.

Once more Falt took the cab seat beside the driver. Hal went back into the body of the van to look at the wounded. One was Morelly Walden; and in the dim interior of the van with its single dim, overhead light, the lines and creases in the heavy face appeared deeper; so that he seemed to have aged another ten years at least into the realm of the truly old.

'It's his leg,' said Joralmon Troy, looking up from where he sat cross-legged beside Morelly's stretcher, perched on its low, dark pile of fertilizer bags. 'When we blew out the door of the warehouse, a big piece got him in the leg and broke it.'

'Did they give you anything for the pain?' Hal asked Morelly, reading the deepness of the facial creases.

'No,' said Morelly, hoarsely. 'No sinful drugs.'

Hal hesitated.

'If you like,' he said, 'there's a way I could massage your forehead and neck to help relieve the pain.'

'No,' said Morelly, effortfully. 'The pain is by God's will. I'll bear it as His Warrior.'

Hal touched him gently on the shoulder and went to look at the other two casualties, a woman who had taken a weapon burn in her right shoulder, superficial but painful, and a man who had been needled in the chest. Both these other two were unconscious, under sedation.

'We're low on painkillers,' murmured one of the women who was sitting beside the stretchers of these other casualties. 'Morelly knows it. He's really not that much of an old prophet.'

Hal nodded.

'I thought so,' he answered in an equally low voice. He turned and went back toward the cab. All three would have to be carried. That meant that if he and they split off from the others, he would have at least a party of nine under his responsibility. By the time he got to the cab, the route as seen through the windshield had narrowed down until there was room only for four vehicles abreast; and the exits were no longer ramps, but simple turnoffs. Falt had unfolded his copy of Rukh's local map, which had been issued to all the group leaders, and was looking at it in the overhead light of the cab. Ahead, beyond the mountains, the stars were beginning to be lost in a sky paling toward the dawn.

'Look here,' said Falt to Hal, as Hal squatted behind his seat. 'Standing orders are that any groups with wounded take priority on the safer rendezvous points over any groups without injured. Since we're the only such group – so far, anyway – that moves us from our prearranged point to this one –'

His finger indicated a starred position higher in the foothills than any others marked there.

'We ought to find more than enough donkeys waiting at that point to carry the light load we've got and sling the stretchers between a pair of beasts apiece.' He turned from the map to look at the driver. 'How long before we get there?'

'Maybe ten, fifteen –' the driver broke off with a grunt. They had just come around a long curve, and he was staring ahead out the windshield. His face had paled, his knuckles gleamed above the steering wheel in the glow from the instrument panel.

Hal and Falt turned to look as he was looking. Ahead – far ahead on the now-straight route – but unmistakable, were lights set up to shine on a barricade closing the road.

'God save us,' whispered the driver. 'I can't turn back. They've seen us by now . . .'

'Drive through,' said Falt.

'I can't,' the driver answered. He was sweating and he had eased off on the thumb-button on the wheel that controlled the throttle. They were slowing gradually, but still approaching the barricade up ahead far too swiftly for anyone's comfort. 'They'll have pylons set up beyond the barricade to turn us over if I try it.'

He stared at Falt.

'What're they doing out here?' His face turned back over its shoulder to look at Hal. 'It's your fault! They don't know anything about the raid – they couldn't! They're out here looking for you – and now they've got us!'

The truck was close enough now so that they could pick out figures in the black uniforms of the Militia on either side of the barricade.

'Go around, then,' said Falt.

'The minute I try that, they'll start shooting!' The driver's face was agonized. 'God save us! God save us –'

Falt took his sidearm from his shirt again.

'Go around,' he said, softly. 'It's the only way.'

The driver threw a quick glance at the weapon.

'If you shoot me at this speed, we'll all crash,' he said bitterly.

Hal put his right hand up with the thumb on one side of the back of the driver's neck, his fingers on the other. He exerted pressure and the driver made a small sound.

'When I snap his spine,' said Hal to Falt, 'you take the wheel.'

'I'll go – I'll go around,' husked the driver. Hal released the pressure on the other's neck but kept his fingers in place.

'At the last moment, only,' Falt said to the driver. 'I'll tell you when to leave the road. Hold steady, now . . . hold steady . . . *now!*'

At the last moment the barricade had seemed to jump at them. The Militia on either side of it had been waving their arms for some time to command the vehicle to a halt.

'Hit it! Up the speed! Hit it – now!' Falt was shouting at the driver.

But the driver had already dug his finger into the throttle button and the truck was off the road and sliding in a tilted curve over the open ground alongside it like a saucer being sailed into a strong wind. Its body rang as power weapons struck the skin of the van with energy bolts that generated explosions of high temperature in the material. The windshield and the window on the driver's side starred suddenly, as if hit by solid birdshot; and the driver cried out, his hands flying up from the wheel. Falt grabbed the wheel and pulled the truck, skittering, back onto the route beyond the barricade and the sharp-pointed pylons anchored in concrete just beyond. His finger pressed down the throttle again, and abruptly they were flying up the route once more, while the barricade, the figures and the pylons behind it dwindled rapidly in the distance.

The driver was huddled against the cab door at his side.

'Where are you hit?' Falt was demanding.

'Oh God!' said the driver. 'Oh God – oh God . . .'

'Howard,' said Falt, 'take a look at this man, find out where he's hit and lift him over the back of the seat, out of my way, if you can.'

Hal stood up, holding to the back of the seat before him and bent over the driver, reaching down to pull him back from the door. A fingernail-sized stain was visible high on the left side of the driver's shirt. Pressing the cloth tight against the man's body as he went, Hal felt for and found wetness on the man's back at a roughly opposite point, then ran his hands over the shirt and the upper areas of the driver's pants, as far as he could reach, bending over the driver as he was.

'Are your legs all right?' he asked the driver.

'Oh, God . . .'

236

Hal put his hand gently once more on the man's neck.

'Yes – yes,' the driver almost yelped. 'They're all right! My legs are all right!'

'You got a single needle through your left shoulder, high up,' Hal told him. 'It's nothing serious. Now . . .'

He massaged the back of the other's neck.

'Now, I'm going to help you up over the back of your seat. I want you to do as much as you can to get over, yourself. Come on, now. . . .'

He reached down with both hands and put them under the driver's armpits. He lifted. The driver scrambled upwards with both arms and legs. Abruptly he screamed and tried to slide back down into the seat again; but Hal held him and half-pulled, half-lifted him over the back of the seat by sheer force. The driver screamed again as the back of his knees bumped over the back of the seat.

'My leg! My leg – oh, God!'

But Hal, with the other already on the floor on his back behind the seats, was checking a stain on the outside of the other's left leg, just above the knee.

'Looks like you've got a needle through the leg, too,' he said. 'Can you bend it?'

The driver tried and did, but screamed a third time.

'Looks like that one could be more serious,' said Hal. 'The needle's hit something in there.'

He felt under the leg.

'And it looks as if it's still in there.'

'Oh God –'

'He's faking,' said Falt clearly. 'There's no way it could be hurting him that much.'

Hal put a hand over the man's mouth.

'You've got a choice,' he said quietly in the other's ear. 'Now I know and you know how that leg of yours hurts. But we also both know it only hurts when you move it; and that you should move it as little as possible. Neither wound is going to kill you. So, lie still; and either you keep quiet or I'll have to make sure you're quiet because you're unconscious. Do you understand?'

Part of his mind was appalled at what he was saying; but another part nodded in bleak approval at this evidence of how well he had learned his lessons once upon a time. For a moment he could almost imagine the harsh, old bass voice of Malachi Nasuno echoing behind his own. He had spoken the words he had just said as if he had read them off a blackboard in Malachi's mind.

But the results were successful. The driver now lay motionless and silent. Hal stood up, clinging to the back of the seat before him; and saw that Falt was now behind the wheel and holding the truck steady as it fled.

'Pick up the map and navigate,' said Falt.

Hal slipped around into the empty seat Falt had vacated. He picked up the map from the cab floor before the seat.

'Are we still on the route?' he asked, glancing ahead through the windshield, for what he looked out on was now a two-lane roadway of crushed gravel.

'No. Two turns off. Local Way Ten – find it there?'

Hal looked.

'Yes,' he said. 'We turn off Way Ten on to Way One Hundred Twenty-three, and off that on to Demming Road – follow Demming Road to the first path, unnamed, turning off to the right. We make a ninety degree left turn off that path after one point eight kilometers, and take out over open country. We go on a compass reading of forty-three minutes, twenty-four seconds, for point six of one kilometer, and that brings us to the gathering point.'

'All right,' said Falt. 'Now direct me.'

They continued according to the directions Hal had spelled out, as the sky brightened above them and the open woods along the back country roads began to emerge into visibility from the solid blackness that had earlier held everything beyond the cast of the truck's lights. Hal glanced back once to check on the driver, who had been silent all this time, and saw him still as he had been, lying on his side with his eyes closed – either unconscious or determined to attract no further attention to himself.

They came to the gathering point finally in the first somber light of the dawn; by then the whole woods were visible around them, although the sun was still hidden behind the mountains to their right. Waiting for them there, shielded from telescopic observation by a tight clump of variform elms, was a pile of packsaddles and related equipment surrounded by fifteen placid donkeys, tethered to the surrounding tree trunks or limbs. There was no one with them. The local farmers were clearly willing to donate their livestock, but only at minimum risk to themselves.

The truck halted. Falt punched the button to open the back doors. He and Hal, with the rest of the team, got out of the truck and began the process of getting the wounded onto their stretchers, once each of these had been slung between two of the donkeys, and loading the remaining animals with the bags of fertilizer as well as the ingots of high-tin solder, which would be cut up and used as payment for equipment the Command would not be able to get by donation along the way.

They were finishing this when a wild voice shouted at them.

'That's right – go off and leave me to die!'

They all looked toward the sound of it. In one of the cab doorways, the driver lay propped on one elbow, the closure of his shirt pulled open halfway by his effort to crawl there, his eyes bloodshot and face contorted. Without a glance at each other, both Falt and Hal walked over to the cab, while the rest of the team turned back to getting the donkey train ready to move out.

'That's right,' said the driver in a lower voice, as they came up to him. He glared at them, his face above the floor of the cab on a level with theirs as they stood outside it. 'Leave me here, all shot up. Leave me here to die.'

'You can drive,' said Falt, flatly. 'It'll hurt some, but I've seen Command members drive half a day in worse shape than you are.'

'And what'll happen when I get home – if I get home?' the driver demanded. 'Because if they've got one roadblock up here, they've got a dozen; and now they'll be looking for this truck after we went around them the way you did! Even if I could get past the roadblocks, even if I could get home, could I go to my family, knowing the Militia'll be searching everywhere and what'd happen to my people if I was found at the farm? Do you think I'm the kind to go back and let them in for that?'

'You can't come with us,' said Falt. 'What else is there for you?'

The driver stared at him for a moment, breathing raggedly.

'There's a place in the mountains I could go,' he said, more quietly. 'But I can't make it alone.'

'I tell you, you can drive, if you want to,' said Falt.

'I can drive!' shouted the driver at him. 'I can drive on a road. I can drive a little ways like this is, from a road. But I can't take this truck ten kilometers back into the woods when I might get jammed between trees or hung up on a rock, or turned over at any minute – and what'd happen to me then? Could I crawl the rest of the way to the cabin?'

'Some might,' said Falt, dryly. But he looked at Hal with a small frown line between his eyes.

'I'll take him to his cabin,' said Hal.

'We can't spare you,' said Falt.

'No reason why not,' Hal said. 'There's no pursuit at the moment. You've got more than enough beasts and the rest of the team's in good shape. I can drive him to his place, and still make it to rendezvous not more than a couple of hours behind the rest of you.'

Falt hesitated. Hal turned to the driver.

'This cabin of yours,' he said. 'What's it doing away off like that, by itself?'

'It's a fishing cabin.' The driver lowered his eyes. 'All right, there's some fishing up here, but not much. It's mainly a place a few of us go just to get away.'

'How few of you? How many know about this place?'

The driver's eyes came up again, defiantly.

'Me, my two next brothers and my cousin Joab,' he said. 'We all live at home together. The Militia couldn't make any of them say anything, anyway. Besides, when I don't come back, they'll think to look for me up there, in a day or two.'

'How far from here is it?' he asked. 'How long to get there in your truck?'

'Half an hour.' The voice of the driver was now eager. 'Just half an hour, and no danger of running into Militia, I swear it.'

'So you'd swear, would you?' said Falt, looking at him, disgust in the older Command member's voice.

The driver colored and looked down at the floor of the cab.

'I only meant . . .'

Hal looked back at Falt.

'There's no reason I can't take him and meet you all at rendez-vous.'

Falt sighed hissingly, between closed teeth.

'Take him then.' He turned his back on the driver. 'Don't take any risks for him. He's not worth it.'

He walked away.

'Move back,' said Hal to the driver. 'Let me in.'

Grunting with pain at each movement of his leg, the other pulled back away from the cab doorway. Hal hoisted himself up inside and took the seat behind the controls. He closed the cab doors, switched the motors from warm to idle, and lifted the truck on its travelling cushion of air from the blowers. Turning the vehicle, he waved through the windshield at the rest of the team who were now watching him, and drove off, toward the road. Behind him there was a good deal of scrabbling and grunting, and the driver at last hauled himself up into the empty seat alongside Hal.

'Which way?' asked Hal, as they came to the road.

'Left.'

They turned on to the road, headed deeper into the foothills, toward the mountains. Hal followed the monosyllabic directions through several turns and changes of roads; and very shortly they were climbing steeply up a track that was hardly more than a donkey-trail. He had expected them to turn off even from this, but instead the track itself came to an end.

'Where now?' Hal asked, seeing the end of the trail approaching.

'Straight ahead for now. Then I'll tell you.'

Hal glanced over at the other man as he followed this latest direction. The driver's face as he stared ahead out the windshield was tight-skinned, his jaws clamped, his eyes hooded and sullen.

'Left now,' he said. They went a short distance. 'Now, right again, between those two large trees and to the left of that boulder. Slow down. The spring thaw makes rocks roll down, and we can run right on top of one of those and get hung up or flipped over before we know it.'

Hal drove. The directions continued. After a short while they came through an opening in some bushes and into a small depression through which a stream ran – a stream too small for fish of reasonable size, but sufficient to provide drinking and washing water for the rather clumsy log cabin with a single drunken eye of a window in its front wall that had been thrown up beside it.

'Here,' said the driver.

Hal stopped the truck. He got out and went around to open the other door of the cab and help the driver out. For a Harmonyite who would not curse, he did a good job of expressing his dissatisfaction with the help he was being given.

'. . . Careful! Can't you be more careful?' he snapped.

'Want to try it on your own?' Hal said. 'I can leave you just where you are, here, outside the cabin.'

The driver became silent. Hal half-carried, half-supported the man in a hopping progress toward the door of the cabin, through it and into the interior – an untidy area of portable camp beds, a woodbox stove, and a large, round table with four chairs, that looked out of place in these surroundings.

'What's the table for – card games?' asked Hal.

The driver flashed a sudden glance that showed a good deal of the whites of the other's eyes; and suddenly Hal realized that by accident he had named the real reason for the existence of the cabin. He aided the driver to one of the camp beds and the driver collapsed on it.

'Is there something clean around here I can fill with water to leave with you?' Hal said. 'And what have you got, a privy somewhere out back? How far is it? By tomorrow you're literally going to have to crawl to get anywhere. You don't have some kind of bucket I can get to put by your bed?'

'There's a water bucket to the left of the stove,' said the driver sullenly. 'And there's a compression toilet under the canvas ground-cloth in the corner. Get my accordion.'

'All right. I'll move the toilet over by your cot,' said Hal. He did so, went out to fill the bucket and brought it back full with a dipper floating in it, to put it by the bedside. 'Now, what about food? Have you got any food here?'

'There's another box on the far side of the stove,' said the driver, sullenly. 'You can bring that over. It's got boxed stuff that keeps in it. You can get some more blankets, too, from the other beds. It gets cold up here, nights.'

'All right,' said Hal. He did so. 'Have you got any medical supplies up here?'

'Emergency kit's around here someplace,' said the driver. 'You'll have to look for it.'

It took eight to ten minutes of searching before Hal came up with the kit. He took it back to the driver, cleaned and spot-bandaged the needle-holes in the man.

'You said the needle's still in my leg,' said the other, suddenly fearful as Hal was doing this. 'What'll it do? What's going to happen to me?'

Hal had to stop and think back to what Malachi had told him.

'If you left it there indefinitely,' he said, 'either your body'd build some kind of shielding tissue around it, or it'd work its way out, eventually – maybe a few years from now. Unless it carried some material in with it , like dirty clothing, it probably won't infect; and gun needles generally don't, because their sharpness sends them through things a slug from missile weapons might push ahead of it into the wound it makes. You'll still want to get it taken out of your leg as soon as you can.'

He considered the man for a moment.

'You'll be all right for a few days, in any case.'

'But I mean –' The driver broke off. The now-strong daylight, coming through the drunken window-eye to push apart the shadows of the cabin's interior, showed his face both crafty and pale. 'You're going to leave me something for the pain, aren't you?'

'Sorry,' said Hal. 'I've got nothing to give you.'

'What do you mean?' the driver's voice rose. 'I saw you put your stuff into the truck. You've got to have painkillers in that med kit in your pack – I know all you Command people carry them for when you get wounded! You've got some and you can give me some!'

Hal thought of Morelly, with the old lines of his face deepened as he lay on the stretcher.

'We carry that sort of thing not for ourselves,' he said, 'but for our brothers and sisters in battle when the time comes that they need it. It's not for you, even if you had to have it – which you don't.'

He turned and went out the door to the truck. He opened its rear doors and, gathering his equipment, began to pack it and put it on. As he did there was a sound from the door of the cabin. Glancing over, he saw that the driver had managed to pull himself as far as the doorway to stand propped up there.

'I suppose you think I owe you some thanks?' the driver shouted. 'Well, I don't! It's all right when our own people want to fight the Militia, but you don't even belong. You with your foreign accent and your pretending to help! What did you do to make them hunt you like that? You made all the trouble. Everybody who got hurt in this got hurt because they were already looking for you! I've got these needles in me because of you – just you. And you think I'm going to thank you? I wouldn't thank you for anything. You know what I say? I say damn on you! Yes, you heard me – I say the damnation in God's name upon you . . .'

He was still shouting as Hal closed the rear truck doors and turned about, fully outfitted at last in his gear, and went away from stream and cabin into the woods. He heard the driver's shouting continue for some distance after he was obviously out of sight. There was a heaviness and a bitterness in him that would not be gotten rid of; even though he exercised his mind as Walter the InTeacher had taught him, to put aside the anger that had surged up in him at the last words of the man behind him. Walking steadily south through the mountain woods, it occurred to him with a touch of wonder that when he had explained to the other why he could not give painkillers to him, he had thought and spoken unconsciously, for the first time in his life, as a Friendly. The thought suddenly wiped clean from him the heaviness and bitterness triggered by the reactions of the driver; the sadness in him that such as Rukh and Morelly – and Child-of-God – should pay the price of the life they had chosen for someone who understood and valued that price so little.

For a little while, he walked through the morning-lit woods, bemused by this new development within him. He had imitated Obadiah, but until now he never reacted in his own right as a Friendly. Like the slow but powerful effects of some heavy shock, he felt an understanding of this stern culture flooding through him – an understanding he had never had before. But even as he realized this, he understood further that he had only begun to grasp that understanding, that he must be content to wait now, to put it aside to be wrestled with at some other opportunity, when the first heavy effects of it would have been absorbed enough to make it possible to stand back and look at the shape of this new comprehension that had just come to him, in detail.

He came finally out into what he had been searching for, an open spot on the mountainside where he could overlook all the foothills and the area beyond where the city of Masenvale sprawled. He glanced down the flank of the earth on which he stood and saw the dished-in, downward swoop of forested slopes that seemed to march to the very edge of the dark oval that was the city. He reached into his pack, took out the field viewer there, and put it to his eye, dialing it into focus on one point, then setting it on automatic adjustment as he swung about to survey the lower area.

With no great difficulty, he picked out the still-smoking fertilizer storage area, then traced the route he and the others had taken in the truck until he came to the point where the barricade still stood. Taking the viewer off automatic to put it on full magnification, he saw that a second row of barricades had been set up on the other side of the pylons they had passed and that the dark-uniformed figures seemed to be keeping a watch now in both directions, instead of merely toward anyone coming out from the city. Beyond this change, the barrier looked as if it had never been encountered – except for a curve of flattened roadside weeds and other small growth that marked the track of the fans of their truck where they had swung out around it; and the addition of a troop carrier truck, that now stood by the far side of the road, looking as if ready to move at a second's notice.

He moved the viewer on, and found the gathering point where he had parted with the rest of the team. The back of his mind, trained early to remember such things, threw up a perfect image of the map he had held to navigate Falt to that point; and he swung the viewer to check the other gathering points that had been marked on it. All but two were now empty of donkeys and equipment; and neither of the teams now loading up in them had Rukh among them.

He began to search forward along the routes he estimated each team would take from the gathering points to the rendezvous deep in the foothills. Once they were under the trees there, of course, he would not be able to see them. He located more than half of the teams, including his own; but was still not able to find the one Rukh was with, although he located the one led by Child. All the teams he could see were close upon the foothills. It looked as if everyone had gotten away safely, he thought; and then a movement on the traffic ways farther down the slope caught his eye as he panned the viewer about.

Focusing in, he located a column of six troop carriers, raising a faint plume of dust along one of the gravel-surfaced Ways as it headed in at an angle to the foothills some kilometers ahead of the rendezvous. Panning the field viewer backwards along the slope, he found three more plumes of dust and focused in on three more columns of carriers. He stood watching them through the viewer. There was no point in their moving in on the foothills in force that way unless the carriers were loaded with armed Militia; and the organization of the pursuit he now saw testified either to the fact that columns and their personnel had been waiting on a standby basis, or that the Militia had been informed of the fertilizer and metals raids ahead of time.

But they could not have been informed ahead of time; not only because of the unlikelihood of anyone connected with Rukh's Command in this effort being a traitor, but because if the Militia had known, they would of course have been set up around the sites of both raids. It would have been far easier to take the members of the Command that way than to pursue them into the foothills.

The only possible conclusion was that they had been on standby – and that the driver had been correct. They had been on standby for the single purpose of capturing Hal; and only one man could set such a large effort in motion for that purpose. Bleys Ahrens must now be sure that he was on Harmony. The tall Other Man must have seen to it that the Militia, planetwide, had been made acquainted with Hal's face; and the Militia officer called Barbage must have recognized Hal and reported seeing him after he had escaped following the ambush of the Command in the pass.

Now Rukh and the rest were being seriously hunted. Because of him. What it amounted to, in the end, was that what the driver had shouted after him had been no more than the literal truth.

CHAPTER TWENTY-FIVE

Drawing lines with a stick in the dirt at his feet to echo the estimated paths of travel of the teams, and the Militia truck units in pursuit of them, Hal came to the conclusion that at his best possible speed he could reach the rendezvous only after the rest had arrived there. But that would still be before the Militia would be dangerously close. He put the viewer back into his pack, erased the lines he had drawn in the earth, and took both a line of sight and a compass reading on the position of the rendezvous, ahead of him in the foothills below.

He began his journey.

He had come a long way back toward good general physical condition in his time with the Command; but he was still not in training for what he might once have done in the way of covering the ground, even back as a fifteen-year-old on Earth. Then, even laden with pack and weapon, he might have chosen to run the whole distance – not at any great speed, but at a steady jog that would have eaten up the kilometers between him and his destination.

As it was, he started out at a fast, smooth walk that was the next best way of covering ground in a hurry. He had had little sleep the day before and he had been up all night. The first two kilometers were work; but by the end of that time his body had warmed to the effort and his mind had moved into the necessary state of mild trance in which he could, if necessary, continue moving until he dropped without really taking conscious note of his fatigue.

This state once achieved, he effectively abandoned the effort of his travel to the automatic machinery of his body and let his mind go off on its own concerns.

Primary among these now was the fact that his presence in the Command was dangerous to it and its members. Treading on the heels of that fact was that Bleys had now located him, and was clearly ready to go to large efforts to lay hands on him. The best assumption from this was that Bleys, at least – and probably the Other Men and Women as a whole – had concluded that he could be dangerous to them. The effort made to find him on Coby might have indicated only something as small as curiosity on Bleys' part. But what was happening now seemed to indicate more than that.

He was conscious of a feeling of being rushed. He had gone to

Coby only to hide out until he was grown enough to protect himself; and until he had a chance to make up his mind as to the specifics of what he wanted to do – with regard to the Others, and to his own life. Now, they were threatening to lay their hands on him and he still did not know how he should fight them, let alone conquer them. His conscience stirred and accused him of letting time slip by these four years, of living in a childish illusion of unlimited time available, until it was too late to decide what had needed to be done from the beginning.

The territory he was passing through was open, for the most part, and his speed was undiminished by the need to go around natural obstacles in his path. From time to time he either took advantage of an open space that gave him a view of the land lower down, or climbed a tree that would offer the same prospect. On his first survey of this kind, he had seen only one of the three Militia vehicle columns out in plain view on a Way. The other two he had to search for; but eventually, he found their vehicles parked and the troops inside them presumably on foot, already penetrating into the hills.

The column that had been still in motion on the Way when he looked the first time had been the column furthest forward, the one that had obviously been intended to cut into the foothills ahead of the fleeing Command. At his second look, this column also had parked, at a point short of being level with the rendezvous; and the Militia in it had taken to the woods. The point from which they had done so reassured him that he would reach the rendezvous, himself, at least a couple of hours before they would be far enough into the wood to cross a trail left by any of the teams on their way there. However, any trails they did cross would be impossible to miss. It was not possible to run donkey trains through an open forest without making it clear even to an untrained eye that they had passed.

He was tempted to step up his pace. But his teaching had been to look ahead in instances like this; and it was plain that merely reaching the Command would not mark the end to his working day. He kept, therefore, to the same steady walk, and let his mind go back to the problem of Bleys' pursuit of him and the question of what his own actions should be under the circumstances.

He was still working with this problem when he finally walked into the temporary camp at the rendezvous site. The day had gone while he had been travelling, and there was no more than a couple of hours of sunlight left. He had been holding fatigue at bay until this moment; but the sight of the tents already set up, the sounds of evening activity and the cooking smells that had gone before to draw him into the camp made him suddenly aware of the weariness in his legs and body.

'Howard!' called Joralmon, spotting him as he walked in. 'We were beginning to worry about you!'

Joralmon got to his feet from the cone rifle he had disassembled and spread out before his tent on a cloth for cleaning. He came toward Hal, followed by everyone else close enough to hear the words, and free enough to break off what they were doing.

Hal waved them aside.

'Where's Rukh?' he asked. 'I need to talk to her.'

Hands pointed. Hal went on toward a tent at the far end of the camp, the others falling back as he turned from them, and paused just outside its closed front flap.

'Rukh?' he called. 'It's Howard. I've got to talk to you.'

'Come in, Howard.'

Her voice was clear and strong from within the tent and he pushed his way in to find her seated on a camp chair at a temporary table that had a map spread out upon it, and Child sitting opposite her. They both looked up at him.

'What is it?' asked Rukh, her eyes on his face.

'Three units of Militia are after us,' he said. 'I saw them from higher up, after I dropped off the driver of our truck at his cabin.'

He told them what he had seen, and what he had estimated.

'Two hours before they cut our trail?' Rukh frowned. 'But how close are they likely to cut it? How much time from then until they find us?'

'No telling,' said Hal.

He leaned over the map, which showed the foothills beyond Masenvale and pointed with his finger as he talked. 'Figuring their travel time through the woods to give them a maximum distance by the time it took me to get here, I drew an arc to cut the trails of our teams, getting here, and the arc cut the closest of the trails almost right here at the rendezvous. But that's looking at the best they'd be able to do. Where they'll really cut one of them depends on the angle to our line of travel, on which they came into the woods. Straight in, at a ninety-degree angle to the Way where they left their vehicles parked, it'd take them two hours to cross one of our trails. At more than ninety degrees, it'd take longer, but then they'd be headed back the way they came, which isn't likely. At a more acute angle, it'd also take them longer, to reach the trail – but they could strike it right on top of us, here.'

Rukh picked up a ruler, set its markings to the scale of the map before them, and measured the distance between the points Hal had indicated.

'Perhaps a third more time to cross our trail at this point here,' she said, thoughtfully, while Child bent his harsh visage above her moving hands. 'A maximum of forty minutes beyond the two hours you figured, Howard. It'll take us at least half an hour to break camp and get on our way; and we won't be ready to travel properly, at that. But there's no choice.'

She looked across at Child.

'James?'

He shook his head.

'No choice.' He looked grimly at Hal. 'Thou hast done well, Howard.'

'I just happened to be in the right spot at the right time,' Hal said. 'If I hadn't driven that truck driver to his cabin, I'd never have had a chance to see what was coming after us.'

'Then we move,' said Rukh. 'James, would you get people started?'

Child rose and went out.

'Howard,' said Rukh, 'go with him and help.'

He stood where he was.

'If I could mention something –' he began.

'Of course.' Her dark eyes considered him. 'You've been coming as fast as you could all day to bring word to us. Forget trying to help. Get half an hour's rest while the packing's going on. Sleep some if you can.'

'That wasn't what I was going to say.' He rested one hand on the back of Child's empty camp chair. Suddenly his weariness was overwhelming. 'I ought to tell you we ran into a road block on our way to the gathering point. It had to have been set up ahead of time. The man who drove us was right in what he said back at the Mohler-Beni farm, when he said I was a danger to you all. The road block had been set up to look for me. That's also why these three units were waiting and could be right on top of us after the raid.'

She nodded, still looking at him.

'The point is,' he said, with effort, 'the man was right. As long as I'm with you, I'm drawing all their attention to this Command. Maybe if I leave, I can draw them off.'

'Do you know why they'd be hunting you?' she asked.

He shook his head.

'I'm not sure. All I know about the Others, directly, is what I told you of what happened at my home. I'm guessing it's Bleys Ahrens, their Vice-Chairman – the tall one of the two that were there that day my tutors were killed – who wants me. But exactly why is another question. At any rate, I think I ought to leave.'

'You heard James at the farm,' Rukh said, quietly, 'when that man suggested it. The Commands have never abandoned their own people.'

'Am I really one of those people?'

She looked at him.

'You've lived and fought with us. What else?' she said. 'But if you want a further reason, think a moment. If they want you badly enough to mobilize the Militia across a countryside, do you think they'd simply let go the Command you were associated with – particularly when that Command had just pulled off two raids within their city limits?'

He did not answer.

'Go rest, Howard,' she said.

He shook his head.

'I'm all right. I'll just get something to eat.'

248

'Get Tallah to give you something you can carry along and eat as we move,' Rukh said. 'Then lie down. That's an order.'

'All right,' he said.

He got bread and bean-paste from Tallah, ate part of it, rewrapped the rest, put it in his pack and lay down. It seemed that he barely blinked his eyes before he was being shaken awake. He looked up groggily into the face of Jason.

'Howard – time to move,' Jason said. He offered Hal a steaming cup. 'Here, the last of the coffee.'

Hal drank the hot liquid gratefully. It was not really coffee, even as Harmony knew it, but a variform of a native plant that had been tamed to make a brewable hot drink. But the sour gray liquid contained a certain amount of chemical stimulants; and by the time he was on his feet with his pack on his back and his rifle in hand, he was ready to move.

The Command travelled as rapidly as the terrain and the donkeys would permit, in the two hours that remained to them before darkness. When the ground became obscure under their feet, Rukh called a halt; and Hal went forward from his position with the donkeys at the tail of the Command to talk to her.

'Going to camp?' he asked.

'Yes,' her voice came out of the blur that was her face, not more than arm's length from him.

He looked up at the sky, which was overcast, but lightly.

'The moon'll be up later on,' he said. 'And the clouds may blow clear from time to time. If we could keep moving we could put a much safer distance between us and that Militia unit. In the daytime, without donkeys to slow them up, they'll begin to gain on us.'

'We'll be out of their district by noon tomorrow,' said Rukh. 'No Militia unit ever follows beyond its own district limits unless it's in a running fight. We ought to be able to stay ahead of them until we're in the next district; and while they get a unit after us from the local Militia there, we ought to be able to lose them.'

'Maybe,' he said. 'In any case, if you want to keep going, there's a way.'

She did not say anything for a second. Then –

'What?'

'There're ways of reading the ground even when it's as dark as this,' he said. 'It was part of my training; and I think I can still do it. We could rope the Command together, in effect, with me in the lead; and if the sky clears and the moon comes out, we can keep going the rest of the night. If we stop, and spread out to sleep, we won't get going again until dawn.'

There was silence from her still figure and invisible face.

'Even with you to lead,' she said, 'how's that going to keep the rest of us from stumbling over ground we can't see?'

'At the very least,' he said, 'I can steer us around things in our way and pick out the more level surfaces to walk on. It works, believe me. I've done it back on Earth.'

Another short silence.

'All right,' she said. 'How do you want the Command roped together?'

It took a full hour to get everyone lined up and connected. Hal made one last tour up and down the line, reminding each one he passed to keep slack in the line connected to the person just ahead. Then he took the lead and started out.

There was nothing in what he was doing that ordinary training could not have developed in anyone. His ability to see his way was based on a number of things, chief of which was the fact that even woods-wise people like the members of the Command instinctively raised their gaze to the relative brightness of even a heavily overcast sky when going through the night-dark outdoors, and lost part of the perception they could have maintained by keeping their eyes adjusted to the darkness at ground level.

What he made use of beyond this was a near-hypnotic concentration of attention on the ground just ahead, reinforced by a similar concentration of his ordinary powers of scent, hearing and balance, to read as much as possible of what was underfoot with these senses as well. All this had been honed by field practice during those early years of his. In fact the largest part of his skill in this was owed to that practice alone. The one danger in what he did was that of running into something above ground level that his downcast eyes had not seen; and to protect himself against this he carried a staff vertically before him, its upper end above his head and its lower end at mid-calf height.

In the beginning of that night trek, the progress of the Command was painfully slow. In spite of his warnings, individuals along the line allowed the rope between them and the person ahead to tighten, with the result that when either of them stumbled or fell, the other was occasionally dragged down as well; and the progress of the whole line halted. But gradually, as with any other physical activity, the members of the Command began to pick up the tricks that made his sort of night movement practical. The falls and the inadvertent stops came less often; and their speed increased. The forward movement of the Command became less like a drunken snake-dance through the dark, and more of a purposeful travelling.

But their speed of straight-line movement was still nothing to be proud of. Back on Earth, practicing this technique with Malachi in the lead and three trained helpers, plus equally trained pack animals, Hal and the others had made almost as good time as they might in broad daylight. Here, the donkeys adjusted to the means of travel faster than the humans in the line, not being cursed with human imaginations and the tendency to guess. But overall, improvement was slow. Rukh, directly behind Hal, was one of the quickest to learn the necessity for a slack line, but there were others, like the woman behind her, who continually forgot.

Hal himself passed quickly into a state of concentration that effectively blanked out everything but his immediate task; and as the evening wore on, the intermediary of his conscious mind cut out entirely. He moved through a maze of perception, navigating through the dark without questioning the impulses that sent him one way or another; almost unconscious of the constant stream of warnings and information about the ground under his feet that he uttered as he went, for the benefit of Rukh behind him, so that there was a steady feed of verbal signals being passed rearward from person to person in the line.

With the waxing of the night hours, the thin new moon rose behind the clouds and the night winds freshened. Breaks in the cloud cover began to come more often; and, even when they did not break, the clouds were thinner, permitting more light to reach the ground. To these changes, Hal paid no conscious attention. He was not even aware of his own ground speed picking up and the progress of the line behind him improving as the illumination of the earth before him improved. He was long past ordinary fatigue, into adrenaline overdrive. He had forgotten his body entirely; and nearly forgotten his senses, as direct instruments of that body and mind. He lived in a universe of varying shades of gray and black; and he swam through that universe, forgetting everything else. Time, the goal toward which he progressed, the reason for progressing, all these were lost to him. Even the thought of those things he turned aside from, as physical obstacles, was forgotten. He turned right and left as he went without understanding why he turned; knowing only that this was his purpose – to move in this careful and intricate fashion, indefinitely.

A jerk on the line connecting him with Rukh eventually stopped him. He rotated blindly to face her.

'We'll stop now,' her voice came strongly to him. 'It's light enough to see by.'

He was aware that the available illumination had increased. He had been able to tell this from the lightening of the shades of gray he saw, the absence of blackness. But for a moment, looking across little more than a meter of distance, caught up still in the concentration of his long navigation, he could not see her. His mind registered her only as one more abstract in varying shades of gray, reflected illumination. Similarly, what she said made no sense to him. His mind registered and identified the words, but could not relate them to the universe in which he was still continuing to feel the way for all of them.

Then sight and understanding flooded back in on him at once. He saw the forest floor, the trees and the bushes about them in the stoic, lean light of pre-dawn; and it finally registered on him that the night, and his task, were over.

He was conscious of falling; but he did not feel the ground when he struck it.

He came slowly back to awareness. Someone was shaking him. With a great effort he opened his eyes and saw it was Rukh.

'Sit up,' she said.

He struggled into a sitting position, discovering that, somehow, a tarp had materialized under him and blankets over him. When he was up he felt something – it was a filled packsack, he saw, on looking – pushed into place behind him, so that he had something to support his back. Rukh put a bowl of undefined hot food – stew, apparently – in his hands.

'Get this inside you,' she told him.

He looked about at trees lit by a late morning light.

'What time is it?' he asked, and was startled to hear his voice come out as a croak.

'One hour until noon. Eat.'

She rose and left him. Still numb in body and brain, he began to eat the stew, using the spoon she had left in the bowl. He could not remember ever tasting anything so delicious; and with each hot bite, life woke more fully in him. The bowl was suddenly empty. He put it aside, got up, folded the blankets and tarp – they were his own, he discovered, as the packsack was his – and stowed them in the pack. But the bowl and spoon were not his. He took them down to the stream by which they had set up camp and washed both items. Around him the rest of the Command were striking their tents or rolling bedsacks, preparatory to getting on their way. He brought the bowl and spoon to Tallah.

'Not the kitchen's,' Tallah said, irritably, over her shoulder as she hurried just-packed equipment onto the backs of the kitchen donkeys. 'Those're Rukh's.'

He took them to Rukh.

'Thank you,' he said, handing them back.

'You're welcome. How are you?'

'I'm awake, he said.

'How do you feel?'

'A little stiff – all right, though.'

'I'm sending the wounded off with a separate party,' Rukh told him, 'with as much of the equipment as we can spare, so as to lighten our load as far as we can. They'll leave us by ones and twos along the line of march today; and hopefully the Militia won't notice their trails in their hot pursuit of ours. Morelly's going leaves us one team leader short. I've talked it over with James and decided it's time we started to use that training of yours on an official basis. I want to appoint you a group leader.'

He nodded.

'There's more to it than that,' she said. 'The other leaders are all senior to you and normally the Command'd have to lose James and myself and all the others before you'd find yourself responsible for the Command. But I'd like to tell the rest of the group leaders something of your special training – with your permission – so that I can also tell them that if you had the experience, James and I would consider you as first in line to be his replacement, as Lieutenant, if anything happened to him. Will you agree to that?'

It took his still-fatigued and sleep-numbed brain a few moments to consider the implications of what she had just asked.

'Since it's an open secret that the Militia want me more than ordinarily,' he said at last, 'there's no reason not to tell them I had special training, and what kinds of training it was. But I'd appreciate it if you didn't tell them the names of my tutors, or anything more than they actually need to know.'

'Of course.'

There was, for a moment, almost a gentle note in her voice; but it was gone before he could do any more than register it; and in fact if it had not been for his memory's ability to replay anything he had just heard, he would have been unsure that he had heard it at all. Standing this close to her, he could feel the outflow of a dark and vibrant living power from her, like a solid pressure.

'You're a sub-officer from now on, then,' she said 'and I'll expect you to come looking for James and myself, whenever we halt, so that we can make use of what you can offer to our planning. For right now, you might note that the Militia are roughly eight kilometers behind us and they're making a kilometer an hour over best pace. Also, what's chasing us now is the first and second units you saw, combined.'

She proceeded to brief him on other details:

Jason and two of the others had been sent off as soon as they had stopped, to climb the side of the mountain they were currently skirting and get enough altitude to check behind them with field viewers for their pursuers.

They had been early enough to witness the smoke plumes rising above the trees from the cooking of a morning meal, barely within viewer range; and make the estimate of the marching time that the Militia would require to catch up with the Command, if it simply stayed where it was. However, the smoke also indicated a force at least double the size of one of the units Hal had seen and described; and later observation, as the Militia broke camp and began to move, had confirmed this fact.

Once the troops were again on the move, it became possible for Jason and the others to make a firm estimate of their rate of march. It

253

was clear that their progress amounted to a strong four kilometers an hour through the open forest. The Command, with its donkeys, was lucky to make three kilometers an hour under the same conditions. In the three hours in which the Militia units had been on the move while the Command was resting, the troops had gained twelve hours of travel time upon them and were now no more than six hours behind them. By twilight, they would catch up – that is if they continued their pursuit at that speed.

'But I think we can shake them about mid-afternoon,' said Rukh.

She explained that they were no more than three hours now from the border of another district.

'And they don't pursue into another district?' Hal asked.

'Legally, only when they're in hot pursuit – which these could consider they were,' she answered, dryly. 'In practice, there's a lot of rivalry between different districts. It goes back to the old sect differences that made us almost into separate countries, once. The Militia of one district don't like the Militia from another coming on their territory. These after us now could keep coming; but the chances are they'll break off and message the Militia of the other district to take up pursuit.'

'If they message ahead before we get there, or if they've messaged ahead already,' said Hal, 'we could be caught between two fires.'

'I said there was a lot of rivalry. If they can't catch us themselves, they aren't usually too enthusiastic about the next district doing it and getting all the credit. The odds are they'll follow us over the border, but only as far as they dare before breaking off pursuit. It's only then they'll message the local Militia; and it'll take the locals two or three hours to get a pursuit going.'

'I see,' said Hal.

'With ordinary luck, we ought to gain eight or nine hours lead time while they're changing pursuit units.' Rukh smiled slightly. 'And by that time we ought to be well on our way to the border of the next district south, where the same thing'll happen and we'll pick up that much more of a lead. This is the way the Commands usually lose pursuit by the Militia forces.'

Her gaze went past his shoulder, into the camp.

'But we're almost ready to go,' she said. 'For the moment, you don't have to do anything but travel with the rest of the Command. I'll check with you later in the day to see how your strength's holding up after yesterday. If you're in shape for it, later on, I might have a special duty for you. Meanwhile, be thinking of who you might want in your team. You'll be taking Morelly's people to begin with, but later on there'll be chance to have the people you want trade off of the other teams on to yours, if everyone concerned agrees.'

Hal went to get his pack.

CHAPTER TWENTY-SIX

The rest of the Command, like Hal, had had a long twenty-four hours before settling down to sleep most of the seven hours just past. At the beginning of this new day's march, they moved doggedly and silently, rather than with their usual accustomed easiness. But, like Hal making the walk from the cabin to the rendezvous the day before, they warmed to the travel as they moved along. They were in good condition from their continual trekking; and they had been eating and sleeping much better than they were used to, these last few weeks among the farm families on their way to Masenvale.

So it happened that they picked up speed as they went along; while the Militia units, for all their full night of rest, began to lag in the heat of the afternoon. Reports from scouts sent up tall trees or nearby observation points, with field viewers, reported evidence that their pursuers had taken to stopping for a ten minute break every hour. At mid-afternoon Rukh sent a runner to call Hal up to the front of the Command to speak with her. He came, and they walked along side by side, a few meters in front of the others for the sake of privacy, Child walking silent on her other side.

'How're you feeling now?' she asked Hal.

'Fine,' he said.

Generally speaking, it was the truth. There was a core of fatigue buried in him; but other than that he felt as well as he would have normally, if not a trifle better. A corner of his mind recognized the fact that he was in overdrive once more; but this was nothing like the extreme state of effort he had worked himself into during the night's travel.

'Then I've got a job for you,' she said.

He nodded.

'According to the best estimate James and I can make,' she said, 'we've just crossed the border into the next district. The Militia behind us'll come at least this far. It'd help in our assessment of the situation if we had any idea of what kind of shape they're in, what kind of attitude they've got toward their officers, and how they're feeling about the prospects of catching us. It's a job for you, bêcause you might be able to get close enough to find out those things without being caught.'

'I ought to be able to,' he said. 'It'd be easier if they were stopped; but then their being on the march gives me advantages too.'

He checked himself on the verge of saying something more, about the general amateurishness of the Militia, since many of the things he had been about to mention would be equally applicable to the Commands. But it was a fact that, by the standards he had acquired from Malachi, both organizations acted in some ways more like children's clubs out on a hike than military or paramilitary outfits.

'Good,' Rukh was saying briskly. 'Take whoever you need, but I'd suggest no more than four or five, for the sake of moving swiftly.'

'Two,' Hal said, 'as fail-safe in case I don't get back. One to carry the word if I don't; and one more, in case the one backing me up has some kind of accident. I'll take Jason and Joralmon, if that's all right.'

For a moment a faint frown line marked the perfect skin between Rukh's dark eyes.

'They ought, probably, to be from your own team,' she said. 'But considering this is a tricky business . . . tell their group leaders I said it was all right.'

He nodded.

'Wait here while we go on and keep the Militia under observation,' she went on. 'That'll let you rest as much as possible; and when they get this far, you can take your chances of getting close enough to observe them then, or follow along until your chances improve.'

He nodded again.

With Jason and Joralmon he set up an observation post some three hundred meters off the estimated line of march of the Militia, and they took turns observing from a treetop the approach of their pursuers, while the Command went on ahead. The troops were now only a couple of kilometers behind them; and they came on steadily.

It was possible to hear their approach well before they became visible as individuals, seen through the leaves of the forest cover, for they were not moving silently. Sitting in the high, swaying fork of the tall tree he had chosen to observe from, Hal silently checked out in his own mind one particular supposition he had been wanting to test. It had been his guess for some time that the Militia – unless they were in some special units organized specifically for pursuit purposes – were composed mainly of the equivalent of garrison soldiers, who were more comfortable with pavement under their feet than the earth of a forest floor.

As those now approaching became more visible, what he saw confirmed that notion. The soldiers he watched looked hot and uncomfortable, like men unaccustomed to this kind of moving over rough country on foot. Their packs were obviously designed to carry gear and supplies for only a short excursion; and at the same time gave the impression that they had been designed at least as much for parade ground looks as for practicality in the field. They were plainly marching under orders of silence for the lower ranks; although the noisily-shouted commands and full-voiced conversations of their officers made a mockery of field-level quiet.

Their column drew close, then stopped, a little more than two hundred meters short of being level with the observation post, for what seemed one of their hourly march breaks. The troops dropped to the ground, loosened their pack straps and lay back with the silence rule apparently relaxed for the moment. Hal slipped down from the tree.

'The two of you stay here,' he told Jason and Joralmon. 'When they start to move again, keep parallel with them but at least this far out and on this side of them. If I don't get back to you in half an hour, or you see some evidence they've got me, get back to Rukh with the information we've already picked up. If I've just been delayed, I'll still catch up with you. But if they've got me, they'll be watching for anyone else and you won't have a chance to get close safely. Understood?'

'Yes, Howard,' Jason said; and Joralmon nodded.

Hal went off toward the Militia's stopping spot. When he got there, he found that it was entirely possible for him to prowl up and down their line close enough to overhear clearly even relatively low-voiced conversation. The column had evidently been marching with no point and no flank guards, and nothing resembling sentries had been set up while they were taking their break. It was an incredible behavior that probably stemmed from the fact that the last thing in the world these domestic troops expected was any kind of counterattack from the Commands they chased – which said nothing complimentary about the Commands, themselves.

He moved up and down the length of the resting column, a handful of meters out from them, hidden by the undergrowth that flanked their line; and, since it was clear he could choose whatever he wished to listen to, he ended up squatting behind some bushes less than five meters from the head of the line, where a sort of officers' council was being held.

There were five men there wearing the better-fitted black uniform of the commissioned ranks, but the argument that was going on seemed to be between two of them, only. Both of these wore the tabs of Militia Captains; and one of them was familiar – it was the officer of the Citadel cells and the ambush in the pass, the one that the driver's information had identified with the name of Barbage.

'. . . Yes, I say it to thee,' Barbage was saying to the other Captain. Barbage was on his feet. The others sat in a row on a log uprooted by some past storm, with the second Commandant at one end of their line. 'I have been given commission by authority far above thee, and beyond that by the Great Teacher himself; and if I say to thee, go – thou wilt go!'

257

The other Captain looked upward and across at Barbage with a tightly-closed jaw. He was a man perhaps five years younger, no more than mid-way into his thirties; but his face was square and heavy with oncoming middle age, and his neck was thick.

'I've seen your orders,' he said. His voice was not hoarse, but thick in his throat – a parade-ground voice. 'They don't say anything about pursuing over district borders.'

'Thou toy man!' said Barbage; and his voice was harsh with contempt. 'What is it to me how such as thee read thy orders? I know the will of those who sent me; and I order thee, that thou pursuest how and where I tell thee to pursue!'

The other Captain had half-risen from the log, his face gone pale.

'You may have orders!' he said, even more thickly. 'But you don't outrank me and there's nothing that says I have to take that sort of language from you. So watch what you say or pick yourself a weapon – I don't care either way.'

Barbage's thin upper lip curled slightly.

'Weapon? What Baal's pride is this to think that in the Lord's work thou mightest be worthy of affront? Unlike thee, I have no weapons. Only tools which the Lord has given me for my work. So thou hast something called a weapon, then? No doubt that which I see on thy leg there. Make use of it therefore, since thou did not like the name I gave thee!'

The Captain flushed.

'You're unarmed,' he said shortly.

And indeed, Hal saw, unlike all the rest of the officers and men here, Barbage was wearing only his uniform.

'Oh, let not that stop thee,' said Barbage, ironically. 'For the true servants of the Lord, tools are ever ready to hand.'

He made one long step while the other still stared at him, to end standing beside the most junior of the officers sitting on the log, laid his hand on the young officer's sidearm buttoned-down holster and flicked up the weather flap with his thumbnail. His hand curled around the exposed butt of the power pistol beneath. A twist of the wrist would be all that would be needed to bring the gun out of its breakaway holster, aim and fire it; while the other would have needed to reach for his own buttoned-down holster before he could fire.

From the far end of the log the Captain stared, suddenly white-faced and foolish, at him.

'I meant . . .' the words stumbled on his tongue. 'Not like this. A proper meeting with seconds –'

'Alas,' said Barbage, 'such games are unfamiliar to me. So I will kill thee now to decide whether we continue or turn back, since thou hast not chosen to obey my orders – unless thou shouldst kill me first to prove thy right to do as *thou* wishest. That is how thou wouldst do things, with thy weapons, and thy meetings and thy seconds, is it not?'

He paused, but the other did not answer.

'Very well, then,' said Barbage. He drew the power pistol from the holster of the junior officer and levelled it at his equal in rank.

'In the Lord's name –' broke out the other, hoarsely. 'Have it any way you want. We'll go on then, over the border!'

'I am happy to hear thee decide so,' said Barbage. He replaced the pistol in the holster from which he had drawn it and stepped away from the young force-leader who owned it. 'We will continue until we make contact with the pursuit unit sent out from the next district; at which time I will join them; and thou, with thy officers and men, mayst go back to thy small games in town. That should be soon. When are the troops from the next district to meet us?'

The other Captain stared at him without answering for a moment.

'It'll take them a few hours,' he said, at last.

'Hours?' Barbage walked forward toward him; and the other stood up swiftly, almost as if he expected Barbage to hit him. 'Why hours? When didst thou message them to meet us?'

'We . . . generally don't message until we're sure the Children of Wrath are going to cross over into the next district –'

'Thou whimpering fool!' said Barbage, softly. 'Hath it not been plain from the beginning that they were fleeing into the next district and beyond?'

'Well, yes. But we might have caught them. . . .'

The other's voice hesitated and ceased.

'Message them *now!*' Barbage's eyes were absolutely unmoving.

'Of course. Of course. Chaims –' he turned sharply to the young force-leader whose sidearm Barbage had laid his hand on, 'get a message off to Hlaber District Command and tell them the situation. Say that Captain Barbage, operating here under special orders, needs a pursuit unit out here to take over from us in one hour. Tell them to check with South Promise HQ on his authority to require that sort of special action. Well? Move! *Move!*'

The junior officer jerked to his feet and ran off down the column.

Hal faded back through the greenery until he was safely enough beyond observation to turn and run himself – for the observation point. Jason, sitting at the foot of the tree with Joralmon above him in the observation post, scrambled upright as Hal reached him.

'I've found out what we need to know,' Hal said, 'and I'm going to be making the best time I can to get the information to the Command. You two follow as fast as you're able to. As we estimated, it's two full pursuit units under Barbage, the captain who ran the ambush on us in the pass. They've just sent for help from the next district; and Barbage is going to keep this bunch coming until they can be relieved – then he'll switch over and travel with the new unit. Share that information with Joralmon, and both of you come after me as fast as you can.'

'Right,' said Jason; and Hal, turning on his heel, set out in pursuit of the Command.

The distance before him now was shorter than that he had had to cover the day before. He ran, therefore, at a steady ground-covering pace through the sunlit afternoon woods, his cone rifle clipped vertically to the harness of the light pack on his back, bouncing rhythmically upon his shoulder blades. When he caught up at last with Rukh and the Command, his shirt was dark and sodden with sweat.

'Jason? Joralmon?' Rukh said, as he stopped before her.

'They're fine. They're behind me. I came ahead to get word to you as soon as possible. Barbage – the officer in the pass – is the one running the pursuit. He's got special authority, it seems. . . .'

Hal ran out of breath. Rukh waited while he got it back.

'He's bullying the local Militia officers to keep after us until they can be joined by a unit from the next district – and they've just now sent for that other unit under pressure of Barbage's special authority, to get it out in an hour. There's not going to be the chance to pick up additional lead time and distance the way you told me the Commands usually do.'

She nodded slowly, listening, and he gave her, word for word out of that perfect recall of his, exactly the conversation he had overheard at the head of the Militia column.

When he was done, she breathed deeply once and turned to Child, who had come up while Hal was talking.

'You heard, James? They're going to stay right behind us.'

'I heard,' he said.

'You've been through these foothills before. How far are we from the next district?'

'A day and a half, thirty-six hours if we go on without stopping,' he answered. 'Up to three full days with normal rest; and thy people are already short of sleep, Rukh.'

'If it weren't for the donkeys we could disperse into the mountains and leave them nothing to chase.' Her eyes studied the ground, thoughtfully, as if she read an invisible map there. 'But if we abandon the donkeys, we also have to abandon the fertilizer and the finished gunpowder we picked up as a primer for it; and with that, over a year's work to sabotage the Core Tap goes down the drain.'

She raised her eyes and looked at Child.

'To say nothing of the lives that have been lost to get it this far.'

'It is God's will,' the older man answered. 'Unless it is thy wish to stand and fight.'

'This Barbage has taken that into account, it seems,' Rukh said. 'With two full units, there're too many behind us now to hope to fight and get away from safely. Presumably, the new Militia replacing these are going to be in the same kind of numbers and strength.'

She turned and walked a few steps away from both Hal and Child, turned and came back again.

'All right,' she said. 'We'll try laying a false trail and see if that can't buy us some time. James, we'll need to give up at least a dozen of the spare donkeys. Rope them three abreast so they leave the most noticeable track; and bring up the rear with them. Luckily, our wounded have gotten away already. Now the rest of us will have to do the same thing, taking off one or two at a time without leaving any sign for the Militia to pick up. Howard –'

'Yes?' Hal said.

'With Jason not back, it's going to have to be you sticking with these particular donkeys until everyone else is gone. Once that happens, keep leading them on straight for at least half an hour more. Then hitch and leave them for the Militia to find, and get out yourself without leaving a trail, if you can. Then come join us at the new rendezvous we'll set up.'

'There's no way to really hide the sign of the loaded donkeys you'll be peeling off earlier,' said Hal.

'I know.' Rukh sighed heavily. 'We'll just have to gamble Barbage is following too hotly after us to look for signs of anyone leaving our line of march; and that the plain tracks of the dozen beasts in the rear makes too attractive a trail for them to suspect anything.'

CHAPTER TWENTY-SEVEN

From nearby in the shadowed woods, as he sat wrapped in a weather cloak on sentry duty on a cool, cloudless night, and some twenty meters from the winking coals of the burnt-down campfires and dark tents of the Command, Hal heard the sound of coughing. But he did not turn. It was Child, gone off a little from the camp into the night – no longer to hide his now-frequent discomfort, but to find a small amount of privacy in which to live with it.

Under the stupidity of his own numbing accumulation of fatigue, Hal's mind was working – slowly, but effectively. He was employing an Exotic technique in which he had been drilled by Walter. In essence, it was like reading a printed page with a magnifying glass that gave him one letter at a time. Plainly, some kind of decision had to be made. Unable to catch them, Barbage and his unlimitedly available Militia forces had settled for harrying them into the kind of exhaustion that would make their eventual capture certain.

Rukh's trick with the donkeys had won them enough of an initial lead on Barbage and the Militia from the second district, so that the Command had been able to get safely over the border into the third district; and there, luck, or an uncooperative local Militia official, had stretched that lead into enough of an edge so that they had been able to get clear of that district and into a fourth one. By that time they were into a different type of countryside; one that worked to their advantage more than it did to that of their pursuers.

Here, the foothills had spread out and become an open, rolling territory of sandy and stony soil replacing the flat, rich farmland they had left behind them. They were no longer penned closely between the lowlands and the mountains; the mountains were far off, blue on the horizon, and the lowlands were lost beyond the opposite horizon, even further.

In this different land of scrub trees, bushes, and narrow streams, was their eventual goal, the city of Ahruma itself, which enclosed the power plant built over the Core Tap they planned to sabotage. There were farms in this territory, too, but they were poor ones, scattered, small, and served with a meager network of roads. For Militia, it was bad country in which to mount a pursuit; but for a Command, it was even worse country in which to survive. As Rukh had said, without their donkey-loads of potential explosive, the Command could have dispersed and effectively ceased to be. But as long as they held tenaciously to the fertilizer and the gunpowder – and therefore necessarily to the donkeys themselves – they could not lose the troops that followed them.

For that reason, they dared not move into Ahruma as planned and contact local sympathizers there for help and to begin mounting their attack on the power plant. The end result of this situation had been that they were continuing to wander the dry hill country around the city at a distance far enough off not to arouse Militia suspicions as to their true destination.

They had stripped the Command to its essentials – those beasts and people without whom the mission could not be accomplished. Now the attrition of being hounded day and night was beginning to wear down both those on two legs and on four. In the end, if this kept up, Barbage would run them into an exhaustion in which they would be forced to stand and fight; and which would give him an easy victory.

The military answer, Hal's early lessons told him, was to attack the Militia camp at night with a small number of the Command; who would then throw their lives away, but do enough damage to render the troops incapable of further pursuit until they could acquire replacements of men and equipment – buying at least twenty-four hours. In that space of time the rest of the Command could force-march to the outskirts of Ahruma and lose themselves, with what their donkeys carried, in the city with their sympathizers.

But the military answer was one that could coldly calculate a certain percentage of an available force as expendable for the purchase of a tactical advantage to the force as a whole. This was unacceptable, in the case of the Command, whose people were as close as members of the same family; and where the Captain would never order such an action.

So the question of what to do came back to turn upon his own actions. Both Barbage and Rukh were trapped in a situation where they could do little but wait for it to wear down. He, on the other hand, should be able to act. And should if he could. But until now, fogged by the arrears of tiredness, his mind had failed to come up with a workable plan.

The sound of coughing had ceased. A few moments later, his ears caught the faint sounds of Child making his way back to his tent. Hal got to his feet. As a sub-officer, he was supposed to be exempt from sentry, kitchen, and other ordinary duties so that he could keep himself ready and alert to his higher responsibilities. But in actual practice, like most of the Command's other sub-officers, he ended up a good share of the time filling in under emergency conditions for one or the other of the members of his own group. Just now he had taken over the sentry duty of one of the team he had inherited from Morelly, who had begun out of excess of exhaustion to nod off on post. But now the man he had relieved had had an extra two hours of sleep; and it was time to return him to his obligations. Hal got to his feet and went into the camp.

He pushed through the flap of a tent and shook the slumbering man.

'Moh,' he said, speaking softly, so as not to wake the three other sleepers in the tent, into the ear visible above the edge of the sleeping sack, 'time to go back on duty.'

The sleeper grunted, stirred, opened his eyes and began wearily to climb out of his bedsack. Hal stayed with him until he was armed and on post, then went to check on the other two sentries posted about the camp.

The others, both women, were awake and reporting all quiet. The Militia camp was only an estimated twelve kilometers from them; and while a nighttime attack by the clumsier, city-trained enemy was possible, it was unlikely. Still, it paid not to take chances. On impulse, Hal went back into the camp, found the tent where Child slept alone, and let himself through the flap.

He squatted beside the Command's now slumbering Lieutenant. For a moment he watched the face, aged a dozen years or more by the exhaustion of the last week, further deepened into a mask of wrinkles and bones by its relaxation into unconsciousness.

'Child-of-God . . .' he said softly.

He had barely breathed the words. But instantly the other was awake and looking up at him, and Hal knew that inside the sack, one bony hand had closed around the butt of a power pistol with a sawed-off barrel, pointing it through the cloth at whoever had roused him.

'Howard?' said Child, equally low-voiced although there was no one at hand to disturb.

'It's close to the end of my watch,' Hal said. 'I'd like to make a quick run, by myself, to the Militia camp – just to see how tired they look; and, with luck, I might pick up one of their maps of this area. We could do with the chance to check our own maps against theirs. Also, with real luck, I could get a map marked with their rendezvous and supply spots.'

Child lay still for a few seconds more.

'That's the thing,' Hal said. 'I'd like to leave now, to make as much use as possible of the darkness that's left. I could wake Falt early, and I don't think he'd object to going on watch an hour or so before his time.'

Child lay still again for several seconds.

'Very well,' he said, 'provided Falt agrees. If he hath objection, come back to me.'

'I will,' said Hal.

He got up and went out. Closing the tent flap behind him, he heard Child, awake once more to the irritation in his lungs, cough briefly.

Falt did not, as Hal had known he would not, object. Hal got his cone rifle and a small travelling pack to supplement his sidearm and knife, blackened his hands and face and left. An hour and eighteen minutes later he was crouching down in the darkness on the bank of a creek behind a stand of young variform willows, having crept up to almost within arm's-length of a pair of young Militiamen. The pair was apparently on watch by a fire at one end of the camp – a watch that presumably took the place of the sentries he had never known the Militia forces to put out.

'. . . soon,' one of these was saying as Hal eased into position. They were both about middle height for Harmonyites, black-haired and fresh-faced – no more than in their late teens. 'And I'll be glad to get back. I have little stomach for this sort of plowing through the woods all the time.'

'Thou hast, hast thou?' The jeer in the voice of the other was obvious. 'It's I *have* little stomach, brickhead! You'll never make a prophet, old or young.'

'You won't, either! Anyway, I'm one of the Elect. You aren't!'

'Who says I'm not? And who told you you were?'

'My folks –'

'*Are we on watch?*' Barbage was suddenly on the other side of the fire, shoulders a little hunched, eyes like polished obsidian chips in their reflection of the firelight. 'Or are we playing the games that childhood hath still left in us?'

The two were silent, staring at him.

'Answer me!'

'Games,' muttered the two, low-voiced.

'And why should we not play games when we are on watch?'

But Hal did not wait to hear the answers of the two as Barbage continued to catechize them. He moved backward, got to his feet, and slipped around the perimeter of the encampment until he was level with the tents of the officers, just a short distance from the fire and easily recognizable by their better cloth and greater size.

There were six of them. Hal slid out of the darkness of the surrounding undergrowth to the back wall of the first in line. With the razor tip of his knife, soundlessly, he made a small slit in the fabric and spread the slit enough to look within. It took a moment for his vision to adjust to the greater darkness within, but when it did he saw a camp chair, a table, and a cot – unoccupied. As the one in effective command of the expedition, Barbage had – as Hal had suspected – taken the first tent in the officer's row.

Hal crept quietly around the side of the tent and looked toward the fire. The rest of the camp slumbered. Barbage, standing, still had his back to his own quarters; and the two he was verbally trouncing would be blinded by the close firelight to something as far away as this tent row, even if all their attention had not been frozen on Barbage.

Softly and swiftly, Hal turned the corner of the tent, lifted its flap, and let himself inside.

He had no time to examine the interior in detail. There was a map in the viewer lying among papers on the table; but to take it would make too obvious his visit. Hal looked about and found what he expected, a map case at the foot of the bed. Opening it, he came up with a full rack of slides for the viewer. Hastily, he took them all to the table, took out the slide already in the viewer and began to check the other slides out in it, one by one.

He found one of the territory roughly three days' march ahead, took it out and replaced it with the original slide, and put the other slides back in the mapcase. Outside the voice of Barbage ceased speaking. Hal stepped to the tent flap and peered out, his fingers lightly grasping the knife hilt.

But Barbage was still standing, silently staring at the two by the fire. A moment later he began to speak to them again; and in a second Hal was in the woods. Another minute put him safely beyond earshot of the voice; and five minutes later he was well on his way back to the Command.

When he returned, daylight was still a full hour off; and Child, when Hal looked into the Lieutenant's tent, was sleeping heavily. Hal went back to his own tent and found his own map viewer. Sitting cross-legged in the darkness while Jason slept undisturbed behind him, he put the stolen slide into it.

The small interior illuminant of the viewer, triggered to life by his finger pressure on its control, made the map leap into white, illuminated relief before him. It showed a stretch of rises and hollows of land, covered with scrub vegetation identical with the area they were now in. To the bottom of its display, a road ran almost horizontally across the map, to intersect with a crossroad near the lower right corner. Marked along the road were three asterisks, with code marks next to them.

The code marks were undecipherable, but a good guess could be made at what they represented. They would give details of the number of trucks and personnel who would be delivering supplies to the points the asterisks marked. It was the delivery of such supplies that allowed the Militia to travel light; and made up for the fact that the Militiamen themselves were, from lack of experience, slow and clumsy compared to the members of the Command. Also, the frequent contact with vehicles at the delivery points allowed for speedy evacuation of sick or hurt men; or any who might, for one reason or another, slow down the pursuit.

Hal mentally photographed the map, took it from the viewer and put it in his pocket. He went to find Falt and pay back the extra hour of watch the other had taken for him.

'You go get some sleep while you can!' Falt said. 'James and Rukh are bad enough without you trying to imitate them and sleep less than half an hour out of the day and night together. I'm fine.'

'All right,' said Hal. He was suddenly unutterably conscious of his own weariness, and of a sort of light-headedness at the same time. 'Thanks.'

'Just get some sleep,' said Falt.

'If you'll wake me as soon as Rukh gets up.'

'Oh? All right, then.'

Hal went back to his own tent. Crawling into his bedsack, with nothing but his boots and harness removed and his pockets emptied, he lay back in the dark, staring at the darkness under the tent roof, with one forearm flung up across his eyes. He realized suddenly that his forehead felt hot; and anger erupted in him. A number of the Command besides Child were beginning to show signs of minor infections as the unrelieved exhaustion exacted its price; but he had assumed that he, of all of them, should be immune to any such thing. He pushed the emotion aside as unprofitable. It was true he had been on his feet, with only brief naps, for several days now. . . .

He woke suddenly to the awareness that he had been asleep, and that Falt, standing back, was shaking his left foot within the bedsack, to wake him. He blinked into full awareness.

'Have I been jumping on people who wake me?' he asked.

'Not jumping – but you do come awake as if you meant to hit first and open your eyes after,' said Falt. 'You'll find Rukh by the kitchen setup.'

'Right,' said Hal, pulling himself out of his bedsack and reaching for the contents of his pocket where he had laid them out earlier. He checked suddenly and looked back up at Falt. 'At the kitchen? How long has she been up? A couple of hours? I asked you –'

Falt snorted, turned and went out.

Hal finished redressing and went out himself. Rukh, as Falt had said, was down where the kitchen had been set up on making camp the night before, standing, plate and fork in hand, to finish her early meal. She looked up at Hal as he approached.

'I made a short visit to the Militia camp early this morning –' he began.

'I know,' she said, scraping her plate clean and handing it, with the fork, back to Tallah. 'James told me he gave you permission. In the future, I'd like you to be a little more specific about why you want to make such a reconnaissance. I've told James to ask you for it.'

'I wasn't too sure what I could find out,' he said. 'As it happened, I was lucky . . .'

He told her about Barbage and the two young Militiamen on watch.

'So I took advantage of the chance to go right into his tent,' he said. 'It's what I suspected. Barbage's not like the others. He's serious military. His tent shows it. Anyway, I got one of the maps from his case.'

He handed her his viewer with the map already in it.

She put it to her eye and pressed the button for the illuminant. For a long moment she stood studying it without saying a word. Then she lowered the viewer, took out the map slide and handed the viewer back to him, putting the map in her pocket.

'It looks like the country up ahead of us,' she said.

He nodded.

'It was in order with the other maps in his map case – I estimated three days march ahead.'

'What good did you think it would do us to have this?'

'For one thing,' he said, 'it lets us check our own maps against it. No offense to the local people you got ours from, but what we have's a lot more sketchy and less accurate than this which has to be from breakdowns of regular survey information.'

'All right,' she said. 'But we might have lost you; and you've become valuable to us, Howard. I'm not sure it was worth the risk.'

'I thought,' he said slowly, 'we might consider hijacking some of those supplies they're sending him.'

Her dark eyes were hard on him.

'It could cost us six to ten people, attacking one of those supply points. Do you think they send out trucks like that without adequate troops and weapons to protect it?'

'I didn't mean at the supply point,' he said. 'I thought we could take just a single truck, someplace along the route, since we know ahead of time where they'll be headed for.'

She was silent.

'We can easily figure out the route a truck'll have to take to the supply point. The old hands in the Command tell me they don't generally send them out in group convoy, but one at a time.'

'That's true,' she said, thoughtfully. 'Normally, they don't worry about a pursued Command having the time to get down to the roads. Also, it's easier to send out each filled truck as it's ready, than to struggle with a convoy of half a dozen to be unloaded all at once and brought back together.'

'If you want . . .' He closed in on her first expression of interest quickly, 'I can figure out the details of taking one of them, and you or Child could decide from there. Almost anything they'd be carrying would be something we'd need.'

She looked at him soberly.

'How much rest have you had lately?' she asked.

'As much as anyone else.'

'Which anyone else? James?'

'Or you,' he said, bluntly.

'I'm Captain of this Command, and James is First Officer. Tonight,' she said, 'you're to be off any duty you're scheduled for. Tonight, you sleep. The next day, if you've slept through, bring me a plan for taking one of the trucks.'

'We'll be only one day away from that map by tomorrow,' he said.

'There're three supply points marked on it, each one at least a day apart. You're not going to lack time to plan.'

There was no reasonable argument against that. He nodded; and was turning away to get something to eat himself, when his mind exploded suddenly with the understanding that had been gnawing its way out of his unconscious into his conscious from the moment in which he had first glimpsed the slide in Barbage's tent.

'Rukh!' He swung back to her. Her eyes stared questioningly at his face. 'I knew there was something wrong! We've got to change route, right away!'

'What is it?' She had tensed, reflecting his tension.

'That slide. I knew something was bothering me about it. You said it yourself just now! It shows supply points for the next three to six days. Why would Barbage have arranged deliveries of supplies up to six days ahead along the road we just happen to be paralleling now? He knows we never move in the same line for more than two days at a time. Six days from now we'd be anywhere but close to that road, and his troops are right behind us!'

He saw understanding register on her. She swung about.

'Tallah!' she snapped. 'Go find James. Pass the word to get moving under any conditions at all. The Militia've sent units into the woods ahead of us to catch us between them and the troops that're after us.'

CHAPTER TWENTY-EIGHT

A scant thirty-one of the Command that had counted over a hundred members when it left the Mohler-Beni farm drove a struggling line of donkeys, of which only two were unloaded, through the dripping woods. The late spring of Harmony North Continent had turned unseasonably cold here at an altitude four thousand feet higher than the rich farmland through which they had passed only a week and a half before; and three days now of intermittent, icy rain had soaked everything human or animal not protected by impermeable coverings, chilling them all to the bone.

They had stripped themselves of anything not immediately necessary. They were down to only a dozen tents, in which they slept three or four together, rather than two, and a few donkey-loads of the kind of food that could be eaten without cooking, out of the hand, on the march. They were nearly all staggering with exhaustion and most were hot with fever. Some respiratory illness had run wild among them since Masenvale; coughing sounded continually up and down their column as, fiery-eyed and dry-skinned wherever the frequent downpours had not found a crevice in their ancient raingear, they plodded through the underbrush of the high foothills.

None of them looked as skeletally close to death as Child-of-God. Yet he continued to move, holding his place in the column and performing his duties as First Officer. The penetrating harshness of his voice had sunk to a near-whisper; but what he said was what he had always said, without difference or admission of weakness.

Of them all, Hal and Rukh appeared to be in the best shape. But they were both among the younger members of the diminished Command to begin with; and each, in his or her own way, seemed to possess a unique personal strength. Hal burned with fever and coughed with the others, but there was a reserve of energy in him that even he was surprised to find – as if he had uncovered a mechanism by which he could continue to burn himself internally for fuel until the last scrap of his bone and flesh had been consumed.

In the case of Rukh, an inner flame that had nothing to do with a self-consummation of her physical body appeared to promise to keep her going until the richly-yellow orb of Epsilon Eridani, now hidden by the weeping cloud cover overhead, should become cindered and cold. Like all the rest of them, she had lost weight, until she might have been the look-alike grandchild of Obadiah or Child-of-God; but this seemed in no way to have lessened her. That inner flame of hers glowing through her dark skin seemed to shine before them like a lamp in the night; and she was more beautiful than ever in her present leanness and fatigue.

They had escaped being caught by the jaws of the trap Barbage had planned to close upon them – jaws that consisted of his own Militia and those he had sent ahead into the woods three days' march before them, to come back and assist his own unit in encircling them beyond any possibility of escape. But the Command had slipped out to freedom by bare meters of distance rather than kilometers. Since then, Barbage had pursued them with an unyielding steadiness, resupplying and remanning his Militia ranks constantly, so that fresh troops were at all times on their heels.

They were given no chance to rest or reorder themselves; and by ones, twos and threes, individual members had faltered in their weariness, or sickened, and been sent away from the main body to try and make their solitary escape as best they might. With them had gone nearly all the spare equipment and donkeys – everything that could be done without, except the bare means of continuing to flee and the sacks of gunpowder and fertilizer that Rukh refused to give up.

She would not admit that escape from this unending hunt was impossible. It seemed that while the lamp burned eternally in her she could not; and her utter refusal to consider any other end to their situation than the accomplishment of their mission hauled the remaining members of the Command forward as if her will was a rope tying them all physically together. Even Hal, who from his Exotic training had the ability to stand aside from her effect upon them, ended by letting himself be deeply seized and moved by it, almost to the point of forgetting his own life and purpose – the purpose he knew must be there, but which he had yet to see clearly – to join in that which Rukh clearly put before all other goals.

Thinking of this, even through the fog of his fever and aching muscles, there came to him finally on wings of insight largely slowed by fatigue the commonplace realization that the great charismatic power of Others like Bleys Ahrens derived not from any special combination of Dorsai and Exotic influences, but solely from the culture of the Friendlies, in its utter absorption with the power to convince and convert. It came as a shock to him, for in spite of knowing Obadiah, he had not been unaffected with the common idea that of the three great Splinter Cultures, the Friendlies had the least in practical powers to offer from the special talents developed by their culture. And – like the final part of a firing mechanism clicking into place to make the whole weapon operative and deadly, it woke in him that in this obvious reason lay the mechanism that had made possible the Others' sudden explosive rise to power behind the scenes on all the worlds except the Dorsai, the Exotics and Earth.

The point that had always puzzled everyone about the achievement of that power had been the repeatedly acknowledged fact that the Others were so very few. Granted, they had chosen to model their organization on the large criminal networks of centuries past, so that they influenced those with power to gain their ends, rather than holding power themselves. Still – in terms of the few thousand that they were, compared to the billions of ordinary humans on the inhabited worlds, even that concept did not explain how they maintained their control. Those they controlled personally were in such large relative numbers that it would be an overwhelming job for the Others just to keep track of replacements being made in their positions, let alone make a fresh effort to convert to an Others-follower each new official. But, thought Hal now, if they could send forth non-Others as disciples, whose own sparks of talent for making such conversions had been fanned by Other efforts into roaring flames, such control became not merely possible, but reasonable.

If that was the explanation for Other success, then it also explained their concern with controlling Harmony and Association, as well as the reason for those two worlds' sudden explosion of activity into interworld commerce within the last twenty or so standard years – an activity which in earlier centuries the Friendlies had scorned except when necessity drove them to a need for the things that only interstellar credits could buy.

Something within the formless movement of Hal's unconscious seemed to register the importance of the conclusion he had just achieved. But there was no leisure to ponder the matter any further, now. If he lived and had the chance, he could check out his discovery. If not, nothing would be changed. Only, he could not bring himself to believe that he would not survive. Either the idea was simply not possible to him, or else his absorption of the uniquely Dorsai attitude of Malachi had dyed the inability to give up into his very bones and soul beyond any laundering. Like Rukh, with her goal of destroying the Core Tap power station, he could not turn aside from the goal he had chosen; and, since death would be a form of turning-aside, death was also not to be considered.

Up ahead of him, the next man in line came to an unexpected, staggering halt; and, having halted, sank down as if his body had suddenly lost all strength in its muscles. Hal moved up and past him. 'What is it?' Hal asked.

The man merely shook his head, his eyes already closed and his breathing beginning to deepen into the slow, heavy rhythm of sleep. Hal went on up, past donkeys and past other members of the team, men and women slumped down where they had ceased moving, some of them already snoring.

At the head of the column, he found Rukh, still on her feet, helping Tallah off with her pack.

'Why the stop?' said Hal, and cleared his throat against the hoarseness in his voice.

'They needed a halt – a short one, anyway.' Rukh got the pack all the way off and bent to examine a hole rubbed in the back of Tallah's heavy checked green workshirt. 'We can pad it,' she said, 'and change the dressing again. But it's turning into a regular ulcer. You shouldn't be carrying a pack at all, with that.'

'Fine,' said Tallah. 'I'll leave it off, then, and the pack can trot along behind me on its own little legs.'

'All right,' said Rukh, 'go see Falt and get a new dressing put on the sore; then you and he figure out what you want to do about putting a better pad on your pack harness. We'll be up and moving again in ten minutes.'

Tallah reached for the straps of her pack with her left hand, lifted it clear of the ground, and carrying it that way at ankle-height, headed back down the column toward Falt.

Rukh's eyes went to meet Hal. They stood, made private for a moment by the distance between them and the next closest members of the Command.

'We had a break only thirty-five minutes ago,' said Hal.

'Yes,' she said, more quietly, 'but in any case we had to stop now, and I didn't want to upset the Command any more than they are already. Come along.'

She led him off into the woods. As soon as the vegetation screened them from sight, she turned left to parallel the column and led the way down alongside it for half a dozen meters. Following her, in spite of the preparation for this moment he had had in events of the past few weeks, it struck Hal like a physical blow to see James Child-of-God, seated on the ground on a rain jacket, with his back propped against the trunk of a large variform maple tree.

Child's face against the rutted bark of the tree, stained dark by the rain, was itself dark and carved, like old wood left too long in the rain and weather. His clothes, even the bulky, outer rain gear, lay limply upon him; so that it was unmistakable how thin he had become in these last few weeks. His forearms rested on his upper thighs, wrists and hands half-turned up, as if they had simply fallen strengthless there under the weight of Harmony's gravity. Legs, arms and body lay utterly still. Only his eyes, sunk deep in their bony hollows beneath the gray brows and above the still-impeccably shaven lower face, showed signs of life and were unchanged. They regarded Rukh and Hal calmly.

'I will stay here,' he said, huskily.

'We can't afford to lose you,' Rukh's voice was cold and bitter.

'Thou canst not wait for me to rest at the cost of letting the Militia catch thee – as they will within the hour if thou dost not move on,' Child said. His words came in little runs and gasps, but steadily. 'And it would be a sin to burden Warriors further with someone useless. It is not as if this is a sickness from which I may recover, if the Command supports me for a while. My sickness is age – that only grows more so as we wait. I could go a little further – but to what purpose? It will be honey to my heart rather to die here, with the enemies of God before me, knowing I still have strength to take more than one of them with me.'

'We can't spare you.' Rukh's voice was even colder and harder than before. 'What if something happens to me? There's no one to take over.'

'How am I to take over now, when I can neither march nor fight? Shame on thee to think so poorly, who art Captain of a Command,' said Child-of-God. 'We are all of us no more than spring flowers, who bloom for a day only in His sight. If a flower dies, any other may take its place. Thou hast known this all thy life, Rukh; and it is the way matters have always stood in the Commands, or with those who testify for the Faith. No one is indispensable. So why shouldst thou miss or mourn me who cannot make a better end than this? It is unseemly in thee, as one of the Elect, to do either.'

Rukh stood, staring at him and saying nothing.

'Think,' said Child. 'The day is advanced. If I can delay those who follow us by only one hour, night will be so close that they will have no choice but to stop where they are until morning. While you, knowing they will not follow, can change your route, now; and, by morning they will have gone at least half a day in the wrong direction before they wake to their mistake. So you can gain a full day on them; and with a day's lead, perhaps, the Command can escape. It is your duty not to let pass that God-given chance.'

Still Rukh stood, unmoving and unspeaking; and the silence following Child's long speech went on and on; until Hal suddenly realized that of the three people there he was the only one who could break it.

'He's right,' Hal said, and heard the words sound tightly in his own throat. 'The Command's waiting, Rukh. I'll give him a hand to make him comfortable here, then catch up.'

Rukh turned her head slowly, as if against the stiff pressure of unwilling neck muscles, and stared at him for a long moment. Then she looked back at Child.

'James . . .' she said, and stopped. She took one step toward him and fell suddenly on both knees beside him. Stiffly, he put his arms around her and held her to him.

'We are of God, thou and I,' he said, looking down at her, 'and to such as us the things of this universe can be but shadows in smoke that vanish even as the eye sees them. I will be parted from thee only a little while – thou knowest this. My work here is done, while thine continues. What should it be to thee, then, if for a short time thou lookest about and seest me not? There is a Command that thou must guard, a Core Tap that thou must destroy, and enemies of God that must be confounded by thy name. Think of this.'

She shuddered in his arms, then lifted her head, kissed him once and got slowly to her feet. She looked down at him and her face smoothed out.

'Not by my name,' she said, softly. 'Thine.'

She gazed down at him and her back straightened. Her voice broke out again, suddenly, whiplashing through the sodden woods under the lowbellied sky with low-pitched intensity.

'*Thou*, James. When the Core Tap is closed and I am free at last, I will raise a storm against those we fight, a whirlwind of judgment in which none of them will be able to stand. And that storm will carry *thy* name, James.'

She wrenched herself around and strode off swiftly, almost running. The two men watched her until low-hanging branches of the trees hid her from sight. Then their gazes came back together again.

'Yes . . .' said Hal, without really knowing why he said the word. He looked about, at the hilly, cut-up, overgrown land surrounding them. A little distance away, a small rise that was almost a miniature bluff showed between the wet-bright, down-turned leaves.

'Up there?' he asked, pointing.

'Yes.' It was more pant than spoken word, and Hal, looking back at the older man, saw how prodigally he had plundered his remaining strength to send Rukh from him.

'I'll carry you up there.'

'Weapons . . .' said Child, with effort. 'My power pistol with the short barrel, to put inside my shirt. My cone rifle . . . rods of cones. Power packs. . . .'

Hal nodded. The older man was now wearing only his customary holstered power pistol with full barrel and a belt knife.

'I'll get them,' said Hal.

He went off through the trees. The Command had just gotten underway once more as he rejoined it; and none of its exhaustion-numbed members bothered to ask why he untied the donkey carrying Child's tent and personal equipment, and led it toward the rear of the moving column.

Reaching the end of the line of people and beasts, he kept going. When vegetation hid him at last from sight of the rearguard, he cut off into the brush and trees once more. A short way back, he found Child sitting where he had been left, and boosted him on top of the load the animal carried.

The donkey dug its hooves in under the double burden, and refused to be led. Hal let the older man off again, and led the animal alone to the little bluff. On top, it was ideal for a single marksman, its surface sloping backward from the edge of the almost vertical, vegetationless face that looked back in the direction the Militia would come. Hal unloaded Child's gear, set up the tent, and laid out food, water and the rest of the equipment within its dry interior. Then, with the donkey's load lightened considerably, he led it back down to where Child still waited.

This time, when the older man was lifted onto its back, the donkey made no objection; and Hal led it back up to the top of the bluff. He spread a tarp before the tent, just back from the lip of rock and earth overhanging the vertical slope, then helped Child down onto it.

'This, if necessary, I could still do myself,' he said, as Hal put him on the tarp, 'but what strength I have, I need.'

Hal only nodded. He brought logs, rocks and tree branches to make a barricade just behind the lip, through which Child could shoot with some sort of protection against return fire.

'They'll try to circle you as soon as they realize you're alone,' said Hal.

'True,' Child smiled a little, 'but first they will stop; and then talk it over before they come again; and when they do come, finally, still they will be cautious. By that time, I need only hold them a little while for the day to end.'

Hal finished laying out the final things, the weapons, a water jug, and some dried food, beside the man who lay on the tarp, his eyes already focused upon the distance beyond the firing gap Hal had left in the barricade. Done, Hal lingered.

'Go,' said Child, without looking up at him. 'There's nothing more for thee to do here. Thy duty is at the Command.'

Hal looked at him for a second more, then turned to go.

'Stop,' Child said.

Hal turned back. The older man was looking away from the firing aperture and up at him.

'What is thy true name, Howard?' Child asked.

Hal stared at him.

'Hal Mayne.'

'Look at me, Hal Mayne,' Child said. 'What dost thou see?'

'I see. . . .' Hal ran strangely out of words.

'Thou seest,' said Child, in a stronger voice, 'one who has served the Lord God all his life in great joy and triumph and now goeth to that final duty which by divine favor is his alone. Thou wilt tell the Command and Rukh Tamani this, in just those words, when thou returnest to them. Thou wilt testify exactly as I say?'

'Yes,' said Hal. He repeated the message Child had given him.

'Good,' said Child. He lay gazing at Hal for a second longer. 'Bless

276

thee in God's name, Hal Mayne. Convey to the others that in God's name, also, I bless the Command and Rukh Tamani and all who fight or shall fight under the banner of the Lord. Now go. Care for those whose care hath been set in thy hands.'

He turned to fix his eyes once more on the forest as seen through the firing slot in his barricade. Hal turned away also, but in a different direction, leaving James Child-of-God upon a small rise in a rain-saddened wood, awaiting his enemies – solitary, as he had always been; but also, as he had always been, not alone.

CHAPTER TWENTY-NINE

It took Hal the better part of an hour to catch up with the Command. Rukh had changed the direction of its march, as Child had suggested; everyone there going off in different directions to regather later at an appointed destination. It required almost twenty minutes for Hal, circling, to pick up their new trail. After that he went swiftly; but still nearly sixty minutes had gone by when at last he caught up with them. In that last half-hour, for the first time since he had left Earth, his mind dropped into certain orderly channels; standing back from the present situation as a detached and independent observer, coldly to chart and weigh its elements. James Child-of-God's last words had had the effect of making the path of Hal's own duty very clear before him; and with that his mind was set free to a hard, practical exercise of the intellect, to which all three of his tutors had trained him, but which until now he had ignored under his involvement in the life of the people around him. Now, however, under the slow abrasion of exhaustion and fever, followed by the final assault of Child's self-sacrifice, his personal emotions vanished from the equation like mist from a mirror, leaving what they all faced, clear and hard in its true dimensions.

As a result, when he at last rejoined the column of the Command, he looked at the men and women trudging along with different eyes. These people were not merely worn out – they were at the furthest stretch of all the extra strength which will and dedication could give them. It might well be that Rukh herself could never be defeated and would never surrender; but these more ordinary mortals who marched and fought under her orders had been used to the near-limits of what was physically and mentally possible to them.

He reached the head of the column and saw at a glance that Rukh had not yet faced this – and would not, could not face it. Like Child, she had an extra dimension of self-use possible to her that ordinary mortals did not have; and she had no real way to appreciate their limits or the fact that these about her now were now very close to them.

Walking at the head of the column, she turned her head to look at him as he came up.

'You did what you could for him?' she asked in a neutral voice. Her face was without expression.

'He sent a message,' said Hal. 'He asked me what I saw; and when I couldn't answer, he told me that what I saw was one who had served the Lord God all his life in great joy and triumph and went now to that final duty which by divine favor was his alone. He asked me to tell you all this.'

Rukh nodded as she marched, still without expression.

'He also asked my true name,' Hal went on, 'and when I told him it was Hal Mayne, he blessed me by it in God's name. He told me as well to convey to the rest of you that in God's name also he blessed the Command and Rukh Tamani and all who fight or shall fight under the banner of the Lord.'

She looked away from him at that and walked in silence for a long minute. When she spoke again, it was still with head averted, but in the same perfectly level voice.

'The Command now lacks a Lieutenant,' she said. 'Temporarily, I'm going to assign that officer's duties jointly to you and Falt.'

He watched her for a second as they walked together.

'You remember,' he said, 'that Barbage's real interest is in me. It's possible that if I were seen to be going away from the rest of you –'

'We talked about that. The Commands don't work that way.'

'I hadn't finished,' he said. 'By tomorrow noon you'll have enough of a lead on the Militia to make some things possible. What I was going to suggest was to let Falt take over the duties of First Officer; and while you're moving forward tomorrow, and even yet today, let me start to slip the loaded donkeys, one by one, off from the line of march. The trail left by the Command will still pull the troops after it; and eventually I'll have all the donkeys away from the rest of you.'

'Leaving them to be found one by one by the Militia, once they pick up our trail again?'

'No,' he said patiently, 'because when I take the last one off I'll head back and pick up the others, and take them off to some rendezvous point. Meanwhile the rest of you keep laying a trail forward for another day or so – then split up. Disappear into the woods individually, so that the trail vanishes into thin air. Later you can all rendezvous with the donkeys.'

She pondered the idea for a moment as they moved forward side by side.

'No,' she said, finally, 'after all this, Barbage won't give up so easily. He'll continue to comb the area generally; and even if he doesn't find us eventually, he'll find the donkeys. No.'

'He won't comb the area unless he thinks when he finds the rest of you he'll find me,' Hal said. 'As soon as I've got the donkeys gathered at the rendezvous, I'll let myself be seen at one of their road supply points – I'll knock out and tie up a sentry and steal a weapon or some food – and once he hears I'm alone and headed away from the area, Barbage'll follow. As I say, it's me he's really after.'

She returned to her thoughts, walking with her head tilted a little down, her eyes fixed on the forest floor a half-dozen steps ahead. The silence stretched out. Finally, she sighed and looked back at him.

'What are your chances of being seen and still getting away safely?' she asked.

'Fine,' he said bluntly, 'if I'm on my own and don't have anyone else from the Command to worry about.'

She looked forward again. There was another little silence. He watched her, knowing he had set her fear of losing the explosive materials against her duty to preserve the lives of those in the Command.

'All right,' she said, finally. She looked squarely at him. 'But you'd better begin right now, as you say. It's going to take time for you to get twenty-one beasts staked out away from the line of march, one by one, going off and then catching up again each time. Go get Falt and the maps from my gear, and we'll pick out a rendezvous point.'

That night and into the dawn hours of the next day, Hal led laden donkeys away from the Command, taking them down the back trail to separate points before entering the woods on one side and then leading each of them far enough off so that it might bray without being overheard by Militia following the trail. By the time the Command was ready to move, he had all the donkeys staked out individually and was ready to part from the rest of its members.

'In five days,' Rukh said. 'Keep a watch out during the day. In five days we'll all meet you at the rendezvous.'

'It'll take you at least that long to get there once you've started to move all the beasts together,' Jason put in. 'It's more than a one-man job. I should really come with you.'

'No,' said Hal. 'Except when I've got the donkeys in tow I can move fastest alone – and if something comes up, I'd rather have only myself to worry about.'

'I think you're right,' said Falt. 'Luck –'

He offered his hand. Hal shook it; and shook hands with Jason also. They were all, including Rukh, wearing trail packs with their essential gear, now that the donkeys were gone.

'You will indeed be careful, won't you, Howard?' Jason said.

Hal smiled.

'I was brought up to be careful,' he said.

'All right,' said Rukh. 'That should take care of the goodbyes. I'll walk off a little ways with you, Howard. I've got a few more things to say to you.'

They went off together, Hal balancing the full pack, heavy on his shoulders, as the power pistol Rukh had now issued him balanced heavy on his right leg and the cone rifle poised in his left hand; so that all those weights could be as easily ignored as the weight of the clothes he wore. The rain had ceased; but the skies were still like gray puddled metal and a stiff wind was blowing from the direction in which the Command was still moving, a wind that picked up the dampness from the leaves and ground, and chilled exposed faces and hands. Once out of earshot of the Command, Rukh stopped; and Hal also stopped, turning to face her.

He waited for her to speak; but, erect and stiff, she merely stared at him, with the look of a person isolated on a promontory, gazing out at someone on a ship that was drawing away from the shore on which she stood. On a sudden impulse, he put his arms around her. The stiffness suddenly went out of her. She leaned heavily against him; and he felt her trembling as her arms went fiercely around him.

'He brought me up,' she said, the words half-buried in his chest. 'He brought me up; and now, you. . . .'

'I'll be all right,' he said to the top of the dark forage cap on her head. But she did not seem to hear him; only continued to hold powerfully to him for a long moment more, before she breathed deeply, stirred and pulled back slightly, lifting her head.

He kissed her; and for another long moment again she held herself against him. Then she broke loose and stepped away.

'You have to go,' she said.

Her voice was almost normal once more. He stood, watching her; knowing instinctively not to reach for her again, but feeling in him, like a sharp ache, her private pain.

'Be careful,' she said.

Without warning, Epsilon Eridani broke through the heavy weight of the clouds over them; and in its sudden rich yellow warmth, her face was clear and young and pale.

'It'll be all right,' he told her automatically.

She reached out her hand. Their fingertips barely touched; and then she had turned and was going away, back through the woods to the Command. He watched her out of sight, then turned away himself, remembering as he did how he had turned from Child, only the afternoon before.

He went swiftly, thinking of the next twenty-four hours, within which so much would need to be done. At the moment he had both eaten and slept recently, enough of both so that he now went easily into the familiar adrenaline overdrive he could always draw upon; and the fatigue, the rawness of his throat and chest, and the headache that had sat like an angry dog in the back of his head on and off since the fever had begun to work on him, effectively were forgotten.

He had not staked out the donkeys individually as he had indicated to Rukh he would; though it had been necessary to lead each of them off the main trail at a different spot, so that the Militia would not realize that there had been a general exodus of the Command's animals. Trail sign of an occasional beast being led away from the line of march was not unusual. Lame or sick beasts would be taken aside before being turned loose, so that they would not be tempted to try and rejoin their fellows in the column. Once Hal had conducted an individual donkey a safe distance from the trail this time, however, he had turned and taken it to a temporary gathering spot, to be staked out there with the others he had already led away from the Command.

It was to this place he headed now. When he got there, the donkeys were patiently grazing at the ends of their long tethers, scattered about a hollow of land screened with trees on the heights surrounding it; and Epsilon Eridani was halfway up toward the noon position overhead, in a sky furnished with only scattered clouds.

He set to work making up his pack train. It was an advantage that the process of filling the trail packs of the Command members had reduced the total amount his animals were carrying, to the point where he now had five of the twenty-five beasts travelling completely without load and available for use as relief pack animals in case any of his loaded beasts could not go on.

Even with that, however, and the advantage of good weather, the handling of a twenty-five animal pack train singlehanded through country like this was a monumental task. He got to work reloading his beasts with the packs he had taken off them on getting them here, and connecting them in a line with lead ropes. It took over three hours before the pack train was ready to go.

When he did at last get under way there were some six hours left in which there would be light enough to travel. He headed almost due east, downslope toward the nearest road shown on his map, which was the closest supply artery Barbage could be using to keep his troops and equipment supplied for the pursuit. In the six hours that remained, he was able to move within half a kilometer of the road. There, he picked a resting spot very like the one in which he had left the donkeys earlier, unloaded, staked them out, and ate. He lay down in his bedsack to sleep, setting his mind to wake him in four hours.

When he opened his eyes, Harmony's moon – as he had expected – was high in the almost cloudless night sky. The moon – called Daughter of the Lord – was half-full now, and the light it gave was more than adequate for the kind of travelling he had in mind.

He made up a light pack with some dried food, first aid kit, ammunition and rain gear, and left his donkeys to the moonlight. Working his way the rest of the distance down to the road, he began a search back along it for one of the Militia's supply points.

He found one within twenty minutes. At night, its two Militiamen on guard were asleep and all ordinary lights were out; but he smelled it before he saw it. Tucked into the side of the road, in an open spot, were a tent, the still red coals of a fire, and some piles of unopened cases and general debris. The odors of woodsmoke, garbage, human waste, and a medley of the smaller, technological smells of such as weapon lubricant and unwashed tarps led him directly to it.

He took off his pack and laid his rifle aside, a few meters back in the trees, and drifted into the sleeping camp on noiseless feet. The night was so still and insect-free here in the high foothills that he could hear the heavy sleep-breathing of at least one of the men. He could possibly have lifted the tent flap in perfect safety to confirm that there were only two of them on duty there; but it was not necessary. The camp shouted forth the fact that no more than a pair of men were occupying it.

He checked the stack of boxes, but short of opening one, there was no way to tell what was in them. The weight of the one he lifted indicated it held either weapons, weapon parts, or some other metallic equipment. The unseal-and-eat meal units on which the Militia were fed in this kind of pursuit would have been packaged up into boxes that were much lighter for their size than these, as would have medical supplies, clothing and most other deliverable items. From the look of the camp and the number of emptied meal unit cartons, it was a good estimate that these two had been holding this supply point for two days already and would be here at least another day yet. They would not be here now – they would have gone back with the last supply truck to reach them – if at least one more delivery to this supply point was not expected. Also, from the marks where the earlier deliveries had been made, at least one full day of sunshine and moisture had been at work on the indented earth where the last truck to visit had shut off its blowers and let itself settle to the ground.

Therefore, there should be at least one truck due tomorrow.

He looked once more about the camp, memorizing the distances between its various parts and its general layout. It was not hard to imagine how it would look and where the men involved would be when a delivery came tomorrow. Having done this, he turned and left as silently as he had come. Only a little more than an hour later, moving on a slant now that he knew the relative positions of the two points between which he travelled, he was once more with his donkeys and in his bedsack, ready for sleep.

He woke before dawn and an hour later was squatting on the hillside a dozen meters above the supply point. He had thought it unlikely that the nearby Militia post, wherever that was, would exert itself to get a supply truck loaded and out before dawn. In any case, he found when he arrived that the two soldiers on duty there were still asleep in their tent; and he was able to listen and watch through the full ritual of their waking and breakfasting.

That day's delivery, he gathered from their breakfast talk, was due an hour before noon and would involve three trucks. His jaw tightened. Three trucks, each with a driver and loader, plus the two Militiamen already here, would be almost too many for him to handle. Ten minutes after hearing this, however, he was on his feet and running back toward his donkeys, having just been gifted with further information. Late in the day there would be another, single truck arriving; but not to make a delivery; and for this reason the two were looking forward to it enthusiastically. It was the truck that would pick them up and return them to barracks life in Ahruma.

The late arrival of this solitary truck offered an opportunity that had been unlikely to hope for – one that could take off some of the hardship his private plans had looked to inflict on the Command. He got back to his donkeys and went swiftly to work loading only the personal gear on as many beasts as were needed to carry it.

Loaded and with the donkeys roped together, he started out for the rendezvous point he had settled on with Rukh.

Left alone as he now was with the problem he faced, caught up in the machinery of the physical job involved in moving nine loaded donkeys in limited time twenty-odd kilometers to the rendezvous point he had originally set up with Rukh, and burning with the fever that had now taken firm hold of him, Hal went almost joyously into a state of self-intoxication in which all things were unreal except the relentless drive of his will.

He had, he estimated, at best seven hours to make the round trip – to get the donkeys there, to get them staked out and unloaded, and to return before the single truck arrived to collect the two Militiamen. It was possible only if everything went without a hitch – which was more than could be expected in the real universe – or if he could manage to move the relatively lightly loaded, if worn-out, donkeys at better than their normal pace.

Somehow he managed to so move them; and the astonished donkeys found themselves at intervals, on downslopes and in open stretches, actually breaking into a trot. For a time that lasted into mid-day, it seemed that fortune would smile on him and not only would he make his schedule, but beat it by an hour or so.

Then without warning, the country turned bad for pack trains. The ground became cut and seamed with gullies, heavily brushed and wooded, so that the last donkeys might be headed down a precipitous – if short – slope, with their hooves digging in to keep them from nosediving forward, while the animals in the lead would be struggling up an opposite slope that was equally steep and tangled with bushes. In the case of a string of beasts of necessity roped together in one long line, this kind of situation produced falls on the part of some of the loaded beasts, and unbelievable tangles. By an hour past mid-day it became clear that, barring a sudden change for the better in the terrain, he had no hope of getting his beasts to their destination and returning in time to the supply point.

284

He did the next best thing. Consulting the map he had copied from Rukh's supply, he located the nearest stream, tied up his donkeys temporarily and prospected for a substitute rendezvous point along it. Having found this, he went back and brought the animals to this point, unloaded and cached the equipment they carried, then staked them out individually on 'clotheslines' fastened at each end, each donkey being tethered to a slip ring that ran up and down the line, so that he could move to reach the stream and available forage.

This done, he cut a generous handful of hair from the tail of one of the donkeys and headed for the original rendezvous. There, he tacked up bunches of the donkey hair on the trunks of several trees, with an arrow carved in the tree just below each bunch, pointing a compass direction to the substitute point where donkeys and equipment were now to be found.

It was all he could do. Rukh and the others were not unaware that under campaign conditions few things went exactly as planned. Not finding the donkeys where they should be, they would instinctively look for them, and for clues left as to where they might be. Unless they had the Militia right on their heels and no time to stop and hunt, a reasonable investigation on their part would find the animals and equipment where he had left them; and this before the donkeys ran out of forage, or fell prey to the kind of accident that could occur to such creatures left tethered alone in the woods for several days. Hal shut his mind to the thought of how Rukh would feel on discovering no explosive among the loads he had cached with the animals.

In any case, he had no time to do more. Leaving the established rendezvous now, he literally ran the more than twenty kilometers back to the supply point.

He arrived no more than three-quarters of an hour later than he had originally planned. The two Militiamen were still there, although their personal gear was packed and ready for their leaving. Puzzlingly, the pile of unopened supplies was also still there; and Hal, sweating and exhausted from the past eight and a half hours of extreme exertion, was left to worry over the possibility that some of Barbage's Militiamen from the pursuit team might appear at any minute to pick them up. If half a dozen more armed men should arrive just when the truck was here to pick up the two on sentry duty, he would be facing an impossible situation.

But there was nothing for him to do but wait; and one of the advantages of waiting was that it gave him a chance to rest before the next demand upon him. He lay on the slope, accordingly, not even bothering to keep an eye on the camp below him, since his ears gave him a clear image of what was going on down there. His only concern now was stifling the urge to cough that, now the excitement and adrenaline of his earlier exertions was over, was threatening to betray his presence to the men below.

In the end it was necessary to use one of the techniques Walter the InTeacher had taught him for emergency control of the body's automatic processes, knowing as he did that he was further draining his strength to do so and putting himself at least partially back into the berserkedness of overdrive. But the exercise effectively silenced the cough for the present; and, after a while, his ear picked up the distant sound of blowers that signalled a truck making its way up the slope of the highway to the supply point.

It was roughly an hour and a half late. He could, if he had known it would be this dilatory, have returned from where he had left the donkeys at no more than a good walking pace. So much for lost opportunities. An hour and a half overdue was almost to be expected in military schedule-keeping; but, he told himself, if he had counted on the truck being late, as surely as this day would end, it would have appeared on time.

The truck came on. The two Militiamen were standing, waiting, out by the side of the road, with their packs and other gear piled behind them. The vehicle was a heavy-framed, military version of the farm trucks the Command had made use of in the Masenvale raids on the fertilizer plant and the metals storage point. It came on, stopped, turned about and backed up to the pile of boxes.

Clearly, it was intended to take back whatever was in the boxes to the supply center. The two Militiamen who had been waiting went back to the boxes themselves, to load. Hal, holding his cone rifle in his right hand and with the flap up on the power pistol holstered on his leg, slipped down until only a small screen of bushes and some four meters of roadside dirt separated him from them. With the back of the truck open now, he could see into the cab. The driver alone was still in the truck, behind its wheel. One other Militiaman had come out of it and was helping the two who had been on duty here to load the boxes.

Hal stepped quietly from the bushes with the cone rifle in his arms.

'Driver, get out here!' he said. 'The rest of you – stand still!'

They had not seen him until the sharp snap of his voice brought their heads around. Inside the truck, the driver's head jerked back to look over the top of his seat. His face stared.

'Back through the truck and stand here with the rest of them!' Hal said to him. 'Be careful – don't make it look as if you're trying anything.'

'I'm not . . .' the driver almost stammered.

He lifted his arms into view beside his head and worked his way clumsily between the two seats of the cab, then came back through the empty body of the truck to jump down and stand beside the other three. Hal turned his attention to the others. One was an older man. The two who had been on sentry duty were plainly only in their teens. Two pale young faces stared blankly at him with the expressionless terror of children.

'Are you – are you going to shoot us?' one of them asked in a high voice.

'Not yet, anyway,' said Hal, 'I've got some heavy work for you to do, first.'

CHAPTER THIRTY

'Take it between those two large trees there. Slowly,' said Hal.

The driver was seated at the vehicle's controls beside him, with the barrel-end of Hal's power pistol touching his ribs. Behind them in the body of the truck, the three other Militiamen sat against one side of it, with their hands in their laps, looking into the small dark circle that was the muzzle of Hal's cone rifle, aimed at them over the back of the seat. Except for the fact that Hal had to keep his attention at once on the route on which he was directing the driver, the driver himself, and the three in the back, the situation was almost comfortable.

'A little farther . . .' said Hal. 'There!'

They emerged into the area holding the donkeys he had not taken to the rendezvous point.

'Over there,' he told the driver, and coughed harshly. 'That stack covered with tarps. Bring the truck up to it, turn around and open your back doors. We'll be loading.'

The driver swung his steering knob and punched keys on his console. The truck's blowers shut off and the vehicle sat down on the ground. Hal herded the driver and others before him out the open rear doors onto the ground beside the pile of explosive materials.

'All right,' he said. 'All of you – yes, you too, driver – start putting everything from that stack into the truck.'

It took the four of them, at gunpoint, only some twenty minutes to load what had taken Hal several hours to unload, pile, and protect from the weather. When it was all in the truck, he set his prisoners to work turning the remaining donkeys loose and shooing them out of the clearing. When the last beast had been chased off, Hal brought the men back to the truck. Leaving them standing on the ground before the open back doors, he climbed back inside alone and went forward to the driver's seat.

Taking the driver's seat, he rested the cone rifle on the back of it, covering them.

'Now,' he said, 'driver, I want your uniform, including your hat and boots. Take it off.'

The driver looked at him grayly. Slowly he began to undress.

'Good,' said Hal, when he was done. 'Throw them here – all the

288

way to me. That's right. Now, the rest of you, take off your boots and toss them in the back of the truck.'

They stared at him.

'Boots,' he repeated, moving the rifle sights from left to right across their line. 'Off!'

Slowly, they began to remove their boots. When the last piece of footwear had fallen with a thump onto the metal bed of the truck, Hal gestured once more with the cone rifle.

'Back off across the clearing until I tell you to stop,' he said.

They backed, lifting unshod feet tenderly high above rocks, sharp twigs and spiny-leaved vegetation.

'That'll do!' Hal called, when they were a good twenty meters from him. 'Now, stay there until I leave. After that, you can make your own way back to the road and either wait for help, or go find it.'

He keyed the truck to life and lifted it on its blowers.

'You can't just leave us out here, without boots!' the driver called. 'You can't –'

The rest of his words were covered by the sound of the blowers as Hal drove off. He watched the four of them in the truck's viewscreen until trees and bushes blocked them from sight; after which he closed the rear doors of the truck and drove with all safe speed to the road.

Bootless and carefully choosing where to set their feet, and with the driver as the only one who had seen the route they had followed from the supply point, the best speed the four could make through the woods on foot would take them at least a couple of hours to find their way back to the highway. After that, they would still have to choose between trying to walk in what was left of their socks, thirty or forty kilometers of this highway down to where it intersected with a more trafficked road; or finding their way back to the supply point and waiting there to be rescued.

In two hours it would be dark and their feet would be very sore. They would almost certainly choose to wait at the supply point. In any case, it would be several hours after dark before their return would be overdue enough to be noticed at the motor pool to which the truck belonged; and the first assumption there would be that, through accident or design, they were simply delayed and would be in by morning. It would probably not be until full morning of the next day that attempts would be made to check on them. Meanwhile, since Barbage would have assumed that by now this point had been abandoned, no one from his pursuit team would be likely to check on it.

So, it should be tomorrow before anyone learned that this truck was in the hands of Hal. He had at least the next ten hours in which to drive, with only the problem of avoiding a routine check on his credentials or his purpose for being on the road with a Militia vehicle.

Just before he turned onto the highway, Hal stopped to replace his own clothes with the driver's uniform. The driver had been both tall and heavy, so that the jacket was only a little tight in the shoulders, though the pants were enormous around Hal's waist; but even the other man's height had not been enough to provide sleeves and pant-legs that were other than obviously, almost ridiculously, short on Hal. Still, wearing the uniform and the cap – which fortunately was only a little loose on his head – and sitting mostly hidden in the cab of the truck, Hal could pass a casual inspection as a Militiaman.

Dressed, he keyed-on the truck's reference screen for a small-scale map of the general area between his present location and Ahruma. The map showed the city at a distance of something over two hundred and ten kilometers, with a spiderweb of roadways multiplying and thickening toward its center.

Somewhere on the city's south outskirts was one of the local people that Rukh's Command had been scheduled to contact, when at last it reached the city, a woman named Athalia McNaughton, who had a small business selling used farm equipment. She might be able to help him – if he could reach her. There would be the truck to dispose of and its contents to hide; and, while he had with him the identification and credit papers he had carried ever since leaving Earth, he would need information on how to use them safely. The only hope of escaping Bleys now lay in getting off Harmony.

Ahruma, he knew, because of its Core Tap and spaceship refitting yards, had a commercial spaceport even larger than that of Citadel, the city at which he had first set foot on Harmony; but any spaceport could be a dangerous place for him to try arranging passage unless he knew where to go and who to see when he got to the terminal.

If she could help, the odds were with him. She could have no idea that he was approaching her without Rukh's approval and orders. It might be a week or more before word of the splitting up of the Command could reach Ahruma partisans. On the other hand, his name and description would be known to her, as one of the Warriors under Rukh's leadership.

He clicked off the reference screen, punched on the trip clock, and having picked his route to the city, drove out onto the highway and turned right.

He drove for half an hour before he ran into any sign of other traffic. By that time he had covered over forty kilometers and was on a double-lane Way headed generally in the direction of Ahruma. The load which had been a full one for nine donkeys was a light one for the truck; and the vehicle hummed along at the legal military speed limit of eighty kilometers an hour. Without problems, he could probably expect to reach the city in about three hours.

Darkness closed in about him as he drove; and as the countryside surrounding the Ways he travelled on became more inhabited, artificial lighting blossomed to challenge it on either side of his route. Seated alone in the cab above the blowers, their breathy roar tuned down by the truck's soundproofing to a steady, soft humming, and with the illumination of the instrument panel softly glowing at him below the dimness of the windshield his alertness began to yield to the lack of that emotional pressure which had kept him keyed up earlier. His body and mind relaxed; and, as it did so, his awareness of the fever, the headache, the cough and the fatigue that rode him like vampires became more and more acute.

For the first time he was able to measure the depths of his own exhaustion and illness; and what he found alarmed him. He would need to be at full alertness, and at something like full strength, from the time he parted company with Athalia McNaughton until he was safely aboard the ship taking him to some other world. The partisans in Ahruma might not know that he had left the Command; but it could not be more than twelve hours before the local Militia would; since he had dealt with the men he had captured so as to make it clear that his hijacking of their truck had been a solitary action.

It might be the better part of wisdom to see if Athalia could provide him with a few hours safe sleep at her place, before he tried the spaceport. He should be relatively safe until dawn. On the other hand, if he could use these same late night hours to get to the spaceport and buy his passage unsuspected, they were probably better utilized that way. Once aboard an interstellar ship, he could sleep as much as he wished.

Mind and body were becoming very heavy. He had to force his gaze to focus on the polished ribbon of the Way, that seemed to roll endlessly out of darkness before his forelights as he went. He debated tapping his overdrive reflex, once more – and once more put it from him. It would be easy and tempting to do, but wasteful of energy in the long run; and his energy was draining fast. He clicked on the reference screen again, and studied the maze of roads before him on the edge of the city. He had been eating up the distance on the open Way; but that sort of travel was reaching its end. Now came the time in which he would have to feel his way through fringe areas of the city by roadsign and map alone, to the front door of Athalia. This close to his goal he could not risk stopping to ask for directions from someone who might later identify him.

The night became one continuing blur of dimly-lit intersection and street signs. He took refuge in focusing down as he had days earlier when he had needed to think effectively toward a decision through the fog of sickness and fatigue; and his vision cleared somewhat. His reflexes were slower, and he slowed the truck accordingly, driving as circumspectly as he dared without drawing attention to a military driver who seemed to be exercising unnatural caution. Time, which had been in generous supply, began to run short. He checked the trip clock and saw that he had been driving now for nearly six hours. The glowing figures of the clock at which he stared made only academic sense to him. Subjectively, the time in the cab seemed to have been, at once, endless and no more than a handful of minutes.

He found himself at last guiding the vehicle down a narrow, fused earth road into the wilderness of a dark suburb, half small farms, half ramshackle cottages or small businesses. There was no light in the buildings he passed until he came to what looked like an abandoned warehouse, with a remarkably tall and new-looking highwire fence about it, and an invisibly large stretch of ground behind it. In one corner window at the front of the building, a window was illuminated.

Hal stopped the truck and got creakily out of it. He walked to the closed and locked pipe-metal gates of the fence and stared through it. The lighted window was uncurtained; but the distance was too great to see if anyone was visible behind it. He looked about the gate for some kind of communicator or bell to announce his presence and found none.

As he stood there, there was the sound of a snarling bark and two dark canine forms rushed the other side of the gate, setting up a savage noise at him. He stared. Like horses, dogs were not usually able to reproduce on Harmony, particularly dogs as large as these. A pair like this would be more likely to have been raised from test-tube embryos of Earth stock, imported by spaceship – and their purchase would have represented a very large expense for a business as small and poor as this one looked. He waited. Perhaps the barking would raise the attention of someone inside.

But no one came, and time – his time, limited as his strength was now limited – was going. He considered getting back into the truck and simply driving it through the locked gates. But that would hardly be the way to begin an appeal to the sympathy and help of Athalia McNaughton, if this was indeed her address. Instead, he sat down cross-legged on his side of the gate and began to croon to the two dogs in a soft, quavering falsetto.

The dogs continued to bark savagely – for a while. Then, gradually, intervals came in their clamor; gradually the volume of their barks lessened and became interspersed with whines. Finally, they fell entirely silent.

Hal continued to croon, as if they were not there.

The dogs whimpered more often, moving about uneasily. First one, then the other, sat down on its haunches. After several minutes, one of them raised its muzzle to the still-dark sky and moaned lightly. The moan continued and increased, developing into a full howl. After a second, the other dog also lifted its muzzle and howled softly.

Hal crooned.

The howling of the dogs rose in volume. Shortly, they were matching voices with him, almost harmonizing, seated on their haunches on the other side of the gates. Time went by; and, suddenly, a crack opened in the dark front wall of the building, next to the window, spilling white, actinic light in a fan of illumination out toward the fence. The dogs fell silent.

A dark, trousered figure occulted the brilliant, newly-appeared opening and advanced across the yard toward the gate, carrying a light in one hand and something short and thick in the other. As it got close, the light being carried centered on Hal's face and blinded him. His available vision became one glare of light. It approached and stopped, close enough that he could have grabbed it, if the bars of the gate had not been between him and the approaching individual.

'Who're you?' The voice was a woman's, but deep-toned.

Hal pulled himself slowly and heavily to his feet. On the other side of the fence, the dogs also rose from their sitting positions, approached the gate and stuck black noses between its pipes, licking their jaws self-consciously with occasional whines.

'Howard Immanuelson,' he said, hearing his own voice echo, hoarse and heavy in the darkness, 'from the Command of Rukh Tamani.'

The light stayed steady on him.

'Name me five people who're with that Command,' said the voice. 'Five besides Rukh Tamani.'

'Jason Rowe, Heidrik Falt, Tallah, Joralmon Troy . . . Amos Paja.'

The light did not move away from his eyes.

'None of these are the Lieutenant of that Command,' said the voice. 'Name him.'

'I'm co-Lieutenant, with Heidrik Falt,' said Hal. 'Both of us, acting only. James Child-of-God is dead.'

For a moment the light held steady. Then it moved away from him to the truck behind him, leaving him lost with expanded pupils in the darkness.

'And this?' The voice came after a moment, unchanged.

'Something I need your help with,' Hal said. 'The truck has to be gotten rid of. Its load is something else. You see –'

'Never mind.' There was a sound of the gate being unlocked. 'Bring it in.'

He turned around, eyes gradually adjusting to the night, fumbled his way to the cab of the vehicle and into it, up behind its controls. Without turning on its forelights again, he drove through the now-open gates to halt just outside the building. When he got down from the cab again, the two dogs pressed shyly forward against him, their noses sniffing at his pants' legs and crotch.

'*Back*,' said the voice; and the two animals retreated slightly. 'Come on inside where I can get a better look at you.'

Within, his vision gradually adjusted to the brightly-lit room behind the window that seemed to be half office, half living room – impeccably neat, but somehow without the forbidding, don't-touch quality that often accompanied such neatness. They stood and examined each other. She was mid-thirties, or possibly a good deal older, straight-backed, wide-shouldered, handsomely strong-boned of face, with heavy, wavy hair, cut short and so rich a brown as to be almost black. Under that darkness of hair, her skin was cream-colored, reminding Hal of a face on a cameo ring he had fallen in love with, once, when he had been very young. Her eyes were also brown and wide-set, he mouth wide and thin-lipped. To only a slightly lesser extent – although they were in no way similar otherwise – she had the devastatingly direct gaze Hal had seen in Rukh; but, unlike Rukh, the challenge of her presence was almost entirely physical.

'You're sick,' she said, looking at him now. 'Sit down.'

He looked about, found an overstuffed chair behind him and dropped heavily into it.

'You say James is dead?' She was still standing over him.

He nodded.

'We've had Militia right behind us for nearly a week and a half now,' he said, 'and there's been some kind of pulmonary disease we've all caught. James got to the point where he couldn't keep up. He insisted on making a rearguard action by himself to give the Command time to change its route. I helped him set up in a position. . . .'

The words Child-of-God had given him to pass on to Rukh and the Command came back to him; and he repeated them now for this woman.

She stood for a moment after he had finished, not saying anything. Her eyes had darkened, although there was no other change in her expression.

'I loved him,' she said at last.

'So did Rukh,' Hal said.

'Rukh was like his grandchild,' she said. 'I loved him.'

The darkness went from her eyes.

'You're Athalia McNaughton?' he asked.

'Yes.' She glanced out the window. 'What's in the truck?'

'Bags of fertilizer – and other makings for the explosive Rukh planned to use to sabotage the Core Tap. Can you hide it?'

'Not here,' she said, 'but I can find a place.'

'The truck needs to disappear,' he said. 'Can you –'

She laughed, dryly. Her laugh, like her voice, was deep-toned.

'That's easier. Its metal can be cut up and sold in pieces. The rest

294

of it can be burned.' Her gaze came back to him. 'What about you?'

'I've got to get off-planet,' he said. 'I've got credit vouchers and personal papers – everything that's necessary. I just need someone to tell me how to go about buying passage at the spaceport here.'

'Real vouchers? Real papers?'

'Real vouchers. The papers are real, too – they just belonged to someone else, once.'

'Let me see them.'

He reached into the inside pocket of his jacket and pulled out the long, lengthwise-folded travel wallet with its contents. She took them from his hand almost brusquely and began to go through them.

'Good,' she said. 'Nothing here to connect you with anyone in Ahruma. No one official's seen these since you left Citadel?'

'No,' he said.

'Even better.' She passed the papers back. 'I can't do anything for you directly; but I can send you to someone who's probably – probably, note – safe to buy from. He's not so safe you can trust him with what you've been doing since you joined Rukh.'

'I understand.' He stowed the envelope with its papers once again in the inside pocket. 'Can I get to him at this time of night?'

She stared at him so directly her gaze was almost brutal.

'You could,' she said. 'But you're ten paces from collapsing. Wait until morning. Meanwhile, I can give you some things to knock down that infection and make sure you sleep.'

'Nothing to make me sleep –' The words were an instinctive reflex out of the years of Walter the InTeacher's guidance. 'What sort of medication were you thinking of for the infection?'

'Just immuno-stimulants,' she said. 'Don't worry. Nothing that does any more than promote your production of antibodies.'

She half-turned to leave, then turned back.

'What did you do to my dogs?' she asked.

He frowned at her, almost too exhausted to think.

'Nothing . . . I mean, I don't know,' he said. 'I just talked to them. you can do it with any animal if you really mean it. Just keep making sounds with your mouth like the sounds they make and concentrate on meaning what you want to tell them. I just tried to say I was no enemy.'

'Can you do it with people?'

'No, it doesn't work with people,' he smiled a little out of his exhaustion. After a second, he added – 'It's a pity.'

'Yes, it's a pity,' she said. She turned away fully. 'Stay where you are. I'll get things for you.'

CHAPTER THIRTY-ONE

He woke suddenly, conscience gripping him sharply for some reason he could not at the moment recall. Then it exploded in him that he had let himself be talked into sleeping rather than continuing on his feet to whoever it was could sell him passage of Harmony.

For a moment, half-awake, he lay on whatever bed he had been given, feeling stripped and naked, as lonely and lost as he had felt in that moment four and a half years before, when he had turned away from the shadows on his terrace and the physical remains of Walter, of Malachi and Obadiah. In this moment between unconsciousness and full awareness, he was once again a child and as alone as he had ever been; and under the massive pressure of the weariness and feverishness that held him, the overwhelming urge in him was to curl up, to bury his head under the covers once more and retreat from the universe into the warm and eternal moment he had just left.

But, far off, like a strident voice barely heard, a sense of urgency spoke against further sleep. Late . . . already late . . . said his mind; and the urgency pulled him like a heavy fish out of deep water back to full awareness. He sat up staring into darkness, finally made out a faint line of something like illumination below eye level and two or three meters from him, and identified it as light coming faintly beneath a closed door.

He got to his feet, groped to the door, found its latch and opened it. He stepped into a dim corridor with light bouncing from around a corner at its far end, to illuminate faintly the walls and floor where he stood. He went toward the light, turned the corner and stepped into the room where he had first confronted Athalia McNaughton, a room now lit from its unshaded windows with the antiseptic light of pre-dawn.

'Athalia McNaughton?' His voice went out and died, unanswered.

He went to the only door than the entrance in the room, and pulled it open. Beyond was a small office stacked with papers and a tiny desk, at which Athalia was now sitting, talking into a phone screen. She switched off and looked over at him.

'So you woke up on your own,' she said. 'All right, let me brief you, feed you, and put you on your way.'

When he rode out through the pipe-iron gates forty-five minutes later, beside her in a light-load truck, the Militia vehicle had vanished from the yard. He did not ask about it and Athalia offered no information. She drove without speaking.

He had no great desire for conversation at the moment, himself. His few hours of rest had only worked to make him aware of how feverish and tired he was. With one voice, all the cells of his body cried for a chance to rest and heal themselves. The immuno-stimulants were hard at work in him, and the fever was down slightly – but only slightly. His throat and chest burned, although the overwhelming urge to cough was now controllable by methods Walter had taught him; and that was something for which he was grateful. He had no desire to draw attention to himself with the sounds of sickness that might cause anyone who came close to him to pay particular attention to him.

Athalia had also made an offer of painkillers and ordinary stimulants. But both would interfere with his own mental control, the effects of which on his weakened body he could judge more accurately than its response to drugs; and on being refused she had turned immediately to the problems of getting him to the person who could sell him the interworld passage he needed. The man's name was Adion Corfua. He was not a native Harmonyite but a Freilander; a small shipping agent who did not sell interworld passages himself, but knew brokers from whom cancelled tickets, or those not picked up within the legal time limit, could be bought – at either a premium or a discount, depending upon the world of destination and the buyer demand.

'I'll drive you to a point close to the terminal,' Athalia told Hal. 'From there you can catch a bus.'

After that, it would be a matter of his following directions to the general shipping office out of which Corfua worked.

The morning had dawned dry and cool, with a stiff breeze, a solid cloud cover, but no prospect of rain. A gray, hard day. Just before Athalia dropped him off at the sub-terminal where he would catch the bus, she drew his attention to a compact piece of tan luggage behind his seat, the sort of case in which interworld employment contracts were carried by those who had business with them.

'The contracts in it are all legitimate,' Athalia said, 'but they're from workers who've made their round trips. They won't stand up to being checked with employers; but for spot inspection, they're unquestionable. Your story should be that you're making a sudden, unexpected courier run. It'll be up to you to come up with a destination, an employer there and a situation in which contract copies are needed in a hurry.'

'Industrial sabotage,' Hal said, 'destroyed some files in an inter-world personnel clearing house on the world I'm going to.'

297

'Very good,' said Athalia, nodding and glancing at him for a moment, then back to the Way down which they were travelling. 'How do you feel?'

'I'll make it,' he said.

They had reached the sub-terminal of the bus line. She handed the case to him as he got out. Standing on the pavement of the sub-terminal with the case in one hand, he turned and looked back at her.

'Thank you,' he said, 'remember me to Rukh and the rest of the Command when you see them.'

'Yes,' she said. Her eyes had darkened again. 'Good luck.'

'And to all those James sent his message to, at the end there,' Hal said, 'good luck.'

The words, once they were spoken, sounded out of place in the hard, prosaic daylight. She did not answer, but sat back in her seat and pressed the stud that closed the door between them. He turned away as she drove off in the truck; and walked over to stand at the point where he would be boarding the bus.

Twenty minutes later he stood instead at the general desk of the shipping office with which Adion Corfua was connected.

'Corfua?' said the man on the general desk. He punched studs, looked into the hidden screen before him, and then glanced off to one side of the room behind him in which a number of desks were spread around. 'He's here today; but he's not in yet. Why don't you take a seat at his desk? It's the third from the wall, second row.'

Hal went over, and settled into the piece of furniture facing the indicated desk. It was not a float seat, but a straight-backed uncushioned chair of native wood, plainly designed to encourage visitors not to linger. But in Hal's present physical state, to sit at all rather than stand was a welcome thing. He sat, therefore, on the edge of dozing; and after some minutes the sound of feet beside him brought him fully awake again. He sat up to see a large, slightly overweight man in his forties with a thick black mustache and a balding head, taking the padded float behind the desk.

'What can I do for you?' said the man who must be Adion Corfua. His smile was a minimum effort. His small blue eyes were large-pupilled and unnaturally steady as they met Hal's.

'I need a passage to the Exotics,' Hal said, 'preferably to Mara. Right away.'

He lifted the contract case from the floor beside him to show briefly above desk level, and dropped it to the floor again.

'I've got some papers to deliver.'

'What's your credit?' asked Corfua.

Hal produced his travel envelope and extracted from it a general voucher of interstellar credit showing more than enough funds to take him to the destination named. He handed these to Corfua.

'It'll be expensive,' said Corfua, slowly, studying the voucher.

'I know what it'll cost,' said Hal; and made the effort necessary to smile at the other man, as Corfua looked over the top of the voucher at him. Athalia had told him approximately what the other should charge for a passage to Mara. In his present feverish and exhausted state he had no interest in bargaining; but to be too unconcerned about the cost of the trip would make people suspicious.

'What's the problem?' Corfua laid the papers on his desk.

'Some papers destroyed by industrial sabotage, there,' he said. 'I'm carrying replacements.'

'Oh? What papers?'

'All I'm interested in with you,' said Hal, 'is finding a passage.' Corfua shrugged.

'Let me talk to some people,' he said. He got up from behind the desk, picking up Hal's identity and voucher. 'I'll be right back.'

Hal stood up also and took the papers neatly back out of the other man's hand.

'You won't need these,' he said, 'and I've got a few things to do. I'll meet you at the central newsstand kiosk in the terminal, in twenty minutes.'

'It'll take longer than that – ' Corfua was beginning.

'It shouldn't,' Hal said. Now that he had actually locked horns with the other man, his head was clearing and his early training was upholding and guiding him. 'If it does, maybe I should find someone else. See you at the kiosk in twenty minutes.'

He turned and walked away without waiting for agreement, out of the shipping office. Once beyond its entrance and beyond the sight of anyone there, he stopped and leaned for a second with one shoulder against a wall. The spurt of adrenaline that had activated him for a moment had died as quickly. He was weak and shaky. Under the jacket of the brown business suit with which Athalia had outfitted him, his shirt was soaked with sweat. After a second he straightened up, put his papers back in their envelope and walked on.

His greatest safety in the terminal, Athalia had not needed to tell him – although she had, anyway – lay in keeping moving. Standing or sitting still, he could be studied. Moving, he was only one more in a continually swarming crowd of faces and bodies that, even to trained observers, could at last all come to look very much alike.

He moved, therefore, about the maze of internal streets, shops and buildings almost at random. Half the Spaceport Terminal was taken up by this Commercial Center, which was like a small city under one roof. The other half was an industrial complex that dealt with the maintenance, repair and housing of both visiting ships and those being worked over in the Core Tap-powered Outfitting Center, only a few kilometers away. Even after three hundred years of interstellar spaceflight, the phase-shift ships, even the smallest courier vessels, were massive, uneasy visitors to a planetary surface. Those landed here were of course completely out of sight of any of the people thronging the Commercial Center. But the awareness of their nearness, and the reminder in that of the great interstellar distances beyond Harmony's atmosphere, shrank the human self-concept and made for a Lilliputian feeling, not only with regard to the crowds filling the Commercial Center, but about the architecture and furnishings surrounding them.

It was with this feeling, superimposed upon the protests of his ill and overextended body and joined to the nervous awareness of a hunted animal, that Hal moved about the Center. He was stripped down to a sensation of being beaten and naked in the midst of enemies, a traitor to all who had trusted him. To save the lives of those in the Command, he had taken it on himself to remove from it not only himself, but the materials for the explosive. In effect, he had betrayed the others, knowing both actions were ones Rukh would never have agreed to, if asked. Only luck could reunite the Command now with what he had carried off in the truck, and lead it to the completion of its planned mission.

But the alternative had been death for all the rest of them; and after the self-sacrifice of James Child-of-God, Hal had found himself unable to face the prospect of more death among these people to whom he had become close.

Perhaps he had been wrong to take matters into his own hands; but there had seemed no other choice. Only, he had never felt so alone in his life – so alone, in fact, that part of him was a little astonished that he still possessed the will to resist capture, control, and possibly death. But yet he was continuing to resist, instinctively and innately. Under his mind-numbing exhaustion, his illness and the sorrow of parting with the first humans he had come to feel deeply at home with since his tutors' deaths – under the desperation of his present situation – an instinct of resistance entirely independent of his will burned steadily with the fierceness of ignited phosphorous.

He pulled himself from the whirlpool of his thoughts and emotions that was sucking him down into himself. It was almost time to meet Adion Corfua at the central newsstand kiosk.

He walked to the end of the interior street he was on and checked the map of the Center. He was only the equivalent of a couple of city blocks from the large central square, edged with sidewalk cafes and filled with plantings and fountains, that held the kiosk. He turned toward the square.

A block from it, he stepped into a clothing shop to buy a blue jacket and gray beret, of the cut he had remembered seeing on New Earth, when he had transferred spaceships there on his way to Coby. Outside the shop, he discarded in a sidewalk trash incinerator the bundle containing the brown jacket he had been wearing when he had met Corfua. Slumping to reduce his height, he went on to the square and began to wander casually around it, observing the kiosk and the people clustered about it out of the corner of his eye.

Corfua was there, standing by a wall of the kiosk and apparently absorbed in reading a news printoff he had just bought. Around the agent there was a little space with no people, the closest one being a man in a green leisure jumper who was scanning a screen with listings of book publications. Hal, who had planned to continue around the square if he had not found Corfua, turned off again up the street at the next corner. He went around that block entirely, coming back into the square at its next corner, turning back and moving in the opposite direction down the side of it he would have gone along next if he had not turned off.

Adion was still there, still seeming to read. The man in the green jumper still scanned the screen. Around them, there was still a small area without any other person.

Hal continued moving. Now that his suspicions had been confirmed, his eyes picked out five other individuals, four men and one woman, standing about the kiosk, who did not fit the normal patterns and movements of the crowd in the square.

The movements of all crowds, Malachi had told him, fell into patterns which were continually changing, but only to related patterns. The old Dorsai had trained young Hal first with a kaleidoscope – a tube with a rotatable end which, when turned, rearranged triangles of color as seen through a prism – then by standing him on a balcony overlooking a shopping center square in Denver, much like this one. The day had finally come when Hal, looking down, could immediately identify all the individuals Malachi had hired to play watchers in the square. It was not by specific actions or the lack of them that Hal had come to recognize those who were anomalies within the patterns. Rather, they had come eventually to jump to his eye, subjectively; as, at first glance, in gestalt fashion, the spuriousness of a fake painting jumps to the eye of an art expert who knows intimately the work of the painter being imitated.

Just so, now, the five men standing about the square jumped to Hal's eye from among the individuals surrounding them. There might well have been others seated at cafe tables, whom with closer study he might have picked out; but what he had now discovered was all he needed to know. He continued casually, but turned off immediately at the same corner he had turned off at before. He began to walk as swiftly as he could without attracting attention.

Once again, the shirt under his jacket was damp with sweat – the sweat of tension and exhaustion. Clearly, the Ahruma area generally had now been warned and his picture made available to anyone selling interstellar passages – and particularly to such as Corfua, who probably worked close enough to the line of legality to be known

301

to the local police. On recognizing him, Corfua, to save himself, would have had no choice but to alert the Militia.

By this time the whole Commercial Center, and possibly the whole terminal, would be under observation and search for him. The only question remaining was whether he could get to the terminal entrance and escape from it before he was noticed, even in his new jacket and beret, and the searching forces closed in on him.

He continued to walk, fast but not so fast as to attract undue attention. He passed nearly a dozen men and women whom he identified as anomalies in the patterns around him; although whether all of them were watching for him or for someone else, was anyone's guess. In a few minutes he had turned a final corner, and one of the entrances to the terminal was before him, with the front end of a line of buses to inner-city Ahruma just visible outside it.

Four black-uniformed Militiamen were checking the papers of everyone entering and leaving through the entrance.

He had altered course automatically, even as he saw them, so that now instead of heading directly toward the entrance, he was headed off to one side of it. He continued, increasing the angle of his change in direction as he went until his route became a curve leading him down a corridor paralleling the front face of the terminal.

It was a temptation to tap his adrenaline reserves once more, if only for a minute or two, simply to forget briefly the physical discomforts that were clamoring for his attention. But he was aware how little his remaining strength was. Effortfully, he put aside the alluring notion of the anesthesia of self-intoxication, and set himself grimly, as he walked, to thinking the situation through in his present fogged and fever-lit mind.

The enemy he faced, he reminded himself, was not the Militia but Bleys. The Militia was only a tool. Bleys must fear him for greater than usual reasons, or the Other Man would not have put into motion this large an effort to capture him. The goal must be his capture, not his death; Bleys could have made sure of his destruction back on Coby by simply arranging the deaths of all those at the mines where Hal was suspected of being. From what Hal had always been given to understand, the use of such bloody means to achieve a relatively small result would not be at all out of character for one of the Others.

Bleys, then, wanted him alive for some specific reason; therefore Hal's goal must be either to keep himself from being captured or make his capture as worthless as possible. It seemed clear that friendless, alone and ill as he was, he stood almost no chance of being able to get away from this terminal without being taken by the Militia. There were things he could and would try, but the fact of his capture had to be faced; and the question therefore was to make that capture as unrewarding as possible.

One way he could do that was to make sure that the credit vouchers and identity papers that made it possible for him to move between the worlds were not taken if he was captured; so that if he had the luck to get free of Bleys and his people, he could regain them and with them the means to escape to another planet.

Still struggling to think of ways to do this, he had paid little attention to where he was going, turning down streets at random. He was only half a block from the square where he had been to meet Corfua, when he suddenly caught sight of a line of black uniforms, a little less than a block distant, across the street and moving toward him.

They were beginning to sweep the interior of the terminal – or the interior of the Commercial Center, at least – for him. The thought of the mobilization of troops required for such an effort brought home to him with a chill more clearly than anything else had done the kind of power that the Others must wield here on Harmony. Idly, he stopped to look into a shop he was passing, gazed for a second, then as idly turned and began to move back the way he had come.

As he did, his steps quickened. He reached the end of the street and turned left, looking for a postal kiosk. A couple of blocks farther down this new street, he found one. A small amount charged against one of the Harmony-local vouchers he had been supplied with as a number of the Command caused a slot in the kiosk to disgorge a large envelope, already stamped with local postage. Hastily, he took his identity envelope from his inside jacket pocket, stuffed it into the envelope, and sealed it. He addressed the envelope to *Amid, Outbond to the Department of History, University of Ceta*. On the bottom in capital letters he printed HOLD FOR ARRIVAL. A screen on the kiosk, questioned, gave him the address of the local Maran Consulate in Ahruma. He memorized it even as he had the kiosk print it on his package. Then he slipped the sealed and addressed package into the mailing tray of the kiosk, which inhaled it with a soft, breathy sound. Empty-handed and momentarily lightheaded with triumph, he turned away from the kiosk.

Now it was only a matter of taking the best of what chances were left to get free of the terminal. There was one means that might allow him to bluff or bully his way past the Militiamen guarding the entrances to the Commercial Center. He might be able to do it if he was addressed as a Militiaman himself – preferably in the uniform of a superior officer. The problem would be to find an officer among those hunting him here whose clothes he could wear with any conviction that they belonged to him. An alternative – the thought struck him suddenly – would be to get the papers of one of the men in civilian clothes that had been stationed around the square and try to make his way out on the strength of those, in his present garb.

He was still only a block from the square. Something like enthusiasm beginning to rise in him for the first time that day, he turned away from the kiosk.

'*There he is – that's him!*'

It was the voice of Adion Corfua. Looking, he saw the pale, large figure, with two men in civilian clothes and five Militiamen, coming toward him from the direction in which he had just been about to go. He wheeled to escape, and saw another line of Militia just entering the intersection at the end of the block behind him.

'Get him!' Corfua was shouting.

There was the pounding of feet on the pavement behind him, and the Militiamen ahead also broke into a run toward him. He looked right and left, but there was nothing on either side of him but the unbreakable glass of shop windows. Choosing, he charged the line of uniforms he was facing.

Almost, he broke through them and got away. They were not expecting attack, and they faltered slightly at the sight of him coming down on them. Nor were they trained as he had been trained. They converged on him and he spun into them as they came close, leaving four of them on the ground and a fifth, still on his feet, but staggering. But they had delayed him just long enough for the Militiamen behind him to catch up; and these swarmed over him, helped by those who could recover from the first group he had hit. Without warning, his momentary burst of strength exhausted itself. There were simply too many of them. He went down, conscious for a little while of blows raining on him – blows hardly, it seemed after a bit, more than light taps; until, after a little while, he did not feel them at all.

CHAPTER THIRTY-TWO

He came to consciousness to find himself lying on his back on some flat, hard, cold surface that tremored slightly; and a second later he recognized the low, steady sound of truck blowers heard from inside a vehicle. His legs and arms ached, and he tried to move them, but they were held – ankles, knees and wrists pressed tightly together. For a moment he threw all his strength against whatever pinioned them, but they remained immovable. He slid back into unconsciousness.

When he woke a second time, he was still lying on his back; but the surface under him was softer and motionless, and there was no sound of blowers. A bright light glaring down into his eyes was in the process of being turned down slightly.

'That's better,' said a memorable, resonant voice he recognized. 'Now take those stays off him and help him sit up.'

With unbelievable gentleness, fingers removed whatever had been holding his wrists, knees and ankles. Hands assisted him to a seated position and put something behind his back to prop him upright. There was a pricking sensation in his left arm that startled him, but not to the extent of betraying him into any sign that he was once more aware. Less than a minute later, however, warmth, energy, and a blissful freedom from pain and discomfort began to flood all through him.

With that, he recognized the ridiculousness of continuing to pretend unconsciousness. He opened his eyes on a small, bare-walled room, furnished like a prison cell, with two Militiamen on their feet and the width of the room away from the narrow bed-surface on which he lay. And Bleys Ahrens, standing tall, loomed close beside and over him.

'Well, Hal,' said Bleys softly, 'now we finally get a chance to talk. If you'd only identified yourself back in Citadel, we could have gotten together then.'

Hal did not answer. He was face to face with the Other, now. The feeling of cold determination that had come on him when he had faced the fact that he was not staying at the Final Encyclopedia, nearly four years before, rose in him again. He lay still, studying Bleys as Malachi had taught him to do with an opponent, waiting for information on which to act.

Bleys sat down on a float beside the bed, which Hal felt to be some cot-like surface, covered with a single mattress of no great thickness. There had been no float beside it when Bleys had started to sit, nor had the Other Man given an order or make any signal Hal had seen. But by the time Bleys had needed it there, the padded float had been in position for him.

'I should tell you how I feel about the deaths of your tutors,' the tall man said. 'I know – at the moment you don't trust me enough to believe me. But you should hear, anyway, that there was never, at any time, any intention to harm anyone at your home. If there'd been any way I could have stopped what happened there, I would have.'

He paused, but Hal said nothing. Bleys smiled slightly, sadly.

'I'm part-Exotic, you know,' he said. 'I not only don't hold with killing, I don't like any violence; and I don't believe ordinarily there's any excuse for it. Would you believe me if I told you that of the three there on the terrace that day, there was only one who could have surprised me enough to make me lose command of the situation long enough for them to be killed?'

Again he paused and again Hal stayed silent.

'That one man,' said Bleys, 'made the only possible move that could have done so. It was your tutor Walter, and his physically attacking me, that was the single action I absolutely couldn't anticipate; and it was also the only thing that could get in the way of my stopping my bodyguards in time.'

'Bodyguards?' said Hal. His voice was so weak and husky he hardly recognized it as his own.

'I'm sorry,' said Bleys. 'I can believe you think of them in different terms. But no matter what you think, their primary duty there, that day, was only to protect me.'

'From three old men,' said Hal.

'Even from three old men,' replied Bleys. 'And they weren't so negligible, those old men. They took out three of four of my bodyguards before they were stopped.'

'Killed,' Hal said.

Bleys inclined his head a little.

'Killed,' he said. '*Murdered*, if you want me to use that word. All I'm asking you to accept is that I'd have prevented what happened, and could have, if Walter hadn't done the one thing that could break my control over my men for the second or two needed to let it all happen.'

Hal looked away from him, at the ceiling. There was a moment of silence.

'From the time you set foot on our property,' said Hal, wearily, 'the responsibility was yours.'

The drug they had given him was holding pain and discomfort at bay, but still he was conscious of an incredible exhaustion; and even turned down, the lights overhead were hurting his eyes. He closed them again; and heard the voice of Bleys above him projected in a different direction.

'Lower that illumination some more. That's right. Now, leave it there. As long as Hal Mayne is in this room, those lights aren't to be turned up or down, unless he asks they be.'

Hal opened his eyes again. The cell was now pleasantly dim; but in the dimness, Bleys seemed – even seated – to loom even taller. By a trick of his fever and the drug in Hal, the Other Man appeared to tower upward above him toward infinity.

'You're right, of course,' Bleys said, now. 'But still, I'd like you to try and understand my point of view.'

'Is that all you want?' Hal asked.

The face of Bleys looked down at him from its unimaginable height.

'Of course not,' said Bleys, gently. 'I want to save you – not only for your own sake but as something to put against the unnecessary deaths of your tutors, for which I still feel responsible.'

'And what does saving me mean?' Hal lay watching him.

'It means,' said Bleys, 'giving you a chance to live the life you've been designed by birth – and from birth – to live.'

'As an Other?'

'As Hal Mayne, free to use his full capabilities.'

'As an Other,' Hal said.

'You're a snob, my young friend,' replied Bleys. 'A snob, and misinformed. The misinformation may not be your fault; but the snobbery is. You're too bright to pretend to a belief in double-dyed villains. If that was all we were – myself and those like me – would most of the inhabited worlds let us take control of things the way they have?'

'If you were capable enough to do it,' Hal said.

'No.' Bleys shook his head. 'Even if we were supermen and super-women – even if we were the mutants some people like to think we are – so few of us could never control so many unless the many wanted us to control them. And you must have been better educated than to think of us as either superbeings or mutants. We're only what we are – what you yourself are – genetically fortunate combinations of human abilities who have had the advantages of some special training.'

'I'm not like you –' For a moment, lulled by Bley's warm, deep tones, Hal had forgotten the hatred in him. It came back redoubled, and a sort of nausea moved in him at the idea of any likeness between Bleys and himself.

'Of course you are,' said Bleys.

Hal looked past him to the two Militiamen standing behind him. With eyes now adjusted to the light, at last, one of them was now recognizable as a commissioned officer. Focusing more closely on the face above the collar tabs, he recognized Barbage.

'That's right, Hal,' said Bleys, having glanced over his shoulder. 'You know the Captain, don't you? This is Amyth Barbage, who'll be responsible for you as long as you're in this place. Amyth – remember, I've a particular interest in Hal. You and your men are going to have to forget he was ever connected with one of the Commands. You're to do nothing to him – for any reason, or under any circumstances. Do you understand me, Amyth?'

'I understand, Great Teacher,' said Barbage. His eyes stared unblinkingly at Hal as he spoke.

'Good,' said Bleys. 'Now, all surveillance of this cell is to be discontinued until I call you to come let me out of here. Leave us, both of you, and wait down the corridor so Hal and I can talk privately – if you please.'

Beside Barbage, the enlisted Militiaman started, taking half a step forward and opening his mouth. But without turning his gaze from Hal, Barbage closed a hand on the other black-sleeved arm. Hal saw the officer's thin fingers sink deeply into the cloth. The man checked and stood still, saying nothing.

'Don't worry,' said Bleys. 'I'll be perfectly safe. Now, go.'

The two of them went. The door of the cell, closing behind him, relocked itself with a soft click.

'You see,' said Bleys, turning back to Hal. 'they don't really understand this; and isn't fair to expect them to. From their standpoint, if another human gets in your way, the sensible thing is to remove him – or her. The concept of you and I as relatively unimportant in ourselves, but as gathering points for great forces, and in a situation where it's those forces that matter . . . that's a thing essentially beyond their comprehension. But certainly you and I ought to understand such things; not only such things but each other.'

'No,' said Hal. There was a great many more things he wanted to say; but suddenly the effort was too great and he ended by simply repeating himself. 'No.'

'Yes,' said Bleys, looking down. 'Yes. I'm afraid I have to insist, on that point. Sooner or later, you're going to have to face the real shape of things in any case and, for your own sake, it'd better be now, rather than later.'

Hal lay still, looking once more only at the ceiling over his head, rather than into the face of Bleys. The tall man's voice sounded like some gently sonorous bassoon in his ears.

'All practical actions are matters of necessity in the light of hard reality,' said Bleys. 'What we – those who're called the Other People – do, is dictated by what we are and the situation in which we find ourselves; and that situation is to be one among literally millions of ordinary humans, with the power to make our lives in that position ones in either a heaven or a hell. Either – but nothing else. Because the choice isn't one any of us can avoid. If we fail to choose heaven, we inevitably find ourselves in hell.'

'I don't believe you,' said Hal. 'There's no reason it has to be that way.'

'Oh yes, my child,' said Bleys softly. 'There is a reason. Apart from our individual talents, our training, and our mutual support, we're still only as human as the millions around us. Friendless and without funds, we can starve, just like anyone else. Our bones can be broken and we can fall sick as easily as ordinary mortals. Killed, we die as obligingly. If taken care of, we may live a few years longer than the average, but not much. We have the same normal, human emotional hungers – for love, for the companionship of someone who can think and talk our own language. But, if we should choose to ignore our differentness and mold ourselves to fit the little patterns of those around us, we can spend our whole lives miserably; and probably – almost certainly – we may never even be lucky enough to meet one other being like ourselves. None of us chose this, to be what each of us is – but what we are, we are; and like everyone else we have an innate human right to make the best of our situation.'

'At the expense of those millions of people you talk about,' said Hal.

'And what sort of expense is that?' Bleys' voice grew even deeper. 'The expense of one Other borne by a million ordinary humans is a light load on each ordinary human. But turn that about. What of the cost to the Other; who, trying only to fit in with the human mass around him, accepts a life of isolation, loneliness, and the endurance daily of prejudice and misunderstanding? While, at the same time, his unique strengths and talents allow those same individuals who draw away from him to reap the benefits of his labors. Is there justice in that? Look down the long pages of past history at the intellectual giants, men and women alike, who've moved civilization forward while struggling to survive in the midst of lesser people who innately feared and distrusted them. Giants, crouching daily to keep their differences from showing and arousing the irrational fears of the small ones around them. From the beginning of time to be human, but different, has been dangerous; and it's been a choice between the many who could carry one lightly on their combined shoulders and the one who must carry the many all alone, with his or her much greater strength, but staggering under the proportionately greater effort; and which of those two choices is fairer?'

Hal's head, under the effects of the fever and the drug together, spun strangely. The mental image of a giant crouching made a grosteque image in his mind.

'Why crouch?' he said.

'Why crouch?' The face of Bleys smiled, far above him. 'Ask yourself that. How old are you now?'

'Twenty,' said Hal.

'Twenty – and you still ask that question? As you've gotten older, haven't you begun to feel an isolation, a separation from all those around you? Haven't you found yourself forced, more and more often lately, to take charge of matters – to make decisions not merely for yourself, but for those with you who aren't capable of making them for themselves? Quietly, but inevitably, taking charge, doing what only you realize has to be done, for the good of all?'

He paused.

'I think you know what I'm talking about,' he said after that moment of silence. 'At first, you only try to tell them what should be done; because you can't believe – you don't want to believe – that they can be so helpless. But, little by little, you come to face the fact that while they may do things right under your continual coaching, they'll never understand enough to do what's necessary on their own, each time the need arises; and so, finally, worn out, you simply take over. Without their even realizing it, you set things in the path they should go; and all these little people follow it, thinking it's the natural course of events.'

He stopped again. Lying still, watching him, a portion of his own mind remote, Hal did not reply.

'Yes,' said Bleys, 'you know what I'm talking about. You've already known it, and started to feel the width and depth of this gulf that separates you from the rest of the race. Believe me when I tell you what you now feel will steadily grow deeper and stronger as time goes on. The experience your more capable mind acquires, at a rate much faster than they can imagine, will continue to widen the gap that separates you from them. In the end, there'll be little more kinship between you and them, than between you and any lesser creature – a dog or a cat – of which you've become fond. And you'll regret that lack of real kinship bitterly but there'll be nothing you can do about it, no way to give them what they'll never be able to hold – any more than you could give an appreciation of great art to monkeys. So, finally, to save yourself the pain that they don't even know you feel, you cut the last emotional tie you have with them, and choose instead the silence, the emptiness and the peace of being what you are – unique and alone, forever.'

He stopped speaking.

'No,' said Hal, after a moment. He felt detached, like someone under heavy sedation. 'That's not a way I can go.'

'Then you'll die,' said Bleys, dispassionately. 'In the end, like those who were like us in past centuries, you'll let them kill you, merely by ceasing to make the continual effort necessary to protect yourself among them. And it'll be wasted, all wasted – what you were and what you could've been.'

'Then it'll have to be wasted,' said Hal. 'I can't be what you say.'

'Perhaps,' said Bleys. He rose to his feet, the float drifting back in mid-air and aside from his legs. 'But wait a bit yet and see. The urge to live is stronger than you think.'

He stood looking down at Hal.

'I told you,' he said. 'I'm part-Exotic. Do you think I didn't fight against the knowledge of what I was, when I first began to be aware of it? Do you think I didn't reject what I saw myself committed to being, only because of what I am? Do you suppose I didn't at first tell myself that I'd choose a hermit's existence, an anchorite's life, rather than make what then I thought of as an immoral use of my abilities? Like you, I was ready to pay any price to save myself from the contamination of playing God to those around me. The idea was as repellent to me then as it is to you now. But what I came to learn was that it wasn't harm, it was good that I could do the race as one of its leaders and masters; and so will you learn – in the end.'

He turned and stepped to the door of the cell.

'Open up here!' he called into the corridor.

'It makes no difference,' he said, turning back once more as footsteps sounded, approaching them from beyond sight of the barred door, 'what you think you choose now. Inevitably, a day'll come when you'll see the foolishness of what you did now by insisting on staying here, in a cell like this, under the guard of those who, compared to you, are little more than civilized animals. None of what your're inflicting on yourself at this moment is really necessary.'

He paused.

'But it's your choice,' he went on. 'Do what you feel like doing until you can see more clearly. But when that times comes, all you'll have to do is say one word. Tell your guards that you'll consider what I've said; and they'll bring you to me, out of here to a place of comfort and freedom and daylight, where you can have time to set your mind straight in decency. Your need to undergo this private self-torture is all in your own mind. Still, as I say, I'll leave you with it until you see more clearly.'

Barbage and the enlisted Militiaman were already at the door of the cell. They unlocked and swung it open. Bleys stepped through and the door closed behind him. Without looking back he walked off, out of sight up the corridor, and the other two followed, leaving Hal to utter silence when the sound of footfalls had at last died away.

CHAPTER THIRTY-THREE

Exhausted, Hal dropped into sodden, dreamless slumber; and the length of his sleep was something he had no way of measuring. But he came struggling back into consciousness to find himself spasming with convulsive shivers that shook him with the power of an autumn gale upon a last dead leaf clinging to a tree.

The cell about him was unchanged. The light still burned with the same muted intensity in the ceiling. Complete silence continued beyond the barred door of his cell. Pushing himself upright again into a semi-sitting position, he saw the thin blanket folded at the foot of his bed, and, reaching out an unsteady hand, caught and pulled it up to his neck.

For a moment the relief of having something covering him almost let him escape again into oblivion. But the blanket was hardly thicker than his shirt; and the chill still savaged him like a dog shaking a rat. Holding the blanket tightly to his chin with both hands, he made an effort to exert some control over his shuddering body, fastening his attention on a point immeasurably remote within his own mind and striving to transfer all his attention to that remote, austere and incorporeal location.

For some minutes, it seemed that he would not be able to do it. The effort at mental control was too great in his worn-out condition, and the wild plungings of his body's reflexes were too strong. Then, gradually, he began to succeed. The shuddering ceased, the tensions leaked slowly from his muscles and his whole body quietened.

He could still feel the urge of his flesh to respond to the frightening chill that had seized him. But now that urge was held at arm's length, and he could think. He opened his mouth to speak but only croaked. Then he managed to clear his throat, take a deep breath and call out.

'It's freezing, here! Turn the heat up!'

There was no answer.

He shouted again. But still there was no response; and the temperature of the cell stayed as it was.

He stayed listening to the silence, and his memory gave him back Bleys' earlier order about all surveillance of the cell being discontinued until the Other should call to be let out. Surveillance must have been resumed when Bleys left and that would mean that there was no need to shout now. Someone must be listening and possibly observing him as well, at this moment.

He lay back under the blanket, still holding down hard on the urge of his body to shiver, and looked up at the ceiling.

'I know you hear me.' With an effort he held his voice level. 'I think Bleys Ahrens told you not to do anything to me – that includes letting me chill to death. Turn the heat up. Otherwise I'll tell him about this, the next time I see him.'

He waited.

Still, no one answered or came. He was about to speak again when it occurred to him that if those watching him had been unmoved by his words, repeating them would do no good; while if he had worried them at all, repetition would only weaken his threat.

After perhaps ten minutes, he heard steps in the corridor. A thin, upright, black-uniformed figure appeared beyond the bars of his cell door, unlocked it and came in. He looked up into the flint-blade features of Amyth Barbage.

'It is well that thou be told,' said Barbage. His voice was oddly remote, almost as if he talked aloud while dreaming.

Hal stared up at him.

'Yes,' said Barbage, 'I will tell thee.'

His eyes glittered like polished chips of hard coal in the dimness of the cell.

'I know thee,' he said slowly, looking down at Hal; and each word was like a drop of icy water chilling the feverish surface of Hal's mind. 'Thou art of that demon blood that cometh before Armageddon – which now is close upon us. Yes, I see thee, if some else do not, in thy true shape with thy jaws of steel and thy head like to the head of a great and loathsome hound. *Wily art thou, a serpent*. Thou didst pretend to save my life, long since, from that apostate of the Lord, the Child of Wrath who would have slain me in the pass – so that I might feel a debt to thee; and so be seduced by thee when thou wert at last, as thou now art, in the power of God's Chosen.'

His voice became slightly harsher, but still it remained distant, detached.

'But I am of the Elect, and beyond thy cunning. It hath been ordered by the Great Teacher that I let no thing be done to thee – nor will I. But there is no need that anything be done *for thee*. Immortal in wickedness and blasphemy as thou art, there is no need to cosset such as thee. Therefore call out as thou wilt – none shall come or answer. This cell is of the temperature it had when thou wert brought in. No one hath altered it, nor will. The lights thou mayest have up or down; but no other thing will be changed or brought about at thy word. Rest thee as thou art, foul dog of Satan.'

313

He turned away. The cell door clicked closed its lock behind him; and Hal was left alone.

He lay still, trying to control his shivering and little by little the effort of doing so became less; not so much because his control was strengthening, as because his fever was once more starting to assert itself and his body temperature beginning again to rise. As he warmed, the need to control his reflexes relaxed; and he drifted once more into sleep.

But it was a light, uneasy sleep, from which he roused suddenly to find his throat so dry and sore it felt as if it would crack open with the simple effort of swallowing. The demand of the thirst upon him was so great that he managed to summon the strength to pull himself up off the bed and on to his feet. He staggered across the room to the washstand anchored to the wall next to the stool. Turning on the single tap there he lowered his head and gulped at the stream of icy water that poured down.

But after only a few swallows he found he could drink no more. The water he had already taken in seemed to fill his gullet full and threaten to nauseate him. He stumbled back to the cot, fell on it and was asleep again instantly – only to wake, it seemed, in minutes; and with the raging thirst that had roused him before once more driving him back to the water tap.

Once more, he made his unsteady pilgrimage to it; and once more he was able to drink only a few swallows before it seemed he could swallow no more. Warned now by his fading strength, he went back to the cot he had been lying on and struggled to pull it across the room until it stood next to the washstand.

The effort of moving the light cot was inconceivable. His head rang and his muscles had the strength of half-melted wax. Jerking the cot first this way, and then that, like an ant trying to move a dead beetle many times its weight, he managed at last to get it next to the washstand and fell back on it exhausted, to sleep immediately.

In some indeterminable time – it seemed only a matter of seconds, though it could have been much longer – he woke again, drank, and fell back to uneasy sleep.

So began a feverish, dream-ridden period which, on the one hand, seemed to encompass no time at all but which, looked at only a little differently, stretched out through an eternity. He woke and drank, drank and slept, woke again to drink and sleep . . . over and over again. While about him there was only stillness; the eternally lighted cell and the silent corridor beyond produced neither the appearance of any watcher nor any change.

He was aware now that the sickness in him was raging with a violence greater than any such he had felt in his life before, and an uneasiness unknown until now stirred deep in him. Periods of fever were alternating with periods of deep chill, with the fever gradually predominating. Little by little, the unnatural states of his body took him over, first the great shuddering chills, then the wild demand of the thirst in him that choked on only a few mouthfuls of water at a time, the ringing headaches and the wakeful periods alternating with snatches of uneasy and nightmare-torn sleep.

He could feel the infection in him gaining on his life-force. The chills gave way at last completely to a light-headed unnaturalness that would have been almost pleasant by comparison if it had not also been ominous. He took it to be one of high fever – but of how high a fever, he had no way of telling. The headaches lessened, temporarily, but his breathing was becoming more and more difficult, as if his lower chest was being slowly stuffed full with some heavy material, forcing him to breathe with only a small space that remained open at the top of his lungs. Gradually, he pulled himself into a sitting position in which breathing was easier, upright at one end of the cot with his back against the rough wall to which the washstand was attached, the washstand on one side of him, the stool on the other.

Somewhere about this time, also, the ability to sleep was lost to him. His head rang and pounded, he breathed painfully in tiny gasps, and a fiery awakeness shut out any possibility of further slumber. The minutes passed as slowly as caterpillars humping their way along a tree limb, but they came endlessly, measuring out hours followed by hours that went on forever. Time itself stretched out endlessly, and still no one appeared at the barred door of his cell.

For the first time he remembered the Coby-built miner's chronometer he normally wore on his wrist, that had been given back to him, among his other belongings, when he and Jason Rowe had been turned loose from the Militia Headquarters in Citadel after Bleys had spoken to them. He had worn it all through the time he had been with the Command. He looked automatically for it at his left wrist now; and, with some surprise, saw the instrument had not been taken from him this time. The current reading of its outer ring of numerals glowed against its metal face like ghost figures of flame to tell him that, somewhere outside this cell, it was eleven twenty-three of the Harmony evening, local time.

There was no telling how long it had been since he had been brought here. But perhaps he could make an estimate. Struggling with his fevered mind to think back, he remembered that it had not yet been noon when he had been captured in the spaceport terminal. He could hardly have been here less than one full day of the twenty-three point sixteen Interstellar Standard Hours that made up the calendar day on Harmony. From that noon, then, to noon of the day following, plus the hours necessary to bring him now almost to midnight of a second day, would make a total of a day and a half since he had been carried in here. Fumbling in his pockets, he came up with everything that had been in his possession when he had been captured, but nothing that could mark on the smooth-painted wall behind him. With the metal case of the watch, finally, he managed to scratch a single vertical line, low down under the washstand, where the shadow of that utility would hide the mark.

They had not brought him food at any time since he had gotten here; but he did not miss it. In the heat of the fever his stomach seemed to have shrunken and contorted upon itself like a clenched fist. The only appetite he had was for water; and, after a swallow or two, that continued to choke him. His single greatest desire now was merely to breathe easily and normally, with the full capacity of his lungs. But his body was denying him that.

The struggle to breathe began to wake all his instincts for survival. On the wings of the fever in him, his total being cranked itself up; his heart hammered in his chest, faster and faster, his mind leaped and dodged and sought for a way out – a way to open his lungs to great gulps of air, to set himself loose from this place. But the lack of oxygen made any additional effort beyond mere existence too great to attempt. Seated bolt-upright, with his back against the cell wall, struggling for air, he was at once physically immobilized and mentally on emergency alert; as his body tuned itself ever higher in an attempt to fight the slow suffocation that was threatening him.

He knew too little of medicine to build a full picture of what was happening inside him. But clearly his struggle to breathe against the congestion of his lungs was triggering off all the instincts and reflexes of his body that could be marshalled against it. He was barely able now to spare breath for the extra physical effort of leaning over to drink from the water tap, but his mind raced at its greatest capacity like a creature afire. Immobilized, but thinking now at life-and-death speed, he sat facing the slow, continuous movement of the hours.

There was no one to help him. Barbage had promised that none would come; and slowly, he was beginning to understand that, barring another visit from Bleys himself, that promise would be kept. For the first time it came to him that Barbage, in his fanaticism, must actually be hoping for his death and doing everything possible within the limits of Bleys' commands to bring it about. If things as they now were with him continued to worsen, then, uncared-for – eventually – he must die.

He found himself facing that prospect at last as an actuality. He could no longer deny that it could happen. All his life until this moment, it had been easier to imagine the death of the universe than his own. But now, at last, his personal mortality had become as real to him as the walls enclosing him. His end could be only a handful of hours away, unless something – some miracle – could prevent it.

His racing mind revolted against that realization, like an animal galloping wildly around and around the circular wall of an abattoir in search of some opening to freedom and life. Deep and far off in him, like the barely-heard trumpet call of an approaching enemy, he felt for the first time in his life the pale, cold touch of pure panic. He made an effort to reach out with the semi-autohypnotic technique he had used when he had passed through the Final Encyclopedia and evoked the images of his three former tutors to help him; but his mind could not be freed sufficiently from the adrenalin released by the instinctive struggles of his body, so that he might be able to find the mental control that would make the evocative technique work.

For a second, realizing this, his panic doubled. Then, coldly, strengtheningly into him came the realization that there was no one to help him now in any case but himself. The years that had passed since the deaths of the three who had raised him had given him experience and information beyond what Malachi, Obadiah and Walter had known in him, while they were alive, and these things he must find how to use for himself.

But the brief moment of logical understanding had steadied him. He had slumped down during the past hours. Now he pushed himself further upright with the wall at his back and set himself consciously to deal with the situation. But the fever still held him like an intoxication and with his best efforts his mind wandered and drifted off from its purpose, in a state of blurred discomfort that left him floating halfway between consciousness and unconsciousness.

Without warning he found himself dreaming with a knife-edged clarity to all his senses, discovering himself on the same mountainside to which his mind had retreated back when he had been newly landed on Harmony and in the Militia's hands before; and Bleys, not recognizing him among prisoners in the room before him, had tried to make them all captive to the Other's charisma.

But this time he dreamed that he was spread-eagled on his back, wrists and ankles manacled tightly to the rough granite upon which he lay and the icy rain, falling steadily upon him, chilled him to his bones. . . .

He forced himself awake to find himself shuddering once again with the great chills that shook his whole body. The thin blanket had fallen from him. He pulled it hastily up around him and huddled down on the mattress, to lie panting with the effort of movement. For what seemed to be a long time he fought for breath and against the shivering fit that shook him, until his fever started to swing upward once more; and – once more without warning – dreams returned him to the moment earlier, in which Bleys had stood towering over him, here in the cell.

'. . . You're right, of course,' he heard the Other saying again. 'But still I'd like you to try and understand my point of view. . . .'

As before, Bleys loomed enormous over Hal. But from somewhere else, out of the far past, the soft voice of Walter the InTeacher rose, reading, as he had once read aloud to Hal, the lines spoken by the fallen Satan in Milton's *Paradise Lost*:

'. . . *The mind is its own place, and in itself*
Can make a Heaven of Hell, a Hell of Heaven.
What matter where, if I still be the same,
And what I should be, all but less than he
Whom thunder hath made greater? . . .'

But Walter's voice dwindled again and was lost while Bleys was still speaking. The Other's deep tones echoed in the fevered vastness of Hal's dream.

'. . . None of us chose this, to be what each of us is,' Bleys was saying once more to him, '– but what we are, we are; and like everyone else we have an innate human right to make the best of our situation.'

'At the expense of those millions of people you talk about.' Hal heard his own answer as if from someone else, speaking far off, at a distance.

'And what sort of expense is that?' Bleys' voice deepened until the whole universe seemed to resonate with it. 'The expense of one Other borne by a million ordinary humans is a light load on each ordinary human. But turn that about. What of the cost to the Other; who, trying only to fit in with the human mass around him, accepts a life of isolation, loneliness, and the endurance daily of prejudice and misunderstanding? While, at the same time, his unique strengths and talents allow those same individuals who draw away from him to reap the benefits of his labors. Is there justice in that? . . .'

The deeply musical voice rolled on, echoing and reechoing until it muttered like distant thunder in the mountains, until in its multi-layered echoes all sense of the individual words was lost. Suddenly, the mountains of his younger years were once more around Hal and he found himself standing again in the water at the edge of the artificial lake on the estate, looking up through the limbs of the bush that hid him at the terrace of the house, seeing the three figures there that he knew so well move suddenly, together . . . and fall.

It seemed he fled from that scene, fled as he had actually fled – to Coby. Once more he lay in his small room in the miner's barracks, that first night at the Yow Dee Mine, feeling that same feeling Bleys had spoken of only hours since, that difference and isolation from everyone else sleeping and awake around him within the plain walls of the building. That isolation, that he seemed to remember knowing also at some earlier time, long, long before Bleys or any Other. . . .

Suddenly, he was back on Harmony, in his dream of rubbled plain; and the tower, far off, toward which he made his slow way on foot. He had known that plain, too, from before, somewhere. He forged on now toward the tower, but his efforts seemed to bring him no

318

nearer to it. Only the conviction held him, like the conviction of life itself, that it was what he must reach eventually, no matter how far it might be, or how difficult the way to it.

He woke from that dream to another – of Harmony and the weeping woods, to the stumbling figures of an exhausted Command fleeing from the relentless Militia pursuit of Barbage. He left the others and by himself carried James Child-of-God up to a little rise, settling him there with his weapons and his slight barricade, leaving him there to die in delaying their pursuers.

'What is thy true name . . .?' James asked again, looking up at him. Hal stared at him.

'Hal Mayne.'

'. . . Bless thee in God's name. Hal Mayne,' said James. 'Convey to the others that in God's name also I bless the Command, Rukh Tamani, and all who shall fight under the banner of the Lord. Now go. Care for those whose care hath been set into thy hands.'

James turned from Hal to fix his eyes once more on the forest as seen through the firing slot in his barricade. Hal turned away also, but in a different direction, leaving James Child-of-God upon the small rise . . .

. . . And woke at last to his silent cell, which took shape around him once more.

CHAPTER THIRTY-FOUR

Here, there was no change. But something in him was aware of having just achieved movement toward some as yet undefined goal. From the dreams just past he had progressed, had gained something that had not been available to him before. Once more aware of the cell about him, he felt for the first time an almost perfect separation of himself into two parts. One part, from which he was withdrawing, was the suffering body, which he now understood clearly but calmly to be losing its battle for life as its temperature mounted and its lungs gradually filled, bringing it closer and closer to the moment when it would cease to function. The other, to which he had drawn nearer, was the mind, now that the tether that normally held it to the demanding feelings and instincts of the body was becoming attenuated under the fierce fire of his struggle to survive. The mind itself burned now, with a brilliance that fed on the heat of that fire.

It was a new sort of brilliance that illuminated things formerly hidden from him. He was acutely aware of the two parts of the structure with which he thought. The but and the ben of it – the front chamber and the rear one. In the front, brightly illuminated, was the long and narrow room of his conscious thoughts, where logic kept order and worked in visible steps from question to answer. But at the back of that room was the doorless wall that separated it from the rear chamber – the vast unordered attic of his unconscious, piled and stored with all the rich lumber of his experience. In just the past few hours of talk and dreams that wall had been burned thin, as the connecting link between mind and body had been thinned by his struggle to survive, so that now it was less a wall than a semi-transparent membrane. Also, the normally blinding lamp of his instinct to survive had been turned down, until with vision adjusted to dimness he could see through that membrane into formerly obscure corners and dark places from which his conscious vision had been blocked before.

Now he saw by the light of that gentler lamp of understanding, which illuminated both chambers alike and shone through the thinned membrane that separated them, until from the dimmed front chamber he could now begin to make out new shapes of patterns and identities amongst all the clutter that the back chamber held.

In that seeking light he could no longer deny what he knew to be true. He had indeed, as Bleys had claimed he must sooner or later, taken matters finally into his own hands. He had lied to Rukh by omission because he knew she would not agree with what he wanted to suggest, the removal of the donkeys and the explosive so that the Command might disperse and survive, the explosives taken by one person to a safe hiding place. He had chosen to do this without consultation with anyone, making the decisions for all of the rest and taking charge by main force. But he had done it with a purpose. A purpose outside himself.

And in that fact lay all the difference in the universe from what Bleys had tried to imply to such an action. For Bleys had spoken of matters taken over by the more powerful individual, alone, for his own survival and comfort. Behind the tall man's words had been the implication that there was no other worthwhile goal but this. But he had been wrong. For there was in fact a massively greater goal – the eternal survival of the race so that it could continue to learn and grow. That purpose was toward life while Bleys' was only toward a brief moment of personal satisfaction, followed by an inevitable death that would leave behind no mark upon the fabric of the universe. The truer instinct to sacrifice a personal life that the race might survive was imaged in the Brown Man he had created as part of the poem he had made in the mountains, reaching out to give form to the understanding already growing within him.

It had been a form constructed by way of the pattern of words, as he had been making such constructs unconsciously with his poetry since he had been very young. Bleys' way had no form, no purpose, no value, only the building of a little comfort for a short while – before the coming of the endless dark.

The way of all those Hal had ever been close to had always been aware of the greater purpose. Malachi, Walter and Obadiah had died to ensure that Hal himself would live, and so perhaps come to this present moment of understanding. Those in Rukh's Command had fought and died for an end they felt too strongly to question, even if the exact shape of it was not visible to them. Tam Olyn had given the long years of his life to guardianship of that great lever for humanity that the Encyclopedia would one day be. And he, himself, had been driven from his earliest beginnings by a similar purpose; even if, as with those in the Command, its exact shape had continued to be hidden from him.

A powerful feeling of being close now to what he had always sought took hold of Hal. In the face of that feeling, the agonies and the approaching death of his body dwindled to unimportance. The fact of the cell about him dwindled. Pushing all things into the background now was the fact that through the near-transparent membrane, between the two compartments of his mind, comprehension was at last beginning to flow back and forth, revealing a possible solution to all problems, a victory the possibility of which had been wholly hidden from him before.

Even now, he still could not see it clearly. But he felt its presence, unmistakably; and, knowing at last that it was there, he mined his way toward it with the twin tools of dreams and poetry, linking the two for the first time to explore, with the illumination of his reasoning front mind, the great store of human experience and unconscious understandings in the mind's darker, older twin beyond the membrane.

A sense of transport uplifted him. He foresaw these tools finally taking him to the distant tower of which he had dreamed, that was his goal and that of humanity since the beginning. The tools only waited for him to fashion them into conscious reality, out of the memories and vision that had been used unconsciously to that purpose since the race first lifted its eyes to dream beyond the prison of its present toward a greater and better future.

All that he needed was there in the cluttered attic of his experience. To isolate each necessary element of it he was only required to follow the two lamps that had lighted the way of every human from his beginning . . . the need, and the dream.

He let his mind take leave, therefore, of his body that was fighting and struggling for the scant breath available to it; and set his perceptions free to go on their search.

Again, he dreamed. But this time on the wings of purpose.

. . . A young man's face looked down at him, with Old Earth's summer sky blue and high behind it. It was an Exotic face, much more youthful than Walter's, the visage of a visitor to the estate. Its owner was a former pupil of Walter's, who had studied under the older man at a time when Walter had still been a teacher on his home of Mara. The pupil was grown, now, and himself a teacher of other Exotics. He wore a dark brown robe on his slim, erect body, and stood with Hal in the woods just beyond the artificial lake. Together, they were watching a sandy patch of ground at their feet and the busy scurrying there of tiny black bodies to and from the opening of an ant hill.

'. . . One way of thinking of them,' the young Exotic was saying to Hal, 'is to think of the whole community as a single creature, so that an ant-hill or a swarm of bees becomes the equivalent of a single animal. The individual ant or bee, then, is just one part of the whole creature. The way a fingernail might be to you, useful, but something that you can do without if necessary, or something for which you can grow a replacement.

'Ants and bees?' echoed Hal, fascinated. The single creature image woke something in him that was almost like a memory. 'What about people?'

The Exotic teacher smiled down at him.

'People are individuals. You're an individual,' he answered. 'You don't have to do what the hive as a whole, or the swarm as a whole wants to do. These have no choice, as you do. You can make individual decisions and be free to act on them.'

'Yes, but . . .' Hal's mind had been captured. The powerful idea that had risen in him was something he could not quite visualize and which his eight-year-old powers of expression were inadequate to describe. 'A person doesn't have to do what other persons want unless he wants to – I know that. But there could be something like everyone knowing the same thing, then each person could make up his own mind about it. Wouldn't that be practically the same thing?'

The Exotic smiled at him.

'I think what you're suggesting is a sort of conversation of minds,' he said. 'It's been speculated about for hundreds of years and called a lot of different names – telepathy is one of them. But every test we've ever been able to make shows that at best telepathy's an occasional phenomenon of the unconscious mind, and there's no way to be sure you can use it when you want it. Most people never experience it at all.'

'But it could be,' said Hal. 'Couldn't it?'

'If it could be, then perhaps you'd be right.' A single, thoughtful crease formed for a second between the eyebrows of the young Exotic. Then it went away and he smiled again at Hal. '. . . Perhaps.'

They turned from the ant hill and went on together to look at other things about the estate. Later, Hal overheard the younger Exotic speaking privately to Walter.

'He's very bright, isn't he?' the visitor was saying.

Walter's reply had been too low for Hal to catch. But he had been fascinated by the compliment implied in the young Exotic's final words – a compliment none of his three tutors had ever chosen to give him. But thinking about it, afterward, the feeling came even more strongly to him than it had at the time, that he had not so much suddenly stumbled then upon the question that had impressed the young Exotic, as found it already there in some part of him with which he was unfamiliar. Now, fascinated by it anew, after all these years, he let go of his dream about the visitor and came back to awareness of the cell.

That one idea was a piece of the whole that had brought him to this moment. It was also – he thought now, with his racing brain – a part of one of the tools of understanding he had just earlier imagined could be forged by a linking of the forward and back parts of his mind. He reached out to develop that idea, trying to touch with his consciousness other knowledges and awarenesses beyond the membrane, things that he could sense were there, but could still not see clearly. However, these still hid from him. It occurred to him once again that these hidden elements might be from a time farther back than his aware memory knew, that perhaps they lay shrouded partly by the darkness of that mystery about himself to which he had always hunted unsuccessfully for an answer, the mystery of who he was and where he had come from.

With that thought, it came to him that the unconscious might know what the conscious did not. Buried within it must be specific memories from before the time when he had been old enough to make conscious observations of what was around him. Memories, perhaps, of what it had been like aboard the old-fashioned courier spaceship on which he had been found as a child. He closed his eyes and leaned back against the cold wall of the cell, willing awareness of his body to depart from him again, reaching out for a vision of the past before the remembered times. . . .

But the picture that he finally summoned up, half dream, half autohypnotic hallucination, was limited in ways that disappointed him. He was able to see something that was clearly like a room, but most of it was shadowy or out of focus. Parts of it – a pilot's chair, some steadily glowing lights on a panel just above his reach – stood out in sharp focus as seen with the unmarred, fresh-born attention of the very young. But the rest was remote or blurred to the point of being unrecognizable. Clearly, he thought, he was looking at the space that had combined the functions of main cabin and control room of the craft in which he had been found. However, he could deduce nothing beyond that fact to help him with the questions in his mind. There was no indication of a particular moment in which he might have been seeing this and no sign of other humans within the remembered range of his vision.

A sharp disappointment woke in him, kindling into near anger. All through the life he could remember, he had dreamed and longed to find out about his origins, imagining a thousand fanciful tales of who he might be and where he might have come from. Now it was almost as if he was deliberately being prevented from that discovery, when it lay at his fingertips. In frustration he turned his mind upon the inmost recesses of his unconscious with all the fury of someone running down empty corridors, pounding on door after unresponsive door. Until, at last, he burst his way through one such door to a point where he found himself brought up short, face to face against a barrier the existence of which he had not expected.

His imagination pictured it for him as a massive, round, metal door, like that on a vault. It was an unnatural barrier, that made no secret of the fact it had been put there by someone so much more capable than his present self, that there was no hope of his forcing it open. It stood, speaking a silent, unyielding message to him from the fact of its very existence.

I will stand open when you no longer need what I hide.

In itself, it represented a defeat. But at the same time it gave a confirmation of what he had often suspected; and that confirmation made it not a defeat but a victory. The barrier's very existence was proof at last that he was, and always had been, something more than his conscious self had realized. Also it meant that the way blocked off was no more than one tried by an earlier self and found to be a dead end. He was being directed by this to find some other path to the goal they had both tried to reach; and a newly possible means for that journey to that goal lay now in the understanding that had just come to him in this cell.

He let himself go back, therefore, to full consciousness of the cell, back to his laboring, suffering body. But with a new freedom now of will and thought, he began consciously to commence the forging of those special mental tools he had imagined earlier when it had come to him how the conscious mind might reach back and tap not only the knowledge but the abilities of the unconscious. He set himself, even as he struggled to breathe, to the building of a poem, sending his desire for that which he needed through the membrane to search among the relationships between the as-yet-unclear shapes and meanings stored back there.

And the search brought those relationships to him finally, in the sharply focused, creative images of the poem itself.

ARMAGEDDON

Yes, they are only deer.
Nervous instincts, fitted with hooves and horns,
That foolishly stamp among these Christian pines
Affixed like seals to the legal foolscap of winter;
And, illiterately facing the line of the snowplowed asphalt
Scrawled by a book-learned hand among these hills.
Cross to the redcapped men.

Armageddon.

Of course. The title and the words of the poem burned in his mind's-eye as the Final Encyclopedia had made his poem about the knight burn amongst the stars that appeared to surround his carrel there. Then, what he had found himself discovering in poetic form had been the irresistible inner force that was to drive him forth from the Encyclopedia, toward his years on Coby and this present moment of realization. Now, with this latter verse he had rendered a picture of the self-created cataclysm toward which the human race was now hurling itself, like a drunken man too intoxicated to realize the consequences of what he did.

Of course. Armageddon – Ragnorak – whatever you wanted to call it, was finally upon all of them. It had caught up all people like an avalanche, gaining speed as it plunged down a mountainside; and there was no one now who could fail to be aware of it on some level or another of his or her senses.

Tam Olyn had told him of it, bluntly and plainly. But he also remembered Sost, in the tunneled corridors of Coby, referring to it. Hilary had talked about it to Jason as he had driven Jason and Hal to their meeting with Rukh's Command . . . and, just a few hours since, Barbage had once more used the term 'Armageddon,' here in this very cell.

Armageddon – the final battle. Its shadow lay with a weight that could be felt on all living humans, even those who had never heard of the word or the concept. Now it was obvious to Hal that each of them, alone, could feel its approach, just as birds and animals under a blue and cloudless sky could yet feel the coming of a thunderstorm. Not only with the thinking top of their minds, but all through their beings, they could sense the buildup of vast forces about to break into conflict above their heads.

And it was a conflict the roots of which stretched back into prehistoric times. Now that Hal had opened his own eyes to its existence, it became obvious how in the last few hundred years the developing historical situation had merely briefly held back the inevitable, coming hour of conflict, while at the same time setting the stage for its final fury.

All of this was there in the poem he had just made, in allegorical form. Now that he looked for it there, he saw each large division of the race represented. The hunters could only be the Others, involved solely with their personal concerns for the brief, secular moments of their individual lives. The deer were the great mass of people like Sost and Hilary, being driven now by pressures they did not understand at last across a dividing line from safety into the hands of the hunters. Finally, there were those who stood back and saw this situation for what it was, with a vantage point like that of a reader of the poem or a viewer of the picture described. Those who could see what was about to happen and who had already dedicated themselves to prevent its happening. People like Walter, Malachi and Obadiah, like Tam, Rukh and Child-of-God. Like –

Without warning, the lighting of the cell and the small section of corridor he could see dimmed almost to total darkness. A shiver ran for some seconds through all around him. At the same time, from nowhere in particular came a deep, rumbling sound that mounted in volume briefly, then died away – as if just beyond the walls enclosing him there had been the passage of that massive, swift-moving avalanche he had imagined as an image for Armageddon.

It was an inexplicable sound to reach his ears, here in the bowels of a Militia Headquarters as this must be, in the center of a city such as Ahruma. Then the lights came back on full again.

He waited for an explanation to offer itself – for the sound of running feet approaching or the corridor-blurred echoes of raised voices. But nothing sounded. No one came.

CHAPTER THIRTY-FIVE

Gradually, he ceased to wait. The hope that someone might come or some sort of explanation appear left him; and his mind, like a compass needle, swung back to the magnetic element of his earlier thoughts. He had been listing in his mind those he had known who were committed to fight the bringers of Armageddon and he had been about to add one more name – his own.

Because he now realized that he also was committed. But there was a difference between him and the others he had thought of. Unlike them, he had been enlisted at some point farther back than his conscious memory could reach. Even before he had been found in the spacecraft, plans must have been laid to make him part of a war what he did not then even know existed.

Once more, he came back to the fact that there were things beyond the membrane, in the shadowy warehouse of his unconscious, that belonged to a past beyond the life his present consciousness knew. He could feel back there answers that had been blocked from him, as the image of the vault door had blocked his earlier searching. But it was no dead end he followed now. A certainty lived in him that the reason he had been committed to this struggle had been with him all this time in his unconscious.

The same tools that had brought him answers so far should continue to work for him now. He closed his eyes and his mind once more to the cell about him and reached out for the materials of another poem that would give him further answers.

But no poem came. Instead, came something so powerful that he lived it beyond the definition of the words dream or vision. It was a memory of a sound once heard. It spoke in his mind with such keen clarity that there was no difference between that and his hearing it with his physical ears, here in the cell, all over again. It was the sound of bagpipe music. And he found himself weeping.

It was not for the music alone he wept, but for what it had meant, for the pain and the grief of that meaning. He followed sound and pain together as if they were a braided thread of gold and scarlet leading him first into darkness and then out once more into a cloud-thick, chilly autumn day, with tall people standing around a newly-dug grave, below willows already stripped of their leaves, and the high, cold peaks of mountains.

The people about seemed so tall, he realized, because he, who was there with them, was still only a child. They were his people and the grave had been filled in though the coffin it held was empty – but the music was now filling it, for the body that should have been there. The man playing the pipes and standing across from him, up near the head of the grave, was his uncle. His father and mother stood behind the gravestone, and his great-uncle stood opposite his uncle. His only other uncle, the twin of the one playing the pipes, was not there. He had been unable to return, even for this. Of the rest of the family present, there was only his one brother, who was six years older than himself, sixteen now and due to leave home himself in two years.

At the foot of the grave were a handful of neighbors and friends. Like the family, they wore black, except for five of them with oriental faces, whose white mourning robes stood out starkly amongst the dark clothing around them.

Then the music ended and his father took a limping half-step forward, so that he could close one big hand over the curved top of the gravestone and speak the words that were always spoken by the head of the family at the burial of one of its members.

'He is home.' His father's voice was hoarse. 'Sleep with those who loved you – James, my brother.'

His father turned away. The burial was over. Family, neighbors and friends went back to the big house. But he, himself, lagged behind and drifted aside, unnoticed, to slip away into the stable.

There, in the familiar dimness warmed by the heavy bodies of the horses, he went slowly down the center aisle between the stalls. The horses put their soft noses over the doors that locked them in and blew at him as he passed, but he ignored them. At the barn's far end he sank down into a sitting position on a bale of new hay from the summer just past, feeling the round logs of the wall hard against his back. He sat, looking at nothing, thinking of James whom he would never see again.

After a while a coldness began to grow in him; but it came, not from the chill of the day outside but from inside him. It spread from a point deep within, outward through his body and limbs. He sat, remembering what he had listened to the day before, with all of the family gathered in the living room to hear from the man who had been his dead uncle's commanding officer, to tell them how James had died.

There had come a point in the talking when the officer, a tall, lean man of his father's age, named Brodsky, had paused in what he was saying and glanced over at him.

'Maybe the boy . . .?' Brodsky said. Small among all the rest, he had tensed.

'No,' answered his father harshly, 'he'll need to know how such things happen soon enough. Let him stay.'

He had relaxed. He would have fought, even in the face of his father's command, being sent away from what the officer had to tell.

Brodsky nodded, and went on with what he had been telling them.

'There were two things that caused it,' he said slowly, 'neither of which should have happened. One of them was that the Director of the Board at Donneswort had been secretly planning to pay us with the help of some pretty heavy funding promised from William of Ceta.'

Donneswort was one of the principalities on the planet called Freiland; and the small war there in which James had died had been one of the disputes between communities on that populous world which had escalated into military conflict.

'He'd kept that from us, of course,' the officer went on, 'or we'd have required a covering deposit in advance. Apparently no one at Donneswort, even the other members of his Board, knew. William, of course, had interests in controlling either Donneswort or its opponent, or both. At any rate, the contract was signed, our troops made good progress from the first into opposition territory and it looked like we were ready to sweep up, when – again, without our knowing it – William reneged on his promise to the Board Director, as he'd probably planned to do from the beginning.'

Brodsky stopped and looked steadily at his father.

'And that left Donneswort without funds to pay you off, of course,' his father said. His father's dark gaze glanced at his uncle and brother. 'That's happened before, too, to our people.'

'Yes,' said Brodsky, emotionlessly. 'At any rate, the Board Director decided to try and hide the news of this from us until we'd got a surrender from our opposition – it looked as if we were only a few days from it, at that time. He did keep it from us, but he didn't manage to keep it from spies belonging to the opposition. As soon as the other side heard, they stuck their necks out, borrowed militia from adjoining states they wouldn't be able to pay for unless they won, and we suddenly found a force three times the size we'd contracted to deal with thrown at us.'

Brodsky paused and he saw the officer's dark eyes glance briefly once more, over at his own small self.

'Go on,' said his father, harshly. 'You're going to tell us how all this affected my brother.'

'Yes,' said the officer. 'We'd had James on duty as a Force-Leader, with a unit of local Donneswort militia. But of course, since he was one of ours, his orders came only down our own chain of command. Because he was new in command and because his militia weren't worth much, we'd held his Force in reserve. But when the Board Director heard of the increase in opposition forces, he panicked and tried to throw all of us, all available troops, into an all-out attack – which would have been suicidal, the way we were positioned at the time.'

'So you refused,' said his uncle, speaking for the first time.

'We did, of course,' said Brodsky, looking over at the uncle. 'Our Battle Op rejected the Director's order, for cause, which he was free to do under the contract, and as he would've in any case. But those companies of militia not under our own officers received the order and followed it. They moved up.'

'But the boy got no order,' said his mother.

'Unfortunately,' Brodsky sighed softly, 'he did. That was the second thing that shouldn't have happened. James' Force was part of a unit positioned off on the left flank of our general position, in touch with the overall Command HQ through a central communications net that was staffed almost totally by local militia. One of these was the man who received the message for the troops in James' area. There, all the units except James' were commanded by militia officers. The militiaman on net communications to their sector made up move orders for all units before someone pointed out to him that the one to your brother could only be sent if it was authorized by one of our own commanders. Because the militiaman was ignorant of the overall situation, and apparently also because it was simply easier for him than checking with our command, he put the name of James' Commander on the order to James without authority, and sent it out over the net to your brother.'

Brodsky sighed softly again.

'James moved his Force up with the rest of the militia around him,' he went on. 'There was a road they'd been ordered to hold; and they made contact with opposition forces almost immediately. James must have seen from the beginning that he and his men were caught up in a fight with numbers and equipment too great for his men to hold. The militia under their own officers on either side of him pulled out – ran, I should say. He checked back with the communications net, but the same militiaman who'd issued the order panicked, just as the Board Director had, and simply told James no orders had come in from the Dorsai command for him to pull back.'

The officer stopped speaking. The silence in the living room was uninterrupted.

'So,' said the officer, 'that's the last contact that was had with his Force. We believe he must have assumed our own people had some reason for wanting him to hold. He could still have pulled back on his own initiative under the Mercenaries Code, of course, but he didn't. He did his best to hold until his position was overrun and he and his men were killed.'

The eyes of all the rest of them in the room were dry and steady upon Brodsky.

'That particular militiaman was killed an hour or so later when the net position was overrun,' the officer said softly. 'We would have dealt with him otherwise, naturally, and also there would at least have been reparations for you as a family. But Donneswort was bankrupt, so not even that much was possible. The rest of us who were there got the funds to return home from the opposition. We threatened to hold the Donneswort capital city on our own, against them, if they didn't pay us what we needed to evacuate. It was a lot cheaper for them to bear the expense of sending us home than to pay the cost of taking the city from us. And if they hadn't taken the city within a week, they'd have been bankrupt themselves, unable to keep the borrowed militia they needed to control Donneswort.'

He stopped speaking. There was a long silence.

'Nothing more than that's required, then,' said his father, harshly. 'We all thank you for bringing us word.'

'So.' It was his uncle speaking, and for once his open, friendly face was no longer so. In this dark moment he was the mirror image of that grim man, his twin brother. 'William of Ceta, the Board Director, and the dead net communicator. We've all three to hold to account for this.'

'The Director was tried and executed by Donneswort, itself,' said Brodsky. 'He got a lot of his own people killed, too.'

'That still leaves –' his uncle was beginning, when his father interrupted.

'It does no good to fix blame now,' his father said. 'It's our life, and this sort of thing happens.'

A deep shock went through him at the words; but he said nothing then, watching as his uncle fell silent and the rest of the family got to their feet. His father offered a hand to the officer, who took it. They stood, hands clasped together for a moment.

'Thank you,' said his father, again. 'Will you be able to stay for the funeral?'

'I wish I could,' Brodsky answered. 'I'm sorry. We've still got wounded coming back.'

'We understand –' his father had said. . . .

– The stable door creaked open now and the scene from the previous day evaporated, leaving him only with the perfect coldness that held him as if he had been frozen into a block of ice. Remotely, he was aware of his uncle coming toward him with long strides down the aisles between the horsestalls.

'Lad, what are you doing here?' his uncle said, in a concerned voice. 'Your mother's worried about you. Come back in the house.'

Hal did not answer. His uncle reached him, abruptly frowned and knelt so that their faces were on a level. His uncle's eyes peered into his own, and his uncle's face suddenly altered into a look of pain and deep shock.

'Oh, boy, boy,' his uncle whispered. He felt the big arms gently enclosing his own stiff body, holding him. 'You're too young for this, yet. It's too soon for you to go this way. Don't, lad, don't! Come back!'

But the words came remotely to his ears, as if they had been addressed to someone other than himself. Out of the coldness in him, he looked steadily into his uncle's eyes.

'No more,' he heard his own voice saying. 'Never any more. I'll stop it. I'll find them and stop them. All of them.'

'Boy . . .' His uncle held him close as if he would warm the smaller body with the living heat of his own. 'Come back. Come back . . .'

For a long moment it was as still as if his uncle was speaking to someone else. But then, in a moment no longer than that of a sigh, the iciness drained out of him. Half-unconscious in the reaction from what he had just been feeling, he fell forward against his uncle's shoulder, and as if in a dream he felt himself lifted up like a tired child in the powerful arms and carried out of the stable. . . .

He woke once more to the cell. For a brief moment, still anesthetized by unconsciousness, he had thought that he was well again; and then an uncontrollable coughing seized him and for a moment he found his breathing completely stopped. Panic, like the shadow of some descending vulture, closed its wings about him and for a long minute he struggled vainly for breath. Then he managed to rid himself of the phlegm he had coughed loose, and momentarily the illusion of being able to breathe more deeply came to him, then was lost in a new awareness of his fever, his violently aching head and his choked lungs.

His sickness had not lessened. But for all that, he felt a difference. A small increase of strength seemed to have been restored to him by the sleep; and he felt a clearheadedness in the midst of the pain and the struggle to breathe that he had not known before. Where he had thought of himself until now as thinking with a fever-fueled over-pressure of brilliance and insight such as he had never touched before, he now, like someone recovering from a massive dose of some stimulant drug, discovered a different and stronger order of perception, an awareness of subtle elements in all of what he had so far perceived and remembered – and the connections between them, that he had been blocked off from previously.

Moreover, with this awareness he found himself caught up for the first time in a tremendous sense of excitement – the excitement of a searcher who has at last stepped over the crest that has been blocking his view and for the first time sees his goal undeniably and clearly. He felt himself on the edge of something enormous, that thing he had been in pursuit of all his life – in fact, for longer than his life, an incalculable amount of time.

Sitting upright once more with his back against the cell wall, he probed the difference this new feeling implied. It was as if all the universe beyond his limited view of the cell and the corridor had suddenly taken a gigantic step toward him. He no longer guessed at the vague shapes of possible understandings just beyond his reach; he knew they were there and that his road to them could not be barred.

So thinking, he let himself go, following the inner compass needle of his will; and passed almost without effort into a condition he had never experienced before. Awake – he dreamed, and was conscious that he dreamed. He could see the cell around him; but at the same time, with as much or more clarity, he could see the landscape of his dream.

He was back in his vision of the rubbled plain and the Tower toward which he had been journeying so long and so painfully on foot; while the Tower itself had seemed to move back from him as each footstep brought him closer to it.

For the first time now, all this was changed. He had taken one great step that brought him close in to the Tower. Now he looked at it from relatively close at hand. Only a short distance separated them. But at the same time he saw that he had covered only the easy half of his journey to it. What remained ahead was less in distance, but so much greater in difficulty that he realized only his training and toughening by the long, arduous travel to this point made it possible for him to hope he could cross the final stretch of forbidding ground that lay between them.

Looking back over his shoulder, he discovered now that his journey to this moment had been subtly upslope, so that only now did he stand on a high point from which he could see what lay before him. Slowly the massive rubble before him began to reveal a form. He stood on the broken and crumbled stones of what had once been the outer ramparts of some great defensive structure, so enormous in extent that the historic Krak des Chevaliers of Old Earth could have been dropped into it and lost, among the very shadows of the massive building stones that had formed its inner structures. It was a castle old beyond memory, and time had all but destroyed it. Only the Tower, which had been its keep, its innermost defense, still stood and waited for him.

It would be among that maze of ruined inner walls and outer walls, of fallen baileys and rubble-choked courtyards, chambers and passageways that he must climb and crawl, to make his way at last to the entrance of the Tower. And it was a journey that would have been inconceivable to him, even now, if it had not been for the changes in mind and body that had come upon him over the years, the counterpart of the hardening absorbed in his dream of the long, solitary trek across the rubbled plain. Now older, more skilled and firm of mind, there had grown in him a relentlessness that he had not recognized until now and that not even what lay before him could halt. As someone might enter hell for some strong purpose, he stepped forward and down off the broken ramparts into the rocky and treacherous wilderness before him; and with that step forward his mind was at last committed and at peace.

Going, he left behind that part of him that had carried him through the long earlier parts of his journey and which he no longer needed. Grown and different, he returned to his self that was still in the cell, where he could now begin to see the work that lay before him and the path he must take to its doing.

CHAPTER THIRTY-SIX

. . . He woke.

It was not a sudden wakening. He came gradually out of deep slumber to the knowledge that he had been sleeping heavily for some little time. With consciousness the awareness of his fever, his weakness and his struggle to breathe came back to him . . . but now there was a difference.

He broke into another heavy fit of coughing, almost strangling, as he had strangled before when the matter in his lungs choked and closed completely the airway that brought him the oxygen of life. But this time the panic that had hovered on dark wings above him as he fought to clear his airways did not materialize. Some new fierceness within him, burning more hotly than the fever itself, more inextinguishably than the attack of whatever microscopic entity was working to destroy him, fought back and routed it.

Gasping, he leaned back limply against the wall. It was strange. Nothing was changed, nothing about his physical condition had improved, but internally he felt as if the universe had swung half a cosmic turn about him and settled in some new order that gave strength and the certainty of hope. Triumph lifted its head in him. Death had been pushed back now, and for some reason, he no longer gave it credit for the power to overcome him.

Why? Or rather, if this was so, why had he ever had a fear of it in the first place? He sat, propped up against the wall of the cell in sitting position, with the thin blanket pulled up over him; and the realization came slowly to him that the difference he now recognized was one of mind and will, rather than of body.

When Barbage had named him a hound of Armageddon, and left him to die, a small part of him had acknowledged a rightness in the Militiaman's attitude. Barbage was what he was. His faith, though twisted, was real. He listened to and was used by Bleys, but only because he believed Bleys spoke with the words of Barbage's own personal God; not, like Bleys' other followers, because he either feared or worshipped the man himself.

Unnaturally turned as it was, still the quality of that faith had had the power to touch and weaken Hal. Because of the strength of it, for the first time in his life he had acknowledged the possibility of his

336

own personal death; and in doing that he had, in effect, accepted the possibility of dying. But now, that acceptance was gone from him. In these last hours of fever-vision and dream-memories he had found and confirmed instead a reason why he could not afford death. There were things to be done first, the most urgent of these being the necessity to translate into clear, conscious terms the unconscious reasonings that had given him the necessity to survive. He cast his mind back.

At first, after Barbage, his journey into understanding had not been toward survival, but away from it. His first dream had been of himself, manacled on the mountainside, slowly being destroyed by the pitiless and invincible rain of Bleys' logic. The words Bleys had spoken had carried the argument Milton had put into the mouth of his Satan in *Paradise Lost* – 'I am greater than either the concept of Heaven or that of Hell.'

And it was true. Only, it was true in that sense not just of Bleys or the Others, but of any human being who was not afraid to face that greatness. It was in his avoidance of that university of possibility that all of Bleys' arguments had betrayed their weakness. The isolation Bleys had spoken of and Hal had remembered feeling on Coby was also true enough, but it was a self-made thing. Nor was it necessary to understand this fact logically in order to put that feeling aside. Anyone with sufficient faith could put it aside without understanding, as James Child-of-God had put aside any consideration of personal cost in the matter of his death on Harmony.

Bleys' arguments, like Bleys' chosen way, were personal and selfish – they closed their eyes to the proven rewards, equally personal but greater, of working not for the self but for humanity as it was personified in one's fellow humans. And it was humanity, the race itself, that was the key to all puzzles. No, not just the race, but the understanding of it as a single creature, concerned with its own survival and apportioning its parts among partisan groups that struggled with each other, so that strengths might be revealed which would point the best direction for future actions and growths by the race as a whole. A race-creature regarded its parts as expendable and unimportant, setting up a web of historic forces that built always forward, containing and controlling the great mass of humanity – that great mass that since time began had been driven like the deer by forces they did not understand, to the waiting, red-capped hunters. Sost and John Heikkila, Hilary and Godlun Amjak, the farmer who had sought reassurance for the future from Child, and had not gotten it – all driven and trapped by the warring factions that had now dwindled to two, the Others and those who opposed them.

And he was one of the opposed. Hal realized suddenly that it was from his understanding of that, that his new strength had just come.

He knew himself now. Once, at some graveside, he had made a commitment; and this present moment in which he found himself was simply an extension of that commitment. He had been barred until now, from knowing his own past, for a reason he could not see. But now he saw.

Until now, the time of this present moment, he who had made the commitment had not known how to get where he wanted to go. It had taken this present life he could remember, up until this moment in the cell, to uncover that way and make it plain. He had seen it now, in allegory in his dream of his path to the Tower – which, that still lost and hidden past of his now whispered, might yet be not dream, but reality. Reality of a different order only, than the here and now.

But it was in the here and now that he presently existed; and so what he must do immediately was translate that unconscious and allegorical understanding of a path into hard and logical understandings of the real forces that must be worked upon to produce the end toward which he had worked all this time. He let the effort of that translation take him and the overriding excitement in his new capacity for understanding flowed purposefully over all that he had mined from his unconscious. The image of the human race as a group entity, an amoeba-like race-animal with an identity and a purpose apart from the individual identities of its component human parts, now stood as a valid model of what he must deal with. The race, pictured as a single creature, a sort of primitive individual with its own instincts and desires – chief among these the instinct to survive as an entity, and a willingness to sacrifice its parts in continuous experimentation to satisfy that instinct – explained all that followed.

Such experimentation would have been a steady process from the time the race-animal became conscious of itself. The drives to develop, through its human components, first intelligence, and later, technology, would have been expressions of that instinct at work. So, too, would have been the twentieth century's probing off the planet of its birth into space, in unconscious search for more living room, the rise of the Splinter Cultures – each an experiment in the viability of human varieties in off-Earth environments – and now, finally, the emergence of the Others.

What made the Others a racial experiment, he understood now, was their need to take over and control all the rest of the race. In that need lay the way to an answer to why the racial animal should have birthed them in the first place. Bleys had answered it himself, in this cell. Whatever else was true about the Others, two things were undeniable. They were human, with all ordinary hungers and wants, including that of always wanting more than they had; and they were very much aware that they were too few to risk the rest of humanity realizing how their sheer lack of numbers made them vulnerable. It was a vulnerability that nothing less than total control of the rest of the race could ever remove; and such control could only be achieved by the establishment of a single unvarying uniform culture. Only such a culture in which all things were permanently fixed and unchanging could release them from the need to stand on guard against those they dominated and turn them loose at last to enjoy their advantage of a natural superiority over the majority of humanity.

And the only way for them to obtain both ends was first to achieve a situation of complete stasis, an end to the long, instinctive upward development of civilization. History must be brought to a halt. To do that they must remove or render harmless to them those other humans who could never accept an end to that development, those who would have no choice but to oppose the Others' building of that stasis.

The strengths of the Others would be first, in their charismatic skills, and secondly, in the fact that individually they were the equals in minds and bodies of the best that could be brought against them. Finally, those strengths would total in that they would be able to marshal most of the total populations of ten worlds to act on their orders. On the other side of their ledger lay their lack of ability to value the future. Other weaknesses. . . .

. . . But so far they seemed to have no other weaknesses. In a strict sense, one thing that could be labeled as a weakness was the smallness of their actual numbers; while the numbers of their opponents included for all practical purposes the total populations of the Dorsai, and the two Exotic worlds; plus, on Harmony and Association, the minority of true faith-holders such as Child-of-God and Rukh. There would also be added, in the long run, a large share of the population of Earth – but any more than that, any hope of getting all the diverse inhabitants of the Home World to join voluntarily together in any kind of effective response to the danger the Others posed, would be wishful thinking.

While the possible numbers of those opposed in the long run, putting Old Earth aside, would equal only a fraction of the fighting strength and resources the Others could raise from the ten planets they effectively controlled even now; if it came down to worlds fighting worlds as in the old days of Donal Graeme. Therefore, from the start, the Others' best tactic had been to work for an Armageddon, a final battle under the cover of which all those they could neither dominate nor persuade could be destroyed or neutralized.

It was easy now for his mind to see how they might aim at this; but hard to see any way by which they could be stopped or turned back. In any case, the war that was beginning even now would not be one fought so much with material weapons for physical territories, but one waged by opposing minds for the support of the driven deer, the mass of uncommitted individuals making up the human race; and, in such a war, the charismatic abilities of the Others ought to make their victory a foregone conclusion.

Hal sat, struggling for breath in the silent cell, his body burning like a live coal, his mind thrusting and dissecting like a surgeon's tool of ice.

What those who opposed the cross-breeds must have, as soon as possible, was first, a long-range plan that promised at least the hope of victory – and, second, a weapon to match the charismatic abilities of the Others. It would have to be a weapon that the Others either did not have, or could not use; any more than those opposing them could probably expect to use charismatic skills successfully against them.

That there must be at least the potential of a counter-weapon was sure, since the Others themselves were an experiment in survival by the racial-animal. It was necessary to look at the racial-animal itself for an understanding of the real forces at work, those historic forces of which the Others, like the Dorsai, the Exotics and the true faith-holders, and like himself, were merely manifestations.

It had been as if the racial-animal – thought Hal – on becoming aware in the twentieth century that space was physically reachable, had been both attracted and frightened by what lay outside the warm, reliable place that was the planet of its birth. History showed at that time two attitudes among people, one that shrank from space, speaking of 'things Men were not meant to know'; and another that was fascinated by it, dreaming of exploration and discoveries, just as dreams of the Indies had moved minds four hundred years earlier, while others foresaw ships sailing off the ocean-edge of the world. When at last it became possible to go into space, and particularly to go beyond the home solar system, both the fears and dreams had spawned thousands of smaller groups, looking for a place to build a society in the pattern of their own desires.

What the racial-animal had wanted, Hal thought now, was proven survivor types, both in the way of individuals and societies; and so it had given free rein to the experimentation of its parts. Out of the diversity of that diaspora had emerged the most successful survivors of the so-called Splinter Cultures; the three greatest, which had been the Dorsai, the Friendlies and the Exotics. These three had flowered for two hundred years during which they performed functions that made the off-Earth, interplanetary society of their time stable, by making war, trade and conflicts safely controllable within the fabric of that society.

Then, with the necessary development of the pattern of that society as its diverse elements were brought under one system of control by Donal Graeme, the need for the Splinter Cultures' special elements dwindled and the cultures themselves had begun to die.

340

Meanwhile, the racial animal, thriftily cross-breeding the new human strains that these Splinter Cultures had developed, so that what had been gained should not be lost, had begun at last to produce the unopposable dominants for which part of its nature had always yearned. So had been rounded out the growth that had gone from development of intelligence – to technology – to the over-population of Earth – to space – to the Splinter Cultures who were experiments with survival types of humans off-Earth – to the recombination of these Splinter types, into the new dominants who called themselves the Others.

Only, these dominants now looked to be unremovable as the new leaders of the race; and the millennia-proven growth of historical progress that had always come from the new human talent of each generation deposing the old from authority was in danger of being ended for all time – unless the Others could be shown, after all, to have a weakness.

So much, then, thought Hal, for the position of the Others. Their opponents' position was simply that, since the coming of the Others to power meant an end to all human change and growth, it was a situation not to be endured. To that part of the racial animal the Others' opponents represented, to cease growing meant a death to all hopes for the future; and to avert that universal death, personal death was a small price to pay.

Something clicked in Hal's mind.

Of course. The reason Earth alone had shown such a resistance to the influence of the Others would be that Earth was still the original gene pool of the race; and its people were full-spectrum human – unspecialized in any of the myriad ways that had resulted from the racial animal's experimentation with the breeding and adaptation of its individual parts for their life on other worlds. Within all of those who were native Earth-born, as opposed to just some of those on the younger worlds, lived not merely a portion, but all of the possibilities of the human spirit, good and bad; and one of those possibilities was a portion with the faith of the Friendlies, the independence of the Dorsai and the vision of the Exotics that could not endure an end to change and growth.

Sudden hope kindled in Hal. Earth, then, was at least part of a weapon the Others could not use.

At least part . . . Hal's leaping mind fastened on a new point. What the Earth's population of native-born, full-spectrum individuals represented to the Others, as to the race as a whole, was genetic insurance, in case their dominance should result in patterns of human specialization that would lack the ability to survive. Some of the variforms of plants and animals had already shown themselves unable to flourish on certain of the Younger Worlds. No one could be sure what several hundred generations from now would produce in human adaptations to the newer planets. Earth was the one world the Others dared not decimate; and also the one they absolutely must control, in order to ensure the survival of their interstellar kingdom once they had established it.

Others, then, equalled stasis. Others-opponents should therefore equal . . . evolution?

Evolution . . . the word rang, like a massive gong hammered once, in Hal's mind. Evolution had been the great dream of the Exotics – their great, unfulfilled dream, that mankind was indeed in process of evolving; and that the Exotic students of mankind would eventually identify the direction of the evolution, foster it, and eventually produce an improved form of human.

But the Exotics were dying now, their dream unfulfilled, if their purpose was still in existence, as was that of the Dorsai and the Friendlies. But meanwhile their place was being usurped, along with that of everyone else, by the Others. The Exotics, like the rest of the Others' opponents, had no solution of their own to the situation. If there had been a way within the reach of the Exotics that would stop the Others, they would have found and used it by now.

But, even though the Exotics were dying off, evolution as a concept still existed – for the moment at least. It was not just the private property of the Exotics and never had been, but a property of mankind in general. In short, all these years that the Exotics had sought it, perhaps evolution and the means for it had been in operation under their noses, unrecognized. Perhaps mankind could have been building toward the future of the race without knowing it, just as for centuries humanity had built toward a home on other worlds without knowing it –

Hal chilled. So profound was the shock of discovery, that even with the candle of his life guttering within him, for a moment he forgot the cell around him, his fever, even his struggle to breathe.

The Final Encyclopedia.

The Encyclopedia was the one weapon the Others did not have, and could not use, even if they had it.

Because it had been designed as a tool for learning that which was not known; and, by definition of the stasis toward which the Others worked, there would be a positive danger for them in a tool that promised the addition of new knowledge, in a culture where they wanted no increase and neither growth nor change.

And that, of course, explained the division and the upcoming conflict.

Because the racial animal was purely concerned with survival, at root it would have no partiality for either side. It was allowing its parts to fight each other only to find out which would win. Therefore, both sides must have been allowed by it to develop unconsciously means and weapons toward the inevitable moment of conflict – not just the side that had spawned the Others. The Final Encyclopedia could be the weapon that balanced the scale for the adherents of evolution against the Others' weapon of charisma.

Hal wiped his forehead with the back of an unsteady hand and it came away damp. With a shock he realized that, in this last burst of mental struggle with the problem obsessing him, something had changed in his physical condition. Strangely, now the chill he had felt at the first shock of discovery was still with him. His fever no longer seemed to burn so fiercely inside him; and even his breathing appeared easier. He coughed; and it was not the dry, struggling cough that it had been before. This cough brought up phlegm more easily and seemed to clear a little extra breathing space in his over-stuffed lungs. His head had almost stopped aching. He put a hand to his forehead, again, wonderingly, and again brought away a palm wet with sweat.

His fever had broken. But so great was the turmoil of discovery in him that he could not yet rejoice.

Within his mind, now, he could feel massive shapes and patterns of understanding beginning to take form, like the underwater ghosts of great icebergs in a murky, polar sea, as known facts fell together with conclusions that suddenly were obvious – all shaping so rapidly that consciously he was not able to read the full meaning of what he was just now beginning to understand. It was as if one block, pulled from a towering and meaningless jumble of other such blocks, had caused an earthquake-like tumbling and rearrangement through the entire pile; so that when the motion at last ceased, as in his last dream of the Tower, the jumble stood as a recognizable structure – complete to the smallest detail; while he stood, with the one removed block still in his hand, and marvelled. Even the charisma must have come from some element buried in the full spectrum of human capabilities. Somewhere perhaps they who would fight the Others could find it and use it equally.

Now that he had found this knowledge – now that he held, safe within him, the understanding that the Final Encyclopedia was indeed the tool he had blindly reached for, the weapon unconsciously prepared over time to be used against the Others – he could hardly believe it. He sat with it in mind, dazed by the fact of his understanding, as Arthur Pendragon who was to be king might have felt dazed at finding the great sword come smoothly from the stone into his hand, deaf to the cheers of the watching multitude in his realization at what he had done.

Now that Hal understood, he realized that this understanding was more precious than anything in the ownership of the race. Now that he had it, he must live to escape from here and get himself and his knowledge to safety.

As this other had been solvable, so that, too, must be.

CHAPTER THIRTY-SEVEN

Sitting exactly as he was, a great sense of accomplishment and relief came over him, like a runner who has raced some incredible distance and won. Still thinking of what he must do, not only to escape with his present understanding but afterward, he fell into a doze, as his worn-out body took advantage of the fact that the fever had now broken and his breathing was slightly easier; and the doze, still without a change of position, became deep and exhausted sleep.

He woke from an apparently dreamless sleep to find that without waking he had slid down into a position flat on his back on the bed and pulled the thin blanket up over him. He struggled up again into a sitting position. The effort brought on a coughing spasm which produced more yellow-green phlegm, but the coughing did not hurt so much; and he found, after the first breathlessness from the effort was over, that he seemed to be more successful at getting air into his lungs now that he had been for some hours; although he was still a long way from normal. About him, the silent cell still showed no change.

His first and most desperate need was to empty his bladder. He threw back the blanket and discovered he had barely strength to get to his feet facing the stool. Finished, he fell back on the bed and lay for a moment, while he collected enough energy to turn, crawl across and raise himself on his knees beside the washstand on the bed's other side. He drank, this time, at last, deeply from its tap, stopping to catch his breath and then drinking again, reveling in again being able to swallow more than a few mouthfuls. Finally, with moisture at least partially restored in him, he sat back against the wall at the head of the bed and put himself to the labor and pain of coming fully awake.

Asleep, he had for a short while forgotten the struggle to breathe; and now for a little while he had attention only for that, and this general weakness and discomfort. But gradually, as he woke more fully, his mind began to gain something of its normal ascendancy over his body; and all that he had thought his way through to, in the long hours just past, came back. The urgency in him reawoke. Even before he remembered fully why it was so, he remembered that he must get out of here.

344

Under the stimulant of that necessity, he began to come back to a normal state of alertness; and his struggle to breathe eased even further, until it was almost possible to ignore it. He coughed and raised a certain amount of phlegm, but the effort ate brutally into his slim supply of strength. He gave up trying to clear his lungs and sat back once more against the wall of his cell. Remembering his chronometer, he looked at it. It showed 10:32 a.m.

His first concern now that he was fully awake was to check the structure of understanding he had built before sleep kidnapped him. But it was still all there, only waiting for deeper examination to give up its details. He was free to devote his attention to getting out of the hands of those who held him.

It was obvious that the situation was one in which it was not practical for him to escape in any physical, literal sense. His only real chance was to persuade his jailers to take him out of the cell. As a last resort, if they would not, he could ask to speak to Bleys; and tell the tall man that he had agreed to think over the possibility that he might be one of the Others.

But it was absolutely a last resort, not because it might not get him out of the cell, or because of any physical danger inherent in it, but because face-to-face contact with Bleys at any time was perilous. Bleys was not only an Other, but – unless matters had changed among his kind – second-in-command of their organization. He was not the kind of individual whom someone possibly ten years younger could confidently expect to delude.

Leaning back against the wall, Hal shut his eyes and let his mind focus down on the question of escape, until everything else was shut out but the edge of his physical misery, niggling on the horizon of his consciousness, and the massive shape of the structure he had conceived, standing mountainous in the background of his thoughts and throwing its shadow over everything.

All together, the physical discomfort, the situation and his new understanding, gave birth to a plan. He opened his eyes after a time, got up from the bed and took two unsteady steps into the center of the room. For a long moment he merely stood there, feeling upon him in his imagination the attentive eyes of the invisible watcher keeping his cell under surveillance.

Then he opened his mouth and screamed – screamed as impressively as he could with the hoarse throat and miserly breath that were all he had to scream with – and collapsed on the floor of his cell.

He had let himself fall as gravity took him; but he had also relaxed in falling, so that the impact upon the bare concrete floor was not as painful as it might have been. Once down, he lay absolutely motionless, and set about doing a number of things to himself internally that either Walter or Malachi had at different times taught him to do.

As individual exercises, most of these were not difficult; and they

345

tended to reinforce each other in the effect he needed. Slowing his respiration was in any case part of the techniques for slowing his heart rate and lowering his blood pressure. These latter two, in turn, helped him achieve the more difficult task of decreasing his body temperature. Taken all together, they decreased his oxygen need, thereby easing the task of breathing with his secretion-choked lungs; and gave him the plausible appearance of having passed into a deep unconsciousness. At the same time the state they helped him achieve made it possible for him to endure without moving the long wait that he expected – and was not disappointed in having – before those watching him finally became convinced enough to send a guard to his cell to see if something had indeed happened to him.

In the end, he lay where he had fallen for over three hours. A small part of his mind kept automatic track of the passage of that time, but the greater part had withdrawn into a state of near-trance; so that he was very close to being honestly in the condition in which he was pretending to be. When his guards finally did reach the point of checking on him, he was only peripherally aware of what was happening. He lay, hearing as if from another room, as the first guard to come into the cell and examine him relayed his conclusions over the surveillance microphones; and after some consultation at the other end, a decision was made to get him to a hospital.

There had been a certain delay, the small, barely interested, watchdog part of his mind noted, resulting from the fact that Barbage was not on duty and his inferiors fretted, caught between their fear of the lean captain's displeasure if they did anything unjustified for the prisoner and their awe and fear of Bleys' reaction if anything happened to Hal. In the end, as Hal had gambled it would – even if Barbage himself had been present – their respect for Bleys' orders left him no choice but to get Hal to someone medically knowledgeable as soon as possible.

It seemed that there had also been another reason for their hesitation, having to do with conditions outside the building; but what this was, Hal could not quite make out. In any case, he eventually found himself being lifted onto a stretcher and carried out of the cell and along corridors to a motorized cart. This took him – now buried under a pile of blankets – for some distance until they passed finally through a tall pair of doors into cold, damp air. He was lifted off the motorized cart onto another stretcher, which was then carried into some sort of vehicle and suspended there, in a rack against one of the vehicle's sides.

A door slammed, metallically. There was a momentary pause, then blowers came to life and the vehicle took off.

Heavily depressed as his body now was, it resisted his efforts to wake it. The resistance was not active but inert, of the same sort that makes an unconscious man harder to lift than a conscious one. The

346

near-trance in which he had put himself had shut out all the pains and struggles of the last few days; and his present comfort drew him the way a drug draws its addict.

It was only by remembering the structure of understanding that he had finally put together in his mind, and its importance, that he was able to rouse himself to push back the torpor he had created. But once he managed to lift the effect slightly, his work became easier. He felt a touch of relief, momentarily. He did not want to bring his body all the way back to normality too soon, in case he should find himself in competent medical hands before he had a chance to take advantage of being out of his prison. There was too much danger of being turned around and sent directly back to his cell.

On the other hand, he needed to be alert enough to take advantage of an opportunity to escape if one should come up. He went back to rousing himself with his original urgency, therefore, toward the point where he believed he would be able to get to his feet and move if he had to; but he could feel that his pulse remained in the forties and his systolic blood pressure was probably still only in the nineties; and his original concern returned. His body was lagging in its response to his efforts to wake it.

With all this, however, he was still becoming once more able to pay attention to what was going on around him, although his emotional reactions to what he saw and heard remained sluggish. He saw that he was alone in the back of what was obviously a military ambulance capable of transporting at least a dozen stretchers hung three-deep along its two sidewalls. A couple of enlisted Militiamen were occupying the bucket seats before the controls up front in the open cab area.

A band of windows ran along each side of the vehicle in the stretcher area; and beside him as he lay on a top-level stretcher the upper edge of the window glass was just below the point of his shoulder. He lay on his back. By turning his head only a little, he could get a good view of the streets along which they were passing. Although it would be early afternoon by this time, no one was to be seen in the streets; and the small shop fronts he passed were closed tight, their display windows opaqued.

It was a dull, wet afternoon. It was not raining now; but the street surface, walkways and building fronts glistened with moisture. He caught only an occasional glimpse of a corner of the sky between far-off building tops when the ambulance passed through the inter-section of a cross-street; but it seemed uniformly heavy and gray with a thick cloud cover. After a little while, he did indeed see one pedestrian who turned his head sharply at the approach of the ambulance and ducked up an alley between two shops.

There was tension in the cab of the vehicle. Now that his senses, at least, were working normally, his woodswise nose could catch in the still, enclosed air of the ambulance, the faint harsh stink of men perspiring under emotional stress. They were also directing the vehicle oddly, travelling only a few blocks in a straight line, pausing at occasional intersections for no visible reason, then turning abruptly to go over several blocks to the right or left before returning to their original direction of travel, as furtive in their movements as the first foot traveller he had seen.

As they went on, their progress slowed, almost as if the man controlling the vehicle had lost his way. Now, they began to see more pedestrians, all in a hurry, nearly all going in the same general direction the ambulance was following. At last, Hal's dead-seeming body was beginning to respond, although it still felt as though it weighed several times its normal amount. He faced the fact that, far from being in danger of recovering too soon, he had underestimated his exhaustion and the effort it would need to lift himself from the attractive state of near-unconsciousness. Elementally, his body was desperate for the rest it felt it needed to survive; and it was resisting being forced back to a higher level of energy-expenditure.

In his concern to get himself back to a state in which, if necessary, he could stand and walk, Hal all but forgot the vehicle around him and the streets through which it was passing. He was barely aware that they were proceeding more and more cautiously; and that more and more often the ambulance halted briefly. Slowly, his stubborn body was returning to life; and at last he was beginning to have confidence that he could raise and move it for a short distance, at least. He lay under the blankets, clenching and unclenching his hands, flexing his arms and legs, shrugging his shoulders and making every movement that was possible without unduly risking the danger of attracting the attention of the two men up front.

He was all but completely occupied with these exercises when the ambulance slowed suddenly enough to slide him forward on his stretcher, then abruptly revved up its blowers for a second before throttling all the way back to idle. The vehicle halted.

Hal stopped exercising and looked out through the window glass beside him.

The ambulance was surrounded by people, a still-gathering crowd not yet so tightly packed that those in it could not move without other bodies moving out of their way. Clearly, it had just become impossible for the vehicle to continue forward; and glancing back the way they had come, Hal saw more people filling in behind them. It was already impossible to turn around and go back.

They were in a large square that was rapidly becoming jammed with people, having apparently just emerged from one of the streets feeding the square. The faces of those around the truck, glancing in at the pair of Militiamen, were not friendly. Hal could now smell more strongly the stink of emotion from the two. He pulled his head back to look forward as far as was possible. Less than thirty meters in front of them, with a solid stand of human bodies in the way, was the entrance to another street that would have led them beyond the square. Clearly, the driver had gambled that he could get across to it before the crowd barred his path completely – and the driver had lost.

The ambulance was trapped like a mastodon in a tarpit. It would remain that way, unless the driver chose simply to bulldoze a way through the people in their path; and that sort of action would clearly be a suicidal thing to try, judging from the scowling faces glancing at the Militia uniforms. With an explosive inhalation somewhere between a sigh and a grunt, the driver cut the blowers entirely and let the vehicle settle to the pavement. The Militiaman beside him was muttering into the vehicle's phone unit.

'Stay put!' crackled an answering voice from the interior speaker unit of the vehicle. 'Don't do anything. Don't attract any attention. Just sit it out and act like you're enjoying it.'

Silence fell inside the cab. The two Militiamen sat, pretending to be engaged in conversation and refusing to meet the dark stares of those who glanced in at them. Looking again out the window glass beside him, Hal saw that their attempted route had been across one corner of the square. They were grounded broadside onto the open space of its middle; and without having to move, he had an excellent view of the central area where the crowd was thickest.

It had pressed in tightly there about a pedestal supporting a stark brownish cross of granite, that towered at least three stories into the air. From where Hal lay on the stretcher, looking out through the moisture-streaked side window of the ambulance, the upper part of the cross seemed to loom impossibly high over them all, giving the illusion of floating against the dark, swag-bellied rainclouds overhead. The figure of a man in a business suit was beginning to climb down from the pedestal, having just finished a speech that Hal had been minimally conscious of hearing from repeaters worn or carried by those in the crowd close around the ambulance.

Applause began, and sounded for a few moments as the business-suited man climbed off the pedestal. After a second another man, this one wearing the familiar bush clothes Hal had seen around him through the past weeks, began to climb up. The ascending man reached the top of the pedestal, took a grip on the upright shaft of the cross to steady himself on the narrow footing, and began to speak. His voice came clearly to Hal's ears; plainly he was wearing a broadcaster which the repeaters were picking up, but from this distance Hal could not see it anywhere visible on his clothing or body. All around the ambulance, the tiny, black repeaters pinned openly to lapels or defiantly held up overhead threw his words out over the listening crowd. They penetrated the walls of the trapped vehicle.

'Brothers and sisters in God –'

Hal's attention woke to a new alertness. The voice he was hearing was the voice of Jason Rowe; and now that he had identified Jason, he recognized the square-shouldered, spare figure standing as he had been used to see it stand.

'– In a moment the one who will speak to you will be Captain Rukh Tamani, who planned the complete blockage of the Core Tap shaft accomplished by her Command, yesterday – who not only planned it; but gathered, with her Command, the materials out of which the necessary explosive was assembled; and trekked those materials halfway across the continent under threat of attack by Militia at all times, and under actual pursuit and attack much of the time. Brothers and sisters in the Lord, we have as of yesterday testified to the fact that our Faith in God remains whole and able to strike at those very points where the Belial-spawn consider themselves strongest. As it was yesterday, so shall it continue to be until the Others and their dogs no longer harry our worlds and our people. Brothers, and sisters, here is Rukh Tamani now, Captain of the Command that sabotaged the Core Tap and shut down the spaceship outfitting station – and *my* Captain, as well!'

A roar built up from the crowd and continued as Jason descended from the pedestal. Then there was a moment in which the cross stood still and alone in the midst of them and the roar slowly died away. Then it began again as a slim figure in dark bush clothes began to climb into view.

It was Rukh – it could be no one else. She climbed up on the pedestal and paused, holding one arm around the vertical shaft of the towering granite cross. It lifted high above her, its polished surface gleaming dully with moisture.

For a moment she stood there, looking like a black wand in the gray light. Gradually, the sounds from the square died away like the sound of surf when a heavy curtain is drawn across an open window. The crowd was silent.

She spoke, and the repeaters carried by people in the square picked up her words and threw them audibly over the heads of everyone there.

'*Awake, drunkards, and weep!*'

It was, Hall recognized, a quotation from the Old Testament of the Bible, from the first chapter of Joel. Her clear voice reached even through the walls of the ambulance to Hal's ears, like a sharp needle prodding him in his efforts to regain full conscious control of his body.

'*All you who drink wine, lament,*' she went on:

'*– For that new wine has been dashed from your lips.*

'*For a nation has invaded my country,
mighty and innumerable;*

its teeth are the teeth of lions,
it has the fangs of a lioness.
It has laid waste my vines
and torn my fig trees to pieces;
it has stripped them clean and cut them down,
their branches have turned white.

'Mourn like a virgin wearing sackcloth
for her young man betrothed to her.
Oblation and libation have vanished
from the house of Yahweh,
the priests, the ministers of Yahweh,
are in mourning.
Wasted lie the fields,
the fallow is in mourning.
For the corn has been laid waste,
the wine fails,
the fresh oil dries up.'

She stopped; and after the clear cadence of her voice, the silence seemed to ring in their ears. She spoke again, slowly.

'When did we come to fear death?' She turned her head, looking at all those about her. 'For you, I see, fear death.'

The silence of the crowd continued. It was as if they had no power to make a sound, almost no power to breathe, until she should finish with them. Hal struggled against the reluctance of his body to return to life.

'Today –' her voice reached him again through the glass window in the ambulance – 'you crowd the streets. Today the Militia does not come out to disperse you. Right now you are willing, in your hundreds, to take up weapons and march against the Belial-spawn and Antichrist.'

She paused, watching them all.

'But tomorrow –' her voice continued – 'you will think better of it. You will not say you will not march; but you will find a thousand reasons to question the time and manner of marching, and so never leave Ahruma at all.

'When did you come to fear death? There is no death to fear. Our forefathers knew this, when they came from Earth. Why do you fail to know it now?'

The crowd neither moved nor made a sound.

'They knew, as we should know,' her voice went on, 'that it does not matter if our bodies die, as long as the People of God continue. For then all are saved, and will live forever.'

Hal got his legs moving, and stirred them quietly on his stretcher, to get the blood moving in them. They made a small rustling sound between the stretcher surface and the covering blankets. But the two

351

Militiamen in the bucket seats up front in the ambulance paid no attention. They were as caught up in Rukh's speaking as the crowd outside.

'There is a man,' went on Rukh; and the repeaters in the crowd flung her words against the concrete fronts of the buildings facing the square on all four sides, 'who has been in this city before today and will be here again, who is called by some the Great Teacher.'

She paused.

'He is a teacher of lies – Antichrist incarnate. But he envies us our immortality – yours and mine, sisters and brothers – for he is only mortal and knows he will die. He can be killed.

'For God alone is independently immortal. He would exist, even if Mankind did not; and because we are part of God, you and I, we are immortal also. But Antichrist, who comes among us now for our last great testing, has no hope of long life except in Mankind. Only if we accept him, and his like, can they hope to live.

'But because Mankind is of God, though the Enemy may slay our bodies he cannot touch our souls unless we give them freely to him. If we do, we are lost indeed.

'But if we do not; then, though we may seem to suffer death, we will live eternally – not only in the Lord but in those who come after us, who will because of us continue to know our God.

'For only if we betray him by giving up the power to choose Him for ourselves, can we lose immortality. If we will not be dogs of Antichrist, we shall be part of our children's children's children – who, because of our faith and our labors, will still belong to our God, our Faith and, therefore, to us, forever. If the race continues free, none of us shall ever die.'

She paused; and for the first time, there was a sighing, no more noticeable than a vagrant wisp of breeze, that travelled across the surface of the crowd and died against the buildings surrounding.

'There are those –' when she went on, her voice had changed slightly – 'who say, 'But what if we should all be killed by those who follow Antichrist?' And the answer to that is, 'they cannot.' For there would then be not enough to serve the Belial-spawn as they wish to be served. But even if it was possible for our enemies to kill all who are steadfast in the Faith, that killing would be useless to them. For even in their slaves the seeds of Faith would still lie dormant, awaiting only the proper hour and the voice of God, to flower once more.'

She paused and once more took a slow survey of the square.

'So, pick up your courage,' she said. 'These who oppose us can only destroy bodies, not souls. Come, join me in putting off our fear of death; which, is after all, only like a child's fear of the dark, and testify for the Lord, praising Him and thanking Him that it is to us, to our generation, that this great and glorious moment has been given. For there is no reward like the reward of those who fight for Him; knowing that they cannot lose because He cannot be defeated.'

She stopped.

'Now,' she said. 'Testify with me, my sisters and brothers in the Lord. Let us sing together that God may hear us.'

She let go of the upright of the cross and stood there balanced upon the narrow upper edge of the pedestal top. Standing so, she began, herself, to sing. Her voice came clearly and joyfully from the repeaters, making the dark hymm Hal had heard led by Child in the house of Amjak into a paean of triumph.

> 'Soldier, ask not, now or ever,
> Where to war your banners go.
> Anarch's legions all surround us.
> Strike! and do not count the blow . . .'

The crowd was singing with one voice. Up in the front of the vehicle, the two Militiamen were silent, but they sat crouched in their seats as if they, too, had been captured by the music. Hal, who had also been caught up in the power and sweep of Rukh's speech, woke suddenly to the fact that he was letting his chance to escape slip through his fingers.

As quietly as he could, he pushed the blankets off him to the window side of the stretcher, swung his legs out over empty air and let himself slip quietly off the stretcher surface until he was standing on his feet.

Up front, the two Militiamen stared out through the side window next to the driver's left elbow, blind and deaf to anything taking place behind them.

Hal swayed a little on his feet. His balance was unsure, and the effort of keeping himself erect was a large one; but he felt a tremendous surge of happiness at being able to stand by himself. He moved as softly as he could to the door in the back end of the ambulance, through which he had been carried in. One step. Two. Three . . . he reached the door.

He put his hand on the rounded, cold, metal bar of its latch lever, ready to push it down; and glanced back over his shoulder at the front of the vehicle. The two Militiamen still sat in profile to him, unnoticing.

He turned to the door again, and pushed down on the lever. It resisted him as if it had been set in concrete. For a moment he thought his weakness was to blame and he threw all his weight upon it to force it down. But it held.

Then his mind cleared. He looked more closely at the latch and saw that it was locked by a horizontal sliding bar that needed to be drawn before the lever could swing down. He took the knob of the bar gingerly in his fingers and pulled. It held as it stuck. He pulled harder. It held for a second more; and then with a rasp and a clang that seemed to echo like a beaten alarm through the ambulance, it sprang back. He seized the lever.

'Stop!' said a tight-throated voice from the front of the ambulance. 'You push that handle down and I'll shoot!'

Still holding the lever, he looked again over his shoulder. The faces of both Militiamen were watching him above the upper edges of their bucket-seat backs; and, down between the seats, its slim, wire-coiled barrel projecting through, was one of the stubby hideout-models of a void pistol. It was aimed squarely at him, held low by the driver so that his body and that of the man beside him would shield it from the eyes of any of the crowd who might happen to look in.

'This doesn't make any noise,' said the driver. 'Go back to your stretcher and get back up on it.'

Hal stared at them and the shadow of the structure in his mind seemed to fall between him and the two of them.

'No,' he said. 'If I fall out of here dead, you two won't live five minutes.'

He pushed the lever down, leaning against the door. The latch released. The door swung half-open under his weight before it was stopped by the body of someone standing in the way; and Hal fell into the opening, which was too narrow for his body to pass but let him get his head outside.

'Help, brothers!' he croaked. 'Help! The Militia've got me.'

He had been braced instinctively for the silent blow of the charge from the void pistol against his back. But nothing happened. He was aware of startled faces turning toward him; then suddenly the door gave fully and he fell through the opening.

He would have tumbled to the pavement, if hands had not caught him and held him upright.

'Help . . .' he said again, weakly, feeling the last of the small spurt of strength he had been able to summon up draining from him in the sudden relief of still being alive. 'They've had me in their cells. . . .'

A fainting spell misted his vision for a few seconds. When it cleared, he became distantly aware of being half-pulled, half-lifted, forward for a little space; then lifted again by many hands to the head-height of the crowd. Dimly, he realized he was being passed along by an unending succession of hands above the heads of the multitude – and, at the same moment, became crazily aware that here and there about the square there were the figures of other casualties of the tight-packed gathering – men, women, and even some children, being passed toward the outskirts of the crowd by the same means.

In his present exhausted, slightly confused state, it was a curious sensation, rather like floating across strangely uneven ground, while receiving innumerable pats on the back; and, strangely, it brought back the dream he had had of startling out on foot, alone, across a plain to a Tower seen far off in its distance. He was conscious mainly of a naked feeling from the cold, wet air cooling him through the thin shirt and trousers that were all his captors had left him to wear in his cell. After a while the number of hands beneath him became less; and, a few moments later, he was let down into an upright position with his feet on the pavemtn of one of the streets leading into the square.

'Hang on,' said a man's voice in his ear.

There were two of them, one on either side of him. He had an arm over the shoulders of each, and they each had an arm about his waist. They half-carried, half-walked him forward through a lesser thickness of people for a little distance, and then abruptly brought him back into warmth, for which he was grateful.

They had helped him up a ramp into the body of a large truck that seemed to have been fitted up as a first aid station.

'Put him there,' said a woman with a stethoscope hanging from her neck, who was working over someone on a cot. Her elbow indicated an empty cot behind her.

Gently, the two men carrying Hal put him down on the cot.

'See if anyone outside knows him,' said the woman briefly.' And shut the door as you go out.'

The two went. Hal lay basking in the warmth and the growing joy of being free. After a while, the medician with the stethoscope came over to him.

'How do you feel?' she asked, putting her fingers on his wrist at the pulse-point.

'Just weak,' said Hal. 'I wasn't in the crowd. I just got away from a Militia ambulance. They were taking me to the hospital.'

'Why?' said the woman, reaching for a thermometer.

'I had a bad cold. A chest cold, that went into bronchitis, or something like that.'

'Are you asthmatic?'

'No.' Hal coughed thickly, looked around for something to spit into, and found a white tray held under his nose. He spat; and the sensor-end of the thermometer was tucked beneath his tongue for a moment, then was withdrawn.

'No fever now,' said the woman. 'But you're still wheezing. You're not moving air well.'

'Yes,' said Hal. 'The last few days. I had a pretty high fever, I think, but it broke early this morning.'

'Roll up your sleeve,' she said, producing a pressure gun and thumbing an ampoule into it. His fingers fumbled clumsily with the fastening of his sleeve cuff, and she laid the gun aside to pull loose the cuff closure and push the sleeve up. He watched the nose of the pressure gun pressed against his upper arm, felt the coolness of a drug being discharged into the muscle, and himself rolled his sleeve down and fastened it once more.

'Drink this,' said the woman, now holding a disposable cup to his lips. 'Drink it all.'

He swallowed something that tasted like weak lemonade. Less than a minute later a blissful miracle took place, as his lungs opened up, and shortly thereafter he became busy coughing up large amounts of the secretions that had clogged his constricted air passages.

The door to the truck by which he had been brought in opened and closed again.

'– Of course I know him,' a voice was saying as it approached him. 'He's Howard Immanuelson, one of the Warriors in Rukh's Command.'

Hal looked and saw the round, determined face of one of Gustav Mohler's grandsons from the Mohler-Beni farm, coming toward him with a man behind him who might have been one of those who had carried Hal in earlier.

'Are you all right, sir?' the grandson asked. Hal had never known his name. 'Is there someplace I can take you to? I drove in earlier this week in one of our trucks, and I can bring it around in a moment. You needn't worry, sir. We're all faithful people of God, here!'

A blush stained his skin on the last words. Hal appreciated for the first time that the urging of the truck driver with the accordion that Hal be put off from the Command, that evening at the Mohler-Beni farm, might have been a source of embarrassment to their host and his family.

'I don't doubt it,' he said.

'He can't go like that,' said the medician sharply, from another stretcher at which she was working, 'unless you want him back down with pneumonia, again. He needs some outdoor clothing. Somebody out there ought to be able to spare a jacket or a coat for a Warrior of God.'

The man who had come in with the grandson ducked back out of the truck.

'Don't worry, sir,' said Mohler's grandson, 'there's lots of people who'll be glad to give you a coat. Maybe I'd better go get the truck and bring it here so you don't have so far to walk to it.'

He went out, leaving Hal to wonder if someone out there would actually be willing to give away an outer garment and expose himself or herself to the temperature Hal had just felt, at the request of someone else who was probably a stranger.

However, the man came back before Mohler's grandson had a chance to return; and his arms were filled with half a dozen coats and jackets. Left to himself, Hal would have taken any one and been grateful for it; but the medician took charge and picked out a jacket with a fleece lining that wrapped him with almost living warmth.

'Thank whoever gave it, for me,' said Hal, to the man who had brought it.

'Sir, he's already thanked,' said the man, 'and proud that a member of Rukh's Command would wear a garment of his.'

He left with the rejected coats. A moment later, Mohler's grandson came in and helped Hal out to a light truck that was now standing in the street beside the first aid truck, surrounded by a considerable crowd that broke into applause as Hal came out, his elbow steadied by the young man.

Hal waved and smiled at the crowd, let himself be helped into the other truck, and sat back exhaustedly in his seat as the grandson lifted the vehicle on its blowers and the crowd made a lane before it to let it move off.

'Where to, sir?' asked the grandson.

'To – I'm sorry, I don't know your name,' said Hal.

'Mercy Mohler,' said the other, solemnly.

'Well, thank you, Mercy,' said Hal. 'I appreciate your identifying me; and believe me when I say I appreciate this ride.'

'It's nothing,' said Mercy, and blushed again. 'Where to?'

Hal had put his memory to work to turn up the address he had written on the mailing envelope containing his papers. Nothing that he wanted to remember was ever forgotten; but sometimes it required a certain amount of mental searching to turn it up. At the last minute, he changed slightly what his memory had given him. There was no need to advertise the fact he was going to the Exotic Consulate.

'Forty-three French Galley Place,' he said. 'Do you know where that is? Because all I have is the address.'

'I'll ask,' said Mercy.

He stopped the truck, lowered the window at his shoulder and put his head out to speak to those in the crowd immediately outside. After a second, he brought his head back in, put up the window and restarted the truck.

'French Galley's right off John Knox Avenue, below the First Church,' he said. 'I know where that is. We'll be there in ten minutes.'

But it took closer to twenty minutes than ten, before French Galley Place was found. It turned out to be a circle of very large, comfortable three-storey houses; and seeing the flags displayed on various of the doorsteps, Hal realized that the Place itself was evidently a favorite location in Ahruma for off-world Consulates. So much for hiding the fact that he had been heading for a diplomatic destination. A somewhat puzzled Mercy dropped him off before a relatively smaller, brown establishment between what were obviously the Venus and New Earth Consulates.

357

'Thanks,' said Hal, climbing out. 'I can't thank you enough. No thanks, I can manage fine by myself. Let me see you safely on your way now – and say hello for me to your grandfather and the rest of your family when you get home.'

'It's been my pleasure – and an honor, sir,' said Mercy; and put the window up between them, before waving and driving off.

Hal waved back and watched the truck continue around the traffic circle on which the houses of the Place were built, and disappear between the trees on either side of the entrance into Knox Avenue. He breathed out, heavily. Merely being polite had drained his small supply of strength.

He turned, and walked slowly and unsteadily around the circle to sixty-seven French Galley Place, four doors away. The walk in from the gate was a short one, but the six steps leading up to the front door were like a small mountain to climb. He reached the top at last, however, and pressed the annunciator button. There was a wait that stretched out to several minutes. He was about to signal the annunciator again when its grille spoke to him.

'Yes?' said a voice from within.

'My name is Howard Immanuelson,' he said, wearily leaning against the doorframe. 'A few days ago I sent some papers –'

The door before him opened. A figure hardly shorter than his own, in a saffron-colored robed but with a full-fleshed, round and ageless face stood framed in the relative darkness of the interior.

'Of course, Hal Mayne,' said a soft, baritone voice. 'Amid asked us to do whatever we could for you; and said that you'd be along shortly. Come in, come in.'

CHAPTER THIRTY-EIGHT

Hal lay, his long body clad in a forest-green Exotic robe, listening to the interweaving of the melody of birdsongs with the sound of a fountain beyond a screen of three-meter-tall, willow-like trees, to the left of the small, depressed sitting area, like a conversation pit, in which he was resting. The harmony that existed in all surroundings created by Exotic minds was soothing to the remnants of a tension that still lived deep inside him. Above, either blue sky or that same sky with a weather screen between himself and it, flooded everything about him with the distant, clear green-tinted light of Procyon A, which shared its energy not only with this world of Mara, but with its twin Exotic planet of Kultis, as well as with the smaller inhabited worlds of St. Marie, half again the distance of Mara out from the sun, and Coby.

He had been reading, but the capsule had dropped from his fingers into his lap, and the words printed on the air before him had vanished. He felt soaked through by that dreamy lethargy that continues to stain for days human bodies recovering from severe illness or great and prolonged physical effort; and his present surroundings, one of those Exotic homes in which it was often uncertain as to whether he was indoors or out, lent itself to a feeling that all eternity was available in which to do anything that needed to be done. At the same time, with the recovering of his strength, a note of urgency, that had kindled in him in the Militia cell, had been growing in insistence.

Something in him had sharpened. He had aged swiftly, these last few weeks. He was not likely now to imagine – as he might have, six months earlier, that the Exotics had smuggled him off Harmony to Mara, here, merely out of kindness or because of a private concern on Amid's part. In principle, the Exotics were kind; but, above all, they were practical. There would be further developments resulting from all this care and service; and, in fact, he welcomed them, for he, himself, had things to talk to his hosts about.

He had not seen Amid except for a few brief visits since he had arrived here, at Amid's home. Before that, from that moment in which he started off Harmony, his contact had been almost solely with a woman named Nerallee, Outbond to Consulate Services on

Harmony. She had been his companion and nurse on the voyage here. Lately now, as he had grown stronger, Nerallee had been less and less in evidence. He felt the sadness of a loss, realizing that she must, of course, soon be returning to her duties on that Friendly World; and that there was little likelihood that he or she would ever meet again.

He lay down, reconstructing the ways by which he had got here. When the door of the Exotic Consulate in Ahruma had opened for him, those within had simply led him to a room and let him sleep for a while. His memory recalled no drugs given to him; but then, while the Exotics had no objection in principle to using pharmacological substances, they preferred to do so only as a last resort. More to the point, he could remember no specific treatment or manipulation of mind or body. Only, the bed surface beneath him had been exactly of the proper texture and firmness, the temperature had been exactly as he would have wished, and the gently moving air about him had been infinitely warm, soft, and enfolding.

He had woken, feeling some return of strength. Staff members of the Consulate had given him quantities of different, pleasant liquids to drink, then padded and dressed him to resemble the tall, portly Exotic who had greeted him at the door.

Nerallee had been involved with him from the first moment; and it was Nerallee who had finally accompanied him out of the Consulate to a closed, official vehicle. This had then delivered them through special diplomatic channels past the usual customs and passport checks, directly to an Exotic-owned ship in the fitting yards, where Nerallee and the supposedly ill Consulate member she had in charge were ushered aboard.

Hal could not remember the ship lifting from Harmony's surface. He could recall the first few ship-days of the trip, but only as long periods of sleep, interrupted only briefly by moments in which Nerallee was always with him and encouraging him to eat. He recovered enough, finally, to realize that she had never left him, ship's-night and ship's day, from the beginning; and that whenever he had woken he had found her in the bed beside him. So, simply and easily, without consciously thinking about it, he had fallen half-way in love with her.

It was a small, wistful, transitory love, which both understood could not last beyond the short time they would have together. Clearly Nerallee was a Healer, in the Exotic tradition, and making herself totally available to him was part of her work. Clearly, also, she had fallen in love with him in return, finding something in him beyond what she had discovered in any other of those before who had needed her ability to repair their bodies, minds and souls – he read this in her even before she told him that it was so.

But, even with her experience and training, she found herself

360

incapable of telling him what it was about him that was different, although they talked in depth about this, as well as many other things. It was part of the requirements of what she did, to open herself to those she ministered to as fully as she attempted to bring them to open themselves to her. One of the things she did tell Hal was that, like all those in her work, she grew – and expected to grow – within herself, with each new person she helped; and that if ever she should become unable to do this, she would have to give up what she did.

Even lying here, listening to fountain and bird-song after several weeks of almost constant association with her, Hal had trouble summoning up in his mind's eye a clear image of her face. Following nearly three hundred years of concern with genetics, there was no such thing as an Exotic who was not physically attractive in the sense of possessing a healthy, regular-featured face and body. But for what Nerallee looked like beyond that, Hal's physical perception had become too buried under his other knowledges of her to tell. She had seemed to him unremarkable, at first, almost ordinary-looking in fact, during their first few days together, but after that from time to time she had appeared to have worn so many different faces that he had lost count. Those faces had ranged from the most dramatic of beauties to a gentle, loved familiarity that washed all ordinary notions of beauty away – the familiarity that finds the faces of parents responded to so strongly by their very young children, or the appearance of a partner who has been close for so long that there is no single memory-picture possible and the person is simply recollected in totality.

But she had been able to do for him what he had so badly needed without having realized that he needed it – absorb his attentions so wholly that she could give him rest. A rest of the sort that he had not known since the death of his tutors. It had been what he had required at the time. But, with his strength now recovered, he was no longer in desperate need of it; and, therefore, Nerallee would be going elsewhere, to others who needed her.

He lay listening to the bird voices and the tinkle of splashing water.

After a while there was the faint scuff of foot-coverings on the floor above the conversation pit, behind him. He turned his head to see Amid coming down the three steps into the pit, to take a seat facing him, in what appeared to be a rock carved armchair-fashion. Hal sat up on the couch on which he had been lying.

'So, we're going to have a chance to talk, finally?' Hal said.

Amid smiled and folded the rust-colored robe he was wearing around his legs. On each of the half-dozen earlier occasions that he had appeared, the former Outbond had spent only a few minutes with Hal before leaving, on the excuse that he had a great deal to do.

361

'The business I've been occupied with,' the small, wrinkle-faced old man said, 'is pretty well taken care of now. Yes, we can talk as long as you like.'

'Your business wouldn't have been caused by my visit here?' Hal smiled back at him.

Amid laughed out loud. In accordance with his age, the sound resembled a dry chuckle, rather than a laugh; but it was a friendly sound.

'You could hardly come to Mara,' he said, 'without involving us with the Others, even if indirectly.'

'Indirectly?' Hal echoed.

'Indirectly, to begin with,' said Amid. His face sobered. 'I'm afraid you're right. For some days now it's been directly. Bleys knows you're here.'

'Here? At this place of yours?'

'Only that you're on – possibly in this hemisphere of Mara,' said Amid. 'Your exact location on this world is something he'd have no way of finding out.'

'But I take it he's putting on pressure to get all of you to give me up to him?' Hal said.

'Yes.' Amid nodded. 'He's putting on pressure; and I'm afraid we'd have to give in to him, if we kept you here long enough. But we don't necessarily have to react right away. For one thing, it'd be rather beneath the dignity of one of our worlds to give in at once to a demand like that, in any case.'

'I'm glad to hear that,' said Hal.

'But not particularly surprised, I take it,' said Amid soberly. 'I gather you realize we've got a particular interest in you, and things to discuss because of it?'

Hal nodded.

'I suppose you've connected me with the calculations Walter InTeacher had run on me when he first became one of my tutors?' he said.

'That,' said Amid, 'of course. Your records were flagged at that time as someone who might be of force historically. Consequently, a record was kept on you that went without interruption until the deaths of your tutors and your entrance into the Final Encyclopedia –'

'Kept with Walter's help?' Hal said.

Amid gazed at him for a moment.

'With Walter's help, of course,' Amid answered calmly: 'After his death and your entrance into the Final Encyclopedia, we lost you; and only traced you to Coby after Bleys' interest pointed you out to us, again. The fact that you've been able to keep out of his hands is, to say the least, remarkable; and it's that, primarily, that's raised our interest in you. Generally speaking, you're someone we've all been keeping an eye out for, lately. When it became obvious Bleys was making a serious effort to flush you out on Coby, we arranged for one of us to be on each of the ships available to you then for off-world escape. I was lucky enough to be on the one you took.'

'Yes,' said Hal. 'I see. You're interested in me because Bleys is.'

'Not because – for the same reason – Bleys is,' said Amid. 'We assume he wants you neutralized, or on his side. We want you made effective in opposition to him. But not just because he's interested in you. We're interested – we've always been interested – in you, simply because our ontogenetic calculations recommend an interest.'

'A little more than recommend, don't they?' Hal asked.

Amid tilted his head a little to one side like a bird, gazing at him.

'I don't believe I follow you,' he said.

Hal breathed slowly before answering. The lethargy was all gone out of him now. Instead there was a sort of sadness, a gray feeling.

'Bleys threatens the very existence of your culture,' he answered. 'I suppose I ought to say that it's the Others who threaten its very existence. Under those conditions, don't your calculations do more than just recommend an interest in me? Or – let me put it a little differently. Is there anyone else they recommend an equal interest in, in that respect?'

Amid sat in the sunlight, looking at him.

'No,' he said, at last.

'Well, then,' said Hal.

'Yes,' said Amid, still watching him. 'Apparently you understand the situation better than we thought you did. You're barely into your twenties, aren't you?'

'Yes,' Hal said.

'You sound much older.'

'Right now,' said Hal, 'I feel older. It's a feeling that came on me rather recently.'

'While you were on Harmony?'

'No. Since then – since I've had time to think. You talked about my staying out of Bleys' hands. I haven't been able to do that, you realize? He had me in a cell of the Militia Headquarters in Ahruma.'

'Yes,' said Amid. 'But you escaped. I take it you've talked face to face with him, since the moment of your tutors' deaths?'

'I didn't talk to him at the time of my tutors' deaths,' said Hal. 'But, yes, a day or two before I got away he came to my cell and we talked.'

'Can I ask about what?'

'He seems to think I'm an Other,' Hal said. 'He told me some of the reasons why he expects me to come over to their side in the end. Mainly, they add up to the fact there's no other position that'll be endurable for me.'

'And I take it you disagreed with him?'

'So far.'

Amid looked at him curiously.

'You're not completely sure he isn't right?'

'I can't afford to be sure of anything – isn't that the principle you've always held to, yourselves, here on the Exotics?'

Amid nodded again.

'Yes,' he said, 'you're older than anyone would have thought – in some ways. But you did mail your papers to me. You did come to us for help.'

'To the best of my knowledge I'm on the opposite side of Bleys and the Others,' Hal said. 'It's only sense to make common cause with those who're also opposed. I had a long time to think in that cell, under conditions where my thinking was unusually concentrated.'

'I can imagine,' said Amid. 'You seem to have gone through a sort of a rite of passage, according to Nerallee.'

'How much did she tell you?' Hal asked.

'That was all – essentially,' said Amid. 'She's got her personal responsibilities as a Healer; and, in any case, we'd rather hear what you wished to tell us about such things, in your own words.'

'At least at first?' said Hal. 'No, I've no objection to your knowing. When I talked to her, I assumed what I said was going to be made available to the rest of you, if you thought you needed to know it. Actually, what I went through isn't the important point. What's important is I came out of it with a clearer picture of the situation than – possibly – even you here on the Exotics.'

Amid smiled a little. Then the smile went away.

'Anything's possible,' he said slowly.

'Yes,' said Hal.

'Then, tell me,' said Amid. The old eyes, set deep in their wrinkles, were steady on him. 'What do you think is going to happen?'

'Armageddon. A final war – with a final conclusion. A quiet war that, when it's over, is going to leave the Others completely in control; with the Exotics gone, with the Dorsai gone, what was the Friendly culture gone, and all progress stopped. The fourteen worlds as a large estate with the Others as landlords and no change permitted.'

Amid nodded slowly.

'Possibly,' he said. 'if the Others have their way.'

'Do you know any means of stopping them?' said Hal. 'And if you do, why be interested in me?'

'You might be that means, or part of it,' said Amid, 'since nothing in history is simple. Briefly, the weapons we've developed here on Mara and Kultis are useless against the Others. Only one Splinter Culture's got the means to be effective against them.'

'The Dorsai,' said Hal.

'Yes.' Amid's face became so devoid of life and motion for a second that it was more like a living mask than a face. 'The Dorsai are going to have to fight them.'

'Physically?'

Amid's eyes held his.

'Physically,' he agreed.

'And you thought,' said Hal, 'that being raised as I've been – so that effectively I'm part Exotic and part Dorsai, as well as being part Friendly – I might be the one you'd want to carry that message to them.'

'Yes,' said Amid, 'but not just that. Our calculations on you show you as a very unusual individual in your own right – it may be that you're particularly fitted to lead in this area, at this time. That would make you much more than just an effective messenger. You must understand how high some of us calculate your potential to be –'

'Thanks,' said Hal. 'But I think you're dealing in too small terms. You seem to be thinking of someone who can lead, but only under your direction. I can't believe that the Exotics, of all people, don't have a clearer picture of the situation than that.'

'In what way?' Amid's voice was suddenly incisive.

'I mean,' said Hal, slowly, 'I can't believe you, of all people, have any illusions. There's no way what you've built here and on Kultis can survive in the form you know it. Any more than the Dorsai or the Friendly Culture can survive as they now are; whether the Others are stopped, or not. The only hope at all is to try to win survival for the whole race at whatever necessary cost, because the only alternative is death for the whole race; and because that's what's going to happen if the Others win. It'll take them some generations, maybe, but if they win, in the end their way will end the human race.'

'And?' The word was close to being a challenge from the small man.

'And so the only way to survival means facing all possible sacrifice,' said Hal. 'What is it you and your fellow Exotics would be willing to give up everything else to preserve – when it comes down to that?'

Amid looked at him, nakedly.

'The idea of human evolution,' he said. 'That, above all, mustn't die. Even if we and all our work in the past four centuries has to be lost.'

'That, yes. I think ideas can be saved,' said Hal, 'if the race is going to be saved as a whole. All right, then. I imagine you've got a number of people you want me to meet?'

He stood up. Amid rose also.

'I believe,' he said. 'we've underestimated you.'

'Perhaps not.' Hal smiled at him. 'I think I'll change clothes first. Will you wait a minute?'

'Of course.'

Hal went back to his sleeping quarters. Among the clothing suspended there, cleaned and waiting for him, were the clothes he had been wearing on Harmony when he had knocked at the door of the Exotic Consulate. He exchanged them for the green robe he had been wearing and went back to Amid in the conversation pit.

'Yes, we did indeed underestimate you,' the old man said, looking at the clothes when Hal returned. 'You're much, much older than when I met you aboard the ship to Harmony.'

CHAPTER THIRTY-NINE

'As it happens,' said Amid, leading Hal through the pleasant maze of rooms and intervening areas that made up his home, 'the people who want to talk to you are already here. While you were dressing, I called around and they were all available.'

'Good,' said Hal.

He strode along beside the much smaller man, holding his pace down to the one that age dictated for Amid. The self-restraint reminded him, suddenly, of how frail the other actually was. Amid must be far up in years, considering the state of Exotic medical science; nowhere near as old as Tam Olyn, of course, but old in any ordinary human terms.

'I've no idea,' Amid said, 'where your knowledge of our ways stops. But I suppose you know that, like the Dorsai, for all effective purposes we don't have governing bodies on Mara or Kultis. Decisions affecting us all become the concern of those in whose field they most clearly lie; and the rest of us, in practice, accept the decision those experienced minds come up with for the situation – though anyone who wants to can object.'

'But they generally don't?' Hal said.

'No,' Amid smiled up at him. 'At any rate, the point is that the four people you're to talk to aren't political heads of areas or groups, but people whose fields of study best equip them to evaluate and interpret your capabilities. For example, my own study of the Friendly Worlds makes me particularly fitted to understand what you did, and what the results may be from what you did, on Harmony. The others are comparable experts.'

'All in fields as applied to ontogenetics?'

'Ontogenetics underlies nearly everything we do –' Amid broke off. They had reached the entrance to what seemed to be less a room than a porch, or balcony, projecting out from a wall of the general house. Beyond the graceful, short pillars of a balustrade there was nothing visible but sky and the distant tops of some deciduous trees. Some empty chairs floats, but nothing else, were visible on the balcony. Amid turned to Hal.

'We're early,' he said, 'and that gives us a moment. Step across the hall with me.'

He turned and led the way into a room with its entrance opposite that of the balcony. Hal followed, frowning a little. The neatness of the opportunity to tell him something was almost suspect. It could be sheer accident, as Amid had implied; or it could be that what the other was about to tell him was something that the Exotics had wanted him to know before they spoke with him, but something they had not wanted him to have too much time to think over beforehand.

'I should explain this, so you aren't puzzled by the fact that some of those you'll be talking to may seem to doubt you unreasonably.' Amid closed the door behind them and stood looking up into Hal's face. 'Walter InTeacher taught you at least the elements of ontogenetics, I think you said?'

Hal hesitated. At fifteen, he would have answered without hesitation that he understood a great deal more than just the elements of ontogenetics. But now, standing at his mature height, after five years of life experience with a number of people on two strange worlds, standing face to face with a born Exotic, on Mara, he found a certain restraint in him.

'The elements, yes,' he answered.

'You're aware, then, that ontogenetics is basically the study of individuals, in their impacts on current and past history, the aim being to identify patterns of action that can help us to evolve an improved form of human?'

Hal nodded.

'And you know,' said Amid, walking over to a small, square table with a bare top, apparently carved of some light-colored stone, 'that beyond its statistical base and its biological understandings, the work's always been highly theoretical. We observe, and try to apply the results of our observation, hoping that the more knowledge we can pile up the more clues we'll find, until eventually, we'll be able to see a clear pattern leading to the evolved form of humanity.'

He paused, now standing beside the tabletop, and looked up at Hal again.

'I suppose you know it was our interest in that sort of piling up of knowledge that led us to supply most of the funds that made the building of the Final Encyclopedia possible; first as an institution in the city of Saint Louis, on Earth, then as it is now, in orbit around that world. Though, as you also must know, neither the Exotics nor anyone else owns the Final Encyclopedia, now.'

'I know,' said Hal.

'Well, the point I wanted to make is that there're innumerable ways to graph individual potential.'

Amid drew the tip of his forefinger from right to left on the tabletop beside him; and a black line sprang into existence in the light, stony material of the surface, following his touch. He crossed the line he had drawn with a vertical one at right angles to it.

'One of the simplest ways to graph ungauged genetic potential for the race at any given moment –' He drew another, horizontal line lifting at a small angle from the base line of the graph, 'gives us what seems to be a slowly ascending curve. Actually, however, this line is only an average derived from a number of points scattered both above and below the base line, where the points above the line refer to historical developments clearly traceable to the action or actions of some individuals –'

'Like Donal Graeme and the fact he made a single legal and economic whole of the fourteen worlds?' said Hal.

'Yes.' Amid looked at him for a moment, then went on. 'But the points can also refer to much smaller historical developments than that even to single actions by obscure individuals whom it's taken us several centuries to identify. However – below the base line the points refer to individual actions that can only probably be linked in a cause-and-effect pattern, with the historical developments that concern us. . . .'

He paused and looked at Hal.

'You follow me?'

Hal nodded.

'As it happens,' Amid turned back to his graph, 'inevitably, when this sort of charting is done, we end up with certain individuals being represented by points above and below the line. Individuals of developing historic effect will often be represented by points below the line before their effect emerges above the line, where their points show a clear relation between their actions and certain historical results. Points below the line, unfortunately, don't necessarily indicate the eventual emergence of points above, for any individual. In fact, points below the line are often achieved by individuals who never show any effect above the line at all.'

He paused again, and looked at Hal.

'Now, all of this may mean anything or nothing,' he said after the pause. 'All work like this, as I said, is theoretical. The results we get this way may have nothing whatever to do with the actual process of racial evolution. However, it's only right that you know this sort of figuring, projected forward, is one of the ways we use to try and estimate the ontogenetic value of any given individual, and the probability of that person having an ability to influence current history.'

'I see,' said Hal, 'and I take it that as of the present moment I'm one of those who charts out with points below the line but none above?'

'That's right,' said Amid. 'Of course, you're young. There's plenty of time for you to show direct influences on the present history. And your effects below the line so far are impressive. But the fact remains, that until you show some direct evidence above the line, your potential to do so remains only that, and estimates of what you may be able to perform in your lifetime are a matter of individual opinion, only.'

He hesitated.

'I follow you,' said Hal.

'I'd expected you to,' said Amid, almost grimly. 'Now I, myself speaking from knowledge of my own particular specialty and seeing what you did in the short time you were on Harmony, estimate you as someone I expect to be highly effective – effective on a scale that can only be compared to that of Donal Graeme in his time. But this is only my opinion. I believe you'll find that some of those you're about to talk to may regard your potential as no more than possible, on the basis of the same calculations that cause me to think the way I do.'

He stopped. For a moment, Hal ignored him, caught up by his own thoughts.

'Well, thanks,' he said at last, rousing himself. 'It's good of you to warn me.'

'There's more,' Amid said. 'I mentioned earlier that you seemed a great deal older than I remembered you on ship to Harmony. As a matter of fact this is something more than a subjective opinion on my part. Our recent tests of you show certain results that we've never found before, except in rather mature individuals – those middle-aged, at least. I was simply confirming this from my own feelings. But if you really are unusually mature, for some reason we can't yet understand, this could be something that might incline some who presently doubt to favor the opinion of someone like myself about your potential effectiveness, provided we can find an explanation for it. Can you think of anything to explain it?'

'When were these tests made?' Hal looked into the eyes of the small man.

'Recently,' said Amid. His returning gaze was perfectly steady. 'In the last few weeks.'

'Nerallee?'

'It's part of our work,' said Amid.

'Without mentioning to the person she's taking care of that she's making such tests?'

'You have to understand,' said Amid, 'a great deal may be at stake here. Also, as a matter of fact, knowledge that the tests are being made on the part of the subject could affect the results of the test.'

'What else did she find out about me?'

'Nothing,' said Amid, 'that you don't already know about yourself. But I asked you if you had an explanation of these indications of an unusual maturity?'

'I'm afraid not,' said Hal, 'unless being raised by three men all over eighty years old had something to do with it.'

'Not in any way we can understand.' Amid was thoughtful for a moment. An abrupt sweep of his hand above the table surface erased the lines on it. 'If you do think of any explanation while we're talking this afternoon, though, I suggest you mention it. It would, I think, be to your advantage.'

'In what way?' said Hal.

Amid turned from the table and went toward the door of the room. Hal went with him.

'We'd be more inclined to trust you – and therefore to help you – with whatever you've got in mind,' said the small man. 'As I keep pointing out, there's something of a division of opinion among those of us who're responsible for making a decision on you. If you seem to be someone on whom we actually can pin our hopes of the future, that could be tremendously useful to you. On the other hand, if – as some of us think – the correct reading on you shows you as at best only a wildly random factor is the present historic pattern, then our two worlds are going to be very reluctant to put ourselves at dependence on your possible actions.'

He led the way through the doorway into the hall; and paused.

'Think about it,' he said, and turned once more toward the door to the balcony. 'The others are probably there by now. Come along.'

Hal followed him. They went out of the room they had been in, crossed the hall and stepped onto the balcony, which now had two men and two women seated on it, in a semi-circle facing the entrance. One of the men, wearing a sky-blue robe, was obviously very old; the other was a reserved-looking, thin man in a gray robe; and, of the two women, one was small and black-haired, wearing green, the other was taller and ageless, with bronze skin, curly brown hair, and an umber-colored robe. Two floats had been left vacant with their backs to the door, completing the circle; and it was to these that Amid led Hal.

'Let me introduce you,' said Amid, as they sat down. 'From left to right, you're meeting Nonne, Recordist for Mara –'

Nonne was the small, black-haired woman in green. She looked to be about in her mid-thirties, her face a little sharp-boned, and her eyes very steady on him.

'Honored,' said Hal to her. She nodded.

'Alhonan of Kultis. Alhonan, Hal, is a specialist in cultural inter-facing.'

'Honored.'

'Very glad to meet you, Hal,' said Alhonan, a narrow man, with a voice as dry and reserved as his appearance.

'Padma, the Inbond.'

'Honored,' said Hal. He had not appreciated at first glance how old indeed the one called Padma was. The Exotic face he looked at now was still relatively unwrinkled, the hands holding the ends of the armrests of his float were not extravagantly shrunken of skin or swollen of vein; but the utter stillness of the body, the unchanging

371

eyes, and other signals too subtle to be consciously catalogued, radiated an impression of almost unnatural age. Here now, indeed, was a man to rival Tam Olyn in antiquity. And the title he bore was a puzzle. Hal had never heard of an Inbond among the Exotics. Any one of them might be Outbond – assigned, that was – to some specific place or duty. But Inbond . . . and to what?

'Welcome,' said Padma; and his voice, neither unusually hoarse nor deep nor faint, seemed somehow to come from a little distance off.

'And Chavis, whose speciality is a little hard to describe to you,' Amid was saying at his shoulder. 'Call her a specialist in historical crises.'

Hal had to tear his eyes away from the gaze of Padma to look at the woman in the umber robe with black markings of random shapes.

'Honored,' he said to Chavis.

'I take that as a compliment,' she said, and smiled. Her age could be anything between late twenties and early sixties; but her voice was young. 'Time may show that it's you who're honoring us.'

'Sit down,' said Amid.

'That'd take some doing,' Hal answered Chavis, as he took his seat. 'I don't think I'm likely to find four Exotics like yourselves brought together on my account, except under very unusual conditions.'

'But it's unusual conditions we've met to talk about here, isn't it?' said the voice of Amid from the float to Hal's left. The two of them sat facing the half-circle of the others. Still, the feeling was plain in the atmosphere of the balcony that Amid was not with Hal, but with those who confronted him.

It was a feeling that triggered another touch of sadness in Hal. With the memory of Walter InTeacher still strong within him, of all the three cultures with which he had grown up believing he had a strong kinship, the Exotics had been those from whom he had expected the most in the way of sensitivity and understanding. But he sat now, intellectually almost at sword-points with those before him. He could feel that concern, first for the survival of their own way of life; and only secondarily with his own interest in the race as a whole. The thought came instinctively to him that it was a rarefied sort of selfishness they were displaying – a selfishness, not for their personal sakes, but for the sake of the principle to which they and their culture had always dedicated their people. It was a selfishness he would have to bring them to see beyond, if there was to be any hope of racial survival.

Looking at the faces around him, Hal's innate confidence in his cause sagged. It might be true, as Amid had said, that tests had shown him to have unusual qualities of maturity. But at the present moment he sat facing a total of several centuries of living and training in those facing him. To deal with all that, all he had to show were twenty years of life-experience, and perhaps sixty hours of intense thought under conditions of exhaustion and high fever.

'How much do you know about the history of the crossbreeds in general?' Nonne's voice roused him from his emotions. Her voice was a very clear contralto. 'I'm speaking specifically, of course, of crossbreeds from the Dorsai, Friendly and Exotic cultures.'

He turned to face her.

'I know they started to be noticed as appearing more frequently about sixty to seventy years ago –' he answered. 'I know very little attention was paid to them as a group until about fifteen or twenty years ago, when they began to call themselves the Other People, show this charismatic skill of theirs, and put together their organization.'

'Actually,' said Nonne, 'their organization began as a mutual-help agreement between two who were both Dorsai-Exotic crosses – a man named Daniel Spence and a woman named merely Deborah, after our own Exotic fashion – who were living together on Ceta, forty-two standard years ago.'

'They were the first to call themselves "Others," ' put in Alhonan.

Nonne glanced at him briefly. 'Like most close partnerships among the crossbreeds,' she went on, 'the physical association didn't last; but the agreement did, and it grew rapidly over the next five years until there were over three thousand individuals involved – an estimated seventy-nine per cent of all crossbreeds from the three major Splinter Cultures who were in existence at that time. Both Spence and Deborah are now dead; and the current top leader of the organization for the past twelve years has been a man named Danno, who led the meeting of Other leaders at your home, the time your tutors were killed.'

'I saw him then, through a window,' said Hal. 'A big, heavy-bodied man – not fat, but heavy-bodied – with black, curly hair.'

'That's Danno,' said Alhonan, in a precise, remote voice.

'He was the son of Daniel Spence and Deborah,' said Nonne. 'Those two also later took in a boy of about eleven, some six years younger than Danno; and the best evidence we can gather indicates that he was a nephew from some other world like Harmony, who had originally been left with some of Spence's relatives there to raise. There may be more to it than that. Bleys insists the former version is what happened. But it's doubtful if even he knows certainly whether it's true or not. In any case, he's a powerful leader; clearly more brilliant than Danno, although he seems to prefer that Danno wear the mantle of supreme leadership. You've met Bleys.'

'Yes,' said Hal. 'Three times, now; and I talked to him this last time, when I was in that prison cell on Harmony. Danno, I saw only once, that first time; but my own feeling is that you're right. Bleys is more capable, and more intelligent – both.'

'Yes,' said Chavis, softly. 'In fact, we've wondered exactly why he seemed content with second place. My own guess has been that he simply doesn't have any great desire to lead.'

'Perhaps,' said Hal. 'Or he could be biding his time.' Like the dark shadow of a cloud, sweeping briefly over his mind, the feverish memory returned of Bleys, seeming to tower enormously above him as he had lain on the cot in the Militia prison. 'But if he's better than Danno, he'll have to lead, in the end. He won't have any choice.'

There was a moment of silence from those around him that stretched out noticeably before Nonne broke it.

'So, you think,' she said, 'that it'll be Bleys we'll be dealing with in the long run?'

'Yes,' said Hal. A wing of the dark cloud still shadowed his mind. 'Even if he has to remove Danno himself.'

'Well,' said Nonne. There was a dry briskness in her voice; and he roused himself to give her his full attention, putting the shadow from him. 'In any case, we've ended up facing something we're not equipped to handle. There was a time when to any of us here the thought of any sociological development arising that we couldn't control would have been unthinkable. We know better now. If we'd moved to control the crossbreeds even two decades ago, we might have succeeded. But some of us were blinded by the attractive hope that they might be the first wave of that evolutionary development of the race we've looked and worked for so hard, during the past four centuries.'

She gazed at Hal grimly.

'I was one of the blind,' she said.

'We all were,' the distant voice of Padma broke in.

Again, there was a silence that lasted a fraction of a second longer than Hal felt was normal.

'However, the end result's been the emergence of a historical force, in the shape of the Others, for which our current interstellar civilization's got no counter and no control,' Nonne went on. 'Organized interplanetary crime was always something that the sheer physical difficulties and expense of interplanetary travel made impractical. It'd still be impractical for the Others, except for the fact that some of them have developed this charismatic skill –'

'If only some can manage it, it needs to be called an ability rather than a skill, doesn't it?' Hal asked, suddenly remembering once more Bleys looming over him in the cell. . . .

'Perhaps,' said Nonne. 'However – skill or ability, it's what makes the organization of the Others effective. With it, even the relative handful of them can manipulate key figures in governments and planets. This gives them political power and financial reserves we can't match. It isn't even necessary for more than a large minority of those in their organization to have this charismatic ability, although they seem to be able to teach it to each other, and even to some of their followers – which, come to think of it, answers your question about why we call it a skill rather than ability –'

'I take it, then, that you haven't been able to duplicate it among your own people here on Mara and Kultis?' Hal interrupted.

Nonne stared at him, her lips closed in a straight line.

'The apparent techniques involved are all Exotic ones,' she answered. 'It's simply that the Others seem to be able to use them with increased effectiveness.'

'The point I'm making –' said Hal, 'is that they can do something that you here on the Exotics can't seem to duplicate. Doesn't that sound like something based on a particular ability?'

'Perhaps.' Nonne's stare was immovable.

'I say that because I think I may be able to tell you why they can,' Hal said. 'I'm beginning to believe that behind their use of those techniques you mention there's a force in operation that's been cultivated only in the Friendly Culture – the drive to preach, to proselyte. Take a look at those followers you mention who've been able to pick up and use some of what you see a minority of Others using. I'll bet you don't find one of them who wasn't either a product of the Friendly Culture to begin with, or the child of at least one parent who was.'

There was another fractionally too long silence.

'An interesting point,' said Nonne. 'We'll look into it. However –'

'If I could get a native of Harmony or Association to come to you for training,' persisted Hal, 'would you be willing to see if you could develop that person into a charismatic of the Other level?'

Nonne and the others traded glances.

'Of course,' said Padma. 'Of course.'

'We'd be glad to,' said Nonne. 'You mustn't think that we're indifferent to what you may be able to suggest to us, Hal. It's simply that time's a factor. We're under strong pressure from Bleys to give you up; and we're either going to have to do that or get you off the Exotics very shortly. In that short time we've got things to talk to you about; and it's to all our advantages if we stick to the point.'

'I think what I've been trying to get at is at least involved in the point,' answered Hal. 'But go on.'

'What I'm trying to do here,' Nonne said, 'is lay out the situation and its history. That, and make sure you understand what our basis for concern is, and what we'd like to do about the situation.'

'Go on,' said Hal.

'Thank you. Wherever the charismatic skill or ability comes from, the fact remains, it's the key to the Others' success. They can't use it, of course, to control us – or the Dorsai people, or at least some of the Friendlies. In addition, a certain percentage of people everywhere seem to be resistant; particularly most of those on Old Earth, for reasons we haven't identified. But if they can use it to control a majority of the race, that's all they need to do. As I started out by saying, our present civilization on the fourteen worlds hasn't any counter to that ability. The result is, the Others have grown in power and wealth to the point where they can win, economically, even against us. They've simply got too many chips to play with. Our two worlds alone can't match their resources in the interplanetary marketplace. As a result, Mara and Kultis are slowly becoming captives of theirs, even though they've made no direct move to dominate us – yet.'

Nonne paused. Hal nodded.

'Yes,' he said. 'Go on.'

'The point I keep making is,' Nonne said, 'we can't do anything to stop them. The worlds they already control obviously aren't going to stop them. Old Earth's people have never all gotten together on anything in their history; and, since they're largely immune to the charismatic influence, themselves, they'll probably simply continue to ignore the Others until they wake up one day to find themselves surrounded by thirteen other worlds, all under crossbreed control, and with no choice but submission. The Friendlies are already half-conquered; and it's only a matter of time until the natives the Others control on Harmony and Association dominate those two worlds completely. That leaves the Dorsai.'

Once more Nonne paused.

'As you say,' said Hal, soberly, 'it leaves the Dorsai, which is slowly being starved to death for lack of off-planet work opportunities for its people.'

'Yes,' said Alhonan, 'but – forgive me, Nonne, but this is my department – such starvation takes time; and that's one world the Others aren't at any time going to try to take over by force. They might be able to do it in the long run, but the cost wouldn't be worth it. In fact, if the Dorsai would be willing to settle temporarily for being a backward planet, lacking the technological and other advantages that dealing with the other settled worlds would give them, they could settle down to a meager but independent existence for a century or more, living on what the oceans and the small land surfaces of their world could provide them. And they're just stubborn enough to do that.'

'In other words,' said Nonne, swiftly, 'for the Dorsai there's still time to act, and that's important; because of all the Splinter Cultures, they alone still have the capability to stop the Others. In fact, they've got the ability to remove the threat of the Others, completely.'

She stopped speaking. Hal stared at her; and the longest of any pause that had occurred so far held the balcony.

'What you're suggesting,' he said at last, 'is unbelievable.'

Nonne looked back at him without answering. Glancing around the circle, Hal saw the others all similarly sitting, waiting. 'What you're suggesting is a Dorsai campaign of assassination,' Hal said. 'That's what you mean, isn't it? That the Dorsai eliminate the Others by sending individuals out to murder them? They'd never do that. They're warriors, not assassins.'

CHAPTER FORTY

Chavis, after a long moment, was the one who spoke.

'We're prepared,' she said, softly, 'to do anything in our power – to give them anything they need or want that we have to give, without reservation, including our lives. If we'll do that much to stop the Others, surely they can put principle aside this once, for this great need?'

Hal looked at her. Slowly, he shook his head.

'You don't understand,' he said. 'It's the one thing they'd never do, just as you'd never give up your faith in human evolution.'

'They might,' it was the voice of Padma, speaking across the great reach of years to him, 'if you convinced them to do it.'

'I convince them –?' Hal looked at them all.

'Can you think of any other way to stop the Others?' Nonne asked.

'No! But there has to be another!' Hal said to her, violently. 'And what makes you think I could convince them to do anything like that?'

'You're unique,' she said. 'Because of your upbringing. In effect, you can speak the emotional languages of all three of our largest Splinter Cultures –'

Hal shook his head.

'Yes,' said Nonne. 'You can. You proved that on Harmony, when you fitted in with one of the resistance groups there. Do you really think the native Friendlies in Rukh Tamani's Command would have taken you in, or kept you for more than a day or two, unless they felt, instinctively, that at least part of you was capable of thinking and feeling as they did?'

'I wasn't that accepted by them,' said Hal.

'Are you so sure?' put in Amid beside him. 'When I talked to you aboard the ship going to Harmony, you could have convinced me you were a Friendly, for all that you knew less about their history and society than I did. There's a particular feel to Friendlies, just as people of other cultures tell us there is to Exotics, and as everyone knows there is to Dorsai. Recognition of that Friendly feel is something I've spent a lifetime acquiring and I don't make mistakes now. You felt to me like a Friendly.'

'You also,' said Alhonan, 'feel to all of us like an Exotic. And to the

378

extent of my specialty, you also feel to me like a Dorsai.'

Hal shook his head.

'No,' he said. 'I'm none of these, none of you. The fact is, I don't belong anywhere.'

'Do you remember,' said Amid, against his ear, 'a moment ago, when you first understood what Nonne was suggesting the Dorsai do about the Others? You answered right away that the Dorsai wouldn't do it. Where did you get the certainty you felt in telling us that? Unless you, yourself, trust yourself to think like a Dorsai?'

The words rang with uncomfortable persistence in Hal's mind. They also, without warning, touched off a sudden, inexplicable, deep sadness inside him; so that it was a moment before he got control of his feelings enough to go on. He made an effort to think calmly.

'It doesn't matter,' he said, finally. 'The idea of Dorsai individuals assassinating the Others, one by one, aside from anything moral or ethical about it, is too simplistic a solution. I can't believe I'm listening to Exotics –'

'Yes, you can,' interrupted Amid. 'Check the Exotic part of yourself.' Hal went on talking, refusing to look at the small man.

'– Whatever else the Others are, they've emerged as a result of natural forces within the human race,' he went on. 'Attempted genocide's no answer to them, any more than it ever was for any situation like this, as long as historic records've run. Besides, it ignores what's really going on. Those same forces that produced them have been building to this moment of confrontation for hundreds of years.'

He paused, looking at them all, wondering how much of what he now felt and realized could be made clear to them.

'When I was in that cell on Harmony,' he went on, 'I had a chance to think intensively under some unusual conditions; and I'm convinced I ended up with a clearer picture of what's going on historically, right now, than a great many people have. The Others pose a question, a question we've got to answer. It's not going to work just to try to erase that question and pretend it was never asked. It's our own race that produced the crossbreeds – and their Other organization. Why? That's what we've got to find out –'

'There's no time left for that sort of general investigation, now,' said Nonne. 'You, of all people, ought to know that.'

'What I know,' said Hal, 'is that there has to be time. Not time to burn, perhaps, but time enough if it's used right. If we can just find out why the Others came to be what they are, then we'll be able to see what the answer is to them; and there's got to be an answer, because they're as human as we are and the instincts of a race don't lead it to produce a species that could destroy it – without some strong reason or purpose. I tell you, the Others were developed to test something, to resolve something; and that means there has to be an answer to

379

them, a solution, a resolution that'll end up doing much more than just taking off our backs what looks now like a threat to our survival. If we can only find that answer, I'm sure it'll turn out to mean more to the whole race than we, here, can begin to imagine.'

He felt his words dying out against the silence that answered him, as calls for help might die against a wall too thick for sound to penetrate. He stopped talking.

'As Amid's pointed out,' said Nonne after a moment, 'you react in part like an Exotic. Ask the Exotic part of yourself, then, which of two answers is most likely to be right – the conclusions you've come to on your own? Or the unanimous conclusion of the best minds of our two worlds, on which the best minds have been sought out and encouraged for nearly four hundred years?'

Hal sat, silent.

'We could, however, ask Hal what alternative he sees,' said Padma. For the first time Nonne turned directly to face the very old man.

'Is there any real point to it?' she asked.

'I think so,' said Padma; and in the pause following those three words of his the silence seemed to gather in on itself and acquire an intensity it had not had until this moment. 'You talked about being one of those who were seduced and blinded by the hope that the crossbreeds were what we had looked for, these hundred of years. Your fault in that was much less than mine, who'd watched them for more years than any of you, and was in even a better position than anyone else to see the truth. I, for one, can't risk being seduced a second time, and blinded by our own desire for a quick and certain solution – a solution which Hal has properly called simplistic.'

'I think –' began Nonne, and then fell quiet again as Padma raised his hand briefly from his lap.

'Not only did I make the mistake of assuming the crossbreeds were something they weren't,' he said, 'unlike the rest of you, I made another mistake, one that still haunts me. Of all Exotics I had the chance, and closed my eyes to it, to find out if Donal Graeme was a real example of evolutionary development. Now, too late, I'm convinced he was. But he was never checked; and I could have had that done at any time in the last five years of his life. If I had only done that much, we'd have been able to read him positively, one way or another. But I failed; and the result was that the chance he might have offered us, eighty standard years ago, was lost forever when he was. I don't want to make another mistake like that.'

The other Exotics looked at each other.

'Padma,' said Chavis, 'what's your personal opinion of Hal's potential then?'

The intensity that had come into the room a moment before when Padma had spoken was still there.

'I think he may be another like Donal Graeme,' he said. 'If he is – we can't afford to lose him; and in any case, the least we can do is listen to him, now.'

The eyes of the other four robed individuals consulted once more.

'We should, of course, then,' said Nonne.

'Then –?' Chavis glanced around at the others, all of whom nodded. 'Go ahead, Hal. That is, if you've got something specifically to suggest that's a workable alternative to our ideas.'

Hal shook his head.

'I don't have any answers,' he said. 'I just believe they can be found. No, I know they can be found.'

'We haven't found any,' said Alhonan. 'But you think you can?'

'Yes.'

'Then,' said Alhonan, 'isn't what you're asking just this – that our two worlds should trust you blindly; and blindly take on all the risks a trust like that implies?'

Hal took a deep breath.

'If you want to put it in those terms,' he said.

'I don't know what other terms to put it in,' replied Alhonan. 'But you do think you, alone, can solve this; and we should simply follow you wherever you want to take us?'

'I've got nothing else to think.' Hal looked at him squarely. 'Yes.'

'All right,' said Chavis, 'then tell us – what would you do?'

'What I decided to do in that cell on Harmony,' said Hal, 'learn what's involved for the race in this situation, decide what's to be done, then try to do it.'

'Calling on us for whatever help you need,' said Alhonan.

'If necessary – and I'd say it will be,' Hal said. 'You, and any others who also want a solution.'

The four before him looked at each other.

'You'll have to give us a specific reason,' said Chavis, gently. 'You must have a basis for this belief of yours, that, even if there's something there for you to find, a reason why you should be the one to find it where we haven't been able to.'

He gazed at her, then at Padma, and finally at Nonne and Alhonan.

'The fact is,' he said, slowly at first but gaining speed and emphasis as he spoke, 'I don't understand why you, with your ontogenetic calculations, don't see it for yourselves. How is it you can't recognize what's under your noses? All that's needed is to look – to stand back for a moment and look at the last five hundred years, the last thousand years, as a whole. It's people building forward – always forward – that makes history. The interaction of their individual forces – conflicting, opposing, mingling and finding compromise vectors for their impinging forces; like an orchestra with millions of instruments, each trying to play a part and each trying to be heard in its own part. If the brass section sounded as if it was dominating the rest of your orchestra, would your solution be no more than eliminating the brass section?'

He paused, but none of them answered.

'That's exactly what you're suggesting, with your idea of setting the Dorsai to destroy the Others,' he said. 'And it's wrong! The orchestra as a whole's got a purpose. What has to be done is find why the brass section's too prominent; and from that knowledge learn to use the whole orchestra better. Because it's not happening by accident – what you hear. It's a result, an end product of things done earlier, things done with a purpose that you haven't yet understood, that the individual players even in the brass section don't themselves understand. It's happening for a reason that has to be found; and it won't be found by anyone looking for it who doesn't believe it's there. So I suppose that's why it has to be me who goes looking for it – not you; and that's why you'll have to trust me until I do find it, then listen when I tell you what needs to be done.'

He stopped at last. The three other faces before him turned to Padma. But Padma sat without saying anything, with no expression on his calm face that would indicate his opinion.

'I think,' Chavis said, carefully, 'that at this point we might do better to talk this over by ourselves, if Hal doesn't mind leaving us.'

Beside Hal, Amid was getting to his feet. Hal also rose, and Amid led him from the balcony. They went left along the hall to a down-sloping ramp, that let them out into a garden which plainly lay below the balcony where the others still sat. A tall hedge enclosed a small pool and fountain, surrounded by deeply-hollowed blocks of stone, obviously designed as seats.

'If you don't mind waiting alone,' Amid said, 'I'm one of them, and I ought to be up there with them. I'll be back, shortly.'

'That's fine,' said Hal, seating himself in one of the stone chairs with its back to the balcony. Amid left him.

The gentle sound of splashing water amid the otherwise silence of the garden enclosed him gently. Looking back over his shoulder and up, he could see the balustrade of the balcony: but the angle of his view was too steep for him to see even the tops of the heads of those still there. By some no-doubt-intentional trick of acoustics, he could hear nothing of their voices.

He looked away from it, back to the leaping water, a jet rising from the center of the pond some fifteen feet in the air before curving over and breaking into feathering spray. Curiously, a feeling of defeat and depression lay like a special darkness upon him.

His thoughts went back to the moment in his cell when he had suddenly broken through to an understanding of all things racial, enclosing him is that moment of his comprehension. The complete picture had been too immense for him to grasp all at once, then; and he still could not do it. During the past weeks he had explored the entity of that understanding section by section, as he might have explored some enormous picture inlaid upon a horizontal area too large to be seen from any one point on it. As he had explored, he had grown taller in knowledge; so that he could see more and more of it from a single point. But, even now, he could not begin to grasp the shape of it as a whole.

However, he could feel it as a whole. He was aware of its totality, the living moment of the great human creation he was now carefully examining bit by bit.

Already, it had become almost incredible to him that the existence of what he could be so aware of, in its immensity, should not equally overwhelmingly, be apparent to everyone else; above all, to seekers after understanding like Amid and the other four upstairs. How was it that the Exotics, all through the three centuries of their existence, had never developed a special study of this great, massive forward progress of the race, that was the result of the interaction of every human individual with its fellows, along the endless road of time?

But they had, of course, he told himself. That was what onto-genetics had been intended to become. Only, apparently it had failed in its purpose. Why?

Because – the answer grew in him slowly out of his new aware-ness of what he now searched, and tried to understand – ontogenetics had been crippled from the start by an assumption that its final answer would be what the Exotics desired as an ultimate goal.

A feeling of depression, a sensation and an emotion such as he had encountered before, was born in him and grew, slowly, undrama-tically but undeniably. The one people he had counted on had been the Exotics clothed in the colors of perceptivity and understanding he had found in Walter the InTeacher. Now, at last, he had been brought to doubt those qualities in them; and, doubting them for the first time, he came at last to doubt himself. Who was he to think that worlds of men and women should listen to him? The task on which he had so confidently launched himself from the cell loomed too great for any single human, even with all things made easy for him. He had little more than twenty years of life's experi-ence to draw on. He was alone – even Amid stood on the other side of the barrier that separated him from all others.

The depression he felt spread to fill him and settle itself in the place of the certainty that had been so much a part of his nature until now. At its base was the dark logic of Bleys, now reinforced by the deaf ears to which he had just been speaking. He lost himself in wrestling with this new enemy and the fountain played. Time passed; and it was with a small shock that he was aware of Amid, once more at his elbow.

Hal got to his feet.

'No,' said Amid, 'no need to go back up. I can tell you what's been decided.'

Hal looked at him closely for a second.

'Yes?' he asked.

'I'm afraid we can't go along with you, blindly,' Amid said. 'I don't believe there's any reason not to tell you, though, that I argued for you as much as I could – as did Padma. And Chavis.'

'That's three out of five,' said Hal. 'A majority in my favor?'

'Something more than a simple majority's needed in a situation like this,' said Amid. 'An element of doubt exists, and eventually we all had to face that.'

'In short, you all ended by deciding against me?'

'Padma took himself out of the decision.' Amid looked up at him; and there was no apology on the small man's face. 'I'm sorry you have to be disappointed.'

'I'm not,' said Hal, wearily. 'I think I expected it.'

'It's still open to you if you want,' said Amid, 'to be our representative to the Dorsai. To go to them with our message to them as it was explained to you. Perhaps you should take the opportunity, even if you don't agree with it. At least you'll be doing something toward dealing with the Others.'

'Oh, I'll do it,' said Hal. 'I'll go.'

Amid looked at him a little strangely.

'I didn't expect you'd agree so easily,' he said.

'As you say,' Hal answered, 'I'll be dealing with the problem of the Others, even if not the way I'd planned to.'

He was suddenly aware that he was smiling tightly. With an effort, he stopped.

'I'm surprised,' murmured Amid. His eyes had never left Hal's face. 'Just like that?'

'Perhaps with one condition,' said Hal. 'After I'm gone, will you remind Nonne and the rest that it was their own assessment that the forces at work right now aren't something I could control, and that they themselves told me time is limited?'

'All right,' said Amid. He seemed to be on the edge of saying something more, when he apparently changed his mind and turned about.

'Come along,' he said. 'I'll help get you prepared and started on your way.'

CHAPTER FORTY-ONE

A brisk chime commanded Hal's attention to the communications screen in one wall of his stateroom. The screen stayed blank, but an equally brisk feminine voice spoke from it.

'Give me your attention, please. Take your place in the fixed armchair by the bed and activate the restraining field. Control is the red stud on the right armrest of the chair.'

He obeyed, a little surprised, aware that activating the field would register on a telltale in the control room, forward. But the order had caught him deep in his own thoughts and for the moment, automatically, he returned to them.

A corner, at least, of that dark shadow of defeat and depression, which had come to touch him in the garden below the balcony at Amid's home on Mara, had stayed with him through these five standard days of ship's time it had taken for his journey to the Dorsai. He had not met the woman who was evidently the pilot of this small courier-class vessel, on which he seemed to be the only passenger; and she had not come back from the restricted control area forward to make any sort of self-introduction. As a result, he had been free to think, uninterrupted, and there had been a great deal to think about.

Now, however, when they must be almost upon the Dorsai . . . he found those thoughts interrupted by the unusual demand that he put his body under control of a restraining field, something ordinarily requested of passengers only when their vessel was docking in space, as the jitney had been when it brought him to and into the Final Encyclopedia.

But this Dorsai light transport was no spaceliner, of course, and the commanders of Dorsai vessels had their own way of doing things, as all the fourteen worlds knew. He reached out and flicked on his room screen to see how close they actually were to going into a parking orbit.

What he saw made him sit up suddenly. They were indeed close enough to go into parking orbit. Blue and white, the orb of the Dorsai loomed large on his stateroom screen, the edge between night and day of the dawn terminator sharp below them. But, far from parking, the ship was still phase-shifting inward toward the surface of the world below. Even fifty years before, the psychic shock of a rapid series of shifts such as these would have required him to medicate himself in advance. But research at the Final Encyclopedia itself had found a way to shield from that shock. So there had been no warning.

It was a second before Hal recalled that the Dorsai – unlike pilots from other planets – had a habit of trusting themselves to shift safely right down into the atmosphere of any world on which they had good data; in fact, to within a few thousand meters of its surface. It was a skill developed in them as part of their normal training in ship-handling, as a practical matter of cutting jitney and shuttle costs on their far-from-wealthy world. The protective restraint was merely a routine precaution against some passenger panicking under such unusual approach maneuvers and getting hurt as a result. In fact, a moment later they came out of a series of very rapid, successive shifts with a jerk that would have thrown him from the chair, if the protective field had not held him anchored.

They were now no more than a thousand meters up, at most, and beginning to descend on atmosphere drive toward a spaceport misted with early morning rain under gray skies; a spaceport larger in area than the small city to which it was adjacent. Clearly, they were about to land at what Amid had earlier told Hal was the intended destination of the ship – the closest thing to a capital city that the Dorsai possessed. This was the city of Omalu, which housed the central administrative offices of the United Cantons, the districts into which the Dorsai had come to be organized for purposes of local self-government.

Actually, however, as Hal knew as well as the Exotics who had sent him here, these offices formed no more than a library and storage center for contractual records; and a contact point for discussion of matters that could not conveniently be discussed and settled locally in or between the cantons concerned. The Dorsai had even less than the Exotic Worlds in the way of a central government.

In theory, the cantonal officers had authority over the individuals and families living within the boundaries of the individual canton; but in actuality even this authority was more a matter of expressing local public opinion than otherwise.

Neighborliness – a word that held a special meaning on the Dorsai – was what made a social unit of this world. The cantons, even in theory, had only a courtesy relationship to the central administrative offices of each island on this world of islands, large and small. And the island offices did no more than communicate with the United Cantonal Offices here in Omalu. It was the only way a world could operate on which families, and individuals in those families, were constantly dealing on a direct and independent basis with off-planet governments and individuals scattered over all other thirteen worlds.

Ironically, Hal had been sent out at Exotic expense to speak to representatives of a world which had no representatives, at least officially. It was ironic because the Exotics, who trusted nothing they could not test and identify, had in this case simply trusted the people of the Dorsai world to bring Hal somehow to those to whom he should speak.

But the spacecraft was now landing at the port, almost as precipitously and economically as it had phase-shifted to within a breath of ground level. As it settled down and became still, the sign winked out over the door. Hal shut off the restraining field. He got to his feet and collected a shoulder bag supplied and filled by Amid, and containing necessary personal clothes and equipment. Amid had reminded him – unnecessarily – that the Dorsai was one world where it was not always possible to buy suddenly needed clothes and other personal necessities conveniently close at hand.

Leaving his stateroom, he had to squeeze his way past crates of Exotic medical machines of various sizes and complexity, stacked even in the central corridor of the craft. A majority of these were new, replacements for worn-out units in Dorsai hospitals; but a fair number were older machines which had been taken back to their designers on Mara for repair or the additions of improvements beyond the training of the local Dorsai technicians doing ordinary maintenance on them. There were even more of these filling the vessel than Hal remembered encountering when he had come aboard. It had been remarkable that a craft this small could lift from the surface, packed with this much cargo.

Finding his way out of the entry port at last, Hal stepped into the cloudy morning and the gusting rain above the landing pad. Descending the ramp to the pad, Hal found at the foot of it a tall, lean, middle-aged woman in gray coveralls, in brisk conversation with a lean-faced, older man riding a small hovertruck.

'– You'll need bodies!' she was saying. 'The way that equipment's packed in there, you're not going to get it out alone, even with hand-lifters. Even the two of us can't do it. We're going to have to lift three things to get one clear enough for you to carry it off.'

'All right,' said the man. 'Back in five minutes.'

He turned his truck and slid off swiftly across the pad toward a blurred line of gray buildings in the distance. The woman turned and saw Hal. Saw him, and stared at him for a long moment.

'Are you Dorsai?' she said, at last.

'No,' said Hal.

'I was about twenty meters away from you, over by the truck, unloading, when they took you on board,' she said. 'You moved like a Dorsai. I thought you were.'

Hal shook his head.

'One of the people who raised me was Dorsai,' he said.

'Yes.' She stared at him for a moment more. 'So, then, you've never had ship-handling. There ought to have been two of us on a trip like this, and I wondered why you didn't come up front and offer to give me a hand. But I had my own hands full; and when you didn't, I took it there was some reason you wanted privacy.'

'In a way,' said Hal, 'I did.'

'Good enough. If you couldn't help, you did just what you should have by staying out of my way. All right, no harm done. I made it here well enough by myself, and you're where you wanted to go.'

'Not exactly,' said Hal. 'Foralie's where I wanted to go.'

'Foralie? On Caerlon Island?' She frowned. 'Those Exotics told me Omalu.'

'They were assuming something,' said Hal. 'I'll be coming back to Omalu here, eventually. But for now, I want to go to Foralie.'

'Hmm.' The pilot glanced over at the buildings. 'Babrak'll be back in a moment. He can give you a ride to the terminal and they can tell you there how you might get to Foralie. You'll probably have to change boats several times –'

'I was hoping to fly straight there,' said Hal. 'I've got the interstellar credit to pay for it.'

'Oh.' She smiled a little grimly. 'Interstellar credit's one thing we can always use these days. I should have guessed you'd have some, since you came aboard on one of the Exotics. Well, as I say, Babrak'll be back shortly. Let's get in out of this weather; and meanwhile, how about giving me a hand clearing enough space just inside the entry port for him to get started?'

Less than two hours later, Hal was airborne in the smallest jitney-type space and atmosphere craft in which he had ever ridden. He sat side by side with the driver before the control panel; there were two more empty seats behind them, and beyond that only a small cargo space.

'It's about a third of a circumference,' said the pilot, a thin, brisk, black-haired man of about thirty in a fur-collared jacket and slacks. 'Take us something over an hour. You're not Dorsai, are you?'

'No,' said Hal.

'Thought for a moment you were. Hold on.' The jitney went straight up toward the upper edge of the atmosphere. The pilot checked his controls and looked over at Hal, again.

'Foralie Town, isn't it?' he said. 'You know someone there?'

'No,' answered Hal. 'I've just always wanted to see Foralie. I mean, Foralie, itself, Graemehouse.'

'Foralie's the property. Graemehouse's the name of the house on it. Which is it, the property or the house you want to see?'

'All of it,' said Hal.

'Ah.'

The driver watched him briefly for a moment longer before

returning his gaze to the stars visible above the far, curved horizon of the daylight surface below, visible beyond the vehicle's windshield. They were headed in the same direction as the rotation of the planet. The brilliant white pinpoint of the local sun, Fomalhaut, which had been behind them on liftoff, began now to catch up. 'You didn't happen to have a relative who was a Graeme?'

'Not as far as I know,' said Hal.

The dry tone in which he was unthinkingly answered had its effect. The driver asked no more questions and Hal was left in the dimness of the jitney's interior to his own thoughts once more. He sat back in his seat and closed his eyes. When he had been very young one of his fanciful dreams had indeed been that his parents might have been related to the Foralie Graemes. But that sort of wishful thinking was long past now. The pilot's question had still managed to touch an old sensitivity.

However, now that he was actually headed toward Foralie, he found himself strangely uneasy with his decision to go there first, before doing anything else on the Dorsai. He had no sensible reason for making this trip now – only his early fascination with the history of the Graemes and the stories Malachi had told him of Ian and Kensie, Donal, and the others.

No, it had simply been that, darkened by the shadow which had come over him in the garden on Mara, he had felt a reluctance to move too swiftly here on the Dorsai – in his execution of the commission that Nonne and the other Exotics had asked him to undertake, or anything else; and in the face of that feeling, on the trip here, he had decided to do what he had always wanted to do since he had been a child, and that was see the Foralie which Malachi had so many times mentioned to him.

The deeper reason was less clear, but more powerful. It was that of all his dreams and fever-visions during the period in the cell, the one that still clung to his mind and moved him most strongly was the dream of the burial. Its events were solid and real in his mind even now – the tearing sorrow and the commitment. He did not need to hunt out points of evidence within that dream to know that it had been about some place and people on the Dorsai. To someone raised as he had been, the fact was self-evident – the very color and feel of what he had dreamed was Dorsai. So powerful had been its effect on him that he felt it like an omen – to be disregarded at his peril; and since Malachi had been the last of his own family, there was no place on that world to which Hal could relate strongly but the household of the legendary Graemes of which he had heard so much in his young years.

It was true, he had always wanted to see the birthplace of Donal Graeme. But something more than that was at work in him, now – something beyond his present understanding of that vision of death and commitment – that was still hidden from his conscious mind and which drew him instinctively toward some place or time strongly Dorsai, for a fuller understanding.

Besides, it was curiously apt that he should go there now. Malachi, or the shade of Malachi which he had conjured up with those of Walter and Obadiah four years past at the Final Encyclopedia, had told him that there would be no reason for him to go to the Dorsai until he was ready to fight the Others. Well, he was at last ready to fight them; and it had been from the starting point of Foralie that Donal Graeme had gone in his time to gain leadership of the whole fourteen worlds. An almost mystic sense of purpose seemed to beckon Hal to the same place of beginning.

Also, he was in a mood that needed support, even mystic support. He had failed dismally to get the Exotics to listen to him or help him. There was no reason to expect the Dorsai to do more. In fact, considering the independence of its people on that harsh world, there was less reason. What had happened to him in Amid's garden as he had waited for their decision had been something outside his experience until that moment. A certain belief in himself with which he had emerged from the Militia cell on Harmony, and which he had then thought impregnable, had been struck and weakened by the blindness of the Exotic attitude.

It had not been merely the fact that they had not listened. That had been only the final assault that had breached the inner fortress of his spirit. But the breach had been made only after a number of recent blows that had already cracked and weakened what he had always thought was unbreakable in him. Where he had once taken for granted that whatever he defended was unconquerable, he now could see defeat as a real possibility.

Granted, there were excuses. The emotional pain of having to trick and abandon his friends in the Command, his illness at the time, his driving of his body far beyond its physical limits and, finally, his rite-of-passage – as Amid had referred to it – alone in the Militia cell, had all had their effect. Even the arguments of Bleys, which, even denied, had weakened him in preparation for this final blow that was the Exotic refusal to hear what he had to say. Of all peoples, he had expected the men and women of Mara and Kultis to understand, to recognize something once it was pointed out to them.

But knowing these things did not help. The grayness, the feeling of defeat remained. He looked at his life and could not see that from the start he had achieved anything. His early dreams, put to the test out on the worlds, had vanished like pricked soap bubbles.

Who was he to think that he was anything but a minor annoyance to the Others – a mouse dodging about under the feet of giants who would sooner or later crush him? He was nothing; not Friendly, not Exotic, not Dorsai. He had no reason even to believe that he had any claim to belong to Earth. That ship in which he had been found could have been coming from anywhere; and been headed to anywhere. What was this present trip to Foralie, but a clutching at a straw floated to the surface of his mind by a dream? He had no real proof that he was not, indeed, a crossbreed, as Bleys had said. He had no identity, no home, no people. He was a stranger in every house, a foreigner on every world, his only known family three old men who had been no actual relations; and even they had only been with him for the first, early years of his life.

He had wanted to stay at the Final Encyclopedia, and his feeling that he must strike back at the Others had driven him from it. He had found a way of life as a miner; then, to save his life, had been forced to run and leave that way of life behind. He had found friends, almost a family, in Rukh's Command; and he had deliberately made the choice to abandon them. The Exotics had had no place or use for him except as a messenger; and there was no hearth waiting for him here on the Dorsai, where there were not even relatives of Malachi's to sit with for a moment and tell about Malachi's death. To have found even one other person who could have shared his grief over the loss of Malachi and the others, would have strengthened him to bear the dry emptiness of his solitary position in the universe.

He drew a deep, slow breath. Long ago, Walter InTeacher had told him how to deal with psychic pain like this; and he had remembered dutifully, if without great interest, seeing that the technique was for something that he could not imagine happening to him. Walter's instruction had been not to fight the depression and the self-condemnation, but to go with them and try to understand them. In the end, Walter had said, understanding could drain the destructive emotion from any situation.

He made an effort to do this now; and his mind slid off into a strange area, without symbols, where he seemed to feel himself tossed about by the vectors of powerful forces he could not see – like someone swept overboard from a ship in a hurricane. It went against his instincts not to fight these pressures; but Walter had emphasized the absence of resistance. Sitting in the thrumming near-silence of the jitney, hurling itself through the space where air and void meet, he forced himself into passivity, searching and feeling for some pattern to the situation that held him. . . .

'Going down now,' said the voice of the pilot, and Hal opened his eyes.

They were back into the atmosphere, descending fast over what seemed open ocean. Then a point of darkness near the horizon became apparent, enlarging as the jitney fell in a long curve toward it, until it was clearly visible as land. A few moments later they were low above mountain meadows and stony peaks; and shortly thereafter they dropped vertically to earth, on a concrete pad at the edge of what had seemed to be a small village beside a river.

'Here you are,' said the driver. He punched a control on the panel before him and the entry to the jitney swung open, steps sliding down and out to the pad surface. 'Just head up that road there. Center of Foralie Town's beyond the trees and the housetops, there.'

'Thanks,' said Hal. He reached for his case of credit papers, then remembered he had paid for this trip before leaving Omalu. He got up, taking his shoulder bag with him. 'Is there a central office or –'

'Town Hall,' said the driver. 'It's always in the center of town. Just follow the road in. You can't miss it and it'll have a sign out front. If you do get lost, ask anyone.'

'Thanks again,' said Hal, and left the jitney, which took off before he had covered half the width of the pad to the road the driver had indicated.

They had flown forward into mid-afternoon. No breeze stirred. The trees that the jitney driver had mentioned were variform maples, and the color on them spoke of autumn. But it hardly needed that to tell Hal of the time of the year in this part of the Dorsai; for the clear, clean light of fall spoke of the season in every quarter. Under an almost cloudless sky, the still air was scentless, cool in the shadow but hot in the sun. The shadows of the trees and, after a bit, the shadows of the wooden buildings when he had passed through the trees and found himself in the streets of Foralie Town itself, seemed hard-edged, they lay so crisply where the brilliant sunlight was interrupted. The colors of the houses glowed, clean and bright, as if all structures there had just been freshly washed and painted against the oncoming winter.

But the town itself was still and quiet, and the relative silence of it touched Hal strangely. He felt an emotion toward its houses and its streets that was an unusual thing to feel to a place never seen before. No one was in the streets through which he walked, although occasionally he heard voices through the open windows he passed. He came after a few moments to a central square; and, facing him at the far end, was a white building of two stories, its lower level half-sunken into the ground. There were two doors visible; one at the top of a flight of six steps to the upper story, the other preceded by a shorter flight, down to the floor below.

The white building plainly showed its difference in design from the obvious homes that fronted on the other three sides of the square. Hal went to it; and as he got close, he saw the word *Library* above the door to the semi-basement entrance. He went up the stairs to the higher door and touched its latch panel. It swung open and he entered.

Inside was a space about ten meters square, divided by a room-wide counter with a gate that marked off the back half of the space into an area with three desks and some office equipment. A thin, handsome boy about ten or twelve years old got up from one of the desks and came to his side of the counter as Hal walked up to the front of it. He stared at Hal for a moment, then visibly pulled himself out of his first reaction.

'I'm sorry,' he said, 'my aunt's the Mayor and she's out in the hills at the moment. I'm Alaef Tormai –'

He broke off, gazing at Hal, penetratingly once more.

'You're not even Dorsai,' he said.

'No,' said Hal. 'My name's Hal Mayne.'

'Honored,' said the boy. 'I'm sorry. Forgive me. I thought – I thought you were.'

'It's all right,' said Hal. For a moment, a sort of bitter curiosity moved in him. 'Tell me what made you think so?'

'I –' the boy hesitated. 'I don't know. You just do. Only something's different.'

He looked embarrassed.

'I'm afraid I'm not too good an observer. After I get through my training –'

'It's not you,' said Hal. 'A couple of adult Dorsai have already had to look twice at me to see what I was. What I'm hoping is to get up in the hills myself and take a look at Foralie. Not for any particular purpose. I've just always wanted to see it.'

'There's no one there now,' said Alaef Tormai.

'Oh?' Hal said.

'I mean, all the Graemes are off-world right now. I don't think any of them are due back for a standard year or so.'

'Is there any reason I can't go up and look around, anyway?'

'Oh, no!' said Alaef, uncomfortably. 'But there'll be no one home. . . .'

'I see.' Hal thought carefully for a second about how to phrase his next question so as not to hurt the other's feelings. 'Isn't there someone close to the Graemes I could talk to? Someone who might be able to show me around?'

'Oh, of course!' Alaef smiled. 'You can go talk to Amanda. Amanda Morgan, I mean. She's their next door neighbor. Fal Morgan's her homestead – do you want me to show you how to get there?'

'Thanks,' said Hal. 'I'll have to rent a vehicle.'

'I'm afraid there's nothing in town here you could rent,' said Alaef, frowning. 'But that's all right. I can slide you up there on our skimmer. Just a minute, I'll call Amanda and tell her we're coming.'

He turned to a screen on one of the desks and punched out call numbers on its deck of keys. A line of printing flooded across the screen in capital letters. Hal could read it from where he stood.

'GONE TO BRING IN THE BRUMBIES.'

'She's gone after wild horses?' Hal asked.

'Not wild.' Alaef turned back to him from the screen and looked embarrassed again. 'Just the stock she's had running loose for the summer in the high pastures. That's what we mean when we say brumbies, here. It's time to bring them in to shelter for the winter. It's all right. We can go ahead. She's got to be back before dark; and she'll probably be home by the time we get there.'

He started out the gate to Hal's side of the counter.

'What about the office?' Hal asked.

'Oh, that's all right,' Alaef said. 'This late in the day, no one's likely to come by. I'll leave word with my aunt on the way out of town, though.'

Hal followed him out, and five minutes later found himself a passenger in an antique-looking ducted-fan skimmer being piloted up one of the slopes enclosing the valley that held Foralie Town, headed toward the high country beyond.

The sun was reaching down toward the mountaintops and a time of sunset, when they came at last over a little rise and Hal saw before them a high, open spot surrounded in front and on both sides by wooded gullies like the one from which they had just emerged; and, beyond that, having a small open field that lifted at the far end to a treed slope, enclosed by the omnipresent mountainsides. In the center of the open area stood a large, square two-story building with walls of light gray stone, accompanied by what seemed to be a long stable, some outbuildings and a corral, all of log construction.

'I guess she isn't back yet, after all,' said Alaef, as he brought the skimmer up close to the house. 'She's left her kitchen door ajar, though, to let people know she'll be right back.'

The skimmer's fan died and the vehicle settled to the grassy earth outside the partly open door with a sigh.

'Do you mind if I just leave you here, then?' said Alaef, looking at Hal a little anxiously. 'It's hardly polite, I know, but I told my aunt I'd be home in time for dinner. Amanda's got to get those brumbies in corral before sundown, so she'll be along at any minute; but if I wait with you I'll be late. You can just go in and make yourself comfortable.'

'Thanks,' said Hal, standing up from his seat in the open skimmer and stepping down onto the earth. 'I think I'd just as soon stand out here and watch the sunset. You get on back; and thanks for bringing me up here.'

'Oh, that's just neighborliness. Honored to have made your acquaintance, Hal Mayne.'

'Honored to have made yours, Alaef Tormai.'

Alaef started up the fans, lifted the skimmer on them, spun it about, waved and slid off. Hal watched him until the vehicle and youngster dipped into a gully and were lost from sight. He turned back to look at the sun.

It was touching the tops of the mountain range with its lower edge and the light was red and full. For a moment the color of it brought back a memory of another sunset-time in which he had been racing the edge of moving sun-shadow across the water and Malachi and Walter had been standing on the terrace of the house. . . .

He shivered, slightly. There was something stark and real about this Dorsai landscape that let the mind and the emotions run full out in any direction that beckoned them. He looked about once more at the edges of the tabletop of land on which he stood, alone with the Morgan house and outbuildings. If this Amanda was indeed sure to be in before dark, she would have to be putting in an appearance very shortly.

Barely a couple of seconds later, his ear caught a sound of distant whooping, followed by an increasing noise of hoofbeats and torn brush and, as he watched, horses boiled up over the edge of one of the gullies, flanked by a blue-capped rider who passed them up and raced flat out before them toward Hal and the clump of buildings.

By this time, somewhere between a dozen and fifteen loose horses were up on the flat, being chivvied forward by two other riders, who looked to be no older than Alaef. Meanwhile, the one in advance had galloped to the corral and was unlatching and swinging open its gate, throwing one quick glance at Hal as she passed.

This, he thought, had to be the Amanda Morgan he was here to see, although she did not look much older than her two assistants. She was tall, with the breasts and body of a grown woman, in spite of her slimness; but an amazing litheness and an indefinable general impression of youthfulness made it hard for him to believe that she was much beyond her middle teens.

She swung the gate wide. The other two riders were already driving the loose horses toward the corral. These thundered past Hal at less than ten meters of distance. One gray horse, with a white splash on its face balked at the gate, dodged and spun about, bolting toward Hal, the house and freedom beyond. Hal ran forward, waving his arms at full length on either side of him and shouting. The gray checked, reared, and dodged aside again only to find its way barred by one of the young riders, who turned it finally back into the corral.

They were all in, and the sun's upper edge disappeared as the gate was swung to and locked. Suddenly shadow and a breath of coolness flooded over all the level land. Amanda Morgan said something Hal could not quite catch to the two younger riders. They waved, swinging their mounts around, heading off at a canter in the direction from which they had come.

Hal, fascinated, watched them down into the gully and out of sight. He looked back, finally, to find Amanda dismounting in front of him. For the first time he got a good look at her. She was as square-shouldered as she was slim, dressed in tan riding pants, heavy black-and-white checkered shirt and leather jacket, with a blue, wide-billed cap pulled low over her eyes as if to still shade them against the direct sunset light that had now left them. Twilight filled the area below the surrounding mountains.

She took off the cap and he saw that her barely shoulder length hair, gathered and tied behind her, was white-blond; her face was slim-boned and regular with a beauty that he had not expected.

'I'm Amanda Morgan,' she said, smiling. 'Who're you, and when did you get here?'

'Just now,' he answered automatically. 'A boy called Alaef Tormai from the Foralie Town Hall office brought me up on a skimmer. Oh, I'm Hal Mayne.'

'Honored,' she said. 'You've got business with me, I take it?'

'Well, yes. . . .'

'Never mind,' she said. 'We can talk about it in a moment. I've got to put Barney here into the stable. Why don't you go into the living room and make yourself comfortable? I'll be with you in twenty minutes.'

'I – thank you,' he said. 'All right, I will.'

He turned and went in, as she led the horse off by its reins toward the long, dark shape of the stable.

Through the door, the interior air of the house was still, and warmer than the first night-coolness outside. The lights in the ceiling came on automatically and he saw he had stepped into a large kitchen. He turned right from it down a short corridor that had a large painting on one wall, apparently of the woman he had just met – no, he corrected his thoughts on stopping to examine it more closely, the woman pictured was at least in her thirties, but so alike to the Amanda Morgan he had met outside that they could have been sisters, if not twins. He went on into another room furnished with large couches, overstuffed chairs and occasional tables all of them articles of solid furniture, with nothing of float construction visible.

At his left as he entered was a wide fireplace, the mantlepiece above it filled with small, apparently homemade bits of handicraft, ranging in artistry from obviously childmade objects such as a long-skirted woman's figure made of dried grass stems tied and glued into shape, to the bust of a horse, its head and arched neck only, carved in a soft reddish stone. The lifelikeness of the horse was breathtaking. Hal was reminded of some early Eskimo carvings he had seen in the Denver museum on Earth, in which an already wave-formed rock had been barely touched by the carver's tool, to transform it into the figure of a seal, or that of a sleeping man. The same kind of creative magic had been at work here, even to the red graininess of the rock evoking the texture and skin-coloring of a roan horse.

In a multitude of small ways, he thought, as he took one of the comfortable chairs, it was the kind of room he had not seen since he left his own home on Earth. Not just the noticeable lack of modern technologies created this feeling. There had been none at all to be seen in the farmhouses that had put him up, together with the other Command members, on Harmony. But there was something different, here. A deliberately archaic feel lived within the walls surrounding him – as if it had been a quality consciously sought for and incorporated by the builders and owners of this place. The same sort of feel had been evident to an extent in Foralie Town also, and might be typical of the Dorsai in general for all he knew, but here, it amounted almost to a fineness, like the warm sheen upon cherished woodwork, lovingly nutured and cared for over the years.

Whatever it was, like Foralie Town itself, it touched and comforted him like a home long familiar to which he was just returning. The emotion it raised in him relieved some of the depression he had been feeling ever since the garden on Mara. Sitting in the armchair, he let his thoughts drift; and they slid, almost in reflex, back into a maze of memories from his own early days, memories that for a change were happy ones, of the years before Bleys had appeared.

So caught up in these memories was he that he only woke from them with the entrance of Amanda into the room, her cap and jacket removed carrying a tray with cups, glasses, a coffee pot and a decanter on it that she set down on a square, squat table between his chair and the one facing it.

'Coffee or whiskey?' she said, sitting down facing him on the other side of the table.

Hal thought of getting used to one more taste-variety of coffee.

'Whiskey,' he said.

'It's Dorsai whiskey,' she said.

'I've tasted it,' he said. 'Malachi – one of my tutors – let me taste some one Christmas when I was eleven.'

He saw her raised eyebrows.

'His full name was Malachi Nasuno,' he added.

'It's a Dorsai name,' said Amanda, tipping some of the dark liquor into a short, heavily-walled glass, and handing it to him. Her eyes studied him with an intensity that tightened the little muscles in the nape of his neck. Her gaze reminded him of the way young Alaef Tormai had stared in the first moment of their meeting at the Town Hall. Then she bent the silver crown of her head and poured coffee for herself, breaking the moment of her glance.

'I had three tutors,' said Hal, almost to himself. He tasted the whiskey, and its fierce burn brought back more memories. 'They were my guardians as well. I was an orphan and they raised me. That was on Earth.'

'Earth – so that's how you know about horses. That – and being raised by a Dorsai, explains it,' she said, looking up and meeting his eyes again. He noticed the color of hers, now. Under the indoor lighting they were a clear, penetrating bluish green, like deep sea waters. 'I took you for one of us at first glance.'

'So have a number of other people since Omalu,' said Hal. He saw her glance was questioning. 'I landed there from Mara, just a few hours back.'

'I see.' She sat back in her chair with the coffee cup, and the color of her eyes seemed to darken as they met his now in the last of the twilight that was flooding the room through its wide windows. 'What can I do for you, Hal Mayne?'

'I wanted to see Foralie,' he said. 'Alaef said none of the Graemes were home, but you were their closest neighbor; and I could talk to you about looking at the place.'

'Graemehouse's locked up now; but I can let you in, of course,' she answered. 'But you won't want to go tonight. Aside from anything else, you'd see a lot more in daylight.'

'Tomorrow?'

'Tomorrow, by all means,' she said. 'I've got an errand to run, but I can leave you there on the way over and collect you on the way back.'

'That's good of you.' He swallowed the rest of the whiskey in his glass, breathed deeply a moment to get his voice back, and stood up. 'Alaef ran me up here, but he had to be back in time for dinner. I don't want to impose on you but do you know anyone I can call for transportation back to Foralie Town?'

She was smiling at him.

'Why? Where do you think you're going?'

'Back to town, as I said,' he answered a little stiffly. 'I've got to arrange for a place to stay.'

'Sit down,' Amanda said. 'Omalu has a hotel or two, but out here we don't run to such things. If you'd stayed in town, the Tormai or one of the other families there would have put you up. Since you're out here, you're my guest. Didn't your Malachi Nasuno teach you how we do things, here on the Dorsai?'

He looked at her. She was still smiling at him. He realized suddenly that, as they had talked, he had completely lost his earlier image of her as a barely-grown young woman. For the first time he began to consider the possibility that her chronological age might be even greater than his own.

CHAPTER FORTY-TWO

He sat at a table in the large kitchen of Fal Morgan while Amanda fixed dinner. It was a square, high-ceilinged room panelled in some pale wood gone honey-colored with time, which reflected the house lights that had seemed to strengthen as the outside twilight faded. It had two entrances; the one to the hall by which he had gone to the living room and by which they had come back in, and one to a presently-unlighted dining room in which Hal could dimly see dark panelling, straight-backed chairs, and part of a long, dark table. In the kitchen the cooking surfaces, the food storage cupboards, and the phone screen hanging high on one wall were modern and techno-logical. Everything else was home-built and simple. Amanda moved about with an accustomed dexterity and speed. His own hands were idle.

'I could give you something to make it look like you're helping,' she had told him as they had come in, 'but there's no point to it. There's nothing you can do here that I can't do faster and better myself. So just sit back out of my way, and we'll talk as I go. More whiskey?'

'Thank you,' he had said. Sitting with a glass in his hand at least gave him the appearance of a reason for sitting still while she worked.

He had expected to feel self-conscious sitting there, nonetheless; but the essential magic of the house, the warmth of the kitchen with her movement about in it, made all things right. Only, for a second, and reasonlessly, watching her now, he felt an unusually sharp stab of that loneliness that had been always part of him these last four years. Then he put that aside too, and merely sat, sipping the dark, fierce whiskey, wrapped in the comfort of the moment.

'What do you like – mutton or fish?' she asked. 'That's our choice, here.'

'Either is fine,' he said. 'I don't eat much.'

Strangely, this had been true since his time in the cell on Harmony. His familiar, oversize appetite had been lost somewhere. On the trip from Harmony to Mara, he had eaten only when meals were pushed upon him; and on Mara itself the indifference had continued. It was not that food did not taste good to him once he began to eat – it was just that hunger and appetite had somehow lately become strangers to him. He did not think of eating until he had been some time without food; and then just enough to take the edge off his immediate need was all he would find himself wanting.

He became aware that Amanda had paused at his answer, and was looking back intently across the room at him from the food storage cupboard she had just unsealed.

'I see,' she said after a second. She went back to taking things from the cupboard. 'In that case why don't we have both? And you can tell me which you like best.'

Hal watched her as she worked. It seemed that Dorsai cookery had something in common with that on Harmony. Here, as there, a little meat was made to go a long way by adding a lot of vegetables. Fish, however, was used somewhat more freely. There appeared to be a fair amount of preparation to all the dishes Amanda made; but each came together and went onto the cooking surface with surprising speed.

'Well, tell me,' she said, after a few minutes, 'why do you want to see Foralie?'

The memory of the burial dream floated unbidden to the surface of his mind. He pushed it back down, out of consciousness.

'Malachi, the tutor I mentioned,' he said, 'told me a lot about it – about Donal and the other Graemes.'

'So you came to see for yourself?'

He caught the unspoken question behind the one uttered out loud.

'I had to come to the Dorsai anyway,' he told her. A desire to be open with her, more than he had intended, stirred in him for a second; but he repressed it. 'Only, when I got here, I found I wasn't ready to get down right away to what I'd come for. So I thought I'd take a day or two and come here first.'

'Because of the stories Malachi Nasuno told you?'

'Stories mean a lot when you're young,' he answered.

She sat down at the table opposite him with a cutting board and began to chop up what looked like variforms of celery, green pepper and chives. Her glance came across the table at him. In the warmly yellow illumination of the lights off the golden panelling, her eyes flashed like sunlight on turquoise water.

'I know,' she said.

They sat in silence as the bright blade of her knife rocked up and down on the board, dividing the vegetables.

'What was it you wanted to see there?' she asked, after a bit, sweeping the chopped vegetables into a pile together and getting up to carry the board with them back across the room.

'The house, mainly, I suppose,' he smiled to himself, talking to her slim, erect back, 'I'd heard so much about it, I think I might even be able to find my way around it blindfolded.'

'Your Malachi may have been one of the officers the twins or

400

Donal used to use a lot on their contracts,' she said, almost to herself. She turned back to face him again. 'I've got to visit one of my sisters tomorrow morning. I'll give you a horse – you can ride, I suppose, from what I saw earlier?'

He nodded.

'I can take you to Graemehouse, let you in, go on to make my visit and come back afterwards. Then after I'm back, if you like, we can go around the house and its land, together.'

'Thanks,' he said. 'That's good of you.'

Without warning, she grinned at him.

'You haven't been here long enough for people to tell you that neighborliness doesn't require thanks?'

He grinned back.

'Malachi told me about neighborliness on the Dorsai,' he said. 'No one since I landed has had time to go into the details for me, though.'

'One of the ways we survive here is by being neighborly,' Amanda said, sobering, 'and we Morgans have survived here since the first Amanda, a good number of years before Graemehouse was even built.'

'The first Amanda?' he echoed.

'The first Amanda Morgan – who built this house of Fal Morgan and brought our name to this part of the Dorsai, nearly two hundred and fifty standard years ago. That's her picture in the hall.'

'It is?'

He watched her, fascinated.

'How many Amandas have there been?' he asked.

'Three,' she said.

'Only three?'

She laughed.

'The first Amanda was touchy about her name being pinned on someone who couldn't live up to it – she was a person. No one in the family named a girl-child Amanda until I came along.'

'But you said there were three. If you're the second –'

'I'm the third. The second Amanda was actually named Elaine. But by the time she was old enough to run about, everybody was starting to call her Amanda, because she was so much like the first. Elaine-Amanda was my great-grand-aunt. She died just four years ago last month; and she'd grown up with Kensie and Ian, the twin uncles of Donal. In fact, they were both in love with her.'

'Which one got her?'

Amanda shook her head.

'Neither. Kensie died on Ste. Marie. Ian married Leah; and it was his children who carried on the Graeme family line, since Kensie died unmarried, and neither Donal nor his brother Mor lived to have any children. But after his sons were all grown and Leah had died – in her sixties – Ian used to be over here at Fal Morgan all the time. I remember when I was very young, I thought that he was just another Morgan. He died fourteen years ago.'

'Fourteen years ago?' Hal said automatically calculating in his head from what he knew of the chronology of the Graeme family. 'He lived a long time. How old was your great-grand-aunt when she died?'

'A hundred and six.' Amanda finished putting the last dish on the cooking surface; and came back to sit down with a cup of tea at the table. 'We live a long time, we Morgans. She was the Dorsai's primary authority on contracts, right up to the day she died.'

'Contracts?' Hal asked.

'Contracts with whoever on other worlds wanted Dorsai to work or fight for them,' said Amanda. 'Families and individuals here have always made their own agreements with governments and people on the other worlds; but as the paperwork got more complicated, an expert eye to check it over became useful.'

'I'd have thought all the contract experts would be in Omalu,' said Hal. The purpose of his being on this world stirred in the back of his mind. 'Who's the leading expert on contracts on the Dorsai, now?'

'I am,' said Amanda.

He looked at her.

'Oh,' he said.

'It's all right to be surprised,' Amanda told him. 'We Morgans not only put in long lives, we tend not to look our age. I'm not as young as I might seem; and the second Amanda saw to it I cut my teeth on contracts. I was reading them when I was four – not that I understood what I read until a few years later. The Second Amanda's also the one who saw to it my parents named their oldest daughter Amanda; and she took me over almost as soon as I was born. In a way, I was always more hers than theirs.'

'If she hadn't pushed it, they wouldn't have given you that name?'

She grinned again.

'Otherwise no member of this family would've risked giving a child that name.'

A timer chimed from the cooking surface and she got up to take care of something.

'Everything's ready,' she said.

Hal got to his feet, turning toward the dining table in the still-unlit room.

'No,' she said, glancing back over her shoulder at him at the scrape of his chair legs on the floor. 'We'll eat in here, since there's just the two of us. Sit down. I'll bring things.'

He sat down again, pleased. The kitchen was more attractive to him at this moment than the dim room with the long dining surface that must have been capable of feeding a dozen people or more.

'That's quite a table in there,' he said.

'Wait until you see the one at Graemehouse,' she said, carrying dishes to the table. She got the food brought and arranged and sat down herself. 'I'll fill a plate for you to start you out since won't know any of these dishes. Eat what tastes good, and tell me what you think. As far as the size of the table goes, when there's a contract to be estimated, even tables like that can be all too small.'

She passed the laden plate to him, and started to fill one for herself from the dishes between them.

'You don't understand?' she said.

'Contract estimating takes space?' said Hal.

'It takes space to work with the sub-contractors,' she answered. 'A large military contract could take a week and more to put together; and during that time everyone's living with it around the clock. Try some of the red sauce on the fish, there.'

Hal did.

'Suppose,' she said, resting her elbows on the table, 'someone like Donal Graeme had been asked by a local government on Ceta if he'd put together a force to take military control of some territory that's currently under dispute; and hold it while its true ownership is negotiated between that government and the other claimants. He'd first sit down and make a general plan of how the job might be done and what he would need to do it – troops, transport, housing, weapons, medical, supply units . . . and so forth.'

Hal nodded.

'I see,' he said.

'Do you? Well, having made his own preliminary, general estimate, he'd then call other individuals, or even families, from around the Dorsai, with whom he may have worked in the past, and whose work he'd liked; and ask each of them if they'd consider working under him on the contract on which he was currently putting together a bid. Those who did would come to Foralie and they'd all sit down together, take his general plan and break it down into particulars. On the Dorsai, every officer is a specialist. We Morgans, for example, tend to be primarily field officers with infantry experience. One or more of us, for example, might take the part of Donal's plan that called for infantry in the field and look at it from the standpoint of what they'd need to do that part of the overall job. They'd tell Donal what they thought would work and what wouldn't, in that area, and how much it would require and cost to do that part successfully. Meanwhile, the other specialists would be working with other parts of the plan . . . and so it'd eventually all be put together; and Donal'd have the hard figures of what it would cost him to fulfill the contract.'

'Not simple,' said Hal.

The food – everything he tasted – was very good. He found himself eating steadily and hungrily as he listened.

'Not even as simple as I make it sound, actually,' said Amanda. 'The fact it, that whole process I just told you about would have to be gone through twice, at least. Because the first figures they'd come up with would have been arrived at according to orthodox military practices; and what that would give them would only be what any responsible mercenary commander would have to charge as a bottom figure – just to break even. But then, once they had that – the competition price – they'd sit down and begin to come up with unorthodox ways of cutting the expenses they'd just figured, or ways of achieving their objective faster, until they'd end with a total that would both underbid any competitor and allow them a profit that made it worth their while to take the contract. It'd take a week or more with the pressure on each specialist there to pull rabbits out of his or her hat; and each bright new idea that was produced could force everyone else to adjust and refigure.'

'I see,' said Hal, 'and all this took place on the dining table?'

'Ninety per cent of it,' said Amanda. 'The table'd be piled halfway to the ceiling with maps, schematics, sketches, models, gadgets, notes . . . and, occasionally, food – when they'd call a break long enough to eat. And all that's only the business use for a large dining room table. It's also the place where the whole family gets together, and family decisions are made. But that's enough talk of tables. What's your preference at this one? The fish, or the mutton?'

'I can't tell you. Both.' Hal came very close to answering with his mouth full.

'That's good,' said Amanda. 'Just help yourself, then.'

'Thank you. You're really a remarkable cook.'

'Growing up in a house with a lot of people to feed every day, anyone gets good at cooking.'

'I suppose . . .' Hal thought for a second of his own solitary childhood. 'You said the Morgans were here even before the Graemes? How did the Morgans happen to come to the Dorsai?'

'The first Amanda,' this Amanda said. 'She's the answer to most questions about the family. She came from Earth in the early days when emigration to the newer worlds first became practical; and when everyone was leaving, or thinking of leaving, to make a new society somewhere.'

'What made her come to the Dorsai?'

'She didn't, at first. Her husband died shortly after they were married. His parents had power and credit; and by pulling legal strings they got her young son away from her. She stole him back, and left Earth so that they couldn't get him again. She emigrated to Newton and married a second time. When her second husband died, Jimmy – the boy – was half-grown. She took him and came to the Dorsai. She was one of the first permanent settlers on this world – the very first in this area. When she came, Foralie Town was only a sort of transitory tent-city headquarters for the out-of-work mercenaries, who were camping out in the hills around here, until they could get taken on by some outfit. . . .'

Hal ate and listened, only occasionally asking questions. It was a strange, dark unrolling of the years that she described for him; the hard times and the hard world gradually producing a people to whom honor and courage were as necessary tools for the making of their living as plow and pump might be to settlers elsewhere – a people shaped by their own history, until it finally began to be said of them, over a hundred years ago, that if they chose to fight as a unit, not all the military forces of the other worlds combined could stand against them.

It was a flamboyant statement, Hal thought now with a part of his mind, listening to Amanda. In the end, numbers and resources could not be withstood in the real universe; and against the military strengths of all the other settled worlds, combined, those of the Dorsai would not be able to win – or even hold out very long. But an odd, small truth within the statement remained. Given that the Dorsai could not win in such a confrontation, it might still be correct to say that the worlds combined would always be slow to test their strength against them. For though the fact that the Dorsai could not win or survive such a test was undeniable, the fact that they would fight against any odds, if attacked, was certain.

Gradually the history of the Morgans, which was also in a sense the history of the Dorsai itself, began to take shape for Hal. The Morgans and the Graemes had lived side by side for generations, had been born together, grew up together, and fought together, with the special effectiveness that such special closeness made possible. They were separate families, but a common people; and, as he touched the life of the Morgans from their beginnings now, in this particularly living way through the voice of Amanda, he found himself brought closer than he had ever been before to the life of Donal, to the lives of Donal's uncles, Kensie and Ian Grahame, to that of Eachan Khan Graeme – Donal's father – even to the life of Cletus Grahame, the ancestor of all of them, who had written the great multi-volume military work on strategy and tactics which had made the effectiveness of the specially-trained Dorsai soldier possible.

'– Now, is there anything else I can offer you?' The voice of Amanda, interrupting herself, brought Hal's mind back from the place into which it had wandered and almost gotten lost.

'I beg your pardon?' said Hal, then realized she was speaking about food. 'How could I eat any more?'

'Well, that's a question, of course,' said Amanda.

He stared at her, then saw the smile quirking the corners of her mouth, and woke to the fact that every serving dish on the table was empty.

'Did I eat all that?' he said.

'You did,' Amanda told him. 'How about coffee and after dinner drinks, if you want them, in the living room?'

'I . . . thank you.' He got to his feet and looked uncertainly at the empty dishes on the table.

'Don't worry about that now,' said Amanda. 'I'll clean up later.'

She got up, herself, put coffee, cups, glasses and whiskey once more on the tray she had carried back from the living room earlier. They went out of the kitchen and down the hall.

The lights in the kitchen went out, and those in the living room went on, softly, as sensors picked up the traces of bodies leaving and entering. Amanda put the tray on a low table before the fireplace and picked up a torch-staff that was leaning against the stonework there. She held it to the kindling and logs already placed. A little flame reached out from the tip of the staff and licked against the shavings under the kindling. The shavings caught. Fire ran among the kindling and along the underside of the laid logs, then blossomed up between them. Amanda leaned the staff back against the stonework.

The new light of the flames had picked out four lines of words carved into the polished edge of the thick slab of the granite mantelpiece. Hal leaned forward to read them. They were cut so deeply into the stone that shadow hid from him the actual depth of their incision.

'*The Song of the House of Fal Morgan*,' said Amanda, looking over his shoulder. 'The first verse. It's a tribute to the first Amanda. Jimmy, her son, wrote it, when he was a good-aged man.'

'It's part of a song?' Hal looked at her.

'It is,' she said.

Unexpectedly, softly, she sang the words cut in the stone. Her voice was lower-pitched than he would have thought, but it was a fine, true voice which loved singing, with strength behind the music of it.

'Stone are my walls, and my roof is of timber,
But the hands of my builder are stronger by far.
My roof may be burnt and my stones may be scattered,
Never her light be defeated in war.'

The words, sung as she had chosen to sing them, triggered off a sudden emotion in Hal so powerful that it approached pain. To cover his reaction, he turned back abruptly to the tray on the table and made a little ceremony of pouring some of the whiskey into a glass and sitting down in an armchair at one side of the fire. Amanda gave herself coffee and sat down in an identical chair facing him on the fire's other side.

'Is that all of the song?' Hal asked.

'No,' said Amanda. Self-consciously, he was aware of her watching him again, closely – and he thought – strangely. 'There're more verses.'

406

'Sometime,' he said quickly, suddenly afraid that she might sing more, and wake again whatever had momentarily touched him so deeply, 'I've got to hear those, too. But tell me – where are all the Morgans and Graemes, now? Graemehouse is empty and you're –'

'And I'm alone here,' Amanda finished the sentence for him. 'Times have changed. For the Dorsai people, life's not easy now.'

'I know,' Hal said. 'I know the Others are working to keep you from getting contracts.'

'They can't keep us from all of them,' said Amanda. 'There aren't enough of them to interfere with all the contracts we sign. But they can stop most of the big ones, the top ten per cent that brings in nearly sixty per cent of our interstellar credit. So, since times are difficult, most of us of working age are either out on the fisheries or at some other job on the Dorsai that ties in with surviving on our own resources. Others have gone off-world. A number of individuals, and even families, have emigrated.'

'Left the Dorsai?'

'Some think they don't have any choice. Others of us, of course, would never leave. But this world's always been one where any adult's free to make his own decisions, without advice or comment unless she or he asks for it.'

'Of course . . .' said Hal, hardly knowing what he was saying.

He was caught up entirely in what he had just heard. Since the hours in the cell on Harmony he had known that the time of the Splinter Cultures was over. But for the first time, with what Amanda had just told him, the knowledge hit deeply within him. The Dorsai world without the Dorsai people was somehow more unthinkable than the same thing on any of the other Younger Worlds. All at once, his mind's eye saw it deserted; its homes empty and decaying, its level lands, oceans and high mountains without the sound of human voices. His whole being tried to push the image from him; and still, in the back of his mind, the certainty of it sat like a certainty of the end of the universe. This, too, had to end; and the concept that had been built here with such labor must finally vanish with it, not to come again.

He roused himself from the feeling that had suddenly crushed him like the grip of some giant's icy hand, into a perfect silence. Across the table with the tray holding glasses, cups, coffee dispenser and whiskey decanter, Amanda still sat watching him almost oddly, as she had watched him in that first moment of their meeting.

He was conscious of something, some current of feeling that seemed to wash back and forth between them, virtually unknown to each other as they were.

'Are you all right?' he heard her ask, calmly.

'I'd kill time if I could!' he heard the words break from him without warning, shocking him with their intensity, 'I'd kill death. I'd kill anything that killed anything!'

'But you can't,' she answered, softly.

'No.' He pulled himself back to something like normal self-possession. The whiskey, he told himself – but he had drunk very little, and alcohol had always had only small power to touch him. Something else had driven him – was still driving him to speak as he just had. 'You're right. Everyone's got a right to his own decisions; and that's what creates history – decisions. The decisions are changing and the times are changing. What we were all used to is going to be put aside; and something new is going to be taking its place. I tried to tell that to some Exotics before I came here; and I thought if anyone would listen, they would.'

'But they didn't?'

'No,' he said, harshly. 'It's the one thing they can't face, time running out. It sets a limit to their search – it means that now they'll never find what they've been looking for, all this time since they called themselves the Chantry Guild, back on Earth. Strange. . . .'

'What's strange?' he heard her ask, when he did not go on.

He was staring into the dark, firelit pool of whiskey in his glass, kneading it between his hands again. He looked up from the glass at her.

'Those who ought to see what's happening – the people who could do something – refusing to see. While everyone who can't do anything about it seems to know it's there. They seem to feel it, the way animals feel a thunderstorm coming.'

'You feel it yourself, do you?' she asked. Her eyes, darker now in the firelight, still watched him, and drew him. He talked on.

'Of course. But I'm of those caught up in it,' he said. 'I've had to face up to what's happening, and will happen.'

'Tell me, then,' said Amanda's voice softly. 'What is it that's happening? And what is it that's going to happen?'

He pressed the hard shape of the whiskey glass between his hands, staring now into the flames of the fireplace.

'We're headed toward the last battle,' he said. 'That's what's happening. No, call it a last conflict, because most of it won't be a battle in the dictionary sense. But, depending on how it comes out, the race is either going to have to die or grow. I know – that sounds like something too large to believe. But we've made it that big ourselves, over the centuries. Only those in the best position to understand how it could happen, wouldn't ever look squarely at the situation. I couldn't see it myself until my nose was rubbed in it. But if you look back at what's been happening in just the last twenty or thirty standard years, you see the evidence all over the place. The Others appearing. . . .'

He talked on, almost in spite of himself. The words ran from him like dogs unleashed, and he found himself telling her about everything that he had come to understand in the cell on Harmony.

She sat quietly, asking a brief question now and then, watching him. He felt a tremendous relief in being able to uncap the pressure of that explosion of understanding. It was a pressure that had been growing steadily in him lately, as his mind developed and extended its first discoveries. His original impulse had been to do no more than sketch the situation for her; but he found himself being drawn, by the way she listened, from that to the people and things that had led him to understanding. He felt captured by her attention; and he heard his own voice going on and on as if it had developed an independent life of its own.

Once, it crossed his mind again to wonder if the Dorsai whiskey had something to do with it. But once more he rejected the idea. It had been in his first year on Coby that he had found that alcohol did not affect him in the same measure as it seemed to affect the other miners. When they had finally drunk themselves into silence and even slumber, he would be still awake and restless, so restless he had been driven to those long, solitary walks of his down the endless stone corridors. It had been as if a part of his mind had withdrawn a little farther with each step his body took toward intoxication; until he had existed apart from the moment, wrapped in a sadness and a sense of isolation that would drive him eventually out, away from the unconscious others to walk those lonely distances.

But what he was feeling now, with her, was if anything the opposite of that sense of isolation; and, in any case, there was a reasonable limit to the strength of alcoholic liquors made for the pleasure of drinking. Beyond a certain proof they were uncomfortable to the palate and throat; and that point the Dorsai whiskey, though strong, had not exceeded. Nor was the amount he had drunk at all great, measured by the meterstick of his experience. . . .

He found himself telling the third Amanda about Child-of-God, and the effect of Child's death upon his own understanding.

'. . . When I first met him,' he was saying, 'I thought he was another Obadiah – I told you about my other two tutors, didn't I? Then, as I got to know him, I began to have less and less use for him. He seemed to be a fanatic and nothing more – not able to care or feel, not interested in anything but the rules of that religion of his. But then, he was the one who spoke up when the local people wanted the Command to send me away; and for the first time I began to see a pattern to what he was; and it was larger – much larger – than I'd thought.'

'You were still young,' said Amanda.

'Yes,' he said. 'I was young. We're always young, no matter how old we are. And then, when he insisted on staying behind to slow down the Militia; and I couldn't stay with him – knew that it wasn't for me to stay with him – and that he understood that, this man I'd thought had no sensitivity, no understanding beyond the church rules he lived by, then it all opened up for me. I knew the difference between someone like him, then, and someone like Barbage, who was my jailer in that Militia cell, the man whose life I'd saved in the mountain pass. . . .'

The lights of the living room blinked once.

'Curfew,' murmured Amanda. 'We save power, nowadays, for those who most need it.'

She got to her feet. The hard fabric of her riding pants whispered lightly, leg against leg, as she stepped to the fireplace once more; and the firelight, reflecting from the polished apron of black stone before it, sent glitters of light into the small wave of her bright hair, where it clung close against the tanned skin of her neck. She lit the stubs of two large candles that stood on supports on either side of it. They looked from their thickness to have been as long as her forearm to begin with; and the stands they rested on were tall, lifting the candle flame even now above Hal's eye level as he sat in his armchair. The candles themselves seemed to be made of grayish-green, waxy-looking seeds, pressed together into sticks. As the generous flames rose from their wicks, the built-in lighting of the room dimmed itself gradually into extinction. Shadow moved in from the corners of the room, until Hal and Amanda were in a little illuminated space constructed by candlelight and firelight alone. A faint, piny odor reached Hal's nostrils.

Amanda sat down again. Even as close as she was to him, the darkness of her outdoor clothing lost itself against the shadows of her chair, so that the whiteness of her face seemed to float in a friendly gloom, watching him.

'You were telling me about someone whose life you saved in a mountain pass,' she said.

'Yes,' he said. 'Barbage's life. I didn't understand then the sort of things the Militia did to anyone from the Commands that they got their hands on; and what Barbage himself must have done to prisoners from the Commands, while he was working his way up through the ranks to Captain. And still, there wasn't anything false about him, either. He was – he is wrong. I think I know why now – but he was what he was. That's why the other Militia officers were afraid of him. I saw him face down another Militia Captain, the one time I managed to get close to their camp . . .'

He talked on. The candles burned lower; and, imperceptibly, he found he had drifted from telling her about those he had met to telling her about himself. Something within him, some small alarm sensor, was trying to catch his attention, but the force pushing him to talk was too great to be denied. Amanda hardly needed to ask questions, now; and in the end he found himself telling her about what it had been like for him when he was very young.

'. . . But what was it, specifically,' she asked, finally, 'that made you identify so with the Graemes?'

'Oh, well,' he said, staring into the fire, his mind adrift in the flame-lit darkness and carried on by the force within him, 'you've got to remember I'm an orphan. I've always been . . . isolated. I suppose I identified with Donal's isolation. You remember how when he was at the Academy, they used to speak of him as an odd boy, different from anyone else –'

– Something happened in the room. He looked up swiftly.

'I'm sorry –' he gazed at Amanda but she was exactly as she had been a moment before. The small alarm sensor was now obvious within him. Deliberately, he forced it from his consciousness. 'Did you say something?'

'No,' she answered. Her eyes were steady on his in the dimness of the room. 'Nothing.'

He tried to pick up the thread of what he had been saying.

'You see he had always been alone inside, always . . .' His voice ran down. He put his hand to his forehead, felt dampness, and took it away again. 'What was I saying?'

'You're probably tired,' Amanda leaned forward in her chair. 'You were saying Donal was always alone. But he wasn't. He married Anea of Kultis.'

'Yes, but that was his mistake. You see, he was hoping then that, after all, he could still live an ordinary life. But he couldn't. He'd been committed so early . . . it was something like the mistake Cletus made with Melissa Khan; although that was different, because all Cletus had to do was finish his book. . . .'

His thoughts slipped away from him once more. He wiped his forehead with his hand and felt the cool dampness of perspiration.

'I guess you're right,' he said. 'I guess I am tired – it's been a long day. . . .'

He was, he realized suddenly, exhausted, sodden with fatigue.

'Of course it has,' said Amanda, gently. 'I'll show you how to get to your room.'

She rose, taking one of the candles from its stand, and led the way into a corridor beyond a further doorway in the wall to the left of the fireplace. He lifted himself woodenly to his feet and walked after her.

CHAPTER FORTY-THREE

His sleep was a dead sleep, so heavy as almost to be exhausting in its own right. He roused once during the night, for only a moment, and lay there in the darkness in an unfamiliar bed, wondering where he was. Remembering, he dropped like a stone back into sleep again.

When he woke again, the bedroom in which he lay was bright with morning sunlight diffused through thin white drapes. He vaguely remembered Amanda as she had turned, candle in hand, to go back down the hall, telling him that there were two sets of window drapes to pull, the light and the heavy. Clearly, he had forgotten to pull the heavy, outer set.

But it did not matter. He sat up, swinging his naked legs over the edge of the bed. He was now up for the day; and he felt fine – except for a mild fuzziness in the head that made his surroundings seem at one remove from him. The room he was in had no lavatory facilities. He remembered something else Amanda had said, put on his pants and found his way down the hall to another door which let him into a lavatory.

Fifteen minutes later, cleaned, shaved and dressed, he walked into the kitchen of Fal Morgan. Amanda was there, seated at the round table, talking on the phone with her sister. Hal took a chair at the table to wait for the end of the conversation. The sister, seen in the screen high on the wall, was more round of face and yellow, rather than white-blond, of hair, but unmistakably a sibling. Like Amanda, she was beautiful, but the intensity Hal had noticed so clearly in Amanda was missing in this other Morgan – or, he thought, perhaps it just did not come through as well on a phone screen.

But his inner senses rejected the latter explanation. The intensity of Amanda was a unique quality, something he had felt in no other human being until now. It was beyond reason to suppose that her whole family shared it.

Amanda had been explaining that she had to take Hal to Graeme-house first before arriving as promised. Now she ended the talk, shut off the phone and looked across the table at him.

'I was just about to wake you,' she said. 'We should be going as soon as you're fed. Do you feel like having breakfast?'

Hal grinned.

'As much as it turned out I felt like having dinner,' he said. His appetite was back to normal.

'All right,' said Amanda, getting to her feet. 'Sit tight. It'll be ready in a minute.'

Fed and mounted, they started off in the morning light of Fomalhaut, a brilliant pinpoint now in the eastern sky, making the snowfields of the mountains just below it glitter like mirrors. It was a cool, clear, still morning with only an occasional cloud in view. The horses fought their bits and waltzed sideways until they were let run to the edge of the tableland on which Fal Morgan stood. At the edge of that flat stretch, however, Amanda pulled the gray under her back to a walk and Hal followed her example.

They plunged over the edge onto a steep downslope thick with variform conifers and native bush forms. The clear ground between the growths was stony and only sparsely covered with small vegetation. They rode through such gullies and alternating stretches of open mountainside for perhaps ten minutes before they came out into an area of high rolling hills covered with the brown, drying grass of late fall. Tucked back up on a high point above these hills, so that it was not visible until they came up over the crest of the slope below it, was a shelf of long, narrow land on which Graemehouse stood.

It was a house of dark timber, two-storied, but low-looking in relation to its length, that seemed to hug the slight curve of the earth on which it and its outbuildings stood. Barely a dozen meters behind it, the ground lifted suddenly in a bare, steep slope toward the mountainside above. They climbed their horses onto the shelf and approached the homestead from the side. The morning sun was ahead of them as they rode toward the buildings; and Graemehouse itself sat at an angle to their line of approach, facing south and downslope toward the lower hill area from which they had just come.

'Not as sheltered as Fal Morgan,' said Hal, almost absent-mindedly, looking at it. Amanda glanced over at him.

'It's got other advantages,' she said, 'Look here –'

She reined to her right and led the way to the edge of the shelf. Hal halted with her. From the edge they could see clear down to the river below and Foralie Town.

'With a scope up on the roof of that house,' Amanda said, 'you can keep a watch on half the local area. And that rise behind cuts off most of the snow and wind that would ordinarily bury a homestead this high up and exposed, when winter comes. Cletus Grahame knew what he was doing when he built it – for all that he called himself a scholar instead of a soldier.'

She turned away from the rim and walked her horse toward the house. Hal rode with her. At the front entrance, they dismounted and dropped their reins. The horses lowered their heads to nibble at the grass of the front lawn.

Amanda led the way to the front entrance, and put her thumb into its lock sensor. The wide, heavy, dark door there swung open. She led the way into a square entry-hall with pegs on the walls, from some of which sweaters and jackets still hung. Straight ahead was an open archway into what seemed a lounge – or, as Amanda had called the equivalent space at Fal Morgan, a living room.

The atmosphere in the house was still and empty, without being lifeless. Amanda turned to Hal.

'I'll leave you now,' she said. 'I'll be back either right around noon, or shortly after. In the meantime, if I get delayed and you want something to eat or drink, the kitchen and storage rooms are at the west end of the house, to your left. Help yourself to whatever's there – that's how we do things here. I don't suppose I need to tell you to clean up after yourself.'

'No,' said Hal. 'But I'll probably just wait to eat with you.'

'Don't hold back out of politeness,' she said. 'The food and drink are there to be used by whoever in this house needs them. You'll also find phones in most of the rooms. My sister's married name is Debigné. Just code for the directory and call me if you need to.'

'Thanks again,' said Hal. A certain awkwardness of feeling came over him. 'I appreciate your trusting me this way, leaving me here alone.'

Her curiously intent gaze held him. Once more, he felt the strange wash of feeling between them.

'I think the house'll be safe enough,' she said; and turned toward the door. 'I'll be back in a few hours.'

'All right,' said Hal.

She went out.

He was left alone in the crystalline stillness of the untenanted home. After a moment, he went into the living room.

It was a large, dark-panelled room, larger than its equivalent at Fal Morgan. The long shape of the house required it to be rectangular rather than square; and there was probably comfortable seating space in it for as many as thirty people. Up to fifty could probably be gathered here, if necessary. Its north wall was nothing but windows, the room-wide drapes upon them drawn back now to the daylight, giving a view of the steep slope behind the house. There would be sensors, he thought, to pull these drapes back each morning, part of the automatic machinery that would manage the purely physical establishment through daylight and dark, summer heat and winter cold, in the absence of its people.

The east wall, to his right, was pierced by a single entrance to what appeared to be a long hallway. The wall itself had only one object on its sober panelling. A full-length, life-size portrait of a man standing, dressed in an old-fashioned military uniform that could have been worn only on Earth, two hundred or more standard years ago. The man was very erect, tall, slim and middle aged. He wore a gray mustache, sharply waxed to points, which ruled out the possibility that it was a picture of Cletus Grahame. Of course, thought Hal, it would not be Cletus. It was a picture of Eachan Khan, the father of Melissa Khan, who had been the wife of Cletus; and from what he remembered about the family, Cletus himself had done the painting. The archaic uniform would be the one Eachan Khan had worn as a general officer in the Afghanistani forces, before he and Melissa had emigrated from Earth.

The south wall, straight ahead of Hal, showed nothing but its panelling, with the entrance from the entry hall in the center of it. The west wall, on his left, had entrances at each end of it. The nearest of these opened on stairs rising to the floor above, with beyond them a hallway which must lead to the kitchen Amanda had mentioned; and the further entrance, lit by the sunlight from the windows in the adjacent north wall, was obviously the entrance to the dining room. He could even see a corner of the dining table Amanda had spoken of, when he had commented on the size of the one at Fal Morgan.

The shortened wallspace between these two entrances was almost entirely occupied by a wide and deep fireplace built of a gray-black granite, including the long and heavy mantelpiece over it; carved into the thick edge of the mantelpiece where the verse had been cut at Fal Morgan was a shield shape, showing three scallop shells upon it. Above the mantelpiece hung a sword in a silver-metal scabbard, as antique as the uniform in the picture of the wall across from it, and plainly also an original possession of Eachan Khan.

Hal sat down in one of the large overstuffed armchairs. The silence of the house around him pressed in on him. He had come here, he had told himself, because he had felt himself unready to speak to the representatives of the Dorsai. Not unready to deliver the message the Exotics had sent with him, but unready to give the Dorsai people his own words, in terms that would make them listen and understand.

How much of this was simple lack of confidence after his failure on Mara, he did not know. He had gone into the meeting with Nonne, Padma and the rest, taking it for granted that they must understand him. He had never felt that sureness where the Dorsai were concerned; and Foralie had drawn him aside from his earlier planned destination like the magnetic North of Earth swinging about to itself the point of a compass needle. The decision to come here first had been born from the moment he had seen this blue and white, ocean-girt world mirrored in the vision screen of his stateroom aboard ship.

Sitting now in the silent living room, it seemed to him as if he could feel the house speaking to him. There was something here that picked him up, body, mind and soul, and held him in a way that was very nearly eerie. As he sat, he could feel the short hairs on the back of his neck lifting and an electric chill starting at the base of his skull and spreading downward, along his spine and across his shoulders. The house pulled at some ancient strings anchored deep within him. A soundless voice called him; and he rose slowly in answer from his chair, and turned to the corridor leading back to the kitchen.

He went down the corridor. It took six paces to traverse, and it was clear within him that he had known it would take that many and no more. It was a little more than twelve meters in length. There were no openings off it until he stepped from its further end into the kitchen. Like the kitchen at Fal Morgan, it was large, perhaps even larger than Amanda's. Like that one, also, another doorway in the wall to his right led into the dining room, giving a glimpse of its end, opposite the one he had seen from the living room.

The corridor he had just come down had paralleled the dining room's length.

In the kitchen here as well, the panelling was dark, unlike that at Fal Morgan, and the kitchen table was not round but octagonal. It was also larger than the one he and Amanda had sat at that morning. But in all important ways, it was a room like its counterpart at Fal Morgan.

He stood for a moment. There was nothing in particular to see, but the intense, high-altitude sunlight beat through the windows to his left and the dark wood of the walls drank up the illumination. There was nothing to hear; but to his imagination it seemed he could almost hear a hum of voices that had soaked, like time, into the panelling, and was now sounding just below his auditory threshold. The unheard sound brought back to him a feeling of the people, now dead and gone, who had sat here living and told each other of their doings and their thoughts.

He stood, feeling the minutes slip past him like stealthy sentinels returning to their posts, until with an effort he broke free and moved across the room to a door let into the north wall of the kitchen. The door opened at a touch and he stepped into the daylight of the morning and the backyard of Graemehouse. Around him and off to his left were the outbuildings that had been hidden by the bulk of the house on his approach, the stable, the stores buildings, the barn and – closest of all – that building that on the Dorsai he knew was customarily called the fieldhouse.

He walked across the short distance of stony and sunlit earth. The fieldhouse was unlocked and he let himself in. It was an unpartitioned building as wide as Graemehouse and almost as long. Its height was greater. Above its walls, the roof arched to a full two stories over the pounded earth of the floor. There were no windows in the walls, but skylights in the arched roof let sunlight down to fill the air of the interior with dancing motes of dust. It was a place for winter exercise; and as Hal knew, it could be heated, but barely to above the freezing point.

Now, it was not yet the season for artificial heat. The sunlight streaming down from the skylight warmed the interior air to a summer temperature; and Hal felt himself touched once more by the ghosts of sounds. To this building Donal Graeme would have come as soon as his infant legs could carry him, following the older members of the family. He would have tottered his unsteady way along the temporary winter passageways set up between the house and the outbuildings to give a weather-protected route. To the young child this building would at first have seemed enormous; and the activities of his elders here magical and frustrating, involving elements of balance, strength and speed that his very young body was not mature enough to imitate.

But he would have tried to imitate, regardless. He would have tried to turn in swift, flowing movement, as his elders turned, to run as they ran, and to struggle in the fashion they struggled with each other in their unarmed practice bouts; and he would have demanded also that they pretend to go through the motions of these activities with him, as they did with each other. By the time he had been five years old, his movements would have begun to resemble theirs, even if more slowly and clumsily.

The memory of that young bright time, in which he had been an instinctive part of his people and thought of himself as no different from them, would have been something Donal would have looked back on often from the standpoint of his later years . . . Hal turned suddenly, and walked on through the fieldhouse, to let himself out by a further door.

Outside, he paused for a second, then turned to go through the other outbuildings, which were also not locked. The interiors of these revealed themselves as clean, neat, and in most cases still stored and fitted with what they would have contained if the house was occupied; but while there was an echo from them of lives lived down the generations, they did not produce the strong effect on him that the house and the fieldhouse had. He was of half a mind to turn back again to the house itself, when he saw a final building that was the stables, with a stand of willows beyond, all but hidden by the stables' bulk. He went forward, stepped through the door into the half-gloom within, and all that he had felt before came back.

Once again, something closed about him and the hair on the back of his neck stood up. The stalls on either side of the central aisle before him were empty. He looked down to bales of hay, neatly stacked at the far end, and that which he had come here to meet stood at last face to face with him.

For a long moment he stood, breathing the dusty, clean-stable odor of the structure; and then he turned and went once more out the door. He turned right and went down along the further length of the stables' outside wall, turned the corner at the end and saw, under the long, gently-downreaching limbs of the willows, the white-painted picket fence that enclosed the private graves of those who had lived here.

For a moment he stopped, only looking at it; and then he went forward to it.

There was a small gate in the fence. He opened it, went through and closed it softly behind him. Each grave had an upright headstone of gray rock the color of the mountains looking down on him. On and between the grave plots the grass was neatly cut. There was space to walk between the graves and the headstones all faced to his left, six across in orderly ranks. He turned to his right and went to the head of the graveyard, where the older plots were.

There he paused, looking down at the names cut in the upright stones. Eachan Murad Khan . . . Melissa Gray Khan Grahame . . . Cletus James Grahame . . . he moved down the ranks . . . Kamal Simon Graeme . . . Anna Outbond Graeme. On his right, Mary Kenwick Graeme and Eachan Khan Graeme, with a single headstone for their graves that lay side by side with no space separating them.

His step faltered. Then he took one more stride forward and looked down. On his right again, Ian Ten Graeme . . . Leah Sary Graeme . . . and Kensie Alan Graeme. Furthest from him, Kensie's grave lay against the far line of the picket fence, so close to the willows there that the branches had grown down until they lightly swept the grassy surface of his grave with their tips, like fingers gently stroking in the little air that stirred about Hal as he stood watching. And in the next rank beyond the graves of Ian and Leah and Kensie were three more identically cut gravestones. His step hesitated again.

Then he stepped forward, turned and looked down. Under the willows beyond Kensie's grave, but untouched by them as his uncle's grave had been touched, was a plot with the name of Donal Evan Graeme upon it. Next to it was the grave of Mor Kamal Graeme, and next to Hal, himself, so close that the toes of his boots almost touched the edge of it, was a stone with the name upon it of James William Graeme. . . .

He could not weep. In the cell, pared thin by fever, exhaustion and the struggle to breathe, he had wept. But here, nearly a century later and in a grown body, he could not. Only his throat clenched painfully and a coldness began to grow in him – not the electric coldness now of the back of the neck and shoulders, but the different, indestructible, unyielding coldness deep in the center of him, spreading out to stain his whole body within. In his mind he felt the powerful arms of his uncle around him once more, heard the voice of Kensie calling on him to come back, come back. . . .

He came back. The coldness went and he turned away from the graves. He went out by the little gate in the picket fence, closing it quietly behind him, and started back up to the house.

He reentered the kitchen door through which he had emerged. It latched softly and he looked at his chronometer. Time had passed. The figures on it now showed less than an hour to noon, the time at which Amanda was due to return.

He went back down the corridor from the kitchen to the living room. Now that he had entered the house for the second time, he felt a difference in his response to it. It was no longer a place in which he was a stranger; and every part of it seemed to have a latent power to kindle emotions in him. The sights and echoes of it were familiar, and the living room, when he came to it, enclosed him like a place well remembered.

He turned his attention to the rest of the building. The stairs off the living room led to bedrooms upstairs, but the bedroom toward which he now felt impelled was down on this level. The corridor opposite the one to the kitchen and leading toward the east end of the house went only a short distance before making a forty-five degree turn to the left for an even shorter distance, then turned back again to its original direction, to run approximately down the center line of the house.

In the left hand wall of the small cross-corridor there was a doorway into a room which was adjacent to the living room he had just left. Hal stepped through the doorway into a library, almost as long and wide as the living room itself. A large writing table of very dark, polished wood stood in one corner near the far windows. As with the living room, the north wall was almost all glass, and the outside daylight lit the shelves of reading cubes and old-fashioned volumes. Low on one shelf near the windows was a long row of tall books, bound in a dark brown leather. Hal walked across to them and saw that they were bound manuscript copies of the volumes of Cletus Grahame's work on Strategy and Tactics. He ran his finger along their spines, but did not disturb them from their quiet order.

He turned and left the room.

Interior lighting went on, down the long leg of the corridor beyond, as he moved through the remaining downstairs part of the house. This section was nearly half of the total building; and the first doors he passed opened on bedrooms to his left, and workrooms like offices to his right. Then the workrooms ended, giving way to bedrooms on both sides. He counted six bedrooms and four offices before the corridor ended at last at a combined master bedroom and office, that took up the full width of that end of the house.

Coming back from the master bedroom, he found the room that

would have been Donal's. Biographies written after Donal's death had identified it as the third back from the master bedroom. Of course. Hal thought, it would be this far back, and this small. The youngest of the family and those ill almost always had the rooms closest to the master bedroom; they would be moved farther from it as the larger, double bedrooms became vacant closer to the living room, through the death or departure of their occupants. Donal had been the youngest in the household at the time he had left home to go out on his first contract; and he had never returned.

It was a very small room, a closet-like space for a single occupant, in contrast to the bedrooms closer to the living room, which were usually occupied by married members of the family. Many other young Graemes would have owned this room since Donal. Neither the furniture nor any object within it could be counted on to have been in his possession during the years of his growing-up.

Nonetheless, Hal stood, gazing about, and the lighter, earlier chill took him again, spreading from neck to shoulders. The walls here were the walls remembered; and the view through these windows of the steep slope guarding the back of Graemehouse was as it had been.

He put out one hand to touch the wood-panelled wall, worn by the cleanings of years to a silky smoothness; and stood, fingertips against the vertical surface, gazing out at the slope seen so many times in the years of Donal's growing up, reaching . . . reaching. For a long moment he stayed as he was; and a fragment of the poem he had written in the Final Encyclopedia came without warning, to him . . .

Within the ruined chapel, the full knight
Woke from the coffin of his last-night's bed;
And clashing mailed feet on the broken stones –
Strode to the shattered lintel and looked out . . .

Then it was as if a wind that was purely of the mind blew through the room and he was suddenly made part of a whole – himself, the wall, and the slope outside, all welded together – caught up in one moment of experience no different from another such moment known many times by the one to whom he reached.

I am here, he thought.

The chill grew, spreading out to take over his whole body. The hair rose again on the back of his neck; and a soundless shrilling, as if the very temporal structure of the moment was in vibration, commenced and mounted swiftly, in and about him, as his identity with the man who had lived here came finally, fully into existence in his mind. He stood – as Donal – in the room; and he looked out – as Donal – on the scene beyond the bedroom window.

CHAPTER FORTY-FOUR

As abruptly as it had arrived, the moment was gone, leaving him unsure that it had ever been. His hand dropped from the wall; and a moment later, when he lifted it to his forehead, he felt the skin there chilled and damp, as if half the strength in him had just been drained away by a massive effort.

For a moment he continued to stand in the room. Then he turned and went back out into the corridor; and turned again toward the living room. Going up the corridor, the drained feeling was strong within him and he recognized its kinship, much greater, but like, to the emptiness and fatigue that had always followed upon the making of a poem that had come suddenly and unexpectedly to life within him, a reaction from the violence of a massive inner effort that had left him forever changed.

But with a poem, he told himself, he had always been left with something accomplished, something solid to hold that he had not had before. While in this case . . . but, even as he thought this, he realized that something had also been accomplished here. A change had taken place in him, so that now he was seeing the house about him with a difference.

Now, as he looked about him, there was a quality of familiarity that lay like a patina on everything at which he looked. As he stepped into the living room, the face of Eachan Khan in the portrait had become one he knew intimately, in all details. With the sword above the fireplace, his fingers and palm seemed to recall the grasp of its hilt, and his mind's eye saw the sudden flash and glitter of its blade, as it was drawn from its scabbard. All about him the rest of the room echoed and reechoed a similar sense of recognition.

He sank into the chair in which he had seated himself when he had first arrived; and sat there, feeling his strength slowly returning to refill the emptiness left by his last coldness at the graveside. All around him, now, the house vibrated with the silent noises of its past. He sat listening to them; and after a while an impulse brought him up out of the chair to his feet. He walked to the corner of the room where the last panel of the east wall touched the windowed north wall. The wood surface was a polished blank before him; but an impulse moved him to put the palm of his right hand flat upon it; and it moved easily, sliding to the right to open a tall, narrow entrance directly from the living room into the library.

He stood, gazing into the opening. He remembered now, hearing it spoken of by Malachi in the stories the old man had told him of Graemehouse. There had been talk of this doorway – and something special about it. For a moment he could not recall just what that was, and then it came back to him. This was the place in which the young Graemes had measured their height as they were growing up.

He looked at the left post of the doorway, from which the panel had slid back. Plain there, now that he gave his attention to it, were thin, neat, dark lines with initials and dates beside them. Looking down, he found Donal's initials, close to the floor, but none any higher than would indicate a measurement had been taken after he had been about five years of age.

Donal had been the smallest among the adult male Graemes of his time. Once he had become conscious of this, it would not have been surprising if the boy had avoided further measurement. Hal looked at the doorway. The patina of recognition lay heavily upon it also, and he remembered something more, how Malachi had told him that in all their generations, none of the Graeme family had ever filled that doorway from top to bottom and side to side, except the twins – Donal's uncles, Ian and Kensie. Hal stared at the doorway with its years of markings; and an emotion compounded of something like fear, mixed with a strange, strong longing moved in him. Ian and Kensie had been outsize, even for Dorsai – and it was Ian he imagined now, dark and massive, standing in the doorway, filling it.

It was foolish to think of measuring himself against the marks here, even in the privacy of this moment that no one else need know about. But the desire grew in him as he stood, until it was undeniable.

The logical front of his mind tried to push the notion aside. There was no real purpose to it. In any case, size alone meant nothing. On the fourteen worlds there must be no end of individuals not only big enough to fill the doorway, but too large to fit themselves into it. But the logical arguments had no strength. It was not a question of his size that was pulling him forward to measure himself, it was part of that same search for Donal in the small bedroom.

He shook off the last objection. What summoned him was only a part of what he had come to Foralie to do. He stepped into the doorway and stood erect there.

With a sudden, cold shock, he felt the underside of the frame's top rail come hard against the top of his head. He stayed as he was, unmoving. For a second his mind denied the implication of that contact with his scalp. He had been aware for years that his eventual height would be far above ordinary. He had even come to take for granted in recent years his looking down at other people. But still, inside him, he shrank from a reality in which his height was also the height of Ian Graeme. The Ian of his imagination had for so long towered like a giant above all others, that for a moment he would not accept what the doorway told him.

Slowly, acceptance came; and only after it had, did he realize that, while he had felt the top rail with his head, he had felt no corresponding touch of the vertical members of the frame against his shoulders. Looking right and left, now, he saw that four to six centimeters of space showed between the shoulder welts of his jacket and the stiles of the doorframe on either side of him. Granted that he still might grow and put on weight, it was hardly likely he could make up that much difference in shoulder width. Ridiculously, a feeling of pure relief woke in him. He was not ready – not yet – to try to be an Ian.

He stepped back out of the doorway. As if its sensors had been only waiting for his leaving, the door slid closed and the wall was whole once more. He turned back to the living room. With the moment of his identification with Donal in the bedroom, his awareness had heightened. But now with his measurement of himself in the doorway, that awareness had been raised near to a point of pain.

The scent of the air in his nostrils, the colors, the shapes, the sounds and echoes of the house as he had moved about it – the light from the windows and the interior lights of the long corridor past the offices and bedrooms – all these had finally built a connection between him and those who also once moved about here; and he finally now felt that, like them, he belonged to the house.

There was no miracle to it. He knew that all he had achieved here so far was humanly quite possible. His recreation of Donal and the others to the point where he literally felt their presence about him was within what he knew of the capability of the human mind and imagination. But nonetheless it felt as if he teetered on the border of something far more awesome; a step beyond the possible into some area where no one had gone before.

He shivered. With the heightened sensitivity had come a clarity of mind that also was close to painful; and with that clarity in him he now identified the one part of the house he had been unconsciously avoiding all this time. The dining room, Amanda had told him, was the area of a Dorsai house where decisions were made, not merely business decisions, but family ones as well. Remembering this, his mind turned him at last toward the dining room, knowing that, if anywhere, he would find there the greatest locus of Donal's being and purpose.

He took a step toward it. But a fear stopped him. He checked himself and sat down in one of the living room's chairs. Sitting, he gazed at the entrance before him, trying to understand the faceless, but very real, terror that had flared at the instant of his decision to go in.

He reached out to grapple with it, as Walter had taught him. Consciously, he made the almost physical effort needed to put emotion apart from him. In his mind he made himself visualize what he feared, as a formless shape standing a little distance from him. Having given it form, he considered it. In itself, it was not important. It was only its effect on him that was important. But to understand that effect, he must understand what it was; and what was it?

It was not the room, itself, nor the thought of what he might find there. It was that irrevocable thing that the finding of it might do to him, that he feared. To enter the dining room in his present state of sensitivity could be finally to discover what part of him was himself and what was Donal. And if he should come to know what he feared to know . . .

. . . He might find himself committed to something from which there would be no drawing back. Perhaps, before him was that boundary of which all men and women were instinctively afraid – the boundary between the possible and the impossible; and if so, once into the impossible he might belong to it forever.

It was an old fear, he understood suddenly; one not merely old to him, but old in humankind. It was the fear of leaving the safeness of the known to cross into the darkness of the unknown, with all the unimaginable dangers that might wait there. And there was, he realized now, only one counter to it – equally old. The great urge to continue, no matter what, to grow and adventure, to discover and learn.

Understanding this at last, he understood for the first time that the commitment he had feared just now was one that he had already made for himself, long since. Faced with the choice of entering the unknown, he was one who would always go forward. Like a messenger, a few lines from a poem by Robert Browning returned to him, out of the depths of memory:

> . . . *they stood, ranged along the hillsides, met*
> *To view the last of me, a living frame*
> *For one more picture! In a sheet of flame*
> *I saw them and I knew them all. And yet*
> *Dauntless the slug-horn to my lips I set,*
> *And blew.* 'Childe Roland to the Dark Tower came.'

The path he had chosen for himself had led him to the cell on Harmony. And the path he had chosen for himself there had led to this house, this room and this moment. He got to his feet and walked across the living room and into it.

Within, the long, silent chamber was in dimness. Here, unlike in those other rooms he had entered, automatic sensors had not pulled the drapes back from the windows. Nor did the drapes pull back as he entered now. They were of heavy but soft cloth, a light brown in color, and the white daylight of Fomalhaut did not so much shine through them as make them glow softly, so that the room seemed caught in a luminous, amber twilight.

In that twilight the long, empty slab of the table and the upright, carved chairs ranked on both sides, with one only at the top end by the kitchen entrance, gleamed in a wood so dark a brown as to be almost black. The ceiling was lower than that of the living room, and beamed, so that the very air of the place, enclosed and populated by stillness, seemed even more hushed and timeless than that in the rest of the house.

On the long wall opposite the windows was the only active color in the dining room. Spaced along it at regular intervals were six small, archaic two-dimensional pictures in narrow frames, showing outdoor scenes; and, offset behind the single chair at the head of the table, to Hal's left as he looked at them, was the entrance from the kitchen.

The light and stillness of the place seemed to flow about Hal, enclosing him from the rest of the house. *All else may alter*, the dining room seemed to say, *I have not changed in two hundred years*. He stepped forward and walked slowly down the wall side of the table, pausing to look at the small framed pictures as he passed.

They were scenes variously showing mountain, lake, glen and seashore, in reproductions which must be as old as Eachan Khan's memory of such places. And they were of Earth. The colors of land and sky, the relationships of slope and level were of the kind that was to be found nowhere else. A thousand tiny, subtle details authenticated the origin of what each represented. For a moment they recalled memories of Hal's that had not come to his mind for a long time; and he felt a sudden, intense homesickness for the Rocky Mountains he remembered from his own youth.

But then the feeling was gone, washed away by the power of the emotion that came from all that surrrounded him. It was an emotion stained into walls and floor, chairs and table, and most of all into those pictures on the wall – the emotion of a family that had lived and died according to its own private code for more than two hundred years. There had been a saying that Malachi had quoted to Hal once when he had been very young – that the Dorsai, more than any other world, was its people. Not its wealth, or its power, or its reputation – but its people. Here, in this long, silent room, that saying stood forward from his memory to confront him.

As those of this family would have stood. Hal walked slowly to the head of the table and stood a little back from the corner of it, there, looking down its length. They had all sat here, at one time or another, since these walls had first been raised. Those whose names he had seen on the gravestones – Eachan Khan, Melissa and Cletus

425

Grahame, Kamal Graeme; Eachan, who had been the father of Donal, Mor – Donal's brother; James, Kensie and Ian – his uncles; Leah – Ian's wife; Simon, Kamal and James – Ian's sons . . . and others.

Including Donal.

Donal would have sat here often before the night of his graduation from the Academy, the night before he was to leave under his first contract. But that one night, after dinner, for the first time, he would have joined those others in the family who had already made their outgoing; those who had left the planet of their birth under contract to fight for other people they did not know. For the first time, then, he would have felt himself one with these older relatives who had already achieved what he had privately feared was beyond any strength and skill he would ever manage. That evening, for the first time, the door to the fourteen worlds would have seemed to stand open to him; and he would have looked through it, and on those beside him, with new eyes.

Hal moved slowly up past the pictures to the head of the table and stood behind the single chair there, looking back down the room. The night before Donal's leaving, who would have been here at Foralie of those who had gone out to the other worlds?

Kamal Khan Graeme – but he would not have been with the rest at the table. By the time of Donal's outgoing, he was confined to his bed. Eachan, of course, who had been home since his right leg had been so badly wounded that field command was no longer practical for him. Hal tried to remember who else might have been here; and, slowly as if of their own accord, the names swam up to the surface of his memory. Ian and Kensie had been home then. And Mor, Donal's oldest brother, had been home on leave from the Friendlies. James had died at Donneswort seven years before.

So . . . there had been five of them at the table after dinner that night. The unchanging twilight of the room about Hal seemed to thicken. Eachan would have been here, at the head of the table – in the chair before Hal. Ian and Kensie, as the two next senior, would normally each have taken the first chair on either side, at Eachan's elbows. But the twins always sat side by side – this night they had sat on Eachan's left, out of the habit of years, with a wall at their backs and both entrances in view. At Eachan's right, then, would have been Mor; and in the chair next to Mor, then . . .

Hal left his station at the head of the table and moved down to stand behind the second chair on Eachan's right, the one Donal would have occupied.

He focused mind and eyes together, rebuilding the scene in his mind. Gazing at the empty chairs, he filled them with the images of the men whose pictures he had seen in the books about Donal. Eachan, tall and gaunt, now that he could not be as physically active

426

as he had been – so that his shoulders looked abnormally wide above the rest of his body, and below the dark, lean face. The face with the deep parentheses around the mouth and the frown-line born of chronic, unmentioned pain deep between his black, level brows.

Ian and Kensie, alike as mirror images – but unmistakably different, with the inner characters that altered their whole appearance. Kensie bright, and Ian dark; both of them taller even than Eachan and Mor and with the massiveness of working muscle that Eachan had lost. Mor, leaner than both his uncles, smooth-faced and younger, but with something lonely and hungry in his dark eyes.

And Donal . . . half a head shorter than Mor, and even slimmer, with the double difference of greater youth and smaller boning, so that he looked like a boy among men at this table.

Eachan, leaning with his forearms on the table, Ian upright and grim, Kensie laughing easily as he always laughed. Mor leaning forward, eager to speak. And Donal . . . listening to them all.

The talk would have been of business, of working conditions for professional soldiers on the worlds they had last left to come home. Ordinary shop talk, but with an ear to Donal, so that they could inform him without directly seeming to give him advice . . .

The sound of their voices had run and echoed off the beams overhead, fast and slow. Statement and response. Pause and speak again.

'. . . The lusts are vampires,' Eachan had said. 'Soldiering is a pure art . . .'

'. . . Would you have stayed home, Eachan,' Mor had asked his father, 'when you were young and had two good legs?'

'Eachan's right,' it was Ian speaking. 'They still dream of squeezing our free people up into one lump and them negotiating with that lump for the force to get the whip hand on all the other worlds. That's the danger . . .'

'As long as the Cantons remain independent of the Council,' said Eachan . . .

'Nothing stands still,' said Kensie.

And with those last three words the whiskey they had been drinking had seemed to go to Donal's head in a rush; and to him it seemed that the table and the dark, harsh-boned faces he watched seemed to swim in the dimness of the dining room and Kensie's voice came roaring at him from a great distance.

About Hal the room was filling with others, other Graemes from before and since, taking the other chairs at the table, joining in the talk, so that the voices rose and mingled, the atmosphere of the room thickened . . . and then, abruptly, the after-dinner gathering was over. They were all standing up, to go to their beds ready for an early start in the morning. The room was full of tall bodies and deep voices; and his head spun.

427

He had to get out, himself. He was very close to something that had now picked him up and was carrying him away, faster and faster, so that soon he would be beyond the power of his strength to get free. He turned toward what he thought was the living room entrance to the dining room, but which he could no longer see for the shapes all around him. He pushed his way between them, stumbling, feeling his strength go. But he could not see the entrance and he did not have the strength to turn and go back the other way –

Strong arms caught him, held him and steered him, on unsteady feet through a mist of wraiths. Suddenly there was fresh air on his face, a breeze blowing against him. His right foot tripped on a downstep and dropped to a yielding surface, and the arms holding him brought him to a halt.

'Breathe deeply,' commanded a voice. 'Now – again!'

He obeyed; and slowly his vision cleared to show him earth and mountains and sky. He was standing on the grass, just outside the front door of Graemehouse; and it was Amanda who was upholding him.

CHAPTER FORTY-FIVE

'I'd better get you home,' Amanda had said.

Dazed and numbed, he had not objected. The sensation had lasted through most of their ride back to Fal Morgan, so that he remembered little of it. Only when they were nearly to Fal Morgan did his head clear and he became conscious of the fact that he felt hollowly weak; drained as if by some emergency physical effort that had taken all his strength.

'I'm sorry,' he said to Amanda, when he had stumbled at last into the living room of Fal Morgan, 'I didn't mean to be a problem. I just seem to be knocked out . . .'

'I know,' she said. Her eyes were steady on him, almost grim, and unfathomable. 'Now, you need rest.'

She turned him about like a child and steered him down the hall, into the room he had used the night before and to a seat on the edge of the bed. Hal did not see her signal the sensors, but the drapes came together over the windows and the room dropped into semi-darkness.

'Sleep now,' said Amanda's voice clearly out of the gloom.

He heard the door close. He was still sitting on the edge of the bed, but now he fell back. Chilled, he turned on his side and reached out to pull over him the heavy quilt that topped the bedding, then fell instantly asleep.

He did not wake until the following morning. Pulling himself out of bed, he dressed and went in search of Amanda. He found her in an office off the living room, at a desk stacked with what appeared to be bound printouts of contracts. She was gazing at a screen inset in the desk surface, stylus in hand, apparently making corrections on what was being shown her on the screen. She lifted her head as he looked in.

'Come along,' she said; and he came in. 'How do you feel?'

'Wobbly,' he said. In fact, he felt as if he had hardly slept at all since dismounting from his horse after the ride back from Foralie.

'Sit down, then,' she said; and herself laid down the stylus she had been holding.

He dropped gratefully into an overstuffed chair. She eyed him keenly.

'You'll have to be quiet for a few days,' she said. 'What can I do for you?'

'Tell me how to arrange for some transportation back to Omalu,' he said. 'I've imposed on you long enough, here.'

'I'll tell you when you've imposed,' Amanda said. 'As far as Omalu goes, you're in no shape to go anywhere.'

'I've got to go,' he said. 'I've things to do there. I've got to go about seeing whoever it is that represents the Dorsai.'

'You want the Grey Captains.'

He stared at her.

'Who?'

She smiled.

'It's an old term,' she said. 'Grey spelled with a "e," incidentally. I don't think anyone knows where it came from, originally. It was back in Cletus' day we stopped using the term Captain as a military rank anywhere but on spaceships. What the name's come to mean here is someone who's a leader, confirmed and accepted, a woman or man other people trust – and trust to make decisions. The first and second Amanda were Grey Captains.'

'And the third?' He looked at her.

'Yes. The third, too,' she said, unsmiling. 'The point is, though, that it's the Grey Captains you want to talk to; and they aren't usually in Omalu. They're wherever they live on the Dorsai.'

'Then I've got to go talk to them individually and get them to agree to get together so I can talk to them all at once.'

She watched him for several seconds without speaking.

'If you were in shape,' she said at last, slowly, 'which you're not, that'd still be the wrong way to go about it. As it is, right now you're not up to talking to anyone. The first thing you do is get your feet back under you – and that means about a week.'

He shook his head.

'Not that long,' he said.

'That long.'

'In any case,' he put his arms on the arms of the chair, ready to get up, 'this can't wait –'

'Yes, it can.'

'You don't understand.' His hands fell away from the arms of the chair. 'To begin with, I've got an important message for the Dorsai people generally, from the Exotics. But, even more important, I've got to talk to these Captains, myself. There's something I've got to make them understand – that what we're headed into may destroy everything the Dorsai's stood for, and most of everything else . . . I don't know how to make you understand –'

'You already have,' she said.

He stared at her with the uneasy feeling that matters were being rushed upon him.

'The first night you were here.' She watched him, unwaveringly, and there was no end to the turquoise depths of her eyes. 'You told me all about it.'

'All about it?' he said. 'All?'

'I think, all,' she said. There was that several second pause, again, as he eyes watched him. 'I know what you need done; and I know – which you don't – the way to do it. Before you can meet with the Grey Captains, they're all going to have to come together at some place. That place might as well be Foralie.'

'Foralie?' He stared at her.

'Why not?' she said. 'It's got the space to handle a meeting that size and it's not being used right now.'

She stopped speaking and sat watching him. He did not say anything for a moment, himself. There was a cold feeling inside him at the thought of his speaking to these people in Graemehouse and for a moment he almost forgot she was there. Then his mind and his eyes came back to her, to find her still watching.

'I can call the Captains for you; and get some help from around the district, here,' she said, 'if it's needed to take care of the situation. It shouldn't take more than a day, unless some of them need to stay overnight before starting home.'

He hesitated.

'You could suggest they come?' he said. 'And you think they'd come?'

'Yes.' It was a blunt statement. 'They'll come.'

'I can't –' words failed him.

'Can't what? Can't impose?' She smiled a little. 'It's for our benefit, isn't it?'

'It is . . .' he said. 'Of course. Still . . .'

'Then it's settled,' she said. 'I'll send the word out to the ones who should be here. Meanwhile, you can get rested up. You need a week.'

'How long does it take to get them together?' he asked, still with the uneasy feeling that matters were being rushed upon him.

'Six hours in an emergency,' she looked at him almost coldly. 'In the case of something like this where there's no emergency, at the very least a week to find a time when most of them can get together. In a week you ought to be able to talk to at least two-thirds of them.'

'Only two-thirds?' he said. 'Is two-thirds enough?'

'If you can convince most of the two-thirds,' she answered, 'you'll have no trouble carrying most of the full number in the long run. Each one is going to make up his own mind; but they're all sensible people. If they hear sense most of them will listen to it and pass it on to their own people.'

'Yes,' he said. He was still unsure about all that she had said; but this talk, mild as it had been, had exhausted him.

'Then I'll take care of it.' She looked keenly at him. 'Can you fix

431

yourself something to eat? I've got my hands full at the moment.'

'Of course,' he said.

She smiled for a second and her face was transformed. Then she was level-mouthed, level-eyed, all business again.

'All right, then,' she said, picking up her stylus again, and turning her attention back to the screen in her desk. 'Don't hesitate to call if you need me.'

He stood looking at her for a second more. There was something odd here. When he had first come, she had been a friendly stranger, polite but open. Now, she was at once much closer and at the same time walled off from him – encased in some armor of her own. He turned and went off to the kitchen, conscious of the rubberiness of his legs and the labor of moving his body along the passageway with them.

He ate and immediately was avaricious for sleep again. He went back to his bedroom and fell on the bed, rousing later, briefly, to eat and sleep once more.

Amanda had been right. It was almost a full three days before he began to feel like himself again. It began to look as if the week until the Grey Captains could be gathered together would be welcome to him after all.

It was a different weakness that had gripped him, this time. Undoubtedly, the remnants of the physical attrition he had endured on Harmony were still with him. Nonetheless, the essential nature of his exhaustion right now did not seem merely physical, but something more – something he considered labelling with the word psychic, then drew back from the term.

What was undeniable was that what had done this to him was the purely non-physical experience in Graemehouse; and his mind, which could never leave anything alone, but was forever digging at things and taking them apart to find out how they worked, would not get off the subject of what had happened to him in the dining room.

There were all sorts of possible explanations.

One that stood up to examination was that he had found exactly what he had gone looking for – an understanding of the Graemes in general, and Donal in particular, so intense that for a moment he had been able, subjectively, at least, to relive an episode out of Donal's life. But there was another one that brought back the chill and the lifted hairs on the back of his neck. He shied away from it, turning back defensively to the first explanation.

Given his training in concentration, and the creative instinct that had led him into poetry, the moments in which he had become Donal, in the bedroom and in the dining room, were not impossible. But still . . . he found he could start comfortably down the route of a sensible explanation – adding together his mental techniques, his young desire to identify with Donal, his hangover of physical exhaustion from Harmony, and the emotional effect of his disappointment on Mara – but in the end he came to a gap, a quantum jump, in which something unknown, something not explainable, had to have happened in addition, to produce what he had experienced.

Something above and beyond knowledge – something almost like magic – had been at work there. And yet, was there not something very much like that sort of quantum jump, or magic, involved in the creation of any piece of art? You could follow down the line of craft and skill only so far – and then something would happen which not even the best craftsman could identify or explain; and the result was art.

In the same way, he had come to a quantum jump-point – first, in his dream of James' burial, back on Harmony, and again in Donal's bedroom, but much more so than either earlier instance, in the dining room – which was unidentifiable and unexplainable. It was easy to tell himself that it had all been the result of a sort of self-hypnosis, a self-created illusion. But deep within himself he did not believe it.

Deeply within himself, he knew better. He knew it the way he knew beyond a shadow of a doubt, sometimes, that the lines of poetry he had just put on paper said something more than the total of their individual words could explain. The poem that worked, that involved the quantum jump, opened a doorway on another universe, which could be felt – as he had felt himself to be Donal.

In the same sense there had been more to the moment in the Graemehouse dining room than all the unconscious memories of what he had heard about the Graemes could account for. Deep within him, too deep for any denial, he knew – as he knew that he lived – that what he had experienced in the dining room was not what could have happened the night of Donal's graduation from the Academy, but what had happened.

In the day or two that followed, as he began to shed his drained feeling, as the inner reservoir of physical and psychic energy began to be replaced, he began to turn more of his attention to Amanda. She was up before dawn, taking care of the house, the stable and everything else around the place. By ten in the morning she would be at work in her office with contracts; and outside of ordinary interruptions in the way of phone calls, meals and other duties around the house, or occasional necessary trips outside it, she worked steadily through until late at night.

Her efficiency was unbelievable. Clearly, she had developed the most economical technique possible for each thing she had to do; and when the time came, she did it swiftly and surely. But none of the things she did were done with the sort of habitual, machine-like response that such a conscious approach often produced. On the contrary, her executions were as easy as breathing, with the unconscious grace of an accomplished artist in the practice of her art.

On the morning of the second day, however, because his conscience bothered him, he cornered her as she started out to the stable.

'Can I help?' he asked.

'I'll tell you if you can,' she said; then, watching him, her voice and expression softened. 'Fal Morgan is mine. You understand?'

'Yes,' he said; and stood aside to let her go.

By the third day his normal energy and strength had largely returned. He had spent most of the time sitting around, reading and thinking; but by that evening a physical restlessness began to build up inside him like water building up behind a dam. After dinner, Amanda went as usual back to her office and he tried again to read; but his thoughts wandered. The teeth of unanswered questions gnawed at him. As the days passed, he had felt something inside himself reaching out to her more and more; and his instinctive perceptions of her had sent back the message that she responded to this reaching out. But if anything, since the day at Foralie, she had drawn more and more back behind the brisk armor of her duties – and the reason for this eluded him.

Also, whatever else had taken place there, he had gone to Foralie with the purpose of finding the truth in his dream; and he had found it, only to realize that it concerned Donal Graeme – and that Donal had been an untypical Dorsai – as Cletus had been before him – and the experience in Graemehouse had been no help in bringing him to feel that he could make himself understood to the Grey Captains.

After nearly three days of circular thinking on these topics, the protest of his body at the long stretch of inactivity that had held him lately rose to an uncontrollable pitch. He put the cube he had been reading after dinner abruptly aside, and went to look through the half-open door of Amanda's office, to see if she was still at work.

She was. He left the office door and went to the closet by the back door of Fal Morgan, where an assortment of work clothing, sweaters and jackets occupied pegs on a wall-long rack. There was no jacket there quite big enough for him, but one of the sweaters, a loosely-knit bulky affair, was ample in size. He put it on, and stepped out into the night.

His intention had been only to go for a walk in the immediate vicinity of the house. But the Dorsai's single moon was nearly full and high in the sky, and the landscape around him showed clear and bright with moonlight. He walked to the edge of the open area in which Fal Morgan sat and looked down into the gully below him. Its tangle of light and dark, and the rocky upslopes beyond, attracted him; and he went down into it.

He had no real fear of getting lost. The surrounding mountain peaks were visible from any position below them; and they made excellent fixed reference points, particularly to someone raised in such territory. He crossed the gully he had chosen and continued up the slope beyond into a bare rock area of small cliffs and passes.

He lost himself in roaming the rocky area. After several days of walking only between rooms, to move freely in the open air was a relief. He had forgotten – even on Harmony when they went through the mountains, he had forgotten – how he had felt as a boy in the Rockies. Now that feeling came back. The peaks above him were not ominous and unknown shapes brooding upon the moonlit horizon; but, as they had been on Earth, sheltering giants within whose shadow he felt a freedom not to be found anywhere else. His stride lengthened, the breath in him came from the depths of his lungs, and from far inside him came a longing to cut loose from all larger duties and purposes and simply work to live, in such a place as this.

He woke, finally, to the fact that he had been walking for at least a couple of hours. Unnoticed until now, the night had chilled; and he had chilled, even with his exercise and clad in the heavy sweater. Also, now that he came down from the feeling that had uplifted him among the mountain peaks, he became conscious of the physical weariness in his not-yet recovered body. He turned back to Fal Morgan.

As he approached the house, he carried the mountains still with him in his mind; and as he laid his hand upon the back door of Fal Morgan to open it, he discovered himself nursing a small, irrational resentment that, self-barricaded from him as she now was, Amanda had become someone he could not tell of his walk and how it had made him feel. He laughed softly and wryly to himself at the disappointment in him at that discovery, quietly opened the door and went in.

The house held the stillness of the hours toward midnight. He thought suddenly to look at his chronometer, and was startled to see that he had been outside almost three hours. Amanda would certainly have finished work by this time and be in bed.

Although there was no danger of her hearing him from the other end of the house, he went softly, out of a touch of conscience, through the kitchen and into the corridor to the living room. As he entered it, he realized that there was still light in the living room – and he hesitated. Then he realized, from the waxing and waning of its illumination, that it must be the light of the fire, still burning in the fireplace; though it was not like Amanda, in her automatic housekeeping, to go to bed with the fire still burning.

She might have left it burning for him; or she might still be up. He went forward quietly, on the chance that the second possibility was correct; and before he was halfway down the corridor he heard the

435

sound of her voice, singing very softly, as if to herself, in the firelit room.

He was suddenly unsure; and he stopped. Then he took off his boots and went forward; not merely quietly, but with the utter silence of his early training in movement. He reached the corner of the entrance to the living room and looked cautiously around it toward the fireplace.

The fire had burned low; but flames still flickered along the dark lengths of the heavy back logs, painting the near floor of the room with ruddy color. Amanda, a half-empty cup beside her which must have originally been full of tea, for it had a milky color and she drank her coffee black, sat cross-legged on the dark red, rectangular carpet directly before the fireplace, gazing into it, her wrists on her knees and her hands relaxed, palm-upwards.

She sat like a slim, erect shadow against the light of the fire. He looked at her almost from the side, but slightly ahead. She was wearing the dark brown work pants and the soft yellow shirt she had had on earlier at dinner; but her shirt had been opened at the neck, and the wings of the collar lay out on her shoulders. Her hair was untied from its earlier, workaday restriction and lay loosely on her neck. Her face was tilted slightly toward the fire, and pensive. Close as he was now, in the silence of the house, he could hear the clear magic of her voice, in spite of its softness, plainly singing:

'. . . *green flows the water by my love's bright fancy.*
Green are the pools at the foot of the falls,
Dark under willow – and past is the sleeping.
Light in the morning, a little bird calls . . .'

He drew back abruptly into darkness, closing his ears to the rest of the song. It was as if he had come upon her naked and sleeping. Silently, he retraced his steps to the kitchen; and stood, uncertain.

From the living room, the murmur of her singing ended. He took a deep breath, stooped to put his boots back on, then stepped back without a sound and reached for the door by which he had entered earlier. He opened it silently, closed it noisily, and walked forward without carefulness through the passage and into the living room.

She was standing by the fire as he entered, looking in his direction as he came through the entrance into the room. Her eyes focused on the sweater he wore and widened a little. He stopped, facing her with a little distance between them.

'I went for a walk,' he said. 'I grabbed this off one of the pegs to wear. I hope that was all right?'

'Of course,' she said. There was a second's hesitation. 'It was Ian Graeme's.'

'Oh, it was?'

'Yes. One he knitted for himself, one winter.' She smiled just a

436

little. 'We tend to keep our hands busy in the winter here, when we're snowed in.'

There was another brief pause.

'You're feeling more lively, then?' Her eyes, darkened in the firelit room, watched him.

'I was. I'm ready for sleep now.' He smiled back at her. Their eyes met for a second, then glanced aside.

'Goodnight,' he said, and went on into the corridor leading to his bedroom, hearing her answer 'goodnight' behind him and leaving the large room, the firelight and her, behind him.

He reached his own room, went in, and closed the door. He was conscious of the weight of the sweater, still upon him. He took it off and proceeded to undress, then lay down on his back on the bed. A wave of his hand over the night table signalled the sensor there to turn off the lighting; and the bedroom around him was plunged in darkness.

He lay there. After a while the sound of her steps came down the hall, passed his bedroom and went on to her own. Silence claimed the house. He continued to lie awake, staring into the darkness, his heart torn by a sorrow and longing he did not dare to investigate too closely.

CHAPTER FORTY-SIX

The following day was Sunday, according to the weekly calendar on the Dorsai. Amanda took Hal with her to visit several of the neighboring homesteads, where there were individuals who had offered to help at Foralie during his meeting with the Grey Captains.

One of these was the Debigné household; and Hal had his suspicions confirmed that the intensity of Amanda was not something shared by her younger sister. What was necessary of Amanda was not something shared by her younger sister. What was necessary was for someone to be in residence at Foralie from the day before to the day after the meeting; and for others to help with meals and maintenance from the time the first of the Captains arrived – as much as an estimated twenty-fours ahead of the meeting time until the last of them left – as much as twenty-four hours after.

On the way back to Fal Morgan after lunch, Amanda took Hal by a route somewhat out of their way to an observation point even higher up than Foralie. It was a patch of grass on a flat ledge hardly large enough to have supported Fal Morgan. They dismounted; and Amanda took a scope out of one of her saddle bags.

'Sit down,' she said to Hal, dropping down herself, cross-legged upon the grass. He settled beside her and she gave him the scope.

'Look there,' she said, pointing. She was directing his attention beyond and below Graemehouse, the roof of which, with the roofs of it outbuildings, was visible perhaps a kilometer below and to the left of them.

Hal put the scope to his eyes and located the spot she had indicated. It was a green patch surrounded by trees somewhat less than eight hundred meters below the house.

'I see it,' he said. 'What is it?

'The site of the original Foralie – the house,' she said. 'Foralie was built by Eachan Khan, in the first place. When Cletus married his daughter, Melissa, he built Graemehouse on Foralie land where you see it now. After Cletus defeated Dow deCastries in his attempt to control all the Younger Worlds with the power of Old Earth, and Melissa went with Cletus to Graemehouse, Eachan Khan began to show his age – he hadn't much before – and Melissa talked him into joining her and Cletus at Graemehouse. He did, and Foralie was left

438

empty – but with everything still in it for a year or two. Eachan didn't seem to be able to make up his mind what to do with it. Then, one night, it caught fire and burned down. Since then Graemehouse has been Foralie.'

'I see,' said Hal. The green space below him was certainly a pleasant place to have put a house, much more sheltered among the trees than Graemehouse on its high perch. He lowered the scope and looked at Amanda.

'We could have ridden down there,' said Amanda,' but there's nothing much to see when you get there; and actually from here you get a better picture of how it was.'

'Yes,' he said; and passed the scope back to her.

'No. Hang on to it for a bit,' she said. 'You can also see Fal Morgan down there – or at least part of its roofs. The trees get in the way, a bit. But you may remember you couldn't see it at all from Graemehouse, for the trees.'

'You're right.' He put the scope to his eyes again and looked. Then lowered it once more to look at her. All this about the original Foralie, and the rest of it, was certainly the sort of thing she might expect him to be interested in; but he could not help feeling that there was a reason behind her obvious one for telling him about this, and showing the original Foralie to him, from this vantage point.

'It was Foralie, the original house, that Cletus came back to after Dow deCastries had moved in with his troops to take over the Dorsai, when all her fighting men were gone,' she said. 'You know about that?'

Hal nodded.

'That was in the early days, wasn't it?' he said. 'Nearly two hundred years ago, when the Earth was split between the Alliance and the Coalition?

And Dow was a Coalition man who got the two governments to combine their forces, under him, so he could take over the newer worlds? I know about it. Cletus Grahame opposed Dow, Dow arranged contracts to drain all the trained soldiers off Dorsai, then moved in here to take the planet over; and those who were left here, the grandparents, the children and the mothers, stopped him.'

He grinned.

'There're still historians who think Dow must have cut his own throat; because noncombatants can't defeat elite troops.'

'Did you ever think that?' Amanda asked.

'No.' He sobered. 'But I heard about it first from Malachi when I was very young. It seemed perfectly natural to me, then, that they could do it, being Dorsai.'

'Nothing happens by reputation alone,' she said. 'Each district – we didn't have cantons in those days – had to decide how to defend itself. Cletus left only Arvid Johnson and Bill Athyer, with six trained men, to organize the defense. . . .'

She fell silent, her eyes gazing down upon the slopes below. He watched her, still trying to understand what she was aiming at. Even seated, her body had an erectness that no man could have possessed without stiffness; and her face had the quality of a profile stamped on a silver coin.

'Amanda . . .' he said, gently.

She did not seem to have heard him; and he felt a clumsiness in himself that made him unsure of prodding her further. Beside her, in his much taller, larger-framed but gaunt, body, thinned down by the experiences of recent months, he felt like some dark bird of earth-bound flesh and bone, bending above an entity of pure spirit. But as he waited, her eyes lost their abstraction and she turned to him.

'What is it?' she said.

It crossed his mind to wonder if perhaps he should avoid further mention of the Defense of Dorsai – as it was called in the histories.

'I was just thinking how much you look like that painting in your hall – was it of the first Amanda? It could be a picture of you.'

'Both the second Amanda and I look like her,' she answered. 'It happens.'

'Does it just happen that she had her picture painted at the same age you are now?'

'No.' She shook her head and smiled, almost mischievously. 'It wasn't.'

'It wasn't?' He gazed at her.

'No,' Amanda laughed. 'That picture in our hall was made when she was a good deal older than I am now.'

He frowned.

'It's true,' she said. 'We age very slowly, we Morgans. And she was something special.'

'Not as special as you,' he said. 'She couldn't be. You're end-result Dorsai. She lived before people like you had been born.'

'That's not true,' Amanda said swiftly. 'She was Dorsai before there was a Dorsai world. What she was, was the material out of which our people and our culture's been made.'

'How can you be so sure of what she was – nearly two centuries ago?'

'How can I?' She turned her head to face him and looked at him strangely. 'Because in many ways I am her.'

The last few words came out without any particular emphasis; but they seemed to ring in his ears with an unusual distinctness. He sat as he was, careful not to move or change his expression, but his inner awareness had just been alerted.

'A reincarnation?' he said, lightly, after a moment.

'No, not really,' she answered. 'But something more . . . as if time didn't matter. As if it's all the same thing; her, there in the beginning of this world of ours; and I, here. . . .'

And now the feeling came clearly to him that her reason was out in the open, that she had told him – warned him, perhaps – of what she had brought him here to be warned about.

'Here at the end of it, you mean?' he challenged her.

'No.' Her turquoise eyes had taken on a gray shade. 'The end won't be until the last Dorsai is dead, and wherever that Dorsai dies. In fact, not even then. The end is only going to be when the last human is dead – because what makes us Dorsai is something that's a part of all humans; that part the first Amanda had when she was born, back on Earth.'

Something – a fragment of cloud across the white dot of the sun, perhaps – shuttered the sunlight from his eyes for a split second. There was some connection between all this she was presently speaking of, the lost house of Foralie, the Defense of the Dorsai and herself, that was still eluding him.

'You think so much of her,' he said thoughtfully. 'But it's the Cletus Grahames and the Donal Graemes that the rest of the worlds think of when they talk about this world.'

'We've had Graemes as our next neighbors since Cletus,' she replied. 'What's thought of them, they earned. But the first Amanda was here before either of them. She founded our family. She cleared the out-of-work mercenaries from these mountains before Cletus came; and it was when she was ninety-three that she held Foralie district against Dow deCastries' troops, who'd landed here, thinking they'd have no trouble with the children and women, the sick and the old, who were all that was left.'

'So, she was given charge of Foralie district?' he said. 'Why her? Had she been a soldier once?'

'No,' she answered. 'But, as I said, during the Outlaw Years here, she'd led the way in clearing out the lawless mercenaries. After she did that, and other things, with just the noncombatants to help her, the rest of the districts followed her example; and law came to the Dorsai. She led when Dow came because she was the one best fit to command in this district, in spite of her age.'

'How did she do it?'

'Clean out the outlaws, or defeat deCastries?'

'Not the outlaws – though I'd like to hear about that sometime, too,' he said. 'No, how did she defeat deCastries when all the experts then and now claim there was no way a gaggle of housewives, children and old people could possibly have done it?'

Amanda's gaze went a long way past him.

'In a way you could say the troops did defeat themselves. Did you ever read Cletus' *Tactics of Mistake?*'

'Yes,' he said. 'But when I was too young to understand it well.'

'What we did was in there – it was a matter of making them make

441

the mistakes, putting our strength against the weaknesses of the invaders.'

'Weaknesses? In first-line troops?'

She looked at him again with the gray tint to her eyes.

'They weren't as willing to die as we were.'

'Willing to die?' he studied her. 'Old people? Mothers –'

'And children. Yes.'

The armor of sunlight around her seemed to invest her words with a quality of truth greater than he had ever known from anyone else.

'The Dorsai,' she said, 'was formed by people who were willing to pay with their lives in others' battles, in order to buy freedom for their homes. It wasn't only in the men who went off to fight. Those at home had that same image of freedom, and were willing to die for it.'

'But simply being willing to die –'

'You don't understand, not being born here,' she said. 'It was a matter of our being able to make harder choices than the soldiers sent in to occupy us. Amanda and the others in the district who were best qualified to decide sat down before the invasion and considered a number of plans. All of the plans meant casualties – and the casualties could include the people who were considering the plans. They chose the one that gave the district its greatest effectiveness against the enemy for the least number of deaths; and, having chosen it, the ones who had done the choosing were ready to be among those who would have to pay for its success. The invading soldiers had no such plan – and no such will.'

He shook his head.

'I don't understand,' he said. 'I suppose it's because I'm not a Dorsai.'

She looked at him for a moment, like someone who considers saying something, then thinks better of it.

'Then you don't understand the first Amanda?' she said. 'I think you'll need to if you're going to talk to the Grey Captains.'

He nodded, soberly.

'How did it happen?' he asked. 'How did she – how did they do it? I have to know.'

'All right,' she said, 'I'll tell you.'

And she did. Sitting there in the sunlight, listening to her talk of a past as if it was something she herself had lived through, he thought again of what she had said about the first Amanda and herself being the same person. The story was a simple one. Dow's troops had come in and bivouacked just beyond Foralie Town. The first Amanda had gotten their commander's permission to continue with a manufacturing process in town that was necessary to the district's economy; and the process, according to plan, had flooded the atmosphere of the town and its vicinity with vaporized nickel carbonyl. One part in

442

a million of those vapors was enough to cause allergic dermatitis and an edema of the lungs that was irreversible. In short – a sure death.

What had lulled the suspicions of the invaders until too late had been that there were inhabitants of Foralie Town also getting sick and dying, just as the soldiers were. Even when at last they understood, it had been unbelievable to Dow's military that townspeople could choose to stay where they were and die, just to make sure that the invaders died with them.

At the last, there had been a situation in which Dow had held Cletus as a captive at Foralie, with healthy troops on guard. An assortment of the older children, armed, plus the eight professionals Cletus had left to organize defenses, and Amanda, had reversed the situation. Amanda, in her ninety-third year, had finally captured the soldiers guarding Foralie by threatening to blow them and herself up together.

Compelling as the story was, it was not so much that which caught at Hal's attention. It was Amanda's way of telling it, as if she herself had been there. More strongly than ever came the impression that there was something she was trying to tell him under the screen of words which he was failing to understand. An anger stirred in him that he should be so unperceptive. But there was nothing to be done but wait and hope for some word that would wake him suddenly to her meaning.

So, he sat with her in the bright sunlight, hearing not merely the story of the defense of Foralie District, but of Kensie's death on Ste. Marie; and about how the second Amanda, who had loved both Kensie and Ian (but Ian more) had decided at last to marry no one. But even when they remounted their horses, he still did not know what it was she wanted him to understand. The afternoon had moved in upon them as she had talked; and Fomalhaut was halfway down the sky by the time they rode once more into the yard of Fal Morgan.

'. . . And I,' she said again at the end of the story, 'am the first and second Amandas over again.'

They did not get the chance to talk again at any length until after the meeting. The next day, Monday, Amanda was gone on a business trip; and on Tuesday she was busy away from Fal Morgan, directing and helping with the preparing of Graemehouse for the meeting. Hal stayed where he was at Fal Morgan, puzzling over her as much as over what he would say to convince the Grey Captains. There was something in him like a superstition – which, strangely, Amanda seemed to understand – that made him unwilling to return to Foralie until the actual meeting time should arrive.

The Captains from furthest away began to arrive late Tuesday; and were welcomed at Graemehouse by Amanda and the neighbors who were helping. She did not get back to Fal Morgan until late evening;

and after a quick meal she sat with Hal over a drink in the living room for only a few minutes before going to bed.

'What was it you said – that I'd need to convince most of those that come?' he asked her as they sat before the fire. 'What percentage is "most"?'

She raised her gaze from the flames, which she had been watching; and smiled a little. 'If you can get through to seventy per cent of those who come, you'll be a success,' she said. 'Those who don't get here will eventually react in pretty much the same proportions, after talking to those who did.'

'Seventy per cent,' he echoed, turning the short, heavy glass slowly in his hands and looking at the firelight through the brown liquid he had barely tasted.

'Don't expect miracles,' her voice said; and he looked up to see her watching him. 'No one, except Cletus, or maybe Donal, in his lifetime, could carry them all. Seventy per cent will give you what you want. Be very happy with that. As I told you – everyone makes up his own mind here, and the Grey Captains more than most.'

He nodded.

'Do you know what you're going to say?' she asked after a moment.

'Part of it. The part that's the Exotic message,' he answered, nursing the whiskey glass between his palms. 'For the rest – it doesn't seem to plan.'

'If you tell them what you told me, your first night here,' she said, 'you'll be all right.'

He looked at her, startled.

'You think so?'

'I know so,' she said.

He continued to look at her, searchingly, trying to remember all of what he had said that first night.

'I'm not sure I remember exactly what that was,' he said, slowly.

'It'll come to you,' she told him. The words lingered on his ears. She got to her feet, carrying her half-empty glass.

'Well, I need sleep,' she said; and watched him for a second. 'Possibly you do, too.'

'Yes,' he said. 'But I think I'll sit here just a little while longer, though. I'll take care of the fire.'

'Just be sure the screen's in place. . . .'

She went off. He sat alone for another twenty minutes before he sighed, reached out to wave his hand over the screen sensor, and stood up. The screen slid tightly across the front of the fireplace, and the last of the flames, cut off from fresh oxygen, began almost immediately to dwindle and die. He drained his glass, took it to the kitchen, and went to bed.

The meeting was not to be held until an hour after lunch time at Foralie. Half an hour before then, Hal and Amanda saddled up and rode from Fal Morgan.

He did not feel like talking, and Amanda seemed content to leave him in his silence. He had expected his mind to be buzzing with possible arguments he could use. Instead, it had retreated into a calmness, utterly remote from the situation into which he was heading.

He was wise enough to let it be. He sat back in the saddle and let his senses be occupied by the sound, scent and vision of the ride.

When they reached the mounded level of the area on which Graemehouse was built, they found a couple of dozen air-space jitneys parked before the main building; and as they dismounted at the corral by the stable, the sound of internal activity reached out to them, through an opened kitchen window. They removed saddles and bridles from their horses, turned them loose in the corral, and went in through the front entrance.

In the living room, they found only two people, seated talking in an adjoining pair of the overstuffed chairs. One was a square, black woman with a hooked nose in a stern face, and the other a pink-faced, small man, both at least in their sixties.

'Miriam Songhai,' said Amanda, 'this is Hal Mayne. Rourke di Facino, Hal Mayne.'

'Honored,' they all murmured to each other.

'I'll go round up people,' added di Facino, getting to his feet, and went off toward the office and bedroom end of the house. Amanda stayed with Hal.

'So you're the lad,' said Miriam, in a voice had a tendency to boom.

'Yes,' said Hal.

'Sit down,' she said. 'It'll be a while before they're all together. Where do you spring from originally?'

'Earth – Old Earth,' said Hal, taking the chair di Facino had vacated.

'When did you leave? Tell me about yourself,' she said; and Hal began to give her something of his personal history.

But they were interrupted by others entering the room in ones and twos, and the necessity of introductions. Shortly, the conversation with Miriam Songhai was lost completely and Hal found himself standing in a room full almost to overcrowding.

'Everybody's here, aren't they?' said a tall, cadaverous man in at least his eighties. He had a bass voice that was remarkable. 'Why don't we move in and get settled?'

There was a general movement toward the dining room and Hal found himself carried along by it. At the entrance to the dining room, for a second only, a small hesitation took him; and then it was gone.

The long room before him was no longer dim and filled with amber light in which ghosts might walk. The drapes had at last been drawn and the fierce white illumination of Fomalhaut reflected off the gray-white surface of the steep slope behind the house and sent hard light through the windows, to carve everything animate and inanimate within to an unsparing three-dimensional solidity. Hal went on, saw Amanda standing beside the single chair at the table's head beckoning to him, and walked forward.

He sat down. Amanda went to seat herself, several chairs from him on his right. The room had filled behind them and empty chairs were rapidly being occupied. In a minute, they had all been filled; and he found himself looking along the polished tabletop, above which thirty-odd faces looked back and waited for him to speak.

CHAPTER FORTY-SEVEN

As they all sat watching him and waiting, an awareness he had never felt before woke suddenly in him.

Later, he was to become familiar with it, but this was his first experience; and it came on him with a shock that there could be a moment in which the universe seemed to stand still, like a ballet dancer poised on one toe; and for a fraction of a second all possibilities were equal. In that moment, he found, a form of double vision occurred. He saw the surrounding scene simultaneously from two viewpoints – both directly, and at one remove. So that he was at the same time both observer and observed; and he became aware of himself, for the first time, as part of something separate and remote. In that transient moment, for a split-second, his detachment was perfect; and his remote, viewing mind was able to weigh all things dispassionately, itself included.

Caught so, he understood for the first time now how those who knew they would be staying in Foralie Town under the vapors of the nickel carbonyl could have made the decision to use it. For at the core of such a moment was a perception tuned too sharply in self-honesty for fear or selfishness to affect decision.

Caught up in wonder at this new perception, Hal did not react for a long moment to the waiting faces as he ordinarily would have; and Rourke di Facino, far down the table on Hal's left, spoke instead to Amanda.

'Well, Amanda? You hinted at some strong reasons for our coming to this meeting. We're here.'

Hal had not realized the quality of the acoustics in the dining room. Di Facino had spoken in no more than a soft conversational tone, but his words had sounded clearly across the length of the space between himself and Hal.

'I said there might be strong reasons for listening to Hal Mayne, Rourke,' answered Amanda, 'and I think there are. One, at least, is the one I told you about – that he's been sent here from Mara by the Exotics, to give us a message. And we could have other reasons for listening to him, as well.'

'All right,' said di Facino. 'I only mention it because – no offense seeing things that aren't there, on occasion.'

'Or perhaps,' said Amanda, 'they merely saw things other people were too blind to see. No offense intended, of course.'

They smiled at each other like friendly old enemies across half the length of the dining room. Still caught in his moment, watching them all, Hal found Amanda standing out among the others as one very bright beacon might stand out in a bank of duller ones. The average age of the Grey Captains was at least in the fifties; and she, in her apparent youthfulness, looked almost like a young girl who has slyly slipped into a solemn gathering of family elders and waits to see how long she can hold her place before being discovered.

'In any case,' the booming voice of Miriam Songhai reached them all, 'We've no prejudice on the Dorsai against people being sensitive, simply because what they're sensitive to isn't easily measured, weighed or tagged – I hope.'

She turned to Hal.

'What's this message from the Exotics?' she demanded.

Hal looked at the waiting faces. There was a quality of difference in those here, compared to the five he had faced on Mara. It was a difference in quietness. The Exotics had not fidgeted physically; but he had been conscious of conflict and uncertainty within each of them. Those sitting at this table with him now radiated no such impression of inner concerns. They were at home here, he was a stranger, and it was their job to decide whatever needed decision. In the hard daylight, here and now, there was no room for the ghosts and the memories he had found in the dining room earlier. He felt isolated, helpless to reach them and convince them.

'I was on my way to the Dorsai, in any case,' he said. 'But as it happened, I got to Mara first; and so it was the Exotics I talked to –'

'Just a minute.' It was a heavy-bodied man in his fifties with a brush of stiff, gray hair; the one person there with oriental features. Hal rummaged in his memory for the name he had heard when Amanda had introduced them. Ke Gok, or K'Gok, was what he remembered hearing her say. 'Why did they pick you to carry their message instead of sending one of their own people?'

'I can tell you what they told me,' Hal said. 'Amanda may have explained to you how I was raised by three tutors, one of them a Dorsai –'

'By the way, does anyone here know of a family named Nasuno?' Amanda's clear voice cut in on him. 'They should have a homestead on Skalland.'

There was a moment's silence, then the cadaverous man – whose name, in spite of the mnemonics of Hal's early training, had freakishly been lost – spoke, thoughtfully.

'Skalland's one of the islands in my area, of course. I know you asked me about that when you called, Amanda. But in the time I had I couldn't seem to turn up any such family. Which doesn't mean they

448

aren't there – or weren't there – a generation ago.'

'It's hardly likely someone could pose as a Dorsai for a dozen years, even on Earth, and get away with it,' said Ke Gok. 'But what I'm still waiting to hear is why the Exotics thought someone tutored by a Dorsai should be particularly qualified to talk to us for them.'

'I was also tutored by a Maran – and by a Harmonyite,' said Hal. 'They seemed to feel the fact I'd been brought up by people from both their culture and yours might make me better able to communicate with you, than one of them could.'

'Still strange,' said Ke Gok. 'Two worlds full of trained people and they pick someone from Earth?'

'They'd also run calculations on me,' said Hal, 'which seemed to show I might be historically useful at this time.'

He had been dreading having to mention this; and he had chosen the mildest words in which to put the information, fearing the prejudice of practical people against anything as theoretical and long-range as Exotic calculations in ontogenetics. But none of those before him reacted antagonistically, and Ke Gok said no more.

'In what way,' said a slim, good-looking woman named Lee, with large, intent brown eyes and gray-black hair, 'did they think you could be historically useful?'

'Useful in dealing with the present historical situation – particularly with the situation created by the Others,' he answered. 'It's that same situation I'm concerned with, myself; and that I'd like to talk to you about, after I've given you the Exotic message –'

'I think we'll want to hear anything you've got to tell us – Exotic message and whatever else you want to talk to us about,' said Lee, 'but some of us have questions of our own, first.'

'Of course,' said Hal.

'Do I understand you right, then?' said Lee. 'The Exotics are concerned about the Others; and they sent you to us because they thought you could do a better job of convincing us to think their way than any one of their own people could?'

Hal breathed deeply.

'Effectively,' he said, 'yes.'

Lee sat back in her chair, her face thoughtful.

'How about you, Amanda?' di Facino said. 'Are you part of this effort to bring us around to an Exotic way of thinking?'

'Rourke,' said Amanda, 'you know that's nonsense.'

He grinned.

'Just asking.'

'Don't,' said Amanda, 'and save us time, all around.'

She looked about at the others. No one else said anything. She looked up at Hal.

'Go ahead,' she said.

Hal looked around at them. There was nothing to be read from their faces. He plunged in.

'I assume there's no point in my wasting your time by telling you what you already know,' he said. 'The interstellar situation's now almost completely under the control of the Others; and what they're after in the long run is no secret. They want total control; and to have that, they've got to get rid of those who'll never work with them – some of the people on the Friendlies, essentially all of the Exotics, and the Dorsai people. The point the Exotics make is that the Others have to be stopped now while there's still time. They think that, of all those opposed to the Others, the Dorsai are the one people who can do that; and they sent me with word that they'll give you anything they have to give, back you in any way they can, if you'll do it.'

He stopped.

The faces around the table looked back at him as if they had expected him to continue.

'That's it?' said Ke Gok. 'How do they think we can stop the Others? Don't they think we'd have done it before this, if we knew how?'

There was a moment of silence around the table. Hal thought of speaking and changed his mind.

'Just a minute,' said the cadaverous old man. 'They can't be thinking – this isn't that old suggestion we go out and play assassins?'

It was as if a whip cracked soundlessly in the room. Hal looked down the room at the hard faces.

'I'm sorry,' he said. 'I was obligated to bring you the message. I told them you'd never do it.'

The silence continued for a second.

'And why were you obligated?' said Miriam Songhai.

'I was obligated,' said Hal, patiently, 'by the fact that delivering the message gave me the chance to speak to you all about what I, myself, believe is the only way to deal with the Others.'

Another tiny silence.

'Perhaps,' said di Facino – very softly, but the words carried through the dining room, nonetheless – 'they don't realize how they insult us.'

'Probably they don't – in the emotional sense,' said Hal. 'But even if they did, it wouldn't matter. They'd have to ask you anyway, because they don't see any other way out.'

'What he's telling you,' said Amanda, 'is that the Exotics feel helpless; and people who feel helpless will try anything.'

'I think you can tell them for us.' said the cadaverous man, 'that the day they give up the principles they've lived by for three hundred years, they can ask us again. But our answer will still be that we don't give up our principles.'

He looked around the room.

'What would we have left, if we did something like that to save our necks? What would the point have been of living honestly, all these centuries? If we'd do assassin's work now, we'd not only not be Dorsai any longer; we'd never have been Dorsai!'

No one nodded or spoke, but a unanimity of approval showed clearly on the faces around the table.

'All right,' said Hal. 'I'll tell them that. But now can I ask, since I've got you all here, what you do intend to do about the Others, before they starve you to death?'

Hal looked at Amanda. But she was still merely sitting, a little back from the table, watching. It was Miriam Songhai who spoke. 'Of course we've no plans,' she said. 'You evidently do. Tell us.'

Hal took a breath and looked at them all.

'I don't have a specific plan, either,' he said. 'But I believe I've got the material out of which a plan can be made. What it's based on, what it has to be based on, is an understanding of the historical situation that's resulted in the Others being so successful. Basically, what we're involved in now is the last act of an era in human development; and the Others are there to threaten us because they stand for one attitude that exists in the race as a whole; and we – you Dorsai, the Exotics, the true faithholders on the Friendlies and some others scattered around all the other worlds – stand for the attitude opposed to it. Natural historical forces in human development are what are pushing this conflict to a showdown. We're looking not merely at the ambitions of the Others, but at an Armageddon . . .'

He talked on. They listened. The light lancing in through the windows made the long, smooth surface of the table glisten like wind-polished ice; and the Grey Captains sat listening in utter still-ness, as if they had been carved in place as they sat, to last forever. Hal heard his voice continuing, saying the same things he had said to Exotic ears; and much of what he must have said to Amanda, that first night here. But there was no sign or signal from this audience to tell him if he was reaching them. Deep within himself, the fear grew that he was not. His words seemed to go out from him, only to die in the silence, against minds that had already shut them out.

He glanced fleetingly at Amanda, hoping for some signal that might give him reassurance; and found none. She did not shake her head, even imperceptibly; but the unchanging gaze she returned to him conveyed the same message. Internally, Hal yielded. There was no point in simply continuing to hold them hostage with words, if the words were not being heard and considered by them. He brought what he had been saying to a close.

There was a moment without anyone speaking. The Captains stir-red slightly, as people will who have sat for some time in one posi-tion. Throats were cleared, here and there. Hands were placed on the table.

'Hal Mayne,' said Miriam Songhai, finally. 'Just what plan do you have for yourself? I mean, what do you, yourself, plan to do next?'

'I'll be going from here to the Final Encyclopedia,' he said. 'There's where most of the information is, that I still need, for an effective understanding of the situation. Once I've got a complete picture, I can give you a specific plan of action.'

'And meanwhile?' said Ke Gok, ironically. 'You're merely asking us to hold ourselves in readiness for your orders?'

Hal felt a despair. He had failed, once more; and there was no magic, no ghosts were here, to save the day. This was reality; the incomprehension of those who saw the universe limited to what they already knew. Unexpectedly, an exasperation erupted in him; and it was as if something put a powerful hand on his shoulder and shoved him forward.

'I'm suggesting that you hold yourself in readiness for orders from someone,' he heard himself answer, dryly.

There was a shock in hearing it. The voice was his own, the words were words he knew, but the choice and delivery of them was coming from somewhere deep within him; as far back as the ghosts he had heard speaking at this table. He felt a strength move in him.

'If I'm fortunate enough to be the one who first gets on top of the situation,' he went on in the same unsparing voice, 'they could indeed come from me.'

'No offense, Hal Mayne,' said di Facino, 'but may I ask how old you are?'

'Twenty-one, standard,' said Hal.

'Doesn't it seem, even to you,' went on di Facino, 'that it's asking a lot of people like ourselves, who've known responsibility on a large scale for twice or three times your lifetime, to take you and what you suggest completely on faith? Not only that, but that we should mobilize a planetful of people in accordance with that faith? You come to us here with no credentials whatsoever, except a high rating according to some Exotic theory – and this world is not one of the Exotics.'

'Credentials,' said Hal, still dryly, 'mean nothing and will never mean anything in this matter. If I find the answers I'm looking for, my credentials are going to be obvious to you, and to everyone else as well. If I don't, then either someone else is going to find the answers, or no one will. In either case, any credentials I have will be very much beside the point. The Exotics knew this.'

'Did they?' said di Facino. 'Did they tell you so?'

'They showed me so,' said Hal. The strange sense of strength in him carried him forward irresistibly. It was as if someone else spoke through him to them; and the exasperation within him had given way now to a diamond-hard sense of logic. 'Sending me here with their message, which they had little hope you'd agree to, guaranteed I'd have a chance to give you my side of things, without their having in any way endorsed it. If it turned out you accepted me, they'd have no choice but to accept me, too, in the long run. If you didn't, they had no responsibility for what I said to you on my own.'

'But,' said Ke Gok, 'we haven't accepted you.'

'You'll have to accept someone, if you're going to deal with the situation,' Hal said. 'You were the one who just said a few moments ago that you'd have stopped the Others before this if you'd known how. The plain fact is you don't know how. I do – perhaps. And there's no time to wait around for other solutions. This late in the day, even all the strength that can be joined against the Others may not be enough. You and the Exotics are in the same camp whether you like it or not – if you don't face that, you and they are going to perish singly, as you're both on the road to perishing now. Only unlike the Exotics, you Dorsai are a people of action. You can't close your eyes to the need for it, when that need crops up. Therefore, the only hope for you and them is that someone will come along who can lead you both, together – and no one has, but me.'

'The necessity to accept someone,' said the cadaverous man, 'hasn't been proven, yet.'

'Certainly it has.' Hal looked directly into the almost-black pupils of the other's eyes. 'The Dorsai is already beginning to starve. Slowly . . . but it's beginning. And you all know that starvation is being caused deliberately by the Others, who are also doing other things to other people. Clearly, this is no problem that can be kept contained between you and the Others, only. It's a case of one part of the human race, spread over many worlds, against the other part. You don't need me to tell you that, you can see it for yourself.'

'But,' said Lee, softly, 'there's no guarantee it has to explode into Armageddon, with what that would mean for all our people – who are the fighters.'

'Take another look if you believe it doesn't have to,' said Hal. 'The situation's been developing for over thirty years. As it develops, it grows exponentially, both in numbers of peoples involved and in complexity. How else can it end except in Armageddon? Unless you and the Exotics and those like you are willing to abandon everything you've believed in, to suit the Others; because that's the only thing the Others'll settle for, in the end.'

'How can you be sure of that?' said Lee. 'Why shouldn't the Others stop before they push it that far?'

'Because if they do, they'll be the ones to be wiped out in a generation; and they know it,' said Hal. 'They're riding a tiger and don't dare get off. There's too few of them. The only way to make life safe for themselves, as individuals, is to make the worlds – note, I said worlds, all the worlds – safe for all of them together. That means changing the very face of human society. It means the Others as masters and the rest of humanity as subordinates. They know that.

For everthing you love, you have to know it, too.'

There was a long moment of silence in the room. Hal sat waiting, still strangely gripped by the clarity and fierceness of thought that had come on him.

'It's still only a theory of yours – this idea of historical confrontation between two halves of the human race,' said Miriam Songhai, heavily. 'How do you expect us to trust something like this, that no one ever proposed before?'

'Check it out for yourselves,' said Hal. 'It doesn't take Exotic calculations to see when and how the Others started, how they've progressed, and where they must be headed. You know better than I how the credit and other reserves of your society are dwindling. The time's coming when the Others'll own the souls of everyone who might hire you, off-world. What happens to the Dorsai, then?'

'But this idea of them as a historical force, with all the dice loaded in their favor against us,' the cadaverous man said, shaking his head, 'that's leaving common sense for fantasy.'

'Would you call it a fantasy, what's already happened on all the worlds but Old Earth? And it hasn't happened there only because the Others have to get the other worlds under control first,' Hal answered. 'The Others' specialty is to attack where there's no counter. There's no present defense against them. How else could they explode the way they have, into a position of interstellar power in just thirty standard years?'

He paused and looked deliberately around the table at all the faces there. There was a strange brightness, almost a light of triumph in Amanda's eyes.

'Against their charisma, and the pattern of their organization,' he went on, 'none of our present cultures have any natural defense. If you could put all of the Others on trial in an interplanetary court right now, I'd be willing to bet you couldn't find legal cause to indict one of them. Most of the time they don't even have to suggest what they want done. They bind to them people with exactly the characters they want, put each in the specific situation each one is best suited for, and each one does exactly what the Others want, on his or her own initiative.'

Hal turned to speak to the table as a whole.

'Look at the large picture, for your own sakes,' he said. 'Think. The Exotics could have handled in its beginning any ordinary economic attempt to dominate all the worlds. You could have handled early any purely military threat. But against the Others you've both been helpless; because they haven't attacked in those forms. They've attacked in a new way, one never anticipated; and they're winning. Because the pattern of human society is changing, as it's always done; and the old, as always, can't resist the new.'

He paused.

'Face that,' he said. 'You, the Exotics, the Friendlies, everyone else who lives by an older pattern, can't resist the Others as you've resisted other enemies until now. If you try going that way, you'll lose – inevitably – and the Others will win. But the possibility is there for you to resist them successfully, and win, if you let yourself become part of the new historical patterns that are shaping up into existence right now.'

He paused again; and this time he waited for comment or objection, a response of any kind. But none came. They sat silent, watching him.

'The Others aren't aliens,' he said. 'They're us, with a difference. But that difference can be enough to give them control as things stand. Again, as I say, it's simply one more instance of the old giving way to the new; only the problem in this case is that the new way the Others want to bring in is a blind alley for the race. Humanity as a whole can't survive in stasis, with one Master to millions of slaves. If it's made to go that way, it'll die.'

He paused. None of them made the slightest movement or sound. They only continued to watch him.

'We can't allow that,' he went on, 'but not allowing it doesn't mean we can keep things as they are. That would also mean stasis – and a race death. So, we have to acknowledge simply what is. Once more, the face of human society is changing, as it's always done; and as always we'll have to change with it or go by the board. Here on the Dorsai you're going to have to be prepared to let go of many things, because you're a Splinter Culture that always held to tradition and custom. But that adaptation will have to be made, for the sake of your children's children. Because, I tell you again, what's at stake isn't the hard-won ways of the Dorsai, or those of the Friendlies or the Exotics, but the survival of the whole human race.'

CHAPTER FORTY-EIGHT

Hal stopped talking at last, and waited for a response. But this time, the silence from his listeners continued. They were looking now at the tabletop before them, at the wall or window opposite them, in any direction, in fact, but at him or at each other.

'That's all I have to say,' he told them, finally.

Their eyes went to him, then. Miriam Songhai sighed.

'It's not an easy picture to look at, the one you've just painted,' she said. 'I believe I need to think this over.'

There was a mutter of agreement around the table. But the cadaverous man got to his feet.

'I don't need to think it over,' he said, looking directly at Hal. 'You've answered every question I could have asked. You've convinced me. But the only answer you have isn't for me.'

He looked for a moment around the table.

'You know me,' he said. 'I'll do anything necessary for my people. But the Dorsai as it is now is what I've lived and fought for all my life. I can't change now. I won't have any hand in making it and its people change. The rest of you can travel this new road we've just been hearing all about, but you'll do it without me.'

He turned toward the door. Two other men and one woman pushed their chairs back also and got up. Ke Gok started to rise, then sat down again, heavily. In the doorway, the cadaverous man stopped and turned back for a moment.

'I'm sorry,' he said to Hal.

Then he was gone and the three others followed him out.

'I gather,' said Hal, in the following hush, 'that most of you, like Miriam Songhai, want to think about what I've said. I can wait on Dorsai up to another week, if any of you want to talk to me further. Then, as I said, I'll be leaving for the Final Encyclopedia.'

'He'll be at Fal Morgan,' said Amanda.

The meeting broke up.

Hal had assumed that he also would now be heading back to Fal Morgan. Instead, he found the living room half-filled with fifteen of the Grey Captains who wanted to talk to him further about the situation as he saw it. Ke Gok, surprisingly, was one of them.

They were, Hal learned from what they had to say, those who had already brought themselves to a belief in the historical situation as Hal had explained it – though not necessarily to him or whatever plan he might develop for dealing with it. He found discussing matters with them to be a clean mental pleasure after the uncertainties and secrecies of the Exotics. They were people who were used to taking problems apart and dealing with them either in section or in whole; and clearly they had accepted him as one who worked in the same manner.

At the same time he was uneasy, conscious of a difference as he talked to them informally in the big living room. For a little while in the dining room he had found himself wearing a cloak of certainty so strong that he had not even needed to think of the words to use. What he had wanted to say had simply come to him out of the obviousness of what they needed to understand. Now, in the living room, with an audience already half-convinced, that diamond-brilliant clarity and conviction was gone once more. His own, usual abilities of expression were still more than adequate to the occasion; but the difference in that from what he had tapped for a short while in the dining room was jolting; and he made himself a promise to find out what it had been that had so touched him then, as soon as he had time to examine his memory of it.

In the end it was five hours later when he and Amanda rode back through the early evening to Fal Morgan.

'What were these strong reasons you hinted at, according to Rourke di Facino?' he asked her, when they and their horses were lost to sight from Graemehouse.

'I told them I was convinced you had greater ties with the Dorsai than it might seem in this situation.'

He considered that answer for a few seconds as their horses walked, side by side.

'And what did you say to the ones who asked you what those ties were?'

'I told them it was a perception of mine, that they were there.' She turned her head as she rode and looked at him squarely. 'I said they could take my word and come, or doubt it and stay away.'

'And most came . . .' He gazed at her. 'I owe a lot to you. But I'd like to know more about this perception of yours, since it's about me. Can you tell me about it?'

She looked away again, back out over the ears of her horse.

'I can,' she said. 'But, in this case, I don't think I will.'

They rode on in silence for a few seconds more.

'Of course,' he said., 'Forgive me.'

She reined her horse to a standstill so sharply it tossed its head against the pressure of the bit. He pulled up also and turned to see her almost glaring at him.

'Why do you ask me?' she said. 'You know what happened to you at Graemehouse!'

He studied her for a second.

'Yes,' he said, finally. 'I know. But how could you?'

'I found you there,' she said, 'and I knew something like it was likely to happen.'

'Why?' he said. 'Why would you expect anything to happen to me at Graemehouse?'

'Because of what I saw in you, your first night here.' Her voice was challenging. 'You don't remember, do you? Do you at least remember telling me that you felt an identity with Donal – because he'd always been considered such an odd boy by his family and his teachers at the Academy?'

The echo of his own words sounded in his memory.

'I guess I did,' he said.

'How did you know that about him?'

'Malachi, I guess,' he said. 'Malachi must have told me. You said yourself he'd probably been involved in contracts taken by the Graemes.'

'Malachi Nasuno,' she said, 'would never have known. The Graemes never talked about each other to people outside the family. They didn't even talk about each other to Morgans. And no teacher at the Academy would discuss a student with anyone but another teacher, or the student's parents.'

Hal sat his horse, saying nothing. There was nothing in him to say.

'Well,' she demanded, at last. 'What made you think Donal was isolated? Where did you get the idea that his teachers referred to him as an odd boy? Are you going to tell me you made it up?'

Still, he could find no response in him. She started walking her horse again. Automatically, he put his in motion to follow her; and they rode on again, side by side.

After a while, he spoke; not so much to her as to the universe in general, staring forward meanwhile at the route they followed together.

'No,' he said, somberly, 'whatever else may be, I didn't make it up.'

They rode on. His mind was suddenly so full it blinded him, and Amanda did not intrude upon his thoughts. When they reached the stable door at Fal Morgan and dismounted, she took the reins from his hand.

'I'll take care of the horses,' she said. 'Go and think things out by yourself for a bit.'

He went into the house. But instead of continuing on down the corridor to the privacy of his bedroom, he found himself turning into the living room. The lights there went on automatically as he entered, and the brightness jarred on him. With a wave of his hand at the nearest sensor, he turned them off. The living room was left dimly lit by only the light from the corridor to the kitchen down which he had just come. The gloom was comforting. He walked in and dropped into a chair before the unlit fireplace, staring sightlessly at the kindling and logs laid waiting there.

There was a strange mixture of emotion in him. Part of it was a large feeling of relief and triumph; but another part was a dark sadness he had never experienced before. Once again, he was conscious of his own isolation from everyone else. The memory of the cadaverous man turning in the doorway to say he was sorry would not leave him. He was inescapably aware of all that the other man had to lose. In fact, he was aware of how they all would lose, if they followed him into the struggle against the Others. But they would lose even more if they did not join him. Still, with him, they would lose much; and he could not turn away from the fact there was no way to temper what would be, just to protect them from their pain.

He heard, with the corners of his consciousness, the kitchen door open and close and the sound of Amanda's footfalls come down the corridor to the living room, enter, and stop suddenly.

'Hal?' Her different, unsure voice erected the hairs on the back of his neck. 'Is that you – Hal?'

He was on his feet, turned about and standing over her, where she had backed against the wall next to the entrance, before he realized he had moved.

He towered over her. He had never before been this aware of his size, in relation to hers; and it seemed to him she had grown smaller, shrunk back against the wall as she was. But he could see nothing to terrify her. They were alone. Their faces stared at each other in the half-light, across a few inches of distance; and his soul turned over in him to see her so frightened.

Gently, he took hold of her shoulders; and was shocked to discover how small the bones and flesh of them felt, wrapped and enclosed by his own large hands. Gently, still holding her, sliding his hands about her shoulders, he stepped aside and behind her, urging her from the wall to one of the chairs facing the unlit fireplace.

'No,' she said, closing her eyes as she reached the chair, pulling away from him and seating herself. He sank down into a chair half-facing hers, and stared at her. His own eyes, adjusted to the dimness, saw the paleness of her face.

'It's all right . . .' she said, after a long moment, in a hushed, breathless voice. She opened her eyes and went on, a little numbly. 'It was just for a moment there. I'd thought you'd naturally go to your room to think. He got thin in the last years, but his hair stayed black – like yours. He . . . sometimes forgot to light the fire; and he used to sit like that, stooped a bit. It was a shock, that's all.'

He stared at her.

'Ian,' he said. 'You mean . . . Ian.'

Out of all his feeling for her came a sudden understanding.

'You were in love with him.' He could not have pulled his gaze from her face with all the willpower he possessed. 'At his age?'

'At any age,' she said. 'Every woman loved Ian.'

A dull knife slowly cut and churned him up inside. The reciprocal feeling for him that he believed he had sensed in her – everything he thought he had understood – all wrong. He had been only a surrogate for a man dead for years, a man old enough to be her great-grandfather.

'I was sixteen when he died,' she said.

– And then he understood. To love and not be able to have, as she was growing up, would have been bad enough. To love and watch the dying would have been beyond bearing. The terrible fire of loss within him was flooded out by love for her and the urge to comfort her. He reached out to her, starting to get up.

'No,' she said, quickly. 'No. No.'

He dropped his arm back, the pain returning. Of course she would not want to be touched by him – particularly now. He should have known that.

They sat in silence for several minutes, he not looking at her. Then he got up, almost mechanically, and lit the fire. As the warmth and the light of the little red flames, moving out and multiplying among the pieces of firewood, began to take over and change the room, he ventured to look at her again. He saw that the color had begun to come back to her face, but the face itself still showed a rigidity from the lingering effects of her shock. She sat with her arms upon the arms of the chair, her back straight against its back.

'You did well, today,' she said.

'Better than I'd hoped,' he answered.

'Not just that. You did well, very, very well,' she said. 'I told you, carrying anything over seventy per cent of them would be a victory. You only lost four out of thirty-one people; and you didn't even really lose them. You convinced them too thoroughly, that's why they left.'

'I suppose,' he said. A little of the earlier feeling of relief and triumph returned for a brief second. 'But I was losing them to begin with, there. And then Rourke di Facino asked that one question and it seemed to trigger off just what I wanted to tell them. Did you notice?'

'I noticed,' she said.

Her brief reply did not encourage him to talk further about the explosion of competence that had come so unexpectedly upon him at the meeting. He turned away to poke the fire; and when he looked at her again, she had gotten to her feet.

'I'd better get us something to eat,' she said; and waved him back as he started to get up. 'No. Stay there. I'll bring it in here.'

She crossed the room quickly to the table with the drinks on it, poured some of the dark whiskey into a glass and brought it back to him.

'Sit and relax,' she said. 'Everything's fine. I'll call Omalu and find out the situation on a ship that can get you out toward the Final Encyclopedia.'

He took the glass, smiled; and drank a little from it. She smiled back, turned, and left the room. He put the glass down on the table beside him.

He had no desire for it, now. But she would notice if he did not drink at least some of it. He set himself to get it down, gradually; and had almost succeeded by the time she came in with two covered hot-dishes on a tray, which she set down on a small table between his chair and the one she had occupied earlier. The tray divided to become two trays; and she passed one over to him, with tableware and a covered dish on it.

'Thanks,' he said, uncovering the dish. 'It smells good.'

'There's a question you're going to have to think about,' she said, uncovering her own dish. 'I called the spaceport at Omalu. A ship's leaving for Freiland, from which you can transfer to one headed for Earth. It leaves tomorrow at mid-day. If you don't take that, the next might be in three weeks – or more. They're not certain. But it'll be at least three weeks. Do you still want to give them a week here?'

'I see,' he said, laying his fork down. She was looking at him with a face on which he could read only the concerned interest of a house-holder with a guest. 'You're right. Perhaps I'd better be on that one, tomorrow.'

'It's too bad,' she said. 'If you could have stayed a week, some of those you met yesterday would've had a chance to talk to you again. There was a time when finding passage out of Omalu to any of the other thirteen worlds was something you could do almost overnight. But not now.'

'It's too bad, as you say,' he said. 'But I'd better take the ship I know is leaving.'

'Yes. You're probably right.' She lowered her gaze to her plate and became busy eating. 'You've got interstellar credit enough for passage, of course?'

'Oh, yes,' he said to her forehead. 'There's no problem there. . . .'

They ate. In spite of the newly empty feeling inside him, his appetite did not let him down; and the soporific effect of the good-sized meal on top of the tensions of the day dulled his emotions and made him realize how tired he was. They talked for a little while about the next day's plans.

'I think some of those who were there today may want to have a last word with you,' she said. 'I'll phone around and see. We could get to the spaceport early and talk in the restaurant, there; if you don't have any objection.'

'No objection, of course,' he said. 'But maybe I should be the one to call them?'

'No,' she said. 'Get some sleep. I'll be up for a few hours yet, anyway, with things I've got to do.'

'All right,' he said. 'Thank you.'

'It's no trouble.'

Shortly, he went to bed; and in the darkness of his room escaped at last into the cave of sleep.

He slept heavily. He was roused by Amanda calling him on the house phone circuit; and he looked up from his pillow to see her face in the screen.

'Breakfast in twenty minutes,' she said. 'We'd better get going.'

'Right,' he said, half-awake.

The kitchen was bright with the first full light of morning as he came into it and took a seat at the table. Thick soup and chunks of brown bread were already waiting for him. She sat down with him.

'How do you want to make the trip to Omalu?' she asked.

He swallowed some bread.

'Is there a choice?'

'There's two ways,' she told him. 'We can hitch a ride, if someone from the area happens to be flying into Omalu today; or, if no one is, which is most likely, we can call for transportation for you from Omalu. In either case, you'll have to pay your way to whoever we ride with. I won't. Of course, I can take you. Because of the work I do, I've got my own jitney.'

He frowned. What she had just said had somehow seemed to end hanging in the air.

'In which case I wouldn't have to pay,' he said, slowly. 'But the Dorsai can use any interstellar credits it can get from me, isn't that right?'

'That's right,' she said. 'If you can afford them.'

'Of course,' he said. 'Just let me know how much I ought to pay you for the ride.'

'We'll go by the fuel used,' she got to her feet. 'I'll go roll the jitney out now. You finish here and collect anything you've got to take with you. Then come down beyond the stable and you'll find me.'

There was nothing that he particularly needed to bring beyond what he had carried in when he had come. What he was carrying away that was important, from the Dorsai and particularly from Fal Morgan and Foralie, was immaterial and interior. They lifted off into the same almost-cloudless sky that had graced all the days he had been there.

– And they descended into an unbroken layer of clouds a little more than an hour later, over Omalu.

Below the clouds it was raining; not heavily, but steadily. They

462

landed on the planetary pad, on the other side of the terminal from the pad for deep-space ships; and ran together through the rain to the side door of the terminal.

When they got to the restaurant on the building's second level, the list on the reservation screen showed the Grey Captains in Cubicle Four. Amanda led Hal through the open central dining area to the private rooms beyond. Cubicle Four turned out to be a room more than adequate to hold the nearly forty people already seated at square, green tables there. Three sides of the room were white-dyed, concrete walls, with the fourth side all window, giving on the downpour over the planetary pad. Heavy white coffee cups were scattered around a number of the tables.

'You've got nearly two hours,' said Amanda. 'Come along. There's at least a dozen people here you haven't met yet.'

She took him off to be introduced. It developed that two of those who had walked out the day before, one woman and one man, had returned, and with them were Grey Captains who had not chosen, or had not been able, to make the first meeting. After Hal had been introduced he took a chair facing a semi-circle of others drawn from the tables and began to answer questions. After a little more than an hour however, he called a halt.

'I don't think we're making much progress this way,' he told them. 'Basically what you're all asking me for are specific answers. This is the very thing I don't have to give you, simply because I haven't got them myself yet. I don't have a specific plan, as I've already told you, several times. That's what I'm going to the Final Encyclopedia to work out. All I can do for you now is what I've done; point out the situation and leave you to look at it for yourselves until I've got more information.'

'No offense intended, Hal Mayne,' said Rourke di Facino. He was sitting in the center of the semicircle, looking small and dandified, with the large, padded collar of his travelling jacket thrown open to the warmth of the cubicle. 'But you've raised a demon among us; and now you seem to be refusing to lend a hand in laying it.'

For a moment it seemed to Hal that the certainty that had visited him in the dining room stirred and threatened to take him over again. Then it subsided; and he kept a firm grip on his patience.

'I'll repeat what I've said before,' he said. 'I've only pointed out to you the situation as it exists; and that was something you actually already knew. You've all made it plain that you won't promise to do anything more than consider what I've told you. On my side, I can't promise anything more than I have, either.'

'At least,' said Ke Gok, 'give us some idea of what to expect, some idea of what direction you're heading in. Give us something we can tie to.'

'All right,' said Hal.' Let me put it this way, then. Would you all be willing to move against the Others if the chance could be offered in the form of ordinary military action?'

There was a general chorus of assent.

'All right,' said Hal, wearily. 'As far as I know now, that's what I'll be trying to find for you. It's your strength; and it's only sensible to work with it.'

'And on that note,' said Amanda, getting to her feet, 'I'm going to take Hal Mayne away. He'll be going directly to his ship. Those of you who want to say goodbye, say it now.'

To Hal's surprise, they all crowded around him. It was not until Amanda had finally extricated him and they were going down a flight of old-fashioned stairs to the ground level, that he thought to look at his chronometer.

'We've got a good ten minutes yet before I'd have had to go,' he said.

'I wanted to talk to you alone,' said Amanda. 'Here, this way.'

She led him off from the foot of the stairs to a small waiting room with a door in its far wall. She led him to the door, opened it and they stepped out onto the spaceship pad.

The door sucked shut behind them under the differential in air pressure between pad and terminal. Weather control had been turned on over the pad, now that liftoff was close. The clouds lay thick above, appearing to be humped up into a dome over the pad by the action of the control; and gray, wavering curtains of rain enclosed the three open sides of the pad. Out here, the air felt damp and thick, with that peculiar stillness found in atmosphere artificially held. The increased pressure and the stillness, together, gave the impression that they were suspended in a bubble outside of ordinary time and space. Eighty meters distant, out on the pad, the spaceship for Freiland lay, lengthwise, enormous and mirror-bright, with her polished skin holding the images of the terminal, the clouds and the rain about her, fuming off the last of the decontaminant gas from her loaded cargo holds.

Amanda turned and began to walk eastward along the blank lower face of the terminal, pierced only by glassless, self-sealing doors like the one that had let them onto the pad. Hal fell in beside her.

'You realize,' she said, 'you've only been here eight days.' She was walking along with her eyes fixed on the rain curtain at the pad edge, two hundred meters ahead of them.

'Yes,' he said. 'It hasn't been long.'

'It's not easy to get to understand someone else in eight days – or eight weeks or eight months, for that matter,' she said. She glanced sideways at him, briefly; then turned her attention once more to the rain at the edge of the pad. 'If two people come from different cultures, they can use the same words and mean two different things; and if their reasons for doing what they do aren't understood, then without planning to, either one of them can completely mislead the other.'

'Yes,' he said. 'I know.'

'I know you were raised by a Dorsai,' she said. 'But that's not the same as being born here. Even born here, you could be wrong about someone from another household. You don't know – and in eight days you couldn't learn to know – the Morgans. Or the Amandas. Or me.'

'It's all right,' he said. 'I think I know what you're trying to tell me. I understand. I simply look like Ian.'

She stopped, turned and stared at him. Necessarily, he also stopped, and they stood, face to face.

'Ian?' she said.

'That's what I found out last night, wasn't it?' he said. 'That he looked in his old age something like me; and you'd been . . . fond of him.'

'Oh!' she said, and looked away from him, back at the rain. 'Not that, too!'

'Too?' He stared at her.

'Of course I loved Ian,' she said. 'I couldn't help loving him. But after he died, I grew up.'

She broke off. Then began again.

'I tried to help you understand,' she said. 'Weren't you listening when I talked to you about the first Amanda, and the second? Couldn't you hear what I was telling you?'

'No,' he said, 'now that you ask, I guess I didn't. I didn't realize you were trying to tell me something.'

She made a small, harsh sound in her throat and walked for a few seconds toward the rain without saying anything more. He went in silence beside her.

'I'm sorry,' she said, after a minute, more gently. 'It's my fault. I was the one trying to explain. If you didn't understand, then it's my responsibility. I told you about the other two Amandas hoping you'd understand about me.'

'What was it I should have understood?' he asked.

'What I am – what all three of us are. The first Amanda had three husbands; but really – even including Jimmy, her first son, who was a special case – what she lived for was her family and people in general. She was a galloping protector.' Amanda breathed deeply, going ahead with her eyes still fixed on the rain curtains at the edge of the pad. 'The second Amanda understood herself. That's why she wouldn't marry Kensie or Ian – particularly Ian, whom she loved best. She gave them both up because sooner or later she knew a choice would come for her, between the one she'd chosen and her duty to everyone else; and she knew that when that happened it wouldn't be him, but everyone else she'd choose.'

She walked a few more paces.

465

'And I'm an Amanda too,' she said. 'So, I'm going to be just as wise as the second Amanda; and save myself and other people heartache.'

They walked on.

'I see,' said Hal, at last.

'I'm glad you see,' said Amanda. She did not look at him.

'Well,' said Hal, after a moment. He felt numb; and in the domed space created around them by the weather control, everything appeared artificial and unreal. He looked at the spaceship. 'Perhaps I ought to be getting on board.'

She stopped, and he stopped with her. She turned to him and held out her hand. He hesitated for a fraction of a second, then took it.

'I'll be back,' he told her.

'Be careful,' she said. Their hands still clasped tightly together. 'The Others aren't going to like what you're doing. The easiest way for them to stop it, is to stop you.'

'I'm used to that,' He stood, looking into her eyes. 'I've been running from them for over five standard years, remember?'

He smiled at her. She smiled back; and with an effort they both let go.

'I'll be back,' he said again.

'Oh, come back!' she told him. 'Come back safely!'

'I will.'

He turned and ran for the spaceship. When he reached the top of the landing ladder and paused to turn his papers and certificate of passage over to the ship's officer, just inside the airlock, he looked back and saw her, made very small by the distance, still standing a little beyond the east end of the terminal building, and looking in his direction, with the curtains of the rain distant behind her, still coming down.

CHAPTER FORTY-NINE

'Tell them,' said Hal, 'that I don't have a pass. But ask them to contact Ajela and give her my name – Hal Mayne.'

He stood in the debarkation lounge of the spaceship that had brought him from Freiland to Earth and which now lay holding its distance at ten kilometers from the Final Encyclopedia. He was talking to the debarkation officer, a slim, gray-haired man; and the two of them were alone in the lounge, now that the hundred and fifty-three other passengers had left for Earth's surface.

At the further ends of the long lounge, the lights had already automatically dimmed themselves to a level of standby illumination; and there was a coolness in the air, because for the few minutes yet the lounge would remain open it was not economical for the heating elements to remedy the drop in room temperature caused by the sudden absence of the large crowd of warm bodies which had abruptly and noisily left it for the landing jitney. The slight chill wrapped around Hal, bringing back to his mind once more the dream from which he had woken in the mountains on Harmony, to find himself trying to strangle Jason Rowe. The dream had come again, ten hours ago, his last night here on shipboard. Again, he had taken leave of those with him, had dismounted and started off alone across the rubbled plain toward the distant tower; only, this time, he had penetrated further into the plain than ever before, and discovered the deception of its appearance.

From its edge it had appeared level and smooth, all the way to the tower. But as he went, he found that the scant grass and hard, pebbled earth of the surface on which he had started had gradually begun to show a change. For one thing, the slope of the ground was deceptive. The fact emerged that the plain actually rose as it approached the tower; and only some trick of perspective had made it seem level, seen from far off.

But, more important, the farther he had penetrated across its bare openness, the more the apparent flatness and smoothness of it had revealed itself to be an illusion. The ground gradually became seamed with cracks enlarging to gullies, the pebbles were superseded by rocks, and the rocks by boulders; and what had been stony soil became only stone; so that his toilsome progress toward the tower had

467

been hindered and slowed to the rate of a man climbing a cliff. . . .

But now, as he stood chilled and separate from the officer who was talking on his behalf with the Final Encyclopedia, it was not his recollection of the struggle across the rocky land, his turnings and back-trackings between the great rocks barring his way, that had been brought back to mind. It was something remembered from very early in the dream and very simple. It had been the creak of his saddle leathers as he had swung down to the ground, the decisive abandonment of the warmth and strength of the horse-body between his knees, the overall feel of leave-taking from all who were familiar, in order to take up the unmarked path of a pilgrimage to some hidden but powerfully attractive goal. Something about this moment and this waiting for entrance this second time to the Final Encyclopedia had brought it back to him. . . .

But the ship's officer had finally gotten into talk with someone at the Encyclopedia who could undertake the conveying of the message Hal had asked sent to Ajela.

'Stand by,' said the male voice of whoever was at the far end.

Silence fell on the speaker grilles by the phone.

'Who's this Ajela, then?' the officer asked.

'The personal assistant to Tam Olyn,' said Hal.

'Oh.' The officer looked down and became busy with a stylus on the desktop screen under his fingers. Hal waited. But in less than a minute, the voice came again.

'No need to pass that request on,' it said. 'I thought I'd seen the name before, so I just checked. Hal Mayne's on the permanent pass list.'

'Thanks,' said the officer in the phone. 'All right. We'll have him straight over to you.'

He cut connection and turned to Hal.

'You didn't know you had a permanent pass?'

Hal shook his head, smiling a little.

'No.'

'All right,' said the officer, into the phone. 'Launch Deck – is the repair boat ready yet?'

'Already on its way.'

'Thank you.'

In fact, the officer had hardly cut connection for a second time before the warning chime from the airlock announced that a boat had docked at it and was unsealing. Hal turned and went to the lock, and the officer came along behind him.

They waited, listening to the sounds of the unsealing process, that carried through the closed inner airlock door. Finally, it swung open; and Hal could look through the matched airlocks to the repair boat's interior, cluttered with machine shop equipment.

'Have a good trip, sir,' said the officer.

'Thanks,' said Hal.

Carrying his small satchel of personal possessions, he ducked through the matched locks, feeling the brief but sudden deeper chill of heat radiated from his body to the cold metal of the lock interiors, and stepped into the repair boat.

'This way, sir,' said a middle-aged, muscular shipwoman in white coveralls. 'You'll have to thread your way through the equipment, I'm afraid.'

'That's all right,' Hal said, following her along a complicated route, around and between the hard-edged pieces of equipment, toward the control cabin in the bow of the boat.

'It's just that the regular ship-to-surface passenger jitney is too big for the entry lock at the Encyclopedia,' she went on over her shoulder. 'That jit is built to carry up to two hundred passengers and crew.'

'They explained that,' said Hal.

'Just so you don't feel snubbed.' She laughed. 'In here, now. . . .'

They entered the cabin and Hal found himself in a room full of control consoles and screens, with three operations chairs up ahead, facing a segmented vision screen. The chair on the far left was already occupied by a shipman, sitting idle.

'Take the seat in middle, if you don't mind,' said the shipwoman.

Hal obeyed. She seated herself to his right and laid her hands on the console before her. Behind them, there was the sound of their airlock resealing and a brief jolt. Then all feeling of motion ceased

'That's it, up ahead,' offered the shipman. He was a wiry man in his forties, smaller than his partner.

Hal looked into the large screen. Its segments at the moment were combined to show a single wide image that spread itself out before them. It was an image of starfilled space; and in the center of it, in full sunlight, floated the small, misty globe of their destination.

The Final Encyclopedia hung there – as they also seemed to hang still, facing it – like a ball small enough for the hand of a young child to hold comfortably. But as Hal watched, it began to enlarge. It swelled and grew before him until it had filled the screen and began to loom, smoke-gray and enormous, over their repair boat, shutting out their view of half the universe.

An opening of bright, yellow light appeared before them as an iris dilated; and they rode through into the same noisy metal cavern that Hal remembered from his first visit, five years before.

The shipwoman got up with him, and steered him back through the equipment in the main cabin of the repair boat and out through the airlock that was already standing open.

He walked down the sloping ramp, his ears assaulted by the clangor of machines moving about on bare metal decking. Ahead of him was the faintly hazy circle that was the entrance to the interior of the Final Encyclopedia; as he stepped through it, the sound behind

469

him was cut off. He stood, and let the moving corridor onto which he had just stepped carry him forward toward a vision screen on the wall to his right, ahead. The screen had been blank, but just before he came level, it illuminated, and the face of Ajela looked out.

'Hal? Take the first door on your right,' her voice told him.

He rode along for another ten meters, saw the door and went through it into another, shorter corridor without a moving walkway. At the end of this was a second door. He pushed it open when he reached it, and went in.

As it sucked shut softly behind him, he saw that he had come into a room half-office, half-lounge. The farthest wall, almost a copy of what he remembered seeing in Tam Olyn's suite, appeared to give on a stream winding through a summer forest; but here the light was like the sunlight of early morning. Ajela was already rising from behind a large desk. Her pink gown rippled as she ran to him, kissed him, then stood back to stare.

'Look at you!' she said.

He had, in fact, been looking at her. After Amanda, and other women he had met on the Dorsai, she gave an appearance of being tiny and fragile – not merely small in stature, by comparison, but more delicate in bone and feature. And yet, he knew that in comparison to the general run of humanity she would not be considered so.

'Look at me?' he answered, triggered by her warm smile to smiling back at her, for no other reason than that she was radiating such happiness. 'Why?'

'You're a monster. A giant!' she told him. 'Twice the size you were when I saw you last, and savage-looking enough to scare people.'

He laughed at that.

'Savage-looking?' he said.

'See for yourself.' She turned him toward the wall at his left, and must have signalled some sensor; for the misty blueness of the wall changed to a mirror surface that gave him back his own image and that of the room around him.

He gazed, startled in spite of himself. He was used to seeing himself every morning as he wiped off the stubble of his beard; and from time to time otherwise, he had caught glimpses of himself in reflecting surfaces like this one. But he had not viewed himself as he now did, with Ajela beside him and in sudden empathy with how she must see him.

The sudden stranger he now saw in the mirror towered above the slim, blond-haired young woman at his elbow. The man's body was lean, broadening from a slender waist to a wide chest, and shoulders broad enough above the narrowness of waist and hips to make him look almost top-heavy. The face above the shoulders was strong-

470

boned, the mouth level, the nose straight; and the eyes, dark gray with a slight difference in color between them, looked out under straight black brows and a wide forehead topped by straight, almost coarse, black hair. But even these features, in total, could not by themselves make for the overall impression that had caused Ajela to call him savage-looking. There was something else, an impression about the figure he stared at which might have been called one of controlled violence, if it had not been for a somber thoughtfulness of eyes, that seemed to overwhelm the general impression of face and body, alike.

He turned from the screen to Ajela.

'Well,' she said. 'You're back to stay? Or is it only a visit?'

He hesitated.

'Both,' he said. 'I'll have to explain what I mean by that –'

'Yes, you will,' she said; and suddenly hugged him again. 'Oh, Tam's going to be so happy!'

She took his hand, towed him toward her desk and pushed him into a padded float beside it.

'How are you?' she said. 'Are you hungry? Can I get you anything?'

He laughed.

'I've still got a pretty good appetite,' he said. 'But let's just talk for the moment. You sit down.'

She perched on the edge of her desk, facing him.

'Let me explain what I meant, just now,' he said; and hesitated, again.

'Go on,' said Ajela.

'I've been thinking about how to explain this to you,' he said slowly. 'I was going to ask you to believe me when I said there's nothing I could imagine myself wanting to do more, than take Tam up now on his offer to work here at the Encyclopedia. . . .'

'And then you realized it wasn't true,' said Ajela, quietly watching him. 'Is that it?'

'Yes and no.' He frowned at her. 'The Encyclopedia pulls me like a moon pulls the tides. I've got things to do here. In the real meaning of the words, it's a tool I've wanted all my life. I know there're things I can do with it, if I had time, that haven't even been dreamed of by anyone else, yet. When I was here before, I really wanted to stay. But you remember I found out I couldn't. There were other things that had to be done. Well, I've still got most of them to do.'

'That's the whole reason that's holding you back from staying with us?' She was watching him closely.

He smiled a bit ruefully.

'That's the immediate reason,' he said. 'But, you're right, to be honest, it isn't all of it. You see, these last few years I've been out among people –'

He hesitated, then went on.

'It's not that easy to explain,' he said, 'put it that I've found I've got

471

things I have to do with people, too; and in any case, right now, there's something more immediate and important. I'd like to talk to you and Tam together, about it. Is that possible?'

'Of course,' she said. 'I haven't told him you're here yet; simply because I wanted a minute or two with you myself, first. The fact is, he's sleeping right now; but he'll be upset if I wait until he wakes up to tell him you're back. Just a second. I'll call him –'

She swung around and reached back over her desk.

'No. Wait,' said Hal. 'Let me give you a general idea of what I'm talking about, first. Let him sleep. There're things with me now I want you to understand, and it'll take me a few hours just to bring you up to date.'

'All right,' Ajela drew her arm back and turned to face him, smiling again. 'Now, are you sure you don't feel like having something to eat?'

Hal laughed.

'Well, maybe . . .' he said.

They went to eat at a table in one of the dining rooms; and Ajela, touching the table's sensor controls, enclosed them this time in something new to him, the privacy of four illusory stone walls.

'Could we have the stars, instead?' Hal asked. 'All around us the way I can have them in a carrel?'

She smiled, moved her fingers over the control pad on the white cloth surface of the table, and abruptly they seemed to float in space, with the large, blue-white circle of Earth appearing to hang only a small distance off to their side, and Earth's moon just beginning to emerge from behind it.

In all other directions were the lights and distances of the universe. Hal looked about and overhead and down below his feet at them, picking out Earth's sister worlds of Mars and Venus; and gazing toward the other suns of the race – Sirius, Alpha Centauri, Tau Ceti, Procyon, Epsilon Eridani, Fomalhaut, Altair. In his mind's eye he saw beneath them what his physical eyes could not, humanity's other thirteen planetary homes – Freiland and New Earth, Newton and Cassida, Ceta, Coby, Ste. Marie, Mara and Kultis, Dorsai, Harmony and Association, Dunnin's World.

Imaginatively, he saw not only them but the people upon them; and for a second he breathed deeply, the emptiness he had felt earlier at the thought of their numbers returned.

'What is it?' Ajela asked, her voice suddenly more soft, her summer-green eyes deeply watching him now.

'Too much to tell at once, probably,' he said, recovering. He smiled to reassure her. 'Anyway, let's have that food, and I'll tell you what's been happening to me.'

They sat among the stars, eating; and he talked. He told her of the mines on Coby and Sost, Tonina and John; and Jason, Rukh and

472

James Child-of-God on Harmony; and of his own solitary break-through in the cell on that world, with everything that had happened since.

'But what is it you think you can find here, to deal with the Others?' she asked, when he was done.

'To deal with the problem of present history, you mean,' he said. 'I'm not sure. But the answer's either here or nowhere. It's not just that I've got to find a way to stop the Others. What I have to find is a way that'll be both obvious and convincing to the Exotics, the Dorsai and anyone else who's needed to fight them.'

'And you really think what you're looking for is here?'

'It has to be here,' he said. 'Didn't Mark Torre originally say that the Final Encyclopedia eventually had to be something more than just a storehouse of knowledge? Hasn't Tam guarded it all these years so that a way might be finally found to do something larger with it than anyone's ever conceived of, yet? If it was my idea alone, I might doubt. But we all can't have been wrong. Three of us – all three – coming to the same conclusion about it, each on his own.'

'But if it's really true that the ultimate use of the Encyclopedia has always been something more –' She broke off, suddenly thoughtful.

'That's right,' he said. 'If it's true, then a lot of things begin to make sense. The historical equation balances, then. Otherwise, the dice have been loaded too overwhelmingly by the race-animal in favor of the Others; and that makes no sense. Because the race-animal isn't out to choose one favorite out of the factions within it to win – it's out to get answers on how to survive. The root causes behind the emergence of the Others go back and back in history; and so do the causes leading to the building of the Final Encyclopedia.'

'How sure can you be of that, though?' she asked.

He gazed at her across the table.

'Did you ever hear of Guido Camillo Delminio, or the Theater of Memory?' he asked her.

'The Theater of Memory?' She frowned. 'I think I have heard that mentioned, or read about it someplace. . . .'

'Mark Torre mentions it in his *Memoirs of Construction*,' Hal answered. 'That's where I ran across it, myself, when I was young, in the library of my home. It was a great library; and back when I was young enough, anything I read about, that sounded interesting, I wanted. So when I read the *Memoirs* and saw the words "Theater of Memory" the first thing I thought of was that I wanted to build one. I went to Walter InTeacher to show me the way to find out how, and he helped me research the actual, historical article.'

Ajela frowned at him.

'There actually was something built that was called a Theater of Memory?'

'Partially built, at least, first in Bologna, and later in Paris with the

473

help of funds from Francis I of France. The Guido Camillo I mentioned conceived of it and spent his life trying to turn it into a reality. That was in the sixteenth century, and his aim was to build a theater where anyone could stand on a stage and look out at art objects ranked on rising levels and put in a certain order, and give speeches calling on all the knowledge in the world, which would be cued by the sight of the art objects before him as he spoke.'

She stared at him.

'Where did he get the idea for something like that?' she said. 'The sixteenth century . . .' Her voice trailed off, thoughtfully.

'He was born about 1480,' said Hal. 'He had a professorship at Bologna, but he was always hard up for funds to build with – that's how he and the Theater came to be connected with Francis I. There was a strong desire in Renaissance times to unify all knowledge and in that way see through it to the very essence of creativity. The idea of objects as mnemonic cues goes back into classical Greece, at least. The early churchmen and scholastics made it a moral practice, and later on Renaissance mysticism saw it as a framework for esoteric enlightenment. It produced Guido's Theater in the sixteenth century; in the thirteenth century it had already produced Ramón Lull's combination-of-wheels device; and that was nothing less than a sort of primitive computer. The same idea affected people from Bacon to Leibnitz, who in the seventeeth century actually did invent calculus. In effect, the Theater of Memory was one of the root causes of later technology and of this Encyclopedia, itself.'

'I see,' she said.

'I thought you would,' he said. 'The point is, the whole chain of effort from the Theater to the Final Encyclopedia represents a struggle, an effort by the race-animal to discover greater possibilities in itself. This is the important truth that underlies the struggle between the Others and everyone else – that's where the real battle-field is and is going to be for a while. So that's where I'll have to be for a time, yet.'

'I see,' she said, again. 'All right. I understand, then.'

She nodded slowly, her eyes abstracted.

'Yes,' she said. 'Yes. I think, after all, the sooner you talk to Tam, the better. If you're through eating, I'll call him and we'll go now.'

'Even if I wasn't through,' he smiled. 'But as it happens, I am.'

They went.

To Hal's eye, it was as if Tam Olyn had not altered in appearance or moved since he had seen the very old man last. Tam's suite, with its illusion of a forest and stream, and all its float furniture – chairs, desk, and everything else – seemed not to have been shifted a millimeter out of place, in the intervening years. Above all, the expression of Tam's face was the same.

But his voice was different.

'Hello, Hal Mayne,' he said; and let Hal come to him to grip hands.

The difference was not great; but Hal's ear registered the barely diminished volume, the slightly greater threadiness of breath behind the words and the infinitesimally increased length of the pauses between them as Tam spoke.

'Sit down here, Hal,' said Ajela, leading him to a cushioned float at no more than arm's length from the one in which Tam was sitting and pulling one up alongside his for herself.

'You've come back,' said Tam.

'Yes,' Hal said. 'But I've come back with something I've got to do that involves not only the Encyclopedia but everything else, as well. What that's going to mean, though, is that I think the Encyclopedia is going to be put to use the way it ought to be, at last.'

'Is it?' said Tam. 'Tell me about it.'

'You were right when you talked to me about Armageddon, when I was here before,' Hal said. 'I've taken nearly six years coming to understand what you meant. When I left here to go to the mines on Coby, I didn't know what I was doing; only that I was running, both because I had to find someplace safe for me and because there were things I had to do. What I didn't know then, I do now.'

'Yes,' said Tam. The deep hoarseness of age with which he spoke seemed to make his words walk under Hal's like those of a ghost speaking from a crypt at their feet. 'You had to find yourself. I knew that, even then.'

'I didn't understand people,' said Hal. 'I'd been brought up under glass. That was why my tutors wanted me to go to Coby. On Coby I began to wake up. . . .'

He told Tam about Walter, Malachi and Obadiah, about Coby, Harmony, and his hours in the Militia cell; with all he had come to understand there and all that had followed from that until now. Tam sat and listened with the motionlessness of face and body that time had brought to him. When Hal finally stopped talking, he did not speak for a long moment.

'And it ends with you back here,' he said at last.

'That much of it ends,' said Hal.

Tam sat looking at him. A younger individual would have frowned, questioningly. But Tam no longer needed gross facial movements to signal his reactions.

'That much was only the beginning,' he went on. 'I can understand the situation, now, I can look beyond the Others and know that they're only a part of the real problem; a symptom, not a cause. The real problem's that we've all of us finally come to the point where there's no longer a choice. Now we've got to take charge – consciously – of what's going to happen to us; instead of going on blundering forward instinctively, the way we've always done ever since we first began to look beyond the next meal, or the next dry place to sleep. And the one tool that can let us do that is here. The Final Encyclopedia's the only thing we've managed to show for all those long centuries of savagery and the short centuries of civilization; that so far've only brought us to the point where a handful of us can kill off everyone else.'

'Yes,' said Tam. For a moment he did not say anything more. His gaze went past Hal and Ajela alike; and when he spoke again, it was clearly to himself as well as them.

'Do you know what it means to try to control history?' he said. He looked back to Hal. 'Do you know the mass and momentum of those forces you're talking about laying your hands on? I tried something like that – and I had power. I raised a social tidal wave against a whole people. A tidal wave that ought to have drowned the Friendlies, forever. And all it took to stop me was Jamethon Black, one man of faith who wouldn't move out of my path. On him all that great force I'd built up broke; and it drained away, in a million little streams, in a million directions, doing nothing, harming no one.'

Ajela leaned forward and put one of her hands over one of his, where it laid on the padded arm of his float. Hal looked at the warm, white young hand over the dark, gnarled one of age.

'For nearly ninety years you've been making up for that,' she said, softly.

'I? All I've done is watch the hearth, keep the candle lit. . . .' His head shook on his shoulders, slightly, from side to side. 'But I know the strength of history when it moves.'

He looked back at Hal.

'And it's what you're talking about working with,' he said. 'Even if you're right about using the Encyclopedia, even if everything you hope for gathers behind what you know needs to be done, you'll still be an ant trying to direct a hurricane. You know that?'

'I think so,' said Hal, soberly.

'God knows,' said Tam, 'I want to see you try. God knows it'd justify me, make me of some worth after all these years to the people I'd have destroyed if I could; and also it'd justify Mark Torre and everyone who's come to work here, after him. But think – you could just as easily close your eyes to where it's all going. You could use your mind and your strength to make a comfortable safe niche out of the storm for yourself and any you might love – for the few years your body still has to give you – just by closing your eyes to what's going to happen eventually to people who'll never really know who you were or what it costs you to try what you want to try. You can still turn back.'

'No,' said Hal. 'Not any more. Not for a longer time than you might think.'

Tam breathed in deeply and pushed himself more upright in his float.

'All right, then,' he said. 'Then you ought to know that you've already got most of ten worlds set in motion against what you want. Bleys Ahrens has put in motion a plan for the mobilization of the credit and the force to take over everything the Others don't already control, by military means if necessary.'

There was a moment's silence among the three of them.

'Bleys?' said Hal. 'What about Danno?'

'Danno died, unexpectedly and conveniently, four standard months ago,' said Tam. 'Bleys controls the Others now. In fact, he may have already for some time since; and plainly he's come to feel he can't risk waiting any longer to act.'

Hal watched the old man, fascinated.

'How do you know that?' he asked. 'How do you know about this plan, this mobilization?'

'It's reflected in hundreds of thousands of ordinary news items,' said Tam. 'All I needed, to pick those out and read them right, was to see the implications of what I read in the neural pathways. What outside scholars come here to do, or what they ask us to tell them, mirrors the state of affairs on their worlds.'

'In the neural pathways?' Hal turned to stare at Ajela.

'I haven't seen it there.' Her face was pale. 'But I told you no one could read the pathways like Tam.'

'Time teaches anyone,' said Tam. 'Believe me.'

The full strength of his grim and cantankerous spirit was in his voice; and Hal believed him. Looking at this man who had held the Final Encyclopedia true to Mark Torre's dream for so long, Hal understood for the first time that to Tam the task had not been just like that of standing sentinel at a vault. It had been like the guarding of a living being. Not simply the fierceness of a dragon crouching above a treasure had ridden in the other man, but an unthinking commitment like that of someone who defends and maintains a child of his or her body. It was not the machinery, but a soul, to which he had given the long years of his life.

'Then time's short,' said Hal.

'Very short,' said Tam. 'What do you plan to do?'

Now that the decision was plainly taken, the strength that Hal had felt in the older man a moment before had given way once more to the great weariness in him.

'First,' said Hal. 'I've got to use the Encyclopedia to trace the roots leading to the emergence of the Others and the emergence of those who may successfully oppose them. It's the process by which knowledge gives birth to idea, and idea gives birth to art, that's the key to the way the Encyclopedia is finally going to be used. But knowledge has to come first. Until I've got a full picture of how the present situation came to be, I'll have no hope of identifying the human elements that are the real things going to war, here. So, while Bleys mobilizes, I'm going to be tracing people and their actions back into the duct of the past. There's no other path I can take to what we need.'

CHAPTER FIFTY

Nearly a standard year had gone by since Hal had come back to the Final Encyclopedia; and the knowledge he had dug out and forged in that time into new tools for his mind weighed far more heavily on his spirit than he could have imagined, twelve months before. It had enabled him to reach deeper into himself than he had thought possible in such a short time but it had also woken inner, sleeping gods and devils that he had not suspected himself of harboring. He understood now not only who he was, but also what he must do, and neither of those understandings were easy burdens to carry.

He sat, his chair float seemingly adrift in space above the eastern hemisphere of the Dorsai. What he looked at was a simulation. No clouds were visible, but innumerable tiny white lights were scattered across the face of the numerous islands that made up the land mass of that sea-girt world; and it was these lights that Hal was considering.

Each of the lights stood for a pad on which a full-sized spacecraft could land and take off – always assuming there was a man or woman of the Dorsai, or an equivalently skilled pilot, at the controls, to justify the risks in handling such a vehicle on and off surface. There were others besides Dorsai pilots who could bring deep space vessels safely to a planetary surface, of course; but it was an uncommon skill.

The great number of pads he now looked at was therefore not surprising, considering the world they were on. Harmony, with its two fitting yards, of which one had been put out of action when he left, and with only two other pads where heavy spacecraft could be landed, was more typical of the other thirteen inhabited planets. Hal rotated the image of the Dorsai to show its western hemisphere; and the lights that signalled pads were as numerous there, as well.

The only other worlds that approached Dorsai in their numbers of landing places were the two Exotic planets of Mara and Kultis; but both of these together did not have as many spacecraft pads as those he had just been observing. The large number on the Dorsai, of course, were attributable to the nearly three centuries in which Dorsai had been not merely a supplier of professional soldiers, but full of training areas for them. Expeditionary forces were normally not only assembled but worked into shape close to the home areas of the officers who had undertaken the contract that would employ all of them.

Hal coded for a list of the pads he had been looking at, with their locations and their distances from nearby concentrations of the Dorsai populace; and as he did so, there was the sound of a single musical chime and a voice spoke to him from among the stars.

'Hal? Jeamus Walters. I can drop in now, if you're ready for me.'

'Come ahead,' said Hal.

He touched the invisible console at his fingertips, staying the list and re-evoking his normal working surroundings. The image of the Dorsai vanished and the small carrel off his own room in the Final Encyclopedia came into existence around him – walls, ceiling, floor, and furniture. The carrel was a tiny place – hardly more than a cubbyhole; and his main room beyond was not much more – almost a single-room office, with bedroom furniture recessed in the walls, and perhaps enough space to gather at most five or six people on floats in close conversation. A moment later, the door chimed on a deeper note than the phone had used to announce Jeamus Walters' call.

'Come on in,' said Hal. The door opened to admit a short, broad man with thin blond hair on a round skull and a pleasant middle-aged face.

'Sit down,' said Hal. 'How much time have you?'

'As much as you want, now,' said Jeamus. 'We were just doing a periodic checkover when you called, earlier.'

Hal touched his console and one side of the room blanked out to show the Final Encyclopedia from the outside; the image was enough to fill the space that had been between ceiling and floor, its gray, misty protective screen looking close enough so that either man could reach out and touch it.

'I haven't had time to learn much about it,' said Hal, looking at the protective screen. 'Periodic checkover, you said? I thought the screen was self-sustaining?'

'It is, of course,' said Jeamus. 'Once created, it's independent of anything else in the universe. Just as the same thing in phase-shift form would have to be independent of the universe, or it couldn't move space-craft around in it. But one of the things that that independence means, is that if we constructed a screen around the Encyclopedia and did nothing more, we'd immediately begin to move out from inside it, as we travelled along with the rest of the solar system, here. So we have to arrange to have it move with us; or we'd destroy ourselves trying to go through it, just like anything else would destroy itself trying to get through it at us. Consequently, we arrange for it to move with us; which takes a certain amount of controlling – as does making irises available, opening and closing them, and all the rest of that business –'

He broke off, looking at Hal.

'You didn't ask me in just to hear me lecture on the phase-screen, though, did you?'

'As a matter of fact, yes,' said Hal. 'I've got some questions about it. How large can you make it? I mean, how large an area can you enclose and protect?'

Jeamus shrugged.

'Theoretically, there's no limit,' he said. 'Well, yes, of course there's the limit imposed by the size of the power source needed to create the protective sphere and keep adjusting it; and you have to keep adjusting, even if you're creating it to be set adrift in the universe; because sooner or later it'd begin to break down under the anomalies inherent in being a timeless system existing in a temporal universe.'

'What's the practical limit, then, approximately?' Hal asked. 'Suppose we just wanted to expand the sphere around us now and keep expanding it as far as we could.'

Jeamus ruffled the thin hair on the back of his head, thoughtfully.

'Well,' he said, 'theoretically, we could make it a number of times as large as the solar system, given the power of our available sun – but actually, as soon as we reached the size of Earth's orbit we'd have the sun inside it with us –' he broke off. 'I'd have to figure that.'

'But,' said Hal, 'there'd be no problem in making it large enough to enclose a single world – practically speaking?'

'Well, no . . . there shouldn't be,' said Jeamus. 'You'd run into some control problems. Something like that's never been considered. We've got some pretty interesting problems even now, just with the Encyclopedia here, as far as ingress and egress go. Also, we have to open irises toward the sun, for example, at regular intervals, to draw power . . . what I mean to say is, the controls for a sphere any larger would have to be very complex, not only for maintenance, but for making irises when and where you wanted them. I suppose you're assuming just about the same proportion of in and out traffic as we have here? Because any differences –'

'No different, for now,' said Hal. 'Could you run me up some figures for a world, say, just a little larger than Earth?'

'Of course,' said Jeamus. He was staring at Hal. 'I suppose I shouldn't ask what all this is about?'

'If you don't mind.'

'Oh, I mind.' Jeamus ruffled his back hair again. 'I'm as curious as the next person. But . . . give me a week.'

'Thanks,' said Hal.

'Don't need to thank me. This is interesting. Anything else?'

'No. And thanks for coming by,' said Hal.

'Honored.' Jeamus got to his feet. 'If you don't hear from me in a week, it'll be because I got sidetracked and bogged down on some

481

maintenance problem. So if I don't get back to you in that time, give me a call; and I'll let you know how I'm coping with this. I suppose you realize, any time this stops being theoretical you're going to have to tell me exactly what you've got in mind if you want any really correct answers.'

'Of course. I understand. Thanks again,' said Hal; and watched the other man leave.

As the door shut, Hal dismissed the image of the Final Encyclopedia and called Ajela.

'How are things?' he asked, when she looked out of the phone screen at him. 'Is now a good time for me to come up and give you both the whole story?'

'Just fine,' she said. 'You'll find us both in Tam's suite.'

'I'll be right there.'

When he stepped through the door into Tam's suite, he found her with Tam, seated in an obviously already prepared group of three chair floats facing each other. He came on in, took the empty float and smiled at Tam.

'How are things?'

'I'm fine,' said Tam. 'Don't waste time worrying about me. You've got the chain of consequences worked out?'

Hal nodded.

'At least as far back as the fourteenth century,' he said. 'Where, for practical purposes, this present historical phase begins with a pivotal figure named John Hawkwood.'

'Ajela told me about him from the time you were here before and wanted to look up Conan Doyle's novelistic hero, Nigel Loring.' Tam's gaze sharpened. 'But Loring was different. He was one of the original Knights of the Garter under the Black Prince, wasn't he? Hawkwood's barely mentioned in Froissart – I know that much.'

'After the Peace of Bretigny, when the Black Prince captured King Jean at Poitiers and England and France were at peace, Hawkwood was one of the leaders of the White Company that went over the mountains into Italy,' Hal said. 'He ended as Captain General of the forces of Florence, two decades later; and he was at least in his forties when he went into Italy.'

'They call him "the first of the modern generals," Ajela tells me,' Tam said. 'Anyway, how'd you get to him? And why've you been so closemouthed about your progress until now?'

'It was one of those situations where I had to have all the pieces before it fell together,' Hal said. 'Until a week ago I was still going largely on faith. That's why I didn't have anything solid to tell you.'

'Faith in yourself,' murmured Ajela.

Tam glanced at her.

'All right,' he said to her. He looked back at Hal. 'Tell us in your own way. I won't interrupt.'

'As you know, I started working from the present backwards,' Hal said. 'The Others are crossbreeds between different Splinter Culture individuals. So they, too, are products of elements in the Splinter Cultures. The Splinter Cultures were a product of elements in the society of Old Earth just before and during the period when the phase-drive began to work and we had the explosion of emigration over less than a hundred years to the presently occupied worlds. The Exotics came from an organization that named itself the Chantry Guild in the twenty-first century. The Friendlies were originally colonies sponsored by the so-called marching societies – and so on and so forth. These, in turn, had their roots in the breakout century – the Chantry Guild of that time grew out of the twentieth century's apocalyptic upsurge of interest in Eastern religions, the occult, and paranormal abilities. The marching societies developed from the reemergence of religious fundamentalism.'

'An apocalyptic time, generally,' Tam grunted. 'In any time of social stress, you've got this sort of hysteria cropping up in biblically-rooted societies. It isn't just with western Christians – the same thing happens with Jews and Moslems, when conditions are right. Lots of historical instances before the twentieth century.'

'But there's a special historical pivot point in the twentieth century,' said Hal. 'It was the time of the acknowledgment of space. The great mass of humanity up until then had ignored, even when they knew of it, the size of the universe outside Earth's air envelope and the insignificance of their little planet compared to it. Suddenly, they couldn't do that anymore, and the psychological shock was profound. Earth had suddenly ceased to be a safe, warm protective shell for the race. They were suddenly naked to the stars. The shock of that made their century unique in human history and pre-history, and they were forced to be aware of that uniqueness. I know – to those people who live in it, their own time is always the supremely important one; but the people in the twentieth really had some reason to think that way. The idea of space shook them up hard, down to the unconscious levels; and consequently, it shook up the then-existing forms of society – all over Old Earth. Those same forms had been shaped by five hundred years of technological development that really became explosive in the mid-nineteenth century . . . and so on. But I'm covering ground too fast, maybe –'

'Did I say you were?' growled Tam.

'No,' Hal smiled at the old man. 'Of course not. What I mean was, I was getting ahead of myself. What I did, working from the present backward, was to key on shifts in historical development, tied to unique individuals. For example, a necessary precursor to the development of the present social conditions that have provided a breeding ground for the rise to power of the Others was the achievement of Donal Graeme in pulling all the fourteen worlds together under one legal system; and putting an end to exploitative opportunities that gave rise to the interstellar barons like William of Ceta –'

'I saw Graeme only once,' the antique way of referring to an individual by surname only rang oddly on Hal's ears, in the harsh old voice of Tam. 'It was at a party for him on Newton. He wasn't particularly impressive to look at.'

'But in any case,' said Hal, 'what Donal did wouldn't have been possible without the emergence of a unique group like the Dorsai; which in the beginning were nothing but a supply of cannon fodder for the intercolony wars of the early centuries of interstellar expansion. And, in turn, what they became, and what Donal achieved would never have been possible without the unorthodox military science developed by Cletus Grahame.'

'Runs in the family, doesn't it?' said Tam, smiling grimly.

'The Dorsai was a strongly hereditary culture,' said Hal. 'It's less surprising on a place like the Dorsai that Donal and Cletus should turn out to be related, than it might have been someplace else. But the interesting thing is that Cletus could not have done what he did without the financial backing of the Exotics, even at that early time, and the Exotics became the Exotics almost exclusively because of –'

'Walter Blunt,' said Tam.

'I don't think so,' said Hal, slowly. 'Walter Blunt was apparently wholeheartedly sincere about his gospel of a cleansing destruction as his cure for whatever ailed the human race. I've got a lot more to learn about Walter Blunt and the Chantry Guild. On the face of it that theory of his is the very antithesis of the search for the evolved human, which the Exotics developed; and yet the Chantry Guild became the Exotics. No, there's another man who comes out of nowhere suddenly, in the late twenty-first century, a mining engineer with one arm who suddenly becomes involved with the Chantry Guild Walter Blunt had founded and rises essentially to challenge Blunt's leadership in a very short time – only to drown almost immediately after that challenge becomes successful, in a small sailboat he was sailing in the Pacific Ocean, offshore. But his brief interaction with the Chantry Guild changes everything about it. After this man – Paul Formain – had been involved, Blunt was left essentially as nothing more than a figurehead; and Jason –'

The chime announcing a phone call interrupted him.

'What's that?' said Tam. 'Ajela, I thought you told them –'

'I said we weren't to be bothered, except for something of the gravest importance,' she answered, reaching for the console on the arm of her float. 'They wouldn't call us unless it was that . . . Chuni?'

'Ajela? We've got a request from Bleys Ahrens to come for a talk with Hal Mayne.'

Ajela's finger lifted from the phone connection. Her eyes, and Tam's as well, went to Hal.

'Yes,' said Hal, after a moment. 'I suppose it was bound to happen. I'll talk to him, of course.'

'Tell Bleys Ahrens he can come on in,' Ajela said over the phone circuit. 'Hal will see him.'

'All right,' answered the voice at the far end. 'And – Ajela?'

'What?'

'We've got another request that came in at almost the same moment, from a jitney that's just docking in B chamber now. An Exotic named Amid; doesn't have a pass, but he also wants to talk to Hal. Bleys Ahrens is holding distance in a private spacecraft. I don't think they know about each other.'

Ajela looked again at Hal.

'Amid first,' said Hal. 'Then Bleys. Amid may have some information for me that'd be useful before I meet Bleys. I told you about Amid; he's the one I mailed my papers to when the Militia caught me finally on Harmony; and he passed the word to the local Exotic consulate to help me if I could get to them, then took care of me on Mara.'

'Let them both in, Chuni,' said Ajela. 'Hal's going to see Amid first. Take him to Hal's room; and if you think they don't know about each other, better keep the two of them separate.'

She glanced at Hal and Hal nodded. She closed off the phone circuit.

'Well,' said Hal, 'I think, under the circumstances, I'd better cut this short. There's too much to tell you to try to rush through it now. The essential point is, the chain leads back to a John Hawkwood, in the fourteenth century. Or rather, it leads back to the Renaissance; and if it hadn't been for John Hawkwood, we might not have had a Renaissance.'

'That's rather a large statement, isn't it?' said Tam. 'You aren't trying to tell us that history goes the way it does not simply because of a chain of social developments, but because of a chain of unusual individuals?'

'No,' said Hal. 'Pressures within the river of historical forces determine the bends and turns in that river; and the unusual individuals are thrown up by those same pressures at the turning points. A different turn or bend would have thrown up a different individual. At least, that's the way it always was in the past. But, beginning about a thousand years ago, the race started to move into an area where certain individuals began to develop a consciousness of the river; and, depending upon how great that consciousness is, each one since has been consciously able to make some at least partially successful attempt to bend the river to his or her will. That's why someone like Bleys with his great awareness of what's now

485

happening can be many times more effective than he could have been in any past period of history.'

He stood up.

'I should go,' he said. 'I want time to talk to Amid without Bleys knowing that I've kept him waiting.'

'What difference would it make if he knew?' Ajela said.

'I don't know. With anyone else I wouldn't be so concerned,' said Hal. 'But I'm cautious about exposing even the corner of any potentially useful data to that mind of Bleys'. I'll talk to you again as soon as I've seen these two.'

Amid, looking almost toylike in a silver-gray robe, was waiting for him when Hal stepped back into his own room. The small Exotic was standing by Hal's desk.

'Sit down,' said Hal, taking a seat himself, away from the desk. 'It's good to see you.'

Amid smiled wryly, and settled himself in a float.

'It's good of you to say so,' he said. 'Are you sure you're that pleased to see me?'

'Of course,' said Hal. 'How long will you stay?'

Amid's face sobered.

'Forever,' he said, quietly. For a moment the lines of his face were sad and older than Hal had ever seen them. 'Or, in practical terms, as long as I can be of any use to you.'

Hal considered him thoughtfully for a moment.

'Should I take it opinions about me have changed on the Exotics?'

'In a sense,' said Amid. 'I'm afraid we've given up. That's why I'm free to come to you.'

'Given up?' Hal sat looking at him. 'That's a little like saying an elephant has given up being an elephant – it makes no sense at all. You don't mean it literally?'

'Literally? Of course not,' said Amid. 'No more than any healthy-minded person means it when he says he's going to give up living. Death is unthinkable; and since the Others mean to kill us off, to acquiesce in that is impossible. No, it's only that our best calculations show us no way out. Effectively, the contest is over. The Others have already won.'

'You can't mean that either,' said Hal.

'No other answer's possible. How much do you know, about what they've been doing lately?'

'Not much,' said Hal. 'We interpret the factors that reach us, particularly with Tam Olyn's understanding of the Encyclopedia to help us; and we get a general picture of the fact that they're mobilizing rapidly under Bleys Ahrens. But it's all inference – even if it's very high level inference. Specific information's what we don't get much of.'

'That's why I'm here. I can help you with that.' Amid sat with

Exotic stillness in his chair, but Hal felt a tenseness in him. 'For example, the situation isn't just that the Others are mobilizing against you; it's that they've already achieved mobilization – past the point where it looks as if they can be stopped. But, about me. With no visible way to go, we're all left free to do what we choose. So, I decided to humor my natural inclinations, and offer you my services, while the Others can still be fought. That's what I meant when I said I could stay forever, if you want. I can stay with you until the end.'

Hal sat back in his float, thoughtfully.

'Oh,' said Amid. 'And, incidentally, we admit now that you and the Dorsai were right. The attempt to assassinate the Others, individually, wouldn't have worked. Each one of them's now got a large partisan population around them, on all the nine worlds they control. Even if they all could be killed, their deaths would only make those populations determined to destroy us in revenge.'

'This is interesting,' said Hal, slowly. 'When I got here, some twelve standard months ago, all I could learn, through Tam Olyn, was that Danno was dead, and that Bleys had taken over, and started to mobilize.'

'When you got away from Bleys on Coby,' said Amid, 'I think you signed Danno's death warrant. We'd known for years that he and Bleys had very different ideas of what the destiny of the Others should be. Danno wanted peace and plenty in his time; and nothing much more. Bleys had a somewhat longer view.'

Hal looked more closely at him.

'You sound as if you're giving me more credit for alarming Bleys than I'd suspected you would.'

'I'm free now to say and do what I want,' said Amid.

'How could Bleys move so fast with this mobilization that all of you on the Exotics would be sure he'd already won?'

'Not – already won,' Amid answered, 'but certain to win. Because of that tremendous leverage on other people that the Others seem to be able to bring to bear. What he's done, in effect, is start a popular movement against all of us who might oppose him.'

'How? On what basis?' Hal said.

Amid smiled, almost wistfully.

'The man's a genius,' he said. 'He simply turned everything inside out. He made the Others' enemies the villains who'd destroy civilization. The popular opinion now becomes that there's a plot on the part of those same people on Earth who always wanted to control the Younger Worlds and their populations. The plot is supposed to be masterminded by those like yourself on the Final Encyclopedia; who, as everyone knows, for two hundred years have been busy developing scientific black magic of great power – the variant of the phase drive that gives you your protective envelope here is visible proof of that. The story goes that the main business of the Encyclopedia

487

has been the development of awesome weaponry all these two centuries, and with these they can sweep all human life from the other worlds, unless those worlds surrender to them. The only hope of the Younger Worlds is that the Encyclopedia isn't quite ready to act; and if they move fast, they can kill the dragon before it gets out of its cave.'

Hal sat for a moment.

'I see,' he said at last.

'The Others have advertized themselves as leaders and organizers of the effort to save the Younger Worlds. According to them, all the historical henchmen of the Encyclopedia, such as the Dorsai, Exotics, and the wrong kind of Friendly, are known to be in with the Encyclopedia in this, helping to soften up the Younger Worlds for Earth's final attack; and so they must also be rooted out at the same time, once and for all.'

Amid paused.

'You'll notice,' he said, 'how neatly this line is set up to be developed later into one that says that, if all people are to have lasting safety, all knowledge, science and related demons must be done away with or strictly controlled; so that they can never rise again in the future, to threaten the ordinary human.'

'How large a proportion of the formerly uncommitted on those nine worlds seem to have been recruited by this, at the present time?' Hal asked.

'Perhaps twenty per cent,' said Amid, 'and that's why we've calculated that there's no hope for us. Effectively, twenty per cent is more than enough to commit an overwhelming supply of cannon fodder for the Others to throw against us. For all practical purposes, twenty per cent might as well be a hundred per cent. It represents so many individuals that they could march upon us, twenty abreast, forever. They'd be self-renewing down the generations, if the war against us could last that long.'

'The Others may have the people,' said Hal. 'But it's something else to mount an attack between worlds with a force that massive, logistically.'

'True,' said Amid. 'So we do have some time. But on the Exotics, our best calculations see the attack eventually, and our destruction, as inevitable.'

His eyes were steady on Hal's.

'So you see,' he went on, after a second. 'Oh, I know. Ten years ago, anything like such a military attempt of worlds upon worlds would have sounded as wild as a fairy tale come to life. But what everyone took for granted was that no people would consider such a tremendous wastage of life and material as would be necessary to gain such an end. But to the Others, the costs don't matter as long as they get the results they want.'

Hal nodded.

488

'Since that's the case,' he said, 'and since I assume you don't find any flaws in the Exotic calculations –'

'No,' said Amid.

'Why bother coming to me?' finished Hal. 'According to what you say, what you and I can do isn't going to make any difference. Under those circumstances I'd expect a mature Exotic to give up philosophically.'

'Possibly then I'm not a mature Exotic,' said Amid. 'In spite of my wrinkles. As I say, I'm free now to do what I want; and, being free, I'm allowing myself to indulge an irrational, unprovable hope that, just as the Others with this charismatic talent of theirs pulled a rabbit out of their hat which nobody'd ever suspected, you just might be able to pull out an equally unsuspected counter-rabbit. Consciously, of course, I have to realize that such a hope is nonsense. But I believe I'll feel better if I go down resisting, so to speak, until the bitter end. So, I'd like to stay as long as I can and be of as much use to you as possible.'

'I see,' said Hal. 'You don't happen to have some Dorsai blood in your ancestry, by any chance?'

Amid laughed.

'I just think I can be useful to you,' he went on. 'You've got your inferences; but I can give you access to specific, hard information, much of it through a network of communication the Exotics have developed and improved over the centuries. If I could set up a communication center for you, here, I think you'd find what I could bring in would be very useful to you.'

'I'm sure I would,' said Hal. 'All right, thanks; and welcome.'

He stood up. Amid in response got to his own feet.

'I'm sorry to cut this short,' said Hal. 'But we'll have time to talk later. I've got someone else to see, now.'

'Perfectly all right,' said Amid.

Hal reached down to the console on the arm of the float he had just left and touched for Ajela.

'Hal?' Her voice came clearly into the room, but without picture on the phone screen.

'I'd like Amid to stay with us,' Hal said. 'Can we arrange quarters for him?'

'If one of the regular rooms for visiting scholars will do, certainly,' said Ajela. 'Tell him to turn right when he steps out of your room and he'll find me through the first door he comes to.'

'Thank you, both of you,' said Amid.

He left. Hal sat down again and touched the phone. This time the face of Chuni, the reception leader who had spoken to them in Tam's office, came on the phone screen.

'Hal?' said Chuni.

'Where's Bleys now, Chuni?'

'He's waiting in the private lounge here by the dock.'

'He's alone?'

'Yes,' said Chuni.

'Send him – no, bring him up yourself, would you please?'

'All right. Is that all?' Chuni looked tensely out of the phone at Hal.

'That's all,' Hal said.

He sat down again. After only a few minutes, the door opened and he got to his feet again.

'Here you are, Bleys Ahrens . . .' the voice of Chuni was saying; and the two of them came through the door, with Bleys in the lead. Chuni stopped just inside the threshold, nodded past Bleys at Hal and went out again, closing the door behind him.

Bleys stopped, three steps inside the room. He stood, lean and tall in a short black jacket and narrow gray trousers tapering into his boots. His straight-boned, angular face with its penetrating brown eyes under straight black brows studied Hal.

'Well,' he said, 'you've grown up.'

'It happens,' said Hal.

They stood, facing, little more than a meter of distance between them; and, strangely, the sight of the Other brought back the memory of Amyth Barbage, standing facing the other Militia captain who had not wanted to keep pursuing Rukh's Command. The feeling struck Hal that the room seemed suddenly to have grown small around them; and he realized that for the first time he was looking at Bleys without the stark emotion of his memory of the day on the terrace, standing like a drawn sword between them. It surprised Hal now – but not as much as he would have been surprised before he had discovered that his head had touched the same top of the doorway as had Ian Graeme's – to discover that he now stood eye to eye, on a level with Bleys. From nowhere, a strange poignancy took him. This individual before him was, in a reverse sense, all he had left of what he had once known; the only one with whom he had any connection from before the moment of his tutors' deaths.

Bleys turned and stepped to Hal's float desk, sitting down on the edge of it, almost as if Hal was the visitor, rather than he.

'A big change to take place in a year,' Bleys said.

Hal sat down in his chair. Perched on the desk, Bleys sat a little above him; but that advantage in position no longer mattered between them.

'The biggest change took place in that Militia cell in Ahruma, in the day or two after you left me,' said Hal. 'I had a chance to sort things out in my mind.'

'Under an unusual set of conditions,' Bleys said. 'That captain deliberately misinterpreted what I told him.'

'Amyth Barbage,' said Hal. 'Have you forgotten his name? What did you do to him, afterwards?'

'Nothing.' Bleys sat still, watching him. 'It was his nature to do what he did. Any blame there was, was mine, for not understanding that nature as I should have. I don't do things to people, in any case. My work is with events.'

'You don't do anything to people? Even to those like Danno?'

Bleys raised his eyebrows slightly, then shook his head.

'Even to those like Danno. Danno destroyed himself, as most people who love power. All I did was give the Others an alternative plan; and in refusing to consider it, Danno created the conditions that led to his destruction at other hands than mine. As I say, I work with larger matters than individual people.'

'Then why come see me?' The almost painfully brilliant, hard-edged clarity of mind that had come on Hal as he sat at the head of the long dining table at Foralie, talking to the Grey Captains, was back with him now.

'Because you're a potential problem,' said Bleys. He smiled. 'Because I hate the waste of a good mind – ask my fellow-Others if I don't – and because I feel an obligation to you.'

'And because you have no one to talk to,' said Hal.

Bleys' smile widened slowly. There was a short pause.

'That's very perceptive of you,' he said, gently. 'But you see, I've never had anyone to talk to; and so I'm afraid I wouldn't know what I was missing. As for what brings me here, I'd like to save you if I could. Unlike Danno, you can be of use to the race.'

'I intend to be,' said Hal.

'No,' said Bleys. 'What you intend is your own destruction – very much like Danno. Are you aware the struggle you've chosen to involve yourself in is all over but the shouting? Your cause isn't only lost, it's already on its way to be forgotten.'

'And you want to save me?' Hal said.

'I can afford what I want,' said Bleys. 'But in this case, it's not a matter of my saving you but of you choosing to save yourself. In a few standard years an avalanche will have swallowed up all you now think you want to fight for. So, what difference will it make if you stop fighting now?'

'You seem to assume,' said Hal, 'that I'm going to stop eventually.'

'Either stop, or – forgive me – be stopped,' said Bleys. 'The outcome of this battle you want to throw yourself into was determined before you were born.'

'No,' said Hal, slowly. 'I don't think it was.'

'I understand you originally had an interest in being a poet,' said Bleys. 'I had inclinations to art, too, once; before I found it wasn't for me. But poetry can be a personally rewarding life work. Be a poet, then. Put this other aside. Let what's going to happen, happen; without wasting yourself trying to change it.'

Hal shook his head.

'I was committed to this, only this, long before you know,' he said.

'I'm entirely serious in what I say,' went on Bleys. 'Stop and think. What good is it going to do to throw yourself away? Wouldn't it be better, for yourself and all the worlds of men and women, that you should live a long time and do whatever you want to do – whether it's poetry or anything else? It could even be something as immaterial as saying what you think to your fellow humans; so that something of yourself will have gone into the race and be carried on to enrich it after you're gone. Isn't that a far better thing than committing suicide because you can't have matters just as you want them?'

'I think,' said Hal, 'we're at cross purposes. What you see as inevitable, I don't see so at all. What you refuse to accept can happen, I know can happen.'

Bleys shook his head.

'You're in love with a sort of poetic illusion about life,' he said. 'And it is an illusion, even in a poetic sense; because even poets – good poets – come to understand the hard limits of reality. Don't take my word for that. What does Shakespeare have Hamlet say at one point . . . "*how weary, flat, stale and unprofitable seem to me all the uses of this world*?" '

Hal smiled suddenly.

'Do you know Lowell?' he asked.

'Lowell? I don't believe so,' answered Bleys.

'James Russell Lowell,' said Hal. 'Nineteenth century American poet.' He quoted:

'*When I was a beggarly boy,*
And lived in a cellar damp,
I had not a friend nor a toy,
But I had Aladdin's lamp . . .'

He sat, matching his gaze with Bleys'.

'I believe you're better at quoting poetry than I am,' said Bleys. He got to his feet and Hal rose with him. 'Also, I believe I'll have to accept the fact I can't save you. So I'll go. What is it you've found here at the Encyclopedia – if anything, if I may ask?'

Hal met his eyes.

'As one of my tutors, Walter InTeacher would have said,' he answered. 'That's a foolish question.'

'Ah,' said Bleys.

He turned toward the door. He had almost reached it, when Hal spoke again behind him; his voice suddenly different, even in his own ears.

'How did it happen?'

Bleys stopped and turned back to face him.

'Of course,' he said, gently, 'you'd have had no way of knowing, would you? I should have seen to your being informed before. Well, I'll tell you now, then. The men we normally use to go before us in situations like that had found two of your tutors already on that terrace and the third was brought to join them a minute or two after I stepped out on to the terrace myself. It was the Friendly they brought. The Dorsai and your Walter InTeacher were already there. Like you, he seemed to be fond of poetry, and as I came out of the library window, he was quoting from that verse drama of Alfred Noyes, *Sherwood*. The lines he was repeating were those about how Robin Hood had saved one of the fairies from what Noyes called The Dark Old Mystery. I quoted him Blondin's song, from the same piece of writing, as a stronger piece of poetry. Then I asked him where you were; and he told me he didn't know – but of course he did. They all knew, didn't they?'

'Yes,' said Hal. 'They knew.'

'It was that which first raised my interest in you above the ordinary,' Bleys said. 'It intrigued me. Why should they be so concerned to hide you? I'd told them no one would be hurt; and they would have known my reputation for keeping my word.'

He paused for a second.

'They were quite right not to speak, of course,' he added, softly.

Hal stood still, waiting.

'At any rate,' said Bleys. 'I tried to bring them to like me, but of course they were all of the old breed – and I failed. That intrigued me even more, that they should be so firmly recalcitrant; and I was just about to make further efforts, which might have worked, to find out from them about you, when your Walter InTeacher physically attacked me – a strange thing for an Exotic to do.'

'Not,' Hal heard his own voice saying, 'under the circumstances.'

'Of course, that triggered off the Dorsai and the Friendly. Together, they accounted for all but one of the men I had watching them; but of course, all three of them were killed in the process. Since there was no hope of questioning them, then, I went back into the house. Danno had just arrived; and I didn't have the leisure to order a search of the grounds for you, after all.'

'I was in the lake,' Hal said. 'Walter and Malachi Nasuno – the Dorsai – signalled me when they guessed you were on the grounds. I had time to hide in some bushes at the water's edge. After . . . I came up to the terrace and saw you and Danno through the window of the library.'

'Did you?' said Bleys.

The two of them stood, facing each other for a moment; and Bleys shook his head, slowly.

'So it had already begun between us, even then?' he said.

He opened the door and stepped through it, closing it quietly behind him. Hal turned back to the nearest float and touched the phone controls.

'Chuni,' he said. 'Bleys Ahrens is on his way out. See that he doesn't go astray.'

493

CHAPTER FIFTY-ONE

Cutting the connection to Chuni, Hal called Ajela.

'I'd like to talk to you and Tam right away,' he said. 'Something new's come up. And I'd like to bring Amid with me, unless there's an objection to it.'

'I'll ask Tam.' Ajela's face looked at him curiously out of the screen 'But I can't imagine any objection. Why don't you just bring him along to Tam's suite? If there's any problem with that, I can meet you at the door and explain to Amid.'

'I'll be there as soon as I can collect him, then,' said Hal.

When the two of them reached the suite, Ajela was waiting, holding the door open. Inside, Tam waved them to chairs.

'I'm afraid this is going to disrupt things,' said Hal, sitting down. 'I'm going to have to leave for a while –'

He glanced at Amid.

'– Taking Amid if he'll go.'

He had said nothing of this to the old Exotic. Amid raised his eyebrows, very slightly, but said nothing.

'Also, I'm going to suggest we tighten security on the Encyclopedia right away. I'm afraid that means all visitors – visiting scholars included – should leave.'

Tam frowned.

'The Encyclopedia's never been closed,' he said. 'Even back when it was on Earth's surface, down in St. Louis, it was always open to those who needed to use it and were qualified to come in.'

'I don't think there's any alternative now, though,' said Hal. 'Otherwise, one of these days a human bomb is going to be walking through an entry port. Bleys can find people willing to give their lives to destroy the Encyclopedia. Closed, we're invulnerable. Only, we'd have to look to the supply situation.'

'That was taken care of long ago,' said Ajela. 'Even in the beginning Mark Torre considered the chance that the Encyclopedia, being what it is, might be isolated one day. We're an almost perfect closed system, ecologically. The only things we'd lack for the next half century is enough energy to see us through that much time. Closed up, we might go half a year to a year on stored power . . . but at the end of that time, we'd have to open irises to collect a fresh supply of solar energy. Of course, I can put Jeamus Walters to work on a way to get solar energy through the shield without opening up . . .'

'I don't think we need to worry about obvious physical attack from outside for some time, yet,' said Hal. 'But for everything else, the available time looks a lot shorter than I'd thought.'

'That's what you found out from Bleys, was it?' Tam asked. 'What did he say?'

'What he told me, effectively, was that he'd like me to resign myself to the fact that his people had already won –'

'Won!' said Tam.

'Unfortunately,' Hal went on, 'What he had to say about it agrees with what Amid came to tell me. Amid, why don't you tell Tam and Ajela?'

Amid did. When he was done, Tam snorted.

'Apologies, and all that,' he said to Amid. 'But I don't know you. How can I be sure you're not someone who belongs to Bleys Ahrens?'

'He isn't, Tam,' said Ajela, softly. 'I know who he is. He's the kind of Exotic who wouldn't be able to work on Bleys' side.'

'I suppose,' Tam growled, looking from her to Amid and back again. 'You Exotics should know each other, of course. But as far as the Others already having won goes, though – well, what did you have in mind to do, Hal?'

'I'm going to have to go back to Harmony, to Mara or Kultis, and the Dorsai. It's become time to get our forces organized,' said Hal. He turned to the small Exotic. 'Amid, you were going to help me with communication. Can you get a message, now, to Harmony ahead of our own landing there? A message arranging a meeting for me with a Leader of one of the resistance Commands, named Rukh Tamani?'

Amid frowned.

'The Encyclopedia can put me in phone communication with the Exotic Embassy in Rheims, down on Earth, can't it?'

'Of course,' said Ajela.

'Good. Let me see what I can do, then,' Amid said. 'If you'll excuse me, I'll go to that room you gave me and do my calling from there.'

'Thank you,' said Hal.

Amid smiled a little grimly, and went out.

'He's a sensitive listener,' said Hal, after the door had closed behind the small man in the gray robe. 'I think he understood I needed to talk to the two of you, alone.'

'Of course he did,' said Ajela. 'But what was it you didn't want him to hear?'

'It's not exactly that I had a specific reason for not wanting him to hear,' said Hal. 'It's just that there's no particular reason for including him, yet; and until there is –'

'Very good. Quite right,' said Tam. 'When we know him better maybe it'll be different. But for now, let's keep private matters among the three of us. What was it you were going to tell us, Hal?'

'My conclusions about Bleys, and his visit,' said Hal. 'Bleys said he came here to see if I couldn't be brought to accepting the fact that his side had won; and I believe that actually was one of his reasons for coming. From which I judge that he's now ready to move against Earth; and that's why I feel the Encyclopedia's now in danger.'

'Why?' demanded Tam. 'What makes you suddenly think he's ready to move against Earth; and why should that suddenly put the Encyclopedia in danger?'

Hal looked from one to the other of them.

'I thought it was obvious. You don't see it?' he said. Ajela, beside Tam, shook her head. 'Well, to begin with, you've got to realize that Bleys is completely honest in anything he says; because he feels he's above any need to dissimulate, let alone lie outright. He told me he'd hate to waste what I could do for the race; and since that's what he said, that's the way he must feel.'

'How,' demanded Tam, 'do you know he's above any need to dissimulate?'

Hal hesitated.

'In some ways I understand him, instinctively,' he answered. 'In some ways, even, I think he and I are alike. That's one of the things I was forced to recognize in the Militia cell on Harmony, when I came to understand other things. I can't prove it to you – that I understand him. All I can do is ask you to take my word for it. What I'm sure of, in this instance, is that if he ever needed to dissimulate, he'd cease, in his own eyes, to be Bleys Ahrens. And being Bleys Ahrens is the most important thing in the universe to him.'

'Again,' said Tam, 'why?'

Hal frowned a little.

'Because he's nothing else. Surely that much has always been obvious about him?'

Tam was silent.

'Yes,' said Ajela, slowly, 'I think it always has been.'

'So,' said Hal. 'Since he doesn't dissimulate and therefore he really was interested in saving me if he could, we're faced with the fact that that reason alone isn't strong enough to bring him here, now. Also, his main reason for coming, whatever else it is, isn't likely to have to do with the Encyclopedia, which he respects but doesn't fear. So it must have to do with Earth. Earth's always been the one world where the Others have been inexplicably ineffective with a majority of the populace.'

'As opposed to the Exotics, the Friendlies and Dorsai, you mean?'

said Ajela, 'where the reasons are plain why most of the people there manage to resist that charismatic talent of the Others?'

'Exactly,' said Hal. 'The people of Old Earth as a whole never have had the sort of commitment to the ideals of their cultures as members of the three great splinter groups have. But in spite of this a majority of the people on Earth seem to be able to shrug off the charisma. The Others know they'll have to control Earth, eventually; but in spite of this mobilization of theirs for what looks like an orthodox military movement against their enemies, their natural preference isn't for that way of doing things. Neither Bleys nor any others of his kind want to spend any large part of their lifetimes playing at being generals. What they really want is to sit back among worlds already conquered and enjoy themselves. So, since Bleys is here now, it has to mean two things at least. One, that he's planning to move soon on Earth, in a non-military manner – since any military effort they could mount is at least logistically unready; and two, Bleys, himself, wanted a first-hand look at the situation there before that effort got under way.'

'All right,' said Tam. 'I still don't see what in this sends you off to Harmony, the Exotics and the Dorsai.'

'The fact that Bleys is different.'

'That's what "Other" means,' said Tam dryly.

'I mean,' said Hal, 'different from the rest of the Others. He heads their cause for a reason of his own I don't yet fully understand; and until I do, I've got to dig for every possible understanding of the situation.'

He stopped and looked at Tam, who nodded slowly.

'And the situation right now requires that understanding,' Hal went on, 'if we're to get any clear idea of what Bleys and the Others are planning for Earth.'

'All right, then,' said Tam, 'just what are they planning, do you think?'

'Well,' answered Hal, 'they know they aren't as successful at stampeding individuals there as they are elsewhere; but on the other hand, Old Earth's people have always been ripe for any emotionally powerful appeal, particularly in an apocalyptic time. You heard Amid. The argument they're already beginning to use in their mobilization on the other worlds – is that individuals on Earth with a traditional desire to dominate all other civilized planets, and armed with new, dark weapons from the Encyclopedia, are about to try to conquer the Younger Worlds. Note that the blame's being laid on individuals.'

'Why's that important?' said Ajela.

'Because, since it's easier to paint individuals as villains than all those on Earth, the most obvious deduction is that Bleys plans to send charismatics to Earth, to preach a crusade in which the

497

common people there will be urged to rise against the Encyclopedia and those supposedly evil individuals who're pushing the plan to take over the Younger Worlds. If they can get a popular movement of any size going down there, then the Younger Worlds can be asked to send help, to take power by force. Meanwhile, it's a good argument to use on Earth's people; and a good plan to gain power for the Others, there. It's using their special talent at one remove; but, given the special character of the old world's full-spectrum peoples, that makes it all the more likely to work.'

He paused.

'Am I making sense to you both?' he asked.

Tam nodded.

'Go on,' his deep, hoarse voice rattled against the walls of the room.

'So it's necessary I carry what we know and what I deduce to the Exotics and the Dorsai; and show the Exotics, in particular, that victory for the Others isn't a foregone conclusion – that they can be fought, if they try what I believe they're going to try. They can be fought and checked right here on Earth.'

'And how are you figuring on fighting them, right here on Earth as you put it?' asked Tam.

'With counter-preachers.' Hal's eyes met the dark old ones levelly. 'What I finally realized in that cell on Harmony was that, at base, those charismatic abilities of the Others are derived from a talent evolved on the Friendlies; where the urge to proselyte has always been strong, powered by the quality of their faith. Rukh Tamani, if I can get to her, can tell me who the Harmonyites are, who're available and would want to come to Earth and oppose those who'll preach this doctrine of the Others. We'll need people who can oppose it with the same sort of force and faith that fuels the charismatic talent. Then, if the Exotics and the Dorsai see reason to hope, we may be able to get all those who ought to be united against the Others working together effectively as a unit – in time to stop Bleys.'

Tam said nothing for a second.

'I see.' He glanced at Ajela. 'The minute you begin fighting him on Earth, successfully or otherwise, you'll force Bleys to fall back on the use of force to win. That's why you think we've got to start protecting the Encyclopedia right now?'

'Yes,' said Hal.

Tam nodded.

'All right,' he said, heavily. He turned to Hal. 'I suppose you've taken into consideration the possibility that Bleys might already have someone, a saboteur, already here, at the Encyclopedia.'

'Yes,' said Hal. 'But it's a long shot. The plans of the Others are too recent for it to be one of the regular personnel; and there's been none of the regulars who've been away from the Encyclopedia in recent years long enough and under conditions where they could be permanently corrupted, by even someone as capable as Bleys himself. That leaves the visiting scholars, as I say; and while it's unlikely one of them could have been gotten at – considering the general level of their ages and reputations – in the last year, we shouldn't take chances. In any case, there's no way I can see that we can check those we've got here now for possible intent to sabotage us, and be sure of what we find.'

'Perhaps there is,' said Tam. 'Come along to the Academic Control Chamber. Let me take a look at the neural chart there and see what our current visitors have been working on in the last twelve months.'

They went. The Control Chamber was as Hal had remembered it from his first visit to the Encyclopedia when he had been brought to it by Ajela. The room, which was large as rooms in the Final Encyclopedia went, was still banked on each wall with the control consoles, with half a dozen technicians in white shirts and slacks moving softly about it, recording the work done by the visitors and surveying it for what was new to the master files and should be added to them.

Tam led Ajela and Hal directly to the mass of red, cord-thick lines apparently hovering at waist level in the center of he room. The one technician beside it moved discreetly back out of view as the old man came to a halt and stared down at the intermittently glowing sections that came and went in the mass of lines. He stood, studying it for a long moment.

'Rotate this overall view forty-five degrees,' he said, almost absently.

'Rotate . . .?' the technician who had retreated came forward, staring. 'But then all our present charting is going to be thrown off –'

He checked himself at the suddenly raised head of Tam and the glare of Tam's eyes. Tam opened his mouth, as if to speak, then closed it again.

'Of course. Right away –' The technician hurried to a console and Tam looked back at the display of the Encyclopedia's neural circuits, as they seemed, not so much to rotate, as to melt and twist into different patterns. After a second, the changes stopped taking place, and Tam considered the shapes before him.

After a moment he sighed and looked at Ajela, then beyond her to the technician, now standing well back by the console he had gone to to rotate the display.

'Come here,' said Tam.

The technician came forward. The other white-dressed figures in the room were not looking, not watching what was going on at the center of it; but they were very still and Hal thought he could see their ears tensed.

'I do my best nowadays,' said Tam quietly to the technician, 'not to lose my temper, but sometimes I'm not too successful. Try and remember that the rest of you don't know all the things I've learned in the last century; and that I get weary of having to make the same explanation over and over again to new people every time I want something done.'

'Of course, Tam,' said the technician hastily. 'I shouldn't have spoken up.'

'No, you shouldn't,' said Tam. 'But now you should also know why you shouldn't have; and from now on you should tell other people, so they know, too. Will you do that?'

'Yes, Tam. Of course.'

'Good.' Tam turned back to Hal and Ajela. 'Jaime Gluck and Eu San Loy. I think both those visitors may have used up their welcome here.'

'Tam –' began Ajela.

'Oh, I can't be sure,' Tam said. 'But let's go on that assumption that I'm right. Better safe than sorry, as Hal pointed out.'

'All right,' said Ajela. She turned to Hal. 'I'll tell them, right away. How soon will you be leaving?'

'Or the first available deep-space transport . . .' But Hal's eyes were on Tam, who had turned back once more to studying the neural display. Ajela's attention followed his and they stood in silence, watching the old man as the seconds slipped past. But Tam was paying attention only to what held his gaze. Finally, slowly, he looked back and around, at Hal, with an expression on his face Hal had never seen before.

'You're doing it,' he said, on a long exhalation of breath.

'Not really,' replied Hal. 'Not yet. I'm just beginning to investigate the possibilities –'

'You're doing it – at last!' said Tam, in a stronger voice. 'What Mark Torre dreamed of – using the Encyclopedia as a pure thinking tool. Using it, by God, the way he planned it to be used!'

'You have to understand,' said Hal, 'this is just a beginning. I'm only trying out poetry as a creative lever. I was waiting to show you until I had some firm results –'

Tam's wrinkled gray-skinned hand closed with remarkable strength on Hal's sleeve.

'This trip,' said Tam. 'Put it off. You've got to stay here, now. Stay, and work with the Encyclopedia.'

Hal shook his head.

'I'm sorry,' he said. 'I'll get at it again just as soon as I can get back. But there's no one else to do what needs to be done on the Friendlies, the Exotics and on the Dorsai. I have to go, if the worlds are to be saved.'

'Damn it, the worlds can take care of themselves, for once!' snapped

Tam. 'This is the doorway, the dawn of a new beginning! And you're the only one who can lead us into it. You can't be risked, now!' The technicians about the room were staring. Tam ignored them. 'Hal!' he said. 'Do you hear me?'

'I'm sorry.' Gently, Hal pulled his sleeve out of the other's grasp. 'I meant what I said. There's no one else to talk to the people who have to be talked to if the worlds are going to survive.'

'Well, and what if they don't – as long as the Encyclopedia survives with what you can learn to do, now – what does the rest matter, then?' raged Tam. 'Let Bleys and his friends have the other worlds, for fifty years – or a hundred years – or whatever. They can't touch you and your work here; and here's where the future lies. Isn't it the future that counts?'

'The future and the people,' said Hal. 'Without the people there wouldn't be any future. What good's a gift with no one to give it to? And you know as well as I do it's only if what I might find here turned out to be no use to anyone else, that Bleys'd leave the Encyclopedia alone. While if he already had all the other worlds and was really determined to get the Encyclopedia, eventually he would. With Newton, Cassida, and the stations on Venus, he'll have some of the best scientific and technological minds in his service. They'd find a way eventually to break through to us. Nothing ever made by humans stops other humans forever. Tam, I have to go.'

Tam stood still. He did not say anything further. But his whole body seemed to hunch into itself, to become less. Ajela stepped to him and put her arms around him.

'It's all right,' she said softly to him. 'It'll work out, Tam. Hal'll come back safe. Believe him – believe me.'

'Yes . . .' said Tam, harshly. He turned slowly away from her and toward the doorway that would take him back to his own suite. 'You don't give me much choice, do you?'

CHAPTER FIFTY-TWO

The first deep-space vessel available to carry Hal and Amid in the right direction took them both only as far as New Earth City on New Earth, from which point they went different ways. Amid, to Mara to talk to his fellow Exotics there in preparation for the message Hal was planning to bring them; Hal, to the city of Citadel on Harmony.

Hal had half a day to himself in New Earth City after seeing Amid off, and he spent it taking note of the differences that had come over that metropolis since he had paused there as a boy, on his way to Coby seven years before. The larger differences were ones that seven years of time alone could not account for. It was the same city, on the same world; and business within it was proceeding much as it had proceeded when he had seen it before; but in the people there, those Hal saw on the streets and in the buildings, a change had come for which ten times seven years would hardly have been enough to account.

It was as if a darkening sense of limited time had moved in upon them like some heavy overcast of cloud, to interdict whatever hope and purpose had formerly shone into their daily lives. Under this gathering darkness, they seemed to scurry with the frantic energy of those who would deny a rapidly approaching deadline when all their efforts would become useless. Like ants who appear to redouble their dashing about in the fading light of sunset, the people of New Earth City seemed obsessed with an urgency to accomplish all their usual activities, both with great dispatch and with a denial that there was any need for that urgency.

But, behind that denial, Hal felt a penetrating and overwhelming fear of an approaching night in which all they had done to prepare would turn out to be useless.

He was glad at last, therefore, to ride up to the ship into which he had transferred to get to Harmony. Arriving at that world, he rode a jitney down to the Citadel spaceport; and landed on a day there that for once was without weeping rainclouds. A watery, but clear, sunlight from the large yellow orb of E. Eridani, that same sol-like star Hal had picked out of the night sky back on Earth as a boy, gilded the stolid brick and concrete buildings of the city outside the port. He took an automated cab and directed it to a destination on that Friendly city's northern outskirts, to a dome-roofed building in the midst of a large, rubbled, open lot among dwelling places set at some little distance from each other. Releasing the cab, he entered the building.

Within, there was nothing to show that time had not stood still since his last visit. The air, barely a degree or two above the temperature of that outside, was as before heavy with the faintly banana-oil-like smell of the lubricant that those living on the Friendlies had harvested by tapping the variform of one variety of native tree they had discovered at the time of their first wave of colonization. Several surface vehicles with their propulsive units exposed or partially dismantled sat about the unpartitioned interior in the pale light through the translucent dome. In the far end of the floor, a stocky, older man in work clothes was head down into the works of one of the vehicles.

Hal walked over to him.

'Hello, Hilary,' he said.

The head of the stocky man came up. Gray eyes from under a tight, oil-streaked skull cap looked at Hal, dryly.

'What can I do for you?' the other man asked.

'You don't recognize me?' said Hal, caught halfway between humor and sadness.

It was not surprising. In the two years since the other had last seen him, Hal had crossed the line into physical maturity . He had been a tall, lean, intense stripling when Hilary had seen him last. Now, although there were no sudden age lines on his face and the twenty extra kilograms of flesh and muscle he now carried on his bones had only reasonably increased his apparent weight, a world of difference had overtaken him. He was no longer just very tall. He was big. Indeed, as he had fully realized at last only when Ajela had confronted him with his own image on his return to the Final Encyclopedia, he was very big.

He read the message of that size in Hilary's response – in the fact that Hilary seemed to tighten up slightly at the first sight of him, then settle in, become even more compact by comparison. It was an unconscious reflex of the other man, part of an indefinable, automatic measuring instinct in him, like that which causes one male dog to bristle at his original glimpse of a strange and larger other, only to lower the hair on back and shoulders when a second glance discovers that the difference in size between them was too great to make any thought of challenge practical.

Hal had encountered similar reactions from time to time, this past year, at the Encyclopedia; and once, turning a corner to find himself face to face with a mirror, in one of those unguarded moments where, for a second, the viewer fails to recognize himself – he had felt it himself. In that moment before recognition and ordinary

503

personal self-consciousness came back, he had seen someone who was not only large physically, but big beyond that size in some indefinable quality that was at once quiet, isolated and forever unyielding. For a fraction of a second there he had seen himself as a man he did not know, and when the recognition had came, it had brought not only a kind of embarrassment, but unhappiness; for until that moment he had been telling himself that he had at last learned to live with that inner difference and isolation of his, some time since. But now, here again with someone who had met him before, he had seen the mark of that difference, unerasable still upon him.

'Hilary, don't you know me?' he said. 'Howard Beloved Immanuelson? Remember when Jason Rowe brought me around and you took us to join Rukh Tamani's Command?'

Hillary's eyes cleared to recognition. He held out his hand.

'Sorry,' he said, 'you've changed a bit. Who are you now?'

Hal gripped hands with him.

'My papers say I'm a Maran named Emer – commercially accredited to trade on Harmony by the Exotic Ambassadorial Office here.'

'You could have fooled me,' said Hilary, dryly, as their hands released. 'Particularly wearing those ordinary clothes.'

'You know Exotics don't always wear robes,' said Hal. 'Any more than Friendlies always dress in black. But, for your information only, you'd better have my real name. It's Hal Mayne. I'm of Earth.'

'Old Earth?'

'Yes,' said Hal. 'Old Earth – and now, of the Final Encyclopedia, as well. I'm up to my ears in something larger than fighting the Militia, nowadays.'

He looked closely at Hilary to read the other man's reaction.

'It isn't just here, or on Association, any longer,' he went on, when Hilary said nothing. 'Now, the battle against the Others is on all the worlds.'

Hilary nodded. The wraith of a sigh seemed to tremble in him.

'I know,' he said. 'The old times are ending. I saw it coming a long time back. What can I do for you?'

'Just tell me where I can find Rukh,' said Hal. 'Some people were looking for me, but they haven't had any luck. For the sake of all the worlds, I've got to talk to her as soon as I can. There's a job only she can do for us.'

Hilary's face became grim.

'I'm not sure I'd tell you unless you had someone to vouch for you. A year can move some people from one side to another. But in this case, it makes no difference. Whatever you've got in mind, you'd better find someone else to take it on,' he said. 'Rukh Tamani's dead – or if she isn't, I'd be sorry to hear it. The Militia have her. They caught up with her three weeks ago.'

Hal stared at the older man.

'Three weeks ago . . . where?'

'Ahruma.'

'Ahruma? You mean she's been there ever since she blew the Core Tap?'

'They had it almost repaired. She was reconnoitering to see if the repair work could be sabotaged. There's a limb of Satan named Colonel Barbage – Amyth Barbage – who's been devoting his full time to running her down. He got word she was in the city, made a sweep, and two of the people he picked up knew where she could be found –'

Hilary paused, shrugged.

'They talked, of course, after he got them back to the Militia Center. And he caught her.'

Hal stared at him.

'I'm going to have to get her out as soon as possible,' he said.

'Get her out?' Hilary stared at him for a long moment. 'You're actually serious, aren't you? Don't you think if prisoners could be got out of Militia Centers, we'd have been doing it before this?'

'And you haven't, I take it,' said Hal, hearing his own voice echoing harshly off the curved walls and roof that were one and the same.

Hilary did not even bother to answer.

'I'm sorry,' said Hal. 'But there's too much at stake. I'll have to get her out, and as soon as possible.'

'Man,' said Hilary softly. 'Don't you understand? Odds are a hundred to one she's been dead for at least a couple of weeks!'

'I've got to assume she isn't,' said Hal. 'We'll go in after her. Who do I see in Ahruma to get help? Are there any of her old Command around here?'

Hilary did not move.

'Help,' he said, almost wonderingly. Moving as if by their own volition, his hands picked up a tan square of saturated cleansing cloth from the mainframe below the windshield of the vehicle he had been working on and started to wipe themselves. 'Listen to me, Hal – if that's really your name – we can't just pick up a phone and call Ahruma. All long distance calls are monitored. It'd take three days to find a courier, a week to pass him or her on through friends who can make transportation available between here and Ahruma, another week to get people there together to talk about trying a rescue – and then they'd all go home an hour later after they heard what you had in mind, because they all know, like me, that any such thing's impossible. You were in a Command. What do you think a handful of people with needle guns and cone rifles can do against a barracks-ful of police inside a fortress?'

'There are ways to deal even with fortresses,' said Hal, 'and as far as a phone message to Ahruma goes, I can probably make use of Exotic diplomatic communications, if the message can be coded safely. Why a week to get a courier there, anyway, when air transportation makes it in two hours?'

'God has afflicted your wits,' said Hilary, calmly. 'Even if we had someone locally who could show airport checkpoints an acceptable reason to make such a trip, it'd cost a fortune we don't have. Remember your Command, I say. Remember how you had to make do with equipment and weapons that were falling apart?'

'Credit's a problem?' Hal reached into his jacket and came out with a folder. He opened it to show the vouchers of balances in interstellar credit within it to Hilary. 'I'm carrying more in interworld credit than you'd need for even a small army – given the exchange rate to Harmony currency. This is mine, and the Final Encyclopedia's. But if necessary, I'm pretty sure I could get more yet through Exotic diplomatic channels.'

Hilary stared at the vouchers. His face became thoughtful. After a second, he walked around the vehicle across which he had been talking to Hal all this time.

'Coffee?' he said.

'Thanks,' answered Hal.

'Hilary led the way to a desk some twenty feet away, with a small cooker holding a coffee pot and a stack of disposable cups. They sat down and the older man poured a couple of cups. He drank slowly and appreciatively from his own, while Hal put his cup to his own lips, then set it down again. He had almost forgotten what Harmony coffee tasted like.

'I'm going to trust you,' said Hilary, putting his own cup back down among the cluttered paperwork on the worn surface of the desk. 'It's impossible, just as I say, but with that kind of credit we can at least daydream about it.'

'Why is it still impossible? What makes it impossible?' Hal asked.

Hilary stared at him without answering.

'You say you're from Old Earth,' he said. 'Not from Dorsai?'

'Old Earth.'

'If you say so.' Hilary nodded slowly. 'All right, then, to answer your questions, weren't you held in the Center here for a day or so before you and Jason came to see me? So do I need to tell you what they're like inside?'

'I didn't see much of it,' said Hal. 'Besides, you said Rukh's in the Center at Ahruma, not the one here at Citadel.'

'They're all built the same,' said Hilary. 'It'd need an army to force its way into one, let alone bring someone out, let alone the Militia'd probably kill any prisoner they suspected we were about to try and rescue.'

'If it needs an army, we'll get an army,' said Hal. 'This is something that concerns all the fourteen worlds. But maybe that much won't be necessary. Draw me a plan of a Center, if they're all alike as you say. Who'd I talk to in Ahruma to help me organize this?'

'Athalia McNaughton – I'd heard you'd met her,' Hilary said briefly. He pushed the paperwork on the desk aside, drew a stylus and a blank sheet from the drawer below the desk's surface. He pushed both things across to Hal. 'I can't draw worth a hoot. I'll tell you, and you draw. There's three main sections inside each Center, the Clerking section, the Militia Barracks, and the Cells section. . . .'

'Just a minute,' said Hal. 'What about finding a courier? We can't spare three days for that –'

'You won't need a courier. I'll go with you,' said Hilary. 'You can try and convince Athalia; and while you're doing that I'll see who I can round up in the local territory to help you, just in case. Now, draw this the way I tell you. The three sections of the Center are always in a single brick building on the end of a city block, as long as the block is wide, and about half that, in its width. The building in Ahruma is going to be less than six stories high, but with at least three levels underground. The Cells section, as you might expect, takes up the bottom levels. . . .'

Together, they caught a late afternoon flight to Ahruma, three hours later; and Hal found himself sitting in the combination outer office-living room of Athalia McNaughton on the outskirts of Ahruma as the summer twilight outside gave way to night. Hilary was in Athalia's small working office, off to the right of this larger room, phoning people from Athalia's records of local resistance members, calling them to a conference. Athalia had remembered Hal but he found her even less ready to entertain the idea of rescuing Rukh than Hilary had been.

'. . . Those funds you've got are all very well,' the tall, brown-haired woman told him, after he had made his initial argument. They were sitting in overstuffed chairs in one corner of the room, facing each other almost like enemies. 'But you're asking me to put the lives of a number of good and necessary local people in danger for a wild goose chase. Hilary told you the straight of it. She's undoubtedly dead by now. The only reason she wouldn't be, would be if someone there had some special use for her.'

'She wouldn't talk easily,' said Hal.

'Don't you think I know that? Athalia flared. 'No Commander of a Command talks easily – and I've known her since she was a baby. But she'd either talk, and they'd kill her when they thought she had no more to tell them; or they'd have killed her by this time trying to make her talk. They aren't set up for keeping prisoners more than a few days – they just don't do it.'

'All right,' said Hal. 'Then let's find out if she's still alive. Don't tell me you don't have some line of contact going inside that Center?'

'Into the Center, yes. Into the Barracks, yes. But into the Cells. . . .' Athalia's words slowed as his eyes remained steady on hers. Her voice became almost gruff. 'All we've ever been able to do as far as the Cells go is sometimes smuggle suicide materials to one of our people who's been caught.'

Hal sat watching her. With Rukh's life or death possibly hanging in the balance, he found himself very quiet within, and certain. As he had when he had come at last to the moment of having to win over the Grey Captains of the Dorsai, he was conscious of tapping skills until now locked away from him. One of these was a sort of intuitive logic that made him very sure of the answers that had come to him. He felt now something like an inner strength that had for a time slumbered, but was now awaking to take hold of him. Athalia, unchanged since he had seen her last, sat as one who has every confidence in her ability to win the argument. Her large-boned, thin-lipped face, strikingly attractive under the dark hair, in spite of her age, waited for him to do the impossible job of convincing her; and watching her, he considered with the recently reawakened part of his mind what would reach her, what would touch her, what would prove what he had to say beyond the possibility of any further disagreement – as he had facing the Grey Captains.

'I know Rukh's alive,' he said.

Only a slight widening of Athalia's eyes signalled that he might have found the right thing to say.

'How?' she demanded.

'Simply take it that I know,' he said, meeting her eyes. And it was true, the feeling was a sureness in him. Although even if he had not felt it, he would have spoken the same words to Athalia, anyway. 'But certainly we ought to be able to find out, if you want outside proof. I can't believe you don't have some way to check on that, at least.'

'I suppose . . .' said Athalia slowly, 'yes, I think we could check that much.'

'Then there's no point in wasting time, is there?' said Hal. 'While you're doing that, everything else can be going forward on the assumption that we're going to hear that she's alive; then we'll be ready to move as soon as possible when we do hear she's alive. Suppose I make an agreement with you?'

He went on before she could have a chance to speak.

'As you know, I've been with a Command. I wouldn't think of trying to buy you, or anyone else. But will you do this much for me? Organize and push forward the preparations for a rescue, including using anyone who'd be involved with that, and if it turns out Rukh isn't still alive I'll reimburse everyone concerned for any time or expense lost they've been put to – if you want to, I'll also donate five hundred credits of interstellar units to the use of your local people – and you know what that works out to in terms of local exchange.'

He paused to take a break and she began to speak, coldly.

'I don't think –'

'But,' he said, overriding her, 'if Rukh is alive, we'll forget about any reimbursement or donations – except for the matter of any expenses your people couldn't afford. Otherwise I'll assume that what this might cost them is no more than what they'd undertake for Rukh's sake, in any case.'

He stopped then and waited for her to speak. But she only looked at him, almost as an enemy might look, for a long second.

'All right,' she said. 'Within reason and within the bounds of what I think is safe for those I'm responsible for, all right.'

'Good,' he said, swiftly, 'then, since I'm willing to pay for it if I'm wrong, there's some things I'd like to put in motion right away. I'll need to know a great deal about that Militia Center, everything you can find our for me, including how many Militiamen and officers they've got there at the moment – I know you won't be able to give me an exact count, but I need to know the approximate number on hand at the time we go in after Rukh. Also, I want to know about deliveries and traffic, in and out of the building. Also, when they unlock the public areas, who those are who don't belong there but are occasionally allowed to go in and out anyway, such as when the building gets its garbage picked up; and what the arrangements are for repair calls by outside workmen, in case they need services of any kind. I need to know the hours of the various shifts on duty, the personalities of the officers in command and the kinds of communication going into the building.'

He stopped.

'You don't want much,' she said. She smiled slightly, grimly.

'There ought to be local people you can ask to find out these things,' he answered. 'Naturally, we also need to know about armament, and locks and security measures. But there's one thing I'd like you to start right now – and it won't commit you or your people to anything. That's to spread the word around the city that Rukh might – just might – still be alive. Then, when we find out she is, that rumor will have the general public ready to accept the information and maybe mount some shielding demonstrations for us.'

Athalia hesitated, then nodded.

'All right,' she said, 'that much can be done.'

'And as soon as we get definite word Rukh's still alive,' he said. 'I want to meet with everyone and explain to them how we can get her out.'

'If you can,' said Athalia.

'We'll see,' he answered.

'All right,' she got to her feet. 'I'll go right now and set the machinery working to find out – if I can get Hilary off that phone for five minutes.'

'How soon do you think we might hear?' he called after her as she headed toward the small office.

'I don't know. Forty-eight hours at least, I'd say,' she answered over her shoulder.

But it was not forty-eight hours. Before noon the next day Athalia heard from the fish dealer who supplied the Barracks section kitchen in the Center and was on easy speaking terms with the mess cook and his staff. Rukh, he had been told, was in an isolation cell; but, as of the previous day, she had been alive.

Eight hours later, as soon as darkness had cloaked the streets for an hour, sixteen people gathered in Athalia's warehouse, around a table of boards set up on trestles for the occasion.

CHAPTER FIFTY-THREE

Hal sat at one end of the table looking down its length at Athalia and at all those between them. Again, as when he had talked to her the evening before, he was strongly reminded of the moment in which he had faced the Grey Captains in the dining room at Foralie. Outside of Athalia herself and Hilary, those at the table were all faces he did not know, with the exception of two from Rukh's Command, the perky, aggressive features of Tallah, and the long face of Morelly Walden. Morelly had evidently healed from his wound, but he had lost weight and now his body was as thin as his limbs. He had supported himself with a stick as he had walked into the warehouse, and he looked twenty years older than the man Hal had known.

If any of the other twelve people Athalia had invited were also members or former members of Commands, they showed no sign of it. It seemed to Hal that with the exception of Tallah and Morelly, he looked at all city faces; hard faces, in some instances, but city ones nonetheless; and his instincts told him that he could expect no help from either of his former comrades, or from Hilary – if Hilary had indeed come to the point of wanting to help – in convincing these others.

Athalia began matters by briefly rehearsing Hal's credentials as a former member of Rukh's group and stating what he wanted.

'. . . and as you all know,' she wound up, 'we did hear earlier today that Rukh was still alive in the Cells at Center – in an isolation cell, but alive. He's made certain offers to us you know about. Now, I'll let Hal have his chance to tell you what he's got in mind.'

'Thanks,' said Hal.

He looked at the men and women he did not know; and their expressions were not encouraging.

'I take it for granted,' he said, 'that there's no one here who'd hesitate at anything I've got to propose, if he or she thought there was a real possibility of getting Rukh free from the Militia. But I'm going to have to ask one uncomfortable question before I start talking to you – is there anyone here who seriously feels that it's a waste of time even listening to me? I'm asking each one of you to examine your own conscience.'

The eyes around the table stared back at him. No one stirred or spoke.

'I ask that,' said Hal, 'because I know many of you feel that simply because no prisoner has ever been recovered from a Center, no prisoner ever could be; and I'm here to tell you not only that that's a belief that's mistaken, but that bringing Rukh safely out of the hands of the Militia is the sort of thing that people like us have done down through history. It's not only possible, it's practical. However, there's not one of you here I can convince of that, if you've already made up your mind there's no point in listening to me. So, I'll ask you again, for Rukh's sake, are there any of you here who've got a completely closed mind on this subject?'

There was a moment of silence and stillness. Then the people about the table looked at each other, and after several seconds there was a screech of metal on concrete, as a tall man in a dark leather jacket, near the far end of the table, pushed back the barrel-like metal container that had been serving him as a seat. He stood up; and at the sight of his rising, a shorter man in a business suit, at the table's very end also stood up.

'Wait,' said Hal.

They paused.

'I honor your honesty,' he went on, 'but please – don't leave. How about sitting in, with the rest of us, after all? Not to join in the discussion, but just to listen?'

The two standing men looked at him. The one who had been the first to rise was the first to sit down. The other followed.

'Thanks,' said Hal. He paused to look around the table before going on. 'Now, let me make one other point first. I've told Athalia, and I believe she's relayed what I said to the rest of you, that the main reason an effort has to be made to free Rukh is there's a job to be done by her no one else on any of the worlds can do.'

'She belongs to Harmony,' broke in a heavy man in a dark green, knitted jacket, seated next to Tallah.

'Right now,' said Hal, 'I could answer that statement by saying the only thing she belongs to is the Militia. But I know what you're talking about – that she's a Harmonyite, one of the Chosen, and that she's got work here. That's true, she does have work here; but she also has it everywhere, now, as well. I'll ask you again, all of you, to keep listening to me with open minds for the moment.'

He paused. Their faces still waited, without expression.

'Stay with me, first,' he said, 'while I go through something you already know, but something that's going to be important in this case. I can't emphasize too much that the Others are only a handful, proportionally speaking, compared to the rest of us, on all the settled worlds. By themselves, no matter what their abilities and powers, they couldn't be a real threat to the whole human race. What makes them a threat is that they're able to use other people, people like your closest neighbors, as a lever to multiply their original strength many

512

times and make it possible to control the rest of us.'

He paused again, waiting for anyone who might want to argue this point, but none of them said anything. He went on.

'They can use others as levers, because they're able to make these people into followers, into believers in them,' he said. 'Everyone knows there are many the Others can't do anything with – people like yourselves who're strong in faith, and the Dorsai, and the Exotics. What's not known so well is that there are also a lot of people the Others can't use among the people of Old Earth –'

'I've heard that,' said the man in the knitted jacket. 'It's hard to believe.'

'The reason you find it hard to believe,' Hal said, 'is because, if true, it sounds like it makes a mockery of your own hard-won strengths, to say nothing of the strengths of those who can also resist on the Dorsai and the Exotics.'

He looked around the table at them all.

'But really,' he went on, 'it doesn't do that at all. It's not even strange. Let me ask you a question. Your forebearers, the ones who emigrated from Earth, and made the first settlements here on Harmony and Association, would you say that they had less faith than you here, and those of your generations of these two worlds, nowadays?'

There was an instant hum of negation around the table.

'More!' came the strong voice of a heavy, middle-aged woman with bright, dark eyes on Hal's left and about five faces down the table.

'Well . . . possibly,' said Hal. 'We tend to remember the best about our ancestors and forget what in any way diminishes them. Let me ask you another question, then. Do you all believe that every person capable of the special faith that you consider makes a Friendly left Earth and came here? Couldn't there have been some who, for personal reasons of anything from finances to a simple preference for Old Earth, stayed there, married and had children of their own there?'

Silence held the table, although he gave them time to speak.

'So,' he said, gently at last, 'is it so unreasonable to think that everyone from Old Earth who might have made a Dorsai went to that world? One more question; and then we'll leave this side matter and get back to the main business. Before any of those emigrants came to any of these worlds, were they any less than they showed themselves to be once they got there?'

Again he waited. Still they were silent.

'Then it's reasonable to assume, isn't it,' he said, 'that there were men and women of faith before Harmony or Association were dreamed of, that there were people of courage and self-reliance before the Dorsai was imagined to exist; and that both men and women dreamed of an ethical ideal and a philosophy for all people from that ethical ideal, when the worlds of Mara and Kultis were not even suspected?'

He paused – only a fraction of a second this time.

'In short, that there were Friendlies before there were Friendly Worlds, Dorsai before the Dorsai was found, and Exotics before the Exotic planets were settled; and that all these others were originally on Old Earth – and that there are people like that there still, part of that original gene pool that's the true reservoir of our race?'

'Granted,' said Athalia sharply form the end of the table. 'As you say, let's get on with the main business that's brought everybody here.'

'All right,' said Hal. 'What all this leads to, is the important point, about Rukh's value to all the worlds. The reason she's needed is because she represents the best of what your culture's been able to produce. People here should be proud of that, rather than jealous of it. But to get to what Athalia's just reminded me is the main business of this meeting. . . .'

He looked around the faces at the table once more and saw some of them, at least, had backed off from their initial hard expressionlessness to looks varying from thoughtfulness to puzzlement. At least, he thought, he was reaching these few among his audience.

'As to how we get her out,' he said – and those words wiped away once more all facial expressions but listening ones – 'the idea that it's impossible to get a prisoner back out of a Center is actually our largest asset. Because that means that the Militia undoubtedly believe it, too; and so they won't be expecting a rescue attempt. That's of the greatest possible help, because to make the rescue we've got to set the stage for it ahead of time; and the Militia's belief in the Center's impregnability is going to work for us to keep them from getting suspicious. Without that, we could still do it, but it'd be a lot more difficult.'

'You still haven't told us anything that makes it possible,' said the man in the knitted jacket.

'It's possible because it's the sort of thing that's been done before,' said Hal, 'as I told you. Simply, it's a matter of creating situations to reduce the opposition we'll run into, once we're inside the Center; reduce it to the point where the rescue party we send in can handle it.'

A thin, fiftyish man across the table and three faces down, with the lines of habitual anger on his face, gave a snort of disgust.

'That's right! All we need are miracles!' the thin man said.

'No,' said Hal, without varying the tone he had used so far, 'all we need is planning.'

He looked at Athalia, at the end of the table.

'I've learned that the number of Militia barracked in your Center here isn't more than four companies of roughly two hundred men each, plus a couple of hundred office and related personnel. In short, the maximum number we can find ourselves up against isn't more than eleven hundred individuals at the outside.'

'And that's a lot,' said the middle-aged woman who had spoken up to deny that the first settlers on the Friendly Worlds had owned less faith than its present generations.

'I know it sounds like a lot,' said Hal, 'But actually, a city on any other world except Association, the Dorsai, or the Exotics would have up to three times that number of police normally, for a city this size. One of the factors working for us is the patterns of your culture which reduce the need for police.'

'That's nice,' said the woman. 'It's a compliment, perhaps; but it doesn't help us in getting Rukh out.'

'Yes, it does,' said Hal. 'Because what it means is that in their duties as police, the Militia here are actually very understaffed to handle a city as big as Ahruma. That was something that didn't matter as long as the Others weren't around and the local populace were cooperative. But now the local people – at least from what I saw the day Rukh spoke in the square, following up the sabotaging of the Core Tap – are anything but cooperative.'

'I still don't see how that helps,' said the man in the knitted jacket.

'Hush, Jabez,' said the woman. 'I think I see. You mean to use the people in the city to help us, don't you, Hal Mayne?'

Hal nodded.

'That's right. I want to use them to draw off the available man-power of the Militia from the Center until it's down to a skeleton crew, before we try going in to get Rukh out.'

'How?' It was Athalia's voice from the head of the table.

'Yes,' said the man in he knitted jacket. 'How? Aside from anything else, if we get people in general involved in this, how are we going to keep the rescue secret? The Militia's got its spies and connections in the city, just like we've got some in the Militia.'

'The people don't have to know – until we want to tell them,' said Hal.

'If they don't know . . .?' the man looked puzzled. 'How can they help? How did you plan to have them help?'

'I want them to start fires, riots, street fights – you name it –' said Hal. 'I want fifty different incidents scattered out all over the city so that the Militia have to keep sending men out to keep order until they're scraping bottom for people to dispatch.'

'But there's no way to get people – I mean ordinary people who aren't Children of Wrath, or otherwise committed to fighting the Belial-spawn – to do all that for you without explaining why you want it done,' half-shouted the thin man with the anger lines on his face. 'And what about the Militia themselves? What's to keep them from getting suspicious when suddenly there's fires and riots erupting all over? They'll smell something rotten and end up by doubling security on the Center!'

Hal looked at him for a moment without speaking.

'When I was here on Harmony before, as Howard Beloved Immanuelson,' he said, finally, 'I was a member of the Revealed Church Reborn. What is thy church, brother?'

The man stared back at him; and the thin face hardened.

'I am of the Eighth Covenant,' he said, harshly. 'Why?'

'The Eighth Covenant . . .' Hal sat back thoughtfully, laying his hands on the table before him and knitting his fingers together. 'Isn't that the Church that was founded by one Forgotten of God? One so steeped in sin and other filthiness that the church to which he was originally born cast him from its doors, forbidding him ever to return, so that he ended by founding his own church, which all know is therefore so steeped in evil and pernicious –'

There was a crash as the barrel that the angry man had been sitting on went over backward loudly onto the concrete floor; and the man himself was on his feet even as his neighbors grabbed and held him from plunging down alongside the table toward Hal.

'Peace! Forgive me! Forgive me, please!' said Hal, holding up his hand, palm out. 'I just wanted to demonstrate what we all know – that arguments between people belonging to different churches can always break out, particularly in a city this size; and if those arguments lead to open fighting, then the Militia is going to have to send out squads to restore order wherever there's trouble, aren't they? So that if the spirit of disputation spreads, we can foresee a lot of Militia squads being sent out from the Center into the city to restore order.'

'I don't understand,' said the man in the knitted jacket; as the angry man slowly and stiffly reseated himself, glaring at Hal.

'I do, Jabez,' said the middle-aged woman with the piercingly dark eyes. 'By starting street fights, we can gradually drain off the interior strength of the Center. All right, Hal Mayne, but the Militia officers'll have figured out ahead of time how many men they can safely spare and not send any more out than that.'

'They'll try not to, of course,' said Hal. 'but our plan would be to give them a gradually escalating situation to deal with, over about a fifty to seventy-five hour period; both to lead them gradually to overstretch themselves and to wear out both them and the men they send out into the streets with lack of sleep. Wear them out until the judgement and reflexes of all of them are less than the best. In fact, what we'll try to do is bring everyone in the Center to the ragged edge of exhaustion. For that, forty-eight to seventy-two hours is about the limit. More than that, and they'll have a chance to adjust. Also, of course, time's critical in getting Rukh out. We know she's

516

alive now, but not what kind of condition she's in; and how much longer she can endure in there.'

Hal paused and took a second to check the expressions on the faces around the table. If nothing else, he had their full attention now, although fury still showed in the expression of the thin man he had provoked earlier.

'It might work,' said the man in the knitted jacket – not to Hal but to the table in general. He turned to Hal. 'Assuming it would, at least to the extent of draining off most of the fighting personnel of the Center, and exhausting them, where do we go from there?'

'When the time's ripe, we send a team into the Center through a service entrance, securing a route as we go through whatever service ways are used to deliver meals to the Cells section or take out anything – from laundry to dead prisoners. This team liberates Rukh and brings her back out the way it went in.'

'And everybody left in the Center is waiting for them when they try to go back out!' said the thin man, harshly.

'Not necessarily,' said Hal. 'Remember, the Militia are going to be thinking primarily in terms of the outside disorders, which by then are going to have escalated to where they begin to look like a potential city-wide riot. Their first thought, when the alarm reaches them that they've been invaded through the service area, will be that this is simply another uncoordinated outbreak of the rioting, a group aiming at damaging the Center, or stealing as much as possible, and then getting away again. There'll be no evidence available to make them suspect that all the rioting is an excuse to get one prisoner – one prisoner only – out of their Cells.'

There was silence in the warehouse.

'A pretty large gamble – that they won't suspect,' said Athalia.

'It shouldn't be,' said Hal. 'For one thing the odds are going to be pared by the fact that just before the team goes in after Rukh, we'll mount a diversionary attack on the front door of the Center. It should look – only look of course – as if the attackers in front are trying to fight their way in; and that ought not only to draw off what Militia strength is left in the building to that front area, but explain any reports that a smaller party has broken in through the service area.'

'You're still gambling on the way the Militia's going to think,' said Athalia.

'We can help the way they think, considerably,' said Hal. 'For one thing, simply by probably dressing up our team going into the Cells and having its members act to give the impression that they're simply a bunch of looters taking advantage of the fact there's an attack going on out front to slip in and grab what they can while the grabbing's good – what's a Militia cone rifle and ammunition worth, sold under the table, nowadays?'

Athalia nodded grudgingly.

'A lot,' she said.

'So,' said Hal, 'I think we can be pretty confident the Militia officers are going to send only a small part of their available strength to deal with what they think must be a lightly armed, untrained bunch off the street, that will run at the first sight of a uniform. Meanwhile, if we move with proper speed, we can have reached Rukh, got her out and be on our way back. We ought to be able to shoot our way through the first opposition they send from the front of the building against us; and be outside the Center by the time reinforcements reach the area where we were. Remember, at least according to the information I've been given, all the important parts of the Center are up front – the Record sections, the Armory, and so forth. The first instinct of Colonel Barbage and his men is going to be to protect that area first, and get around to mopping up the incursion through the service area when they've got more time.'

He stopped talking. His own first instinct had been merely to give them a moment to let them think over what he had just said. But a fine-tuned perception in him now told him that he had, in fact, achieved more than he had hoped for, at this stage.

'Excuse me a minute,' he said. 'I'll be right back.'

He turned and walked out through the door that connected the ware-house proper with Athalia's living quarters. Even as he passed through and shut it behind him, he could hear their voices break out in sudden discussion which came, blurred but unmistakable, through the wooden panel of the door behind him.

Let them discuss it among themselves, he thought. Let them talk. He glanced at the chronometer on his wrist. Give them five minutes and then he would go back in . . .

He wandered about the main room of Athalia's home, killing time. His thoughts drifted, and he thought of Rukh in the Militia Center. The image of her as he had first seen her came back to him, the whole scene of it caught between the tree-shadow of the conifers by the little stream, and the sunlight; with the green moss and the brown, dead needles underfoot – and overhead the wind-torn clouds, black and white, against the startling blue of the open sky – and Rukh and he and all the rest standing looking at each other, in that moment.

He remembered how he had thought then that she had looked, tall, slim and erect, in her bush-jacket, woods trousers and gunbelt – like the dark blade of a sword in the sunlight. He thought of her again now, as he had seen her in that moment, and that image was followed by another, one of her in the hands of the Militia; and it was as if something broke in him, without warning, like a small, hard explosion high in his chest near his throat, that spread its effect outward through all his body and limbs, chilling him.

He stood, chilling . . .

A door opened noisily behind him, and he whirled about like a tiger. Athalia stood framed in the opening to the warehouse.

'What's keeping you?' she said. 'We're all waiting.'

'Waiting?' he echoed. He glanced at his chronometer, but he could not remember what it had said when he had looked at it just a short while before.

'It's been more than ten minutes,' said Athalia, and jerked her head toward the warehouse interior behind her. 'Come along. We've got a lot of questions for you.'

CHAPTER FIFTY-FOUR

Opening the door into the warehouse, he found a change in those waiting there; and a change in the very atmosphere of the wide, chill, echoing enclosure. For a second, the faces at the table looked up at him in a savage eagerness, with the glitter of excitement found in the eyes of starving people held back too long from food spread plainly before them. It came to him then that he had forgotten how many years people like these had suffered from the Militia, without a chance to strike back in equal measure. It was small credit to him after all, he told himself, that he should be able to move them now to the point of action for Rukh and against such an enemy.

They dropped their heads, turning their eyes away from him as he stepped through the door and began to approach the table; but the caution was useless. To anyone trained by life as he had been, the fire in those seated there could be felt as plainly as the radiation from a metal stove with a roaring blaze in its belly.

'The question is,' said the man in the knitted jacket to Hal, as Hal retook his seat, 'whether we've got anything like the number of people you've planned for to do something this big. How many men and women do you think you'll have to have?'

'For which part of the operation?' asked Hal. 'To go into the prison section of the Center and bring Rukh out won't take more than a dozen people – and half of those are there only to be dropped off at points along the route, to give us warning if any force is sent against us from the front part of the Center. Any more than six people in on the actual rescue – that's five, including me – would get in each other's way in any small rooms or corridors. Our real protection's going to be in getting in fast and getting out again before the Center's officers realize what's happened.'

'Only twelve?' said the tall man who had gotten up to leave, earlier. 'But who's to back you up outside, once you've brought Rukh Tamani out?'

'Maybe a dozen more,' said Hal, 'but those don't need to have combat experience, like those I'll take inside; and in fact, the only really trained help I'll need are going to be the five with me. Give me five former Command members and the others can be anyone you trust to have courage and keep their heads under fire.'

– Or give me just two Dorsai like Malachi or Amanda, the back of his mind added. He put the thought from him. Nothing was as useless as wishing for what was not available.

'But you want us meanwhile to staff a full-scale assault on the front of the Center –' began the man in the knitted jacket.

'Thirty people who can actually hit most of what they shoot at,' said Hal. 'Plus as many more as you've got weapons for and can be trusted not to kill themselves or their friends. But by the time the assault starts, you ought to be able to use those you put to work to stir up the riots and fights, earlier. I'll say it again – the attack on the Center from its front is only for the purpose of occupying the attention of the Militia in the building, for the twenty minutes or so it takes us to get Rukh out. Don't tell me a city area this size can't come up with a hundred hard-core resistance people.'

He stopped speaking and looked down the table at all of them. For a moment none of them answered. They were all looking at the tabletop and elsewhere to hide their satisfaction with his answers.

'All right,' said Athalia, once more from the far end of the table where she had reseated herself. 'We'll have to talk over the details, of course. Why don't you wait in your room until I bring you our answer?'

Hal nodded, getting to his feet. He left the room and all of them to what he was fairly certain was already a foregone conclusion. But instead of going to his room, he stepped out the front door of Athalia's establishment into the darkness and the cool night air of the yard. Three low shapes, heads down and tails wagging solemnly, moved in on him. He squatted on the dirt of the yard and held his arms out to them.

Above them, the cloud cover of the night sky was torn here and there to show the pinpoints of stars. The dogs pressed hard against him, licking at his face and hands. . . .

The next day fighting broke out in the city, here and there, at first between individuals and then between the congregations of various churches. A few fires erupted. The day after there were more fires, fighting was more common and mothers did not send their children to school. By afternoon of the second day, the only people seen on the streets in Ahruma were adults armed with clubs, at the least, and squads of Militia, who ordered them back inside whatever buildings belonged to them, then went on to help the overburdened firemen of the city deal with the conflagrations that seemed to be erupting everywhere. The tempers of the Militiamen had shortened with exhaustion; and the reactiveness of the civilians had risen to match.

'It's out of hand,' said Morelly Walden, coming into Athalia's front room late on that afternoon. The slack skin of his aging face was pulled into a shape of sad anger. 'We're not controlling it any longer. It's happening on its own.'

'As it should,' said Hal.

Athalia's front room had been made into a command headquarters;

but she and Hal were the only people other than Morelly there at the moment. Morelly looked from Hal to her.

'The city doesn't have a single district left that doesn't have at least two or three fires,' he said. 'It could end with the whole area burnt down.'

'No,' said Hal. 'The firebugs who've been tempted to go to work on their own are getting tired, just like the Militia and the rest of us. Dawn tomorrow, things will begin to slack off. There's a pattern to riots in cities that's existed since there were cities to riot in.'

'I believe you,' said Morelly, and sighed, 'since I know you from the days in the Command with Rukh. But I can't help worrying, anyway. I think we ought to make our move on Center now.'

'No,' said Hal. 'We need darkness – for psychological as well as tactical reasons. If you want to worry about something, Morelly, worry about whether both the rescue teams and the ones who'll be attacking the front of the Center are getting some rest so as to be ready for tonight. Go check on them. The attackers shouldn't move into position until full dark; and the rescuers mustn't move until the fighting's been going on up front for at least a couple of hours; long enough to draw as many of the Militia in the building as possible up to the front of it.'

'All right,' said Morelly.

He went across the room and through the door leading back into the warehouse where the cots had been set up for those not presently needed on the streets.

As the door closed behind him, Athalia looked directly across the room at Hal.

'Still,' she said, 'isn't it about time you were waking those who're going in with you?'

'They already know all I know about what we'll run into,' answered Hal, nodding at the plans on the table, plans drawn from the information they had been able to gather from Athalia's contacts with the Center, of the corridors and passageways leading to Rukh's cell. 'From here on, it'll be a matter of making decisions, and their following the orders I give. Let them rest as much as they can – if they can.'

Shortly after sunset, word came back to Athalia's front room that sniping at the front of the Center building had begun. Hal went into the warehouse to gather his two teams; the one that would penetrate the building and the one that would guard the service courtyard where deliveries were normally made, at the back of the building, where the first team would go in through the barracks kitchen entrance. Of the twenty-five men and women he sought, he found all but one of them awake, sitting up for the most part on the edge of their cots and talking in low voices. The exception was a slim, dark-skinned man dressed in the rough bush clothing that was the informal uniform of those in the Commands – a last minute replacement for one of the interior team whom Hal had not met yet, slumbering face-down.

Hal shook a shoulder and the other sat up. It was Jason Rowe, who had led Had originally to the Commands and to Rukh Tamani.

'Jase!' said Hal.

'I just made the last truck in,' Jason said, yawning hugely. 'Greetings, Brother. Forgive me, I've been a little short on sleep lately.'

'And I was giving you credit for being the one person here with no nerves.' Hal laughed. 'How much sleep have you had?'

'Don't worry about me, Howard – Hal, I should say – I've had six –' Jason glanced at the chronometer on his wrist –'no, seven hours since I got here. I heard about you being here and thought you'd need me.'

'It's good to see you – and good to have you,' said Hal. Jason got to his feet. Hal looked around and raised his voice. 'All right, everyone who's with me! Into the front room and we'll get ready to leave.'

As the trucks that carried them got close to the Center, they heard the whistle of cone rifles from a couple of blocks away, and when they were closer yet, the tall faces of the buildings on either side of the street brought them echoes of the brief, throaty roars of power weapons, like the angry voicings of large beasts.

The trucks turned into a street along one side of the Center; and the metal gates to the service courtyard entrance, almost to the rear of the block-long building, stood wide open. Whatever Militia Guards had kept their post here, normally, there was now no sign of them. Instead, four men and one woman in civilian clothes and holding power rifles, with two still figures in uniforms lying against the rear courtyard, and the gates closed behind them.

'Everyone out!' Hal called as the trucks stopped.

He got out himself and saw the riders in the main bodies of the trucks dismount and sort themselves into two groups. He turned to the seven men and five women he would be taking inside with him; and saw that they had already congregated about Jason, as a recognized Command officer.

'Power sidearms and rifles, only, inside,' he told them. 'Who's got the cable?'

'Here,' said one of the men, partially lifting the small spool of what seemed only thin, gray wire, at his belt. The wire was shielded cable for a phone connection between the invaders which the communication equipment in the center would not register, let alone be able to tap.

'Stretcher?'

'Here,' answered a woman. She held up what seemed to be only a pair of poles wrapped in canvas.

'Good,' said Hal. He looked for the four people who had been guarding the black metal gates when the trucks arrived, and saw one of them, a man, standing a little apart from the two groups. 'Anyone in the kitchen there, as far as you know?'

'We were inside,' said the man, shifting his power rifle from one arm to the other. 'There was just one person on duty. She's tied up in a corner of the main room.'

That would mean, thought Hal, that the kitchen attendant on duty was a civilian. If she had been of the Militia, they would have killed her.

'All right,' Hal turned back to his dozen people. 'After me, then. If you fall out of touch with me, or something happens to me, take your orders from Jason Rowe, here. Keep together; and you observers take posts in the order we talked about earlier today. Report anything – anything at all out of the ordinary you see or hear – over the phone circuit. Come on.'

They went in, with Hal in the lead. Inside, the kitchen was only partially lighted over the sinks at one end and smelled heavily of cooked vegetables and soap. Hal saw a bundle of dark blue cloth under the furthest sink that must be the bound and gagged attendant.

'First observer, here,' he said. One of the two women in his group, taller and leaner than the other and in her forties, stooped and took the end of the cable from the drum slung from the shoulders of the man beside her, clipping it to a wrist phone on her right arm. The detailed map of the Center's interior, which Athalia had provided for Hal to study, was printed in his mind. He led the rest off through a doorway in the wall to his left, down a long, straight corridor where the odors, by contrast, were dominated by the sharp smell of some vinegarish disinfectant.

Dropping off observers at the points already picked out on the map he had studied, Hal led deep into the interior of the block-square building and quietly down three flights of ramps. At the base of the last of the ramps, a man in black Militia uniform snored lightly on a cot beside a bare desk and just to the left of a barred door leading to a corridor lined with metal doors that could be seen beyond. The Militiaman slept the utter sleep of exhaustion, and only woke as they began to bind his arms and legs to make him a prisoner.

'How do I open the door to the cells?' Hal asked him.

'I won't tell you,' said the Militiaman, hoarsely.

Hal shrugged. There was no time to waste in persuading the man, even if he had preferred doing so. With his power pistol he slagged the lock of the barred door, which had not been designed to resist that sort of assault. Kicking the still-hot bars of the door to open it, Hal led the six who were left, including the team member with the reel of cable, into the corridor lined with cell doors. The last of the observers was left behind with the trussed and gagged Militiaman.

The doors of the cell, like the door on the cell Hal had shared with

Jason, long before, in Citadel's Militia Center, were solid metal with only a small observation window which could be covered with a sliding panel. The observation windows on the cells they passed were uncovered; and as Hal glanced into each, he saw it was empty. They reached the end of the corridor where it ran into another corridor at right angles, running right and left.

'Shall we split up, Hal?' Jason asked.

'No,' said Hal. 'Let's try to the right, first.'

The leg of the cross corridor to the right offered more empty cells – but also three inhabited ones. They slagged the locks on these and released two men and one woman who turned out to have been arrested the day before in the course of the rioting. All three had been badly treated; but only one of the men required assistance to walk; and this the other two gave him. Hal sent them back to the room where the last observer waited with the bound Militiaman, with orders to follow the cable wire from there to the kitchen and freedom.

In the same way Hal and his team proceeded through eight more corridors and cross corridors, releasing over twenty inmates, only one of whom had been there before the riot; and who had to be carried out by his fellow-rescuers on a makeshift stretcher. Still, they had not found Rukh; and a coldness was settling into existence, deep inside Hal, at the thought that maybe they were half a day too late – perhaps she had died and her body had been taken out to be disposed of by whatever methods were used in Centers like this one.

'That's the end of it,' said Jason Rowe at Hal's left shoulder.

They had come to the end of a corridor and the wall that faced them was doorless and blank.

'It can't be,' said Hal. He turned about and went back to the room before the entrance into the cell block.

'There are other cells,' he said to the captured Militiaman. 'Where?'

The white face of the bound man in the black uniform stared up into his and did not answer. Hal felt something like a breath of coldness that blew briefly through his chest. A living pressure went out from him and he saw the man on the cot felt it. He stared down.

'You'll tell me,' he said; and heard – as a stranger might hear – a difference in his voice.

The other's eyes were already wide, his face was already pale; but the skin seemed to shrink back on his bones as Hal's stare held him. Something more than fear moved between the two of them. In Hal's mind there came back a long-age echo of a voice that had been his, telling a man like this to suffer; and now, in front of him, the Militiaman stared back as a bird might stare at a weasel.

'The second door, in the first corridor to the right – it isn't a cell door,' the man answered, huskily. 'It's a stair door, to the cells downstairs.'

Hal went back to the cell block. He heard the footfalls of Jason and the others on the concrete floor behind him, hurrying to keep up. He came to the door the Militiaman had mentioned and saw that the window shield of it was open. The view through it showed an ordinary, empty cell. He tried the door handle.

It was unlocked.

He swung it wide; and it yawned open to this left. Stepping through, he turned and saw a picture screen box fastened over the window on the inside face of the door. Beyond were wide, gray, concrete stairs under bright illumination, leading downward. He descended them swiftly, through the door at the bottom, and stepped into a corridor less than fifteen meters in length, with cell doors lacking windows spaced along each side of it.

Where the windows might have been were red metal flags, and these, on all the doors but one, were down. Hal took five long strides to the one with the flag up and reached for its latch.

It was locked. He slagged the lock. Holstering his pistol, he tore off a section of his shirt, wadded it up to protect his hands, and, grasping the handle above the ruined lock, swung the door open.

A sewer stench struck him solidly in the face. He stepped inside, almost slipping for a second on the human waste that covered he floor. Inside, after the brilliance of the light in the corridor outside, he could see nothing. He stood still and let his senses reach out.

A scant current of moving air from some slow ventilating system touched his left cheek. His ears caught the even fainter sound of shallow breathing ahead of him. He stepped forward cautiously, with his arms outstretched and felt a hard, black wall. Feeling down, at the foot of the wall, his hands discovered the shape of a body. He scooped it up; and it came lightly into his arms as if it weighed no more than a half-grown child. He turned and carried it out the doorway into the light.

For less than a second the thin, foul-smelling bundle of rags he held in his arms could have been someone other than Rukh. She was almost skeletal; bruises and half-healed lacerations and burns had distorted her features and her hair was matted with filth. But her dark eyelids, which had closed against the light as he stepped through the doorway, opened slowly, and the brown eyes that looked up at him were untouched and unchanged.

With effort, her dry lips parted. Barely, he heard the whisper that came from her.

'I testify yet to thee, my God.'

A memory of a day in which he had stood to his neck in water, looking through the screening branches of a waterside bush, returned to Hal. Through the delicate tracery of brown twigs and small green leaves, he remembered seeing in the distance – now, for the first time, clearly – three old men on a terrace, surrounded by young men in black with long barrelled pistols and a very tall, slim man; and his arms pressed the body he held close to himself, tenderly and protectively, as if it was something more precious than the universe could know. Deep within him, the breath of coldness that had woken in him momentarily in Athalia's outer office came back, coalesced to a point, and kindled into icy fire.

'Here,' he said, putting Rukh gently into Jason's arms. 'Take her out of here; and give me your rifle.'

His hand closed about the small of the butt of Jason's power rifle, as the other man handed it to him. The feel of the polished wood against his fingers was strange – as if he had never touched such a thing before – and at the same time, unforgettably familiar and inescapable. He holstered his own power pistol and turned to one of the others who carried a rifle.

'And yours . . .' he said.

He grasped the second rifle in his other hand and looked again at Jason.

'If I'm not outside with the rest of you when you've loaded the trucks.' he said, 'don't wait for me.'

He turned and went off before Jason had time to question him. He heard the footsteps of the others begin and follow. But the sound of their feet died away quickly behind him, for he was moving with long strides, up the stairs, out of the cell block and through the entrance room. He passed the final observer there without answering her as she tried to question him about the still-bound Militiaman, and went on up the corridor beyond.

The chart he had studied of the Center's interior layout was burned sharply into his memory. As he approached the next to last observer she stared at him and at the two rifles he carried nakedly, one in each hand.

'Monitoring equipment from the yard just called to say they think a party's been sent from the front of Center to deal with us –' she began.

'Jason and the rest have Rukh,' he interrupted, with breaking stride. 'Go with them as soon as they reach you.'

He continued straight down the corridor, parting company with the cable, which here made a ninety degree turn into a cross corridor, on its way back to the kitchen and its exit.

'But where are you going, Hal Mayne?' the observer called after him.

He did not answer; and the echoes of her question followed him down the corridor.

He went on, following the chart in his head now, turning at the second cross corridor he came to, heading toward the front of the building. Inside him, the point of coldness was expanding, spreading out through all his body. All his senses were turned to an acuteness

527

wound to the edge of pain. He saw and remembered each crack and jointure in the walls that he passed. He heard the normally silent breathing of air in the ventilating system through the gratings in the ceiling beneath which he stepped. His mind was focussed on a single point that ranged ahead of him, reaching through the walls and corridors between the Center's front offices, where the majority of the black-clad Militia would be, their officers with them and Amyth Barbage, among those officers.

Now, the coldness possessed him totally. He felt nothing – only the purpose in him. He turned into a new corridor and saw, ten meters down it, three Militiamen pushing a small, wheeled, power cannon in his direction.

He walked toward them, even as they suddenly noticed him and stopped in stunned silence to stare at him, striding toward them. Then, as one of them roused at last and reached for the power cannon's firing lever, the rifles in his hands roared briefly, the one in his left hand twice – like the coughings of a lion – and the three men dropped. He walked up to them, past them, and on toward the front of the building.

'Report!' rapped a harsh voice from a speaker grille in the ceiling of the corridor. 'Sergeant Abram – report!'

He walked on.

'What's happening there, Sergeant? Report!' cried the speaker grille, more faintly over the increasing distance between it and him. He walked on.

He was all of one piece, now; with the coldness in him that left no room for anything else. Turning into another corridor he faced two more Militia men and cut them down also with his rifles; but not before one of the counter discharges from the power pistols both carried cut a smoking gash in the jacket sleeve of his upper left arm. He smelled the odor of the burned cloth and the burned flesh beneath, but felt no heat or pain.

He was getting close to the front of the building; and the corridor he was on ended a short distance ahead in another cross corridor. Already, there was a difference in what he saw around him. The doors, that were now of glass, to the dark offices he passed had become more widely separated, indicating that the rooms they opened on were larger than those he had passed earlier. Half a dozen steps from its end, the corridor he was in abruptly widened, its walls now faced with smooth stone where up to this point they had been merely of white-painted concrete. The floor had also changed, becoming covered with a pattern of inlaid gray tiles in various shapes, highly polished; and his footsteps rang more sharply upon this new surface. To the abnormal acuteness of his vision, under the now-hidden but even brighter illumination from overhead, the invisible atmosphere about him seemed to quiver like the flesh of a living creature.

He had been moving under the impetus of something neither instinct nor training, which directed him from the back, hidden recesses of his mind. Now he felt this impetus, like a hand laid on one of his shoulders, stop him, turn him and steer him into one of the dark offices. He closed the door behind him and stood to one side in the interior shadows, looking out through the transparency of the door at the empty corridor ahead.

For a few seconds he heard and saw nothing. Then, from a distance there came a growing sound that was the hasty beating of many feet, rapidly approaching; and, within a minute, fully a dozen fully-armed Militiamen burst into sight around a corner of the cross corridor and ran past him back the way he had come. He let them go. When they were out of sight, he stepped back into the passageway, and continued, turning left into the cross corridor in the direction from which they had just come.

A short dogleg in this direction, and then another turn, brought him to a final cross corridor busy with men in black uniforms hurrying back and forth between doorways. These glanced at him puzzledly as he walked among them; but no one stopped him until he came at last to an open doorway on his left, looked in, and saw a large room with a long, fully-occupied conference table and blackout curtains over tall windows in a far wall. Two Militiamen privates with cone rifles stood guard, one on each side of the entrance; and when he turned to enter, they stepped to bar his way, the rifles snapping up to cover him.

'Who're you –' began one of them.

Hal stuck out right and left at both men. The butt of a power rifle crashed into the forehead of one, the barrel end across the throat of the other, and they dropped. Hal stepped inside, closing the door behind him.

Those at the conference table within were already on their feet. Still moving swiftly, he saw clearly what his first glance through the doorway had made him suspect, that the uniforms of all of them there showed officer's rank.

Two reached for holstered pistols at their belts; and the rifles in his hands coughed. They fell; and the other officers stood staring. A hand turned the doorknob from the corridor, outside.

'Stay out!' shouted the officer at the far end of the table.

'Where's Amyth Barbage?' Hal asked – for the man he had come to find was nowhere in the room. He continued to move as he spoke around the walls of the room, so that he could cover with his weapons not only those at the table but the closed door through which he had just come.

No one answered. Still moving, and approaching the table, Hal swung the muzzle of the rifle in his left fist to center on the senior officer present, a squarely-built major in his fifties, at the end of the table farthest from the door, under the curtains of one of the windows.

'He's not here –' said the Major.

'Where?' demanded Hal.

The Major's face had been pale. Now the color came back.

'No one here knows,' he said, harshly. 'If anyone could tell you, even, it'd be me – and I can't.'

'But he's in the Center,' said Hal; for Athalia's people had reported Barbage returning to the Center some hours past, and that he had no gone out again.

'Satan take you!' said the Major. 'Do you think I'd tell you if I knew?'

But to Hal's hypersensitive hearing in this moment, there was a note of triumph in the officer's voice that convinced him not only that the other was lying and knew where Barbage was, but that something had been achieved by the other since Hal had entered the room.

The words of the second to last observer on the cable line came back to Hal, telling him that the monitoring equipment in the kitchen courtyard had called with the suspicion that an earlier party had been sent from the front of the building to deal with the team sent out to rescue Rukh. The Major's hands were in open sight on the tabletop, but he was standing with the middle of his body pressed against the table-edge before him. Hal moved swiftly forward and knocked the man backward. Cut at an angle of forty-five degrees into the table's edge and covered until now by the bottom edge of the Major's uniform jacket was a communications panel as long as Hal's hand, but hardly wider than a ruler.

The door to the room smashed open the armed Militiamen erupted inward.

'Take him now!' The Major's order came out more scream than shout. Around the table, the officers who had not yet drawn their sidearms were reaching for them.

Malachi Nasuno, or anyone who had ever had Dorsai training, could have pointed out their error. Their very numbers were the cause out of which their failure could be certainly predicted. Moving thinkingly and surely around the table, using the bodies of those who would kill or capture him as shields, Hal disabled or threw into the fire of the weapons aimed at him all those with whom he came in contact. Finally, as the room began to be empty of people still on their feet, panic took those of the Militia who were still unharmed; and there was a sudden, general rush for the still-open door.

Hal found himself standing alone, the passage beyond the open doorway empty.

But, caught still in the coldness that held him, he was aware that the victory was a transient one; and that the way out of the still-open door was no safe escape route for him. Turning, he pointed his power pistol at one curtained window and blew out both curtain and window. The thick but ragged edge of the window material showed through the tatters of the curtain. It had been heavy sandwich glass, which would have frustrated even the energy of a power pistol at any greater distance than the point blank range at which he had used the one he held.

He knew from the plan in his memory that the window from which he was escaping was near one end of the building's front, closest to that same side which, further back, held the courtyard and the kitchen entrance. He dropped onto concrete sidewalk, behind the line of Militia cars parked along the front curb of the street. Having landed, he stayed flat on his belly at the foot of the front wall of the Center; and had this sensible decision rewarded by hearing the whistle and pock of impacts on the wall above him, of cones fired by the resistance people in buildings across the street.

Undoubtedly, among those rounded up to maintain a steady fire on the Center's front, there were responsible individuals who would realize that someone not in Militia uniform, exiting out a smashed window of the building, was hardly likely to be an enemy. But they would be too few and too scattered to get that understanding passed quickly to all the excited amateurs with weapons surrounding them.

The cone rifle firing continued – but, as he had foreseen, the line of vehicles parked parallel to the curb shielded him from the direct view of the resistance people, and from any shots that came close. While his position up against the base of the wall, under the narrow outcropping of the decorative stone window ledge over which he had just come, protected him from observation and fire from above the building. Almost immediately, he began to wriggle along the base of the wall toward the corner of the building, only a few scant meters from him.

He reached it and turned the corner. Rising to his feet he ran down the empty, lamplit street toward the lights of the kitchen courtyard.

There was a silence about the courtyard as he got closer that made him slow his steps and begin to move more quietly, himself. There had not been time for the rest of the team to get loaded into the trucks and away, yet. He went swiftly but softly until he came to the beginning of the courtyard wall. Ignoring the gate, he found finger-cracks enough where the building wall joined that of the courtyard, climbed to the top of the wall and dropped down inside.

The trucks were still there, close enough to him so that they blocked his view of most of the rest of the courtyard. He drew the power pistol and went with it in his hand around the back of the nearest truck . . . and breathed out with relief.

The team was just now loading, ready to depart. But some-thing – it may have been their first sight of Rukh as she now was – seemed to have impressed them to a degree he himself had not been able to, earlier. They were moving as silently as they could, and communicating by hand signals wherever possible.

Rukh was just now being brought to the back of the nearer truck. He holstered his gun and stepped forward into the midst of them. Ignoring the astonishment of the others, to whom he must have seemed to have appeared out of empty air, he walked to the side of the stretcher on which they carried her.

Her bearers checked themselves, just short of handing the stretcher up to those waiting to receive it, behind the raised tailgate of the truck; and Rukh herself looked up at him. The nurse they had had among those waiting with the backup team in the courtyard had possibly already gives her medications to ease and strengthen her; but the eyes looking up into his were now more widely open and her voice, though still whispering, was stronger than he had heard it in the cell block.

'Thank you, Hal,' she said.

For a moment the coldness moved back from him.

'Thank the others,' he said. 'I had selfish motives; but the others just wanted you out.'

She blinked at him. Her eyes were moist. He thought she would like to say something more; but that the effort was too great. Hastily he spoke himself.

'Lie quiet,' he said. 'I'm taking you clear off-planet to Mara; where the Exotics can put you back together, body and mind, as good as new.'

'Body only . . .' she whispered. 'My mind is always my own. . . .'

Hal felt his right sleeve plucked. He turned and saw Athalia standing just behind him with a face shaped by cold anger. He allowed her to pull him back out of earshot of Rukh.

'You didn't tell us anything about taking her off-world!' Athalia whispered savagely in his ear.

'Would you have risked lives to rescue her, if I had?' he answered grimly, but with equal softness. 'I told you she had a value to the whole race, above and beyond her value to all of you here on Harmony. Now that she's free, do you suppose anything less than off-planet can be safe for her, or safe for anyone who might try to hide her?'

Athalia's hand fell from his sleeve.

'You're an enemy, after all,' she said, bitterly.

'Ask yourself that a year from now,' said Hal. 'In any case, the Exotic Embassy can help get her off Harmony, which none of you can do; and once she's known to be on another world, the pressure from the Milita, turning you all upside down to find her, will let up.'

'Yes,' Athalia said. But she still looked at him savagely as he turned away from her.

They had begun to lift the stretcher's far end so as to pass it to those in the truck. There was a pause as they made the decision to lower the tailgate first, after all. In the moment of that pause, a voice struck at them from the kitchen entrance of the building.

'So!' it said, hard, loud and triumphant in the silence of the lamplit courtyard, 'the Whore of Abomination has friends who would try to steal her from God's justice?'

Everyone looked. Amyth Barbage, stick-thin in his close-fitting black Militia colonel's uniform, stood alone in the entrance to the kitchen. He carried a power rifle, generally pointed at all of them; and Hal's eyes, without moving, saw that – like himself – none of the rest had weapons in hand and ready for use.

Alone and apparently indifferent to that fact, Barbage walked three steps forward from the doorway. His power rifle pointed more directly toward the stretcher bearing Rukh, and those who stood closely around it.

'Carry her back inside,' he said, harshly. 'Now!'

The coldness returned to Hal with a rush; and from the same place that it came from in him, came other knowledge he had not known he had.

A wordless shout that erupted like an explosion in the stillness of the courtyard tore itself from him. It came from every nerve and muscle of his being, not merely from the lungs alone, the utmost in sound of which his body was capable; and it went out like a bludgeon against the thin, white-faced man, a wall of sound directed against Barbage alone. For a moment the other seemed stunned and frozen by it; and in that same moment, Hal leaped aside from the line of aim of the Militia officer's rifle, drew his own pistol and fired.

The knowledge, the actions, were all as they should have been. But Hal's body had not been trained relentlessly from birth and never allowed to fall out of the ultimate in fire-tuned conditioning. The early years with Malachi and the last couple of years of self-exercise at the Encyclopedia could not give him what the years of his lifetime would have given a body born and raised on the Dorsai. The energy bolt from his power gun struck, not Barbage at whom it was aimed, but Barbage's rifle, spinning it from that officer's hands to skitter across the rough paving of the courtyard with the last few millimeters of its barrel's muzzle-end glowing a dull red heart.

And Barbage – where Hal had been less than he should, Barbage was more. Barbage, who should have been doubly immobilized, first by the killing shout, and then by the loss of his weapon, recovered before Hal had fully regained his balance. Bare-handed, he plunged toward the truck and Rukh on her stretcher.

Hal threw up the muzzle of his pistol to fire, found too many bodies in the way, and dropped his sidearm on the pavement. He leaped forward himself to meet Barbage, just as the other reached the tailgate of the truck. Hal's hands intercepted and closed on the furious, narrow body, at waist and shoulder, and lifted it into the air. It was like lifting a man of cloth and straw.

'No!' Rukh said.

The volume of her voice was hardly more than the whisper in which she had spoken a moment earlier; but Hal heard it and it stopped him. The coldness held him in an icy fist.

'Why?' he said. Barbage was still in the air, motionless now above the paving on which his life could be dashed out.

'You cannot touch him,' said Rukh. 'Put him down.'

A quiver like that which comes from overtensed muscles passed through Hal; but he still held Barbage in the air.

'For my sake, Hal,' he heard her say through the coldness, 'put him back on his feet.'

Slowly, the coldness yielded. He lowered the man he held and set him upright. Barbage stood, his face frozen, staring not at him, but at Rukh.

'He must be stopped,' Hal muttered. 'A long time ago, James Child-of-God told me he had to be stopped.'

'James was much loved by God, and by many of the rest of us,' said Rukh. With great effort she raised herself slightly from the stretcher and looked Hal in the face. 'But not even the saints are always right. I tell you you cannot touch this man. He is of the Elect and he hears no one but himself and the Lord. You think you can punish him for what he did to me and others, by destroying his body. But his body means nothing to him.'

Hal turned to stare at the white face above the black uniform collar, that did not see him – only Rukh.

'Then what?' Hal heard himself saying. 'Something has to be done.'

'Then do it,' said Rukh. 'Something far harsher than destroying his mortal envelope. He will not hear his fellows. Leave him then to the Lord. Leave him, by himself, to the voice of God.'

Hal was still staring at Barbage, waiting for the other man to speak. But to his wonderment, Barbage said nothing. Nor did he move. He simply stood, gazing at Rukh, as she sagged back on to the stretcher.

For a moment there was no movement anywhere in the courtyard. Then, slowly, the resistance people began to continue bringing Rukh fully aboard the vehicle and themselves mounting into it and the other one that waited for them. Hal stood, continuing to watch Barbage, waiting for him to make a leap for the fallen power rifle. But Barbage still stood motionless, his expression unchanged, staring into the darkness under the canvas hood of the tuck into which Rukh had now disappeared.

The motor of that truck started. Then the motor of the other vehicle.

'Hal! Come on!' called the voice of Jason.

Slowly, still keeping an eye on Barbage, Hal stepped back two paces and picked up his power pistol from where it had landed when he had flung it down. Careful not to turn his back on the Militia officer, he swung himself up into the back of the truck which held Rukh. Once up, he turned, and stood above the again-raised tailgate, holding the pistol ready at his side as the truck he was in slowly pulled out of the courtyard and until the wall about it finally cut off his view of its interior.

But Barbage had not moved from where he stood.

CHAPTER FIFTY-FIVE

The best ways between the stars were not always the direct ways; and the fastest route for Hal to the Dorsai turned out to be to accompany Rukh to Kultis, transship and proceed from there to his own destination.

So it was that he landed once again at Omalu. There, in the terminal after the long trudge across the landing pad, through cool air and the blinding sunlight from the white-hot dot in the sky that was Fomalhaut, he found someone waiting for him. It was Amanda; and he felt a sudden, great, rush of relief and love as without planning, thought or warning, his arms went around her.

Her body was slim and strong and real against him. In almost the same second, her own arms wrapped his body and she held him, strongly. They pressed together wordlessly, ignoring the rest of the universe. He had not realized until this moment how transient and uncertain by comparison were almost all the other things of his life. He did not want to let her go. But he could not, after all, stand in the middle of a busy terminal forever, holding on to her. After a long moment, he released her. She released him, and stepped back.

'How'd you know I was coming?' he asked, incredulously.

'The captain of your ship sent word you were aboard when he called in from solar orbit,' she told him. 'You're a passenger who's noticed, nowadays.'

'I am?' he said. He had not been aware of the Exotics aboard the ship affording him any special notice. But then Exotics were hardly likely to fuss over anyone.

'Yes,' she told him. She turned and they moved off through the terminal together. She was wearing a knitted dress of brilliantly white wool that clung to the narrowness of her waist. At her throat was a necklace, small, coiled with seashells, also a clean white outside, but with a delicate pink rimming the inner lips of each shell opening.

'You're dressed up,' he said, with his eyes on her.

She smiled, looking straight ahead.

'I had some business in Omalu today, to get dressed up for,' she answered. 'You brought luggage, this time?'

'A travel case, that's all.'

She walked with him toward the baggage delivery section; and they did not quite touch as they went, but he was conscious of the living warmth of her body beside him.

'I wrote to Simon Khan Graeme – the senior living Graeme – about you,' she said. 'He's still on New Earth doing police organizational work; and his estimate was that he hasn't more than another few months before the influence of the Others squeezes him out of a job, even there. But he'll be staying as long as he can earn interstellar credits. Of the other two left in the family, the younger brother – Alistair – is consulting on Kultis, and their sister, Mary, is on Ste. Marie for some border dispute, so the place is still empty. But Simon said you're welcome to stay there anytime you're on Dorsai.'

'That's good of him,' said Hal.

She opened the small hand-case she was carrying and passed him a thumb-stall with a fingerprint reproed on the end.

'You can use my print to unlock the front door,' she said. 'But you'd better register your own when you get there, so you won't need to carry a copy of mine. You'll find the lock-memory just inside the front door to the left – look under the sweaters and jackets hanging up there, if you don't see it at first.'

He smiled at her and took the stall, putting it in a breast pocket of his gray jacket. She moved along beside him, appraising him gravely as she went.

'You've come into your full size,' she said. 'The house will feel right, having you there.'

There was a moment of silence between them.

'Yes . . .' he said. 'Will you thank Simon Khan Graeme for me?'

'Of course. But it's nothing unusual, this inviting you to stay,' she smiled again, an almost secret smile. Her white-blonde hair was longer now; and she shook it back over her shoulders as she walked. 'Hospitality's a neighborly duty, after all. Besides, as I say, I told him about you. There's hardly a Dorsai home that wouldn't put you up.'

'With its people not there?'

'Well . . . maybe not with their people not there,' she said; and smiled back at him.

'I appreciate your thinking of my staying there,' he said slowly. 'I may not get another chance.'

She sobered, looking away from him, toward the baggage area.

'I thought you'd want to,' she told him. 'Have the flyer you hire take you right to the house. There's no need to go in through Foralie Town unless you want to; and people there are busy. Everyone's busy, right now.'

They walked on in silence. When they reached the baggage area, luggage from the ship Hal had come in one had not yet been delivered.

'When you're done in Omalu, today, you'll come by and visit me?' he said.

'Oh, yes.' She met his eyes squarely for a moment. 'Here comes your luggage, now.'

The wall had dilated an iris in itself, to give entrance to an automated luggage carrier. It drove up to the distribution circle before them and the baggage began to feed off from it into the chutes that would sort their contents into the stalls where the passengers waited. Hal slid his passage voucher into the sensor slot of the stall in which he and Amanda were standing. Seconds later, the check stub attached to his case having shown that its torn edge matched the torn edge of Hal's voucher, the case slid up through a trapdoor before them, onto the floor of the stall.

Hal picked it up and moved away toward the local transportation desk. Amanda went with him. They did not talk as they walked. Hal felt himself full of words that would not sound right, said here and now.

But at the local transportation desk it developed that all the long-haul jitneys based at the spaceport had already been put under hire for the day. He would have to take ground transportation to Omalu and pick up one at the Transportation Center, there.

'We can go to town together, then,' he said to Amanda, feeling suddenly as light as a reprieved prisoner. She frowned.

'I hitched a ride out,' she answered. 'I shouldn't – on the other hand it's your interstellar credit, if you want to buy me a seat on the bus.'

'Of course I want to,' he said firmly.

They rode in together, sitting in adjoining seats three rows back in an otherwise empty surface bus. He put his hand on hers, and she squeezed his fingers briefly, then slid her arm through his and brought their hands together again, so that they sat with forearms on the armrest between them, arms intertwined and hands clasped. Their forearms pressed again each other, he thought, like those of two people about to take a blood oath, mingling the fluid in both their veins with the single cut of a knife.

But the knife and oath were unnecessary, here. It seemed to Hal, as they sat holding to each other in this unremarkable way, as if the life-sustaining conduits of their flesh had long since been joined into one system; so that each beat of his heart sent his blood through her arteries as well as his; and that each of hers must direct that of both of them back through his own body.

There was still a great deal to say but no hurry to say it now. The silence of the moment was itself infinitely valuable. He watched her clean profile etched against the windowed view of the countryside through which their vehicle was passing. There was a glow of a quiet peace and happiness in her that had not been present when he had been here before, a warmth independent of and at odds with the season of his coming. His last visit had been at the crisp end of summer. The second time, a year and a half later, he was arriving early in the spring. Beyond the windows of the bus it was cold, clear and bright. The unsparing illumination of Fomalhaut lit all the landscape like a late and final dawn.

Under that light there was a northern look to what he could see outside the windows of the bus, that had not been there on his earlier visit. Now, in the nakedness of spring, it was clear that the land had just emerged from an icy winter and was hurrying to adapt to the march of seasons. In the earth and the growing things he read a race to survive under the sword of time. The few homesteads they passed were as neat as those he had seen before; but fields that had obviously been under cultivation the previous year had not been prepared this spring for sowing. Flower beds before the houses they passed were bare and empty.

Even in the wild fields the light green of the grass stems lay over toward the ground under the breeze, showing the brown tint of the earth through their own color. Against the dark branches and twigs of the trees, the young leaves were darker green than the grass; but tiny and stiff, as if they huddled on the stems that held them. Above, the upper wind sent scattered clouds scudding forward visibly, harrying them toward the close, jagged horizon of the surrounding mountains. The little creeks that the bus occasionally crossed were gray-blue of surface and sharp-edged where their brown banks met the blue water, the earth not yet with new vegetation to soften the sharp line where their earth ended at streamside.

At the Transportation Center in Omalu, he arranged for a jitney and Amanda parted from him. He wanted to remind her of her promise to see him after her business here was done; but he was half-ashamed to make such a point of it. The jitney he had hired lifted him high above the surface of the world, into the blue-black of near space, and dropped him down again in the front yard of Graemehouse.

He let himself in, as the jitney took off again into the upper skies. Within, the house was as ready for habitation as ever; but the stillness of the air there shut out the strange winteriness he had seen everywhere on the way here and wrapped him with a feeling of suspended time. He reached, without looking, brushed aside a jacket and put his hand on the plate of the lock-memory, his fingers coding it to remember his thumbprint. He walked through the house, dropped his luggage case on the white coverlet of the bed that had been Donal's and left it there, coming back to the living room.

He opened the door that led from the living room to the library and stepped into the opening. His head brushed the top bar of the frame, his shoulders brushed against the uprights on both sides of him. Amanda had been right – he had come into his full size. He was conscious of what was himself, small, silent, and alone, inside the big body.

'An odd boy. . . .'

He went into the kitchen, opened the storage units there and made himself a meal of bread, goat cheese and barleylike soup, which he ate seated at the kitchen table and looking out on the same steep hillside that was visible from the window of Donal's bedroom. Afterwards, he cleaned up the debris of his eating and went back to browse through the book-shelves of the library. They were old, familiar books, and he lost himself in reading.

He woke from the pages before him to see that the sun was low on the mountains and afternoon had grown long shadows. Loneliness stirred in him; and to put it away from him he got up, returned his book to its place, and went out through the front door of the house.

It would be sunset shortly and Amanda had not come. He turned away from the house and wandered toward the outbuildings. As he came close, a horse neighed from the stable. He went in and found two of them in the stalls there. Their long noses and brown eyes looked around at him as he came up behind them.

One was Barney, the gray Amanda had been riding when he had first seen her, and during their rides together afterwards during his first visit. The other was a tall bay gelding, large enough to carry someone of his size and weight comfortably. Saddles, bridles and blankets were hung on the wall of an adjacent stall.

He smiled. Both horses whickered and moved impatiently, watching him over their shoulders for some sign that he would take one of them out for a ride. But he turned away and went back out again.

He moved about the grounds, stepping into each of the outbuildings in turn, standing and listening to the walled quiet inside them. As the sun was setting he went back to the house. It was time for the end-of-day news on any technologized world; and he sat watching that news on the communications screen in the living room. For the first few minutes, as on any unfamiliar world, what he saw and heard of people and their actions made little sense. Then, gradually, the forces behind what he watched became more apparent. The Dorsai world was mobilizing – it was as he had expected when he had decided it was time to come here once more.

He became engrossed in what he watched and followed, as the sunset moved on around the planet and the source of the broadcast moved with it. There was a uniqueness, an attention compelling magic in the interior life of a people – any people. Waking at last from this, he suddenly realized it was almost ten p.m. and Amanda had neither come nor called. Outside, it had been dark for several hours.

He sat, recalled once more to the emptiness and silence of the house about him. He stood up and stretched. A fatigue he had not noticed until this moment sat between his shoulder blades. He dimmed the light in the living room to a nightglow and went to the room where his travel case waited.

Lying in bed, he thought at first that in spite of the fatigue he would not sleep. But he put disappointment from him and slumber came. It was at some unknown time later that he was roused by the faintest whisper of movement and opened his eyes on the darkened space around him.

He had swung wide the windows and left the drapes drawn back so that outside breeze could come freely through. In that moving air, the bottom ends of the glass curtains now flowed inward, moving between the dark pillars of the pulled drapes. In the time he had been asleep the moon had risen and moved into position to shine strongly into the middle part of the room, away from his bed. The air was cool – he could feel it on face and hands, only, the rest of him warm under the thick coverlet; and in the center of the room stood Amanda, half-turned from him, undressing.

He lay, watching her. She would be too good at moving silently not to have deliberately made the slight sound that she knew would waken him. But she went on now with what she was doing as if unaware his eyes were on her. He lay watching; and the last piece of clothing dropped to her ankles and lay still. She straightened, and stood for a second like some warm and living sculpture of ivory, bathed in moonlight, drowned in moonlight. The light turned the curve of hip and buttock, outlining them against the further darkness of the room and her breasts shone full in the moonbeams. Her hair was like a cloud with its own interior illumination, haloing her head. Beneath its light, her calm face was like the profile on some old coin; and from shoulder to feet the length of her body reflected the moonlight. Balanced there like a wild thing that had just raised its head from drinking at something heard far off, she turned and he saw the flare of her hips widen below the narrow waist as she came toward him. Lifting the coverlet, she slid beneath it, turning to face him.

A harsh, ragged sigh of relief tore itself past the gates of his throat and his arms went around her, one hand closing about the soft turn of hip, one sliding beneath her to cradle her upper body, his forearm beneath her shoulder and his fingers in the softness of her hair. With one simple effort, he lifted her to him.

'You came . . .' he said, just before their lips met, and their bodies pressed strongly together.

He returned, after a while, to the rest of the universe – he came back gradually, drifting back. They were lying side by side now on the bed, with no cover covering them; and the moon had moved some

541

distance in the sky, so that its light had abandoned the center of the room, and now shone full upon them.

'Now everything is different,' he said.

He lay on his back; and she lay half-turned toward him, her head on the pillow, so that he could feel her eyes watching him even though he stared at the ceiling and the moonlight.

'Is it?' she said, softly. Her right arm lay above her head and the fingers of that hand wandered caressingly, through his own black, coarse hair. Her other arm lay across his chest, white against the darkness of the matted hair there. She moved closer to him, fitting her head into the hollow of his shoulder; and he turned toward her, laying his left arm over her. He saw his own thick wrist and massive hand lying relaxed upon the gentle rises of her breasts and felt a wonder that she should be here, like this; that out of all times and places they should find each other in this moment when the worlds were beginning to burn about them.

The wonder grew in him. How was it that at a time like this he could feel so close to someone else and happy; when only a handful of days past on Harmony –

He shuddered suddenly; and her arms tightened swiftly about him.

'What is it?' she said.

'Nothing . . .' he said. 'Nothing. An old ghost walking over my grave.'

'What old ghost?'

'A very old one,' he said. 'Hundreds of years old.'

'It's not gone,' she said, 'it's still with you.'

'Yes,' he said, giving up. The core of him was still cold, even though she warmed him with her arms; and the words came from him almost in spite of himself.

'I've just come from the Friendlies,' he said. 'I'd gone there to get a Harmonyite named Rukh Tamani – did I tell you about her when I was her before? There's a work she's needed for on Earth, for all the worlds. But when I got there the Militia at Ahruma had her in prison.'

He stopped, feeling the coldness grown within him.

'I know about the Militia on the Friendlies,' Amanda said.

'I got the local resistance people to get her out. We went into the Militia Headquarters after her. When I found her, she'd been left in a cell. . . .'

The memory grew back into a living thing, about him. He talked on. The coldness began once more to grow in him, as it had then, spreading out through his body. The bedroom and Amanda seemed to move away from him, to become remote and unimportant. He felt himself reentering the memory; and he grew even more icy and remote. . . .

'No!' It was Amanda's voice, sharply. 'Hal! Come back! Now!'

542

For a moment he teetered, as on a sharp-crested rock, high above a dark depth. Then slowly, clinging to her presence, he began to retreat from the place into which he had almost gone a second time. He returned, farther and farther . . . until finally he was back and fully alive again. The coldness had melted from him. He lay on his back on the bed and Amanda had him in her arms.

He breathed out once, heavily; a sound too great to be called a sigh; and turned his head to look at her.

'You know about it?' he said. 'How do you know?'

'It's not uncommon here,' she said, grimly. 'The Graemes had their share of it. It's called a cold rage.'

'A cold rage . . .' He looked back up at the shadowy ceiling overhead, The phrase rang with familiarity in his ears. His mind took what she had just told him and ran far into the interior of his own thoughts, fitting it like a key to many things in himself he had not yet completely understood. He felt Amanda releasing the fierce grip she had maintained on him until now. She let go the tension of her arms and lay back a little from him. He felt her watching him.

'I'm sorry.' The words came from him in a weary gust of air. He was still not looking at her. 'I didn't mean to put it off on you, that way.'

'I just told you,' she answered – but her tone was more gentle than her words, 'it's not uncommon here. I said the Graemes had their share of it. How many nights out of the past three hundred years, do you think, has one of them, man or woman, laid talking to whoever was close enough to tell, as you did now?'

He could think of nothing to say. He felt ashamed . . . but released. After a little while, she spoke again.

He closed his eyes. Her question struck heavily upon him at his recognition of a knowledge he had not expected her to have. There was nowhere he could turn to hide the rest of things from her – now that he had just tried to go as far as human mind could take him from her and she had brought him back in spite of himself.

'Donal,' He heard his voice say it, out loud in the night silence. 'I was Donal.'

His eyes were still closed. He could not look at her. After a long moment he asked her: 'How did you know?'

'Knowing runs in the Morgan line,' she answered. 'And the Amandas have always been gifted with it, even more than the others in the family. Also, I grew up with Ian around. How could I not know?'

He said nothing for a little while.

'It's Ian you look like,' she said. 'But you know that.'

He smiled painfully, opening his eyes at last and gazing up at the ceiling. The relief in having it out in the open was so great that adjustment to it came hard.

543

'It was always Ian and Kensie I wanted to be like – when I was growing up – as Donal,' he said; 'and I never could.'

'It wasn't Eachan Graeme? Your own father?'

He laughed a little at the thought.

'No one could be like Eachan Graeme, as I saw it then,' he said. 'That was too much to expect. But the twins – that seemed just barely possible.'

'Why do you say you never were?' she said.

'Because I wasn't,' he said. 'As the Graemes go, I was a little man. Even my brother Mor was half a head taller than I was.'

'Two lifetimes . . .' she said. 'Two lifetimes bothering over the fact that you were shorter than the other men in your family?'

'Three lifetimes,' he corrected her, 'and if you're male, it sometimes matters.'

'Three?'

He lay silent again for a moment, sorting out the words to say.

'I was also a dead man for a time,' he said at last. 'That is, I used the body and name of a man who'd died. I had to go back in time; and there was no other way to do it.'

It was the last thing he had meant to do, but he heard the tone of his own voice putting up a wall again further questions from her about that second lifetime.

'How long have you known who you were . . . this last time?' she asked.

He had been speaking without looking at her. But now he opened his eyes and turned toward her; and, her own eyes, pure blue now in the moonlight, drew him down to her. He kissed her, as someone might reach out to hold a talisman.

'Not until these last two years – for certain,' he said. 'I grew up until I was nearly seventeen years old on old Earth, not knowing. Then later, when I was in the mines on Coby, I began to feel the differences in me. Later, on Harmony, there began to be moments when I did things better than I should have known how to do. But it wasn't until I got here to Graemehouse on my first trip – when I was in the dining room there –'

He broke off, looking down into those eyes of hers.

'You must have known, then,' he said, 'or suspected, when you found me there when you came back, and saw how I was.'

'No,' she said. 'It was the night before, that I felt it. I knew then, not who you were, but what you were.'

He shook slightly, remembering.

'But I wasn't really sure then, myself. I didn't even understand how it could be,' he said, 'until this last year at the Final Encyclopedia. Then, when I began to use the Encyclopedia for the first time as a creative tool, the way Mark Torre had hoped and planned it would be used, I put it to work to hunt back and help me find out where I'd come from.'

'And it showed you,' she said, 'that you'd come from the Dorsai?'

A coolness – different from the coldness she had rescued him from before, but equally awesome, blew through him.

'Yes,' he said, 'but also much more than that, very much, much farther back than that.'

She watched him.

'I don't understand,' she said.

'I'm Time's soldier,' he said softly. 'I always have been. And it's been a long, long campaign. Now we're on the eve of the last battle.'

'Now?' she asked. 'Or can it still be sidestepped?'

'No,' he said, bleakly. 'It can't be. That's why everyone's in it who's alive today, whether they want to be or not. I'll take you to the Encyclopedia one day and show you the whole story as it's developed, down the centuries – as I've got to show it to Tam Olyn and Ajela as soon as I get back.'

'Ajela?'

'Ajela's an Exotic – only about my age.' He smiled. 'But at the same time she's Tam's foster-mother. She's in her twenties now, and she's been taking care of him since she was sixteen. In his name she does most of the administrating of the Encyclopedia.'

CHAPTER FIFTY-SIX

Amanda asked nothing more, for the moment. A temporary silence closed around them and by mutual consent they turned back to each other and into the universe and language that belonged only to the two of them. Later they lay companionably quiet together on their backs, side by side, watching the last of the moonlight illuminating a far corner of the room; and Amanda spoke.

'You didn't expect it at all, then, that I'd be waiting for the space-port when you came back?'

He shook his head.

'I couldn't expect that,' he said. 'It would have been like expecting to grow up to be like Eachan Khan Graeme – too much to imagine. I just thought that when I came I'd look you up, wherever you were. I only hoped. . . .'

He ran down into silence. Amanda said nothing for a moment.

'I've had more than a year to think about you,' she said.

'Yes,' he smiled, ruefully. 'Has it been that long? I guess it has, hasn't it? So much has been going on. . . .'

'You don't understand.'

She raised herself up on one elbow and looked down into his face.

'You remember what I tried to tell you when you were here the last time?'

'That you were like the other two Amandas,' he said, sobering. 'I remember.'

He looked up at her.

'I'm sorry I was so slow to realize what you meant,' he went on. 'I do now. You were telling me that, like them, you're committed to a great many people, too many to take to the possible conflict of an extra commitment to someone like myself. I understand. I've found out how little I can escape from my own commitments. I can hardly expect you to try to escape from yours.'

'If you'll listen,' she said, 'I might be able to tell you what I'm trying to tell you.'

'I'm listening,' he answered.

'What I'm trying to say is that I had a chance to think about things after you were gone. You're right, I sent you off because I didn't think there was any room in my life for anyone like you – because I thought I had to be what the second Amanda had been; and she'd sent Ian away. But with time to think about it I started to realize there was a lot there I hadn't understood about both the earlier Amandas.'

He lay waiting, listening. When she paused, he merely continued to look up at her.

'One of the largest shocks was realizing,' she said, almost severely, 'how little I'd understood about my own Amanda, the second one, in spite of being raised by her. I told you I grew up with Ian around the house so much of the time that as a young child I thought he was a Morgan. He and Amanda were both at a good age then, his children were grown and had children of their own; and his wife, Leah, was dead. He and Amanda, eventually in their old age, had come to be what life and their own senses of duty had never let them be until then – a love match. This was all right there, under my nose, but I was too young to appreciate it. Being that young and romantic-minded, all I could see was Amanda's great renunciation of Ian when she was younger, because of her obligation to the people of the Dorsai.'

She paused.

'Say something,' she demanded. 'You are following me, aren't you?'

'I'm following you,' he said.

'All right,' she went on. 'Actually, when I began to see Ian and Amanda as the human beings they really were, I was finally able to see how there'd been a progression at work down the Amanda line. The First had her obligation only to her family and the people of this local community. My Amanda had hers to the Dorsai people as a whole. The obligation I carry, I think, is the same as yours, to the human race as a whole – in fact, I think that's one of the forces that's brought us together now, and would have brought us together, sooner or later, in any case.'

He frowned a little. What she had last said was an obvious truth that had never occurred to him.

'I realized finally,' she was going on, 'that, far from our personal commitments making us walk separate roads, they probably do just the opposite. They were probably going to require us to walk the same road together, whether we wanted to do so, or not; and if that was so, then there was no problem – for me, at least.'

She stopped and looked down at him with an almost sly smile he had not expected and did not understand.

'Are you still following me?' she demanded.

'No,' he answered. 'No, to be honest, now you've lost me completely.'

'My, my,' she said, 'the unexpected limits to genius. What I'm telling you is, I decided that if it was indeed inevitable that the factors involved were going to bring the two of us together, then it was just a matter of time before you came back here. If you never did, I could simply forget about the whole matter.'

'But if I did come back? What then?' he asked.

She became serious.

'Then,' she said, 'I wouldn't make the mistake I'd made the first time. I'd be waiting for you when you got here.'

They stared at each other for a long moment; and then she took her weight off her elbow, lay down and curled up against him, her head in the hollow of his shoulder. He put his other arm over and around her, holding her close. For a moment or two neither of them said anything.

'The last thing in the universe I expected,' he commented, at last, to the ceiling. 'It took me two tries at life to realize I had to develop the ability to love, then a third try from a standing start to actually develop it. And now, when I finally have, at a time when it ought to have been far too late to do me any good – here you are.'

He stopped talking and ran the palm of is hand in one long sweep down her back from the nape of her neck to the inner crook of her knee.

'Amazing,' he said thoughtfully, 'how you can fit yourself so well to me, like that,' he said.

'It's a knack,' she answered, her lips against his chest. There was a second's pause. 'Except all these hairs you have here tickle my nose.'

'Sorry.'

'Quite all right,' she said, without moving. Another momentary pause. 'I won't ask you to shave them off.'

'Shave them off!'

She chuckled into his chest. They held each other close for a little while.

'I shouldn't do that sort of thing,' she said in a different voice, after the time had passed. 'I don't know what makes me want to tease you. It's just that it's like being able to ride a wild horse everyone is afraid to get close to. But I can feel something of what it must have been like for you, all those years and all those lives. It's so strange it doesn't show on you more, now that you know who you were and what you did.'

'Each time was a fresh start,' he said, earnestly. 'It had to be. The slate had to be wiped clean each time so there'd be no danger of what had been learned before getting in the way of the new learning. I set myself up fresh each time. That way I could be sure I'd only remember what I'd known before after I'd progressed beyond needing it in my newer life. I've been learning – learning all the way.'

'Yes, but hasn't it been strange, though?' she said. 'Everybody else starts at the bottom and works up. Actually, what you've done is start at the top and work down. From Donal, controller of worlds,

548

you've struggled your way down to being as much like an ordinary person as you can.'

'It's because the solution's got to be for the ordinary person level – or it's no solution. Donal started out to mend the race by main force; and he learned it didn't work. Force never really changes the inner human. When Genghis Khan was alive, they said a virgin with a bag of gold could ride from one border of his empire to the other end and no one would molest her, or it. But once he was dead, the virgins and the gold started moving again under heavy armed guard, as they always had before. All anyone can ever do for even one other human being is break trail for him or her, and hope whoever it is follows. But how could I even break trail for people unless I could think like them, feel like them – know myself to be one of them?'

His voice sounded strange in the quiet nighttime room and his own ears.

'You couldn't, of course,' Amanda said gently. 'But how did Donal go wrong?'

'He didn't really,' Hal said, to her and the shadowy ceiling. 'He went right, but without enough understanding; and it may be I don't have enough understanding, even yet. But his start was in the right direction and what he dedicated me to as a child is still my path, my job.'

'Dedicated you?' she said. 'You mean, as Donal, as a child, you dedicated yourself to what you're doing now? How – so early?'

A remembered pain moved in him. A memory of the cell on Harmony closed around him once more.

'Do you remember James Graeme?' he asked her.

'Which James?' she asked. 'There've been three by that name down the Graeme generations since Cletus.'

'The James who was Donal's youngest uncle,' he answered. 'The James who was killed at Donneswort when I – when Donal was still a child.'

He paused, looking at her calm face, resting now with the one cheek against his chest, looking back at him in the remains of the moonlight.

'Did I tell you the last time I was here about my dreaming about a graveyard and a burial, while I was in the cell on Harmony?' he asked.

'No,' she said, 'You told me a lot about the cell and what you thought your way through to, when you were there. But you didn't mention any dream of a burial.'

'It was when I was just about to give up,' he said. 'I didn't realize it then, but I was just on the brink, finally, of finding what I'd sent myself out as Hal Mayne to find. What I'd come to understand began to crack through the barrier I'd set up to keep myself as Hal from knowing what had happened to me before, and what came through

549

was a memory of the ceremony at Foralie held over James' grave, when I was a boy. . . .'

His voice was lost in the pain of remembering for a moment, then he brought it back.

'That was the moment of Donal's decision, his commitment,' Hal went on. 'James had been closer to him than his own brother – it sometimes happens that way. Mor was between us in age, but Mor –'

His voice did not die this time, it struck. Mor's name blocked his throat.

'What about Mor?' Amanda asked after a moment. Her hand moved gently to touch his, her fingertips resting on the skin at the back of his hand as it lay on the bed.

'Donal killed Mor,' he said, from a long distance away.

He could feel her fingertips as they touched the naked nerves below the skin and reached up along them to touch the innermost part of his identity.

'That's not the truth.' He heard her voice a little way off. 'You're making more of it than it is, somehow. It's right, but not that right. What is true?'

'Donal was responsible for Mor's death,' he answered, as if she had commanded him.

The feeling of her reaching into him withdrew.

'Yes,' she said. 'That's all right, then, for now. You were telling me about James' death and how it brought about Donal's commitment to what's driven you all these lifetimes and all these years. What happened?'

'What happened?' His mind pulled itself back from the vision of Mor, as the finally-insane William of Ceta had left him, and came back to the vision of James' burial. 'They just accepted it. Even Eachan – even my father – he just accepted James' being killed, reasonlessly, like that; and I . . . couldn't. I – he went into a cold rage – Donal did. The same sort of thing you brought me back from a little while ago.'

'He did?' Amanda's voice broke on a note of incredulity. 'He couldn't – he was far too young. How old was he?'

'Eleven.'

'He couldn't at that age. It's impossible.'

Hal laughed, and the laugh rang harshly in the quiet bedroom.

'He did. Kensie felt the same way you're feeling . . . when Kensie found him, in the stables where he'd gone after the ceremony, when all the rest had gone up to the house. But he could and did. He was Donal.'

With the last word, as if the name had been a trigger, he felt within him a return, not only of the coldness, but of a sweep of power that woke in him without warning, threatening to carry him off like a tidal bore sweeping up in its wall of water anything caught in its naked channel at high water time.

'I am Donal,' he said; and the power took and lifted him, irresistible, towering –

'Not Bleys.'

Amanda's quiet voice reached out and cut the power off at its source. Clear-mindedness came back to him, in a rush of utter relief. He lay for a few seconds, saying nothing.

'What have I told you about Bleys?' he asked her, then, turning to look through the gloom at her.

'A great deal,' she answered, softly, 'that first night you were at Fal Morgan, when you talked so much.'

'I see.' He sighed. 'The sin of the Warrior, still with me. It's one of the things I still have to leave behind, as you saw . . . when I remembered Rukh's rescue. No, thank God, I'm not Bleys. But at eleven years old, I wasn't Bleys either. I only knew I couldn't endure that nothing be done about James' unnecessary death, about all such unnecessary evils in the universe – all the things people do to each other that should never be done.'

'And you committed yourself then, to stop that?'

'Donal did. Yes,' he said. 'And he gave all his own life to trying. In a sense, it wasn't all his fault he went wrong. He was still young. . . .'

'What did he do?' her voice gently drew him back onto the path of what he had been about to tell her, earlier.

'He went looking for a tool, a tool to make people not do the sort of things that had caused James' death,' Hal said. 'And he found one. I call it – he called it – intuitive logic. It's either logic working with the immediacy of intuition, or intuition that gets its answers according to the hard rules of a logic. Take your pick. Actually, he was far from the first to find it. Creative people – artists, writers, composers of music, musicians themselves, had used it for years. Researchers had used it. He only made a system for it and used it consciously, at his will and desire.'

'But what it is?' Amanda's voice prodded him.

'It can't be explained – in the same sense as mathematics can't be explained – in words,' he said. 'You have to talk the language in which it exists to explain it – and even before that, your mind has to begin by making the quantum jump to a first understanding of that language, before you can really start learning what it is. I can give you a parallel example. You'll have seen, at one time or another, some great painting that reached out and captured you, heard a piece of music that was genius made audible, read a book that was beyond question one of the everlasting books?'

'Yes,' she said.

'Then you know how all those things have one element in

common, the fact you can come back and back to them. You can look, and look again, at the painting without ever exhausting what's to be found in it. You can listen to the music over and over, and each time find something new in it. You can read and reread the book without ever getting out of it all that's there for you to discover and enjoy.'

'I know,' she said.

'You see,' he told her, 'what makes all your returning to these things possible is their capability of triggering off in you an infinity of discoveries; and they can do that because there is an infinity of things to be discovered put into them by the creator. That infinity of possibilities could never be marshalled together consciously by one human mind and put to work in one piece of canvas, one succession of sounds, one succession of printed words. You know that. But still, there they are. They did not exist before, and now they do. There was no way they could have come into existence except by being put there by the human being who made each of them. And there was only one way he or she could have accomplished that – the maker had to have built not only with his conscious mind, which is precise but limited in how much it can conceive at any one time, but also with the unconscious, which knows no limits, and can bring all life's observations, all life's experience, to bear on a single rendered shape, sound, or word, placed just so among its fellow shapes, sounds or words.'

He stopped speaking. For a second, she did not reply.

'And that,' said Amanda then, 'is what you call intuitive logic?'

'Not quite,' said Hal. 'What I was talking about there was creative logic, which is still operating under the control of the unconscious. If the unconscious is displeased with the task, it refuses to work, and no power of will can make it. What Donal did was move that control fully into the conscious area, that's all, and put it to work there manipulating the threads of cause and effect. Then, when he was still so young, he didn't realize how much he was drawing on what he had learned from reading the works on Strategy and Tactics by his great-grandfather.'

'By Cletus Grahame, you mean?'

Hall nodded.

'Yes. You remember, don't you, that Cletus had actually started out with the idea of being an artist? It was only later on he became caught up in the physics of military action and reaction. He used creative logic to build his principles; and in fact, from what's there to be seen in his work, he may have crossed the line himself from time to time, into a conscious control of what he was making.'

'I see,' Amanda seemed to think for a moment. 'But you don't know if he ever did? You seem to know that Donal did.'

'I was never Cletus.' Hal smiled, more to himself than to her. 'But I was Donal.'

'And you say creative logic was why Cletus was able to win the way he did, against Dow deCastries and an Earth so rich in everything all the Younger Worlds seemed to have no chance against it? And it was symbolic logic then that brought Donal to the title of Protector of the fourteen worlds, including Earth, before he was in his mid-thirties?'

'Yes,' said Hal, somberly. 'And having done it, Donal understood the lesson of the virgin with the bag of gold, after the death of Genghis Khan. He looked at the peace and law he had enforced on all the civilized planets and saw that he'd done nothing. He hadn't changed a single mind, a single attitude in the base structure of the human animal. It was the nadir of everything he had reached out for since that moment when he was eleven years old.'

Her hand reached out and caressed his arm.

'It was all right.' He smiled again, this time ruefully. 'He lived through it. I lived through it. Being who I am, I can't give up. That's really what operated in that Militia cell. My conscious mind and body were ready to give up and lay back to do just that – but they weren't allowed to. That that's in me pushed me on, anyway. Just as it pushed Donal on, back then. As Donal, I saw I'd been wrong. The next step was to amend that wrongness – to correct, not an errant humanity, but the overall historic pattern that had made humanity errant.'

'And how did he think he could do that?' her voice led him on to talk, and the talking was the slow unloading of an intolerable burden he had carried for so long he had forgotten that he had ever been without it.

'By turning his tool of intuitive logic not just upon the present, but on what made it, the causes behind the effects he saw around him and the causes behind those causes, until he came back to a point at which something could be done.'

'And he found it.'

'He found it,' Hal nodded. 'But he also found that what needed to be done was not something he could do as he had done things up until then. It wasn't something he was yet equipped to do. To operate upon what he needed to operate upon he himself had to change, to learn. To grow.'

'So,' Amanda said. 'And your second life came from that. Can you tell me about that, now?'

He was conscious of all the burden he had already laid aside for the first time in his life, in talking to her here and now.

'Yes,' he said. 'Now I can.'

He reached his free hand across to lay on the living incurve of her belly. He could feel her ribs rise and fall, slowly and fully with her breathing. He stared into the shadows about him.

'The problem had several sides,' he said. 'Humanity couldn't, as he thought he saw it then, be changed from where he stood at the moment, just like you couldn't do much about a tree that was already grown. But if you went back to the time of its planting and made changes that would be effective upon the environment in which it would grow to what it would be in the present. . . .'

He stopped.

'Go on,' Amanda said.

'I'm trying to work out the best way of telling you all this briefly,' he answered. 'And it takes a little thinking. You'll have to take my word for it that by using intuitional logic and working back from the then present effects to the causes he already knew for them, or could discover, he found he could trace back to the closest point in history where all the elements he hoped to alter were available at a single time and place for changing. He found that first point in the twenty-first century, just on the eve of the practical development of the phase drive, just before the diaspora to the Younger Worlds, in a time when all the root stocks of what would later become the Splinter Cultures were to be found together within a single environment – that of Old Earth.'

Amanda rose on her elbow again to look down into his face.

'You're going to tell me he actually went back in time, to change the past?'

'Yes and no,' Hal said. 'He couldn't physically travel back in time, of course. He couldn't actually change the past. But what he found he could do was work his consciousness back along the chain of cause and effect to the time he wanted and there try to make the necessary changes, not in what actually happened then, but in the possible implications of what happened. He could open up to the minds living in that time possibilities that otherwise they might not have seen.'

'How did he think he was going to communicate these possibilities – by stepping into people's dreams, then, or speaking to them, mind to mind?'

'No,' he said, 'by interacting – but as someone who actually did not exist at the time. To make the story as short as possible, he ended by reanimating a dead body, a mining engineer of the twenty-first century, who had drowned, named Paul Formain. As Paul Formain, he influenced people who were the forerunners of the Dorsai, the Friendlies and others – but most of all he influenced the people making up something that was then called the Chantry Guild.'

'I remember that from history.' said Amanda. 'The Exotics came from the Chantry Guild.'

'Yes,' said Hal. 'In the Chantry Guild and seed organizations of other Splinter Cultures, he introduced possibilities that were to have their effect, not in Donal's time, but in our present day. Now.'

'But when did Donal manage to do this?' Amanda said. 'He was in the public eye right up to the moment of his death – when he took that courier ship out alone and was caught by the one-in-a-million chance of not coming out of phase shift.'

'He didn't die,' said Hal. 'It was simply assumed he'd died, when he didn't arrive where and when he was supposed to and no trace of his ship could be found. He hid in space for over eighty years, until it was time to let the ship be found, drifting into Old Earth orbit.'

She said nothing for a long moment.

'With a baby aboard,' she said. 'A very young child – that was you?'

'Yes.' Had nodded. 'It's something the mind can do with the body, if it has to. Even Cletus mended his crippled leg with his mind.'

'I know that story,' said Amanda. 'But the Exotics helped him.'

'No,' said Hal. 'They just provided the excuse for him to believe in his own ability to do it.'

She said nothing, looking at him.

'We've had miracle cures reported all down the centuries,' he said, 'Long before the Exotics. They, themselves, have quite a library on such incidents, I understand. So, I hear, has the Final Encyclopedia. I believe I was dying in that cell from the pneumonia or whatever it was I had, until I realized I couldn't afford to die. Shortly after that realization, my fever broke. Of course, it could have been coincidence. But mothers have stayed untouched in the midst of epidemics as long as they were needed to care for their sick children.'

'Yes,' she said, slowly. 'I do know what you mean.'

'That, and taking over a dead body as life leaves it, are only two aspects of the same thing. But I don't want to get off on that business now. The main point is, Donal went back and became Paul Formain, so as to change the shape of things to come – and to change himself.'

'Will you sit up?' Amanda said. 'Then I can sit up, too. I can't lie propped on one elbow indefinitely.'

They arranged themselves in seated position, side by side, with their backs protected by pillows from the metal bars of the bedstead behind them. The narrow width of the single bed left them still close, still touching.

'Now,' said Amanda. 'You said – "and to change himself." Change himself how?'

'Donal'd seen how he'd gone astray in his own time,' Hal said. 'He felt it was because he had failed to feel as he should for those around him – and he was right, as far as that went. At any rate, he went out to learn the ability to feel another's feelings, so that he could never again fall into the trap of thinking he had changed people when actually all he'd done was change the laws that controlled their actions.'

'Empathy? That was what he wanted?'

555

'Yes,' said Hal.

'And he found it?'

'He learned it. But it wasn't enough.'

Amanda looked at him.

'What is it bothers you so about this time Donal – no, not Donal – when you were this animated dead man . . . what was his name?'

'Paul Formain,' Hal said. 'It's not easy to explain. You see as Formain, he – I – did it again. Donal'd played God. He hadn't done it just for the sake of playing God, but that's what the effect he'd had on the populations of fourteen worlds had amounted to. Then when he saw what he'd done; it sickened him, and he decided whatever else he did, he wouldn't be guilty of doing it again. Then, as Paul Formain, he went and did just that.'

'He did?' Amanda stared at him. 'I don't see why you say that – unless you call it playing God to plant the possibilities of our present time. . . .'

Her own voice ran down.

'No!' she said, suddenly and strongly. 'Follow that sort of reasoning and you end up with the fact that to try to do anything for people, even for the best of reasons, is immoral.'

'No,' Hal said. 'I don't mean that. What I mean is that once again, he realized he'd acted without sufficient understanding. As Donal he hadn't considered people at all, except as chess pieces on a board. As Paul Formain, he considered people – but only those with whom he learned to empathize. He was still trying to work with humanity from the outside – that was what hadn't changed in him.'

He paused, then went on.

'He faced that, after he'd done what he'd gone back to the twenty-first century to do. He'd set in motion the very factors that are now bringing the internal struggle of the race animal out into the open and forcing everyone to take sides, with the Others or against, for the survival of us all. But he'd done it, in a sense, with a certain blindness; and it was because of that blindness that he couldn't foresee someone like Bleys and the growth of power behind him. After he returned Paul Formain's body to the ocean bed from which he had lifted it, he realized how he had gone wrong – although he couldn't yet foresee the consequences, that hold us in a vice right now. But he understood enough finally to see what his great fault had been.'

'His great fault?' said Amanda, almost harshly. 'And what was that great fault?'

'Just that he'd never had the courage to give up the one apart corner of himself, to abandon standing apart from everyone else.' Hal turned his head to look directly at her. 'He'd been the "odd boy," according to his teachers. He'd been the small and different ugly duckling among the Graemes. He'd been born with the same sort of mind that led Bleys Ahrens to put himself lightyears apart from the rest of the race. Donal, too, had been born an isolated individual, suffered from that isolation, and come to embrace it, as Bleys had embraced it. With his development of empathy, Paul Formain could begin to feel what someone else might be feeling, but he felt it as any human being might feel a frog's hunger for a passing fly. The soul of him still stood alone and apart from all those he had thought early had cast him out.'

Again, he paused.

'I was afraid to be human, then,' he said. He did not look at her, but he felt her arm go around his waist and her head come to rest on his shoulder.

'Not any more,' she said.

'No.' He heaved a very deep sigh. 'But it was literally the hardest thing I ever had to do. Only there was no choice. There was the commitment. I had to go forward – and so I did.'

'By coming back as a child,' she said.

'As a child,' he agreed. 'Starting all over again without memory, without strength, without the skills of two lifetimes to protect myself with in an arena I'd built and didn't know I'd built. So I could finally learn, once and for all, to be like everybody else.'

'Was it so absolutely necessary to do that?' he heard her asking from the region of his shoulder.

'It was critical,' he said. 'You can lead or drive from the outside, but you can only show the way from inside. It's not just enough to know how they feel – you have to feel it with them. That was the mistake I made being Formain and thinking empathy alone was going to give me what I needed to get the work done. And I was right – all the years of being Hal Mayne have proved how right I was, this last time. I was born Donal, and nothing I can do can ever leave him behind, but I can be a larger Donal. I can feel as if I belong to the community of all people – and I do.'

He stopped and turned his head to look down into her face.

'And, of course,' he said, 'it brought me you.'

'Who knows?' she said. 'You might've come to it anyway by a different route, eventually. I still feel things – the historic forces, as you call them – would've brought us together in the long run, the way or another.'

'I thought you'd thought it could go either way, and you'd just left it up to fate,' he said.

'I did,' she answered. 'But looking back on it, I was certain you'd be back. I've learned to trust myself in things like that. I know that I'm right. Just as I know . . .'

She did not finish the sentence.

'Know what?' he asked.

'Nothing. Nothing worth talking about, right now, anyway.

Nothing to worry about.' He felt her shake her head, briefly. 'In ancient times they would have called feeling like that second sight. But it's not giving me anything you ought to be concerned about. Tell me something else. When you talk about the race-animal, do you really mean some entity, actual and separate from us all?'

'Not separate,' he said. 'Oh, I suppose you could call it separate in that it might want something that you or I as part of it doesn't want. No, as I say, it's just the self-protective and other reflexes of the race as a whole, raised to the level of something approaching a personality because it's now the reflex-bundle of an intelligent, thinking race, as opposed to the same sort of thing in the case of the race, or genus or species of, say, lions or lemmings – or you name them.'

'And that's all it is?' she said. 'Then how do you justify talking about it as if it was a sort of wilfull individual personality that had to be dealt with?'

'Well, again, that's the difference that's come into it because we, who make it up, while we're a race of intelligent individuals, are also a conglomeration of wilful individuals. Because we think, it thinks – after our fashion. Try this for an explanation. It's a sort of collective unconscious, as if all our individual unconsciousnesses were wired together with something like telepathy – again, there's been evidence for that sort of wired-togetherness in the past.'

'Yes,' she said thoughtfully. 'The empathy between twins. Or between parent and child, or any two adults in love, that allows them sometimes to feel at a distance what's happening to the other. I can agree with that. You know, we – you and I – have that, I think.'

'All right, then,' he said. 'But there's one difference from us in the lower orders – particularly in the examples of the bee hive or the ant hill – in our case. It's that we can not only want something different from what the race-animal wants, we can actually try to change its mind and its course, by convincing the unconsciouses of our fellow-individuals. If we can get enough of them wanting what we want, the race-creature has to turn that way from whatever other route it's chosen.'

'How do you convince the unconsciousness of others, though? There's nothing there to take hold of. The conscious mind of someone else you can talk to. All right, I know the Exotics do a beautiful job of mending sick minds by talking to the conscious and getting the corrections filtered down to the unconscious. And, for that matter, Bleys' charisma and that of the Others – that's working directly with the unconscious of others. So's hypnosis. But none of those thing have a lasting effect unless what's being put into the subject really agrees with what was there in the unconscious in the first place. There's no direct way to hold converse with another human's unconscious.'

'Yes, there is,' he said, 'and it's a way that's been used at least since

558

a prehistoric people lived in the caves of the Dordogne, back on Old Earth – you can talk to the unconscious of other people through the mediums of art.'

'Art . . .' she said, thoughtfully.

'That's right,' he said. 'And you know why? Because art – real art – never tells anyone something. It only lays it out there for whoever comes to pick up.'

'Perhaps. But it certainly makes whatever it has to say as attractive as possible to whoever comes along. You have to admit that.'

'Yes, all right. If it's good. And if it isn't good, it doesn't offer anything to the unconscious of a viewer, reader, or listener. But the difference between that and conscious attempts to persuade is the difference between an order and a demonstration. The maker of the piece of art doesn't convince the person experiencing it – the person experiencing it convinces himself or herself, if they decide what's laid out in the art is worth picking up. That's why I worked my way back down the ladder from Donal, as you put it. All of Donal's strength couldn't move the race one millimeter from its already chosen path. But if I go first and leave footprints in the snow, some may follow, and others may follow them.'

'Why?' she said. 'I'm not against you, my love, but I want to see the reasons plainly. Why should anyone follow you?'

'Because of my dreams,' he said. 'Donal dreamed at James' death of a time when no more James' would be killed for stupid or selfish reasons. I've come to dream farther – I see the old dream of the race as a whole, now possible.'

'And what does a race dream of?' she asked, so softly that anywhere but in this quiet and private room he would not have been able to hear her.

'It dreams,' he said, 'of being a race of gods. From the beginning, the individual part of the race, shivering in the wet as a stone-age savage, said, 'I wish I was a god who could turn the rain off,' and, finally, generations and millennia later, he was such a god – and his godlike power was called weather control. But long before that the urge to command wetness to cease had produced hats, and roofs and umbrellas – but always the push in the human heart went on toward the original dreams of being able to just say, 'rain, stop!' and the rain would stop.'

He looked down through the dimness at her.

'And that's how it's been with everything else the individual, and therefore the race-animal, dreamed of – warmth when it was cold, coolness when it was too hot, the ability to fly bird-like, to cross great distances of water dry-shod, to hear and talk at as great or even greater distances, to block pain, defy disease and death. In the end, it's added up to one great desire. To be all-mighty. To be a god.'

He paused, having heard his voice grow loud in the room and went on more quietly.

'And always the way to what was wanted's been found in a dozen small and practical ways before the single command, the wave of a godlike hand, was developed that could simply make it happen. But always the dream has run in advance. Hunters and cities, conquerors and kings, all succeeded in being and were superceded. The dream was always achieved first in art, time and again, and never forgotten until it was made real. Slowly, the human creature was changing, from a being that lived and died for what was material, to one who lived and died – and fought and died – for what was immaterial; for faith and obligation and love and power, power over the material first and then power over fellow-creatures, and finally, last and greatest, the power over self. And the dreams have gone always ahead, picturing what was wanted as something already possessed; until it became a truism to the race-animal that what could be conceived, could be had.'

He stopped talking, finally.

'And you say these dreams were kept in the language of art?' she said.

'Yes,' he answered, 'and still are. The footprints I want to leave in the snow lead off toward the reality of what has only been barely dreamed of yet. The universe in which to understand a thing is to have it. Do you want a castle? You can have it merely by wanting it – but you have to know and own the materials it's to be built of, the architecture that'll ensure it'll stand, not fall, once it's built, and the very nature and extent of the ground on which it stands. If you know that much, you can have your castle right now, by means already known. But you want more than just the physical structure. Your castle must have those immaterial qualities that made you desire its castleness in the first place. These are not to be found in the physical universe, but in the other one that we all know and reach for, unconsciously. So, such a universe offers much more than the fulfillment of material dreams, it offers satisfaction of that original dream to be a god – the chance to cure all ills, to learn all mysteries, and finally to build what has never been dreamed of by any of us before now.'

'You want everyone to dream your dream,' Amanda said.

'Yes,' he said. 'But my dream is their dream, already – unless they shut it out as Bleys and his kind have done. I just articulate it.'

'But maybe it never will be articulated, except in your own individual mind,' she went on. 'And when you're gone, it'll be gone.'

'No,' he said, strongly. 'It's there in other minds as well, too strongly for that. It's there in the race-creature itself, along with the fear of trying for it. Haven't you felt it yourself – haven't you always felt it? It's too late now to hide it or kill it. Four hundred years ago, the race-animal was forced to face the fact that the safe, warm world it was born on was only an indistinguishable mote in a physical universe so big that anything conceivable not only could, but almost certainly must, exist in it. It could try to close its eyes to what it had been brought generally to know, or it could take the risk and step out into the alien territory beyond its atmosphere.'

'It hadn't any choice,' she said. 'Overpopulation of Old Earth, for one thing, drove it out.'

'Overpopulation was a devil it knew. The unlimited universe was one it didn't. But it went – in fear and trembling, talking of things *'man was not meant to know,'* but going; and it scattered its bets as best it could by turning loose all the different cultural varieties of itself society had produced up until then, to see which, if any, would survive. Toward whatever survivors there were, it would adapt. Now that time of adaptation is on us; and the question is, which of two choices is it going to be? The type that'd stop and keep what he had – or the type that'd go on risking and experimenting? Because the human equation that's involved can stand for only one solution. If the dominant survivor is the Bleys type, with its philosophy of stasis, then, for the first time since we lifted our eyes above the hard realities of our daily lives, we stop where we are. If it's yours and mine, and that of those like us – we go on reaching for what may make us or destroy us. The race-creature waits to see which of us will win.'

'But if the choices are either-or,' she said, 'then maybe the race-creature – you know, I've got trouble with that clumsy double word you thought up, you really should try to come up with something better – would be doing the right thing in going with Bleys and the Others if they win.'

'No,' said Hal, bleakly, 'it wouldn't. Because it's a creature made up of its parts, and its parts aren't gods – yet. They and it can still be wrong. And they'll be wrong to choose the Others, because neither they nor it seem to realize that the only end to stasis is eventual death. Any end to growth is death. Never having stopped growing from the beginning, the race-creature's like a child who can't really believe he'll ever come to an end. But I know we can.'

'You could still be the one who's wrong.'

'No!' he said again. He stared down at her. 'Let me tell you about this last year. You know I went back to the Final Encyclopedia; and with what I know now as Paul Formain and Hal Mayne this time I use it as Mark Torre dreamed of it being used – I made poetry into a key to unlock the implications of the records of our past – and the dream of godhood I've been talking about, personal godhood for every individual human, is there in the record. It explodes for the first time, plainly, in the constructs of the Renaissance. Not just in the art, but in all the artifacts of human creation from that period on.'

He stopped and looked hard at her.

'You believe me?' he asked.

'Go on,' said Amanda, quietly, 'I'm still listening.'

'Even today,' he said, 'there's a tendency to think of the Renaissance only in terms of its great art works. But it was a time of much more than that. It was a time of a multitude of breakings-out, in the forms of craft innovations and social and conceptual experimentation. I told you about the Theater of of Memory which prefigures the Final Encyclopedia, itself. It wasn't just by chance that Leonardo da Vinci was an engineer. Actually, what we call the technological age had already begun in the pragmatic innovations of the later Middle Ages – now it flowed into a new consciousness of what might be possible to humans. From that, in only six centuries came the step into space . . . and everything since has followed. In each generation there were those who wanted to stop where they were, like Bleys, and consolidate. But did we? At any time along that uncertain and fearful upward way, did we stop?'

He himself stopped.

'No,' said Amanda. 'Of course, we didn't.'

She turned and darted upwards slightly at him – and he jerked his head away from her. He stared grimly at her.

'You bit my ear!' he said.

'That's right.' She looked at him wickedly. 'Because that's enough of that for now. There'll be time yet to worry about the enemy before he starts beating at our gates. For now, I'm hungry and it's time for breakfast.'

'Breakfast?'

Involuntarily, he glanced at the window and what she had just said was true. They – or rather he, he thought ruefully – had talked the moon down; and the darkness outside was beginning to pale toward day. He could see the grayish scree of the slope behind the house more clearly, looming like a slightly more solid ghost of the future.

'That's what I said.' She was already out of bed, had seized his wrist and was hauling him also to his feet. 'We've had a large night and we've got a large day ahead of us, starting not many hours off. We'll eat, clean up, and then if you can nap, you take a nap. Your meeting with the Grey Captains is set for noon.'

'Meeting?' he echoed. He watched her begin to dress and mechanically reached for his shorts to follow her example. 'I didn't even ask you yet about setting one up.'

'A notice was sent out to all of the Captains as soon as the Commander of the ship that brought you in sent word you were aboard,' she said. 'That was what kept me in Omalu yesterday, putting the last minute finish to the paperwork for the meeting. I brought some meat up here with me, Hal Mayne. Not fish this time – meat! How about a rack of lamb for a combination breakfast and the proper dinner you probably didn't get around to having last night?'

CHAPTER FIFTY-SEVEN

Amanda lifted her little air-space jitney off the ground of Foralie with the two of them aboard; and Hal watched Foralie fall and dwindle swiftly away below them, feeling an emptiness in him. It was a moment before he associated the emptiness with how he had felt on his first days on Coby, and how he had felt as Donal, leaving this same house to go out to the stars.

'I'd thought I'd be staying at least a week,' he said. Her profile was sharply sculpted against the steel-blue sky beyond the jitney's side window. 'But if I can settle things with the Grey Captains today, I'd better get moving as soon after that as possible. Can we stop at the Spaceport by Omalu long enough for me to find out when the next ship is due to be headed back toward Sol and the Final Encyclopedia?'

'That won't be necessary,' said Amanda. She was wearing a dark blue linen suit of skirt and jacket, light blue blouse and a single strand of small blue-gray coral beads; and somehow her dress today gave her distance from him and authority. 'We're giving you a courier ship and pilot.'

He was jolted. It was not the cost of a private ship to Earth that startled him. He could draw interstellar funds to handle that, from the Encyclopedia or probably even from the Exotics, if necessary. Very soon, such funds would have little use, in any case. It was the realization that other people had already begun to think of him in terms of someone whose work was now important enough not to be slowed down by the delays of commercial spaceship schedules. As he was still absorbing that idea, Amanda reached forward to the hand-luggage compartment in the firewall of the jitney; and, without looking down, brought out a sheaf of papers which she tossed into his lap.

'What's this?' he asked, picking it up. The set of pages made a stack at least three centimeters thick.

'A copy of the contract for you to read on the way to Omalu,' she answered, with her eyes on the cloud layer ahead above which the jitney was now climbing.

Contract . . . he smiled sadly to himself. Laying the paper on his knees, he started to read. Such documents would also soon have as little use and purpose as funds of interstellar credit. But at the same time it was touching and a little awesome to hold the commitment of a world of people in his hands, in so small a form as a handful of printed sheets.

When they got to Omalu, Amanda landed the jitney beside others in the parking lot of the Cental Administrative Offices. Here, rain had moved in once more; and the skies above them were an unbroken, dull-colored mass. They went in the wide, double-doored main entrance and Hal, looking up, saw the two stanzas of A. E. Housman's poem *Epitaph on Army of Dead Mercenaries* cut into the stone of the wall just above the doors. The four somber lines of the first stanza caught in his mind, as always, as he passed underneath them.

> *These, in the day when heaven was falling,*
> *The hour when earth's foundations fled,*
> *Followed their mercenary calling*
> *And took their wages and are dead . . .*

The room in which the meeting was to be held turned out to be one of the general audience rooms, where matters of concern to large areas of the Dorsai, if not to the planet as a whole, were debated. It was a chamber that could hold at least several hundred people and it was needed for the number who had come this day.

'That many Grey Captains?' Hal said softly to Amanda, as she led him to the platform at the center of the semi-circular room; from which he looked out at the curved ranks of seats, each with a continuous table running in front of it, lifting to the back of the room.

'Active, reactivated, and also all those others who may not be Captains but have become responsible in what we're to do now,' she answered, as quietly. 'There's no one here who's not involved.'

She stood with him on the platform at the lectern, until the conversation in the room died and all eyes came on them.

'I think you all recognize Hal Mayne,' she said; her voice reaching clearly to the walls under the excellent acoustics of the chamber. 'Rourke di Facino is Chairman of this meeting. I'll leave it to him, now.'

She stepped down from the platform and went to sit in the only seat left empty in the first row. Hal recognized the pink, older face of Rourke di Facino in the center of the second row, directly opposite him. He also saw that the second row, and therefore Rourke himself, was directly level with him, leaving the first row, where Amanda sat, slightly below him and all rows from the third upwards, above.

For a moment a touch of impatience stirred in Hal. He could see so clearly now what must be done, without other choice, that meeting like this seemed redundant, a waste of valuable time. Then, surging up in him, came the understanding that this gathering was not less important a ritual than the service and the bagpipe music at the grave of James. He realized that he was listening to the deathsong of a people and his impatience was lost in shame.

He was still standing at the lectern. To his left were also a table and chair, the chair pulled back invitingly, the table empty. But he continued to stand. He put his copy of the contract, which he was still carrying, on the lectern's sloping face before him, and waited. Surprisingly, Rourke did not leave his seat in the audience area, but spoke from there.

'This meeting is now in session,' said the small man; his tenor voice beat sharply upward upon the general silence of the room. 'I'll announce the time for general discussion when that time comes. Until then, matters will proceed according to the schedule set up by your steering committee.'

He stared at Hal.

'We're honored to have you with us again, Hal Mayne,' he said.

'Thank you,' said Hal.

'Is there anything in particular you want to say before we get into the planned business?'

Hal looked at him and around the room.

'Just . . . that I see you've anticipated me,' he said.

There was a difference in attitude about those he now watched from the lectern, a difference from what he had seen and felt, facing the smaller number of Grey Captains he had talked to at Foralie. What he sensed now was part of the larger difference he had observed earlier in the unplanted fields and all the other changes he had noticed on the Dorsai since he had arrived.

The awareness of it struck him with a sharpness and a poignancy he had not expected to feel. It drew him to identify it and the source of its power upon him; and so, in that moment between his answer to Rourke and Rourke's response to it, he saw more clearly the details of what was before him.

It was as if the moment put itself on pause; as if time held its hand, briefly. But it was not really time holding or being held, but his own mental processes that had been enormously speeded up. Donal had known how to do that; and with the reawakening of Donal inside him, the ability came back to him.

So in that stretched-out second he noticed the clothes worn by those there, while still individual and casual for the most part, were, like Amanda's this morning, yet more formal that what he had seen the last time he had faced the Captains.

In a subtle way, although what they were dressed in varied from individual to individual, there was a preponderance of quiet earth colors, blues and grays, and a majority of open-throated upper garments with collars that laid down neatly, and a fresh cleanliness showed about everything they had on, that gave the impression that they were in a common uniform.

But then he saw that the impression had deeper roots than clothes alone. There was also an innate commonality in the way they sat and in the state of their bodies. All of them, even the older ones present, had the appearance of being healthy and in good physical condition. There was no excess fat to be seen, even on the more thick-boned and thick-chested of those present. They sat easily, upright and square-shouldered in their seats; and they sat still, with the relaxed stillness of those who have themselves under complete control.

. . . And there was also something even deeper in them than clothes and bodies that made them seem alike, for all their faces were the most varied, one from another, of the faces in any gathering he had seen on the Younger Worlds or Old Earth. No two, from the pink of Rourke's, to the hard black of Miriam Songhai's, to the lightly turned whiteness of Amanda's, were in any way the same. But still the likeness sat on them all; and he recognized its source finally in a similarity of attitude that gave them all a kinship.

For the first time, then, he saw something he had not caught earlier. A bleakness lived in them all, a bleakness that was so deep in each that it lay buried, below actions, below appearance, even below speech.

It was a bleakness hiding a silent and dry-eyed grief. A grief so intense and personal that they did not even speak of it to each other. A grief so fenced apart by custom and responsibility that it could be more easily seen in an unplowed field and unplanted flowers, than by anything said or done by these people. He felt it also in his own soul, recognizing it with that powerful empathy for which he, as Donal, had put off his flesh and returned to the body of a dead man in the twenty-first century, in order to acquire.

Feeling it, he suddenly understood why he had shrunk from talking even to Amanda about that second existence of his as Paul Formain. Each time he had needed to start life again, either as Paul or as Hal, the process of abandoning the life in him that had been, and the beginning again, had been traumatic.

The first time, when he had become Paul Formain, had been hardest of all. To strip the mind naked of knowledge and recollections, to throw the body into an unknown environment trusting it to survive without all that had been a familiar anchor in reality – to accept the very universe as a plastic and changeable thing – had taken more courage than even Donal had realized, until the actual moment of his changing. He had gone on, then, only because there had been no other choice.

Remembering that pain, he came abruptly to a full understanding of the pain in those he faced. It was not from what they would lose personally, or the destruction of their world and way, that they had labored to build for over three hundred years. It was from something even harder to bear; the knowledge that what they had lived with, and once thought of as secure for all foreseeable time, was now passing, would never come again, would in time be all but forgotten and buried forever.

The pride and dream of the Dorsai, like the dream of the Round Table before it, was to pass; and they were witnesses to its passing.

'We will proceed.' The voice of Rourke was dry and emotionless in the room.

He shuffled together the papers lying before him on his section of the long table.

'We've lived by contracts for three centuries, here on the Dorsai,' he said, briskly. 'We'll die, if necessary, by proper contract. I take it you've had a chance to read the copy Amanda Morgan furnished you?'

'Yes,' said Hal. 'I should say, to begin with –'

The uplifted hand of Rourke stopped him.

'We can discuss the actual contract in a moment,' Rourke said. 'As it happens, this isn't an ordinary coming to terms; but an agreement which goes in many ways beyond anything any of us have entered into before. So with your permission, we'll ask you a few questions first; and if the answers to those are satisfactory, we can move to direct discussion of the contract, itself.'

'By all means,' said Hal.

'Good,' said Rourke.

He glanced right and left, as if he would have paused to gather the eyes of all his fellow Dorsai there, if that had been possible without his standing up and turning around. Then his gaze came back to Hal's.

'There are provisions in the contract,' he said, 'to require operating income for those engaged in the work of the contract, for the care of their dependents and for themselves in case of death or disabilities received in the course of work, as well as some further provision for everyone from this world who's to be engaged in that work. But in the ultimate sense, there's no currency or credit in which payment can be made for the kind of service that's being asked of us, here. I believe you can agree with me on that?'

'Yes,' said Hal. 'It's true.'

'Then,' said Rourke, 'on behalf of all of us, let me ask you the soldier's question. Under that circumstance, why should we risk everything we've ever had, to fight and die for people who can't or won't fight for themselves?'

'I don't think you'll find them unwilling to fight,' said Hal slowly. 'Some, right from the start, and more as time goes on, are going to come and join you. In fact, I'd be surprised if you hadn't already made provision for that.'

'We have, of course,' said Rourke. 'But my question still needs an answer.'

'I'll try to answer it . . .' said Hal. He stepped back mentally to let that in him which was Donal respond, and – as had happened involuntarily to him on his previous meeting with the Grey Captains – felt his earliest self take over.

'It's an old question, isn't it?' he heard himself say. 'Never answered once and for all. The Classical Greek who drank hemlock, the Roman who fell on his sword, had reason for what they did. More to the point, the blind king, John of Bohemia, had his reasons nine hundred years ago when at fifty-four, he went to help King Philip of France against the English at the battle of Crecy; and had his squires lead him into the thick of battle, that August twenty-sixth in the year 1346, a battle in which he had to know he would be killed.'

He paused, searching the faces before him. But there was no puzzlement or uncertainty there, only a waiting.

'In my own case . . .' he went on, 'it's clear to me why I'm going to give everything that I've got – not just my life and all I've ever had, but any future there is for me – to what has to be done, now. I could give you my own reasons for doing that. Or I could make out a list of reasons for that ancient Greek I talked about, that old Roman, and the blind king of Bohemia. But in the end, each set of reasons would total up to the fact that what was done was done because the person doing it was who he or she was. I do now what I do because I am what I am. You, all of you, will do what you choose to do because as individuals and as a community you are what you are; and have been what you are, since the race began.'

He stopped speaking.

'That's all the answer I've got for you,' he said.

'Yes,' said Rourke unemotionally. 'The other question is – where are you going to want us to fight?'

Hal's eyes met his on the level.

'You know I can't answer that,' he said. 'In the first place, that where is going to be decided by what happens between now and the moment in which we all commit ourselves to action. In the second place – you know that I don't doubt your security. But in a matter like this, with the life and future of people on a number of worlds concerned, that's one piece of information I can't share with anyone until the time is right. When the moment comes for your involvement, I'll tell you; and at that time, if you want, you can make your decision to go along with it or not, since there'll be no way in any case that I could make you agree to go along with my plans if you didn't want to.'

There was silence in the general audience room. Rourke had a stylus in hand and was making notes on the screen inset in the table surface before him. A strange feeling of having been through this

568

before took Hal, followed by another, even stranger sensation. Abruptly, it seemed to him that he could feel the movement of this small world around its distant sun of Fomalhaut, the movement of Fomalhaut amongst its neighboring stars, the further movements of each of the human-inhabited worlds under their suns; and beyond even these he seemed to feel the great sidereal movement of the galaxy, wheeling them all inexorably onward to what awaited them further in time and space.

'I've so noted that in the contract,' Rourke said, looking up again at Hal; 'and that ends the questions we had for you, at this moment. Do you have any to ask us?'

'No,' said Hal. 'I'm sorry, but yes. You've made this a contract between all of you and me, with only the Final Encyclopedia to back me up. You'll have to understand that there's no way I'd ever be capable of ensuring the obligations this contract requires me to have toward you all. Even the Encyclopedia doesn't have the kind of resources that would allow it to guarantee what's set down there as due to you in certain eventualities. Matters like rehabilitating this entire world, for example, if parts of it should be destroyed or damaged by enemy action in retaliation for your work under the contract; that's beyond the capabilities and wealth of several worlds, let alone something like the Encyclopedia – to say nothing of being beyond the resource of an individual like myself.'

'We understand that,' said Rourke. 'But this contract is made for the historical record, as well as for legal reasons. It's the whole human race we're serving in this instance; and there's no legal machinery that would be capable of binding the human race as a whole, to these obligations. But an opposite party to a contract is a necessary element in an agreement like this. We consider that what's set down here will bind both you and the Final Encyclopedia morally, to the extent of what resources you do have, to observe its provisions. More than that, we can't expect – and don't.'

'I see.' Hal nodded. 'On that basis, of course. Both Tam Olyn, for the Final Encyclopedia, and I will be more than willing to agree to it.'

'Then,' said Rourke, 'it only remains for this assembly to go through the contract itself with you, paragraph by paragraph, and make sure that the language of it means the same thing to you as it does to us.'

So they did. The procedure took over three hours, local time, and when Hal at last stepped down from the lectern, he found himself stiff-legged and light-headed. Amanda collected him from a number of the Captains who had come up to clasp hands with him; and led him toward the back of the room.

'I've got someone to introduce you to,' she said.

She preceded him through the crowd of rising and departing people, many of whom also interrupted his passage to clasp his hand as he went up the levels toward the back of the chamber. As they got toward the back, the crowd thinned, and he saw a man standing by one of the entrances looking in their direction. For a moment Hal's gaze sharpened; for it was almost as if he was seeing one of the Graeme twins alive again, as his Donal memory recalled them.

But when he got closer, he saw the differences. The man waiting for them was undeniably a Graeme – he had the straight, coarse black hair, the powerful frame and the dark eyes; but he was shorter than Ian or Kensie had been – shorter by several centimeters, in fact, than Hal himself. His shoulders sloped more than had Ian's or Kensie's and there was a more solid, less mobile, look about him. The impression he gave was of power and immovability, rather than of the rangy agility that had belonged to the twins, for all that this latter-day Graeme stood with all the balance and lightness of his lifetime's training. He was perhaps in his early thirties; and his eyes watched Hal with a controlled curiosity that Hal could understand, knowing how he, himself, must look to the other man.

But whatever his curiosity, the other was clearly too polite in Dorsai terms to ask direct questions of Hal when Amanda halted the two of them before him.

'Hal,' said Amanda, 'I want you to meet the driver of your courier ship. This is the current head of the Graeme household I told you about – Simon Khan Graeme. He just got in from New Earth, after all.'

Simon and Hal clasped hands.

'I'm indebted to you for letting me be at Foralie,' Hal said.

Simon smiled. He had a slow, but strongly warming smile.

'You did the old house honor by stopping there,' he said, softly.

'No,' Hal shook his head. 'Foralie is something more than any single person can honor.'

Simon's grip tightened briefly again before he released Hal's hand.

'I appreciate your saying that,' he said. 'So will the rest of the family.'

'Maybe a time will come when I can meet the rest of the family,' said Hal. 'You'll be Ian's great-grandson, then?'

It was an incautious question, coming from someone who bore the family resemblance as plainly as Hal; and Hal saw a certainty wake and settle permanently in Simon's eyes.

'Yes,' Simon answered. The words he did not speak – *and your own relationship to Ian, is . . . ?* hung on the air between them.

'I'm ready to go this moment if you want,' Simon said. 'There's nothing in particular for me to stop home for. Would you want to lift right away?'

'I'm afraid time is tight,' said Hal. 'I need to leave for Mara as soon as possible, now things are settled here. Now, about the costs involved in your services and this ship –'

'No, Hal,' said Amanda, 'any costs are part of Dorsai's obligations under the contract, now. Simon'll take you where you need to go and stay with you from now on. Any expenses concerned with him or the ship should be routed back through our Central Accounting.'

'Why don't all three of us have lunch, then,' said Hal, 'and after that, you can take care of whatever last minute details there are with the ship? It'd give us a chance to talk, Simon.'

'You did say you wanted to leave as soon as possible?' Simon asked.

'I'm afraid so.'

'Then I think I'd better go directly to see about the vessel,' said Simon. 'I had a late breakfast in any case, and we'll have time to talk on our way, Hal Mayne. You two don't mind eating by yourselves, do you?'

Hal smiled.

'Of course not. Thank you,' he said.

'Not at all,' said Simon. 'I'll see you at the ship, then. Excuse me.'

He swung away. Hal felt Amanda's hand close on his, down between their bodies.

'He's thoughtful,' said Hal. 'I think he knew I wanted you to myself for a little longer.'

'Of course,' said Amanda. 'Now, come along. I know where we'll eat.'

The place she took him to was within the terminal itself; but except for the occasional, muted sound of a liftoff or landing and the sight of the spacepad beyond the one wall that was a window, the small room was as remote from the business of travelling as any restaurant they might have found in Omalu. It held only four tables; but whether because of arrangement by Amanda, or chance, the other tables were all empty.

The four tables sat next to a balcony on a sort of terrace which occupied most of the room; and looked down across a small reflecting pool at the window wall that showed the landing pad and space vehicles ready to lift. Among them, in the middle distance, Amanda pointed out the small silver shape of the courier ship assigned to Hal.

'I was found in a ship that size,' said Hal, half to himself, 'a much older model, of course.'

He looked back to her from the field in time to see her draw her shoulders slightly into her body, as if she had felt a sudden chill.

'Will you ever have to do it again, do you think?' she asked.

Her voice was very nearly a whisper; and her eyes were focused not on him but past him. She gazed at some point in infinity.

'No,' he answered, 'I don't think so. This time I should go on being Hal Mayne until I die.'

Her eyes were still fixed on that far, invisible point. He reached across the table and took her hand, that lay on the table's surface, into his own.

Her fingers tightened about his and her eyes came back to his, watching him strangely and longingly, like someone watching a loved one on a ship which is at last pulling out from shore.

'It's going to be all right,' he said. 'And even if it shouldn't, it wouldn't make a difference for us.'

Her fingers tightened. They held together, as in the night just past, building a moment around themselves that made time once more seem to stand apart. And so they continued to sit, their fingers interlocked, with the clean air, the reflecting water and the field beyond the window's transparency enclosing them.

Again, as he had sensed it standing before the Grey Captains just a little while past, he felt the turning of the universe, the inexorable sweep of events forward into a future. That sweep was all about them now but it did not reach them. They stayed, as two people standing upon a floating hub might stay, unmoved by the spinning of the great wheel surrounding the place on which they were temporarily at rest.

CHAPTER FIFTY-EIGHT

In the sunlight of Procyon, Mara floated below the courier ship like a blue ball, laced with the swirling white of clouds. Its resemblance to Earth, and the thought of Earth, itself, touched off a loneliness and sadness in Hal, mingled with the secret and bitter knowledge of guilt. If it had not been for the lack of a moon there would be little to identify Mara as not being Earth, the two worlds were so close in appearance and Mara so slightly larger. Even knowing it was not Earth, Hal was tempted to imagine that he was watching the planet on which, only a handful of years back, he had grown to physical maturity; and it came to him for the first time how deep was the emotional bond that tied him to the Mother World.

They had been holding on station for some twenty minutes; now the vessel's speaker system woke with the voice of a surface traffic control unit.

'Dorsai JN Class Number 549371, you're cleared for self-controlled descent to referenced intersection, access code Cable Yellow/Cable Orange, private landing pad. Link for coordinates, please.'

Simon Khan Graeme tapped the white access button of the vessel's navigation equipment to link it to the control unit's net; and under his hands, the small ship began to drop toward the surface far below. Hal had all but forgotten the advantage of a Dorsai ship and pilot that could take him to the very doorstep of his destination on any world, rather than hanging in orbit around a world and making him wait for shuttle service. He looked at the long, powerful fingers of Simon, resting their tips lightly upon the direct control keys, touching . . . pausing . . . touching again.

The face of Mara came up toward them. Then they were suddenly through a high cloud layer, over blue ocean and slanting in toward a coastline. They were over land and dropping, and without warning, there was snow in the air about them. Below, dusted with snowcover, were rolling woodlands from horizon to horizon, with only the occasional white patch of a meadow-clearing to interrupt them; and their ship fell at last toward the still, ice-held ribbon of a minor river, and to what looked like an interconnected clump of graceful, pastel-colored buildings sitting back a small distance from its bank.

They sat down at last on a small weather-controlled pad, showing the bare concrete of its surface to the clouded sky. Hal stepped out, followed by Simon, and found Amid, in a light gray robe, waiting for them.

'Amid, this is Simon Khan Graeme,' Hal said, stepping aside to let Simon come forward. 'He's driving me around these days, courtesy of the Dorsai.'

'Honored to meet you, Simon Khan Graeme,' said Amid.

'And I, you,' said Simon.

In the Exotic fashion, Amid did not offer his hand; and Simon did not seem to expect it. Hal had forgotten how tiny the older man was. Seeing him now, as he stood looking up at Simon's face, Hal registered their difference in size with a mild emotional shock. It was almost as if Amid had aged and dwindled since Hal had last seen him. Standing together on the pad, there was only still dry, warm air surrounding them; but, beyond, about the house, over the river and above the trees, the snow was quietly sifting down in large, soft flakes.

It was strange to see it. Somehow, Hal had always thought of the two Exotic worlds as caught in an endless summer of the blue skies and green fields. With Simon, now, he followed Amid off the pad and into the house – if that was really the right word for such a wandering and connected collection of structures – and almost immediately found himself, as usual, without any way of telling whether he was indoors or outdoors, except for an occasional glimpse of snowy surface beyond a weather shield.

Simon was left behind in a suite of rooms that would be his until he left; and Amid took Hal on to find Rukh.

They located her after a little while, wrapped in what looked more like a colorful, antique quilt than anything else, seated by the side of a free-form pool surrounded by tall green plants that arched long, spade-shaped leaves over the lounging float upon which she was stretched out.

She threw off the quilt and sat up when she caught sight of them, her float adjusting to her new posture. She was wearing an ankle-length Exotic robe of maroon and white, the ample folds of which helped to hide how she had lost weight. Her olive skin looked sallow but her face, in its gauntness, was more beautiful than ever. They came up to her and Hal reached down to kiss her. It was still a wire-strong young body that his arms enclosed; but thin, thin . . .

He let go of her as Amid brought up floats for the two of them; and they sat down together.

'Thank you, Hal,' she said.

'For what?' he asked.

'For being God's instrument to set me free.'

'I had reasons of my own for doing it.' His voice sounded roughly over the quiet pool – but hid, and effectively reburied, the chill of fury momentarily reawakened in him by the sight of how frail she was. 'I needed you – I have plans for you.'

'Not you, only.' She looked at him closely. 'You're a lot older, now.'

'Yes.' A soberness in him had replaced the first stirrings of remembered emotion. 'I still need to explain to you, though, why it was I did something different than I told you I was going to do – back when the Militia was after us all, there outside Ahruma.'

'You don't have to explain.' She smiled. 'I understood it, later. How you'd taken the only way there was to protect the rest of us and get the explosives safely into Ahruma, out of the Militia's reach. Once I understood, we scattered, and lost them. We stayed scattered until it was time to gather together again to destroy the Core Tap. But by doing what you did for us, you delivered yourself up to the Militia.'

And she put one narrow hand softly on his arm.

'They carried me around on a silver platter in that jail –' he said, suddenly and bitterly, 'compared to what they did to you!

'But I was enguarded of God,' her voice reproved him, gently. 'You were not. There was no way they could touch me with anything they might do; any more than anything you might have done could have touched Amyth Barbage in the courtyard there, afterwards.'

An uncomfortableness moved in him – something as yet not understood, as the scene she spoke of came back to him. But she smiled at him again, gently and tolerantly, the way a mother might smile at a child who did not yet understand some completely ordinary matter, and the uncomfortableness was forgotten.

'You say you had reasons for doing what you did?' Her brown eyes watched him gravely. 'What reasons were these?'

'I've still got them,' he said. 'Rukh – there's a place that needs you more than Harmony does.'

He had expected her to object to that, and he paused, waiting. But she merely continued to look at him, patiently.

'Go on,' she said.

'I'm talking about Old Earth,' he told her. 'The Others have been holding back from an all-out effort at getting control of the people there, because so many show that strong, apparently innate resistance to their charismatic talent. You know about that. So Bleys and the rest have been marking time, hoping they could figure out a way around the problem, before trying to move in. But time's getting short for them, as well as us. They'll have to start pushing onto Old Earth, any time now.'

'But they've already got people there, haven't they?' Rukh asked. 'We were told on Harmony that a secret group of unknown but influential Earth locals are afraid of them; and that these've been running a campaign to prejudice the general mass of Earth's people against them?' She looked at him closely. 'Or was that report just a divide and conquer technique, on Bleys' part?'

Hal nodded.

'But if they're not going to be able to convert any important percentage of the populace there, in any case,' she went on, 'why worry about them? Even if they put on what you call a push, it wouldn't look at if they'd have much luck.'

'I'll tell you why.' Hal sat back on his float. 'When they had me in that Militia cell, I was running a high fever and I hit a decision point in my life. The result was, I went into what you might want to call a sort of mental overdrive; and I realized a number of things I hadn't been able to see earlier.'

She reached out to put her hand on his, softly, for a moment.

'You don't need to feel for me,' he told her gently in return. 'I told you they carried me around on a silver platter there, compared to what they did to you.'

'No one seems to understand you – how you fight in a battle larger than any of ours,' she murmured. 'But I know.'

'Some of us have some idea, I think,' murmured Amid.

Hal curled his fingers around hers.

'One of the things I suddenly understood, then,' he went on, 'was that the charismatic talent, instead of being some special gift of genetic accident, given only to those who were Others, was really just a developed form of an ability that had been already sharpened to a fine edge on your own worlds, Harmony and Association. It was the ability to proselyte and convert – worked over, refined, and raised to a slightly higher power. The only ones among the Others who really have it are those like Bleys Ahrens who are at least partial products of the Friendly Worlds.'

'Friendly? The records say Bleys is a mixture of Dorsai and Exotic,' Amid put in.

'I know he's claimed that; and that that's what the records say, as far as they say anything about him', answered Hal; 'and I've got no hard evidence to the contrary. But I've met him; and in some ways I think I know him better than anyone else alive. He's all three Splinter Cultures –'

He broke off, abruptly. He had been about to say – just as I am myself – and had stopped just in time. Somehow, since the night with Amanda, he was not only more open to the universe, but also less self-guarded. But neither Rukh nor Amid seemed to notice the check in what he had been about to say. He went on.

'The point is,' he said, 'your culture, Rukh, like the cultures of the Exotics and the Dorsai, ties back into Old Earth cultures at their roots; and there've been times in history before this when the faith-holders have managed to stampede the general culture around them. Look at the rise of Islam in the Near East in the seventh century, or the Children's Crusade, in the thirteenth. The Others won't need to control the Exotics directly, any more than they'll need to control the Dorsai, as long as the rest of the inhabited worlds are under their direct control. But Old Earth is a different problem from the Dorsai or the Exotics. It's like the Friendlies in that the Others can be satisfied there with a division of opinion about them that effectively keeps the world as a whole from organized opposition. But on Earth, unlike Harmony or Association, the Others can't afford open civil war. A peaceful Old Earth is still necessary as an economic pivot point for interworld commerce – which will have to go on. But if they can prevent Earth from becoming a potential enemy, short of crippling her economic roles, they'll control absolutely the inter-world trade in skills – the base of our common interplanetary credit system that's let all our worlds hold together in one common community of humanity this long.'

He looked at Amid.

'The Exotics have always known that, haven't they, Amid?'

The wrinkles in Amid's face rearranged with his smile.

'We've known it for three hundred years,' he said. 'That's why, from the first, we made it our major effort – in a secular sense – to dominate interplanetary trade, so as to protect ourselves.'

He sobered.

'That's why, Hal Mayne,' he said, 'you'll find us probably more hard-headed about this situation with the Others than anyone else. We know what it'll mean to have them in power, and we've known it from the first move they began to make as a group.'

Hal nodded, turning back to Rukh.

'So,' he said, 'you see. The one world it's absolutely necessary for the Others to neutralize is Earth. The reason they've got to do that goes beyond the obvious fact that, in spite of the way the Old World was plundered and wasted in the early years of the early centuries of technological civilization, it's still far and away the most populous and resource-rich of the inhabited planets. The further reason's that, quite literally, it's the storehouse of the original gene pool, the basic source of the full-spectrum human being, from which we all came.'

He stopped, and waited to see if she wanted to respond to all this he was saying, but she simply sat, relaxed and still, waiting for him to go on.

'If successful opposition to the Others is possible from any people at all, in the future,' he went on, 'it's most possible from the people of Old Earth. They've got their past all around them – there's no way they can be blinded to what the Others would take from them. Also, as their history shows, they're intractable, imaginative and – if they have to be – capable of giving their lives for what they consider a necessary goal, practical or otherwise. For the Others, the necessity is obvious – Earth is the one citadel which must be taken and controlled, to ensure a permanent end to all opposition to them. As a last resort – but only as a last resort – they'll destroy it rather than have it go against them. They've got no choice, if it comes to that.' He paused. Rukh watched him. Amid watched him.

'In the long run, the Dorsai can be starved to death. The Exotic Worlds can be rendered helpless. The Friendlies can be kept fighting among themselves to the point where they never emerge as a serious threat. But Earth has to be either cancelled out or destroyed, if it's to be taken out of the equation at all. Nothing less's going to answer for what the Others need.'

He stopped talking, hearing the echo of his own words in the following silence; and wondering if he had gone too far into rhetoric, so that Rukh would instinctively recoil from him and from what he was about to ask her to do. But when he paused she still merely sat silent, her gaze going a little past him to the greenery around the further bend of the pool, then turned her eyes back a little to look into his.

'There's only one way for them to do this, as things stand,' he told her. 'They've got to work inside the social structure and pattern of Earth if they want to bring about a large enough division of opinion there to keep its people as a whole stalemated. And that's what they've been trying to do from the start with the individuals they've already got there, talking up their cause. But with things on all the other worlds moving to a showdown –'

He paused and shrugged.

Somewhere in the depths of the garden a soft chime rang once, and a small sound in Amid's throat intruded on the silence. Hal turned to look at the smaller man.

'I'm afraid I've been waiting for a chance to tell you something,' Amid said. 'You remember, you wanted it arranged for you to talk to the Exotics as a whole. A gathering of representatives from both Mara and Kultis are here, now; and they're ready to listen to you as soon as you can talk to them; by using single-shift phase, color code transmission, we're going to try to make it possible for everyone of both worlds to see and hear you as you talk – this may not work, of course.'

'I understand,' said Hal. As phase shifting went, the distance between the two worlds under the sun of Procyon was easily short enough to be bridged in a single shift. But the problem here would be the tricky business of ensuring that the distance between disassembly point and reassembly point of the transmitted data was bridged exactly at all moments during transmission. Even with no more than a single shift, and orbital points whose positions were continuously calculated from outside referrents like that of Procyon itself, keeping precise contact over that distance for any period of time at all would be a staggering problem.

'However, what I really have to tell you is that Bleys Ahrens is here, here on Mara – here with us.' The voice of Amid held no change of expression. 'He seems to be remarkably lucky at making guesses; because he apparently assumed you'd be coming to speak to us at this time. Under the circumstances, the sooner we finish talking here and let you go to that talking, Hal, the better. Everyone's ready, including Bleys. He's asked for a chance to address us, himself. We said yes.'

'I wouldn't expect you to do anything else,' answered Hal. 'As far as his ability to guess my being here to talk, he could be using an intuitional logic, like the one Donal worked with.'

Amid's eyes narrowed, and his gaze sharpened.

'You think the Others have that, too, now?'

'No . . . not the Others as a group,' Hal said. 'Bleys alone might – but almost certainly no one else. Or, he could just have made a lucky guess, as you say. It doesn't disturb me that he's going to talk. Before me – or after me?'

'Which would you prefer?' Amid's voice was still expressionless.

'Let him speak first.'

Amid nodded; and Hal turned back to Rukh.

'As I was saying,' he went on, 'there's no real alternative for the Others, then. They're going to have to send to Earth some of their own number, plus as many disciples as they can who seem to be able to use something of the charismatic talent. With these they can try to make an all-out effort to enlist enough of Earth's population to build a division of opinion large enough to block anything that might be done by Earth people who could realize what the Others' control of the civilized worlds will mean.'

She nodded.

'So,' he said, 'Bleys knows he's got people with the talent to do that; and his assumption will be we've got no one to stop them. But we do – we've got you Rukh; and those like you. I escaped from the Militia by getting out of an ambulance that was taking me to the hospital; and the reason I could escape was because the ambulance was caught in the crowd listening to you speak in that square at Ahruma. I heard you that day, Rukh – and there's nothing permanent in the way of changing minds Bleys or any others of his people can do, talking to an audience, that you can't match. In addition, you know other true holders of the Faith who could join you in opposing the crowd-leaders Bleys will be sending to Earth. Those others like you are there – on Harmony and Association. They'd never listen to me, if I tried to convince them to come. But you could – by coming yourself first and sending your words back to those who're left behind you as well as those you'll be speaking to on Earth.'

He stopped speaking.

'Will you?' he asked.

She sat, looking at and through him for a little while. When she did begin to speak, it was so softly that if he had not been straining to hear her answer, he would have had difficulty understanding her.

'When I was in my cell alone, there, near the end of the time I was prisoner of the Militia,' she said, talking almost as if to herself, 'I spoke to my God and thanked Him for giving me this chance to testify for Him. I resigned myself once more to His will; and asked Him to show me how I might best serve Him in the little time I thought I had left.'

Her eyes came back and focused penetratingly only on him.

'And His answer came – that I should know better than to ask. That, as one of the Faith, I already knew that the way I must travel at any time would always become plain and clear to me, once it was time for me to take it up. When I accepted this, a happiness came over me, of a kind I hadn't felt since James Child-of-Gold left the Command to die alone, so the rest of us might survive. You remember that, Hal, because you were the last to speak to him. I understood, then, that all I had to do was wait for my path to appear; for I knew now that it would do so, in its own good time. And I've been waiting, in peace and happiness, since then –'

She reached out to take Hal's hand.

'And it's a special joy to me, Hal, that you should be the one to point it out to me.'

He held her hand; wasted, weak and fragile within his own powerful fingers and wide palm; and he could feel the strength that flowed between them – not from him to her, but the other way around. He leaned forward and kissed her again, then got to his feet.

'We'll talk some more as soon as I've done what I came here for,' he said. 'Rest and get strong.'

'As fast as I can.' She smiled; and smiling, she watched them go.

The amphitheater into which Amid brought Hal was deceptive to the eye. Hal's first impression was that it was a small place, holding at most thirty or forty people in the seats of the semicircle of rising tiers. Then he caught a slight blurring at the edges of his vision and realized that in any direction in which he looked, the faces of those in the audience directly in focus were clear and sharp; but that beyond that area of sharpness and clarity, there was a faint ring of fuzzily visible faces. He seemed to be looking across an enormous distance at mere dots of people. With that he realized that the smallness of amphitheater and audience was a deception; and that a telescopic effect was bringing close any area he looked at directly to give the impression of smallness to an area that must hold an uncountable number of individuals – who each undoubtedly saw him at short distance.

Padma, the very aged Exotic he had met before, was standing on the low platform facing up at the seats of the amphitheater, dwarfed by the slim, erect, wide-shouldered shape of Bleys, now dressed in a loose, light gray jacket, over dark, narrow-legged trousers, and towering over the aged Exotic. The illusion Hal had encountered so frequently – of Bleys standing taller than human – was here again; but as Hal himself approached the two men, it was as if Bleys dwindled toward normal limits of size. Until at last when they were finally face to face, as it had also happened the last time they had met, he and the leader of the Others stood level, eye to eye, the same size.

It registered in Hal's mind that Bleys had changed since that last meeting, in some subtle way. There were no new lines of age in his features, no obvious alteration in any part of his features. But nonetheless there was an impression about him of having become worn to a finer point, the skin of his face drawn more taut over its bones. He looked at Hal quietly, remotely, even a little wistfully.

'Hal Mayne,' said Amid at Hal's elbow, as the two of them reached Padma and Bleys, 'would prefer that Bleys Ahrens speaks first.'

'Of course,' Bleys murmured. His eyes rested for a moment longer in contact with Hal's. It seemed to Hal that in Bleys' expression, there was something that was not quite an appeal, but came close to being one. Then the Other's gaze moved away, to sweep out over the amphitheater.

'I'll leave you to it, then,' said Hal.

He turned and led the two Exotics back off the platform to some chair floats that were ranked on the floor beside it. They sat down, the back of their floats against the wall that backed the platform. They sat, looking out at the amphitheater and the side and back of Bleys.

Standing alone on the stage, he seemed once more to tower, taller than any ordinary human might stand, above audience and amphitheater, alike.

Unexpectedly he spread his long arms wide, at shoulder height, to their fullest extent.

'Will you listen to me?' he said to the Exotic audience. 'For a few moments only, will you listen to me – without preconceptions, without already existing opinions, as if I was a petitioner at your gates whom you'd never heard before?'

There was a long moment of silence. Slowly, he dropped his arms to his side.

'It's painful, I know,' he went on, speaking the words slowly and separately, 'always, it is painful when times change; when everything

581

we've come to take for granted has to be reexamined. All at once, our firmest and our most cherished beliefs have to be pulled out by the roots, out of those very places where we'd always expected them to stand forever, and subjected to the same sort of remorseless scrutiny we'd give to the newest and wildest of our theories or thoughts.'

He paused and looked deliberately from one side of the amphitheater to the other.

'Yes, it's painful,' he went on, 'but we all know it happens. We all have to face that sort of self-reexamination, sooner or later. But of all peoples, those I'd have expected to face this task the best would have been the peoples of Mara and Kultis.'

He paused again. His voice lifted.

'Haven't you given your lives, and the lives of all your generations to that principle, ever since you ceased to call yourselves the Chantry Guild and came here to these Exotic Worlds, searching for the future of humankind? Not just searching toward that future by ways you found pleasant and palatable, but by all the ways to it you could find, agreeable or not? Isn't that so?'

Once more he looked the audience over from side to side, as if waiting for objection or argument; and after a moment he went on.

'You've grown into the two worlds of peoples who dominated the economies of all the inhabited worlds – so that you wouldn't have to spare time from your search to struggle for a living. You've bought and sold armies so that you'd be free of fighting, and of all the emotional commitment that's involved in it – all so you'd have the best possible conditions to continue your work, your search. Now, after all those many years of putting that search first, you seem ready to put it in second place to a taking of sides, in a transient, present-day dispute. I tell you frankly, because by inheritance I'm one of you, as I think you know, that even if it should be the side I find myself on that you wish to join, at the expense of your long struggle to bring about humanity's future, I'd still stand here as I do now, and ask you to think again of what you have to lose by doing so.'

He stopped speaking. For a long moment there was no sound at all; and then he took a single step backwards and stood still.

'That's all,' he said quietly, 'that I've come here to say to you. That's all there is. The rest, the decision, I leave to you.'

He stopped speaking and stood in silence, looking at them a moment longer. A long moment of silence hung on the air of the amphitheater. Then he turned and walked off the platform to the chairs from which Hal, Amid and Padma rose to face him.

Behind him, in the amphitheater, the silence continued.

'I'd like to speak privately to those people,' said Hal.

Bleys smiled, a gentle tired smile, nodding.

'I'll see to it,' said Amid, answering even before Bleys had nodded. He turned to the Other. 'If you'll come with me?'

He led the tall man out by the door in through which he had brought Hal, a short few minutes earlier. Hal stepped up on the platform, walked to the front of it and looked at the audience.

'He doesn't hope to convince you, of course,' Hal said to them. 'He does hope he might be able to lull you into wasting time which his group can put to good use. I know – it's not necessary to point that out to you; but having been in the habit of being able to take the time you need to consider a question sometimes makes it hard to make decisions in little or no time.'

He was searching his mind for something to say that would reach them as he had finally reached the Grey Captains at Foralie; and he suddenly realized that what he was waiting for was some response from them to what he had already said. But this was not a single room with a handful of people all within easy sight and sound of his voice. Here, he must simply trust to his words to do the job he had set them, as Bleys had been forced to do a few moments before. He remembered the mental image that had come to him in his final moments before parting with Amanda – of being for a brief time at the hub of a great, inexorably turning wheel. But this place in which he now stood was no longer at that hub – nor were these who sat here as his audience.

'The river of time,' he said, 'often hardly seems to be moving about us until we see the equivalent of a waterfall ahead or suddenly find the current too strong for us to reach a shore. We're at that point now. The currents of history, which together make up time's current as a whole have us firmly in their grip. There's no space left to look about at leisure for a solution, each in his own way. All I can do is tell you what I came to say.

'I've just come from the Dorsai,' he said. 'They've made their preparations there now for this last fight. And they will fight, of course, as they've always fought, for what they believe in, for the race as a whole – and for you. What I've come to ask you is whether you're willing to make an equal contribution for the sake of what you've always believed in.'

He suddenly remembered the first stanza of the Housman poem, carved above the entrance on the Central Administrative Offices in Omalu on the Dorsai. He shook off the memory and went on.

'They've agreed to give up everything they have, including their lives, so that the race as a whole may survive. What I've come to ask of you is no less – that you strip yourselves of everything you own and everything you've gained over three hundred years so that it may be given away to people you do not know and whom you've never spoken to; in the hope that it may save, not your lives, but theirs. For in the end you also will almost surely have to give your lives – not in war, like the Dorsai, perhaps – but give them up nonetheless. In return, all I have to offer you is that hope of life for

583

others, hope for those people to which you will have given everything, hope for them and their children, and their children's children, who may – there can be no guarantee – once more hope and work for what you hope now.'

He paused again. Nothing had changed, but he no longer felt so remote from his audience.

'You've given yourselves for three hundred years to the work and the hope that there's a higher evolutionary future in store for the human race. You haven't found it in that time; but the hope itself remains. I, personally, share that hope. I more than hope – I believe. What you look for will come, eventually. But the only way to it now is a path that will ensure the race survives.'

The feeling of being closer to his audience was stronger now. He told himself that he was merely being moved by the emotion of his own arguments, but nonetheless the feeling was there. The words that came to him now felt more like words that must move his listeners because of their inarguable truth.

'There was a time,' he said, 'in the stone-age, when an individual who thought in terms of destruction could possibly smash in the heads of three or even four human beings before his fellows gathered about him and put it beyond his power to do more damage. Later, in the twentieth century, when the power of nuclear explosive was uncovered and developed for the first time, a situation was possible in which a single person, working with the proper equipment and supplies, could end up with the capability of destroying a large metropolitan area, including possibly several millions of his fellow human beings. You all know these things. The curve that measures the destructive capability of an individual has climbed from the moment the first human picked up a stick or stone to use as a weapon, until now we've come to the point where one man – Bleys – can threaten the death of the whole race.'

He took a deep breath. 'If he achieves it, it won't be a sudden or dramatic death, like that from some massive explosion. It will take generations to accomplish, but at its end will be death, all the same. Because for Bleys and those who see things as he does, there is no future – only the choice between the present as they want it or nothing at all. He and those like him lose nothing in their own terms by trading a future that is valueless for them for a here and now that sees them get what they want. But the real price of what they want is an end to all dreams – including the one you all have followed for three hundred years. You, with all the wealth and power you still have, cannot stop them from getting what they want; the Dorsai can't stop them, nor, by themselves, can all the other groups and individuals who are able to see the death that lies in giving up dreams of the future. But all together we can stop them – for the saving of those who come after us.'

584

He let his eyes search from one side of what he saw as the amphitheater to the other.

'So I'm asking that you give me everything you have – for nothing in return but the hope that it may help preserve, not you, but what you've always believed in. I want your interstellar credit, all of it. I want your interstellar ships, all of them. I want everything else that you've gained or built that can be put to use by the rest who will be actively fighting the Others from now on – leaving you naked and impoverished to face what they will surely choose to do to you in retaliation. You must give it, and I must take it; because the contest that's now shaping up can only be won by those who believe in the future if they work and struggle as one single people.

He stopped talking.

'That's all,' he said, abruptly.

He turned and left the platform. There was no sound from the audience to signal his going. Amid had returned and was standing waiting for him with Padma.

In silence they left the amphitheater through a doorway different from the one by which they had entered. Hal found himself walking down a long, stone-walled corridor, with an arched roof and a waist-high stretch of windows deeply inset in the full length of wall on his right. They were actual windows, not merely open space with weather control holding the cold and the wind at bay; and their glass was made up of diamond-shaped panes leaded together. The stone was gray and cold-looking; and beyond the leaden panes, he could see in the late-afternoon light that the white flakes were still falling thickly, so that the snow was already beginning to soften and obliterate the clear outlines of trees, paths and buildings.

'How long, do you think, before the vote will be in, from both worlds?' Hal asked Amid.

The small, old face looked sideways and up at him.

'It was in before you landed.'

Hal walked a few steps without saying anything.

'I see,' he said, then. 'And, when Bleys appeared, it was decided to hold up the results until everyone had heard what he had to say.'

'We're a practical people – in practical matters,' said Amid. 'It was that, of course. But also, everyone wanted to see and hear you speak, before a final announcement of the decision. Wouldn't you, yourself, want to meet the one person who would deal with the end of everything you'd ever lived for?'

'All the same,' said Hal, 'the option was reopened for them to change their minds, if Bleys was able to bring them to it. Well, was he?'

'Except for a statistically insignificant handful, no, I'm told.' Amid's eyes rested on him as they walked. 'I think that in this, Hal Mayne, you may fail to understand something. We knew there was nothing Bleys Ahrens could say that would change any of us. But it's always been our way to listen. Should we change now? And do you really think so badly of us that you could believe we'd fail to face up to what we have to do? We here have our faith, too – and our courage.'

Amid turned his gaze away from him, looking on ahead to the end of the corridor, to the double doors of heavy, bolted wood, standing ajar on a dimness that baffled the eye.

'It'll take a day or two for our representatives to get together with you on details,' the small man went on. 'Meanwhile, you can be discussing with Rukh Tamani your plans for her crusade on Old Earth. In three days, at most, your work will be done here, and then you'll be free to go on to wherever you've planned to, next. Where is that, by the way?'

'Earth . . .' said Hal.

But his mind was elsewhere; and his conscience was reproaching him. He had felt a small chill on hearing that Bleys was here; and that chill had come close to triggering an actual fear in him when he saw the man standing before those assembled in the amphitheater, and heard him speak. It was no longer a fear that Bleys might have the talent and the arguments to out-talk him; but a fear that the Exotics, even recognizing the falsity of Bleys' purpose, would still seize on what the Other said as an excuse not to act, not to join the fight openly until it was too late for them and everyone else.

He had been wrong. From the time he had been Donal, he thought now, one failing had clung to him. With all he knew, he could still find it in him to doubt his fellow humans; when, deeply, he knew that anything that was possible to him must be possible to them, as well. For a little while, there in the amphitheater, he had doubted that the Exotics had it in them to die for a cause, even for their own cause. He had let himself be prejudiced by the centuries in which they had seemed to want to buy peace at any price; and he had forgotten their dedication to the purpose for which they had bought that peace.

Now he faced the unyielding truth. It was far easier for anyone simply to fight, and die fighting; than calmly, cold-bloodedly, to invite the enemy within doors and sit waiting for death so that others might live. But that was what the people of Mara and Kultis had just voted to do.

Amid had been right in what he had just said.

With this last act, all of them, including the unwarlike little man now walking beside him, had demonstrated a courage as great as any Dorsai's, and a faith in what they had lived for during these last three centuries, as great as that of any Friendly. Out of the corner of his eyes he watched Amid moving down the corridor; and in his mind he could see – not himself – but the ghosts of Ian and Child-

586

of-God walking on either side of his ancient and fragile companion.

'Yes,' he said, breaking the silence once more as they came to the double doors. 'Earth. There's a place there I've been trying to get back to for a long time now.'

CHAPTER FIFTY-NINE

They went on together, passing from the light of day into the relative obscurity of the space lying beyond the double doors, which closed behind them.

Within, warmly lit by an artificial illumination that in here was more than sufficient, but which had been unable to compete with the cloudy brightness of the late winter afternoon beyond the leaded windows, was a hexagonal room with a slightly domed ceiling, under which nine Exotics were seated about a large, round table. Their robes warmed the interior space with rich earth-colors in the soft light. Two floats at the table sat empty; and it was to these that Amid brought Hal and himself.

Sitting down, Hal looked about at those there, four of whom he recognized. There were the old features of Padma, the small, dark ones of Nonne, the dry ones of Alhanon and the friendly expression of Chavis – all of those who had talked to him on his last visit here, sitting with him and Amid on a balcony of Amid's home. The others he saw were strangers to him; strangers with quiet, Exotic faces having little to make them stick in the mind at first glance.

'Our two worlds are at your disposal now, Hal Mayne,' said the age-hoarsened voice of Padma; and Hal looked over at the very old man. 'Or had Amid already told you?'

'Yes,' said Hal, 'I asked him, on the way here.'

Nonne started to say something, then stopped, looking at Padma.

'I won't forget,' said Padma, looking briefly at her. 'Hal, we feel you ought to understand one thing about our future cooperation with you. We don't sign contracts like the Dorsai, but three hundred years of keeping our word speaks for itself.'

'It does,' said Hal. 'Of course.'

'Therefore,' Padma put his hands flat on the smooth, dark surface of the table before him as if he would summon it to confirm his words, 'you have to understand that we've chosen to go your way in this struggle, simply because there was no other way we could find to go. What's ironical is that the very calculations we'd been using to find out if you ought to be followed, now unmistakably show that you should be – primarily because of the effect of our own decision on the situation.'

The hoarseness in his voice had been getting worse as he talked. He stopped speaking and tapped the tabletop before him with a wrinkled forefinger. A glass of clear liquid rose into view; and he drank from it, then continued.

'It's only right to tell you that there was a great feeling of reservation in many of us about following you,' he said, '– not in me, personally, but in many of us – and that reservation was a reasonable one. But you should know us well enough to trust us, now that we've voted. Effectively, those reservations don't exist any longer. Irrevocably and unchangingly, we're now committed to follow wherever you lead, whatever the cost to us.'

'Thank you,' said Hal. 'Knowing what that voting has to have meant to you all. I appreciate what you've done.'

He leaned forward a little over the table, becoming suddenly conscious of how his greater height and width of shoulders made him seem to loom over the rest of them.

'As I said out there, what I'll probably have to ask your two worlds to give me,' he said to them all, 'to put it simply, is everything you have –'

'One more moment, if you don't mind,' Padma broke in.

Hal stopped speaking. He turned back to Padma.

'We know something of what you've got to tell us,' Padma said. 'But first, you ought to let us give you some information we can share with you now; we couldn't tell you, earlier, before we were committed to working with you.'

There was a small, tight silence about the table.

'All right,' said Hal. 'Go on. I'm listening.'

'As I just said, what we have is yours, now,' said Padma. 'That includes some things you may know we have, but which are possibly a great deal more effective than you might have guessed.'

His old, dry-throated voice failed him again. He reached for the filled glass on the table before him and sipped once more from its contents. Putting the glass down, he went on more clearly.

'I'm talking,' he said, 'of our ability to gather information – and our techniques for evaluating it. I think you'll be interested to hear, now, what we've concluded about both you and Bleys Ahrens.'

'You're right.' Hal stared hard into the old eyes.

'The result,' Padma went on with no change in his tone, 'of that gathering and evaluating gave us a pattern on each of you that could help you now to define the shape of the coming conflict.'

He paused.

'The pattern on Bleys shows him aware of his strength and determined to use it in economical fashion – in other words, in such a way that he and the Others can't lose, since they'll simply operate by maintaining their present advantage and increasing it when they can, until there's no opposition to them left. This is the sort of dealing from strength that seems particularly congenial to Bley's temperament. He seems to believe he and his people are fated to win; and, far from glorying in it, he seems to find a sad, almost melancholy pleasure in the inevitability of this that suits his own view of himself and reality. Apparently, he regards himself as being so isolated in the universe that nothing that happens in it can either much raise or lower his spirits.'

'Yes,' murmured Hal.

'This isolation of his bears an interesting resemblance to your own isolated character,' said Padma, gazing at Hal. 'In many ways, in fact, he's remarkably like you.'

Hal said nothing.

'In fact,' Padma went on, 'to a large extent he's justified in his expectations. The ongoing factors of history – the forces that continue from generation to generation, sometimes building, sometimes waning – now seem to be overwhelmingly on the side of the Others. Our own discipline of ontogenetics, which we evolved to help us solve such problems as this, instead simply produces more and more proofs that Bleys is right in what he believes.'

Hal nodded, slowly; and Padma took a moment to drink once more.

'If Bleys is the epitome of all that is orthodox aiming to win and moving to that end,' Padma went on, 'you, who should in any sane universe be the champion of what has been tried and established, are just the opposite. You are unorthodoxy personified. We have no real data on you before the time you were picked up as a mystery infant from a derelict ship in Earth orbit. You show no hard reason why you should emerge as the leader of an effort to turn back something like Bleys and the Others; but somehow all those opposed to Bleys have enlisted to follow you – even those of us on our two worlds, who've striven to think coolly and sensibly for three hundred years.'

He paused and drew a deep breath.

'We,' he said, 'of all people, don't believe in mysteries. Therefore, we've had to conclude that there must be some mechanism at work here in your favor that we can't see and don't understand. All we can do is hope that it's equally invisible to, and equally beyond the understanding of, Bleys Ahrens.'

'Assuming you're right,' said Hal, 'I'll join you in that hope.'

'Which brings us to your pattern – what we know of it,' said Padma. 'What we have, in fact, concluded from the information we've processed – and we assume that someone like Bleys must have also come to the same conclusions – is that the only course open to you is to use the Dorsai as an expeditionary force against whatever military forces the Others may be able to gather and equip.'

He paused and looked at Hal.

'Go on,' said Hal, levelly. 'What you've said so far's only an obvious conclusion in the light of the present situation. It doesn't call for any special access to information, or a Bleys-like mind, to read that as a possibility.'

'Perhaps not,' said Padma. 'However, it's equally obvious then that, either way, such a use on your part can't end in anything but failure. On the one hand, if you hold back your Dorsai until the forces that the Others are capable of gathering are ready to move, then not even the Dorsai will be able to handle that much opposition. Am I right?'

'Perhaps,' said Hal.

'On the other hand,' Padma went on, 'if you spend this irreplaceable pool of trained military personnel in raids to destroy the Others' forces while those forces are forming and arming, the gradual attrition of even such experienced fighters as the Dorsai in such encounters will eventually reduce their numbers to the point where there won't be enough of them left to pose any real opposition to the Others' strength. Isn't that also an inescapable conclusion?'

'It's a conclusion, certainly,' Hal answered.

'How, then,' said Padma, 'can you hope to win?'

Hal smiled – and it was not until he saw the faint but unmistakable changes of expression on the other faces around the table that he realized how that smile must appear to them.

'I can hope to win,' he said slowly and clearly, 'because I will not lose. I know those words mean nothing to you now. But if it was possible for you to understand what I mean by that, there'd be no war facing us; and the threat posed against us by the existence of the Others would've already been solved.'

Padma frowned.

'That's no answer,' he said.

'Then let me offer you this one,' said Hal. 'The forces of history are only the internal struggles of a human race that's determined, above all, to survive. That much you ought to be able to understand yourselves, from your own work and studying to understand what is humanity. Apply that understanding equally to the large number of forces that seem to operate in favor of the Others and to the relatively small number that seem to operate in the favor of the survival of us – we who oppose them – and you'll see which forces must wax and which must wane if survival for the race as a whole is to be achieved.'

He stopped, and his words echoed in his own ears. I'm talking like an Exotic myself, he thought.

'If what you're saying is the truth,' Nonne broke out as if she could not hold herself silent any longer, 'then the situation ought to cure itself. We don't need you.'

He turned his smile on her.

'But I'm one of those forces of history I mentioned,' he said, '– as

Bleys is. We're effects, not causes, of the historical situation. If you got rid of either one of us you'd simply have a slightly different aspect of the same problem with someone else in replacement position. The truth is you can't get rid of what each of us represents, any more than you can get rid of any of the other forces at work. All you can do is choose your side; and I thought I'd just point out to you that you've already done that?'

'Hal,' said Amid softly at his side, 'that was an unnecessary, if not somewhat discourteous, question.'

Hal sobered, turning to the small man.

'Of course. You're right. I withdraw it – and apologize,' he said to Nonne. He looked at Padma. 'What else have you got to tell me from this body of information you've gathered and evaluated?'

'We've got detailed data from all the sites on the worlds where the Others are gathering and training their soldiers,' said Padma, 'and from all the areas where work is going on to produce the spaceships and material to equip them. Hopefully, this will be sufficient for your needs, although of course there's information we can't get –'

'It's not that so much,' said Hal, almost unthinkingly, 'as that there's other information I have to gather for myself.'

'I don't understand,' said Padma.

Around the table they were regarding him oddly.

'I'm afraid,' said Hal slowly, 'I'd have trouble explaining it to your satisfaction. Basically, it's just that I'll have to see these places and the people working in them for myself. I'll be looking for things your people could never give me. You'll just have to take my word for it, that it's necessary I go and see for myself.'

The concept of the Final Encyclopedia had been forming like a palpable mass in his mind as he spoke and the sense of the immeasurably vast, inchoate problem with which he had been wrestling these last years crouched like a living thing before him. There was no way of explaining to Exotics that the battleground he now envisioned encroached literally upon that territory which encompassed the human soul.

'You'll simply have to trust me,' he repeated, 'when I say it's necessary.'

'Well,' said Padma heavily, 'if you must . . . we still have courier ships making the trips back and forth between these two worlds of ours and our embassies on the other worlds. We can supply you with a ship.'

Hal breathed out evenly and lowered his gaze to the polished pool of darkness that was the tabletop.

'A ship won't be necessary,' he heard himself say, as if from some distance. 'The Dorsai've already given me one – and a driver.'

He continued to stare into the darkness of the tabletop for a moment longer, then slowly raised his eyes and looked back once more at Amid. He smiled again, but this time the smile faded quickly.

'It seems that trip of mine to Old Earth is going to have to wait a little longer, after all,' he said.

His perception was correct. Nearly four months later, standard time, he had still not stepped within the orbit of Earth; and he was running for his life through back alleys of Novenoe, a city on Freiland.

The months of visiting most of the Younger Worlds, slipping in with his Dorsai courier ship and going secretly to make first-hand observations at the factories and installations in which the Others were putting together the soldiers and material they would use in their war effort, had worn him thin – almost as thin as he had been on Harmony when the Militia had caught him.

But this was a different thinness. With his admission at last to Amanda of his first identity as Donal Graeme – that identity that had been withheld from him deliberately by his Donal-self until he should pass through the learning process of growing up as Hal Mayne – he had finally come very close to replicating Donal's old physical abilities and strengths, though he still necessarily fell short of the strength and skill of an adult Dorsai who had maintained his training daily since birth. Still, what he had accomplished flew in the face of all physiological experience among the Dorsai. That after twenty-odd years of living untrained by Dorsai standards (even giving him credit for what Malachi Nasuno had taught him up into his sixteenth years) it was simply beyond reason that in only a few months he had been able to achieve reflexes and responses that came at all close to being as effective as Simon Graeme's, for example.

Simon himself had commented on it. It had been impossible to hide the development in Hal from the other man, under the conditions of the close-knit existence they shared aboard the courier vessel with Amid. The old Exotic had been riding with them as a necessary living passport for Hal to the Exotic embassies from which they drew information and assistance. That development was, as Simon hinted, at once impossible and an obvious fact, and Simon had compared the achievement with that of some of the martial artists down through history who had become legendary in their own times. Beyond that comment, the current titular head of the Graeme family seemed content to leave the matter for later explanation. Hal had no choice but to do the same; although to him, too, it was a cause for wonder and a puzzle not as easy to accept as it seemed to be for Simon.

His own temporary conclusion was that it could be some sort of psychic force at work upon him in response in Donal's emergent identity; a psychic force that could shape even bone and muscle, if necessary. Cletus Grahame, nearly a hundred years before, had been supposed to have rebuilt a damaged knee of his by some such means. At the same time, something in Hal strongly insisted that there was more to it than the simple term 'Psychic force' implied; and the unknown element nagged at him.

But there had been no time to ponder this currently; and there was certainly none at this present moment. Running easily but steadily, like a hunger-gaunted wolf dodging through the dark and odiferous passages that hardly deserved the names of streets and alleys in this quarter of ruined buildings, Hal felt the intuition that had been Donal's numbering and placing in position about him the pursuers that were now closing in.

He had gotten inside the spaceship yards he had gone to Freiland to see; and identified the vessels being built there as military transports. But after these many months the forces controlled by the Others on all their worlds were alerted and on watch for him; and he had been both identified and pursued by the so-called 'executive' arm of the Novenoe police. His only hope of escape from them lay in the courier ship waiting for him in the yard of a decayed warehouse. He was leading his pursuers toward it now, simply because he had no other choice. The invisible calculations of intuitive logic that had woken in him from the Donal part of himself told him there was no way he could reach the vessel before those hunting him would close in on him.

His estimate was that there were between thirty and forty of the 'executives' – and they would know this part of Novenoe better than he did.

He ran on – steadily, still at three-quarter speed, saving his strength for the moment in which he would need it. The last leg of his journey led over broken, but still high, security fences; and across forgotten yards full of abandoned equipment rusting in the darkness. As, still running, he reached the last fence but two, flung up a hand to catch its stop edge and vaulted over, he heard ahead of him the small, impatient sounds of at least two police in wait for him in the darkness of the littered yard.

He crouched down and went like a ghost, feeling his way ahead and around the debris, large and small, that littered his way. His aim was to bypass those in wait for him if he could; but one of them – evidently cramped and weary with waiting – rose and blundered directly into his way as Hal tried to pass.

Hal felt the heat of the body approaching and both smelled and heard the other's breath. There was no time to go around, so he rose from the ground and struck out, swiftly.

The 'executive' dropped, but grunted as he fell; and immediately a thin, rapier-like guide-beam of visible light, of the sort used to direct the night-firing of a power weapon, began playing about the yard like a child's toy searchlight. Hal snapped a shot with the silent, but low-powered, void pistol that was the only weapon he carried, at the source-point of the light and the beam vanished. But the damage was done. The darkness now would be alive with the electronic screaming of alarms and communications, pinpointing his position to his pursuers.

He went to full speed. Even then, clearing the fence before him into the yard next to the one where the courier ship waited, his senses of hearing and smell counted five of those who sought him, on hand to block his way. They were too many to slip by. He could hear each now, plainly, while they would not be able to hear him; but they would have heatsensing equiment and with it could see him as a glow amidst the scattered junk filling the yard; a glow imprecise in outline and occulted by the shapes of the junked vehicles and trash filling the yard, establishing his general position, nonetheless.

The choice was no choice. If he wanted to reach the ship, there was no way to do it unobserved. He must fight his way through those who were here to take him. He dropped to the gritty earth underfoot to catch his breath for a second.

It needed little enough though to see how he had to do it. His position was hardly different from that of a man in a river, and about to be swept over a waterfall, who calls to a friend safe on the bank to jump in and help him. But the hard facts of the matter were, he knew he was more important to the large work yet to be done than was Simon Graeme. Nor would Simon – or any other Dorsai – thank him for not calling for help when it was needed, under such circumstances.

Savagely, he pressed the button at his waist that would send out a single gravity pulse to the ship's sensors and summon Simon to his aid.

Having called, he gave himself wholly over to survival, dropping flat in the dirt of the yard and squirming his way forward toward the further fence. He could hear the five men closing in upon him; and knew that they would shortly be reinforced. He stopped, suddenly, finding himself boxed. To move in any direction from the ruins of a tractor behind which he was presently sheltering was to put himself into the open field of fire from one of the 'executives.' Now, he must make gaps in their circle about him, if he wanted to pass through.

He did not need a visible guide-beam for the weapon he carried. He could aim accurately by ear; and the silentness of the void pistol in use would help to hide the point of origin of its killing pulse. He shot one man, and shifted quickly into the gap this made, only to find himself boxed again. And, so it began. . . .

It was an ugly little battle, fought in the dark, at point-blank range, with his opponents' numbers being reinforced faster than his accurate fire could clear them out of his way. A bitterness stirred inside him; the bitterness of someone who has had to fight for his life for too many years, on too many occasions, and who is weary of the unceasing attacks that give him no rest. Crouching and moving through the dark, he felt for the first time in his experience the burden he carried – not the physical but the emotional weight of his three lifetimes.

He had fought his way now for half the remaining distance between him and the last fence. He was less than five or six meters from it; and the number of his enemies in the yard had grown to more than fifteen. He stopped in passing over the body of one of those he had just taken out of the action and picked up the heavy shape of the power rifle the man had been using. And at that moment, Simon came over the wall from the ship.

Hal heard him come; and knew who he was. The 'executives,' hearing nothing, suspecting nothing, were caught by void pistol fire from a new angle and assumed that Hal had reached the fence. They changed direction to move in on the position Simon now held.

Hal gave them a slow count of five. Then, standing up in the darkness and holstering his nearly depleted void pistol, he triggered the power rifle he had picked up onto continuous fire; and swept it like a hose of destruction across the front of those making the sounds of movement through the yard.

There was sudden, appalled inactivity among the weapons of those still left unhurt among the attackers. In that moment, Hal threw the power rifle from him, far across the yard, to where the clatter of its fall would draw any fire well away from Simon and himself – and ran for Simon's position, hurdling the barely-seen obstacles in his path.

They were suddenly together, two patches of darker dark in the gloom.

'Go!' grunted Simon.

Hal went up and over the fence, without pausing, checked on the far side, and swung about, void pistol held high over the fence to cover Simon as the other followed, landing beside him. They ran together for the courier ship. The outer airlock door yawned before them, with Amid ducking hastily back out of their way, then closed behind them. Simon hurled himself at the controls; and the courier ship bucked explosively into motion – upward into the night sky.

There were police craft holding station overhead, in positions up to four kilometers of altitude. But barely above the rooftops, Simon went into phase shift; and suddenly the silence of orbital space was around them. Hal, who had been standing, holding to the back of the co-pilot's seat against the savage acceleration off the ground, let go and sagged limply backward into one of the backup seats of the control compartment.

He felt a touch on his elbow, turned his head to look into the face of Amid, standing beside him.

'You need sleep,' said Amid.

Hal glanced again at Simon, but Simon had already finished his plot for a second shift, and the stars jumped as they watched, to a new configuration in the screens about them. Ignoring them, Simon reached to the plotting board for the next shift and Hal stood up.

'Yes . . .' he said.

He let Amid lead him back into his own compartment and stretched out in the bunk, unprotestingly letting Amid pull off his boots and his heavy outer jacket. Exhaustion was like a deep aching, all through his body and mind. He lay, staring at the gray metal of the compartment ceiling, a meter and a half above his bunk; and Amid's head moved into his field of vision, between him and it, looking down.

'Let me help you sleep,' said Amid; and his eyes seemed to begin to grow enormously as Hal watched.

'No.' Hal shook his head, fractionally. It was a great effort even to speak. 'You can't. I have to do it for myself. But I will. Just leave me.'

Amid went, turning out the compartment lighting, closing the door behind him. Hal stared up into sudden lightlessness; feeling again the weight of his lifetimes, which had come upon him in the darkness of the yard. He turned his mind like a hand holding up the stone of consciousness, letting that stone fall from the grasp that held it, fall into darkness . . . and fall . . . and fall . . . and fall. . . .

It took them five days, ship's-time, to make Earth orbit. Most of that time Hal slept and thought. The other two left him alone. When they parked at last in Earth orbit, Hal called up a jitney to take him down to the planet's surface.

'And Amid and me?' asked Simon. 'What do you want us to do? Wait here?'

'No. Go and wait for the me at the Final Encyclopedia,' answered Hal. 'I'll be a day – at most two, No more.'

CHAPTER SIXTY

Riding the upcurrent above the brown granite slope of the mountainside in the late afternoon, high above the grounds of the Mayne Estate, the golden eagle turned his head sharply to focus his telescopic vision on the flat area surrounding the pool behind the building. There had been movement there – animal movement different from the movement of grass and twigs in the wind – where there had been no movement for a very long time.

His eyes fastened on a dark-clad, upright man-shape, tiny with the distance between them. There was no profit to be found in this, then, for a knight of the air like himself. The eagle cried harshly his disappointment and wheeled off, away from the estate and the mountainside, out over the thick green of the upland conifer forest.

Hal watched him go, standing on the far edge of the terrace overlooking the lake. A little, cold breeze rippled the gray surface of the water; and, above him, in the declining afternoon light, the blue of the sky was the blue of ice. Here, in this northern temperate zone of Old Earth, summer still held to the lowlands; but up in the mountains the first cutting blasts of winter's horn could be faintly heard. The cold, moving air chilled the exposed skin surfaces of his body and out of old days and memories came a piece of a poem to fit itself to the moment . . .

> O what can ail thee, knight at arms
>   Alone and palely loitering?
> The sedge has withered from the lake,
>   And no birds sing . . .

It was the first verse of the original version of *La Belle Dame Sans Merci* – 'The Beautiful Lady Without Mercy' – a poem by John Keats about a mortal ensorcelled by a fairy, but without the limiting term to that ensorcelment found in its poetic ancestor – *True Thomas*. The older poem had been written by Thomas of Erceldoune back in the thirteenth century, from even older versions of the legend passed down by word of mouth.

For that matter, he thought, the coming of the technological age five hundred years ago had brought the old tale to a newer version still; the concept of the Iron Mistress, that artifact of work that could capture a human soul and never let it loose again to live naturally among its own kind.

It was an update of an Iron Mistress, that historic purpose, which held him captive now; and had held him from his beginning.

He shook off the self-pitying notion. Ever since he had been last on the Dorsai, he had been missing Amanda, deeply and unyieldingly. The pain of not having her within sight and hearing and touch was a feeling of deep wrongness and loss, like the pain of an amputated limb that would not grow again. No, he corrected himself, it was as if the pain and sense of loss from an earlier amputation had finally made him aware of it. The feeling was something that could be buried temporarily under the emergencies of the moment, during most of his waking hours. But at times when exhaustion stripped him down to bones and soul, as aboard the courier ship leaving Freiland recently, or when he was alone, as now, it came back upon him.

What were the later six lines in Keats' poem – about the hillside and the pale kings and warriors, with their warning? Oh, yes . . .

> . . . *The latest dream I ever dreamed*
> *On the cold hillside.*

I saw pale kings, and princes too,
Pale warriors, death-pale were they all
Who cried – 'La Belle Dame Sans Merci
Hath thee in thrall!'

'. . . *The Iron Mistress hath thee in thrall! . . .*'

Once more, he pushed the feeling of depression from him. There was no need for this. The time would not be too long before he and Amanda would be together, permanently. It was not like him to waste time on gloomy thoughts, fantasies of despair summoned up out of old writings. He made an effort to examine why he should be acting like this, now; but his mind shied away from the question.

It was only his coming back here and finding the estate so empty, he told himself. For that matter, when poetry could hurt, poetry could also heal. The heart of the same ancient story had been dealt with less than thirty-four years later by another poet, Robert Browning, in the first volume of his *Men and Women*. Browning had written *Childe Roland to the Dark Tower Came*, a poem similar in subject – but with all the difference in the universe, in theme. As an antidote to the earlier verse, Hal quoted the last verse of Browning's poem to himself aloud, softly, into the face of the chill river of air coming at him across the cooling water of the lake –

> . . . *There they stood, ranged along the hillsides, met*
> *To view the last of me, a living frame*
> *For one more picture! in a sheet of flame*

599

> *I saw them and I knew them all. And yet*
> *Dauntless the slug-horn to my lips I set,*
> *And blew.* 'Childe Roland to the Dark Tower came.'

Browning had been a Childe all his life – an aspirant to a greater knighthood – although that part of him had passed, invisible before the conscious eyes of almost everyone, with the exception of his wife. As Hal was, himself, a Childe now, though in a different time and place and way, and never as a poet. It was no Iron Mistress that drove Browning, and perhaps even himself, after all, but the fire of a hope that would not let itself be put out.

At the same time, even with this small bit of understanding, the emptiness inside him that reached for Amanda echoed back the emptiness of this place he had known so well, but from which the three old men who had given it life and meaning were now departed. The estate had not become strange to him. He had become a stranger within it.

But an instinct had drawn him back to spend the night here; and spend it, he would. He turned back from the terrace and toward the French windows that would let him into the house, glancing through them, instinctively, down into the library where already the automatic lighting had gone on; and where, the last time he had looked in, he had seen Bleys and Danno standing toe to toe.

He opened one of the windows and stepped through, closing it behind him. The warmth of the atmosphere within, guarded by that same automatic machinery that had kept the place so well that all these years its caretaker had needed only to glance occasionally into the surveillance screens in his own home, five miles away, to make sure all was well, wrapped itself around him. He was enclosed by the still air, the smell of the leather bindings on the hundreds of old-fashioned books, dustless and waiting still on their long shelves of polished, honey-colored wood. He had read them all in those early years, devouring them one after the other, whenever he had the chance, like some starving creature fallen into a land of plenty.

Now that he was within doors, he was made aware of the darkening of the day beyond the windows. In just these last few moments the sun had gone behind the mountains. He walked to the fireplace at the end of the room. It, too, was waiting; laid ready for firing. He took the ancient sparker from its clip on the mantelpiece and with it touched the kindling under the logs alight.

Flames woke and raced among the shavings and the splinters beneath the kindling, reaching up to make the bark on the logs spark and glow. He seated himself in one of the large, overstuffed, wing-backed chairs flanking the hearth and fastened his eyes on the growing fire. The flames ran like small heralds among the dark structure of the wood, summoning its parts to holocaust. The heat of the burning reached out to warm him; but he could still feel the emptiness of the house at his back.

He had not been so conscious of being alone since he had run for the Encyclopedia, after the killing on the terrace beyond these windows. In all that time since, except for the moment in the Harmony prison when they would not come, he had never made the fully necessary effort to summon up self-hypnotically the images of his three dead tutors. But now, feeling the hollowness and darkness at his back, he reached within himself, keeping his eyes on the fire, and let the mental technique, in which Walter the InTeacher had coached him as a child, channel the force of his memories into subjective reality.

When I lift my eyes from the fire, he thought, they will be there.

He sat, gazing at the fire which was now sending flames halfway up inside the squared central pile of logs; and after a bit, he felt presences in the room behind him. He lifted his head, turned and saw them.

Malachi Nasuno. Obadiah Testator. Walter the InTeacher.

They sat in other chairs of the room, making a rough semi-circle facing him; and he turned the back of his own chair to the fire, in order to look directly at them.

'I've missed you,' he told them.

'Not for a long time,' said Malachi. The massive torso of the old Dorsai dwarfed the tall carved chair that held him; and his deep voice was as unyielding as ever. 'And before that, only now and then, at times like this. If you'd done anything else, we'd have failed with you.'

'And that we did not,' said Obadiah. Scarecrow thin, looking taller than he was by virtue of his extreme uprightness as he sat in his chair. 'Now you've met my own people, as well as others, and you understand more than I ever could have taught you.'

'That's true,' said Hal. He looked at Walter the InTeacher and saw the Exotic's old, blue eyes quiet upon him. 'Walter? Aren't you going to say hello?'

'I was thinking, only.' Walter smiled at him. 'When I was alive, I would have asked you at a moment like this why you needed us in the first place. Being only a figment of your imagination and memory, I don't have to ask. I know. You needed us to help you do the kind of learning that was only possible to the open, fresh mind of someone discovering the universe for the first time. But do you even know now where the end of this journey of yours lies?'

'Not where,' said Hal. 'But in what. Like all journey, it has to end in accomplishment – or I've gone nowhere.'

'And if it should turn out you have?' asked Walter.

'If he has,' Malachi broke in harshly, 'he did well – he did his best while he could, at the trying of it. Do you always have to make things difficult for him?'

'That was our job here, Malachi,' said Walter, 'to make things difficult for him. You know that. He knows that – now. When he was

Donal Graeme he saw himself growing away from the soul of human-kind. He had to come back – and the only way was a hard way.'

He smiled at his two fellow tutors.

'Otherwise why arrange with your intuitive logic that your trustees would choose three like us?'

'I'm sorry,' said Hal. 'I used you all. I've always used people.'

'Maudlin self-pity!' snapped Obadiah. 'What weakness is this, after all we taught you, and now that you're face to face at last with what you set out to do?'

Hal grinned, a little wanly.

'You sent me out to become human, after you were killed,' he answered. 'But you also put me on the road even before you sent me out. Can't you let me be a little human now, from time to time?'

'As long as you get your job done, boy,' rumbled Malachi.

'Oh,' Hal sobered. 'I'll get it done, if it can be done. There's no changing or stopping the juggernaut of history, now. But, you know what the real miracle is? I wanted to start Donal over again, to get him right this time. But what I did worked even better than I could have dreamed. I'm not Donal, redone. I'm Hal; and even all of what Donal was, is only a part of me, now.'

'Yes,' said Malachi, slowly. 'You've put away all armor. I suppose you had to.'

'Yes,' said Hal. 'The passage ahead's too narrow for anyone wearing armor.' He lost himself for a moment in thought, then went on, 'And all those who come after me are going to have to come naked, likewise, or they won't get through.'

He shivered.

'You're afraid,' said Walter, quickly, leaning forward intently in his chair. 'What are you afraid of, Hal?'

'Of what's coming,' said Hal; and shivered again. 'Of my own testing.'

'Afraid,' said a new voice in the room, 'of me. Afraid I'll prove him wrong about this human race of ours, after all.'

The tall figure of Bleys moved out of an angle in the bookcases and stepped forward to stand between Obadiah's chair and that of Malachi.

'Playing with your imagination, again?' he said to Hal. 'Making up ghosts out of the images of your memory – even a ghost of me; and I'm still very much alive.'

'You can go,' said Hal. 'I'll deal with you another time.'

But Bleys continued to exist, standing between the chairs holding Malachi and Obadiah.

'Your unconscious doesn't want to dismiss me, it seems,' he said.

Hal sighed and looked again into the fire. When he turned back to the room, Bleys was still there with the rest of them.

'No,' Hal said. 'I guess not.'

602

None of the subjective images replied. They stayed; the three sitting, the one standing, looking at him, but without words.

'Yes,' said Hal, after a time, looking back at the fire. 'I'm afraid of you, Bleys. I never guessed there would be someone like you; and it shocked me to find you, in real life. If I've evoked your image now, it is to make me see something in myself I don't want to see. That's why you're here.'

'My similarity to you,' said Bleys. 'That's what you don't want to see.'

'No.' Hal shook his head. 'We're really not that similar. We only look that way to everyone else. But that doesn't make us alike. If all the people on all the worlds had in common what you and I have, we wouldn't look alike. Our differences would show, then; and we'd look as unlike – as we actually are.'

He glanced briefly into the fire again.

'Unlike as two gladiators pushed into a ring to fight each other,' he said.

'No one pushed either of us,' said Bleys. 'I chose my way. You chose to fight it. I offered you all I had to offer, not to fight me. But you decided to anyway. Who could push either of us, in any case?'

'People,' said Hal.

'People!' There was a strange note of anger in Bleys' voice. 'People are mayflies. It's no shame or sin in them; it's only fact. But will you die – and that magnificent, unique engine that's yourself be lost, for a swarm of mayflies? Leaving aside the other fact that the only one who can certainly kill you is myself; and you know I won't do that until it's plain you've lost.'

'No,' said Hal. 'You know you'd lose, not gain, by killing me before that. As a dead martyr either one of us would make sure of victory for our side – and perhaps wrongly, by that means. No, it's the contest that's important, not ourselves. A chess Grand Master could shoot his opponent dead before the game between them was done. But the fact the other couldn't finish would prove nothing to the watchers, when it was vital to know whose game was best and who should have won. The watchers might even assume that the one who shot did because he knew he was going to lose – and that might not be true.'

He paused. Bleys said nothing.

'I've understood you couldn't afford to kill me,' Hal went on, more gently. 'You admitted that when you didn't take advantage of my being your prisoner, back in the hands of the Militia on Harmony. You talk of mayflies; but I know – maybe I'm the only one who knows – that you care for the race as a race, in your own way, as much as I do.'

'Perhaps,' said Bleys, broodingly. 'Perhaps you and I only need them to fill the void around us. In any case, the mayflies aren't us.

603

Tomorrow there'll come another swarm of them, to replace what died today, and tomorrow after that, another. Give me one reason you want to sacrifice yourself for what lives only for a single day.'

Hal looked at him, bleakly.

'They break my heart,' he said.

There was silence in the room.

'I know you don't understand them,' Hal said to Bleys. 'That's the one great difference between us, the one reason I'm afraid. Because you represent only one part of the race; and if you win . . . if you win, the part I know is there can be lost forever, now that the race-animal's decided it can't live divided any longer. I can't let that happen.'

He stopped speaking for a moment, looking at all four of his subjective images, then back at the shade of the tall Other.

'You don't see what I see,' he said, 'you can't see it, can you Bleys?'

'I find it,' said Bleys slowly and quietly, 'inconceivable. There's nothing in them – in us – to break any heart, even if hearts were breakable. We're painted savages, nothing more, in spite of what we like to think of as some thousands of years of civilization. Only our present paint's called clothing and our caves called buildings and spaceships. We're what we were yesterday, and the day before that, back to the point where we dropped on all fours and went like the animals we really are.'

'No!' said Hal. 'No. And that's the crux of it. That's why I can't let the juggernaut go the way you want. It's not true we're still animals; it's not true we're still savages. We've grown from the beginning. There was never a time we weren't growing; and we're growing now. Everything we face in this moment's only the final result of that growing, when it broke loose into consciousness, finally, a thousand years ago.'

'Just a thousand?' Bleys' eyebrows lifted. 'Not five hundred or fifteen hundred – or forty, or four thousand?'

'Pick the when and where you like,' said Hal. 'From any point in the past, the chain of events run inescapably forward to this moment. I've chosen the nexus in the fourteenth century of western Europe, to count from.'

'And John Hawkwood,' said Bleys, smiling thinly. 'The last of the medieval captains, the first of the modern generals. First among the first of the condottieri, you'd say? Sir John, in northern Italy. You see, like these others here, I can read your mind.'

'Only the shade of you I summon reads my mind,' said Hal. 'Otherwise, perhaps I could make you see some things you don't want to see. It was John Hawkwood who stopped Giangalleazo Visconti in 1387.'

'And preserved the system of city-states that made the

Renaissance possible? As I just said, I know your mind.' Bleys shook his head. 'But it's only your theory. Do you really think the Renaissance could have been stopped by one summer's military frustration of a Milanese Duke who was still in pursuit of the kingship of all Italy when he died, about a dozen years later?'

'Probably not,' said Hal. 'Giangalleazo's later tries didn't work. Nonetheless, the historic change was in the wind. But history's what happened. The causal chain I picked to work with links forward from Hawkwood. If you see that much, why can't you see people as I do?'

'And have them break my heart too?' Bleys watched him steadily. 'I told you I found that inconceivable. And it's inconceivable to me that they can break yours – or that hearts can break, as I said, for any reason.'

'It breaks mine, because I've seen them in actions you don't believe exist.' Hal met the other man's gaze. 'I've been among them and I've watched. I've seen the countless things they do for each other – the extraordinary kindnesses, the small efforts to help or comfort each other, the little things they deny themselves so that someone else can have what they might have had. And the large things – the lives risked and laid down, the lifetimes of unreturned effort, the silent heroisms, the quiet faithfulnesses – all without trumpet and flags, because life required it of them. These aren't the actions of mayflies, of animals – or even of savages. These are the actions of men and women reaching out for something greater than what they have now; and while I live I'll help them to it.'

'There's that,' said Bleys, remotely. 'Sooner or later, you'll die. Do you think they'll build a statue to you, then?'

'No, because no statues are needed,' Hal answered. 'My reward never was supposed to be a recognition of anything I've done; but only my knowing I'd done it. And I get that reward every day, seeing the road extend, seeing my work on it and seeing that it's good. There's a poem by Rudyard Kipling, called *The Palace* –'

'Spare me your poems,' said Bleys.

'I can spare you them, but life won't,' said Hal. 'Poems are the tool I've been hunting for all these years, the tool I needed to defeat those who think the way you do. Listen to this one. You might learn something. It's about a king who was also a master mason, who decided to build himself a palace like no one had ever seen before. But when his workmen dug down for the foundations they found the ruins of an earlier palace, with one phrase carved on every stone of it. The king ordered them to use the materials of the earlier palace and continued to build – until word came to him one day that it was ordained he should never finish. Then, at last, he understood the phrase the earlier builder had carved on each stone; and he told his workmen to stop building, but to carve the same phrase on each stone he had caused to be set in place. That phrase was – *"After me cometh a builder. Tell him I too have known!"* '

Hal stopped talking. Bleys sat still, silent, watching him.

'Do you understand?' Hal said. 'The message is that the knowing is enough. No more is needed. And I have that knowing.'

'*Shai* Hal!' murmured Malachi.

But Hal barely heard the old Dorsai praise-word. His mind was suddenly caught up by what he had just said; and his mind wheeled outward like an eagle, seeing further and further distances lifting over the horizon as his wide wings carried him toward it.

The fire crackled and burned low behind him, unnoticed.

When he looked up, all four of the shades he had summoned from the depths of his mind were gone.

CHAPTER SIXTY-ONE

Sometime in the hours of the night he exploded into wakefulness, sitting up, swinging his legs over the side of the bed and getting to his feet in one swift, reflexive motion.

He stood utterly still in the darkness, his senses stretched to their limits, his eyes moving in steady search of the deeper shadows, his ears tensed for the faintest sound.

As he stood, his recently sleeping mind caught up with his already roused body. The hard electric surge of adrenaline was suddenly all through him. There was an aching and a heaviness in his left side and shoulder, as if he had slept with it twisted under him so long that a cutoff of circulation had numbed it. He waited.

Nothing stirred. The house was silent. Slowly, the ache and heaviness faded from his side and shoulder, and his tension relaxed. He got back into the bed. For a little while he lay awake, wondering. Then sleep took him once more.

But this time he dreamed; and in his dream he had come close at last to that dark tower which he had been approaching in his earlier dreams, across a rubbled plain that had become a wild land of rock and gullied earth. Now, however, he was in a place of naked rock – a barren and blasted landscape, through which wound the narrow trail he was following.

He came at last to a small open space in which stood the ruins of a stone building with a broken cross on top of it. Just outside the shattered doorway of the building was a horse with a braided bridle, a saddle with a high cantle and armor on its chest and upper legs. It stood tethered to the lintel. When it caught sight of him, it threw up its head, struck its hooves on the broken paving beneath them and neighed three times, loudly. He went to it and mounted it; and rode on, for now the trail had widened. It led him along and between the rocks, sometimes by way of a scant ledge with sheer stone to his right, a sheer drop to his left; and then again between close rocky walls on either side. As he rode, the day, which was gloomy already, darkened even further until it was as if he rode at twilight.

What little illumination there was seemed to come from the sky in general. It was more light than starglow or moonglow, but not much more; and no trace of sun was visible, so that the dimness enclosed everything. Down among the rocks as he was, he could no longer see the tower, and the trail wound backward and forward, turning to every quarter of the compass. But he did not doubt that he was still headed for the tower, for he could feel its presence, close now ahead of him.

He let the reins lie slack, because the horse seemed to be determined to carry him on, whether he controlled it or not; and in any case there was only one route to follow. From the first moment he had seen it at the chapel it had shown its eagerness to be ridden by him, and in this one direction.

Together, they continued a little ways; and then he saw, ahead and on his right, a break in the rock wall filled by a pair of locked gates, made of dark metal bars overgrown with green vines. Through the bars was revealed an area of stony wilderness in which nothing seemed to live or move; and pressed against the far side of the gates, gazing through them at Hal as he approached, was a slim figure that was Bleys Ahrens.

Hal checked his horse opposite the gate. It tossed its head impatiently against the pull of the bit, but stood; and for a moment the two men were face to face.

'So,' said Bleys, in a remote voice, 'we have the ghosts of those three tutors of yours, do we, raised again by you, and crying out against me for vengeance?'

'No,' said Hal. 'They were only creatures of history, just as you and I are. It's everyone who lives now, crying out to be freed from the chains that always held them.'

'There's no freedom for them,' said Bleys, still in the remote voice. 'There never was.'

'There is, and always has been,' said Hal. 'Open the gate, come through and let me show you.'

'There is no gate,' said Bleys. 'No trail, no tower – everything but this land about us here is illusion. Face that, and learn to make the best of what is.'

Hal shook his head.

'You're a fool,' said Bleys, sadly. 'A fool who hopes.'

'We're both fools,' said Hal. 'But I don't hope, I know.'

And he rode on, leaving Bleys standing, still leaning against the other side of the locked gate, until a turn in the narrow trail lost him to sight.

. . . Hal was roused again, this time by the chiming of a call signal, and opened his eyes to the phone screen at his bedside glowing white. Groggily he pushed himself to full awareness; and with that, suddenly, he was fully alert. No one except a few people at the Final Encyclopedia, such as Amid, Simon, Ajela and Tam, knew that he was here – or even had any reason to think that the estate was occupied.

He flung out an arm and punched on the phone. The screen cleared to show Ajela's face, tight with an unusual tension.

'Hal,' she said. 'Are you awake? They've tried to assassinate Rukh!'

'Where? When?' He pushed himself up on one elbow and saw himself screen-lit, imaged in a mirror across the room, the dark hair tumbled forward over his forehead, the strong-boned features below it scowling away the last numbness of slumber. The hard-muscled, naked torso above the bed covers was the brutal upper body of a stranger.

'A little over forty minutes ago, standard time,' said Ajela. 'The word is she's only wounded.'

'Where is she?' Hal swung his legs over the edge of the bed, throwing the bed-covers back. 'Will you get Simon down here to the estate for me right away?'

He got up and stepped past the screen, reaching for his clothes, from long automatic habit laid close and ready. He began dressing.

'We can't get traffic clearance down there for a courier ship,' Ajela's voice came from the screen, behind him. 'Not even for you, under Earth's regulations. An aircar'll pick you up and take you to Salt Lake – a shuttle'll be held there for you. It'll bring you straight to the Encyclopedia.'

'No.' He was almost dressed now. 'I'll go directly to Rukh.'

'You can't – where are you now?' Ajela said – and he moved back to sit on the bed and face the screen. 'Oh, there you are! You can't just go to her. Her own people with her rushed her off and hid her after it happened. We don't know yet where they've taken her.'

'I'd still be better on the scene, helping to find her.'

'Be sensible.' The tone of Ajela's voice was hard. 'The most your being there could mean would be finding her a few minutes earlier. Besides, you've been out of touch with us and Earth, except for messages, for almost a year. You're needed here, to catch up. No one grudged you a day to make the trip you're on; but if it gets down to hard choices, your duty's here, not with Rukh.'

He took a short breath.

'You're right,' he said. 'I need to talk to you all as soon as I can. The aircar's on its way?'

'Be with you in fifteen minutes. It'll land on that small lake behind your house.'

'I'll be out there waiting,' he said.

'Good.' Ajela's voice softened. 'It's all right, Hal. I know she'll be all right.'

'Yes,' said Hal, hearing his voice as if it came from someone else. 'Of course. I'll be outside waiting for the aircar when it comes.'

'Good; and we'll all be waiting for you when you get here. Come right to Tam's quarters.'

'I will.'

The screen went dark. He rose, finished dressing and went out.

In the open air behind the house, frost held the grounds and mountain areas beyond. In a cloudless, icy sky, the stars were large and seemed to hang low overhead. A nearly full moon was bright. The cold struck in at him, and his breath plumed straight upwards from his lips in the moonlight as he stood by the dark water's edge at the house end of the lake. After a while a dark shape scudded across the sky, occulting the stars, and dropped vertically to land on the water at the center of the lake. It turned toward him and slid across the watery surface to where he stood. The passenger door opened.

'Hal Mayne?' called a male voice from the lighted interior.

'Yes,' Hal said, already inside the car. He dropped into a seat behind the driver as the door closed again and the vehicle leaped upward.

'We ought to make Salt Lake Pad in twenty minutes,' said the driver, over his shoulder.

'Good,' said Hal.

He sat back, letting his mind slip off into a calculation of the probabilities involved in Rukh's situation, using all of Donal's old abilities in that area. It was true enough, if she had not been killed outright and there was any decent sort of medical help available, she was almost sure to survive.

If.

He forced his mind to turn, coldly and dispassionately, to what it would mean to the confrontation with the Others if she had not lived; or had, but would no longer be able to lead Earth's people to an understanding of the cost of an Others' victory. The messages about her of which Ajela had just now spoken had, he knew, been painting a picture of strong successes, for Rukh and for those others she had recruited from Harmony and Association to speak elsewhere about Earth. He had been counting on those successes, taking them for granted.

If her help was now to be lost . . . it was true that he had fallen out of touch with the situation here on Earth, while he had been out scouting Bleys' military preparations on the Younger Worlds. What he had seen out there had not only confirmed his worst forebodings but driven the more immediate problem of controlling Earth from his mind. His losing touch with the Encyclopedia and Earth had, in a sense, been unavoidable – he could not be in two places at once – but its unavoidability did not alter the danger in which it had possibly put them all. The open contest with the Others here at humanity's birthplace was one in which lack of knowledge could guarantee defeat. Now that he knew what he knew, there was nothing for it but to move as swiftly as he could.

Ajela had been more right than she knew, in insisting he come back to the Encyclopedia just now. The breakpoint was upon them.

How close upon them, he had not realized himself until the past evening. But the full implications of the realization was something to be explored later, when time was available. For now, even if Rukh had been no more than scratched, it was not. Every standard day now that he delayed in putting to work the information he had gained, more of its usefulness would leak away.

The shuttle, empty of passengers except himself, slid into the metal-noisy, bright-lit entry port of the Encyclopedia. Simon Graeme was waiting for him as he stepped out of the vehicle.

'I'm to take you to Tam Olyn's quarters,' Simon said.

'I know.'

They went quickly, bypassing the usual passage that led past the center of the Encyclopedia and stepping almost immediately through a side door into a quiet corridor that, by the internal magic of the Encyclopedia, led them only a dozen steps to Tam's entrance door.

Within, Tam's office-lounge was as Hal had remembered it, with the illusion of the little stream and the grove of trees. But both the temperature and humidity of the place were higher; and Tam, seated in one of the big chairs, looked further shrunken and stilled by the hard hand of age, into a final motionlessness in which there seemed to be no energy left for any movement or emotion.

Besides Tam, the office held Ajela and Jeamus Walters, the Engineering Chief of the Encyclopedia, standing facing Tam, one on either side of his chair. They turned together at the sound of the door-chimes; and both their faces lit up.

'Hal!' Ajela turned quickly to Tam. 'You see? I told you. Here he is, now!'

She turned back to hug Hal as he reached her. But almost immediately she let him go again and pushed him toward the chair with the old man in it.

'Hal!' said Tam. His voice rustled like dry paper; and the fingers he put out for Hal to grip were leathery and cold. 'It's good to have you here. I can leave it to you and Ajela, now.'

'Don't,' said Hal, brusquely. 'I'm going to need you, for some time yet.'

'Need me?' Tam's darkened eyes found a spark of life and his papery voice strengthened.

'That's right,' Hal said. 'I've got something specific to talk to you about as soon as there's a minute to spare.'

He turned to Ajela.

'No more word on Rukh?' He saw the answer in her face before she could speak. 'All right. What's the situation here that I need to catch up on?'

'Amid, Rourke di Facino and Jason Rowe were to be signalled the minute you landed,' she answered. 'They'll be here in minutes.

Then we can go over the full situation. Meanwhile, sit down –'

'If you don't mind.' The interruption by the short, broad Chief Engineer was soft-voiced, but insistent. 'While you've got a minute to give me, Hal, I've got something wonderful to tell you. You know this phase-shift-derived communication system of the Exotics? The one by which they've been able to transmit simple messages via color-code across interplanetary distances with at least forty-per cent effectiveness –'

'Jeamus,' said Ajela, 'you can tell Hal about that later.'

'No,' said Hal, watching the serious, round face under the thinning, blond hair, 'if you can tell me in just a few words, go ahead, Jeamus.'

'We didn't know about their method, here,' said Jeamus; 'because they were so good at keeping it secret; and they didn't appreciate the fact that here on the Encyclopedia we know more about collateral uses for the phase-shift than anyone else, including them. Also, they didn't have experience or the capacity to do the running calculations necessary to maintain a steady contact over light-years of distance; which is why they'd never succeeded in using it across interstellar space. After all, the problems involved were like trying to make a spaceship hop the distance from here to any one of the Younger Worlds in a single shift –'

'Jeamus,' said Ajela, gently, 'Hal said – "a few words." '

'Yes. Well,' Jeamus went on. 'The point is, we took what they already had; and in seven months here, we've come up with a system by which I can link with an echo transmitter on one of the Younger Worlds and give you this-moment, standard time, sight and sound of what the echo-transmitter's viewing. Do you understand, Hal? It's still got some problems, of course; but still – you can actually see and hear what's going on there with no time lag at all!'

'Good!' said Hal. 'That's going to be a life-saver, Jeamus. It's something that'll be useful –'

'Useful?' Jeamus took an indignant step toward Hal. 'It'll be a miracle! It's the greatest step forward since we put the shield wall around the Encyclopedia, itself. This is doing the impossible! I don't think you appreciate quite what –'

'I do appreciate it,' Hal said. 'And I realize what you and your people've done, Jeamus. But right now we're under emergency conditions when other thing have priority. We'll talk about this communication system in a little while. Now, what progress have you made on setting up that planet-sized shield-wall I asked you to work up?'

'Oh, that,' said Jeamus. 'It's all done. There's nothing to doing something like that, as I told you, except to make the necessary adjustments for the difference in size between the Encyclopedia and a planet. But this phase-shift communication –'

'Done?' said Hal. 'In what sense done?'

'Well,' there was an edge in Jeamus' voice, 'I mean done – it's ready to go. I've even got the support ships equipped for it and their crews trained, ready to take station. It turned out we needed fifteen spaceships for a wall the size you wanted; and they've been set up. They'll take position around whatever world you want . . . and then it's done. Once the wall's up, they'll act as inner control stations to open irises, just as the Encyclopedia does – only of course larger and more of them – to the star around which the planet is orbiting, for energy input. They're parked now in close proximity orbit, staffed and ready to go, as soon as you tell them where. Not that they haven't got a pretty good idea where. They had to practice taking station, and everyone knows there's only one world larger than Earth that fits the specifications you gave me –'

The door to Tam's quarters chimed and opened. Nonne came in, moving swiftly in a dark brown robe that swirled about her feet as she strode forward. Her face was thinner and older-looking; and she was followed by both Jason Rowe and Rourke di Facino. Jason was wearing a thin, blue shirt and the sort of light-gray work slacks common in the unchanging, indoor climate of the Encyclopedia; clothes which had obviously never been fabricated on either Harmony or Association. In them, rather than his Harmony checked bush shirt and trousers, he looked, by contrast with Nonne, even smaller and younger than Hal remembered him. Rourke, however, was unchanged – still in his Dorsai wardrobe; as dapper, as crisp of manner and as unchanged as ever.

'Good,' said Hal, turning from Jeamus. 'I'm sorry to have been gone so long. Sit down and we'll talk. Jeamus, I'll catch up with you a little later.'

Jeamus nodded dourly, and went out.

Ajela had pulled up one of the antique, overstuffed chairs. Nonne took the only other such one, turning it so that she faced Hal, as he pulled in a float from behind him and sat down next to Tam. Jason took another float, a little back from Nonne's and alongside it. He smiled at Hal and sat back in the float. Only Rourke continued to stand, behind and between Nonne and Jason. He folded his arms and looked keenly at Hal.

'I'm honored to see you all again,' Hal said, looking about at them, 'and my apologies for being out of touch with everyone this length of time. There wasn't any other way to do it; but I appreciate what it's been like for the rest of you. Why don't we go around the circle; and each of you tell me what you most want to talk to me about?'

Silence gave assent.

'Tam?'

'Ajela can tell you,' said Tam hoarsely.

'Ajela?'

'The Final Encyclopedia's as ready as we're ever going to be, for whatever you've got in mind,' said Ajela. 'Earth's another matter.

Rukh and her people have been working miracles I honestly didn't expect, myself. They've already raised a powerful wave of popular opinion all over the world that's ready to back us. But there's still a majority down there who're of a few thousand other sets of minds, or who're blithely ignoring the whole situation on the basis that whatever happens, Earth always comes out all right – by which I mean they simply assume there won't be changes in their backyards.'

'What's your opinion of what's going to happen, now that Rukh's been at least hurt and maybe killed?' Hal said.

'Now . . .' Ajela hesitated and took a deep breath. 'Now, until we can find out about her, and until word of how she is reaches the general Earth populace, it's anyone's guess.'

She stopped speaking. Hal waited for a moment.

'Anything more?'

'No,' said Ajela. 'That's it. If you want anything more, you ask the questions.'

Hal turned to Nonne.

'Nonne?'

'Both Mara and Kultis are prepared,' she said gravely. Her hands smoothed the gown over her knees. 'We've turned over to the Dorsai, the Encyclopedia here and to those Friendlies who oppose the Others, anything they said they needed and we had to give, as you told us to do. Those on both our worlds now are waiting for the next step – ready and waiting. It's up to you now to tell us what's next. Beyond that, as Ajela said, if you want details you've only to ask me.'

Hal nodded; and was about to move his gaze to Jason when she spoke again.

'That doesn't mean there aren't a multitude of things I've got to discuss with you.'

'I know,' said Hal softly. 'I'll get to that with all of you, in time. Jason?'

Jason shrugged.

'Those who oppose us still hold the cities and much of the countryside, on both Harmony and Association,' he said. 'But you don't need to be told that the Children of the Lord aren't ever going to stop fighting. There's little we can do for you, Hal, but go on fighting. I can tell you what we hold and where our strengths are; and if you can give me specific targets to aim at, we'll aim at them. As everybody else here says, beyond that you'll have to ask me questions – or let me ask you some.'

Hal nodded again and looked finally at Rourke di Facino. But the spare, dandified little man answered before Hal could speak his name.

'We're ready to move,' he said.

His arms were still folded. He stood, unaltered, as if the four words he had just brought forth were the sum total of anything that he could contribute to the conference.

'Thank you,' answered Hal.

He looked at the others.

'Thank you all,' he said. 'To give you my own information in capsule form, Bleys has going what'll amount to an unending capability to attack us. He's got more than enough bases, more than enough material, more than enough people to arm and throw at all our capabilities for resistance. It's only a matter of a standard year or less; then he can begin that attack any time he wants; and, if pushed, he could begin it this moment. Being Bleys, I expect him to wait, until he's fully ready to move.'

'I take it,' said Nonne, 'you want to force his hand, then?'

Hal looked soberly at her.

'We have to,' he said.

'Then let me ask you a question,' Nonne said. 'I said there were a multitude of things I wanted to discuss with you. Let me ask you about one.'

'Go ahead.' Hal looked at her thoughtfully.

'We seem to be heading inevitably for the point,' said Nonne, 'where it's going to boil down to a personal duel between you and Bleys. For the sake of my people I have to ask you – do you really think you can win a duel like that? And if so, what makes you think so?'

'I'm not sure at all I can win,' answered Hal. 'There're no certainties in human history. As an Exotic, of all people, you should realize that –'

He checked himself. Ajela had just made a small sound in the back of her throat as if she had begun to speak and then changed her mind. He turned to her. She shook her head.

'No,' she said. 'Nothing.' She was looking hard at Nonne.

'We've got to go with what advantages we've got,' Hal went on, 'and in most cases that means turning the advantages of the Others to our use. Did you ever read Cletus Graeme's work on strategy and tactics?'

'Cletus –? Oh, that early Dorsai ancestor of Donal Graeme,' said Nonne. 'No. My field was recordist – character and its association with activity or occupation. Military maneuvers didn't impinge.'

'I suppose not,' said Hal. 'Let me explain, then. Bleys is the most capable of the Others – you know that as well as I do. Otherwise he wouldn't be leading them. Someone more capable would have taken the leadership from him before this. So we've no choice who we've got to fight – we either defeat him, or lose. All I can tell you about my winning any duel with him is that if it ever comes down to that, I intend to be the winner; and as to why I think I might, it's because I've at least one advantage over him. My cause is better.'

'Is that all?' Nonne's face was completely without expression.

'That can be all it takes,' said Hal, gently. 'A better cause can mean a better base for judgment; and better judgment is sometimes everything in a close contest.'

'Forgive me,' said Nonne, 'if I boggle at the word everything.'

'Think of two chess masters playing opposite each other,' said Hal. 'Neither one's going to make any obvious mistake. But either one can misjudge and make an obviously right move a little too early or a little too late. My job's going to be to try to avoid misjudging like that, while trying at the same time to lead Bleys into misjudgments. To do that, I'll be taking advantage of the difference in our characters and styles. Bleys has all the apparent advantages in this contest of ours. He can lead from strength. Earlier than anyone else among the Others, I think, he perceived that about the situation from the beginning. Certainly, his use of that fact has been the major factor in his being accepted by the rest of the Others as their most capable member. Since his recognition of this has worked for him so far I believe his perception of it is going to continue to lead him, as I said earlier, to wait until he's fully ready before he moves against us.'

He broke off.

'Am I making my point clear to you?' he asked.

'Oh, yes,' said Nonne.

'Good,' answered Hal. 'Now, then, it'd be bad strategy for him to change tactics that are winning for him without a strong reason, in any case. But I think we can count on this other factor in his thinking, as well. So, this leaves the initiative with us – which he will be aware of, but doesn't worry about. However, that same initiative can give us an advantage he may not suspect, if we can use it either to lull him into waiting too long to make a move, or startle him into moving too soon. It'll all depend on how good the plans are we've made.'

'Then I take it you feel you've made good plans?'

He smiled gently at her.

'Yes,' he said. 'I do.' He turned to Ajela. 'I shouldn't have sent Jeamus away,' he said. 'Could you get him back here?'

Ajela nodded and reached to the control panel set in the arm of her chair. She touched one of the controls, murmuring to the receptor in the panel. Hal had turned back to the others.

'When you say you're ready to move,' he said to Rourke, 'do you mean just combat-ready adults, or all adults, or the whole population?'

'Nothing's ever unanimous,' said Rourke, 'and least of all, on the Dorsai, as I'd expect you to appreciate, Hal Mayne. A fair percentage of the population is going to stay. Some because age or sickness gives them no choice, some because they'd rather wait in the place they were born for whatever's going to happen to them. Nearly all of those of service age are ready to go.'

'Yes,' said Hal, nodding, 'that was pretty much what I'd expected.'

The voice of Jason sounded almost on the echo of his last word.

'Go where, Hal?' asked Jason.

'You didn't know?' Nonne looked across at the young Friendly.

'No,' said Jason slowly, looking from her to Hal. 'I didn't know. What was it I was supposed to have known?'

Instead of answering, Nonne looked at Hal.

'In a minute, Jason,' Hal said. 'Wait until Jeamus gets here.'

They fell silent, looking at him. For a moment, as they sat waiting, Hal's mind went away from the immediate concerns.

He was aware of the four of them as individual puzzle-boxes, unique individual universes of thought and response, through which must be communicated what those they represented would need to understand. Once, as Donal, he would have seen them only as units, solid working parts of an overall solution to an overall problem. His greatest interest in them would have been that they should execute what he would direct them to do or say. Their objections would have been minor obstacles, to be laid flat by indisputable logic, until they were reduced to silence. The tag-end of some lines from the New Testament of the Bible, spoken by the Roman Centurion to Christ, came back to his mind, '*I say to one, go, and he goeth and to another come, and he cometh . . .*'

That sort of thinking could indeed produce a solution on the Donal level. But he had lived two lives since then to find something better, something more lasting. It had been his awareness of the need for that which had bothered Donal near the end of his time, as he stood, finally in charge of all the worlds and their workings, looking out at the stars beyond the known stars. He had seen the future clearly, then, and the fallacy in the idea that it could be won, even to a good end, by strength alone.

It had never been enough to make people dress neatly, walk soberly and obey the law. Only when the necessary improvement had at last been accepted by the inner self, when the law was no longer necessary, had any permanent development been accomplished. And if he could not show to these people here in this room with him now what would need to be done and achieved, then how was he going to show it to the billions of other individual human universes that made up the race?

It was not that they were not willing, any of them, to move to a higher and better land. But each of them, one by one, individually, in their billions, would have to make the trip by himself or herself when the time came; and for that, they would need to be able to see the way clear and the goal plain and desirable before them, so that each would move freely and on a personal determination to find it. Because the goal was not one that could be reached by intellectual decision alone. In the case of each person, it would require combined effort of the conscious and the unconscious minds, of which only a handful of people in each past century had been capable. But now the way would be marked. Those who really desired to reach it could do so – they could all do so. Only, they would first have to see the marking of the way; and grow into a belief in their own abilities that would make them set their feet with utter confidence upon it.

And as yet that way was cloudy, even to him. He must go first, like a pioneer into new territory, charting as he went, making a road for the rest to follow – and that road began with these here, with Rukh and these others who had shown some desire to listen to him and follow him –

The chiming of the annunciator and the opening of the door to Tam's suite to let in Jeamus interrupted that train of thought.

'Come in, Jeamus,' said Hal. 'Take a seat if you like. I want to explain to these people what I asked you to design, in the way of a planetary shield-wall.'

'Isn't this wasting valuable time?' Nonne broke in. 'We all know he's been working on a shield-wall, and where it has to go –'

'I don't,' said Jason, interrupting in turn. The eyes of the rest turned to him, for there was a strength and firmness to his voice that none of them, except Hal, had ever heard before. 'Let's hear that explanation.'

Jeamus had reached the circle by this time. His eyes rested for a second on the standing figure of Rourke, and he ignored the float that was within arm's reach of him.

'More than a standard year back,' he said, 'Hal asked me to look into making a phase-shift shield-wall, like the one we have around the Encyclopedia here to protect it, but large enough to protect a world. He specified a world slightly larger than Earth. We've done that. Once the ships to effect it are in proper position about that world, and in proper communication between themselves, it can be created instantly.'

He looked at Hal.

'Do you want me to go into the principle of it and the details of its generation?'

'No,' said Hal. 'Just tell them what it'll do.'

'What it'll do,' said Jeamus to the rest of them, 'is enclose what it surrounds in essentially a double shell which from either side will translate anything touching it into universal position – just as a phase-shift drive does. Only, in this case, the object won't be retranslated into a specific position again, the way a phase-drive does. I suppose all of you know that the phase-drive theory was developed from the Heisenberg Uncertainty Principle –'

'Yes, yes,' said Nonne. 'We know all that. We know that the Principle says it's impossible to determine both the position and velocity of a particle with full accuracy; and the more accurate the one, the more uncertain the other. We know that in phase-drive terms this means, for all practical purposes, that in the instant of no-time in which velocity can be absolutely fixed, position becomes universal. We know this means anyone or anything trying to pass a shield-wall like the one around the Encyclopedia would be effectively spread out to infinity. We know that Hal Mayne plans to set up a garrison world with such a shield-wall around it – as no doubt Bleys Ahrens also does – and defend it with the Dorsai, and that world is to be our Exotic world of Mara –'

'No,' said Hal.

Jeamus' head came around with a jerk. Ajela leaned forward, her face suddenly intent. Nonne stared at him.

'No?' she said. 'No what? No, to which part of what I said?'

'It won't be Mara,' said Hal gently. 'It's to be right here – Earth.'

'Earth!' burst out Jeamus. 'But you told me larger than Earth! The dimensions you gave me –'

He broke off, suddenly.

'Of course!' he said wearily. 'You wanted to enclose the Encyclopedia in it. Of course.'

'Earth?' said Nonne.

'Earth,' Hal repeated.

He touched the control panel on the edge of his float and one side of the room dissolved into a view of the Earth as seen from the orbit of the Encyclopedia. A great globe, blue swathed with white, it hung before them. Hal got up and walked toward it until he stood next to the view, seeming to the rest of them almost to stand over the imaged world, as someone might bend above something infinitely valuable.

'But this makes no sense!' said Nonne, almost to herself. 'Hal!'

At the sound of his name he turned from the screen to face her across the small distance that now separated them.

'Hal,' she said. 'Earth? What's the point of defending Earth? What kind of a strong point can it make for you when more than half the people there don't care if the Others end up in control? You haven't even got their permission, down there, to put a shell around them, like the one we've been talking about!'

'I know,' said Hal. 'But asking first would've been not only foolish, but unworkable. They'll be surprised, I'm afraid.'

'They'll make you take it down.'

'No,' said Hal. 'Some will try, of course. But they won't succeed. The point is, they can't. And in time they'll come to understand why it has to be there.'

'Wishful thinking!' said Nonne.

'No.' He looked at her for a second. 'Or at least, not wishful thinking in the sense you mean. I'm sorry, Nonne, but now, for the first time, we're at a point where you're going to have to trust me.'

'Why should I?' Her answer was fierce.

He sighed.

619

'For the same reason,' he said, 'that's been operative from the time you first heard of me. You, your people, and everyone else who hopes to escape the Others hasn't any other choice.'

'But this is madness!' she said. 'Mara's willing to have you put a shield-wall around it. The people on Mara are even expecting it. The people on Mara are behind you to a person. They're ready for sacrifice; they've faced the need to sacrifice in order to survive. Hardly enough individuals to count on Earth have even thought of opposing the Others, let alone the cost of it.'

'Something more than that, Nonne,' put in Ajela. 'Rukh's crusade has been a real crusade. They've been flocking in their thousands and hundreds of thousands to listen to her and the other people she brought in to carry the message.'

'There's several billions of people on Earth!' said Nonne.

'Give Rukh time,' said Ajela. 'The process is accelerating.'

'There's no more time,' said Hal; and the eyes of all of them came to him. 'Bleys has moved faster than any of you realize. I've just spent the last months seeing the evidence of that. A decision has to be made now. And it has to be for Earth.'

'Why?' demanded Nonne.

'Because Earth holds the heart of the race,' said Hal, slowly. 'As long as Earth is unconquered, the race is unconquered. A man once said, talking to an Irishman in a hotel at five o'clock in the morning, back in the twentieth century, 'Suppose all the poets, all the playwrights, all the songmakers of Ireland were to be wiped out in an instant. How many generations would it take to replace them?' And before he could answer his own question, the Irishman held up one finger, as the answer the man had been about to give.'

He looked at them all.

'One. One finger. One generation. And they were both right. Because not only the children who were still young would grow up to have poets and playwrights and songmakers among them; but those adults presently alive who'd never written or sung would suddenly begin to produce the music that had always been in them – in response to the sudden silence about them. Because the ability to produce such things never was the special province of a few. It was something belonging to the people as a whole, in the souls of every one of them, only waiting to be called forth. And what was true at the time of that conversation, and before and since, with the Irish people, is true as well, now, for the people of Earth.'

'And not for the people of the other worlds?' asked Jason.

'In time, them too. But their forebears were sent out by the hunger and fear of the race, to be expendable, to take root in strange places. For now, they stand – all of you stand, except Tam – at arm's length from the source of the music that's in you, and the future that's in you. You'll find it – but it would come harder and

620

more slowly to any of you than it would for any of those down there –'

He gestured at the blue and white globe he had displayed.

They sat watching him, saying nothing. Even Nonne was silent.

'I told the Exotics,' Hal went on, in the new silence, 'I told the Dorsai – and I would have told your people, as well, Jason, if I'd had the proper chance to speak to them all – that in the final essential, they were experiments of the race. That they were brought into being only to be used when the time came. Now, that time's come. You all know the centuries of the Splinter Cultures are over. You know that, each of you, instinctively inside you. Their day of experimentation is done. Your kind lived, grew, and flourished for the ultimate purpose of taking one side of the great survival question of which road the race as a whole is going to follow into its future among the stars. Not to you and your children, unique and different, but to the children of the race in general, the future belongs.'

He stopped. They still said nothing.

'And so,' he said, tiredly, 'it's Earth we have to end by protecting; Earth with all its history of savagery, and cruelty, and foolishness and selfishness – and all its words and songs and mighty dreams. Here, and no place else, the battle's finally going to be lost or won.'

He stopped again. He wanted them to speak – if only so that he would not feel so utterly alone. But they did not.

He looked back at the blue and white globe of Earth.

'And it's here the question of the future is going to be decided,' he said, softly, 'and such as you and I will have to die, if that's our job, to get the answer needed for that decision to be made.'

He stopped speaking and looked again at the imaged Earth. After a second or two, he was conscious of another body close behind him, and turned, lifting his eyes, to see that it was Ajela.

She put her arms around him; and merely held him for a minute. Then she let him go and went back to her seat by Tam.

'You give us reasons,' said Nonne to him, 'which aren't military reasons, and may not even be pragmatic, practical reasons. My point remains that Mara's a better base for a stonewall defense than Earth is. You haven't really answered me on that.'

'This isn't,' said Hal, 'exactly a war we're entered into for pragmatic and practical reasons – except in the long run. But the fact is, you're wrong. Mara's a rich world, as the Younger Worlds go; but even after centuries of misuse and plundering of its resources, Earth is still the richest inhabited planet the human race knows. It's entirely self-supporting, and it still maintains a population twenty times as large as that of any other inhabited world, to this day.'

He broke off abruptly, holding all their eyes with his. Then he went on.

'Also, there's a psychological difference. Enclose any other world,

621

cut it off from contact with the other inhabited worlds, and emotionally it can't escape the feeling that it may have been discarded by the community of humanity, left behind to wither and die. As time goes on, it'll become more and more conscious of its isolation from the main body of the race. But Earth still thinks of itself as the hub of the human universe. All other worlds, to it, are only buds on its branch. If all those others are cut off, whatever the cost may be otherwise, emotionally the most Earth will think of itself as having lost are appendages it lived without for millions of years and can do without again, if necessary.'

'That large population's no benefit to you,' said Nonne, 'particularly, if – as it is – it's full of people who disagree with what you're doing. They're not the ones who're rallying to the defense of Earth. You're planning to defend that world with the Dorsai.'

'In the beginning,' said Hal, 'certainly. If the battle goes on, I think we'll find people from Earth itself coming forward to man the barricades. In fact, they'll have to.'

He turned to the old man.

'Tam?' he said. 'What do you think?'

'They'll come,' said Tam. The rattly, ancient voice made the two words seem to fall, flat and heavy in their midst, like stones too weighty to hold. 'This is where the Dorsai came from, and the Exotics, and the Friendlies – and everyone else. When defenders are needed from the people, they'll be there.'

For a moment no one said anything.

'And that,' said Hal, with a deep breath, 'is another reason for it to be Earth, rather than Mara. In time, even your Marans would produce people to stand on guard. But they'd have to go back into what lies below their present character to do it.'

'But they could and would,' said Nonne. 'In this time, when everything that's been built up is falling apart, even Maran adults would do that. Even I'd fight – if I thought I could.'

A little smile, a not-unkindly smile, twitched the corners of Rourke di Facino's lips.

'Dear lady,' he said to her. 'That's always been the only difference.'

The remark drew her attention to him.

'You!' she said. 'You stand there, saying nothing. Did your people bargain to defend Earth where the people have never understood or appreciated what the Younger Worlds mean – least of all, your kind? Are you simply willing to be their common fodder, without at least protesting what Hal Mayne wants? You're the military expert. You speak to him!'

The little smile went from Rourke's lips, to be replaced by an expression that had a strange touch of sadness to it. He came slowly around from behind the chairs of the rest where he had been standing and walked up to Hal. Hal looked at the erect, smaller man.

'I've talked to Simon about you,' Rourke said. 'And to Amanda. Who you are is your own business and no one discusses it –'

'I don't understand,' interrupted Nonne, looking from one of them to the other. 'What do you mean – who he is, is his own business?'

For a second it seemed that Rourke would turn and answer her. Then he went on speaking to Hal.

'But it's the opinion of the Grey Captains that we've got to trust your judgment,' he said.

'Thank you,' said Hal.

'So,' said Rourke, 'you think it should be Earth, then?'

'I think it always had to be,' said Hal. 'The only question has been, when to begin to move; and as things stand now, Bleys gets stronger every standard day we wait.'

'I repeat,' said Nonne. 'You don't have a solid Earth at your back – you don't begin to have a solid Earth at your back. Rukh may have been gaining ground fast – as you say, Ajela – but now she's out of the picture and the job she set out to do isn't done. If you move now, you're gambling, Hal, gambling with the odds against you.'

She looked back at Hal.

'You're right,' said Hal. He stood for a second in silence. 'But in every situation a time comes when decisions have to be made whether all the data's on hand, or not. I'm afraid I see more harm in waiting than acting. We'll begin to garrison Earth and lock it up.'

Rourke nodded, almost as if to himself.

'In that case,' he said, 'I'll get busy.'

He looked over at Jeamus.

'I can use that new communications system of yours now, Chief Engineer,' he said, turning and heading for the door. Jeamus looked at Hal, who nodded, and the balding man hurried after the small, erect back of the Dorsai.

Before either one reached it, however, the sound of a phone chime sounded. They stopped, as Ajela reached out to touch the control panel on the arm of her chair and all of the rest of them turned to look at her. A voice spoke from the panel, too low-pitched for the others to hear.

She lifted her head and looked at Hal.

'They've located Rukh,' she said. 'She's at a little place outside Sidi Barrani on the Mediterranean coast, west of Alexandria.'

'I'll have to catch up with the rest of you later, then,' Hal said. 'Everything down below depends to some extent on how much she's going to be able to go on doing. Ajela, can you set up surface transportation for me while I'm on my way down to the shuttle port nearest Sidi Barrani?'

Ajela nodded. Hal started toward the door, looking over at the young Friendly.

'Jason,' he said, 'do you want to come?'

'Yes,' said Jason.

'All right, then,' Hal said, as Rourke and Jeamus stood aside to let him out the door first. 'We'll be back in some hours, with luck. Meanwhile, simply begin what you'd planned to do, once the decision to move was taken.'

He went out the door with Jason close behind him.

CHAPTER SIXTY-TWO

Sidi Barrani lay inland from the shore of the Mediterranean, across one of those areas which had been among the first to be reclaimed from the North African desert, over two hundred years before. Tall still-towers had been built and water from the Mediterranean had been pumped into them, to be discharged within their tops and allowed to fall some hundreds of meters to great fans in their bases, which then blew the moistened air back up and out the tops of the towers to humidify the local atmosphere.

That humidity had made lush cropland out of the dry earth surrounding; and, as the years went by, a resulting climatological change had altered the fertile areas, pushing inland from the shoreline the edge of the desert Rommel and Montgomery had fought over in the mid-twentieth century. The desert's edge had been forced to retreat some hundreds of kilometers, until it had been finally overwhelmed and vanquished entirely against the green borderland surrounding the newly formed Lake of Qattara; a large body of water formed when the Nile, backed up by the massive Aswan Dam, had at last found a new channel westward into the Qattara Depression.

It was to the shore of that lake and to a hotel called the Bahrain, therefore – an inconspicuous, low, white-walled structure in a brilliantly flowered and tropically aired landscape – that Hal and Jason came finally in their journey to find Rukh.

But for all the peace and softness of the physical surroundings, stepping through the front door of the hotel was like stepping out into a bare field when lightning is in the air. Hal shot a quick glance at Jason, who, after his years in the Harmony resistance, could be sensitive enough to feel the field of emotional tension they had just entered, but might not yet be experienced enough to react wisely to it.

However, Jason's face was calm. Possibly a little more pale than usual – but calm.

The sunken lobby under the high-arched white ceiling before them showed no one occupying the overstuffed floats hovering around a small ornamental pool. The only visible living figure to be seen was what, here on Earth, must be a desk clerk hired for purely ornamental purposes. His gaze was directed downward behind the counter of the reception desk, as he appeared busy, or pretended to be busy, at something. Otherwise there was no sign of anyone human within sight or hearing – but the feeling of tense, if invisible watchers, all around them, was overwhelming.

The desk clerk did not look up until they had actually reached the counter and stopped on their side of it. He was a slight young man with a brown, smooth skin and a round face.

'Welcome to the Bahrain,' he said. 'Can I be of assistance?'

'Thanks, yes,' said Hal. 'Would you tell the lady that Howard Immanuelson is here to see her?'

'Which lady would that be, sir?'

'You've only got one lady here that message could be for,' said Hal. 'Please send it right away.'

The clerk put both hands on the counter and leaned his weight slightly on them.

'I'm afraid, gentlemen,' he said, 'I don't understand. I can't deliver a message until I know who it's for.'

Hal looked at him for a second.

'I can understand your position,' he said, gently. 'But you're making a mistake. We'll go and sit down by the pool, there; and you see that message I gave you gets delivered. If it doesn't . . . perhaps you'd better ask someone who'd know, who Howard Immanuelson is.'

'I'm sorry, sirs,' said the clerk, 'but without knowing who you want to contact, I've no way of knowing if that person is even a guest here, and –'

But they had already turned away, with Hal in the lead, and his voice died behind them. Hal chose a float with his back to the desk; and Jason moved to sit opposite him so that between them they would have the whole lobby in view. Hal frowned slightly; and, after a split second of hesitation, Jason took a float beside him, facing the same way.

They sat without talking. There was no sound from the desk. Hal's eyes and ears and nose were alert, exploring their surroundings. After a moment his nose singled out a faint, but pervasive and pleasant, scent on the air of the lobby; and an alarm-signal sounded in his mind. Out on one of the Younger Worlds such a thing would have been highly unlikely; but here on Earth, where riches made for easy access to Exotic weapons, and disregard for even the most solemn local laws and international agreements were not to be ruled out, it was not impossible that an attempt was being made to drug them by way of the lobby atmosphere.

It would not call for a drug capable of making them unconscious. All that would be needed would be slightly dull to one or more of their senses, or blunt the fine edge of their judgment, to give the unseen watchers a dangerous advantage.

On the other hand, the scent could be no more than it seemed. One of the services, or grace notes, a place like this might provide to make its lobby pleasant to guests.

There was only one way to find out which it was. The single ability most vulnerable to any kind of drugging was the meditatively creative one. The gossamer bubbles of memory or fantasy, blown by the mind, and all the powerful release of emotion these could entail, were invariably warped or inhibited by anything alien to the physiological machinery supporting them.

He let the meditative machinery of his mind sink momentarily below the surface level of that watchful awareness which still continued to be maintained automatically by the outward engine of his consciousness; and allowed himself to slip back into recall of his childhood years, to a time when all emotions had been simple, pure and explosive.

It had been, he remembered, a time when excitement had had the power almost to tear him apart. Sorrow had been unbearable, happiness had lit up the world around him like a sheet of lighting, and anger had swallowed up all things – like one sheet of flame devouring the universe.

There had been a time, once, when he had been about five years old, that Malachi Nasuno had refused him something. He could not now remember what it had been without digging for the information and for present purposes so much was not necessary. He had wanted to handle some tool or weapon, that the old Dorsai had considered beyond his years and ability; and Malachi had refused to let him have it. A fury at all things – at Malachi, at rules and principles, at a universe made for adults in which he was manacled by the unfairness of being young and small, had erupted in him. He had exploded at Malachi, shouting out his frustration and resentment, and run off into the woods.

He had run and run until breath and legs gave out together; and he had dropped down at last at the narrow edge of a stream which had cut its way through the mountain rock, bursting into unexpected tears. He had cried in sheer fury; determined never to go back, never to see Malachi or Walter or Obadiah again. Wild visions of living off the land in the mountains by himself billowed up like smoke from the bitter fires of frustration inside him.

And gradually a new despair came over him; so that he lay by the stream, silent in the misery of the thought that it seemed he could never be either what he wanted to be or what Malachi and the others might want him to be. Inwardly, he accused them of not understanding him, or not caring for him – when they were all he had, and when he had tried with every ounce of strength he owned to be what they wanted.

. . . And in that moment, as he huddled lost on the ground, two

627

massive, trunklike arms closed around him and brought him gently against the wide chest of Malachi. It was infinitely comforting to be found after all, held so; and he sobbed again – but now in relief, wearing himself out into peace and silence against the rough fabric of Malachi's jacket. The old man said nothing, only held him. He could hear, through jacket and chest wall, the slow, powerful beating of the adult heart. It seemed to him that his own heart slowed and moved to match that rhythm; and, just before he slipped into a slumber from which he would not wake until hours later, in his own bed, he felt – as clearly as if it had been in himself – the pain and sorrow that was in his tutor, together with an urge to love no less powerful than his own. . . .

He came back to full awareness of the Bahrain lobby, still wrung by the remembered emotions, and the achievement of that first rung on the ladder of human understanding, which had made life different for him from that moment on; but reassured by the successful summoning up of that ancient emotion that whatever perfumed the air around him was nothing with any power to inhibit either his body or his mind.

There was the sound of shoe soles on the hard, polished surface of the floor, approaching behind them. They turned to see the desk clerk.

'If you'll go up to room four-thirty-nine, gentlemen?' said the clerk. 'It's the fifth door, to your right as you step out of the lift tube.'

'Thanks,' said Hal, rising. Jason was also getting to his feet; and they went toward the bank of lift that the clerk was indicating with one hand.

The soft, white walls of the corridor of the fourth floor stretched right and left from the lift tube exits there, but bent out of sight within a short distance in either direction. Clearly it was designed to wander among the rooms and suites available. They went to their right; and, as they passed each door, it chimed and lit up its surface. As they went by, the number faded.

'Vanities!' said Jason under his breath; and Hal glanced at him, smiling a little.

Perhaps thirty meters from the lift tubes, a door glowed alight with the number 439 as they came level with it. They stopped, facing toward it.

'This is Howard Immanuelson,' said Hal, clearly, 'with someone who's an old friend of all of us. May we come in?'

For a moment there was no response. Then the door swung silently inward; and they entered.

The room they stepped into was large and square. The whole of the side opposite the door by which they had come in was apparently open to the weather, with a balcony beyond; but the coolness and stillness of the atmosphere about them told of an invisible barrier between room and balcony. Green-brown drapes of heavy material had been pulled back from the open wall to their limit on each side. Framed by these, the blue waters of Lake Qattara, with three white triangles that were the sails of one-person pleasure rafts, looked inward to the room.

There was no one visible, only a closed door in the wall to their left. The entrance, which had opened behind them, closed again. Hal turned toward the closed door in the side wall.

'No,' said a voice.

A thin, intense figure with the long-barrelled void pistol, favored for its silence and deadliness on an Earth where there was little call for long-range accuracy, and where the destruction of property could have a higher price tag than that of human lives, stepped from behind the bunched folds of the drape three steps down the wall from the side door. Bony of feature, frail and deadly, incongruous in khaki-colored, Earth-style beach shorts and brightly patterned shirt with leg-o'-mutton sleeves, was Amyth Barbage; and the pistol in his hand covered both Hal and Jason with utter steadiness.

Hal took a step toward him.

'Stop there,' said Barbage. 'I know of what thou art capable, Hal Mayne, if I let thee come close enough.'

'Hal!' said Jason, quickly. 'It's all right. He's Rukh's now!'

'I am none but the Lord's, weak man – nor ever have been,' replied Barbage, dryly, 'as perhaps thou hast. But it's true I know now that Rukh Tamani is of the Lord and speaks with His voice; and I will guard her, therefore, while I live. She is not to be disturbed – by anyone.'

Hal stared with a touch of wonder.

'Are you sure about this?' he said to Jason, without taking his eyes off the thin, still figure and the absolutely motionless muzzle of the gun. 'When did he change sides?'

'I changed no sides,' said Barbage, 'as I just said. How could I, who am of the Elect and must move always in obedience to His will? But in a courtyard of which you know, it happened once to be His will that a certain blindness should be lifted from my eyes; and I saw at last how He had vouchsafed that Rukh should see His Way more clearly than I or any other, and was beloved of Him above all. In my weakness I had strayed, but was found again through great mercy; and now I tell you that for the protection of her life, neither you nor anyone else shall disturb her rest. Her doctor has ordered it; and I will see it done.'

'Amyth Barbage,' said Hal, 'I have to see her, now; and talk to her. If I don't, all the work she's done can be lost.'

'I do not believe you,' said Barbage.

'But I do,' said Jason, 'since I know more about it than you, Old Prophet. And my duty to the Lord is as great as yours. Count on that, Hal –'

'Wait!'

629

Hal spoke just in time. He had read the sudden tensing in the man at his side, and understood that Jason was about to throw himself into the fire of Barbage's pistol so Hal might have time to reach the other man and deal with him. Jason slowly, imperceptibly, relaxed. Hal stared at the man with the gun.

'I think,' he said slowly, 'a little of that blindness you talked about is still with you, Amyth Barbage. Did you hear what I said – that if I didn't see and talk to Rukh now, all her work here could be lost?'

His eyes matched and held those of Barbage. The seconds stretched out in silence. Then, still holding the void pistol's muzzle steadily upon them, still watching them unvaryingly, Barbage moved sideways to the door in the side wall they had been facing, softly touched and softly opened it, then stepped backward through it. Standing one step inside the further room, he spoke in so low a voice they barely heard him.

'Come. Come quietly.'

They followed him into a curious room. It was narrow before them as they stepped into it and completely without furniture. Its far end was closed by drawn draperies of the same material and color as those in the room they had just left; and the wall to their right seemed to shimmer slightly as they looked at it.

As soon as they were inside and the door had closed automatically behind them, Barbage held up his free hand to bring them to a halt.

'Stay here,' he said.

He turned and walked through the wall with the shimmer, revealing it for the projected sound-barrier image that it was. Hal and Jason stood silently waiting for several slow minutes; then suddenly the imaged wall vanished to show a large, pleasant hotel bedroom with the drapes drawn back and a bed float contoured into a sitting position – and, propped up in it, Rukh.

Barbage was standing by the bedside, frowning back at them.

'Her strength must not be wasted,' Barbage said. 'I do this only because she insists. Tell her briefly what you have to say.'

'No, Amyth,' said Rukh from the bed, 'they can talk until I ask them to stop. Hal, come here – and you, too, Jason.'

They stepped to the bedside. Clearly, Hal saw, Rukh had never recovered from the thinness to which her ordeal at the hands of the Harmony Militia had reduced her; and now, with her upper left side and shoulder, farthest from them, bulky with bandages under the loose white bed dress she wore, she looked even more frail than when Hal had seen her last. But her remarkable beauty was, if anything, more overwhelming than ever. In the green-blue light reflected into the room by the vegetation and water outside, there appeared to be a translucency to her dark body, framed by the pale buttercup shade of the bed coverings.

Jason reached out to touch the arm of her unwounded side, gently, with the tips of his fingers.

'Rukh,' he said softly. 'Thou art not in pain? Thou art comfortable?'

'Of course, Jason,' she said, and smiled at him. 'I'm not badly hurt at all. It's just that the doctor said I was needing a rest, anyway –'

'She hath been close to exhaustion for some months, now –' began Barbage harshly, but checked himself as she looked at him.

'It's all right,' she said. 'But Amyth, I want to talk to Hal alone. Jason, would you forgive us . . .?'

'If this is thy wish.' Barbage lowered the pistol, turned to the shimmering image wall and passed through it. Jason turned to follow.

'Jason – I'll be talking to you, too. Later.' Rukh spoke hastily. He smiled back at her.

'Of course. I understand, Rukh – whenever you want to, I'll be here,' he said, and went out.

Left alone with Hal she lifted her good right arm with effort from the bedspread covering her and started to reach out to him. He stepped close and caught hold of her hand with his own before hers was barely above the covers. Still holding it, he pulled a chair float up to her bedside with his other hand and sat down close to her.

'It occurred to me you'd be showing up here,' she said, with a smile. Her hand was warm but narrow-boned in his own much larger grasp.

'I wanted to come the moment I heard,' he said. 'But it was pointed out to me that there were things to do, decisions I had to make. And we didn't know where you were until a few hours ago.'

'Amyth and the others decided I ought to vanish,' she said, 'and I think they were probably right. This is an area where the people like me.'

'Where they love you, you mean,' said Hal.

She smiled again. For all its beauty, it was a tired smile.

'Duty kept you from searching for me right away, then,' she said. 'Did duty bring you now?'

He nodded.

'I'm afraid so,' he said. 'Time can't wait for either of us. Rukh, I had to make a decision to start things moving. We're out of time. I've sent word to the Dorsai they're to come here; and a phase shield-wall, like the one about the Final Encyclopedia, is going to be thrown around the whole Earth – including the Encyclopedia, in orbit. From now on, we're a fortress under seige.'

'And the Exotics?' she said, still holding his hand, and searching his eyes. 'All of us thought it would be one of the Exotics you'd chose to fortify and defend, with the help of the Dorsai.'

'No.' He shook his head again. 'It was always to be here, but I had to keep that to myself.'

'And Mara and Kultis, then? What happens to them?'

'They die.' His voice sounded unsparing in his own ears. 'We've taken their space shipping, any of their experts and valuables, and

631

whatever else they could use. The Others will make them pay for giving us those things, of course.'

She shook her head slowly, her eyes somberly upon him.

'The Exotics knew this would happen?'

'They knew. Just as the Dorsai knew they'd have to abandon their world. Just as you and those others from Harmony and Association who came here knew you came here not for a few months or years, but probably for the rest of your lives.' He gazed for a long second at her. 'You did know, didn't you?'

'The Lord told me,' she said. She drew her hand softly from within his fingers and put it around them, instead. 'Of course, we knew.'

'All things were headed this way from the beginning,' he said. His voice had an edge like the edge found in the voice of someone in deep anger. He knew he did not have to lay the cold truth out for her in spoken words, but his own inner pain drove him to it. 'In the end, when the choosing of sides came, the Dorsai were to fight for the side of the future, the Exotics were to make it possible for them, at the cost of everything they'd built. And those of you from the Friendlies who truly held faith in your hands were to waken the minds of all who fought on that side so they could see what it was they fought for.'

Her fingers gently stroked the back of his hand.

'And Earth?' she said.

'Earth?' He smiled a little bitterly. 'Earth's job is to do what it has always done – to survive. To survive so as to give birth to those who'll live to know a better universe.'

'Shh,' she said; and she stroked his hand gently with her thin fingers. 'You do the task that's been set you, like us all.'

He looked at her and made himself smile.

'You're right,' he said. 'It doesn't change how I feel – but you're right.'

'Of course,' she said. 'Now, what did you come to ask from me?'

'I need you back at the Encyclopedia,' he said, bluntly, 'if you're able to travel at all. I want you to make a broadcast to all of Earth from the Encyclopedia; and I want all of Earth to know you're speaking from the Encyclopedia. I need you to help explain why the Dorsai are coming here and why a phase-shield-wall's been put around this planet, both without anyone asking the Earth people's permission. I can talk to them at the same time you do and take any responsibility you'd like me to spell out. But no one else can make them understand why these things had to be done the way you can. The question is – can you travel?'

'Of course, Hal,' she said.

'No,' he replied deliberately. 'I mean exactly what I say – are you physically able to make the trip? You're too valuable to risk losing you for the sake of one speech, no matter how important it is.'

She smiled at him.

'And if I didn't go, what would happen then, when the Dorsai start arriving down here and they discover the shield-wall?'

'I don't know,' he said. His eyes met hers on a level.

'You see?' she said. 'I have to go; just as we all have to do what we have to do. But don't worry, Hal. I really am all right. The wound's nothing; and otherwise there's nothing wrong with me a few weeks of rest won't cure – once the Dorsai are here and the shield-wall's up. There's no reason I can't have time off then, is there?'

'Of course there isn't.'

'Well, then –'

But what she had started to say was cut off by the sudden eruption through the wall of a man of ordinary height with thin, fading brown hair, a bristling gray mustache and a face that seemed too young for either. He was wearing a sand-colored business suit that looked as if he had been sleeping in it and had just been wakened. The expression on his face was one of bright anger. Amyth Barbage was right behind him.

'You!' he said to Hal. 'Get out of here!'

He swung to face Rukh, on the bed.

'Am I your doctor or not?' His voice beat upward under the pale, white ceiling of the quiet room 'If I'm not, tell me now; and you can find yourself someone else to take care of you!'

'Of course you are, Roget,' she said.

CHAPTER SIXTY-THREE

Dawn came up bright and hard on the waters of Lake Qattara, with a little chop to the waves and an on-shore breeze. With dawn came also a man in his fifties with a tanned, sharp-boned face and bright, opaque eyes, who wore his civilian suit like a uniform and was called Jarir al-Hariri. It appeared he was the equivalent of Police Commissioner for the large district surrounding the lake. With his coming the hotel began to swarm with activity. The instincts of Hal and Jason on entering the hotel had not lied to them. The great majority of guests who now appeared were plainly Earth-born and non-military; but their protective attitude toward Rukh was more like that of the members of her old Command on Harmony than that which might have been expected from casual converts to the message she had been preaching.

Hal himself was up before dawn. He had sat with Rukh until her breathing deepened into heavy slumber, then eased himself gently and with great slowness from the position in which he sat holding her. Detached, finally, he had laid her gently down in the bed and covered her up, leaving her to sleep.

Back in the room to which the clerk in the hotel led him after Amyth had called down to the lobby, he dropped onto his own bed; and slept heavily for nine hours – coming awake suddenly with a clear mind and drugged feel to his body that told him he was still far from normally rested. He rose, showered, ran his clothes through the room cleaner, and ate the breakfast he had ordered up to his room.

Then he went in search of Jason and Amyth, found them deep in consultation with Roget the physician over the problem of moving Rukh safely, and was himself drawn into the talk. But by nine in the morning, local time, the move was underway. They would go from the hotel to the spacepad outside Alexandria, some two hundred and seventy-three kilometers distant, by surface transportation. Medically, Roget had reservations about an air trip. These were slight, but existed nonetheless. There were, however, very strong security reasons for sticking to the ground. Any atmosphere craft could be vulnerable to destruction by a robot drone with an explosive warhead – something any wild-eyed fringe group could put together in an hour or so – given the materials – out of any number of

634

industrial atmosphere-operating robots, doing the work in any handy back room or basement.

Spacepad security would destroy any such drone automatically at its perimeters, so there would be no worries once the spacepad was reached; and beyond the umbrella of that security any shuttle on its way to the Encyclopedia would be either too high or moving too swiftly for a drone to reach it.

Once in the Encyclopedia, of course, Rukh would be utterly safe.

'I take it,' Hal had said to Jarir al-Hariri, early in this discussion, 'security's been strict about letting the information spread beyond these walls that Rukh's leaving today?'

The stony, bright eyes had met his almost indifferently across the table at which they sat with cups of coffee – real Earth coffee, pleasant but strange now to Hal's taste buds.

'There has been no leak through my people,' Jarir had said.

The pronunciation of the words in Basic were noticeably mangled on the Commissioner's tongue; surprising in the case of anyone speaking a language that had been the majority tongue of Earth, as well as that of the Younger Worlds for three hundred years; particularly when teaching methods had been in existence at least that long which made it possible for nearly everyone to learn any new language quickly, easily and without accent.

Jarir was evidently one of those rare linguistic exceptions who had trouble with any tongue he had not been born to. The Commissioner turned to Roget and spoke to him rapidly in what Hal recognized as Arabic. Hal did not speak that particular language himself, but he caught the word '*Es-sha'b*' which he identified by the Exotic cognate methods Walter the InTeacher had taught him, as meaning 'people' in Arabic.

Roget answered with equal rapidity in the same language, then broke back to Basic, looking at Hal.

'I go in and out of this hotel all the time,' he said. 'None of those with Rukh have left it since you came in; and the hotel staff is as loyal to her as anyone else.'

There was a casualness with which both of them seemed to dismiss the problem of necessary secrecy that disturbed Hal. No doubt what both had just said was true enough. Nonetheless, he had seen people beginning to congregate there at first light, outside the low white stone wall with its wide, low gates, that marked the limits of the hotel's grounds before its entrance.

Later, when their convoy of vehicles finally drove out through those same gates, the crowd assembled there was several hundred people in size, standing closely massed on both sides of the road. As the gates opened and the convoy of vehicles moved out, they waved – still silently, at the opaqued windows of the ambulance in the center of the convoy line. While their appearance was friendly, it was impossible that so many should have known to gather there unless there had been little or no attempt to keep word of the trip from them; and if Jarir's security was so lax in that respect, what did that promise for the other areas of possible danger they might encounter on their way to the Alexandria spacepad?

The waving hands were clearly directed at Rukh; but in fact, Rukh was not in the ambulance. She rode on the curved banquette seat of the rear compartment of one of the following police escort cars, seated between Hal and Roget, with Jason occupying the single facing seat. The transparent safety window between the rear and driving compartments was up and locked, additional and effective enough shield against any small arms fire short of that from power rifles or handguns – which were unlikely to be found outside the hands of the military or paramilitary here on Earth.

Through the window as the convoy left the hotel, Hal could see the countryside before them, framed between the backs of the heads of the police driver and Jarir. As they went through the gates, Jarir glanced back for a second at Rukh, and through the transparency, Hal saw the stony eyes go soft and dark. Only half a kilometer or so down the road the wayside was free of people watching and waving, and the convoy speeded up. Ahead, the roadstead was a wide strip of closely-growing dwarf grass, green as spring leaves between the low white siderails that warned off pedestrians. Hal could see even this short, thick grass flatten beneath the supporting air cushions of the vehicles as they picked up speed.

The green road ran in a long curve steadily toward the horizon, bordered on each side by open fields interspersed with the low transparent domes of hydroponic farms. Occasionally a few people were to be seen, standing waiting for the convoy to pass and waving as it did so.

'So much for security about Rukh's leaving the hotel,' commented Hal.

'I can sympathize with those who leaked the word, though,' said Jason. 'Particularly after those news broadcasts last night.'

'What news broadcasts?' Hal looked at him.

'You didn't – no, that's right, you went to bed early.' Jason's face lit up. 'You don't know, then!'

'That's right,' said Hal, 'I don't. Tell me.'

'Why,' Jason said, 'evidently it took about ten hours for news about the assassination attempt to sink in around the world. Then some groups in a few of the major cities – you know, it's just like back home, here. The people outside the cities are all on our side. It's in the cities that they don't care – but as I started to tell you, some of these groups who'd picketed Rukh's talks and spoken and written against her came up with the idea of celebrating the fact that someone'd tried to kill her. And that triggered off the landslide.'

'In what way?' demanded Hal.

636

'Why, it brought out all the people who'd heard her, and understood her, and had faith in her!' Jason's face was alight. 'More people than anyone'd imagined – more people than we'd believed or imagined. News services came out with large stories on her side. Government bodies started to debate resolutions to protect people like her from other assassination tries like that. Hal – you actually hadn't heard about this until now? Isn't it unbelievable?'

'Yes,' said Hal, numbly.

He felt like someone who had been preparing to move a mountain out of his way by sheer strength of muscle, only to have it slide aside under its own power before he could lay a finger on it. He had gambled, making the decision to move the Dorsai in and put up the shield-wall, hoping only that enough of Earth's population could be brought to listen – only listen – when Rukh spoke, so that she would have a reasonable chance of convincing them that what had been done had needed to be done.

Now, apparently, there was to be little problem in getting a majority of them to listen. He sat back on the banquette, his mind teeming with wonder and sudden understandings. No wonder Jarir, and even Roget, had seemed to dismiss so lightly his concern over keeping secret Rukh's drive to the Alexandria spacepad. Given the kind of attention that had erupted all over the world, it would have been foolish to imagine that all of those there, including the staff of the hotel, could be kept from letting out word of the trip to those closest to them. Also, those now lining each side of the roadstead were security themselves, of a not inconsiderable kind.

As they approached the coast the number of people on either side of their way, held back by the white barriers, became more and more numerous; until there was an unbroken double band of humanity ahead of them as far as the eye could see. When they began at last to come into the built-up areas surrounding the spacepad, so that storefronts and other structures enclosed the route, leaving only a narrow walkway between themselves and the barriers, that space was filled four and five bodies deep – all that the walkway would hold – with those waving as they passed.

But it was when finally they passed out from between the buildings, into the open space required by law in a broad belt outside the high-fenced perimeter of the spacepad itself, that the shock came. The tall structures had held them in shadow; so that they burst out at once into sunlight and into the midst of a gathering of people so large that it took the breath away.

Looking out across the heads of this multitude, Hal saw the brilliantly cloudless sky overhead dim fractionally and a gray sparkle seem to come into it.

'Jason,' he said. 'Take a look at the sky.'

Jason withdrew his staring eyes reluctantly from the crowd of faces on his side of the vehicle and glanced upward.

'What about it?' he asked. 'It's as clear and fine a day as you'd like – and nothing up there that looks dangerous. Besides, we're practically inside the perimeter, now.'

Rukh had been dozing quietly most of their trip. Like Morelly and others Hal remembered from the Command on Harmony, her faith led her to avoid medication if at all possible. She was no fanatic about it; but Hal had noticed that apparently the same kind of discomfort touched her that he had seen in people raised under strict dietary laws and who no longer lived by them but could not bring themselves to eat with any relish what had once been forbidden. So she had refused the mild sedative Roget would have given her for the trip; and the physician had not insisted. Her general exhaustion, he had told Hal, would keep her quiet enough.

But now, the sudden glare of the sunlight through the one-way windows of the vehicle on her closed eyelids, plus the excitement in Jason's voice, roused her. She opened her eyes, sat up to look up and saw the crowd.

'Oh!' she said.

'They're here to see you pass, Rukh!' said Jason, turning to her exultantly. 'All of them – here for you!'

She stared out the windows as the convoy slid along through the air, plainly absorbing what she saw and coming fully awake at the same time. After a moment she spoke again.

'They think I'm in the ambulance,' she said. 'We've got to stop. I've got to get out and show them I'm all right.'

'No!' said Roget and Hal together.

The doctor glanced swiftly at Hal.

'You promised to save your strength!' Roget said, almost savagely. 'That was your promise. You know, yourself, you can't step outside there without going right into full gear. Is that saving your strength?'

'Besides that,' said Hal. 'All it takes is one armed fanatic there, willing to die to get you first; or one armed idiot who hasn't thought beyond killing you if the chance comes; and the fact that all these other people'll tear someone like that to pieces afterwards won't bring you back to life.'

'Don't be foolish, Hal,' said Rukh. Her voice had strengthened. 'How would any assassin know we'd stop along here, when we didn't know we were going to do it, ourselves? And Roget, this is something I have to do – something I owe those people out there. I'll just get out, let them see me and get right back in. I can lean on Hal.'

She was already reaching forward to press the tab that signalled the front compartment of the vehicle. Jarir's head turned back and the window slid down between him and them.

'Jarir,' said Rukh. 'Stop the convoy. I'm going to get out just long enough for these people to see I'm all right.'

'It's not wise –' Jarir began.

'Wise or not, do what I tell you,' said Rukh. 'Jarir?'

The Commissioner shrugged. Once more the stony eyes had gone liquid and soft.

'*Es-sha'b*,' he said to the driver, whose inquiring face was turned toward him. He turned to the panel in front of him, touched a stud and spoke in Arabic.

The convoy slowed and stopped, the vehicles which composed it settling to the bright turf underneath them.

'Now,' said Rukh, to Hal. 'If you'll give me your arm, Hal. Open the door, Jason.'

Reluctantly, Jason unlocked and swung open the rear compartment door on Hal's side of the car. Hal stepped out, turned and reached back in to help Rukh emerge. She stepped out and down to the ground, leaning heavily on his arm.

'We'll step out between the cars where they can see me,' she said.

He led her in that direction. For the first three steps she bore most of her weight upon him; but as they left behind the vehicle they had been riding in and passed out into the thirty meters of space that separated it from the next car in line she straightened up, stretched her legs into a firmer stride, and after a pace or two let go of him entirely to walk forward by herself and stand straight, alone and a little in advance of him, facing the crowd on that side of the road-stead.

All along the route the people had waved at their passing in silence. At first this had felt strange to Hal, even though he realized those along the way must think that Rukh in the ambulance could not easily hear them if they did call out of her, and that in any case she should have to endure as little disturbance as possible. But he had grown accustomed to the lack of shouting as they went along and all but forgotten it, until this moment. But now, standing beside Rukh and looking out at those thousands of faces, the waving hands together with the quiet was eerie.

For a moment after they stopped and stood waiting, there was no change in those out at whom they looked. The eyes of everyone had been fastened on the ambulance; and few of them had even noticed the two figures that had come from one of the escort cars.

Then, slowly, the waving hands of those nearest Rukh and Hal began to hesitate, as the people became aware of them. Faces turned toward them; and gradually, like a ripple going over some wide and fluid surface, the attention of each one in the crowd was brought, one by one, to fasten upon them – and at last Rukh was recognized.

The hands had fallen now. It was a sea of faces only that looked at Rukh; and with that recognition, starting with those closest to her, the first sound was heard from the people as a whole. To the ears of Hal it was like a sigh, that like a wave washed out and out from them until it was lost in the farthest part of the gathering, then came rushing like a wave back in again, gathering strength and speed, rising to a roar, a thunder that shook the air around them.

Rukh stood facing them. She could not speak to them with the noise they were making. She could not even have spoken to them if they had stopped making it. The closest were twenty meters from her; and a few of them would have come equipped with repeaters to pick up her words and rebroadcast them to those further back. But she slowly raised both her arms, stretched at full length before her, until they were at shoulder level, and then slowly she spread them wide, as if blessing them all.

With the lifting of her arms, their voices began to die and by the time she had finished sweeping them wide, there was no sound at all to be heard from that vast gathering before her. In the new quiet, she turned about to face the other side of the roadstead; and repeated the gesture there, bringing these, too, into silence.

In that silence, she turned back toward the car and Hal moved quickly to catch her as she almost staggered once more, leaning heavily against him. He helped her back and half-lifted her into the vehicle, following close behind her.

With the closing of the door after them, and the starting up once more of the vehicles of the convoy, the voices broke out again; and that thunder beat steadily upon them, now, following them as they moved down the road past those who had not yet seen them up close, until they passed through the entrance in the high fence, past the unusually heavy perimeter guard of the spacepad in their trim blue uniforms and heavy power rifles, and went on into the relative emptiness of the pad, heading not for the terminal but for the shuttle itself, better than four kilometers distant across the endless gray surface of the pad.

Hal leaned forward and spoke to Jarir through the openness where the window between the compartments remained rolled down.

'You'll have to take my word for this,' he said. 'It's something I just noticed. A protective shield we've been planning to put around all of the Earth at low orbit level's just been set in place. The world is going to be hearing all about it in a few hours. But for now, if we don't get Rukh aboard that shuttle, and it off the ground in minutes, its pilots may find themselves ordered by the Atmosphere and Space authorities not to lift.'

Jarir's eyes met his from a distance of only inches away, and held for a long moment. They had gone back to being bright stones again.

'She will be aboard,' he said. 'And it will lift.'

CHAPTER SIXTY-FOUR

As Roget had predicted to them all in their pre-dawn session in the hotel, by the time the shuttle entered a bay at the Final Encyclopedia, Rukh was exhausted and sleeping heavily. Hal carried her off in his arms into the clanging noise and brightness of the bay and handed her over to two of the people from the Encyclopedia's medical clinic, who had brought a float stretcher. Almost beside him, the Number One pilot of the shuttle was close to shouting at the bay commander.

'I tell you I got word from the surface to turn around, to head back!' he was saying, 'and I talked them out of it! I was the one who told them if they let me go on, I could get some answers up here. We could see it plain as day, coming in at this altitude – like a gray wall above us, stretching everywhere, out of sight. If it isn't all around the world and it isn't the same thing you've got around the Encyclopedia, I'll eat it –'

'Pilot, I tell you,' said the bay commander, a small, black-haired woman in her thirties with a quiet, oriental face, 'everything's on emergency status here at the moment. If you want to wait, I'll try to get someone down from the Director's staff to talk to you. But I can't promise when anyone'll come –'

'That's not good enough!' The pilot's voice lifted. He was a large, heavy man and he loomed over the commander. 'I'm asking you for an answer in the name of the Space and Atmosphere Agency –'

Hal tapped the man on the shoulder, and the pilot pivoted swiftly, then stopped and stared upward as he found himself facing Hal's jacket collar tab.

'There'll be broadcasts from here explaining this to the whole world, shortly,' Hal said. 'There's nothing you can be told now that you and your superiors won't be hearing in a few hours, anyway.'

The pilot found his voice again.

'Who're you? One of the passengers, aren't you? That's no good. I want someone who knows what's going on, and I want whoever that is, now!' He swung back to the bay commander. 'I'm ordering you, if necessary, to get someone here in five minutes –'

'Pilot,' said the bay commander, wearily, 'let's be sensible. You've got no authority to order anyone here. Neither has Space and Atmosphere, or anyone else from below.'

Hal turned away, his leaving ignored by the pilot. With Jason close

641

behind, he headed toward Tam's suite, pushing his way gently through the turmoil and confusion he encountered along the way.

As he stepped through the door of the suite he found a broadcast of the sort he had promised the pilot already underway. The room was crowded. Not only were Amid and Nonne there, as well as the head of every department in the Encyclopedia except Jeamus, but there were at least half a dozen technicians, apparently concerned with the technical details of the broadcast.

It was Tam who was speaking. A desk float had been moved into position in front of his favorite non-float armchair and he looked across the unyielding gleam of the oak-colored surface as he spoke. Ajela stood to one side, behind him, just out of picture range. Her head turned to the door as Hal and Jason entered; and when she saw who it was she smiled at them. A smile, it seemed to Hal, of strong relief.

He went quietly to her along one wall of the room. It was neither a quick nor a steady journey. Everyone else in the room, it seemed, was utterly caught up in what Tam was saying in his deep and age-hoarsened voice. Hal would move a step or two, find his way blocked, and whisper in the ear of whoever was in the way. Whoever it was would turn, start, smile at him a little strangely, then move aside with a matching whisper of apology.

'. . . times without precedent sometimes require actions without precedent,' Tam was saying to the picture receptors – and the whole Earth beyond.

'. . . And because we have access here at the Encyclopedia to equipment that does not, to my knowledge, exist anywhere else, I've been forced to make an emergency decision on the basis of information which we'll shortly be making available to all of you; but on which I felt I had to act at once.

'In brief, that information is that Earth is in danger of being attacked without warning and finding itself stripped of its historic freedom as an independent and autonomous world. My decision was that an impregnable barrier should be placed in position without further delay around our Mother World to make sure this could not happen.

'Accordingly, I gave an order which has since been carried out by personnel of the Encyclopedia; that a phase shield-wall, similar to the one that's preserved the independence of this Encyclopedia itself for more than eighty years, be placed completely about our planet, to lock out any possibility of armed attack from other human worlds.

'This phase shield-wall, as it's now configured, has been structured with all the necessary irises – or openings to outer space – that may be needed by space shipping to enter or leave the territory of Earth's space and atmosphere. These irises can be closed at will; and they will be, at a moment's notice, in the case of any threat against us. Once they are closed, nothing in the universe can penetrate to us without our permission.

'Even fully closed, however, this phase shield-wall, which is an improved model of that which guards the Final Encyclopedia, has been designed to allow through it all necessary sunlight or any other solar radiation required for normal and customary existence. The physical condition of the space it occupies and the space it separates us from has been in no way altered by its existence.

'It's also within the capabilities of our crews generating this shield-wall to open irises at any other points that may be necessary, now or at any time in the future. Eventually they will do so in accordance with the desires of the general population of Earth.

'In short, nothing has been imposed upon, or taken away from the ordinary quality of life on our Earth by the establishment of this protective barrier. As you know this world of ours is a closed and self-sustaining system that requires only the solar energy which will continue to reach us in order to exist indefinitely as we know it.

'Additional details on both the shield-wall and the threat that caused me to order it constructed will be made available to you shortly. There is no intention here on the part of those of us who staff the Final Encyclopedia to set ourselves up in any way as a form of authority over Earth or its peoples. In any case, we lack the skills and numbers of personnel to do so, even if this community of scholars and researchers were so inclined. Simply, we have been required by circumstances to take a single, vitally necessary, specific action without having time to consult with the rest of you first.

'For that action, I take sole and individual responsibility. For taking it without consultation with you all, I apologize, repeating only that the necessity existed for doing so. I ask you all to wait until all the information that led us to generate it is also in your possession; and you are individually in a position to judge the emergency that led us to take this action.

'Having said that much, I have only one more thing to tell you. It's that this is my last official act as Director of the Encyclopedia. As I imagine most of you know, I have held this post far longer than I'd planned, while the search has gone on for a qualified successor. Now, I'm happy to say, one has finally been found – I should, more correctly, say the Encyclopedia itself has found one, since the man I speak of has passed a test by the Encyclopedia itself that only two other human beings in its history have passed – those two being myself and Mark Torre, the founder of this great tool and storehouse of human knowledge.

'The individual who now replaces me is a citizen of Old Earth, named Hal Mayne. Some of you have already heard of him. The rest of you will shortly, when he speaks to you from here in the next day or two.'

He stopped. His voice had been weakening steadily; and now it failed him. After a second he continued.

'Bless you, people of Earth. I think more than a few of you know me by reputation. I'm not given to compliments or praise unless there's no doubt it's been earned. But I tell you, as someone who's watched you for over a century and a quarter now, that as long as you remain what you've been no enemy can hope to conquer you, no threat can hope to intimidate you. I have been greatly privileged, through a long life, to guard this precious creation, this Encyclopedia, for you. Hal Mayne, who follows me as its guardian, will keep it as well and better than I have ever been able to . . .'

For a moment he stopped and occupied himself only with breathing. Then he went on, raggedly.

'To you all, goodbye.'

He sank back into his chair, closing his eyes, as the operating lights on the picture receptor went out. The room erupted with voices, all talking to each other around him and for a moment he was ignored, sitting shrunken and still in the big armchair.

Hal had reached Ajela's side, behind Tam's chair, some seconds back. At the sudden introduction of his own name into the speech he had looked down into Ajela's face and had been answered by something that could only be described as a hard grin.

'So,' he said, as the talk rose around them. 'You and Tam just went ahead and appointed me.'

'You've been doing what's necessary without asking, when there wasn't any time to ask,' she retorted. 'So now we've done the same thing. You knew Tam's finally gone as far as he can –'

A shadow of pain darkened her eyes for a second.

'You're drafted,' she said. 'That's all. Because there's no one else around for the job.'

He nodded slowly. It was true; moreover, he had been expecting Tam and Ajela to do some such thing as this. They knew as well as he did that he had to take on the title of Director of the Encyclopedia eventually; and that he would need it to give him a position from which to deal with the people of Earth in the future now upon them. Reflexively, he had left it to the two of them to push the job upon him, so that it would come to him only at the time when Tam was fully ready to let go. He had, he thought, been fully prepared for this moment.

But now that it had come, he felt a sudden chill to the mantle of authority that had just been draped about his shoulders. He tried to push the feeling away. He had always wanted to be a part of the Encyclopedia; and the work he had still to do required him to be here. But still, with Ajela's words, it was as if a shadow had fallen across his soul and he looked up to see tall walls closing about him. He felt an ominous premonition that he imagined as somehow being connected with Amanda.

'I won't have time to run it,' he said, as he had known he would say at this time to either Tam or Ajela.

'I know,' she answered, as he had known she would. 'I'll do that part of it, as I – as I'm used to doing.'

The door to the suite opened and Rourke di Facino came quickly in, followed by Jeamus. Hal, whose height allowed him to see over the heads of others in the room, caught sight of them immediately; and Ajela, following the sudden shift in direction of his gaze, turned and saw them also.

'Hal –' Rourke had caught sight of him. 'Jeamus' system is working and we've just got a picture of the first transports beginning to lift from the Dorsai –'

He had needed to speak across the room and over the sound of the crowd. His words reached everyone; and he was suddenly interrupted by a cheer. When it died, Rourke was still talking to Hal.

'. . . come and see for yourself?'

'Pipe it in here!' shouted a female voice; and the room broke out in a noise of agreement.

'No!' Ajela's clear voice rode up over the voices of them all. 'Everybody out, please. You can watch it in one of the dining rooms. Out, if you don't mind.'

'Hal –' it was Tam's voice, unexpectedly. 'Wait.'

Hal checked his first movement to leave and stepped around to face the chair. Ajela had already moved around on the other side of it. Behind them, the suite was clearing quickly. Tam reached out and Hal now felt his hand taken between the two dry knobby ones of the old man, the bones of which felt too large for the skin enclosing them.

'Hal!' said Tam. He seemed to struggle for words a moment, then let the effort go. '. . . Hal!'

'Thank you,' said Hal softly. 'Don't worry. I'll take good care of it.'

'I know you will,' said Tam. 'I know you will. . . .'

He let Hal's hand slide from between his own, which dropped back down on his knees. He sighed deeply, the burst of energy gone, sitting back in the chair with his eyelids sagging almost closed. Hal's eyes lifted and met those of Ajela. She moved her head slightly and he nodded. Quietly, he turned and went toward the door as she sank down on her knees beside Tam's chair.

As he went out, Hal looked back. Tam sat still, his eyes completely closed now. Still kneeling, she had put her arms around his waist and laid her head against his chest.

Hal closed the suite door and went off down the corridor outside. The second dining room he tried held everyone who had been in Tam's suite and a great many more of the people momentarily off duty in the Encyclopedia, all of them watching the one side of the room Jeamus had used as a stage for the projection equipment of his communications system.

Jason was standing just outside the entrance to the room, obviously waiting for him.

'Hal?' he said, as Hal came up to him. 'There's a lot to be done. . . .'

'I know,' said Hal. He closed one hand briefly about the nearer of Jason's lean shoulders. 'I'll only step in for a minute.'

He went past the other man through the doorway, and stepped aside from it to put his back to the wall and watch the projected scene over the heads of those between him and the stage area. The images projected were not perfect. A halo of rainbow colors encircled the pictured three-dimensional action, which it seemed was being recorded from some distance. The images went in and out of focus as the Encyclopedia's capacity to calculate strove to keep pinpointed the exact distance between it and the light-years-distant transmitter, continually correcting with small phase shifts, as a ship might have to do to hold a constant position in interstellar space, relative to any other single point. The sound was irregular also – one moment clear and the next blurred.

The scene showed the large pad at Omalu where Hal had last parted from Amanda. The pad was full of spaceships, now; most of them obviously Dorsai but a fair number identifiable as having been built to Exotic specifications. The ship in closest focus at the moment had a large group of people slowly boarding it; mostly young adults and children, but here and there an older face could be seen among them. The scene blurred in, blurred out of focus, the sound wavering; and Hal found himself caught by what he watched as if he had been nailed to the wall behind him.

'They're singing something, but I can't catch the words,' whispered the man just in front of him to the woman beside him. 'Clea, can you make out the words?'

The woman's head shook.

Hal stood listening. He could not make out the words either, but he did not have to. From the tune he was hearing he knew them, from his boyhood as Donal. It was the unofficial Dorsai anthem, unofficial because there was no official anthem, any more than there was an official Dorsai flag or the armies the anthem spoke of; the Dorsai they were singing about was not the Dorsai they were leaving, but the Dorsai each one of them was carrying within them. He turned and went back out the door to find Jason waiting for him.

'All right, now,' he said to the other man, as they went off down the corridor together. 'What's most urgent of the things you've got in hand?'

CHAPTER SIXTY-FIVE

'The things I had in mind can wait,' Jason said. 'I just got a call from Jeamus. He's been trying to locate you, quietly.'

'Jeamus?' Hal glanced toward the dining room where people were still watching the images from the Dorsai.

'Jeamus isn't there,' Jason said. 'It seems he got called back to Communications as soon as he stepped out of Tam Olyn's suite. He had a crew with him to set up the reception – he'd hoped to do it in the Director's suite, too – and he just left it to them to carry on the dining room with it. He went back down to Communications himself, and he's just called me from there.'

'He didn't say what about?'

'Just that he wanted you to come down there as quickly as possible, without telling anyone he'd called you.'

Hal nodded, and led off down the corridor in which they were standing with long strides.

Within the door of the Communications Department, Jeamus, his face tight, caught sight of them the minute they entered, and came to hurry them into the privacy of his own small, personal office.

'What is it?' asked Hal.

'A signal,' said Jeamus, 'from Bleys. It just came in, via orbit relay private for me. I don't have a written copy because he asked me not to make one. The call came in without identification, to me, by name. I didn't even know he knew I existed. He said you'd know the call was authentic if I referred to him as one of the two visitors you once had in your library; and he gave me a verbal message for you.'

Jeamus hesitated.

'You're Director now,' he said. 'It's only fair to tell you that fifteen minutes ago I'd have checked with Tam before passing this message along to you.'

'That's all right,' said Hal. 'I assume you thought there might be something in it that might affect the security of the Encyclopedia. Fine. I'll appreciate your having the same sense of responsibility toward me now that I'm Director. What's the message?'

Jeamus still hesitated. He looked at Jason.

'It's all right,' said Hal. 'Jason can stay.'

'Forgive me,' Jeamus said. 'Are you sure . . . I mean, this might affect more than the Encyclopedia. It might affect everything.'

'I know Bleys; better, I think, than anyone else.' Hal's eyes fastened on Jeamus' brown ones. 'Any secrecy he's concerned about is only going to matter with those who're uncommitted – to being either for or against him. Jason can stay. Tell me.'

'If you say so,' said Jeamus. He took a deep breath. 'He wants to meet you, secretly – here.'

'Here in the Encyclopedia?'

'No. Close to it,' Jeamus said.

'I see.' Hal looked about the small, neat office. 'Tell him yes. Have him signal you, personally, once he's here. Then you yourself see to it that an iris no bigger than necessary to let him, personally, in is dilated in the shield-wall close to here. I'll meet him inside the shield-wall.'

'All right,' said Jeamus.

'And of course you'll tell no one,' Hal said. 'Including Ajela. Including Tam.'

'I –' began Jeamus, and stuck.

'I know,' said Hal. 'The habits of years aren't easy to change in a minute. But I'm either Director or not; and you're either the head of my Communications Department or not. You expected me to go to Tam or Ajela as soon as you'd told me this, didn't you?'

'Yes,' said Jeamus, miserably.

'Tam's out of it now,' Hal said. 'And Ajela I'll tell myself, in my own time. If you're tempted to go to either one in spite of what I've just said to you, stop first and think who'll take the Encyclopedia over if I don't. Ajela can keep it going; but I think you've heard Tam say often enough it's meant for more than this.'

'Yes.' Jeamus sighed. 'All right, I won't say anything to either of them. But –' he looked suddenly up into Hal's face – 'you'll tell me when you've told Ajela?'

'Yes,' said Hal. He turned to Jason. 'Come on. Didn't you have a whole list with you of things you wanted me to attend to?'

Jason nodded.

'Thanks, Jeamus,' said Hal; and led Jason out of the Communications Section.

In the corridor outside, Jason stared at him as they walked.

'Can I ask?' he said. 'What does it mean, this business of Bleys wanting to talk to you secretly?'

'I think it means he discovered he'd made a misjudgment.' Hal answered. 'Now, weren't you the one who told me how much work we had to do?'

The work was real enough. It was nearly four days, local time at the Encyclopedia, before Rukh was strong enough to make her address to the world; and Hal chose to put off his own first speech as Director until it could also act as an introduction to what Rukh would say. Meanwhile, the days were frantic ones, with the Encyclopedia like a fortress under siege. A full third of the non-specialist staff was busy in shifts around the clock, fielding queries from the surface of Earth from governmental bodies or planetary agencies like Space and Atmosphere.

The primary difficulty for the staff was the keeping of tempers. From sheer habit the various governments and authorities below had begun by demanding attention and answers. Only slowly had they come to realize that not merely was there no way they could force or threaten the shield-walled, independently powered and fully supplied Encyclopedia to do anything, but there had not been for the last eighty years. So they had finally backed off the path of bluster to the highway of diplomacy; but by that time the damage to the frayed patience of the Encyclopedia's relatively tiny staff had been done.

'Who'd have thought it'd be like this?' Ajela said exhaustedly to Hal at mid-morning of that fourth day. Like everyone else, she had been operating on little food and less sleep since Tam's speech. 'Ninety per cent of this is unnecessary. If some of those people in control down there would only face reality – but I suppose there's no hope of that.'

'They actually are facing reality; and, in fact, it actually is necessary,' said Hal.

They were in Ajela's office suite, and Ajela had just been talking to the Director of the planet's Northwest Agricultural Sector, who had been only the latest of a large number of officials needing to be reassured that the interposition of the shield-wall between the particular area of his responsibilities and the sun would not somehow have an adverse effect on the ripening grain of that year's upcoming harvest. It was clear he had no idea what kind of adverse effect this could be, but rather, hoped Ajela could tell him of one.

She frowned at Hal; suddenly he was emphatically conscious of how exhausted she was. In anyone but a born Exotic that frown would have been an emotional explosion. He hurried to explain.

'A man like that one you just heard from,' Hal said, 'is struggling to make an adjustment to the concept of the Encyclopedia as not only a politically potent, but a superior entity. This is a situation that even a week ago was as far-fetched as it was inconceivable. But now we've become the main power center, up here. So it's necessary for each member of the power network below to make contact with us and make sure we know they, personally, are also on the political map.'

'But we haven't got the staff to play those kinds of games!' said Ajela. 'That isn't what's important, anyway. What's important is handling four million Dorsai as they get here and seeing to their resettlement; and even if that was all we were trying to do, we don't have staff enough for it, now that the ships have started arriving; even if we do have all that wealth from the Exotics and can use the Encyclopedia as if it was an automated bureaucracy!'

'All right,' said Hal. 'Then let's have a communications breakdown.'

She stared at him.

'I mean a breakdown as far as conversations with the surface is concerned,' Hal said.

Ajela was still staring. She was, Hal realized, more tired than he had thought.

'We can simply simulate an overload, or a power failure – Jeamus'll know what to do,' he said. 'Either respond to all calls from below as if our phones were tied up, or simply not answer at all with anything but static. We can have the difficulty clear up just as soon as I've made my speech and Rukh begins hers; and that leaves you free to fold up from now until I start talking. That ought to be good for at least four hours sleep for you.'

'Four hours,' she echoed, as if the words were sounds in some peculiar, unknown tongue. Then her gaze sharpened and she frowned at him again.

'And are you going to fold up too?'

'No,' he said. 'I don't need to. You've been running things, not me. All I am is ordinarily tired. In fact, it'll give me the chance I haven't had to work on my speech – which is my main concern.'

She swayed a little as she sat at her desk, puzzling over what he had said, instinctively feeling the deception in it; but too dulled by fatigue to pinpoint the lie.

'You really think . . .' she began at last – and ran down.

'I do,' he said. He rose and went to her; and over her protests literally lifted her from her float by her elbows. Setting her on her feet, he steered her into her adjoining personal suite and made her lie down on her bed. He sat down in a float beside her.

'What are you doing there?' she demanded, drunk with the exhaustion that was taking her over completely, now that she had let herself admit to it.

'Waiting to make sure you fall asleep.'

'Don't be ridiculous,' she said. 'I'm wound up like a spring. I'm not going to fall asleep just like that. . . .'

She stared at him fiercely for all of twenty seconds before her eyes fluttered, closed, and she slept. He set the temperature control above her bed and left.

He went directly to his own quarters, now enlarged into a suite to provide space for the kind of conferences his new obligations as Director required; and sat down to put in a call to Rukh, Nonne, Rourke, Amid and Jason.

'Conference in two hours,' he told them. 'Here.'

Having passed that message he went to the same bay into which he, Rukh and Jason had arrived less than a week before. The same bay commander was on duty.

'Chuni,' he said to her, 'I need a skidder to go visit the Dorsai transports parked in orbit.'

A shuttle was unloading; and a man in a pilot's uniform had just stepped out of the airlock among the passengers. She broke off to shout at him.

'No, you don't! Back in there! Passengers only. No crew allowed off the transport at this end!'

Her voice was considerable. He would not have thought it of her. She turned back, saw him watching her and looked, for a second, a little flustered.

'We've all changed, I guess,' she said. 'You want a driver?'

'No.'

'If you want to go up to the front of the bay, out of the passenger area, I'll have one unracked and brought up to you right away.'

Five minutes later Hal drove out of the Encyclopedia in his mosquito of a one-man craft and headed toward the parking area of the spaceships from the Dorsai. The gray orb of the Encyclopedia dwindled swiftly behind him at steady acceleration until his instruments warned him he was at midpoint from the nearest of the still-invisible ships. Then he flipped the power segment beneath his seat and rode in toward his destination on metered deceleration; as, with his viewscreen ranging ahead on normal telescopic setting, the first of the spacecraft which had just crossed twenty-three light-years of interstellar emptiness began to come into view.

These, lying ahead of him at protectively spaced intervals, were some of the largest vessels, troop transports of the Dorsai and luxury spaceships that had followed regular schedules between the stars under Exotic ownership. The hundreds of smaller craft that would also be making the trip would lift later from the outlying, smaller community centers like Foralie; and even from personal spacepads built by Dorsai families such as the Graemes who had mustered and trained soldiers on their own land for specific off-Dorsai contracts. But first had come the big ships, loading up from the few cities and larger population centers.

They were fully visible now on his screen in a scan that compensated for the distance they covered, their parked ranks stretching away from him in a long curve that was part the illusion of distance and space, part actuality. They lay in sunlight translated through the screen, next to the great, apparently vertical wall of it on his right, that stretched upwards and downwards from his viewpoint until all view of it was lost in the blackness of space.

To his left, also in bright sunlight, floated the white-swatched blue orb of the Earth, looking close enough in the compensated view of the screen so that he could reach out at arm's length and touch it.

Unimportant in the space that went also between them, and seeming only to crawl along, his tiny skidder crept up on the nearest of the huge vessels. Far ahead, and far behind, where the gray of the shield-wall seemed to vanish, the blackness of space showed the lights of stars, which from that angle and distance were perceptible through it.

A stillness took him. He felt the presence of the universe that dwarfed not only men and women but ships, planets and stars – even galaxies that were no more than scatterings of dust across its inconceivable face. The universe that knew nothing and cared less for the microscopic organism called the human race, that in its many parts tried so hard for survival. It was all around him, and its remoteness and vastness confirmed the isolation of his own spirit. Not on Earth, nor in sky nor space, he floated apart, even from his own kind. A crushing loneliness closed around him; but the call of what he had seen, what Donal had seen, gazing out at the unknown stars in that moment when Padma had at last had a chance and failed to recognize him for what he was, drew him on. With the failure of Padma he had set aside all hope of being touched again by human understanding as one touched one in the race of his birth; and he had left it set aside through two lives since . . . until this one. Until now. . . .

He had come close enough finally to the first of the parked ships – a wide-bodied transport – to hit its metal skin with a spot communicator beam of light.

'Sea of Summer!', he said into his phone grille. 'Sea of Summer, this is Hal Mayne of the Final Encyclopedia, en route from the Encyclopedia by skidder to the Olof's Own. I'm transmitting my personal image for identification. Repeat, this is Hal Mayne. Can you direct me to Olof's Own? I ask, can you direct me –'

His screen lit up suddenly with a lean-faced young man wearing a ship's officer's jacket, who seemed to peer at him through the screen.

'Hal Mayne?' he said. He glanced briefly off-screen then back at Hal. 'I'm third officer, duty shift. Mika Moyne. Want to identify yourself by telling me where you last outvisited on the Dorsai?'

'Foralie Town, Mika Moyne,' said Hal. 'Honored.'

'The honor's mine.' The lean face grinned. 'Hal Mayne, the Olof's Own was the next to the last arrival last time I checked. We're going through Fleet Locator now . . . all right, she's now in Station 103 – not far down the line at all.'

'Thank you, Mika Moyne.'

'My pleasure, Hal Mayne.'

He signed off and went on. Fourteen hundred kilometers down the line, he found the Olof's Own, identified himself and was invited aboard.

'I understand one of your passengers is Miriam Songhai,' he said, when he was inside. 'I'd to talk to her for a moment if she wouldn't mind.'

'We'll find her and ask,' said the *Olof's Own* captain. 'Do you want to wait in the Officers' Duty Lounge? It shouldn't take more than a few minutes to find her for you.'

He took Hal into the Duty Lounge. Less than ten minutes later, Miriam Songhai pushed open the door of the lounge and stepped in. Hal and the captain stood up from the floats on which they had been seated.

'Excuse me,' said the captain. 'I've got to get back to the control area.'

He left them in the empty lounge.

'It's good of you to see me,' said Hal. 'Honored.'

'Nonsense,' said Miriam Songhai. 'I was only twiddling my thumbs, anyway, and I'm the one who's honored. What did you want to see me about?'

She sat down and Hal reseated himself.

'I've been watching for Amanda Morgan to turn up,' he said. 'So far I haven't found anyone who knows when she'll be coming. I've talked to a few of the Foralie area people, but they say she's been spending all her time in Omalu these last weeks – which makes sense. She mentioned once that you, too, had duties that put you in Omalu, a lot. So I thought I'd ask you if you knew anything.'

Miriam shook her head.

'I haven't seen her for a couple of weeks, at least,' she said,' and then only to talk business about ways and means of getting official records packed and shipped. I've no idea when she was leaving. But the responsibilities of most of us in Omalu are over, now that the ships are actually lifting. She ought to be along any time now.'

'I hope so,' said Hal, and smiled.

He stood up. She stood up, also.

'Well, thank you,' he said. 'It was a long shot – but I appreciate being able to ask you.'

'Nonsense, again,' she said. 'I'm just sorry I didn't have anything definite to tell you. But, as I say, she'll be along.'

They went to the door of the lounge together. As it slid back automatically for them both, they stepped through; and just outside, she stopped – and checked him also with a hand that closed on his arm. He felt a strange shock go through him at her touch, as if a powerful electricity charged her. Her blunt, dark fingers held his arm strongly.

'Don't worry,' Miriam Songhai said, firmly. Her gaze was direct and unyielding. 'She'll be all right.'

'Thank you,' he said.

She released him; and he watched her go off down the corridor toward the aft section of the ship. He turned back into the control area and was greeted by the captain.

'Had your talk?' said the captain. 'Anything else we can do for you, Hal Mayne?'

'No. Thanks very much,' said Hal. 'I'd better be starting back for the Encyclopedia.'

Once more in the little skidder, he increased his acceleration to shorten the trip back. But when he finally reentered his suite, it was almost time for the conference he had called – and Ajela was waiting for him there in one of the non-float chairs, which, like Tam, she favored.

'That's interesting,' he said, closing the door behind him. 'Can you let yourself into anyone's living quarters whether they're home or not?'

'I can to yours,' she said. 'Because you're the Director; and I'm Special Assistant to the Director; and in case of emergency I have to have access to any place the Director might be.'

She stared at him.

'– And as a matter fact, yes,' she went on, 'I could let myself into the quarters of anyone here at the Encyclopedia, only I wouldn't.'

'Only into the Director's quarters?'

'That's right.'

He sat down opposite her and looked at her critically.

'How much sleep did you get?'

'An hour – an hour and a half. Never mind that,' she said. 'What's this conference you'd have had me miss out on?'

He shook his head at her.

'The most important topic for discussion,' he said, 'is undoubtedly going to be an announcement that I'll be insisting on being a free agent; so I can do my own work in my own carrel, here. The rest of them are going to have to run matters without my looking over their shoulders. But this is something you already know about. The others are going to find it something of a shock, I think.'

'That – and what else.'

'That and a few other things. The most important of those is that Bleys is coming secretly to have a talk with me.'

She sat up suddenly in the arm chair.

'What about?'

'I'll find out when he gets here.'

The door annunciator spoke with the voice of Rourke di Facino.

'Hal, I'm here.'

'Open,' said Hal to the door; and Rourke walked in to take a seat with them.

'Nonne's on her way. So is Jason,' Rourke said. 'I haven't seen Amid.'

He looked penetratingly at Ajela.

'You need rest,' he said.

'Later,' she answered.

'Then close your eyes and lean back until the rest get here,' said Rourke. 'You won't think it's helping, but it will.'

She opened her mouth to answer him, then smiled a little and did as he had just suggested. Almost immediately, her breathing slowed and deepened.

Hal and Rourke looked at each other and said nothing by mutual consent. Hal got up, walked to the door and set it wide open. As the others he had called in appeared at it, one by one, he held his fingers to his lips and beckoned them in. Finally, however, they were all there – including Amid; and it was not possible to put off conversation any longer.

'We've just got time,' said Hal, 'to go over a few things before I go on general broadcast to the Earth to announce I've taken over as Director up here and introduce Rukh.'

He looked across the seated circle of their gathering at Rukh, who returned his gaze calmly. The few days of rest for her here at the Encyclopedia had been absolute, simply because there was no means by which news that might disturb or rouse her could reach her without the active cooperation of the Encyclopedia's Communications Center, which Hal had refused to allow. Roget had all but danced in the corridors at the results that now showed. She was still as thin and fragile in appearance as she had been when Hal had seen her down at the hotel beside Lake Qattara. But the look of transparency had vanished from her. She was fully alive once more; and the aura of personal strength that had always been part of her was back.

He paused to look over at Ajela; but she had not woken at the sound of his voice. She continued to slumber, half-curled up with her head tucked into the angle between one of the wings and the back of the chair.

'I want to make sure you all understand fully what that appointment is going to mean, both for me and for the rest of you,' Hal went on. 'To begin with, I take it I don't have to explain why there's no question of my refusing it? There's no one else; and Tam isn't up to continuing other than under ordinary conditions. If Ajela was awake, she'd tell you that Tam first spoke to me about taking over here eventually some years ago; and both of us knew it had to happen eventually.'

He looked around at them for possible comment. No one said anything, although Nonne's face was absolutely expressionless.

'Why you, especially, Hal?' asked Rukh.

'I'm sorry,' he answered. 'With all else that's been going on, I took it for granted Ajela or someone else might have told you. They didn't? But they did take you all past the Transit Point as you came in here the first time?'

All other heads, except Ajela's, shook.

'I didn't know that,' Hal said. 'There's a spot in the Encyclopedia at its centerpoint. I invite you all to ask one of the staff to show you where it is and go and stand there for a second. If you hear any voices speaking, get in touch with me at once; because it means you've also got one of the qualifications that's needed in whoever takes over the Encyclopedia. In all the years since it became operative, everyone who's come here's been led past that centerpoint; and I apologize for the system breaking down now. You all should have been tested as a matter of routine. In nearly a century only Mark Torre, Tam Olyn and myself have heard voices at that spot.'

'You heard voices' said Nonne. 'When, if you don't mind my asking?'

'The first time I came here, when I was not quite seventeen years old,' said Hal.

'And not since?'

'Yes.' Hal smiled at her. 'I went back and stood there for a moment, as soon as I could get off by myself after Tam announced I'd be succeeding him.'

'And the voices were still there?'

'Still there,' said Hal.

Nonne's expressionlessness of face did not change.

'And this is supposed to mean . . . what?'

'That the Encyclopedia was meant to be something more than a supremely effective library and research mechanism,' he answered. 'Mark Torre, who planned and built it, had a conception of something greater; a tool for the innate improvement of mankind. He built the Encyclopedia on the faith of that idea and nothing more; but the faith was justified when Tam also heard the voices. Until then Mark Torre had kept quiet about his reasons for running everyone who came through the centerpoint. After that he spoke up. It was the one proof that came in his lifetime, that there was a greater purpose and use for the Encyclopedia than anyone else had believed; a purpose and use we can't see clearly even yet, but that send out signals of its possibilities in something more than ordinary physical terms.'

'And you'd like to be the one who puts it to that greater purpose? Nonne asked.

'Nonne,' said Rukh. 'It strikes me at this point that Ajela'd have a question for you. Since she's still sleeping, I'll ask it for her. Amid –'

She glanced across at the older Exotic.

'You told me Nonne'd been one of those Exotics who'd originally been against Hal being trusted and backed by your people. From what I've been told by Ajela, so far, and from what I've seen in the short time I've known you, Nonne, you seem to have gone from having reservations about everything thing Hal's done to an outright antagonism toward him. Maybe it's time you tell the rest of us why.'

Nonne's expressionlessness vanished. A little color tinted the smooth skin over her cheekbones.

656

'I didn't approve of Hal being given a blank check by my people, no,' she said. 'Amid was the one who did, as you say. As a result, it was decided by the rest of us studying the matter that since Amid was in the best position to act as liaison for us with Hal, he ought to be counterbalanced by someone who had an opposite point of view to his. You might call him the supportive angel and me the critical one –'

'That'd be the Exotic way,' said Rourke, dryly.

Nonne turned on him.

'Actually, I find those not from Mara or Kultis often seem to tend to consider me rather untypical as an Exotic,' she said. 'However, that's a mistake on their part. My point of view represents one rather more common among our people than most of you realize. It's just one non-Exotics don't often see.'

'You haven't explained this antagonism of yours,' said Rukh, 'only confirmed it.'

'Very well,' said Nonne. She looked back to Hal. 'I'd have expected Hal to ask me about this, rather than one of you. But it doesn't matter. I'm not convinced you know what you're doing, Hal. You said essentially, the last time I questioned you about something, that you and Bleys were like master chess players, too skilled to make the wrong move, and only liable to the danger of making the right move either too early or too late.'

'That's what I said.' Hal nodded.

'Then I have to say I've seen no evidence of that level of competence, on your side at least, Hal. All I've seen is the Dorsai uprooted and brought *en masse* to fight for a world that doesn't even know they're coming; my own people –'

There was a momentary, almost unnoticeable catch in her voice.

'– stripped of everything they ever earned and accomplished and then abandoned, Earth turned into a walled fortress without being asked for its permission, and its people expected to commit themselves to a possibly endless war with an enemy that has all the strength, all the wealth, all the material and all the advantage – when only a minority of those Earth people ever showed any understanding of the situation with the enemy, or a will to fight him in the first place –'

'You forget,' Jason broke in, 'how they've been educated, and their opinion changed, since Rukh and our other truth-speakers started telling their own personal stories of how it's been for us all on Harmony and Association. You forget how they've reacted down there, these last few days since news of her nearly being assassinated got out. I hear from our speakers daily. They're all being overwhelmed now with people who want to hear more of what they have to say. We've got a majority of opinion down below in favor of Hal's actions, now, not a minority!'

'Hardly in favor of Hal's actions,' said Nonne. 'They don't know about his actions. Emotionally, for Rukh and your people and mine, certainly – but that's a fire that can go out as quickly as it's been lit, the minute they find out their own lives and their own world have been thrown into the table stakes. Meanwhile, with all the population and resources of nine other worlds, Bleys goes on growing stronger daily; and I come to this suite now, only to hear Hal tell us he's seriously planning to split his energies even further by adding the Encyclopedia to his responsibilities.'

She looked at Hal.

'Besides,' she said, 'it was none of the rest of you I've been waiting to hear some answers from. It's from Hal. Tell me, then, Hal. How do you justify adding something like the Encyclopedia to everything else you're supposed to be taking care of?'

'That's a question at a good time,' said Hal, 'because one of the things I was about to tell you was that my work with the Encyclopedia here is going to have to take priority over anything else, in the days and years to come. In other words, the defense of Earth is now set up. I'm going to be leaving it to the rest of you to handle.'

Nonne stared at him.

'This is insane!' she said, finally.

'No,' said Hal. He found himself feeling suddenly weary. 'It's what's necessary. This battle between the Others and ourselves isn't going to be won with weapons at a shield-wall, or even on the face of any of the inhabited worlds. The only place it's ever going to be won is in the hearts and minds of men and women, on all the worlds; and the only source of the means to win that non-physical war lies here, in the potential of the Final Encyclopedia. This is where the meaningful battle is going to be fought, and won or lost; and this is where I'm going to have to do my real work.'

Nonne still stared at him.

'Think,' he said to her. 'What else, or what thing different, could have been done to give us any chance at all before the inevitable growth of the Others to an overwhelming power that could threaten to make us prisoners of their philosophy? The only hope we ever had to resist them, and the worlds they owned, was for this planet and the other ones we still owned to combine their forces at one strongpoint. Because, unlike us, the only way the Others can win is to win utterly. And I explained to you once, I think, that the numbers of Earth's population and its existing physical resources made it the only reasonable choice for a citadel world, a world to garrison against the force that's going to be brought against us. How could we have asked in advance for Earth's permission to do this, making the possibility a matter of public debate for years, at least, without giving Bleys and his people the opportunity to move in while discussion was going on, and defeat us within at the same time as they were marshalling to take us over from without? As it was, Bleys saw the move we've just made, but moved to defend against it too late – the fault I explained to you earlier, Nonne. And so, we've stolen a march on him.'

She opened her mouth as if to reply, but he went on without stopping.

'So tell me,' he said, 'given those imperatives, how could anything else have been done? Simply, from the beginning we've all been called upon to give whatever we had to give. The Dorsai, their strength; you Exotics, your wealth and information; Earth, its resources of people and material; and the Friendlies, their unyielding faith in an ultimate victory to hold all the rest of us together. Called upon that way, what could we have done differently? Give me the alternatives.'

He paused again. But she had closed her mouth again and now sat silent.

'Your argument,' he went on after a moment, more gently, 'isn't with me, Nonne. It's with the forces of history – the movements of people that cause further movements; and so on, and on, until we finally have a situation like this that can only be dealt with in a single way. The choices have all now been either raised up and answered, or ignored. This is a final confrontation in the terms of our present moment; but every generation in its own time has had an equivalent confrontation, in its own terms. People have followed me in this, not because of what I say, or who I am, but because this is the only way things seem to have a chance of working out. There's no other path visible. Can you see one? If so, tell me what it is.'

He stopped speaking.

She sat for a moment longer; and then when it became clear that he was not going to go on without an answer, she closed her eyes for a minute and sat blindly, tense and upright, in her chair for a long moment. Then she opened her eyes.

'You're right,' she said. Her voice was brittle. 'I've got no alternatives to offer. Go on, then – there's nothing more I can say, at this time.'

'Thank you,' said Hal in the following silence. He looked back around the gathering. 'All right, we've already used most of our time before I'm to say my piece and introduce Rukh. I take it you understand the process by which the Dorsai are to be resettled here on Earth, with the help of the financial resources of the Encyclopedia and what we've been given by the Exotics? If not – if want details – will you ask Rourke for them?'

He looked over at Rourke, who nodded at them all.

'We've no intention of announcing ourselves as coming here to be a defense force of Earth,' Rourke said. 'Our activity in that regard is only the subject of a private contract between our people and the Final Encyclopedia. We'll only fight for Earth if asked by the people of Earth, themselves; and with the Final Encyclopedia's permission, of course, which we take it won't be refused. So we'll wait until Earth asks us for help – if indeed that's what they want. All Rukh is going to say about us in her speech now – and she'll be the one to explain to Earth why we're here – is that we're refugees from the expansionism of the Others; and that the Exotics sacrificed all they owned to make sure we'd be refugees who'd be able to pay their own way and not be a burden on Earth –'

He broke off. The door annunciator had chimed.

'Forgive me, Hal,' said the voice of Jeamus. 'I've got some urgent messages for you.'

'Bring them in,' said Hal. 'Go on, Rourke.'

'That's all, actually,' answered Rourke.

Hal turned back to the others.

'As I think I've said, I'm going to give the barest minimum of speeches,' he said. Jeamus had entered and was circling the room to come up quietly at his shoulder. 'I'll simply confirm the fact that Tam has given me a chance to take over the Directorship from him and I've agreed – thank you, Jeamus –'

Jeamus had slipped him a sealed envelope and a folded sheet of the single-molecule material used for hard copies in the Encyclopedia.

'The envelope's personal to you, brought by hand from the Dorsai,' Jeamus whispered in his ear. 'It's from an Amanda Morgan. The message is a picture-copy of a public letter Bleys had published on New Earth less than a standard day ago. It's even got his name signed to it. The Exotic Embassy on New Earth got hold of and sent it here by the new communication system. They also messaged they think that same letter's also being issued on those other worlds the Others control.'

'Thanks,' said Hal.

He slipped the letter from Amanda into his jacket's inner pocket and opened the folded sheet on his knee to read the message.

'Sorry again to bother you all,' said Jeamus; and slipped out.

CHAPTER SIXTY-SIX

As the door closed behind Jeamus, Hal was glancing over the sheet on his knee.

'I'll read this to all of you,' he said. 'It's a dispatch from an Exotic Embassy, which is still functioning in the city of Cathay on New Earth. Jeamus just got it over the new phase communications system. It's a copy of a letter to the New Earth people published by Bleys, and, the embassy thinks, to the peoples of the other worlds under Other control.

' "To all who believe in the future for ourselves and our children:

' "I have been reluctant to speak out, since it has always been my firm belief that those like myself exist only to answer questions – once they have been asked, and if they are asked.

' "However, I have just now received information from people fleeing Old Earth which alarms me. It speaks, I think, of a danger to all those of good intent; and particularly to such of us on the new worlds. For some hundreds of years now, the power-center world of the Dorsai, with their lust for warlike aggression, the Exotics, with their avarice and cunning, and those the Friendly people have so aptly named the Forgotten of God – these, among the otherwise great people of the fourteen worlds, have striven to control and plunder the peaceful and law-abiding cultures among us.

' "For some hundreds of years we have been aware that a loose conspiracy existed among these three groups; who have ended by arrogating the title of Splinter Cultures almost exclusively to themselves, when by rights it applies equally, as we all know, to hundreds of useful, productive, and unpredatory communities among the human race. We among you who have striven quietly to turn our talents to the good of all, we whom some call the Others but whom those of us who qualify for that name think of only as an association of like minds, thrown together by a common use of talents, have been particularly aware of this conspiracy over the past three hundred years. But we have not seen it as a threat to the race as a whole until this moment.

' "Now, however, we have learned of an unholy alliance, which threatens each one of us with eventual and literal slavery under the domination of that institution orbiting Earth under the name of the Final Encyclopedia. I and my friends have long known that the Final

Encyclopedia was conceived for only one purpose, to which it has been devoted ever since its inception. That purpose has been the development of unimaginable and unnatural means of controlling the hearts and minds of normal people. In fact, its construction was initially financed by the Exotics for that purpose; as those who care to investigate the writings of Mark Torre, its first Director, will find.

' *"That aim, pursued in secrecy and isolation which required even that the Encyclopedia be placed in orbit above the surface of Earth, has been furthered by the Encyclopedia's practice of picking the brains of the best minds in each generation; by inviting them, ostensibly as visiting scholars, to visit that institution.*

' *"Also, it has continued to be financed by the Exotics, who, records will show, have also had a hand in financing the Dorsai, who were from the first developed with the aim of becoming a military arm that could be used to police all other, subject worlds.*

' *"That unholy work, over the last three hundred years, has now borne fruit. The Encyclopedia and its backers – including the people of Old Earth themselves, whose early, bloody attempts to keep all the newly settled worlds subject to them – were only frustrated by the courageous resistance of the peoples on all those worlds, after a hundred years of unending fighting; as you all know from the history books you studied as children.*

' *"Now the people of Old Earth, under the leadership of the Final Encyclopedia, have finally thrown off all pretense of innocent purpose. They have withdrawn the unbelievable wealth accumulated by the Exotic Worlds by trade and intrigue from such people as ourselves, moving it to their treasury on Earth. They have also, openly, in one mass movement, evacuated the Dorsai from their world and brought them to Earth; to begin building the army that is intended to conquer our new worlds, one by one, and leave us enslaved forever under the steel rule of martial authority. And they have begun to ready for action those awesome weapons the Encyclopedia itself has been developing over three centuries.*

' *"They are ready to attack us – we who have been so completely without suspicion of their arrogant intentions. We stand now, essentially unarmed, unprepared, facing the imminent threat of an inhuman and immoral attempt to enslave or destroy us. We will now begin to hear thrown at us, in grim earnest, the saying that has been quietly circulated among the worlds for centuries, in order to destroy our will to resist – the phrase that not even the massed armies of all the rest of mankind can defeat the Dorsai, if the Dorsai chose to confront those armies.*

' *"But do not believe this –"* '

Rourke snorted.

'He can say that again, right here and now,' he said in an undertone, unfortunately a little too loudly not to interrupt Hal's reading, 'and keep on repeating it until it penetrates a few thick skulls down on Old Earth!'

His eye caught Hal's.

'Sorry. It's just that we're all braced to hear a loud group down there, saying, "but what do we need to do anything for? We've got the Dorsai; and they like to fight." '

He coughed.

'Sorry, again. Go on, Hal.'

' "... *Do not believe this,*" ' Hal continued, ' "*It was never true, only a statement circulated by the Exotics and the Dorsai for their own advantage. As for massed armies, as you all know, we have none –*" '

'Not true,' commented Amid. 'Sorry. My turn to apologize, Hal. Go on.'

' "... *we have none. But we can raise them. We can raise armies in numbers and strengths never dreamed of by the population of Old Earth. We are not the impoverished, young peoples that Old Earth, with Dow deCastries, tried to dominate unsuccessfully in the first century of our colonization. Now, on nine worlds our united numbers add up to nearly five billion. What can be done against the courage and resistance of such a people, even by the four million trained and battle-hardened warriors that Old Earth has just imported from the Dorsai –*" '

Rourke snorted again, as the number was mentioned, but this time contained himself and said nothing.

' "... *United, we of the nine worlds are invincible. We will arm, we will go to meet our enemy – and this time, with the help of God, we will crush this decadent, proud planet that has threatened us too long; and, to the extent it is necessary, we will so deal with the people of Old Earth as to make sure that such an attempt by them never again occurs to threaten our lives, our homes, and the lives and homes of those who come after us.*

' "*In this effort, I and my friends stand ready to do anything that will help. It has always been our nature never to seek the limelight; but in the shadow of this emergency I have personally asked all whom you call the Others, and they have agreed with me, to make themselves known to you, to make themselves available for any work or duty in which they can be useful in turning back this inconceivable threat.*

' "*The unholy peoples of Old Earth say they will come against us. Let them come, then, if they are that foolish. Let us lay this demon once and for all. How little they suspect it will be the beginning of the end. for them!*

' "... *Signed, Bleys Ahrens.*' No title, just the signature.'

Hal handed the message over to Rukh, who was closest to him. She scanned it and passed it on around the circle of listeners.

'That business of four million battle-ready veterans!' Rourke said. 'I tell you, I can see trouble coming from Earth about that. We'll have hell's own job to make them understand that we brought in families – families! If there's six hundred thousand battle-age and combat-fit adults among them, we're lucky; and at least two-thirds of those are going to have to be sleeping and eating, not to mention out, sick or disabled, at any given time. Not to mention where the replacements are going to come from when we start taking losses.

And they expect us to guard a perimeter considerably larger in area than the planet Earth, itself? Wait'll they discover they're going to end by putting more of their own people than our whole population into the firing line to defend an area that size.'

'That's something the future'll have to take care of,' said Hal. 'Once they realize what's needed to survive, there'll be those who'll be ready to help. But my hope is that we can find another way to win, here in the Encyclopedia, itself, than by trying to match, one for one, the literally millions of soldiers he'll need to, and can, raise in order, to put any iris we open in the shield-wall instantly under an attack that won't be halted until we close it again. But never mind that, too, for now. If you've all had a look at that message sheet –'

They had. Even Nonne had studied it.

'So there's another instance of what you meant by Bleys possibly making the mistake of moving too soon or too late!' burst out Jason. 'He waited too long to come out with this letter, didn't he? If he'd brought if out even a month ago – certainly if he'd come out with the same sort of talk about a coalition against us, even if he hadn't been able to cite the Dorsai moving to Earth – he could have sowed a lot of doubt down below and panicked a lot more of Earth's people into taking hard positions, that could have shut out the Dorsai before they could get here –'

He broke off. His eyes were bright on Hal.

'And that's why you were working so hard to set up the idea that the Dorsai were going to move to one of the Exotic Worlds!'

'It's true,' said Rukh, 'that this letter's going to be all it takes to solidify public opinion on Old Earth against the Others. It's what was really needed to make them realize down there what the Others are after. We probably could have managed without it; but now that it's here, it couldn't have come at a better time. Hal, I think I ought to read it as part of my speech.'

'Yes,' said Hal.

'He must have jumped the gun when he heard we were coming in here –' Rourke broke off, thoughtfully. 'No, he wouldn't have had time to have found that out and still get this published so that we'd have a copy, now.'

'Yes, he would,' said Amid. 'One way on Mara and Kultis we used to get information between the worlds in a hurry, faster than anyone thought it could be done, was to set up a chain of spaceships holding position between any two worlds at an easy single phase shift apart. When there was a message to be sent, a ship would lift off one world with it, make one jump to rendezvous with the first ship in line, and pass the message on to it. The second ship'd make one jump and pass it on to a third jump – and so on. There'd be little search-to-contact time in the target area of each jump, since each one was so short; and the necessary calculation would already have been made by the ship

664

ready to go; and because each pilot made only one jump, there'd be no problem with the psychic effects of enduring too many phase shifts close together. The only requirement of the system was that you needed to be able to afford to tie up a lot of ships, standing idle in your message line and waiting. We could, then. Bleys can afford it, now.'

'Hmm,' said Rourke.'

'Yes,' and Amid, looking at him, 'I understand Donal Graeme also came up with the same system, independently, in his later years after he had the ships to do it. At any rate, if Bleys had been keeping a watch like that on all worlds potentially hostile to him, he could've known within twenty-four hours, standard, when the first of the Dorsai transports lifted; and in the same amount of time when the first of them began to appear above Earth. And he'd have already known that none were appearing above Mara or Kultis.'

'So he panicked and moved too soon,' Jason said. 'I thought that letter didn't sound like him.'

'I wouldn't call it panic, with someone like Bleys,' Hal said. 'His plan would have been to beat the news of the Dorsai moving to Old Earth with his own announcement. He'll have gained that – it's just that he's lost in another area – and if he'd decided Old Earth was lost for now, in any case, he may have simply written off the effect his letter would have there – though he couldn't have expected Old Earth's people to read it so soon.'

He paused.

'As for sounding like him,' Hal went on, 'there are sides to him that none of the worlds have seen, yet.'

He had captured their attention. He went on.

'I've got one more thing to tell you,' he said. 'Bleys has also sent a message asking me to meet him secretly; and I told him I'd do it – inside the shield-wall. I've been interested in why he'd want to talk just now. This –'

He pointed toward the message sheet, which now lay on a table beside Rourke's chair.

'– tells me what he's after. He'll need to sound out the effect of the successful move of the Dorsai to Earth on my thinking. As soon as Jeamus lets me me know he's here, I'll be going to meet him; and that could be at any time now.'

'But if he had to get the message, then leave from New Earth –' Rourke interrupted himself and sat musing.

'He may not have been on New Earth,' said Amid. 'Even if he was, with Sirius at under nine light-years of distance from here, he could make the trip by crowding on the phase shifts and using the old crutch of drugs, in two standard days.'

'How would he know we knew about it yet?' demanded Rukh.

'I don't think there's much doubt he knows we have some newer, faster means of communicating,' said Amid. 'He just doesn't know how we do it, yet.'

'It's almost time for us to talk,' Rukh interrupted. 'Hal, have you got your speech ready?'

'I don't have it written out, but I know what I want to say,' Hal answered, as the others began to move their chairs and floats back out of picture range. He pressed a stud on the arm of his chair.

'Jeamus,' he said. 'Any time the transmission crew's ready, we'll get going on those speeches.'

'We've been waiting outside in the corridor,' Jeamus' voice answered from the door annunciator. 'We'll come in now, then?'

'Come ahead,' said Hal.

The technical crew entered.

'Are you going to wake up Ajela?' Rukh asked Hal. 'If she's going to introduce you in a minute or two, she'll need a few seconds to come to.'

'I suppose so,' said Hal, reluctantly.

He got up, went over to Ajela and stroked her forehead. She slumbered on. He shook her shoulder gently. For a moment it seemed she would not respond even to that; but then her eyes opened suddenly and brightly.

'I haven't been sleeping,' she said.

Her eyelids fluttered closed and she went back to breathing deeply.

'Jeamus can introduce me,' said Hal. He picked up Ajela, carried her into one of the two bedrooms of his suite and laid her on the bed. She woke as he put her down.

'I'm not sleeping, I tell you!' she said crossly.

'Good,' said Hal. 'Just keep it up.'

'I will!' She closed her eyes firmly, turned on her side and dropped off again.

Hal went out, closing the bedroom door behind him. Her sat back down in his chair, and looked at the technical crew. 'You alone first, Jeamus,' said one of them, holding up one finger. 'Ready . . . go!'

The small lights went on in the receptors aimed at Jeamus, who was standing beside Hal's chair.

'My name is Jeamus Walters,' Jeamus said. 'I'm the Chief of the Communications Section at the Final Encyclopedia; and I'm honored today to introduce the new Director of the Encyclopedia, about whom you'll be reading in the information releases just authorized by the Encyclopedia.

'May I present to you, peoples of Earth, the Director of the Final Encyclopedia. Hal Mayne!'

The lights winked out. Jeamus stood back. The lights went on again. Hal looked into their small brilliant eyes, shining now on him.

'What I have to say today is going to be very brief,' he said, 'since we're particularly busy here at the moment at the Final Encyclopedia. There'll be details on what's keeping us occupied in the releases Jeamus Walters mentioned; and I believe Rukh Tamani, who'll be speaking to you in a moment, may also have something to say about it.

'I've been honored by being chosen by Tam Olyn, Director of the Encyclopedia for over eighty years, to follow him in that post. As you all know, the only Director before Tam Olyn was Mark Torre; the man who conceived of, planned and supervised the building of this great work from its earliest form, earthbound at the city of St. Louis in the northwestern quadrisphere of this world.

'Mark Torre's aim, as you know, was to create a tool for research into the frontiers of the human mind itself, by providing a storage place for all known information on everything that mind has produced or recognized since the dawn of intellectual consciousness. It was his belief and his hope that this storehouse of human knowledge and creativity would provide materials and, eventually, a means of exploring what has always been unknown and unseeable – in the same way that none of us, unaided, can see the back of his or her own head.

'To that search, Tam Olyn, like Mark Torre before him, dedicated himself. To that same faith that Mark Torre had shown, he adhered through his long tenure of duty here.

'I can make no stronger statement to you, today, than to say that I share the same faith and intent, the same dedication. But, more fortunate than the two men who dedicated their lives to the search before me, I may possess something in addition. I have, I believe, some reason to hope that the long years of work here have brought us close to our goal, that we are very near, at last, now to stepping over the threshold of that universe of the unknown which Mark Torre dreamed of entering and reaping the rewards of exploring it – that inner exploration of the human race we have never ceased to yearn towards; unconsciously to begin with, but later consciously, from the beginning of time.

'When the moment comes that this threshold is crossed the lives of none of us will ever be the same again. We stand at perhaps the greatest moment in the known history of humanity; and I, for one, have no doubt whatsoever that what we have sought for over millennia, we will find; not in centuries or decades from now, but within our lifetimes and possibly even in a time so close that if I could tell you certainly, as I now speak, how long it would be, the nearness of it would seem inconceivable to us all.

'But in any case, I give you my promise that while I am Director of the Final Encyclopedia, I will not allow work toward that future to be slowed or halted, by anything. There is no greater pledge I can offer you than that, and I offer it now, with all the strength that is in me.

'Having said this about myself and the Directory, I will now turn from that subject to introduce someone who I think means so much to so many of us, that this, too, would have seemed inconceivable a short year ago.

'Peoples of Earth, it's my pleasure and honor to introduce Rukh Tamani.'

The lights went out before Hal and on before Rukh. He got to his feet and went quickly to stand beside the door to his suite, so that he would be easily and silently reachable from the corridor, during her talk. Standing with his shoulder blades against the wall, he found himself captured immediately by what she was saying. Whenever Rukh spoke in this fashion, everyone within hearing was caught and held; and he was no exception.

'I am sorry to have caused you grief,' were her first words to the world below.

'I have been told that many of you believed me dead or at least badly hurt in recent days; and because you believed this you grieved. But you should not grieve for me, ever.

'Grieve instead for those things more important under Heaven. For any who may have shared their lives with you and now suffer or lack. For your angers which wound, your indifference which hurts of kills, more than any outright anger or cruelty does.

'Grieve that you live in yourself, walled and apart from your fellow women and men. Grieve for your failures in courage, in faith, in kindness to all.

'But, grieving, know that it is not necessary to grieve, for you need not have done or been that which causes you to grieve.

'. . . For there is a great meaning to life which each of you controls utterly for yourself; and which no one else can bear you from without your consent . . .'

There was a touch on his shoulder.

'Hal –'

It was Jeamus, whispering beside him. Hal followed the Communications head out into the corridor and down it a little ways, away from the doorway they had just left.

'He's here,' said Jeamus. 'Standing off outside the shield-wall above us in a spacecraft. I didn't talk to him. Someone from his ship called in to tell me they were there and that he'd meet you as soon as you were ready.'

Hal nodded. He had felt this moment coming close in time. All the instincts of his nature, all the calculations of intuitive logic had made it sure that he would not hear the end of what Rukh was now saying.

Jeamus was still talking.

'. . . I told whoever it was I was speaking to that you'd said you'd be right along the moment you heard he was here. I also told him how Bleys was to find the iris in the shield-wall and how he should enter it and act after he was inside – I particularly warned him about the danger of touching the walls. The iris is open now, and we've run a floor the full length of it. You'll want someone to drive you to the meeting, won't you?'

'No,' said Hal; and then changed his mind. 'I'd like Simon Graeme to drive me. Would you find him?'

'Yes,' said Jeamus. 'Your craft's ready, with suits in it and everything else you need, in Number Three bay. Why don't you go directly there; and I'll have Simon along to you in a minute. I explained to the man I was talking to how he should park whatever small transportation he has well clear of the iris opening at their end; and how Bleys should enter it . . .'

'Good,' said Hal. 'It sounds as if everything's set and fine. You get Simon for me. I'll go ahead.'

The craft Jeamus had ready was a ten-passenger Space and Atmosphere vehicle. Hal had barely entered it and sat down in the Second Pilot's seat up front when Simon and Jeamus entered the craft.

Simon sat down at the controls without a word.

'Jeamus told you about this?' Hal asked him.

'On the way here.' Simon nodded. He powered up and looked around at Jeamus; but Jeamus was still delaying his exit from the craft.

'You're sure you understand everything?' he asked Hal.

'Go over it again, if you like,' said Hal, patiently.

'All right,' said Jeamus, relieved. 'The shield-wall is actually two walls – two phase shift interfaces set at varying widths apart so there'll be room for protective personnel when we open irises under the attack conditions to let ships in or out. When we open an iris, we'll essentially make a tunnel varying in width up to anything we want and anywhere from fifty meters to several kilometers in length, depending on how far apart we want to set the two walls at that point –'

'Make it brief, if you can, Jeamus,' said Hal.

'I will. I am. What I want to be sure you understand are conditions at the iris openings and inside that tunnel. The openings in this case will each have a non-physical, pressure airseal. You know those from experience. It'll be like any air-door, you just push your way through it. Inside, we'll have been able to build up a breathable atmosphere, not only for your sake and Bleys', but so we can super-saturate that atmosphere with moisture to reduce the chance of static charges to either one of you from the walls. A static link between you and the wall could be as bad as touching the wall of the tunnel physically. Stay in the middle of the tunnel at all times. Now the super-saturation will cause a lot of heavy mist. Follow the line of where the mist is thinnest, accordingly, and you'll be sure you're in the tunnel's center at all times. We've passed the same information to Bleys. We've also floated in that floor I mentioned for the two of you to walk on. It'll be gravity-charged.'

'Good,' said Hal. 'Thank you, Jeamus. Simon, we'll go as soon as Jeamus closes the door –'

'You must – *must* – remember!' said Jeamus, backing to the door of the craft. 'Any contact with the tunnel wall will be exactly like a contact with the shield-wall itself. You'll be instantly translated to universal position, with no hope of reassembly.'

'I understand. Thanks, Jeamus. Thank you.'

Jeamus stepped out of the vehicle and closed the door behind him. Simon lifted the craft and they floated out the bay entrance, which opened before them.

CHAPTER SIXTY-SEVEN

As they slid through the pressure airseal of the entrance, Hal was already back up on his feet and putting on one of the vacuum suits. It turned out to be the one provided for Simon and therefore too small for Hal. He took it off and put on the other suit instead. Once donned, it was hardly noticeable, like transparent overalls of thin material, except for the heavy, dark power belt around the waist. He left the rigid, but equally transparent, bell of the helmet thrown back.

'There it is,' said Simon as Hal came back to the front of the craft.

Hal looked in the front screen and saw what looked like a bright, opaque, circular hole in the grayness, perhaps ten meters in diameter. A thick, dark line cut a chord across its bottom curve – the end of the floor provided.

'Nicely illuminated,' he said. In fact, the innumerable moisture droplets of the mist filling the tunnel opening seemed to cause its interior to glow as they individually reflected the lighting built into the upper and lower surfaces of the panel that was the floor.

'My directions from Jeamus were to park a good fifty meters off,' said Simon. 'I can run out a landing ramp for you right up to within half a meter of the iris opening – or would you rather use your power belt and jump?'

'I'll jump,' said Hal. 'If Jeamus wants you fifty meters off, poking a ramp in close to it might not be the brightest idea.'

'There's no problem about my holding the craft steady,' said Simon.

'I know you can do it,' said Hal. 'Still, let's play the odds. If I jump, I'll only have to be thinking about myself.'

Simon parked. Hal closed his helmet and went out through the double doors of the vehicle, now on airlock cycle, and stepped toward the entrance to the iris, correcting his course as he approached with small bursts from the power belt.

At the doorway itself there was a little tension to be felt, like that of breaking through an invisible, and thin but tough membrane, as he penetrated the pressure airseal and let himself down, feet first on the mist-hidden floor. In fact, it was easy to imagine that he could feel the coolness of the white fog around him, even through the impermeable fabric of the vacuum suit. The suspended water droplets hid not only the walls of the tunnel and the floor beneath his feet, but floated about him in clouds of varying thickness.

He threw back his helmet and breathed in the moisture-laden atmosphere. It felt heavy as water itself in his lungs; and he knew that the feeling was not simply imagination, as the super-saturation under these abnormal conditions would be well above what Earth surface-pressure air could normally be induced to carry in the way of moisture.

He went forward.

After a hundred or so steps, he caught sight of a bobbing darkness through the mist ahead, which swiftly became the shape of a tall man, also suited, also with helmet thrown back, coming toward him.

Three more steps brought them face to face and they stopped. Through the transparency of Bleys' vacuum suit, he could see the other man was wearing his customary narrow tousers and jacket – but still, there seemed to be a difference about him.

For a moment the difference eluded Hal, and then he identified it. The tall man was as slim as ever, but in the vacuum suit he gave the appearance of being bulkier and more physical. His shoulders had always been as wide as Hal's but now they seemed heavier. His face was unchanged; but his body seemed more heavy-boned and powerful.

It was only a subjective alteration in appearance, but oddly important, here and now. And yet it was not as if the Other had put on weight. Eerily, it was as if he and Hal had grown more alike physically. Their eyes met. Bleys spoke, and his voice went out and was lost against the walls of the tunnel, its crispness blurred by the heavy air and the mist.

'Well,' said Bleys, 'you've got your Dorsai and everything you want from the Exotics locked up, here. I take it, then, you're determined to go through with this?'

'I told you,' said Hal, 'there was never any other way.'

Bleys nodded, a trifle wearily.

'So now the gloves come off,' he said.

'Yes,' answered Hal. 'Sooner or later they had to, I being what I am and you being what you are.'

'And what are you?' Bleys smiled.

'You don't know, of course,' said Hal.

'No,' said Bleys. 'I've known for some time you're not just a boy whose tutors I watched die on a certain occasion. How much more, I still don't know. But it'd be petty-minded of me to hide the fact that I've been astonished by the quality of your opposition to me. You're too intelligent to move worlds like this just for revenge on me because of your tutors' deaths. What you've done and are doing is too big for any personal cause. Tell me – what drives you to oppose me like this?'

'What drives me?' Hal found himself smiling a little sadly – almost a Bleys type of smile. 'A million years of history and prehistory drive me – as they drive you. To be more specific, the last thousand years of history drive me. There's no other way for you and I to be, but opponents. But if it's any consolation to you, I've also been surprised by the quality of your opposition.'

'You?' Bleys' face could not bring itself to express incredulity. 'Why should you be surprised?'

'Because,' said Hal, 'I'm more than you could imagine – just as you've turned out to be something I couldn't imagine. But then when I was imagining this present time we live in I had no real appreciation of the true value of faith. It's something that goes far beyond blind worship. It's a type of understanding in those who've paid the price to win it. As you, yourself, know.'

Bleys was watching him intently.

'As I know?'

'Yes,' said Hal, 'as you, of all people, know.'

Bleys shook his head.

'I should have dealt with you when you were much younger,' he said, almost to himself.

'You tried,' said Hal. 'You couldn't.'

'I did?' said Bleys. 'I see. You're using faith, again, to reach that conclusion?'

'Not for that. No, only observation and fact.' Hal was still watching Bleys as closely as Bleys was watching him. 'Primarily, the fact that I'm who I am, and know what I can do.'

'You're mistaken if you think I couldn't have eliminated a sixteen-year-old boy if I'd wanted to.'

'No, I'm not mistaken,' Hal said. 'As I say, you tried. But I wasn't a boy, even then when I thought I was. I was an experienced adult, who had reasons for staying alive. I told you I've learned faith, even if it took me three lives to do the learning. That's why I know I'm going to win, now. Just as I know my winning means your destruction, because you won't have it any other way.'

'You seem to think you know a great deal about me.' The smile was back on Bleys' face. It was a smile that hid all thoughts behind it.

'I do. I came to understand you better by learning to understand myself – though understanding myself was a job I started long before you came along.' Hal paused for a fraction of a second as a surgeon might pause before the first cut of the scalpel. 'If you'd been only what I thought you were the first time I saw you, the contest between us would already be over. More than that, I'd have found some way by this time to bring you to the side of things as they must be for the race to survive.'

Bleys' smile widened. Ignoring it, Hal went on.

'But since that day at the estate,' he said, 'I've learned about myself, as well as more about you, and I know I'll never be able to bring you to see what I see until you, yourself, choose to make the effort to do so. And without that effort, we're matched too evenly, you and I, by the forces of history, for any compromise to work.'

'I'm not sure I understand you,' said Bleys, 'and that's unusual enough to be interesting.'

'You don't understand me because I'm talking of things outside your experience,' Hal said. 'I came to talk to you here – as I'll always be willing to come to talk to you – because I've got to hang on to the hope you might be brought to consider things beyond the scope of what you look at now; and change your mind.'

'You talk,' said Bleys, now openly amused, 'like a grandfather talking to a grandson.'

'I don't mean to,' said Hal. 'But the hard fact is you've had only one lifetime from which to draw your conclusions. As I just said, I've had three. It took me that long to become human; and because I've finally made it, I can see how you, yourself, fall short of being the full human being the race has to produce to survive the dangers it can't even imagine yet. Like it or not, that experience is there, and a difference between us.'

'I told you you were an Other,' said Bleys.

'Not exactly,' said Hal. 'If you remember, you left me to infer it. But I'm splitting hairs. In a sense you were right. In one sense I am an Other, being a blend of all that's new as well as all that's old in the race. But I'm not the kind of Other who's Everyman. Your kind, if it survives, are at best going to be a transient form of human. Mine, if it does, will be immortal.'

'I'm sorry,' said Bleys, gracefully, 'I don't have a kind. I'm my own unique mixture of Exotic and Dorsai, only.'

'No,' said Hal. 'You did have an Exotic and a Dorsai as parents of your father. But your mother's family, which raised you on Harmony, was pure Friendly, and it's that which dominates in you.'

Bleys looked at him as if from an impossible distance.

'In what records did you find that fairy tale?'

'In none,' said Hal. 'The official records of your birth and movements all show what you fixed them to say.'

'Then what makes you say something like this?'

'The correct knowledge,' said Hal. 'An absolute knowledge that comes from joining together bits and pieces of general records that hadn't been tampered with – because there was no reason to tamper with them – at the Final Encyclopedia. I put them together only a year ago, and then made deductions from them using something I taught myself during my self trial of life. It's called intuitive logic.'

Bleys frowned slightly. Then his frown cleared.

'Ah,' he said; and was silent for a long moment, looking a little aside from Hal. When he spoke again, his voice was thoughtful and remote. 'I believe what you're talking about may be what I've been calling interval thinking.'

'The name hardly matters,' said Hal.

674

'Of course not. So,' Bleys' gaze came back to him, openly, 'there's more to learn about you than I'd imagined. But tell me, why place so much emphasis on the fact that part of what I am by inheritance and upbringing may be Friendly?'

'For one reason, because it explains your ability of charisma, as well as that of those Others who have it to some extent or another,' said Hal. 'But I'd rather you called yourself faith-holder than Friendly. Because, more than anyone of all the world's suspects, it's a form of faith-holding that rules you. You never were the bored cross-breed whose only concern was being comfortable during his own brief years of life. That was a facade, a false exterior set up in the first place to protect you from your older half-brother, Danno – who would have been deathly afraid of you if he'd suspected you had a purpose of your own.'

'He would, indeed,' murmured Bleys. 'Not that I'm agreeing with these fancies and good-nights of yours, of course.'

'Your agreement isn't necessary,' said Hal. 'As I was saying, you used it first to protect yourself against Danno, then to reassure the rest of the Others that you weren't just using them for your own private purposes. Finally, you're using it still to blind the peoples of the worlds you control to that personal goal that draws you now more strongly than ever. You're a faith-holder, twisted to the worship of a false god – the same god under a different mask that Walter Blunt worshipped back in the twenty-first century. Your god is stasis. You want to enshrine the race as it is, make it stop and go farther. It's the end you've worked to from the time you were old enough to conceive it.'

'And if all this should be true,' Bleys smiled again. 'The end is still the end. It remains inevitable. You can think all this about me, but it isn't going to make any difference.'

'Again, you, of all people, know that's not so,' answered Hal. 'The fact I understand this is going to make all the difference between us. You developed the Others and let them think that the power they gained was all their own doing. But now you'll understand that I'm aware it was mainly accomplished with recruits who were simply non-Other, native-born Friendlies with their own natural, culturally developed, charismatic gift to some degree, working under your own personal spell and command. Meanwhile, covered by the appearance of working for the Others, you've begun to spread your own personal faith in the inevitably necessary cleansing of the race, followed by a freezing of it into an immobility of changelessness.' Hal stopped, to give Bleys a chance to respond. But the Other man said nothing. 'Unlike your servants and the Others who've been your dupe,' Hal went on, 'you're able to see the possibility of a final death resulting from that state of stasis, if you achieve it. But under the influence of the dark part of the racial unconsciousness whose laboratory experiment and chess piece you are – as I also am, on the other side – you see growth in the race as the source of all human evils, and you're willing to kill the patient, if necessary, to kill the cancer.'

He stopped. This time there was a difference to the silence which succeeded his words and lay between the two of them.

'You realize,' said Bleys at last, softly, 'that now I have no choice at all but to destroy you?'

'You can't afford to destroy me,' said Hal, 'even if you could. Just as I can't afford to destroy you. This battle is now being fought for the adherence of the minds of all our fellow humans. What I have to do, to make the race understand which way they must go, is prove you wrong; and I need you alive for that. You have to prove me wrong if you want to win, and you need me alive for that. Force alone won't solve anything for either of us, in the long run. You know that as well as I do.'

'But it will help.' Bleys smiled. 'Because you're right. I have to win. I will win. There's got to be an end to this madness you call growth but which is actually only expansion further and further into the perils of the physical universe until the lines that supply our lives will finally be snapped of their own weight. Only by putting it aside, can we start the growth within that's both safe and necessary.'

'You're wrong,' said Hal. 'That way lies death. It's a dead end road that assumes inner growth can only be had at the price of giving up what's made us what we are over that million years I mentioned. Chained and channeled organisms grow stunted and wrong, always. Free ones grow wrong sometimes, but right other times; because the price of life is a continual seeking to grow and explore. Lacking that freedom, all action, physical and mental, circles in on itself and ends up only wearing a deeper and deeper rut in which it goes around and around until it dies.'

'No,' said Bleys; and his face, his whole body seemed to shrug off Hal's words. 'It leads to life for the race. It's the only way that can. There had to be an end to growth out into the physical universe, and a change over to growth within. That's all that can save us. Only by stopping now and turning back, only by stopping this endless attempt to enlarge and develop can we turn inward and find a way to be invulnerable in spite of anything the universe might hold.

'It's you who are wrong,' said Bleys; and his face, his whole body seemed to harden and take on a look of power that Hal had never seen it show before. 'But you're self-deluded. Besotted with love for the shiny bauble of adventure and discovery. Out there –'

He stabbed one long finger back into the gray mist that obscured his end of the tunnel, at the upper side of the shield-wall.

'– out there are all things that can be. How can it be otherwise? And among all things have to be all things that must be

676

unconquerable by us. How can it be otherwise? All they that take the sword shall perish by the sword – and this is a sword you keep reaching for, this so-called spirit of exploration and adventure – this leaping out into the physical universe. Is the spirit of mankind nothing more than a questing hound that always has to keep finding a new rabbit to run after? How many other races, in this infinity, in this eternity, do you think haven't already followed that glittering path? And how many of those do you suppose have become master of the universe, which is the only alternative ending to going down?'

His eyes burned on Hal's.

'What will be –' he went on, 'what I'll see done will be a final reversal to that process. What you'll try to do to stop it is going to make no difference in that. You've made a fortress out of Old Earth. It makes no difference. What human minds can do by way of science and technology other human minds can undo. We'll find a way eventually through that shield-wall of yours. We'll retake Earth, and cleanse it of all those who'd continue this mad, sick, outward plunge of humankind. Then it'll be reseeded with those who see our race's way as it should be.'

'And the Younger Worlds?' Hal said. 'What about all the other settled planets? Have you forgotten them?'

'No,' said Bleys. 'They'll die. No one will kill them. But, little by little, with the outward-seeking sickness cured, and the attention of Earth, of real Earth, on itself as it should be – these others will wither and their populations dwindle. In the long run, they'll be empty worlds again; and humanity'll be back where it began, where it belongs and where it'll stay, on its own world. And here – as fate wills it – it'll learn how to live properly and exist to the natural end of its days – or die.'

He stopped speaking. The force that had powered his voice fell away into silence. Hal stood, looking at him, with nothing to say. After a long moment, Bleys spoke again, quietly.

'Words are no use between us two, are they?' he said, at last. 'I'm sorry, Hal. Believe what you want, but those who think the way you do can't win. Look how you and your kind have done nothing but lose to me and mine, so far.'

'You're wrong' said Hal. 'We haven't really contested you until now; and now that we're going to, we're the ones who can't lose.'

Bleys reached out his hand and Hal took it. They did not grasp in the ordinary fashion of greeting, but only held for a moment. The Other's flesh and bones felt strange in Hal's hand as if he had taken the hand of a condemned man. Then they both turned and each went off his own way, in opposite directions into the mist.

CHAPTER SIXTY-EIGHT

His mind was so full of the conversation just past, that he was hardly aware of reaching the end of the tunnel, making the jump into the airlock of the vehicle waiting, and being driven back to the Encyclopedia. Once parked back in the bay again, he thanked Simon absentmindedly and went off towards his own suite, brushing aside the people he encountered along the way who had matters they wanted to talk to him about.

He reached his suite, stepped in, and drew a breath of relief on finding it empty as far as he could see into it. He went through to the spare bedroom, saw Ajela was still asleep in the same position, and left her, going through his own bedroom to the small room beyond – the carrel in which his private work here at the Encyclopedia would be done.

He stepped into the carrel, closed the door behind him and sat down within the four walls that were all screen. He touched a stud on the control panel before him and suddenly, as far as the eye could tell, he hung floating in space – beyond the Earth, beyond the Encyclopedia and beyond the shield-wall.

The unchanging stars looked back at him.

Alone at last, he was free to remember the letter from Amanda; and with that all thought of Bleys and related matters was plucked from his mind. He reached into his inside jacket pocket and brought out the envelope waiting for him there.

For a moment, with the stars around him, he held it unopened. The sight of it had suddenly brought, on the intuitive wings of his mind, an unusual feeling of sorrow and apprehension. The Dorsai-made, thick, slightly grayish paper of the envelope reminded him of the mist in the iris tunnel.

He slipped his thumb under the sealed flap and tore the envelope open. Within it was a sheaf of pages, and the first one was dated five days, absolute, just past.

He read.

May 36, 342 Dorsai/2366 Absolute

My dearest:

I kept avoiding telling you when I'd be coming to Earth in the

Exodus, because I had a decision to make. Forgive me. But it's now made, and I will be standing by it.

We belong to our duties, you and I, for some little time yet. Yours is there, in the Encyclopedia; but mine isn't there with you, much as I'd give anything I have or may have – except you – to be where you are.

At Earth, I could be no help in the things that are going to need to be done, except to provide one more body to the ramparts. My real usefulness now is anywhere but there. At this moment, we're entering a time in which there'll be nothing in the large sense but two things, the citadel and the territory of the enemy outside it. My usefulness is also outside, in that enemy territory.

In the years that will be coming, as important as it'll be to hold the citadel against all attack, it's going to be equally important to make sure those who're now under the will of the Others don't forget what freedom is. The human spirit will never endure chains long, any more than it ever has; and there are going to be spontaneous uprisings against the rule of those like Bleys, in addition to those left on the Dorsai and on the Friendlies, who'll hide out in the back country and other areas from which they will be difficult to dislodge; and they'll continue to fight, perhaps indefinitely.

From Earth, you'll be sending out people and supplies to help support groups like these on all the Younger Worlds. You'll also need people already out there who know how such fighting and surviving should be done; and who you know are going to think the way you do, in terms of what has to be accomplished to prepare for the day when you can come back out of the citadel and take back what's been lost.

If you've thought at all about the needs to come, as I know you must, you've already recognized the need for people to go out now to advising and organizing such groups and that the natural choice for such people would be from our ranks on the Dorsai. We faced that necessity ourselves early here, in making our general plans for the Exodus; and a number of us have already volunteered for this work, myself among them.

By the time you get this letter, I'll be between the stars; on my way, or already at, a destination that I've no way at this moment of knowing; and I'll have already begun my work, using contacts provided for me through Friendlies, Exotics and other people generally, who understand what needs to be done to help those who will still want to resist, outside Old Earth. But wherever I am when you read these words, you'll know at that moment, as always, I'll be carrying the thought of you and my love for you like a fireside warmth inside me, to warm me always, wherever I go and whatever I do.

If and when you find yourself in contact with those of us who are out there and can send a message to me, write and let me know that you understand what I've done and why I did it, in spite of all it would have meant to be there with you. I won't need to hear from you to know you understand, but it's going to strengthen me to read that you do, just the same.

And now, let me tell you how I love you . . .

The page blurred before his eyes. Then it cleared, and he sat reading the letter, page by page, as if the words on them had the power to draw him down into them. At length, he reached the end of it; and sat gazing down at it with the eyes of the stars upon him.

The last five lines above her signature burned themselves into the patterns of his mind and soul.

You know I've loved you, and we've loved each other, longer than others would ever understand. You know as I know that nothing can part us. You know we are always together, no matter where our bodies may happen to be. Reach out at any time and find me. And I will do the same to you.

> All my
> love,
> Amanda

He reached.

Amanda . . .?

It was as if one wave spoke to another, a call from the one washing the eastern shore of one continent reaching the one washing the western shore of another, half a world apart, but joined by the ocean to which both waves belonged.

Hal. . . .

Her response returned to him, and they touched across the vast space between them, touched and held. It was not in words that they spoke, but in surges of feeling and knowing.

After a time, they parted; and he felt her withdraw. But the warmth of her, like the fireside warmth she had spoken of early in her letter, stayed with him, strengthening him.

He looked at the stars and down at the control panel under his hands. His fingertips began to move and words lighted themselves into existence against the dark and stars' points before him.

In morning's ruined chapel, the full knight
Woke from the coffin of his last night's bed . . .

The poem drew him into the work, and the work enlarged in him, taking him over at last completely. He grew to be part of it as it grew in him; and gradually, alone with the stars, he left behind all else except the warmth of the link to Amanda, and became fully occupied with what at last held and engrossed him, beyond all other things.

Afterword
The Door into Darkness
by
Sandra Miesel

'Verily, verily I say unto thee, except a man be born again, he cannot see the kingdom of God.'

– John 3:3

All creation is in flux. Every particle of matter, every living person is a pilgrim in a fluid universe. Each child's growth in body, mind, and spirit retraces that immeasurably ancient racial arche-type, the Way. However many seasons wheel onward to mark the years, our progress from birth to death still shapes the myth we live by. All of us are destined to make the night-journey, endure the difficult passage, and seek entry through the narrow gate.

The first clear footprints on this path appear during the Ice Age, 25,000 years ago. In those days, Paleolithic cave-dwellers would crawl for hours through labyrinthine corridors to reach ceremonial chambers deep in the stony womb of Mother Earth. The life-defining rituals they celebrated there have left us trail markers in the form of splendid art at Lascaux, Altamira, and hundreds of other sites.

As millennia passed, initiation became the universal story, the tale, of the hero of a thousand faces. The initiate's path rose in stages: to the plateau of tribal membership, up the heights of some specialized skill, ending on a lone peak of spiritual perfection. The higher one climbed, the farther one could see – and be seen as a scout by those below.

This age-old symbolism survives in the teachings of historic religions. The West speaks of passing over from bondage into freedom, the East of escaping the sorrowful wheel of existence. But whether the road be described as linear, cyclic, or spiral, salvation remains fundamentally a *transit*. Our quest for transcendence began as soon as human consciousness emerged. Pursuing it has made us what we are and suggests what we may become.

This is the message of Gordon R. Dickson's Childe Cycle. An evolutionary epic planned in twelve volumes, the Cycle treats the entire human species as one multi-celled organism undergoing initiation. This communal experience culminates in one man's pilgrimage across the centuries and among the stars. Like the race for which he stands, the hero is a squire – a *child* – seeking knight-hood. Through the victory of a single member, the whole body triumphs.

The man who came into existence as Donal Graeme is a worthy model for others to follow, because his three lives have been successive courses of initiation. Even heraldry proclaims his destiny. The three scallop shells adorning the arms of Graeme, as well as those of Sir John Hawkwood, Donal's historical forerunner, signify pilgrimage, rebirth, and the waters of limitless possibility.

First as Donald Graeme the Dorsai Warrior (*Dorsai!*, 1959), then as Paul Formain, the proto-Exotic (*Necromancer*, 1962 and for the forthcoming *Chantry Guild*), and finally here as Hal Mayne, the adopted Friendly Faith-holder, he explores three fundamental roles. These are the three points that determine the circle of his being. When he has finally integrated the separate lessons of each life – intuition, empathy, and creativity – his initiation as an evolved, ethically responsible person will be complete. Remembering what he learned as Donal and as Paul enables Hal to begin mastering the cosmic wheel. No longer a victim bound to it, he will eventually turn it himself, becoming the axis about which it willingly revolves.

But no hero's path to glory is smooth. Like Christ before His public ministry and the Buddha prior to his Enlightenment, Hal must withstand the blandishments of a tempter. Hal's satanic opponent, Bleys Ahrens, is a princely, titanic fiend out of *Paradise Lost*, an archangel noble even in his ruin. (The Miltonic inspiration is obvious and acknowledged, since Milton is to be the subject of a Childe Cycle historical novel.)

Biblical overtones resonate in Bleys. He is the corrupting serpent of Genesis and the whole hellish trinity of Revelation. Like Satan in the Book of Job, Bleys is the adversary who tests the just man nearly to destruction. But the trials thus inflicted inspire virtue that would not have emerged otherwise, even as Bleys' challenge triggers Hal's self-discovery. Satan's overtures to Christ in the desert are probes to discern His mission as well as lures to mislead Him, for Satan expects a Messiah in his own image. Likewise, Bleys attempts to examine as well as enlist Hal. He cannot imagine Hal being anything except an Other – darkness cannot grasp light. The captor remains imprisoned within walls of his own making while his captive breaks free.

Bleys' guileful tactics also parallel those of Mara, the Buddhist Lord of Death who lures men into fatal snares. When the treacherous god's threats and blandishments fail to dissuade the Buddha from seeking Enlightenment, the tempter disputes his very right to search for a new direction. But Mother Earth herself bears witness for the Buddha. He perseveres in his crucial meditation and, in the course of a single night, finds his Way to Liberation. In the same fashion Bleys ridicules Hal's agonizing pursuit of a path different from the Others'. But fundamental reality confirms the quest and thus Hal crosses nightfall into dawn.

The supernatural being Bleys most resembles in personality is Iblis, the melancholy Islamic Satan. They share the same fondness for sad songs and somber dress, the same grave manner that cloaks self-pity. Each strikes the pose of a scapegoat blamed for the failings of jealous inferiors. Each justifies himself as acting according to his inborn nature. Both beings suffer the predestined but no less tragic, fault of single-eyed vision: they recognize power, not love. Bleys' fascination with Hal is like Iblis' longing to be overcome by the Perfect Man. Each instinctively seeks the defeat that will make him whole. Meanwhile, both Bleys and Iblis serve a greater purpose. As a Persian poem says, 'Shadow makes clear the brilliance of light.'

Thus Bleys Ahrens is an ancient Enemy poets knew of old. His very name marks him as a 'wrongful blaze' that sheds 'no light, but rather darkness visible.' Preferring to 'reign in hell than serve in heaven,' he is the lord of endless twilight, the woeful 'son of morn in weary night's decline.' The infernal constancy of 'a mind not to be chang'd in place or time' traps him in a dismal maze of his own design: 'for within him hell he brings, and round about him, nor from hell one step no more than from himself can fly.' Though 'graceful and humane; . . . he seem'd for dignity composed and high exploit,' his venomously sweet tongue can lick truth itself into deceitful shapes. Much as he professes to deplore bloodshed, 'the dragons of the prime . . . were mellow music matched with him' for nothing in his arid heart 'shares the eternal reciprocity of tears.' He is the everlasting negation whose stubborn choice of stasis over growth makes potential heaven accomplished hell.

Since Bleys impedes the pilgrimage to transcendence Hal incites, they collide like immovable object and irresistable force. But their clash is necessary as well as inevitable for, as the Greek philosopher Heraclitus puts it, 'Out of discord comes the fairest harmony.' The racial organism cannot pass from youth to maturity until its conscious and unconscious aspects are properly developed and fully integrated into a single self.

Humanity's contrary impulses to hold fast and reach out wage random war with each other until mystically divided by Hal's earlier incarnation Paul in *Necromancer*. This intervention allows the nascent Splinter Cultures to go their separate ways among the stars. Then the new planets' right to independence is assured by Cletus Grahame in *Tactics of Mistake* (1970). Generations later, Cletus' descendant Donal Graeme imposes interstellar peace in *Dorsai!*

683

Now the experiment is nearly complete. The garden planted by Paul and cultivated by Donal ripens for Hal to harvest. The special gifts that bloom best in the Splinter Cultures have begun to wither. But as they fade, they cross-fertilize one another. When traits mingle and perceptions change, mystical Dorsai, brave Exotics, and wise Friendlies emerge. When intermarriages multiply, the Others appear. Unless the new variants are grafted back on Earth's old roots soon, the entire species will perish in a final winter that never sees spring.

Curiously, despite the utter opposition between the sides Hal and Bleys lead, the rival paladins are obscurely alike, as if they were the right and left hands of a single entity. Cunning Bleys is quicker to spy an affinity and add this notion to his tempter's bag of tricks. But Hal denies any likeness so vehemently, the very force of is revulsion impels him towards understanding.

Nevertheless, the haunting issue remains. Mere disbelief cannot drive the demon from the mirror. Indeed, his mocking image grows clearer over the years as Hal reaches full adult size. By the time he hurls his solemn *défi* at Bleys, their physical resemblance is unmistakable.

What might brotherhood between these enemies imply? Past situations offer parallels. The starkest tragedies Hal witnesses as Donal are deaths of brother-figures: the slaughter of his uncle James (his father's counterweight), the assassination of his uncle Kensie (dark Ian's bright twin), and the murder of his elder brother Mor (a hostile shadow of himself). Meanwhile, in *Soldier, Ask Not* (1965), young Tam's malice destroys three men who could have been his brothers and thereby fill the chasms of his lonely heart. Thus fraternity can fail through too much closeness or too much distance. Ian and Kensie are doomed from the very beginning when fate cleaves them into separate persons instead of the one they would afterwards yearn to be. Death renders the lifelong gap between Mor and Donal forever unbridgeable, leaving Hal a legacy of guilt for his part in the fatal estrangement.

Instinct and memory also breed imagery that inspires art. For example, Hal's vision of himself and Bleys confined in membrane-walled compartments not unlike amniotic sacs is transformed and incorporated into his poem 'The Enchanted Tower': 'And now, through double glass I see/My brother's image darklingly.' This poem, quoted in *Necromancer*, will become a psychic vehicle to bring their sundered selves together face to face in *Childe*. Nourished by the Final Encyclopedia's vast resources, Hal's innate sensitivity to mythic symbols will equip him to place his predicament in a universal context. For as anthropologist Claude Lévi-Strauss proposes, 'The aim of myth is to furnish a logical model for solving a contradiction.'

Likeness and likeness define existence. Their interplay pulls the cosmos apart and brings it back together. Thus although we perceive our world through pairs of opposites such as Light and Darkness, we also long to transcend these oppositions once and for all. Various solutions are possible. Light may ultimately over-whelm its twin Darkness (Persian) or coexist with it in dynamic harmony (China) or coincide with it (India). Many cultures see a cryptic kinship beyond appearances, making deities and devils interchangeable poles of some primordial unity. ('God and Satan are brothers,' says a Romanian proverb.) But if Light is active Darkness and Darkness potential Light, what reconciliation waits when when they meet at midnight noon?

The growing understanding that leads Hal from rejection to recognition of Bleys as his counterpart transforms their relation-ship. Hal's road to wisdom retraces the tradition-hallowed path of heroes – separation, initiation, return. (Tam, ever the pioneer, travels this route earlier in *Soldier, Ask Not*.) The process also repeats Hal's experiences with the trio of elderly men who are his prototypes.

Since his origins are unknown, young Hal strives to identify with his tutors, each of whom speaks to one portion of his full-spectrum self. As age-patined relics of their cultures' peak years, Walter, Obadiah, and Malachi are worthy of emulation. But in order to surpass them, Hal must leave them. The child grows to manhood relearning his foster-fathers' lessons from models he initially tries to resist.

Tam, the Earthman with Exotic links, had been a demonic force in Donal's day, before his polarity was reversed in blood. Hal is unready to assume the mental task Tam offers him at the Encyclo-pedia because the promotion is premature. He needs to understand how his precursor anticipates him in the evolutionary adventure. Recognizing Tam as the age-gnarled taproot and himself as the ripening fruit of the same tree shows Hal why the newly selected strains of humanity need the adaptable hardiness of the old.

At first, Hal and Child-of-God are totally at odds despite their significantly parallel names. Not only does 'Child' pun *childe*, the Friendly's messianic surname is equivalent to 'Immanuelson,' Hal's alias on Harmony as a member of the Revealed Church of God Reborn. (And note that Donal's beloved uncle and surrogate brother is also called James.) But suffering in a common cause brings the two men together. The same inflexible Ironside who would have barred Hal from the Command in the beginning, demands he be retained at the end. 'Unshaken, unseduc'd, unterri-fied,' Child is the unyielding die that stamps Hal into shape as a Friendly. His example of fidelity unto death teaches Hal to live by faith, the sole weapon that can match the Others, though might and mind falter. This spiritual transfiguration completes the circuit of the hero's lives and readies him for his saving task.

Initially, Donal's filial piety inhibits Hal's reaction to Ian because young Donal could scarcely imagine equaling his revered uncle's prowess. Although he later surpasses Ian's military record, he never matches the older man's towering stature. But Hal's recreated body does approximate Ian's as Amanda swiftly recognizes. Her spell-song 'Green Water' has finally sung back Ian's springtime after years of heartbreak. Graemehouse itself bears witness to the chieftain's return, like Celtic talisman stones welcoming a high king. When Hal can fill the measuring doorway as completely as Ian once did, he is ready for Amanda and the rest of Ian's unfulfilled potential. In life, Ian was the Dorsai ideal incarnate, the knight with the purest heart. Through Hal, his protective spirit will reach out to enfold Earth's besieged walls.

Thus by identifying with Tam in mind, Child in spirit, and Ian in body, Hal inherits the young woman who loves each of these aged men. Whereas Donal and Paul meet danger and disapointment in their relations with females, femininity enriches Hal's life on every level. He is fully immersed in feminine influences, both real and symbolic. This is only fitting, since goddesses are the traditional guardians of creativity, the boon Hal is destined to win for all human beings.

In Ajela lives the 'dearest freshness deep down things' for she is the last flower to bloom before Fimbulwinter. Hers is the nurturing glow of golden sunlight. As handmaiden of the Final Encyclopedia, she is a living link between Hal and Tam as Tam's late wife Lisa was between Tam and Mark Torre, the first Director. Like Lisa, she is an unconventional Exotic, an idealist with a capacity for deep and lasting attachments. Her romantic fixation on Tam has gradually come to terms with reality. By sharing his work she possesses the man of her dreams, the splendid titan untouched by time. But it is a partnership of mind alone – Ajela is no bedwarmer for an enfeebled king.

Ajela's wholesome relationship with Tam reverses – and thereby redeems – the harmful one between Kantele and Walt in *Necromancer*. Kantele became the ancestress of the Exotics that are; Ajela will be the ancestress of the Exotics yet to come. Though unmated, Ajela mothers Tam, her staff, and eventually all Earth's children. Thus she is a doublet for the Encyclopedia itself, just as a priestess shares the identity of the goddess she serves.

Immovable as the roots of the mountains, Rukh has none of Ajela's softness. She is the Lord's terrible swift sword tempered in her own blood. Zeal is in her very bones because she is descended from the same North African stock that earlier had produced Jamethon Black in *Soldier, Ask Not*. Their Berber ancestors' ferocity blazed brightest under Islam. Not only did this folk breed fanatical fighters (they were the Almoravid foes of that proto-Dorsai El Cid) but they also revered 'living saints' like the Elect of Harmony among whom Rukh is numbered.

Pain seals this quinstessential Woman of Faith into the vocation she was born to follow, for she is a female version of Isaiah's Suffering Servant. She 'can speak to the weary a word that will rouse them' for she has been called 'for the victory of justice, . . . a convenant of the people, a light for the nations, to open the eyes of the blind, to bring out prisoners from confinement, and from the dungeon, those who live in darkness.' Nevertheless, she is also merciful, unwilling to quench a smoking wick. (Her name means 'bright' but in Persian mysticism signifies the Gracious Attributes of God.) Her mercy toward her tormentor Barbage has unexpected consequences – and incidentally prevents Hal from committing the 'sin of the warrior' that blemishes Donal. In her prophetic function, she foreshadows the eventual transmutation of denial to affirmation in the Friendly spirit. Rukh is a torch to light candles in the darkness and those she enkindles with her inner fire are her virgin-born children.

In Amanda, 'the shadows of the stars have mingled with the sea.' Like a Celtic goddess, she is linked with horses, birds, and water as well as being a triplet of her other selves, the First and Second Amandas. From a broader view, the three Amandas comprise a Great Goddess – Maid, Mistress/Wife, Crone – bracketting each of Hal's three lives. Moreover, Amanda III traces the whole circle herself. She was a virgin warrior, is a lover, and will be a mother to a new kind of human. In Hindu terms, she plays Mahadevi to Hal's Mahadeva.

Fal Morgan, the house built with its foundress's 'heart for the hall's foundation stone' is an extention of the Amanda-persona herself. She made it, not it her, as in the case of Ajela and the Final Encyclopedia. As the pattern repeats itself through time, she extends the scope of her embrace – from family to planet to species. Her breadth of experience prepares her for fulfillment. Amanda I had three husbands and Amanda II none but Amanda III is joined to a perfect soulmate. By adding her ancestresses' traits to her own she is a full-spectrum Woman of Faith, Philosophy, and War and thus a properly royal consort of Hal.

Not only do Ajela (Mother), Rukh (Maid) and Amanda (Mistress) themselves constitute a Great Goddess, they fit like tabs of differing shape into corresponding slots in Hal. Their special loves help grow beyond the limitations of his solely masculine upbringing. In contrast, Tonina's aid is merley practical. She is the crippled counterpart of the other three, since, despite a few good intentions, she fails in her successive feminine roles. This barren woman stands for a dead-end universe badly in need of opening. Like the counterfeit gardens of Coby, she stirs a hunger for genuine beauty others will satisfy.

Once Hal has settled into his carrel at the Encyclopedia, his three women colleagues actualize what he inspires. This division of labor is efficient since each of them is more skilled in some area than he. But it is also symbolically significant that the women take conventionally 'masculine' leadership roles on Earth, in low heaven, and in deep space – the three domains of Indo-European sky *gods*.

Meanwhile, Hal stays englobed within an artificial moon spinning webs of past, present, and future fate from the Encyclopedia's threads of data just like a lunar *goddess*. By his three seashell-marked births from the maternal waters of possibility, he has developed conventionally 'feminine' traits of intuition, empathy, and creativity.

Thus, Hal, Ajela, Rukh, and Amanda are complementary within as well as among themselves. By crossing the traditional boundaries between the sexes, they expand the scope of their being so that each encompasses the full circle of *yang* and *yin*. Thus when Hal and Amanda come together 'each is both' and their union is all the closer for it.

But Bleys in his terrible angelic neuterness cannot experience this. He is both a null sum within himself and uncompleted by anything outside himself. As Arthur Machen observes, 'Evil in its essence is a lonely thing, a passion of the solitary, individual soul.' Devoid of family or friends or helpmate, Bleys could not help but envy Hal and Amanda 'imparadis'd in one another's arms.' Although he senses kindship with Hal, he will not open himself the slightest crack to claim it. The Other's imprisoned ego cannot be an 'I' unless it allows another to be a 'Thou.'

While Bleys remains a bleak monad, alone in his unsatisfying excellence, Hal makes his way into full membership in the human family. Hal's broken-hearted compassion for everyone mystifies unbreakable Bleys who cannot conceive of suffering on anyone's behalf save his own. These differences determine their styles of leadership: Bleys is a cattle-drover heading his beasts into a pen but Hal is the soaring point of a hurled spear.

Learning how to love and be loved is Hal's particular triumph – he yields to overcome. As Donal he tries to push and pull persons around like building blocks, arranging his subordinates below him like the supporting pillars of an arch. But Hal instead persuades his comrades to form an encircling wall of linked arms around him. The lonely godling has become human so that other humans can become godlike.

The kinds of associates Hal draws to him make interesting

contrasts to Donal's contemporaries. Because the Splinter Cultures are eroding, the men are lower peaks in the same mountain ranges their predecessors dominated: Jason is a lesser Jamethon, Amid a lesser Padma, Simon a lesser Ian. But women like Athalia (Friendly/Exotic), Nonne (Exotic/Dorsai), and Miriam (Dorsai/Friendly) are subliminally crosscultural for the tectonic plates that uphold established mountains are shifting.

The company is shaped by the struggle it agrees to undertake at Hal's side. His apocalyptic message poses cruel choices that divide single homes and whole societies. Yet once made, these decisions also open unexpected avenues to reconciliation between cultures sundered from birth. The process affects both groups and individuals. Hostile sects on Harmony join hands against the common foe. Ajela, Rukh, and Amanda each resolve previous conflicts between their public roles and private selves. Above all, it touches the racial animal. What Paul divides into conscious and unconscious halves, Hal labors to rejoin. Only prior separation makes reunion possible.

But before the peace, the war. Hal and his companions form a whole constellation of light to confront a prince of darkness. This tension between Light and Darkness is a recurring thematic marker to characterize persons or situations – or even both at once. Rukh and Child radiate like glowing coals; Bleys bedims like a gloomy cloud. Hal's will to live is a blinding lamp but the shades of his tutors are burnt-out candles. Coby's lighting is cruelly steady and the Encyclopedia's responsively fluid just as Bleys is a Tyrant Holdfast and Hal a champion of change.

But light is not automatically equated with Good nor darkness with Evil. Either condition can express either quality. In their first trial of will, Hal draws strength to resist the storm of darkness that is Bleys by envisioning both an eternal flame and a dark stone altar. Brunette Rukh with her dusky Mediterranean complexion is faery-fair Amanda's match in loveliness and heroism. Mystic shadows matter as much as the luminous reason that dispels them. Cool darkness coceals Hal's flight home but hot brightness signals danger during his brawl with a fellow miner. Turning his eyes from the light lets Hal lead the Command through the night-shrouded forest to safety.

The alteration of bright and dark shapes days and seasons to signal shifting moods. Though autumn evening dies on Earth and winter falls on Mara, which once had seemed a summer country of the mind, one last defiant Dorsai springtime promises rebirth. But until that destiny is fulfilled, light and darkness wait 'in order serviceable' for the climax of Hal's creative struggle. Within the Encyclopedia he strives alone, enveloped by silent, starry space no Lucifer could endure.

Passages between Darkness and Light delimit human life. Three pairs of transits made by one persona bring forth Donal, Paul, and Hal in turn. But their lives do not simply retrace the same round. Since each of these avatars undergoes a whole series of initiations, their collective experiences form a winding gyre of many small turns between the three great ones. This unique spiral ascent opens a path the whole race will follow. Then nothing that once comes into light will thereafter go into darkness forever.

Day and night have measured enough lifetimes. A long evolutionary gestation stretching back to the first germ of sentient awareness draws near its term. A new and more perfect human condition is about to emerge. Soon, ethically mature mankind will be able to believe, think, and act responsibly, with conscious and unconscious impulses permanently reconciled. While 'the whole creation groaneth and travaileth in pain together' awaiting this consummation, recurring images of conception, pregnancy, and birth convey Hal's role in bringing it forth.

From the time Donal recreates himself as an infant inside his personal spacecraft until the full-grown man takes his place in the Encyclopedia, Hal passes through a bewildering variety of wombs. The circumstances of his escape from Earth immediately set the tone. Note the Freudian femininity of the 'eggshell' canoe, lake, shed, house, bus, and space ferry. Thereafter, a sequence of real or visionary chambers are places where transforming lessons are learned and prodigious growth achieved. Sessions in a healer's cozily uterine bed restore him so he can proclaim the enlightenment he won in prison. (He then plays midwife in Rukh's delivery from the same confinement.) These enclosures may be as grand as the Dorsai assembly hall or trivial as the mail kiosk that receives his identity papers with a soft, orgiastic sigh. In his end is his beginning and in his beginning, his end: only a return to the ancestral womb of Graemehouse establishes his true nature and bonds him to the partner best suited to appreciate it.

But the two most significant incubators are so utterly unlike as to be mystically the same. Coby and the Final Encyclopedia are Night and Day faces of Motherhood – Devourer versus Nourisher – but Mothers nonetheless. The moonlet and the planetoid are both hollow, inhabited bodies that spacecraft actually penetrate to service. Their mazy inner recesses hold vital resources everywhere in demand. However, Coby grudgingly yields ore to sweaty, competitive miners while the Encyclopedia freely offers knowledge to cooperative scholars. The one society is oppressed, deprived, and brutal; the other is liberated, affluent, and kindly. The infernal Mother kills her children but the celestial one preserves them.

Hal enters the mines with the utmost reluctance. His alias 'Tad Thornhill' sounds a boy's phallic defiance in the midst of a fearsome rocky womb. Yet even in the belly of the beast he finds gold and friendship for there is no darkness wholly barren of light. Refined raw materials from Coby may be incorporated into the subtle fabric of rhe Encyclopedia; unpromising people may be converted by compassion. The lowest is potentially the highest nor can the highest stand without it.

Thus Coby is a necessary stage in Hal's pilgrimage to the Encyclopedia, not a detour away from it. The long way round is really the shortest route – a spiritual great circle. On Coby Hal begins learning that progress comes paradoxically. Neither force nor reason suffices for making the difficult passage. One leaps through the clashing rocks by faith or not at all. Only by embracing the Hag does Hal win the Queen for both are the same woman in different guise.

The same underlying principle can resolve Hal's impasse with Bleys. They are two rival futures struggling like Jacob and Esau in the womb of Time – their final meeting-place at the Encyclopedia's boundary is a kind of birth-canal – and Necessity is closing around them like uterine contractions. Vast causal chains of choice have brought them to this crisis. Liberty loving Dorsai that he is, Donal assumes his actions are completely free. But after contemplating his past lives, Hal gradually realizes that historic forces have determined his decisions. Held fast by his dilemma, he has yet to discover how opposites like Freedom and Necessity or Self and Other can be identical. Until the path through paradox opens, Time will labor in vain without hope of living issue.

It is only fitting that the age-old conflict be concluded in and around the Final Encyclopedia, the ultimate man-made womb. Here is the matrix of transcendence for Hal and for all humanity through him.

First, the Encyclopedia is a marvelous artifact, begun on Earth and completed in orbit. This evolutionary instrument is designed to shine light into the dark corners of the racial mind just as a woman might 'show a man the back of his head.' On the personal scale, its womanly vitality reverses the negative feminine symbols that haunt Tam in *Soldier, Ask Not*. In place of a cryptlike house, the ruined Parthenon, and his victims' graves, it gives him a loving home, a temple of learning, and a font of life.

Moreover, the Encyclopedia is the heavenly computer, antithesis of *Necromancer*'s hellish Super Complex. That sentient subterranean device is a Terrible Mother who castrates, crushes, and controls her children to keep them infantile forever. Super Complex threatens mankind until Paul defangs it; the Encyclopedia cannot save mankind unless Hal joins it.

Furthermore, the Encyclopedia is both an 'elementary' and a 'transformative' Mother figure as defined by mythologist Erich Neumann. On the one hand, it is a container for implanted knowledge. Its mission to guard the sum of recorded experience later expands to encompass the physical defense of Earth. (Thus did the medieval Virgin of Mercy spread her sheltering cloak over people of every class and condition.) On the other hand, the Encyclopedia also shapes what it holds, knotting strands of data into new webs of understanding. (Likewise the Biblical Holy Wisdom, Yahweh's docile agent, 'covered the earth like a mist' and 'encircled the vault of the sky' tirelessly 'ordering all things for the good.') Taken together, the Encyclopedia's twin functions of keeping and transmuting link it back to its Renaissance prototype, the Theater of Memory. There, encoded knowledge was catalogued to spark mystic enlightenment. (Paleolithic cave art may have served a similar purpose.) But what the past failed to produce, the Encyclopedia will deliver.

As the promise of that wondrous future made flesh, Hal is self-conceived in his fruitful virgin mother's metal womb and is coupled to his creative work within her. But Bleys, the solitary autarch, enjoys no such parent or partner's care. Tomorrow's gates are locked against his keyless hand.

Meanwhile, Hal has literally found his 'final encyclopedia.' His third lap around life's circuit of instruction is to be his last. The long initiation hastens to its close. The child is nearly a man; the *childe* is almost a knight. 'Darkness within darkness,' says the *Tao Te Ching:* 'the gate to all mystery.' But the pilgrim bold enough to brave rebirth finds the Door into Darkness a passageway to boundless Light.

From the Hugo and Nebula award-winning author

TIME
PATROLMAN
by POUL ANDERSON

DEFENDER OF THE PAST . . .

The creaking Phoenician ship slowly approached its destination. Everard gazed out over the sparkling water at the ancient port of Tyre. "A grand sight indeed," he murmured to the captain, glad of the easy electrocram method of learning the language. His gaze went forward again; the city reminded him not a little of New York.

Time patrolmen like Everard guard the past. No matter how good or evil an event, it must be held inviolate. The slightest slip, and Time would become Chaos, and all that has ever been or will ever be will tumble into darkness. When the Birth of Civilization is endangered by the malign counter-emperor Varagan, the patrol must be on its mettle . . .

SCIENCE FICTION   0 7221 1290 4   **£2.50**

Also by Poul Anderson in Sphere Books:

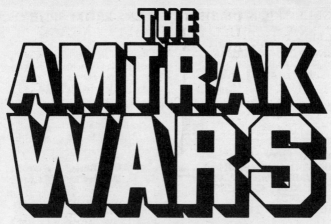

THE AMTRAK WARS

BOOK 2
First Family
The second volume of
a futureworld epic

PATRICK TILLEY

The ultimate struggle to rule earth . . .

After countless years of fighting – of pitting sophisticated
technology against the primitive surface-dwelling people who
seemed to possess supernatural powers – the Federation was
still no nearer to ending the battle with the Mutes. But then a
lone flier was hauled into one of its underground bunkers – a
man whose very existence was a challenge to the all-
pervading wisdom of the First Family. A man whose destiny
would determine the future for both the Federation and the
Mutes . . .

General Fiction   0 7221 8517 0   **£2.25**

A SELECTION OF BESTSELLERS FROM SPHERE

FICTION

DUNN'S CONUNDRUM	Stan Lee	£2.95 ☐
GOLDEN TALLY	Pamela Oldfield	£2.95 ☐
HUSBANDS AND LOVERS	Ruth Harris	£2.95 ☐
SWITCH	William Bayer	£2.25 ☐

FILM & TV TIE-IN

BOON	Anthony Masters	£2.50 ☐
LADY JANE	Anthony Smith	£1.95 ☐

NON-FICTION

THE FALL OF SAIGON	David Butler	£3.95 ☐
THE AMBRIDGE YEARS	Dan Archer	£2.50 ☐
THE SUNDAY EXPRESS DIET BOOK	Marina Andrews	£2.50 ☐
THE PRICE OF TRUTH	John Lawrenson and Lionel Barber	£3.50 ☐

All Sphere books are available at your local bookshop or newsagent, or can be ordered direct from the publisher. Just tick the titles you want and fill in the form below.

Name _____

Address _____

_____

Write to Sphere Books, Cash Sales Department, P.O. Box 11, Falmouth, Cornwall TR10 9EN

Please enclose a cheque or postal order to the value of the cover price plus:

UK: 45p for the first book, 20p for the second book and 14p for each additional book ordered to a maximum charge of £1.63.

OVERSEAS: 75p for the first book plus 21p per copy for each additional book.

BFPO & EIRE: 45p for the first book, 20p for the second book plus 14p per copy for the next 7 books, thereafter 8p per book.

Sphere Books reserve the right to show new retail prices on covers which may differ from those previously advertised in the text or elsewhere, and to increase postal rates in accordance with the PO.